PRAISE FOR **ADVENTURES OF V**

With a few brush strokes, Reid creates a whole world. It's like magic –
the reader is sucked into that world, instantaneously. V swirls us into an
extravaganza, a detailed, delightful, dystopic, alien, familiar future – primal,
ferocious, and gratifying.
– Susan S. Senstad, author of *Milk and Venom* and *Music for the Third Ear*

Vivacious, vampish, victorious, voluptuous, vibrant, villainous … An
eternal 19-year-old, gorgeous vampire, monster-vixen named "V" – a pagan
Goddess, reborn as a super-heroine beauty who lives off the blood of the
bad, to rescue the souls of the good. Irresistible hijinks!
– Ed Cowen, producer, impresario

A wild ride into adventure, fantasy, and chills, V gifted me with glimpses of
arcane current and historical knowledge. Not for years have novels been as
much fun and enlightening.
– Chuck Shamata, actor

Utterly engrossing, rich, dark, and deep, Gilbert Reid creates worlds within
worlds of vivid, bold adventure.
– Bernice Landry, artist

Gilbert Reid's prose is so sensuous and evocative! When he takes you down
unfamiliar paths, and into situations that excite suspension of disbelief, you
follow him because the energy of V's personality is so witty and alluring, she
charms you into the universe the author has created. Vivid, complex, wildly
imaginative.
– Diana Leblanc, actor, director

PRAISE FOR OTHER BOOKS BY GILBERT REID

PRAISE FOR OTHER BOOKS BY GILBERT REID

PRAISE FOR *LAVA AND OTHER STORIES*

Very powerful, poetic and nasty and tough.
– Anna Porter, publisher, writer

The writing is terrific. The characters are glamorous, decayed, old, young, loved, unloved. Reid inhabits each one. His raw, elegant prose, his vivid and sensuous images leave one breathless, with recognition and terror.
– Diana Leblanc, actor, director

The women, how they speak, what they confide, and omit, what they expose about each other! It's as if only sexuality happened that summer.
– Susan S. Senstad, author of *Milk and Venom* and *Music for the Third Ear*

PRAISE FOR SO *THIS IS LOVE: LOLLIPOP AND OTHER STORIES*

Reid's stories are in the great traditions of Alice Munro or Mavis Gallant.
– Margaret Macmillan, historian, author

Powerfully rendered and suspenseful.
– Joyce Carol Oates, critic, publisher, writer

An unerring and compelling examination of aggression and compassion.
– *The Vancouver Sun*

One of the 100 best books of the year.
– *The Globe & Mail*

EXTINCTION

BOOK 2

REVOLT OF THE ANGELS

ADVENTURES OF V: VOLUME 6
"The Goddess is back. Her hour has come."
– Jules Cashford

EXTINCTION

BOOK 2

REVOLT OF THE ANGELS

by
GILBERT REID

TWIN RIVERS
PRODUCTIONS

Issued in print and electronic formats
ISBN 978-1-7771580-7-1: *Extinction Book 2, Revolt of the Angels:* Paperback
ISBN 978-1-7771580-6-4: *Extinction Book 2, Revolt of the Angels:* EPUB
ISBN 978-1-9994790-3-9: *Extinction Book 2, Revolt of the Angels:* Kindle
ISBN 978-1-7773141-5-6: *Extinction Book 2, Revolt of the Angels:* Amazon paperback

Cover and text design by Counterpunch Inc. / Linda Gustafson
Illustrations by Nick Vitacco

Published by
Twin Rivers Productions
20 Bloor Street East
PO Box 75070
Toronto, Ontario, M4W 3T3

To receive a free book or novella, sign up at:
https://gilbertreid.com

In memory of Michael Treadwell
And for Florence

Man is the cruelest animal.
  – FRIEDRICH NIETZSCHE

Evil begins when you begin to treat people as things.
  – TERRY PRATCHETT

CONTENTS

CAST OF CHARACTERS

Alex Moro – Deputy Commandant of Camp Terminus

Ben Faulkner – technician, working in Camp Terminus

Ben McAdams – father of Billie Jo McAdams

Bernard Milosevic – underground guard in Camp Terminus

Billie Jo McAdams – lover and unwilling companion of The Boy

Bob Norton – Australian Cosmos, Head of Security at Camp Terminus

Boy – The Boy, also El Niño, emanation of the Force of Evil

Buck Thornton – Billie Jo McAdam's childhood enemy

Caliban – Prince of the Mutant Kingdom, aka Tarzan of the Desert

Cassandra – political prisoner, infected with tailor-made leprosy

C Emerson Caldwell III – businessman, obsessed with Claire

Charlie – Jane Fox's pet desk bio-robot

Claire V Jacobs, V's clone, model, fashion designer Hybrid-HZ-3

Demi Pfeiffer – Cosmos First-Class, executive and CFO

Eve Schmidt – aka Golden Hybrid, a prisoner in Camp Terminus

Flick Churn – Cosmos Oligarch

Freddy – killer hybrid, prisoner in Camp Terminus

Fred Ho – engineer, working in Camp Terminus

Gloria – 9-year-old girl, born a prisoner in Camp Terminus

Golden hybrid – aka HZ-10, prisoner in Camp Terminus

Great High Priest – chief celebrant of the Religion of Dolly

Hector Cramer – young man who meets V in a subway car

Helen Guerrera – aka Hybrid HZ-8, prisoner in Camp Terminus

Hilmar (Hilly) Loritz – Commandant of Camp Terminus

Hugo – highly trained Border collie security dog

HZ-2 – aka Sabrina Jacobs, ex CEO of Andromeda Corp

HZ-7 – aka Sarah James, ex Secret Service officer

HZ-8 – aka Helen Guerrera, ex Chief Counsel, Andromeda Corp

Jake – 12-year-old boy, prisoner in Camp Terminus

Jane Fox – camp doctor at Camp Terminus, lover-slave of Loritz

Jim Rahv – engineer, working in Camp Terminus

Judith McAdams – mother of Billie Jo McAdams

Julian Harvey – engineer, working in Camp Terminus

Kit Candy – 16-year-old Sub, house cleaner for Nikki Hughes

Lance Chase – underground guard in Camp Terminus

Major Emily Rodriguez – V's alias as a Centurion Cosmos officer

Mind-Child – Spirit of the World Mind crystalized as a child

Miranda Hughes – daughter of Nikki Hughes

Ms. Agnes – prisoner in Camp Terminus

Ms. Chang – prisoner in Camp Terminus

Nikki Hughes – Cosmos First-Class, Goddess of the Mutants

Preacher – leader of a Fundamentalist Sect

Professor Philip January – inventor of torture technologies

Rick Mills – rare metals analyst, working in Camp Terminus

Robyn – technician, mind partially erased as punishment

Rodriguez Carpenter – engineer, working in Camp Terminus

Sabrina Jacobs – aka Hybrid HZ-2, prisoner in Camp Terminus

Sal Handler – technician working in Camp Terminus

Sally – incubus or ghost of a dead terrorist bomb expert

Sally Ho – prisoner in Camp Terminus

Sammy Franks – underground guard in Camp Terminus

V – aka Hybrid HZ-1, Queen of the Hybrids

Valerie Joffre – Cosmos First-Class, a geologist, scientist

Wolf Ritz – engineer, working at Camp Terminus

PROLOGUE – WHISPERING

Lieutenant Kat Jackson gunned the Cosmos Centurion bike up a dizzying sixty-degree slope. At the very last instant, at the towering crest of the dune, she swiveled the bike into a right-angle turn, and, in a spray of sand, she skidded to a stop, right on the dune's sharp edge. She killed the motor.

Suddenly – silence.

A crystal-clear, utterly black sky twinkled with a myriad of stars. The full moon shone, peaceful brilliance – an illusory image of paradise.

Below the dune, the Great Central Desert – the Deadlands – once the heartland of the United States of America – stretched away for hundreds of miles.

V let go of Kat's waist, stepped off the bike, and wiggled her shoulders. Reaching towards the sky, she stretched, up on tip-toes. Then, her hands on her hips, taking a deep breath, she gazed at the distant horizon – dunes and more dunes, sculpted in silver moonlight, and, far away, a few dark, low, jagged escarpments.

Kat kicked the prop into place. She jumped off the bike and shook herself, shimmying, twisting her shoulders. Raising her arms straight above her head, she spun around, tip-toe, like a ballerina. In the silk-smooth, skintight black body armor, her slender figure rippled in the moonlight. "Why are we stopping? We're exposed out here. It's dangerous."

"Listen."

"To what?"

"Just listen."

"Yes, ma'am!" Kat grinned and sketched a courtly little bow. She snapped to attention, saluted, and stood absolutely still, listening. The moonlight glinted on her full dark lips, black satin-smooth skin, and dark wraparound visor. A moment passed.

"Damn it!" Kat frowned. "I hear it too. It's inside my head, a rustling – like a murmuring of leaves." She pushed up the visor. Her face, suddenly naked, turned to V.

"Yes. A murmuring of leaves ..." V nodded.

"It's like ... It's like ..." Kat's eyes glistened. She blinked away the threat of tears. "A child crying ... many children, crying."

"Yes, a lamentation."

Kat bit her lip. "Oh, God! I don't know what's worse, V – becoming a hybrid and losing my humanity ... or feeling this suffering, hearing things, things flooding in, inside my head; I don't know if I can stand –"

"You haven't lost your humanity, Kat." V pushed up her wraparounds. Drops glistened, silver sparkles, on her jet-black lashes. Her eyes reflected flashes of moonlight. "Those sounds – I think ..."

"What?"

"The hybrids ... are waking ... waking up."

"Hybrids? So, they're not dead ...?"

"Maybe not – not entirely dead. For fourteen years, there has been silence – and now ... this sound, this whimpering ..." V frowned. She didn't know what to make of it. When hybrids thought, their thinking was always brilliant, lucid, incisive, fast, and merciless – but this ... this lamentation was ... primitive, lost, confused, childlike, hardly intelligence at all. If these mental messages came from hybrids, what horrible thing had happened to them? Had they been lobotomized?

V turned away. She blinked away the tears. An icy foreboding chilled her heart.

"And now, they are waking up ..." Kat took a deep breath. This was bad. This could be very bad. If the hybrids woke, it would be a catastrophe – for humanity, for the ruling Cosmos, such as herself. But, of course, she was now a hybrid, an exile from her own kind. The horror and betrayal resided in *her* heart. She swallowed. "It looks so peaceful. It looks unreal."

The stars reached down to the horizon. The air was perfectly clear – no haze, no mist, and no smoke. Nowhere were there signs of life, of human civilization – no lights, no buildings – nothing. And there was no sign of the deadly zombie-bats, either. If the bats did come, they would hunt, swooping down from the sky. Out here, on the naked land, she and V were easy prey.

"Yes, it is – peaceful." V turned to Kat.

"Life is wonderful!" Startled, Kat blinked. Whatever had possessed her to say such a thing?

"Yes, it is wonderful."

"So, we get to Camp Terminus, and if the hybrids really are alive, we liberate them."

"Not only the hybrids …"

"People too." Kat nodded. Somehow, she knew there must be people too. If it was a prison camp, there would be human prisoners. Then, again not knowing what possessed her, she kissed V on the cheek.

V's smile grew. She gazed, blinking, into Kat's eyes. After a moment, she whispered, "Thank you, Kat."

They climbed on the bike. Kat turned to V, "Miranda Hughes is unique, isn't she? She and Nikki and Caliban are special. I mean, they are much more than what they seem to be."

"Yes, yes, they are." V leaned forward and wrapped her arms tight around Kat's waist. "They are the future. I think they are the future."

"The future …" Kat clutched the pure steel between her thighs. She gunned the motor. The bike sped off under the resplendent moon and shimmering starlight. It raced downward, to the foot of the dune, and out into the deadly beautiful silence of the Great Central Desert.

"Camp Terminus," Kat frowned. The very name was somber, final, redolent of death.

"Yes, Camp Terminus." V's echoing thought was laden with melancholy, and, even, with terror, "Yes, Camp Terminus."

PART ONE – DARK TIDE

CHAPTER 1 – BUGS

Camp Terminus – the end of the line.

"Bugs!!" Hilly Loritz tossed back and forth – writhing on his side of the king-size bed, its thin mattress, its creaking, rusty springs. "Bugs! Fuck! Bugs!"

Click, click, click …

On the ceiling, the rusty paddles of a sixty-year-old fan rotated, ticking off a sluggish, rhythmic *click-click-click* and casting a flickering shadow. It never stopped, *click, click, click …*

"Damn it!" Jane Fox turned on her right side, then on her left. "Damn it!" She flipped over and lay flat on her back. She stared at the rotating fan. She exhaled a ragged sigh. It was fucking impossible to sleep!

Stretching her body out full length, straining every sinew, she arched her back into the air. Taut as a violin string, she shook herself and yawned. It was past midnight. Inside the bedroom, it was at least 105 degrees Fahrenheit – 40 degrees Celsius. The air-conditioning had given up the ghost, sputtering into silence, four months, three days, and two hours ago, if Jane's reckoning was accurate. Jane possessed, perched inside her head, a sort of pitiless, scrupulous, time-keeper accountant. It took note of every passing minute, every passing second.

"Bugs!! Bugs!! Oh, God – Bugs!" Hilly screamed.

"Fuck! Hilly," Jane whispered, in a quiet, carefully controlled, clinical voice, "You're driving yourself nuts." She yawned and licked her lips. Yuk! Cruddy, salty, dry lips – dehydrated – disgusting! She picked at the flakes of crud. "You're driving me nuts too!"

She stretched her arms above her head, wrists slack, as if handcuffed, pressed against the metal bars of the ancient brass headboard. She stared at the ceiling. It had been cream-colored. Now, it was a dun gray, flaking, peeling. She counted the rotation of the ceiling fan's paddles – *one, two, three, four* … Laboriously, they clicked their way around the infernal circle, creating hardly any breeze at all, *click, click, click* … Worse than useless!

Jane left the handcuffed fantasy behind – her body helpless and offered up to pleasure – and levered herself up on her elbows. She glanced at her tummy. The flat, tense, sweaty midriff rippled with oily reflections. Great washboard abs! Neat, cupcake tits too. Pretty good shape! She sniffed and blinked at the gray darkness. *Fuck!* How many hours had she been lying there, naked, beaded in gluey sweat, crucified, on top of the sheets? Giving up, she had tossed and turned, tense as a twanging violin. Desperate for sleep. Fucking impossible! No, she was not going to get any sleep, not tonight. Goddamn it to Hell!

"Bugs!" The man screamed.

"Hilly!" Jane growled, evenly, between her teeth, "Shut the fuck up!"

Exiled to his half of the bed, Camp Commandant, Hilmar Loritz – his buddies called him "Hilly" – well, that was when Hilmar Loritz still had buddies – had kicked and thrashed, groaning and screaming – the whole goddamn night.

"Fuck!" Jane swiveled around, and sat up, the soles of her bare feet touching down on the rough unvarnished wooden planks of the floor. Even the wood sizzled. Dripping sweat, hunched forward, sitting on the edge of the bed, she stared into space. Her fists clutched the mattress so hard her knuckles turned white. What a dreary fucking godforsaken place!

The pithead and security perimeter lights glared through the torn, fly-spotted muslin curtain. Everything in the room was cast in a gray-silver ghostly hue. Jane glanced down. Her legs were pasty chalk – pale, vampire-like, the skinny legs of an anemic virgin. *A virgin! Now that would be something! A virgin! Pshaw!*

"I can't help it!" Hilly groaned. Even if the man did fall asleep, he still thrashed, fighting the bugs. The damned things crawled all over him. Every inch of the man's skin swarmed with bugs.

Maybe half an hour ago it was: He leaped out of bed, tore off his underpants, scampered around the goddamn room, stark naked, out his fucking mind. His voice had zipped up a few octaves, shrill, totally unlike the old Hilly. He scratched everywhere, jumping up and down, some strange high-kick dance, screaming, "Bugs, bugs, bugs, bugs!"

"Goddamn it, Hilly," Jane had sighed. "Enough already! It's all in your goddamn head! There are no bugs!"

The man saw bugs everywhere, and reported his sightings to Jane in gory sadomasochistic detail. A glistening drop of water running along a pipe was a scurrying, skittering, flesh-eating centipede. A wrinkle in the sheets was a marching line of bed bugs, each equipped with huge jaws and a stinger an inch long. Bugs popped out of the corner of Hilly's eyes. When he slapped them, they scattered into his hairline.

Bugs rippled through what little hair he had left. Their itchy, sticky, little feet beat out a tattoo on his cadaverous, waxy scalp, native tom-toms in some entirely imaginary heart of darkness. The bugs were underneath his skin. They moved in ripples in his flesh, nibbling like a cancer at his sphincter. They tunneled into his anus. They wiggled up inside his penis. They spiraled into his brain.

How to cure Hilly? Jane had no idea. She was a fucking flesh-and-bones doctor, not a goddamn psychotherapist.

She stood up, stretched, and walked to the window. She was acutely aware of herself – barefoot, naked, edgy, pissed off, soaked in sweat, dog-tired, but, even now, her body quivered with energy. It was a wiry, thin body, smooth and chalk-white, with neat little buttocks, perfect champagne-glass breasts, shapely legs, a tight, muscular belly, and a narrow, stubborn back.

She wiggled her shoulders. That damned stiffness in her neck! She pushed aside the tattered curtain. Above the dark buildings, the monstrous pit-head towered. A line from one of William Blake's poems rose up from some obscure forgotten place in her mind: *And was Jerusalem builded here, among these dark satanic mills?*

Fuck!

Jane put her finger on the window pane. William Blake was a goddamned prophet: *And they built a hell in heaven's despite ...*

This hell hole was, so the secret briefing documents said, the front line in defense of the New Jerusalem, the Cosmos Empire, the ethereal hanging cities, the new Babylon, the Cosmos Paradise, the domed cities – all built on mountains of cadavers. This was the Satanic Mill that protected Cosmos. held the monsters at bay.

Beyond the soaring pithead, garish floodlights lit up security fences and guard towers. Beyond the fences and towers, the stripped-down ground stretched away into darkness. It had been leveled flat. No undetected approach was possible.

The windowpane trembled. Jane pressed the palm of her hand against it, quieting the rattling. *We're in a prison, just as much as the prisoners.*

The *thump, thump, thump!* The steady vibration of pumps came from far below. They were the massive machines, desperately struggling to keep the mine alive: *Thump, thump, thump.* Air went down, more than a mile, far more. Water and clayey sludge came up, hundreds of tons of it. It was ancient machinery. Everything was archaic, improvised, cobbled together – and brittle. Jane feared the fragility. If the pumps and ventilators failed, the whole thing would implode – an utter catastrophe.

She pressed her hand harder. Beyond the glass, the coal-black pithead silhouette was, truly, an image from Hell. Encrusted with grease and soot, the tower soared up, a tentacular, rusty excrescence, a giant spider, crouching over the desert. Yellow catwalk lights reflected on shadowy braces, struts, columns, and beams. The whole monstrous thing was merely the tip of an iceberg, the visible projection of a vast underground labyrinth – streets, and alleyways, mile-deep shafts, tunnels and passages, many going down much farther than a mile, and lakes and rivers, an underground city, an invisible concentration camp. The pithead was the dark tip of Dante's Inferno.

Far below – more than a mile down – the enemies of humanity, the enemies of Cosmos, were buried. That was where they would remain, hopefully, forever – until they died, if they ever did die – and rumor had it that, if they really existed, the hybrids were immortal, or nearly so.

It was a hell tailor-made for immortal monsters!

Jane had never seen the hybrids. It was said they were demons from someone's idea of Hell, crafty, evil, strong, pitiless and bloodthirsty.

For the outside world, Camp Terminus didn't exist. The world thought the hybrids were all dead or had never existed. They were like the human dissidents who became non-people. They were *los desaparecidos* – "the disappeared."

The officially non-existent hybrids, had, it was generally maintained, been all killed off – if they had ever existed at all – in the great – and victorious – confrontation between humanity and the hybrid-aliens and those SINs, or Synthetic Individuals, years ago, in the Culling – the Culling, part myth, part reality. Or maybe it was all an urban myth. Who knew what was true or real anymore? *Reality* had been scrubbed away. Truth was a dirty word, it was an obscene stain, snidely dismissed from polite conversation, from the media, from the language. *Of some things, one does not speak.*

Jane ran her fingernail down the glass. This was her world. This would be her world until she died. She knew too much; they all knew too much. None of them would ever leave Camp Terminus alive.

The giant wheel of the main elevator winch was turning. Jane shivered. The cables went down thousands of feet, pulling up a tiny elevator cage, containing its fragile human cargo, and creaking, groaning, swaying.

It was dangerous. A small rusty cage being hauled up thousands of feet – with two or three humans. The whole place was a museum of ancient, decaying, patched-up technologies. She pressed her fist against the window-pane, and took a deep breath. Camp Terminus was a ticking time bomb, a catastrophe waiting to happen.

It would take twenty minutes for whoever it was in that antique elevator cage to get to the top. They would come up, sweaty and filthy, exhausted and almost certainly terrified, from the vast ramified steamy muddy labyrinth, the inferno, far below, where they guarded and supervised the prisoners – well, "prisoners" was a euphemism. "Monsters" was the more appropriate term, or so people said.

Jane had been down in the pit twice. Twice was enough. Once she'd gone down to tend to a guy who'd broken an arm, lots of blood, and he couldn't be moved; the other time, was to give first aid to a guy who'd been electro-cuted – burns over most of his body – when he backed up against a live cable that was spitting sparks. He survived the incident, but with neuro-logical damage and lots of scar tissue. She'd never met any of the prisoners, human or hybrid.

So, she'd never seen a hybrid.

Maybe they weren't there.

Maybe the hybrids really were just some crazy fairy tale, a boogeyman to scare the serfs – the Subs, the Burbites, and the Outlanders – into submission. An urban legend exploited by the Cosmos to consolidate the power of the Cosmos elite. Terror will justify anything.

Maybe, if they'd ever existed, the hybrids were all dead.

Then there were the human prisoners. More horror stories! Some of the human dissidents, she'd been told, had been infected with disfiguring or fatal time-release diseases, set to go off at a certain time in the future; or diseases that could be triggered on cue, triggered electronically from a distance, years, or even decades, later, if the dissident misbehaved, say, or contacted another dissident, or accessed a restricted file, or whatever ... Then you could pull the trigger, and kill the dissident, or incapacitate them, turn them into a cripple, a disfigured monstrosity, or a drooling idiot. "Tick-Tock Mutilation" – or "Bespoke Maiming" – it was called, she had been told, by those cynical enough to be in the know.

These were just rumors, of course. She didn't want to know more than she knew. Though, when she thought about it, from a scientific point of view, it would be interesting. How did the non-infectious, time-release, quick-action leprosy or smallpox or dementia or total paralysis work? How did the time-release mechanism click on? Was the action sudden or slow? And, even more important: Could such tailor-made pathogens evolve, escape, and become infectious? People were playing with some goddamned dangerous toys.

Yes, come to think of it – it would be interesting. Maybe she should screw up her courage, go down into the pit, and try to meet some of those lepers or smallpox carriers, these man-created *monsters* that she had heard about. If they existed, then there were probably some of them down there, a mile down, or more, right under her feet. If they let her publish any research – and they wouldn't – she might be able to make something of such creatures if they existed – *Tailor-Made Freaks* – an article by Doctor Jane Fox, published in some prestigious Cosmos revue.

No, "*freaks*" was as inaccurate as it was unkind.

Those two times she'd been down there were terrifying – it was steamy, clayey, sulfurous, a fit home for demons, for hybrids, those half-alien invaders who had attempted to usurp humankind's dominion over the earth – again, if they really existed.

Luckily, both times she'd only been down there for fifteen minutes, maybe a half an hour max.

Jane laid the palm of her hand against the window. It trembled.

Behind her, Hilly was grumbling, "Goddamn bugs! Jesus! Jesus! Jesus!"

Jane bit her knuckle, leaving a mark. She stared at the red marks, her incisors. It wasn't the bugs; it was the whole place, The whole of Camp Terminus was eating at Hilly, devouring him from within; it was the fact of being out here, isolated, with all the evil of the world bottled up, more than a mile underground; and then, the recent spate of mutilations and murders made the place seem even more horrible, enough to spook anybody. And, then, too, maybe Hilly's past, his evil past, was eating at him. Hilly was a hollow man, disintegrating from within.

Hilly had been a killer. Hilly was a murderer. "I put the gun to the back of her neck," he'd told her once, "She was kneeling, I put the gun to the back of her neck, and I pulled the trigger, and I walked up and down the whole row of them, they were all kneeling, adults, children, hybrids, humans, Synthetic Individuals, those beautiful SINs. And I shot them all, one after the other, one after the other."

That's what he told her – months, years, ago.

"I can't help it." Hilly was trembling, sitting on the edge of the bed, hunched over, covered in sweat.

Without turning to face him, Jane shrugged. "It's a phobia, Hilly; it's irrational. Bugs are not the problem. There are no bugs."

No bugs ... She ran her fingers over her breasts, down to her belly. In this place, she and her body had devolved, become primal, a dripping, slimy, hot-skinned creature of wet clay; her belly and breasts felt gluey, drooling sticky sweat. Her back was beaded in bubbles of it. It trickled between her shoulder blades, ran down her spine, into the crack of her ass – ticklish and squirmy, like one of Hilly's bugs. She shook herself – it didn't work, of course. The rivulet of sweat was still there, thicker than before, insinuating – weirdly, horribly, sensual, the caress of a clammy serpent. Surely, it guilt was eating at Hilly. He was a murderer, more than a murderer.

"God!" she twisted her lips and pressed her knuckles tight against the glass. I am going to go crazy out here, utterly mad, bonkers, clean off my fucking rocker!

There had been a week-long pause in Hilly's madness. But in the last two days, the hallucinations had returned, and with a vengeance. They were getting worse – the craziness had powered up, accelerated – it was as if some evil genius was pulling his strings, turning Hilly into a puppet, jerking him around.

"You should let me give you an *Erasure Subcutaneous*." She turned away from the window and faced the shivering gray figure crouched on the edge of the bed. "Or, if you let me, I could do a partial *electro-erasure* of the trauma, get rid of the memories, if I can locate them."

Officially, Jane was "Doctor Jane Fox." She was the medical officer at the camp. As best she could, she looked after the personnel – the guards, the pit-head personnel, the underground personnel, the cooks ...

It was not what she'd had in mind when she studied medicine, paying her way through school by working nights as a half-naked or – depending on the clientele and the tips – naked – sequin-coated server-girl in an Elysium Sin Zone strip bar, studying all day, getting three hours of sleep a night – using pills to stay awake, souped-up caffeine capsules to concentrate, selling herself, briefly, to a Professor of Anatomical Reconstruction, a true Cosmos, so she could afford to study and to buy the memory implants – anatomy, physiology, neurology, and basic bio-tech.

She had been ambitious, once upon a time, young Jane, truly ambitious. She was going to be the best and to have the best. But, above all, she was determined to *be* the best – she wasn't going to go for black-market copies or cheap mind-implant knockoffs; they could screw up your brain, and so to pay for first-class mind-implants she fucked the professor, or, more accurately, he fucked her, over, and over, and over.

She'd imagined herself, if everything went according to plan, practicing in a big hospital or a small clinic, in one of the domed cities, safe, with a husband and then, after a year or two, with kids, maybe graduate up the social echelon, maybe even cease to be a Sub, and become a *Cosmos,* maybe even a *Cosmos First Class.* Dream on! Social mobility was not what it used to be. In fact, it was rumored that there no longer was any social mobility. Horatio Alger stories belonged, truly, to the 19th century.

She made one mistake, and it all came tumbling down. She'd been caught visiting – and it was only once – a website critical of the regime – there was a cartoon depicting the Glorious Leader in his underwear – he did look sort of sexy! She rather admired the man, truth be told, and he was bloody handsome, no doubt about that. *Hail, Hail, All Hail!*

At the end of her five-minute-long secret trial, held in a dank sweaty basement far underground in Elysium City, she'd been given a choice: Either permanent *total mind erasure* – electrochemical removal of her personality and all her knowledge and memories, both personal and general; or a stint in a wastelands prison camp, as medical officer, for a five-year contract, renewable at the government's discretion to ten, and then to fifteen years. The camp was not named, and she was not told what kind of camp it was.

To be obliterated as a person and be reprogrammed as somebody else – as a sex puppet or worker-slave – which was equal to death – or to survive, in exile, but still conscious, still herself. That was the choice.

So here she was, at Camp Terminus!

She was one of only two females on site – the other, recently arrived, was an ice queen, Valerie Joffre, a blond, blue-eyed geologist – a gorgeous stunner,

Jane had to admit – and a *Cosmos, First Class*, goddamn it. The woman was here only for a week or two to do a scientific study. Joffre kept to herself and rarely talked to anybody. She was civil, carefully polite, but she avoided getting close. Jane had a theory: Joffre knows she will be leaving, and we won't, she doesn't want to get intimate, it would make the difference even more painful. We are dirt, she is gold; we are dead, she is alive.

Four years ago, on the very first day Jane Fox arrived, Hilly – Camp Commandant Hilmar Loritz – had claimed Doctor Jane Fox for his own.

"Follow me."

"Okay! Yes, sir."

"You'll sleep here – with me."

Hilly was a big man, tanned, thick black hair greased back, strong dark eyebrows, broad shoulders, a barrel chest, and he was the chief.

"Okay, boss," she'd said, putting down her small battered suitcase – bought second-hand in a bazaar in the Sin Zone in Elysium City – cheap stuff from down there, where she'd shimmied in sequin glow paint and strutted her stuff – miming orgasm, over and over, and miming making out with another girl, a cute but desperate fellow Sub, 19-year-old Phoebe Monroe, a brilliant student in quantum molecular biology – and bloody hard work it was too – among the weirdoes and slumming *Cosmos* and inveterate sinners. She had one other suitcase – she'd left it in the infirmary – a collection of antique books and electronic books and study programs; she intended to study while here; she still wanted to be a real doctor in a real place, not an indentured slave in this godforsaken hole, lost hundreds of miles out in the Dead Lands.

"You'll sleep here, with me," Hilmar Loritz repeated.

"Okay, boss," she looked down at her toes, then up, into his eyes.

She had made a quick judgment, figuring this was maybe the best way to survive: Being with the Big Man would mean the other men would have to leave her alone. She'd been raped before, gang-raped; she didn't want to repeat the experience. Whenever she thought of it, she cringed, shivering, unable to stop. Four undergraduate medical students, sons of bigwig *Cosmos*, powerful, dangerous people, they'd trapped her in a dark side alley, gagged her, and kidnapped her on her way home from the strip joint.

After their little party with her, it lasted more than twelve hours, in an abandoned subway tool room, she had limped, bowlegged and pigeon-toed, for a week and the bleeding didn't stop not for a long time, but she didn't file a complaint.

"Forty electro-lashes for soliciting outside the Sin Zone," one of the students warned her, "Us four *Cosmos* as witnesses against you – and you're nobody." His hand squeezed her jaw, jamming her mouth shut, twisting her face into a grotesque rubber mask. "You're filth. You are Sub Excrement. You disgust me." He spat in her eyes, twice, and let her go.

One of the other guys, the tall, skinny, shy one, stared at her. "Next time, we'll leave real scars." He drew his hand along her cheek, and pressed his index finger – long fingernail like a claw – really hard, like the tip of a razor, from the corner of one of her eyes, down across the bridge of her nose, to her jaw, and down to her throat, and back up and across her eyes. She was trembling. But she stared straight into the guy's eyes, not flinching, not for a nanosecond. If she ever got a chance, she'd rip his guts out.

"Call me Hilly," Hilmar Loritz had said. He took her by the shoulders, kissed her full and hard on the mouth, and then he forced her down, onto her knees, in front of him. "Humor me," he said, "Pleasure me."

That was four years ago.

Strangely, once those introductions were over, he had been a good lover – he seemed to know what would touch her to the core, excite her, conquer her: a slow hungry delicate nibbling kiss on her earlobes, a sliding gentle warm kiss on the nape of her neck up to and along the hairline, a subtle then violent pressure on the small of her back and those oh so sweet kisses – her breasts and her belly and then and then …

He had a good mouth, a wise and skilled mouth – lips and tongue.

There were no limits to him, no shame, he dared go everywhere.

He was a giant of a man … and when he came into her …!

What more could a girl ask?

Now, forty-eight months later, leaning against the window, she turned and faced him, faced what had become of her man, of Camp Commandant Hilmar Loritz.

Shrunken and wizened, perched on the edge of the bed, the creature was a shadow of the old Hilly. Hunched, skeletal, ghostly pale, he was a specter, coated, ape-like, in white, wispy, fluffy body hair, lit up with a phosphorescent glow by reflections from the pithead. Hilly's body hair used to be – just weeks ago – strong, virile stuff, stuff that she'd first forced herself to accept– then learned to like – and then loved to stroke and caress. Now it was insubstantial, fine as gossamer, wispy as ash. He'd hollowed out. His muscles had withered, his chest had caved in. And – it drove her *crazy* – he walked bent forward, his head hanging, shameful, all virility gone, and all pride. In a few weeks, Hilly had become ancient, a shuffling, drooling duffer.

By now, she pitied him. And she was angry, angry at him, and angry at herself, at her impotence. There was nothing she could do, no way to comfort him, no way to save him. Against her will, and against every principle she swore by, she'd begun to love the guy – even knowing he was a killer, a rapist, a mass murderer, a cold-blooded executioner, and even knowing he was the chief of a vast concentration camp, a camp where she, of course, worked. She bit her lip. I am an accomplice, she thought, I too am guilty.

"I had a dream." Hilly turned his baleful gaze on her.

"Oh, shit," she wanted to turn away from his stare, but she didn't. The dreams were worse than the bugs. Hilly was not the only one with the dreams. In the last two months, most of the men had reported the dreams – nightmares – and asked for heavy-duty biorhythm sleeping patches to knock them out. Even she had had the dreams.

"Yeah," he blinked up at her, sheepishly. Cruelty and pride had been burned out of the man, and desire. Not a shadow of his overwhelming libido remained, not a trace of healthy cruel macho lust. "You've been good to me," he said, staring at her.

"I try." Jane suddenly saw herself as he must have seen her, at least when he first saw her, when he still desired her. She was slender – though she thought of herself as skinny – and pale, with a narrow face, thin, sharply etched lips, a surprisingly quick, bright smile, gray eyes, people said looked intelligent, a rapid, darting glance, sometimes locked into owlish concentration. She had small, perfect breasts, ultra-sensitive nipples, a glossy, neat, coal-black triangle between her legs, and straight black shoulder-length hair, which she usually pulled up and tied with a twined elastic band making a perky ponytail that bounced when she walked. In spray-on sequins, or naked, she'd been a hit.

She knew the guards thought she was sexy in a brusque, boyish, scholarly, scolding, schoolmarm sort of way; she was aware that they fed their lurid fantasies on her, even more than they did on the recently arrived ice queen, who was certainly a looker – but the newcomer was a *Cosmos, First Class,* strictly out of bounds to the rabble. *Don't you dare even think it,* that lady's cool glance seemed to say.

So, Jane Fox was the repository of the men's dreams, their icon.

Janie, they called her, when they dared, *Janie.*

Not "doctor," no, of course not, although, "Doc," yes, they'd use that!

Come on, Janie, I've got a real bad cold!

Doc, I gotta come and see you!

Janie, I got these erections, I can't control!

Doc, you gotta look at this rash, right down here, yeah, right there, in the groin. I swear, I can't work, I …

Some of the guys would invent any excuse to come to the infirmary to have Jane fuss over them and tease them.

"You really are a cry baby, Leonard!"

"Aw, don't say that, Doc, or I really am gonna cry!"

Out-of-date vintage Net Porn from decades ago, stored on the isolated Terminus internal net, was not enough. And nobody in Camp Terminus was allowed direct access to the Net – or to any outside communication – except Bob Norton, the head of External Security. Even Hilly had to go through Bob to send out a message. And all incoming messages were filtered through Bob.

So, all the erotica was decades old. Synthetic sex dolls with personalities and working parts were not always enough either. Aside from Jane and the *Cosmos* geologist, there weren't any women in Camp Terminus, real women that is – there were, down below, or so it was said, female monsters and freaks and animals and terrorists, and up above there were a couple of robotic sex toys – but no Synthetic Individuals, otherwise known as SINs, who often used to work as prostitutes. The problem was SINs had personalities. In fact, Jane wouldn't have minded having one or two female SINs around for female company, she'd heard they could be ultra-charming and highly intelligent, but they were of course illegal and, so far as she knew, all SINs had been terminated and incinerated and were dead. And the monsters, hybrids, dissidents, and so forth, however sexy they might be, were far below, sealed away, in a hellish world of their own, food for fantasy maybe, but …

In Jane's imagination, demons, female and male, were all around, haunting Camp Terminus, and haunting the desert out there, the stony desolation under the moon. But, mostly, the demons weren't available for sex, except in nightmares, though some of the men certainly did claim to fantasize about the monsters down below, but, even in confession, they were vague on details, on what they actually imagined they were doing, or having done to them by those monstrous diabolical and quite possibly mythical females, the hybrids. It sometimes made Jane smile, *boys, boys, boys …*

"I'll make some coffee," she said, giving up on the idea of sleep, and moving toward the coffeemaker that stood on a narrow shelf beside the bathroom door. If it goes on like this, the man will soon be dead.

Just two months ago, Hilly had been wound up, tight, full of energy, randy as a wild monkey, his body tanned, like burnished gold, thirsting after her with a violence and eagerness and delicacy that was scary and flattering and sometimes verged on the dangerous. Unquenchable lust that seemed almost like love: him – his big hands, his bulging muscles – pulling her down, ripping off her clothes, crawling on top of her, laughing, rolling over, carrying her with him, a real sport; and then she was on top of him, or crouching, lying, or sitting, or him forcing her down onto the floorboards, exploring every inch of her with his hands, his lips, the bare rough wood floor hard under her hands and knees or under her back and ass, as he whispered, "You are mine, my darling little bitch, you are mine and nobody else's!"

"Yes, Master," she'd say, biting her lip, tilting back her throat so he could kiss her neck, vulnerable and offered up to him, the delicate side of her face just along the edge of the cheekbone, and the tender lobe of her ear, with his hand under her the small of her back, fingers pressing on her vertebrae, arching her body up, tightening, cantilevering the angle as he entered her, *Oh, so Big, Oh, God, so Big,* again, and again, and again …

Thrust, thrust, thrust …

Now, Hilly never approached her sexually. At night, he lay curled like a child against her back, his big body inert, passive, clinging to her, his arms sometimes wrapped around her, in what a Sub girlfriend of hers – also banished to a concentration camp somewhere – used to call, in days gone by, "the spoon position," his big flaccid calloused hand lying flat and limp against the soft smoothness of her belly, and his furry chest – all that dying old-man's fluff that covered in furry gossamer his thin, drooping, old-man's arms, all that damned fluff tickling her, so bloody irritating, she had to bloody well make a huge effort just to lie still, and it took her a long time to fall asleep, partly from irritation at the lack of sex and energy, partly from roiling anger at his passivity, since, yes, she had to admit, with rage in her heart, she'd become addicted to his violent love-making, now a thing, alas, of the past …

Often, now, he whimpered; he cried out, "Oh, God, Oh God!"

And, "Bugs, bugs, bugs!"

She could easily despise him, and maybe she did – his weakness. He was no longer a man.

"We need coffee." She snapped open the espresso cubes, and looked down at him. "Supplies are low."

"Yeah," he murmured, "I dreamed of the bodies …"

"Well, that's hardly a dream, Hilly, the bodies are real enough." She watched for the water to boil so she could plop the instant espresso cubes into the ancient machine the moment the water was ready. Bodies – human and animal – had been found just beyond the security perimeter, chopped up, half-devoured, crawling with maggots, sparkly with iridescent buzzing flies.

Someone or something was out there. It was killing people and animals, dismembering, and eating them.

"Yes …" Hilly sat on the edge of the bed, his big hands, wrists limp, dangling between his legs. His broad shoulders, shrunken, hunched forward. How quickly the flesh could wither! If only she had the tools to cure him, the knowledge to cure him …

Her request to Headquarters, relayed through Bob Norton, that Hilly be evacuated, had been turned down flat.

"Sit tight," Bob Norton read her the gist of HQ's reply: "There are no resources available for personal or personnel problems. Highest security is to be maintained … Real and imminent dangers been reported, alert levels world-wide are at Dark Orange."

"Dark Orange?"

That was the second-highest level of alert.

And then there was more bureaucratic bullshit: the gist was: Stay where you are; you don't count for anything; we don't care if any of you live or die, we'll let you know when we let you know.

"Sorry, Jane," Bob Norton said, handing her a print-out. "I backed you up. Hilly is a serious security risk. I told them. I underlined it ten times. But HQ is not listening." Bob Norton was a 42-year-old Australian mercenary, ex-Australian-Indonesian Special Forces, a good, level-headed, fair-minded guy for a Security Chief. He was also a Cosmos First Class, and he was the Camp Censor – no communication was allowed with the outside world, except through him.

Two days later, Jane was informed that her request for pardon had been refused; they imposed a five-year extension of her sentence – if she complained, her term would be extended to thirty years, in other words, life.

"Sorry again, Jane, this is more bad news," Norton said, showing her a hard copy of the message, "This is no place for somebody like you."

"It's not a place for anybody," she said.

"Your right, Doctor Fox. You're damned right," Norton gave her a grim smile. He turned and stared out the armored window of his office – the sun was a huge blotch over an endless expanse of sand and dunes and hardscrabble gravel – "You know, Jane, I think we are in for some trouble, bad trouble – I don't know exactly what, or why, but I have a feeling, an itchy feeling. Call it intuition. Keep your eyes open, will you."

That had been three days ago.

Hilly, seated on the edge of the bed, rocked back and forth, groaning, his fists clutched tight between his shrunken thighs, hiding his shriveled penis, his withered testicles.

Jane plopped the espresso cubes into the water, watched them swirl, and dissolve. The dead bodies, beyond the perimeter, out in the wasteland, were a puzzle. She was not a forensic pathologist – but no one had been sent to investigate the mysterious murders. Norton had asked her to examine the bodies. She did so, and prepared the reports and, through Norton, sent them on to HQ of North American Cosmos Imperial Security.

She wasn't sure that anyone read any of their reports; things seemed to be falling apart. It was as if rot had set in, even at the center, even among the militarized, highly-disciplined Cosmos; and there was a feeling of revolt in the air, an electric unease – she sensed it, somehow even out here, even cut off from everything, she sensed it. Norton was right – something horrible was brewing, some catastrophe was in the offing, but what it might be ...

She watched the water darken and thicken, and she sniffed in the heady perfume of synthetic coffee. Supplies were flown in by RoboCopters once a month – everything was valuable. Being in the heart of the Dead Lands or the Great Central Desert was like being on another planet.

"Here," she handed Hilly a half full cup; if she gave him a full cup, he'd spill it. His hand trembled. The coffee sloshed. He looked up at her, woeful, empty eyes, a beaten dog.

"Drink it, Hilly, drink it." She took her own cup, brimming full, from the machine, holding it in both hands. "Drink it, drink it."

She turned away, went back to the window, and stood there with her trim little back turned to the room, letting the outside lights play in patterns on her skin, arms, breasts, belly. It was still deepest night; the bleak dark pithead soared up; the lights glared down. Far out, the ghastly bright phosphorescence of the perimeter shone like a mirage.

Nothing was what it seemed. The last few months, some of Norton's high-intelligence guard dogs that patrolled beyond the perimeter had been torn apart; then, some of Norton's men, perimeter security guards, out in their Desert Bugs, had found two wild desert cats – a sort of cougar – ripped to shreds. Finally, a number of illegal migrants, lost in the desert – how the hell had they gotten there – had turned up dead, less than three miles away from the perimeter, their skeletons picked clean.

That one time, the skeleton was still fresh, streaks of flesh on the bones, just dried out by the pitiless sun.

Who or what was doing this?

With Norton standing over her, holding his laser gun ready, Jane examined the remains in situ, crouching on the sand under the blazing sun – every month, the sun seemed to get bigger and hotter.

Guards were standing around in a circle, facing outward, machine guns ready, protecting her. It almost made her feel important. The dust and heat and glare swirled around them. Blinding it was, really. She had to goddamn blink away the sweat and the shimmering glare.

She'd injected herself with solar protection so the UV would not burn her and so the light would not tan her. Since the ozone layer had collapsed, the sun was a real and mortal danger – breaking down DNA faster than a butcher hacking into the carcass of a dead rabbit – creating cancers that proliferated in a matter of weeks. Jane was determined to remain immune, nocturnal, chalk-white, virginal – larval, as if not yet born, an underground creature, immune to the seductions of the light. It was her protest, her way of remaining herself: *I am what I am.*

"Oh, boy," she'd whispered. She'd just noticed, from the shape of the wounds and the scrapings that, in the killing and feasting, tools had been used – primitive tools.

"What?" Norton leaned close, crouching, his gloved hand on one of his knees, brilliant sunlight reflecting on his wraparounds. "What did you find?"

"Tools, weapons, they used tools." She squinted up at him. "Whoever – whatever – did this, they used tools."

"Interesting." Norton slipped up his wraparounds and gave her his steely blue, eye-piercing stare. He squatted lower. "Show me," he said.

She brushed away some sand from the small row of serrated chisel marks on the hipbone, and from the knife-like scraping marks on the tibia and from one of the fractures, a crushed joint, as if hit by a hammer. "There, there, and there."

"Hmm, yes, it looks like a knife, maybe a chisel, yes, and a hammer or a club." Norton stood up. "Good work, Doctor. Get as much detail as you can, analyze as much as you can. And, Jane, don't be afraid to make an educated guess – or just a wild guess. Anything is possible." Norton glanced around, scanning the horizon.

Jane was still squatting, the small archeologist's brush in her hand. A guess? An educated guess? A wild guess? Who am I to make such a guess? There are so many wild forms of life out there … Who had done this – humans, mutants, animals …?

The tools had been used to scrape off the meat, to gouge out the brains, and there were footprints that were almost human around the site, though the wind had blown most of the traces away.

Jane had at first thought that maybe the hybrids had gotten out, somehow, and went hunting at night, or when they should be sleeping, whenever that was; of course, five thousand feet underground, there would be no night or day. But that was impossible, Hilly said, when she asked. The hybrids, he told her, were traceable every instant of the day and night; they were all accounted for all the time. No hybrid had gone missing, ever. The system was foolproof and linked straight to the World Mind Cloud or World Hive System. "Their minds have been neutered. They are too stupid to escape, much less to go hunting up on the surface." Hilly grinned. It was his special, cruel, self-satisfied grin – the grin of a sadist, the grin of a killer.

"Hybrids," Norton said, when he and Jane were at another death site, and the guards were about 50 meters away, facing outwards, toward the eerie endless flatness baking, shimmering in the sun. The skeleton had been stripped of flesh and neatly laid out as if for a ceremony, "Hybrids, well, Jane, hybrids are geniuses in chains, that's what they are."

"Really?" Jane was crouched over the remains. The skeleton had its arms stretched straight up over the skull, wrists crossed, like a ballerina doing a pivot, legs close together, ankles crossed. It was very dainty, really. Someone or something had carefully placed the bones this way – a message, a ritual, a symbol, a work of art?

"And, in their own way, they are beautiful."

"Really? The hybrids are beautiful?" Sweat was getting in her eyes. Jane poked with a scalpel: just beside the skeleton, there was something almost completely buried in the sand; it glittered. Jane probed and carefully lifted the sparkling object free; it was a finely wrought gold chain, with a crucifix; the skeleton was a girl; and the girl had been Catholic, probably. She was being smuggled north, almost certainly; she was about 14 years old, Jane figured, not yet fully grown; she must have gotten lost, separated from the group, or abandoned – people-smugglers often robbed and raped and murdered their flock, or just abandoned them. Being left out here, alone, was a death sentence, equivalent to murder; and then, whatever had found the girl, had found her, and …

"Yes, hybrids are beautiful. But I didn't say it, Jane. It's strictly between you and me," Norton said, turning his smooth, evenly tanned warrior face and cool blue eyes on her.

"Yes, strictly between you and me," said Jane, looking up, nodding, holding his gaze, steady and hot, the glare of the sun blazed into her eyes and made a halo around Norton's shoulders.

"So, it's not hybrids," she said, motioning toward the bones.

"No, it's certainly not hybrids," Norton crouched down beside her, his voice quieter now, and softer.

It wasn't the hybrids – but it was something humanoid, something with rudimentary intelligence, or more …

And, yes, the footprints were almost human – a bit elongated, a bit ape-like, but essentially – almost – human.

Jane took photographs of the footprints.

And she took photographs of the victims' bones – how they were scattered, how they were broken or shattered, how they and been scraped with something, something like a knife. How some of the remains had been laid out with care, with something like love …

Mutants …? Could it be mutants?

Now, in the clammy bedroom, standing with her arms crossed over her breasts and with her coffee cup set down on the windowsill, Jane stared out the window. Yes, things were happening, bad things.

Three days ago, Norton had again confided in her. Bad news, he said, really strange news in any case – an uprising in the west, a strange rumor of weird winged creatures; Los Angeles and much of the West Coast blacked out and hiccups of some kind in the World Mind. It was reported, too, that a Presidential plane had crashed in the Dead Lands, and a couple of expeditions, Cosmos convoys, had been lost, or so the preliminary reports said. "I've been told not to discuss this with anybody, not even Hilly."

"I understand."

"Keep your eyes open, Jane, even for little things, any detail, or any incongruity, anything strange or out of the ordinary. You are one of the few sane people around here."

Whatever is happening, she thought, we will be the last to know about it. We've dropped out of the universe. We no longer exist.

Jane pressed her hand flat against the windowpane. She thought of so many things that for her were no more: life in the big city; the smells of tenement buildings in the Burbs, the shouts, the insults in many languages, the lives glimpsed behind closed doors, the kids hanging out on the front steps, the wild extravaganza and kinky weirdness in the Sin Zone, the grit and wit of so many fellow Subs she had known. She missed a lot of things.

Maybe, she thought, it was *life* she was missing.

She shook herself. For her, the world she missed – the wild, wacky fallen world of the Burbs and – a total contrast – the ethereal perfumed towers, where the Cosmos lived, under the climate-proof Dome of Elysium City – it was all gone forever; it was a fading dream. She would never see it again.

A trickle of sweat meandered down her backside. All those memories belonged to the past. The past was dead. She was idealizing; none of that existed anymore, and, in the past, it hadn't even been what it seemed to be.

The smells of food, of chili powder, pizza, curry, hamburger, lamb, spices, of fresh-baked bread, of rain on a sidewalk, on leaves, the perfumes of ...

Here, at Terminus, on the surface, it smelled of dust and sand and burned air and salty ozone and heated grease and sun-seared metal. Down below, in the mine, and exhaling from the mine, the smells were different – musty and fecund, raw and earthy, clayey and slimy. It was as if something inside the earth was breathing, a big humid beast, crouching down there, breathing, secretly, and messily, fornicating, getting ready to rise up, to destroy ...

And then, up top, it smelled, too, of dust when the great sandstorms swept through, turning the air yellow and amber – and unbreathable. At night, during a sand blizzard, the air turned pure black: you couldn't see your hand in front of your face; you couldn't breathe; the air was like sandpaper. You ran; and, with a handkerchief or mask protecting your mouth and nostrils, you took refuge inside, slamming the double-lock power doors against the rasping roaring wind; still, the sand leaked in, through windows, cracks, and under doors and around doorframes. It was all so shoddy and ancient.

Sometimes some of the surface machinery would grind to a halt, and the engineers would be busy for a week or two clearing the sand from the ancient gears and winches and pulleys.

What a god-awful shitty place! Jane clenched her fists. If only she could escape, if only she could get away from here.

She stood staring out the window, arms crossed tight over her breasts, listening to the distant, comforting, heavy throb of the pumps – the water pumps that kept the mine dry, the clay pumps that moved the sludgy semi-liquid clay from the various storage reservoirs up to the top reservoir, and the big ventilator pumps that kept air circulating in the mine, pushing air down and pulling it up, circulating breathable air down a mile and more, into and out of shafts and drifts and cross-drifts and caverns and tunnels and enormous bore-holes, something like 25 to 30 miles in total, a labyrinth …

It was vast, really, all this machinery, and yet, in the great scheme of the universe, it was a tiny thing too.

The dark silhouette of the giant wheel of the main shaft elevator was turning slowly, hauling up that small, fragile passenger cage. It was frightening, all the dark and diabolic machinery, somehow it seemed like the Power of Evil Incarnate. *Dark satanic mills …*

So, she stood at the window, a slender, wounded, naked woman – *I am a snail without a shell, a fragile fragment of flesh, I am nothing, nothing* – Her arms folded across her chest, she hugged her breasts. *I will become my own lover.* Humans are such raw defenseless solitary creatures, what will become of us, whatever will become of us?

Alone, she felt terribly alone.

In the past, Hilly would have come over, put his arms around her, slid his big strong, rough-skinned hands up and down her body, cupping her breasts, stroking her rib cage, and coming to the soft downward swelling and slope of her belly, and resting those big strong hands there, gently pressing in on her, while he whispered sweet and bitter nothings, nibbled at an earlobe, breathing a gentle breeze in the hairs at the nape of her neck; but not now.

Now Hilly sat on the edge of the bed, passive, frightened, and empty. It was weird – it was obscene, really – to see a strong man fall apart like that.

She licked her lips. "Hilly, it's not your fault there is some mad creature out there doing this; there are mutants all over the place, and it's probably some mutant doing the killing."

"I'm afraid," he mumbled, "I'm afraid."

His nightmares disturbed her more than she let on. Hilly was not alone. It was an epidemic. Even she had had the cannibalistic nightmare. The other guards – and some of the engineers – had reported the same nightmare.

Rodriguez, one of the technical guys, was sick in the infirmary, and he too reported the dream, a vivid cannibalistic nightmare. His dream was perhaps the most vivid of all. Jane had given him extra-strong wide-spectrum antibiotics, just in case there was some weird infection at work behind the psychosis.

Jane dictated detailed notes of the dreams. Something interesting, but inexplicable was going on: if they were all having dreams, and many of the dreams were similar or the same, so she thought, if she ever got out of this place, if she ever survived, there might be a learned article in this and perhaps some sort of minor career as a scholar-doctor, anything would be better than being …

Jane had had her own version of the nightmare – the strange twist was that she dreamed *she* was the monster. She had become a hunchbacked, clawed, hideous, chalk-white, slimy thing. Dripping with mud, she rose up out of the muck of a steamy swamp. She skulked through the night, in a sort of forest. It was weirdly voluptuous, a crescendo of excitement, her loins, and fangs tingling in anticipation. She came upon a young couple making love by moonlight in a clearing and she watched them for a time, envy and hunger and lust rising, wanting to be the girl, wanting to be the boy, wanting to be both of them, wanting to be the tangle of intermingled limbs, of interpenetrating bodies, and realizing with rage that she never could be them, that she was an outsider, a *monster*! She leaped. The lovers didn't have time to scream. She tore them apart. It was so easy! Her claws ripped through them – like a saber slicing through half-melted butter. She squatted on the ground, feasting on the remains, and a quivering excitement rippled through her naked loins. The gory, bloody flesh was delicious, against her tongue, under her fangs … *I am a hybrid,* she thought, *I am a demon, or I am even worse … I am a …*

Oh, God, no, not that!

I am a ghoul!

I am a ghoul!

A ghoul is what I am!

She woke up trembling with the taste of blood in her mouth. There was a lingering erotic delight from the nightmare that was horrifying and yet …

She told no one of her dream. Somebody had to remain strong; somebody had to remain sane.

She had the dream only once – five nights ago.

If it returned and became part of a series, she would get truly worried. She did not want to take pills or use implants or injections; she did not want to erase part of her mind.

Standing at the window, she took a sip of the coffee, holding the warm cup against her lips – this was real, tangible, and human: a cup of coffee – dense hot coffee, caffeine, her one drug. *Proof of humanity and civilization.*

Then – as she held the cup against her lips – *something changed.*

What was it? Panic rippled in her belly. Her muscles tightened.

The elevator cables had stopped!

She blinked. The giant winch wheel, outlined against the night sky, was not turning. It was still. That was weird. Maybe the elevator had already reached the top. Soon it would be time for the dawn shift. She glanced at her watch. No, it was too early. The shifts worked like clockwork. There must be a glitch, a serious glitch. *Something was wrong.*

The lights at the perimeter and on the towers, blinked, went off, came on, went off, and came on again.

Something was wrong!

Something was definitely wrong!

"Hilly, something's wrong." In one gulp, she swallowed the rest of the coffee. There was a drill for emergencies, and, in typically thorough and obsessive fashion, Jane had memorized the drill, all the steps that she should take.

Let's see: Getting dressed would take less than a minute – panties, T-shirt, jeans, socks, and boots. Getting to the infirmary and control center would take three to four minutes – across the trestle bridge to the main tower, then, inside the control center, five floors down a spiral staircase, and through three security doors, each with its own code, to her infirmary on level four – total: six minutes.

"What, Jane, what's wrong?" Hilly looked up at her, his eyes pale, panicked, characterless, all color long since drained away.

"Maybe it's nothing, but …"

The security lights at the perimeter blinked and went out. Jane put her hand to her throat. A shiver of fear. Goosebumps rose on her arms. Something was happening. Some dark infernal beast was slouching toward them, some ... The security lights blinked back on; then they went off.

Camp Terminus plunged into darkness.

Sirens wailed.

A suave automatic female voice said, "Red Alert, this is a Red Alert, this is not a test, this is not an exercise, this is a Red Alert, Red Alert ..."

More sirens wailed.

Jane Fox grabbed for her clothes.

When the alarm sounded, and the lights of Camp Terminus blinked several times, and then went dark, Security Chief Bob Norton was eight kilometers outside the brightly lit, fortified perimeter, in his Desert Bug, with just three guard dogs and four bio-drones for company.

Even the few minutes preceding the blackout had been exciting – Oh yes!

The first sign of trouble came from the mini-bio-drones. On Norton's dashboard drone-locator, all the little green lights that indicated the drone positions had suddenly gone red. Then they went blank.

This was weird. Norton pushed the backup circuit button.

Nothing.

Then the two mini-bio-drones that had been flying just in front of the Bug, at about 20 meters – sniffing and scanning for danger – had suddenly turned, and headed straight at the Bug, on a kamikaze mission – they aimed to kill their erstwhile master, Bob Norton.

Somehow Norton saw them in time.

"Hold on, mates!" Norton gunned the armored Desert Bug and swerved out of the way. The drones swerved when he swerved; they looped around when he veered again; finally, getting a bead on him and coming too fast for him to avoid them, they tried for the open window of the side door, but, as he swerved again, they smashed full tilt against the armored glass windshield. They had been aiming straight for him. Splat! Each drone left a crimson star-shaped bio-splatter on the glass.

Norton wiped his brow. He had tried to avoid them – but they had chased him – which was uncanny – it looked like something had taken over control of the drone minds, something hostile – and deadly. Something that knew what it wanted: Norton dead. Two drones down. What had happened to the other two drones?

The glass was cracked, but it had not shattered.

Norton felt violated. It was as if part of his own body had revolted against him. He'd come to depend on the drones, and almost thought of them as family, like the patrol dogs. The drones had tried to kill him, but they merely managed to commit suicide. The drones were soft bio-matter, specialized intelligences, insect-like, with a light, shelled carapace, and a titanium alloy center, designed for reconnaissance only, not weaponized. Still, they had tried to kill him, and, for special missions, they did contain poison, a lethal cocktail of high potency biomaterial. Getting even splashed in the face – particularly in the eyes – by one of those things would be fatal.

"Sorry about that, mates!" Norton glanced back at the three patrol dogs that had been tossed around – just a bit, they were belted in – when he had swerved the Bug and then slammed it to a stop.

The high IQ dogs barked a friendly bark – confirming that they were okay. Hugo, the lead dog, was his favorite. Maybe Hugo was Norton's best friend in Camp Terminus, and the others were solid friends too. If he had to make a last stand, he'd pick the dogs as allies, and Doc Jane certainly, then maybe Alex Moro Deputy Commandant, and a few of the underground guys – Julian Harvey, maybe Jimmy Rahv – Fred Ho, the engineer, and, yes, if she were still around – but she'd be gone soon – that geologist, Cosmos First Class, damn her extraordinary, icy beauty, a danger for discipline, but she was cool and tough and principled. What was her name? Ah, yes, Valerie Joffre, with a string of letters behind her name, M.Sc., Ph.D., FRS, FGSA … and so on …

The Bug had skidded to a stop on a low rise of sand and gravel eight kilometers from the brightly lit outer perimeter of Camp Terminus.

Norton glanced at the drone-locator screen. It had lit up again and now indicated the position of the inert drones; yes, there were two more drones out there. He slipped on a protective mask, took out his laser pistol, and cautiously opened the Bug's Door.

"Wait here," he whispered.

The dogs watched him, wagged their tails, their eyes bright in the dimly lit interior of the Bug; they didn't bark.

Norton closed the Bug's door and secured it. He walked over to where one of the two remaining drones should be.

He shone a beam of light in front of him, a wavering, narrow-focused brilliance of pebbles, drifted sand, more sand, sand piled up into a small drift, and, yes, there it was – one of the drones.

He held his laser gun steady, pointed at the drone.

He knelt down, feeling very vulnerable.

The drone was on the ground, blinking feebly. It looked like a very large dragonfly, about six inches long; its multifaceted eyes turned toward him, reflecting the beamed light, iridescent prisms; its antennae and sensors twitched; its wings fluttered in a short spasm; it rose slightly off the ground, and then it fell back.

Norton pulled the trigger and vaporized the drone.

The bright flash blinded him for a second, and then his vision returned; he turned off the light beam. The vast night was silent, stars overhead, distant horizon as flat as a pool table, emptiness.

Norton was suddenly aware of himself as a piece of flesh, vulnerable, alone, in the desert, the armored Desert Bug nearby, all its lights off, all windows closed, and his three canine pals inside, ready, eager, friendly.

He walked around to the other side of the Bug, where the last of the drones should be, where its last signal had blinked then faded on the locator screen. His boots crunched on the sand and gravel. A drone would locate him easily. Using its night vision, its sound direction detector, its infrared bio recon array, it would instantaneously know where he was, tracking his every step. But he wouldn't know where it was. He just hoped the last drone hadn't recovered from whatever ailed it. An angry or crazy drone, however small, could be a deadly foe, a suicidal six-inch-long projectile.

He flicked on the light beam, a bright circle of sand, pebbles, coarser sand, mixture of quartz and granite; he shifted the beam right and left, more sand, ripples of sand like you see at a beach, underwater; and, then, there it was: the drone.

It didn't look damaged at all. It was standing upright, wings slowly moving as if it were readying itself for takeoff. Its eyes were watching him; the facets sparkled, a rainbow kaleidoscope in the beam of light; its feelers flexed themselves in the air; its mandibles moving as if anticipating a meal, designed as it was to feed off the land, anything organic was fuel, so that once released a bio-drone could go on virtually forever.

"Well, mate," said Norton, holding the laser pistol steady, "What's the problem then?"

The drone twitched slightly and tensed its six limbs: take off was imminent, "Kill, kill, kill," it said, the tiny synthetic voice sounding like a tin can cartoon figure whispering, "Kill, kill, kill."

They rarely used their voices.

"I see," Norton said. He hesitated. He'd prefer to neutralize the drone, take it into the camp for vivisection and analysis, and try to discover what had happened to it, but …

It took off.

Norton pulled the trigger.

The drone went up in a flash – and its burning biomaterial fell in a melting tangle to the ground.

The smoky vapors smelled like burned beef.

Norton probed the embers with his boot. He switched off the light beam and stood still. It was quiet, more than quiet – not a whisper, not a breeze, not a rustle. Nothing much lived out here, though there were people-smugglers, mutants about fifty kilometers away, and rattlesnakes everywhere, and a few small animals – the desert cats for instance – and the hunter cannibals that had killed some of his dogs and that poor young girl, and others; the cannibals were ghouls, he guessed, probably ghouls … He hadn't told Jane; he didn't want to frighten her; she had enough on her plate, poor girl, and if it were ghouls … then … then …

Then that meant more problems.

Norton walked back to the Bug, opened the door, got in, and closed the door, locking it. The dogs shifted, tongues hanging out, excited, radiating the feeling that they were glad to have him back.

"Well, lads, well Hugo," Norton said, "Strange things are afoot, lads, strange things …"

The dogs shifted, eager. They were highly intelligent, but action was their forte, not analysis, not talk.

Norton left the inside lights off; he stared at the dashboard: all World Mind-Linked systems, dependent on residual surviving satellites and land towers, were down.

"Bugger!" Norton tightened his grip on the steering wheel. This had never happened before, not like this; there had been flickers in the system three days ago; for about an hour everything, all signals, just disappeared, and that Presidential superliner – the president wasn't on it apparently – had gone down, and there had been trouble, it was said, worse than trouble, if you read between the lines, with some Cosmos regiments, attacked or lost in the Dead Lands; since then link-ups and info-flows had been dodgy, but not a full failure, not like now.

"Well, what shall we do then, lads?"

Hugo growled; in the circumstances, a comforting human reaction.

Norton liked being alone with only the patrol dogs for company. He liked to get away from Camp Terminus, and he liked to go out at night, under the stars and the moon, the vast empty space.

Also, there was that little question of dead bodies turning up, munched down to the bones. Yes, ghouls, probably, was Norton's guess, the new version of ghoul he'd been briefed about two weeks ago – "Confidential, Top Secret."

Some forms of ghoul had been around for a long time, decades, it seemed, but now more were appearing, it was an epidemic of some kind, hundreds of them in the last couple of months: a virus that quickly morphed people into … monsters.

Top Secret! Your Eyes Only!

Nobody else in Camp Terminus knew about the ghouls, not even Hilly, not even Doc Jane, though she had probably guessed something close to the truth. Then, there was that weird plague out west, and the collapse of some of the Cosmos Domed cities, and … lots of the men were having dreams, weird nightmares …

Norton swiveled the driver's seat around and turned on the Bug's independent – non-World Mind Dependent – infrared, audio, and radar sensors. He had a hunch, or a feeling, or a suspicion – hard to put a word to it, really. Maybe just call it a creepy feeling. Using the full array of sensors, he scanned the crest of a low limestone ridge that was about thirty kilometers away.

"Something's fishy out there, mate," he mumbled, partly to himself, and partly to the dogs, particularly to the lead dog. Hugo was an eight-year-old, IQ-and Communications-genetically-enhanced, a black-and-white Border collie. Hugo wagged his tail and waited, his tongue hanging out, eager for a mission. He and the other dogs were used to Norton's soliloquies.

When the drones went haywire, Norton had already been examining the crest of that ridge 30 klicks to the west. Was there any connection, he wondered, between the ridge and the fact that the drones had gone bonkers, just when he was scanning the ridge?

Even thinking it sounded crazy!

He rolled down the window and put multi-function binoculars to his eyes. The binoculars focused, scanned, enlarged, gave visuals, and infrared.

Yes, there was definitely something weird out there: there were human shapes, but the infrared heat signature was not right – higher than it should be – a very active, over-active metabolism – and, in the profile, it looked like these creatures had, it looked like they had … well, it looked like they had wings.

"Mutants with wings!" Norton took a deep breath. "Bloody hell, Hugo!"

He glanced at the Bug's sensor screens. Were they seeing the same thing he was seeing?

Yes, they were. Some of the humanoid figures – five feet tall, six feet in some cases – were rising into the air, and then sinking down again, circling, and then landing. Yes, if it wasn't an illusion, it must be some new form of mutant – a mutant that might be able to fly. Norton didn't like the look of them. He didn't like the look of them at all.

Maybe they were those new flying creatures he'd heard so much vague buzz about. Flying zombies …

He tried to zoom in with the binoculars. Suddenly it went all blurry. The image wavered, smeared, and then faded: blank, totally blank.

Ah, ah, so these things were hiding – they had protection, an electro-screen of some kind, so technology was involved, high technology.

"Give me schematics," he said.

The Bug's screen shifted to schematics mode – a quick architectural-drawing outline of something that looked like a large bat, with a huge wingspan, and with …

The Bug's sensor screens turned to static.

"Give me schematics," Norton pushed the manual command too, more in frustration than anything.

Nothing: all of the Bug's sensor screens remained in static mode.

Norton turned on the engine. It was time to get back to base; something bad was going to happen, and it was going to happen soon.

Those things were not ghouls – they were something worse, and they were undoubtedly *much* worse …

Then, out of the corner of his eye, Norton noticed the perimeter lights of Camp Terminus flicker, go off, then go on again, bright, extra bright it seemed, and then go off.

He glanced at the Terminus Systems Monitor in the Bug. Strangely, it was still working. And what it showed was bad: The Central Systems of Camp Terminus were down; the elevator winches were not working – little red blinking light – and, worse, much, much worse: The pumps and ventilators in the mine were not working ... Tons of liquid clay and water being pumped each minute, and ...

And ...?

What about the mind-collars the hybrids wore? For security reasons, the collars were linked to the World Mind, powered by the World Mind, and if the World Mind were disconnected, or failed to function, then ... when the mind-collar backup batteries ran out ...

"Well, Hugo, we've got trouble on our hands!"

Norton flicked the Bug's defenses to full security mode, put it in gear, gunned the motor, and took off, spurting up a wave of sand and pebbles.

About 500 meters beyond the perimeter and just outside the perimeter minefields, Norton screeched the Bug to a halt. The hatch swung open, the seat belts snapped open, and the dogs jumped out.

"Okay, lads, do the night patrol, and then if anything hostile comes up, transmit what you can, and just run, get the hell back to base as fast as you can, right. In particular, lads, watch for flying things," Norton doubled the message by using the sign language hand movement for "flying danger."

The dogs looked at him, wagged their tails.

Norton gave them a smile; they sensed danger, potentially extreme danger. "And, mates, if you can, save your valuable skins, okay!"

The dogs wagged their tails again; then, they were gone, shooting off into the darkness, each one heading away to cover his special patrol route.

The main perimeter lights were still off; emergency lights shone dimly on the pitheads and giant hangers and administrative buildings and on the clay and gasoline reservoirs and on the walkways. The big winch wheel was stopped too – and at this hour, there'd be men in the elevator ...

Norton accelerated; he used the code to neutralize the mines in the mine-field, but, not trusting to any electronics at the moment, he zigzagged his way along the clear path through the outer minefield, a path he had memorized – just in case. *You never know, mate, you never know!*

"Well, I'm here," Hilly Loritz pushed his way through the security lock into the Control Room. The main lights were still off. Emergency lights made things look even more ghastly than they were.

Hilly stood there, suddenly hesitant, his eyes round. It was like he didn't know where he was. When he spoke, his voice was strange, shrill and squeaky.

It had gone up an octave or two. It was the voice of a fussy eunuch or ancient, hysterical witch.

Alex Moro, Deputy Commander of Camp Terminus, swallowed, swiveled around in his chair and stared at the man. God, how Hilly had aged in a couple of months, even days, even hours! He'd shriveled. His shirts and pants were too big – his trousers were slipping down. His Adam's apple stood out like a buzzard's beak. His hair had turned dirty, streaked greasy gray, and started to thin. God, he was half bald! When did that happen? Whole slices of his scalp had gone all bleached, oily-shiny like the melted white candle wax in a church, in front of those musty old icons of saints and the Virgin Mary, where Alex's mother had forced him to kneel, oh, decades ago. May God have mercy upon her soul! I may have to take over. Maybe Hilly can't hack it anymore. I should talk to Norton.

Alex tried to keep his gaze steady, his expression friendly. Could Janie be poisoning the guy? Maybe she was wearing him out with too much acrobatic sex? Dream on, Alex! No, Janie wouldn't poison anybody; she was a good sport, a great girl, as honest as the day was long. I'm jealous, is all. It can drive a man mad being cooped up here for years … and, aside from Jane, who was beautiful in a skinny, perky, pouty, tomboy sort of way – she really did *love* to scold – there were no women – not even to talk to, except the new arrival, the visitor, scheduled to leave in a week, Valerie Joffre, the ice-goddess geologist, but she was a *Cosmos, First Class*, and, though she was polite in a guarded frosty sort of way, she was careful not to really talk to anybody: even her most casual glance said, albeit with downcast eyes and a slight almost shy smile, "Don't even think about it!"

Valerie Joffre Ph.D., etc., was going back to the world of the living; the rest of us aren't and probably never will; when you were out here at Camp Terminus, you might as well be dead, at least as far as the rest of the world was concerned.

"Norton's on his way," Alex said.

"Good," Hilly slumped into his seat; he closed his eyes. He put his hand down on a tabletop; it looked like he was steadying himself. His hand, even flat down on the tabletop, shook. His lips trembled. They were slick with saliva. Hilly was ghostly pale; he did not look good, not good at all.

Alex swiveled back to face the monitors, dead blank surfaces of inert dark glass. Yeah, he'd better get Janie up here, get her to give Hilly a shot, maybe get Hilly to lie down. The man was in no shape to command. Alex wiped his brow. It was worrisome, all of this: Hilly's hand was trembling and there was a wild look in the man's eyes. He didn't like that wild look at all. We've got enough crazy, Alex thought, we don't need any more crazy.

Suddenly, the lights went back on. The computer screens came alive. The security monitors lit up. Alex stared. Monitor number one showed two guys, Jim Rahv and Julian Harvey, trapped in the elevator 300 feet down. They were making mouths at the camera, but there was no sound; landline hooks up and cellular nets were not working. Well, if the elevator didn't start up, the guys would have to climb. They'd figure it out.

Monitor two, the drone map, was supposed to show where all the drones were and what they were doing. None of the internal drones seemed to be working. It looked like they were all dead! That was weird! Usually, the little things – not many, about ten – buzzed up and down the shaft and patrolled the tunnels, keeping tabs on the guards and hybrids, right down to level Z-7. But there were no signals, no signals at all. All the drone channels were just static.

As for the hybrids: On level Z-13, a hybrid was loading a cart with blocks of clay, okay, so far so good. On level Z-11, two hybrids were working pulling a cart. On level Z-7 that idiot Sammy Franks was snapping his electro-whip at hybrid-HZ-2, and the hybrid was cowering. Well, that was normal. Little Sammy Franks was a sadist. Down in the lowest level of Inferno – Alex's private name for the world below Shaft-1 of Camp Terminus – the human prison sector, where the drones didn't go, the great metal door to dissidents' cave was closed, no alarm bells there, no monitors inside the dissident cavern, no drones inside the dissident cavern. The humans – well, they were too weak and confused to be a danger, and if they drowned, maybe nobody would really miss them; they had little value. But the hybrids were dangerous and were classified as valuable top-grade national security DNA material, behavioral research reserve, and potential weaponized resource, so, if the hybrids were all behaving, cowering and obedient, then the mind-collars had not failed, not yet; but if the mind-collar batteries were low, without the feed from the World Mind, the mind-collars would soon fail. Then Sammy Franks and everybody else might get a little surprise. The hybrids would wake up.

The vehicle park monitor showed that Norton had come into the compound. He would be here in a few minutes; so much the better.

"Norton's almost here," Alex said, just for something to say.

"Good," Fred Ho, the engineer, was just coming in through the security lock, "I checked the elevators. We've got a few working at various levels, the old stuff, the ones with internal combustion motors, non-electronic power and manual controls; maybe we can use those to get down into the mine if we need to."

"Down into the mine?" Alex gulped. "For Christ's sake!"

"I'm just saying," Ho looked sheepish, embarrassed by what he was about to say, "We might need to evacuate – everybody, hybrids, prisoners … But if we're going to evacuate, we'd need more power, more gasoline, maybe hook up the old tanks and …"

"*I'm drunk, and I want to go to bed,*" Hilly sang. It was a half-comprehensible mutter. He stared at the tabletop in front of him. He ran his fingers through his hair, and came out with a thick handful of greasy, gray-black locks. He stared at the clumps of hair, but didn't say a word. He hummed to himself. He chomped on the hair.

"Hilly …" Ho started to say. Alex gave him a look. Ho shut up, maybe realizing – hopefully realizing – that they were dealing with something not normal here; something potentially dangerous – one wrong word, and Hilly would explode. Ho was a good guy, idealistic, a true engineer, well-meaning, Mr. Fix-it, brilliant even, but, when it came to the darker sides of life, the human sides, Ho was a bit naïve. But it looked like he got it: Camp Commandant Hilmar Loritz was a ticking time bomb.

Norton had better hurry. Norton would have the authority to do whatever had to be done.

Norton was an Aussie, so an Outlander, and a fucking Cosmos First Class too for God's sake, ex-military. He showed a weird tenderness for hybrids, but he was as solid as a rock, and clever. And, boy, God knows, they were gonna need clever!

Ah! Good! Norton came through the security lock. The doors hissed shut behind him. And just as they did, and just as he said, "Well, lads, how are things?"

WHAM!

The computers and monitors faded; the lights went out; everything was dead.

The garish emergency lights sputtered back on.

Alex blinked. Even Norton looked like a cadaver.

Jane glanced at her wristwatch. Had she made record time? Yes, exactly 6 minutes from the alarm!

Tucking the bottom of her T-shirt into her jeans, she pushed open the door to the infirmary. *Phew! Thank God!* The emergency lights had gone on, each light powered by its own individual battery.

It was a garish little scene. Everything was there. But, in the livid emergency light, it all looked strange, alien – unrecognizable.

Her desk with its computer and the row of medical books above the desk, and the swivel-chair, and the ancient rotating desk fan, and her diagrams of human anatomy and her antique wall charts of symptoms and remedies, all seemed weird, as if she were seeing them for the first time.

She gave Charlie a chuck under the chin. He was her pet desk bio-robot – he looked like a miniature pink rabbit with rotating ears and bright sympathetic eyes. He looked up, bowed, bounced, and blinked, "Hello, Jane, this is an unusual hour for a visit."

"I know, Charlie."

"But I am delighted to see you, of course, Jane."

"Thank you."

"I am always delighted to see you, Jane."

"I know, Charlie; thank you."

Jane pulled back a curtain and looked in on her one and only patient – Rodriguez Carpenter, an engineer, specialized in rare clay metals separation, who'd been working down below the deepest level of the Main Shaft – in some of the outlying caverns and abandoned drifts – and who'd suffered what Jane at first surmised was a nervous breakdown; later, she had begun to have doubts.

Three days ago Rodriguez had been found at the bottom of the main shaft, lying in a puddle of engine oil, stark naked, and screaming about mutants, chalk-white cannibalistic mutants, "*ghouls*," he called them, and he screamed that they had bitten him and that he was going to become a ghoul himself, and that he would rather die, and that these mutants ghouls were all around them, that they were worse than the hybrids, that they could invade your mind, that they were about to invade the world, that they were the midwives of nightmares, that they were a portent of things to come, that they had come from God, from a false Ghoul of a God, a God called the Boy, el Niño, that the world was about to end, that humans were obsolete, way beyond the end of their shelf life, that …

Jane went into his cubical.

Rodriguez lay flat on top of the covers – his body beaded in sweat – wearing only underpants.

Jane bent over him. She had kept him under constant gentle sedation. It looked like he was asleep.

She blinked and swallowed. In the few hours she had been away, Rodriguez had changed, changed horribly. He was not the same person she had left in the infirmary at six p.m., less than eight hours ago.

His skin glowed, a chalky, translucent white. The veins shone, snaky blue lines, pulsating close to the surface. She put her hand on his forehead. He was burning up. Over the last few days, she'd given him a series of wide-spectrum antiviral shots and immune boosters. Nothing worked.

She glanced at the readings: the computer was dead: *no readings.*

Damn it!

Jane got an old-fashioned in-the-armpit thermometer from her desk, wiped it with sterilizer, and inserted it under his arm.

The reading was 42 degrees centigrade.

That was impossible. And, yet, the man was still breathing.

He was apparently asleep, but, as Jane was writing down her notes, his arms and legs suddenly jerked as if he were a puppet, and somebody was pulling his strings. Jane wrote down the temperature and again laid her hand on his forehead – her palm met a thick layer of gluey sweat. He was burning up. So, it was not just a nervous breakdown. It was, as she had begun to suspect two days ago, a true illness, or worse than an illness – a curse.

No, Jane Fox, that does not bear thinking about.

She wiped her forehead. She would do some additional tests. In any case, she had to be on duty in the infirmary whenever there was an emergency – it was standard procedure – but she didn't think there'd be much business; the whole fuss was probably a problem with the computers. She might as well use the time to explore what was wrong with Rodriguez Carpenter.

Also, she'd give herself another shot – a wide-spectrum antibiotic and a super-plus immune system booster; *you never know …*

She got out the kit and prepared to inject herself.

The emergency lights flickered off, then on, then off, then on again; this time, they stayed on – a funereal glare.

Jane stuck out her arm and plunged the needle.

Hilly growled. He slurped saliva. It was thick, gooey, delicious. The humans – despicable creatures – were in the middle of their "Crisis Control Meeting." Hilly was dying to dance a jig, right there, right now, on the tabletop, or maybe a bit of a soft shoe – the Rapture was coming! And It was good!

He frowned, tried to concentrate. He scratched his armpits. He shook his shoulders. *I must get rid of the damned bugs!* And, with that part of his mind that was still thinking, and still human, he thought: I have to fight this madness. I must remain myself, Camp Commandant, Hilly Loritz. Okay, let's see! With the World Mind down, all the camp systems and all the mine systems will cease to operate, unless …

Norton, that arrogant Aussi First-Class Cosmos, was gabbling on and on about something. Blah, blah, blah! "Have we got any extra independent circuits that are still able to function?"

That spineless imbecile Fred Ho looked like a fucking ghost. His lips were moving. He too was prattling, endless fucking meaningless words, "A few, maybe, most of them, particularly those down in the mine, are dormant – haven't been used for years."

Norton, the sanctimonious prick, too handsome for his own good, leaned forward, elbows, big tanned forearms on the table, "Can you activate anything? We're blind here, and we've got a bunch of hybrids and maybe 30 human terrorists and a whole lot of dissidents a mile and even deeper underground, we've got ventilation that's not working, and we've got pumps that have failed …"

Blah, blah, blah! Who the fuck cared! Hilly wiped his mouth. He stared. His fingers were covered in thick clumps of greasy gray hair. Where did that come from?

Boom! The computer screens flashed on; the lights lit up; the control panels shone brightly, green lights, red lights, and little graphs.

Rows of red lights began to blink – alarm, alarm, alarm.

"Well, well," Norton said, "Looks like we're on the *Titanic.*" Norton had a sort of grin, Hilly thought, like he was pleased by the challenge. Maybe it was the grin of the conqueror, the Master Race, the Cosmos, the guy who knew whatever challenge it was, he could meet it if any human being could meet it. *Cosmos, despicable Cosmos, Humans, despicable humans …*

"On the what?" Alex raised an eyebrow.

"Old boat that sank," said Fred Ho, "Centuries ago."

"Right, Fred," Norton's blue eyes lit up, "old boat, hit an iceberg, centuries ago, and it sank; thing is, up on the bridge, when they saw those little red lights blinking, they saw that there was just *one too many* of those little red lights blinking, and so they knew one too many of the ship's watertight compartments had been slashed by the iceberg, one too many compartments was flooding, which meant too much water, so they knew they were going to sink; they knew they were doomed long before, hours before, it became evident to the passengers – or to most of the crew. And we've got this picture here, something similar, I'd say."

Graph One showed that water levels were rising at the lower levels; the underground river was no longer being diverted and pumped off.

"So, that's one little danger – water," Norton raised his index finger as if he were going to count off, schoolmarm fashion, the different disasters rushing toward them.

Graph Two: Liquid clay was still pouring, from past loads, into the underground silo on the first level, but not being pumped out, so that …

Fred Ho cleared his throat, "If the clay silo gets more than three-quarters full, it'll explode and flood the shafts."

"Really? I figured as much. A flood of clay." Norton raised another finger: two catastrophes.

"Yes," Ho coughed, "it's really ancient. I protested, but …"

"Requests were made," Alex said.

"Requests were made …" Norton repeated. His smile was even, thin-lipped, and his teeth were bright. "I know – requests were made. I put them through – multiple times, top priority, but …"

"HQ doesn't listen," Alex Moro muttered, his shoulders slumping, "The silo and pump system hasn't been repaired in decades."

Hilly fidgeted. He suddenly realized that the liquid clay could flood the main shaft. Part of his mind, the shrinking human part, screamed: God! Why didn't we plan for this? But the rising monster within him tickled his spine and chuckled:

They will all die, oh, how wonderful, Hilly, they will all die!

Shut up!

I won't shut up, Hilly, because I am you, I am the real you!

You are not me!

I am so you, Hilly, naughty boy, I am the real you, the new you, the about-to-be-born you, the you of the future, the imminent, impending, immediate future!

Shut up!

"Let's see," Hilly said. They all turned to look at him. Sweat dripped from his forehead. The inner voice nattered on below his own words. He tried to speak slowly to keep himself steady, "Down in the mine, carbon dioxide and Carbon monoxide levels are rising, if these monitors are right."

"Carbon monoxide and no oxygen," Norton raised two more pedantic schoolmarm fingers: the third and fourth catastrophes.

"Yeah, and if the pumps don't come back on, the mine will collapse." Alex stared at the schematics. "There's the water reservoir on level two; if it gets full, it'll fail, then there's the liquid clay, which we talked about, on level three, the silo has a gravity feed, so it will keep filling, if the silo gets more than two thirds full, its seams will crack and … All these structures are out-dated junk …What are we going to do?"

Norton sat back. He watched Hilly closely; maybe the man was pulling himself together; maybe he could be saved.

"I don't know." Hilly got up and walked over and stood at the window. For just a second, he'd forgotten about the bugs. It was pitch dark out beyond the garish lights of the perimeter. This was the middle of nowhere. They didn't have many guards because it was assumed the electronics and robots could control any situation that arose. Out behind the perimeter, a monster was wandering, or perhaps deep underground.

Am I that monster?

Yes, you are, Hilly, you are definitely that monster!

No!

Oh, yes, Hilly, you are going to kill them all – Jane, Fred, Alex, Norton, all of them!

No!

You will even kill Hugo and the dogs!

No!

The perimeter lights, five stories below Hilly and about 300 meters away, had gone on again. They glared over the desert and rough ground, scrub, and stones, and sand – and nothingness. They were still on. At least, *they* were still on. Hybrids and terrorists down below and something out there in the desert that was tearing dogs, coyotes, and humans apart …

Hilly shivered. Danger was everywhere, gathering like an invisible storm. This collapse of the system was not natural, he was sure of it; it was not an accident. And then there was this voice in his head. *Yes, yes, Hilly, that voice is you. I am you, Hilly, the new godlike you!* Hilly turned to Norton, "I think we should … evacuate the mine, get the hybrids and prisoners out …"

The lights went off.

The computers blinked … and failed …

Emergency lights again went on, made everybody look like ghosts.

Maybe we are ghosts, thought Hilly. The thought gave him a shiver of pleasure. I am no longer me. Now I am free. Now I can be anything and do anything and be anybody and even be dead and kill them all, and it won't make any difference, no difference at all …

Jane took a deep breath.

This was spooky.

What the hell was going on here?

Whenever Jane turned her back, she somehow knew that Rodriguez opened his eyes and stared at her. His gaze drilled into her flesh. It ran up and down her spine. It tingled – lingering on the fragile, slender nape of her neck.

She had spent the dead time – waiting for the emergency to end – examining the Rodriguez test results. They didn't make any sense. Whatever afflicted Rodriguez, it was unique. Nothing in the literature described anything like it. Finally, in frustration, she gave up and sat down at her desk and started reading old articles she'd meant to read. "Are you feeling, okay, Jane?" Charlie, the robot asked. "I'm fine," she said, "Just tired, and frustrated." "You should get more rest, Jane," said Charlie, nodding his head sagely. "I know," Jane glanced at the robot, "Thank you!"

The emergency light was not pleasant, but it made quite a good reading light.

Every few minutes, she glanced at Rodriguez. He pretended to be asleep. But she knew he was spying on her. It was a creepy feeling, visceral and physical, as if a spider were crawling up her back. The damned idiot was playing cat-and-mouse. He was the cat. She was the mouse. Her skin prickled. Strands of hair stood on end. She shivered, twisted her shoulders this way and that, and smoothed the rebellious tendrils down.

She got up and looked out the window. Nothing. The great wheel of the pithead was dark. She turned away from the window, sat down at her desk, and tried to concentrate on an article about lead and clay poisoning in ancient mines. Charlie gazed at her with benevolent unthinking eyes. She gave Charlie a little wave. Charlie blinked and bowed a short little bow.

"Buck up, Jane," Charlie said.

"Thanks, Charlie; it's good to have a friend."

"I'm always eager to help, Jane."

She took a deep breath. Maybe Rodriguez was no longer Rodriguez. It was a weird, overpowering thought. A question popped into her mind: *Who, precisely, is playing cat-and-mouse with me, Rodriguez or something or somebody else?* She felt for the pistol in its holster, snug against her hip, she patted it. But ... against whatever Rodriguez had become, would a 9mm automatic be of any use?

She stood up, stretched, and walked to the window. The emergency lights were shining dimly on the towers of the pitheads. The perimeter lights, though, were still bright, a ghastly white glare, far away, out there.

Still conscious of Rodriguez, and watching him – his body sketchily reflected in the dirty windowpane, Jane stared into the night.

She put her hand up, touching the glass. It was smooth, dusty, and not at all cool. Nothing was cool. They were roasting, roasting to death. It must be close to 95 degrees Fahrenheit. Above the main shaft pithead were the dark silhouettes of the huge winch wheels – one for each elevator.

The wheels weren't moving. They were just big black wheels against the vague starlight. The motors were off, the electricity was off, and the main computer systems were off.

Close to her face, reflected in the windowpane, looking ghastly under white glare of the emergency lights, Rodriguez seemed to glow.

She turned around. Rodriguez's eyes fluttered – she could have sworn it – and then they were closed; there were blue veins on the eyelids which seemed to have become almost transparent. Wait a minute! He no longer had eyelashes.

When the fuck had that happened?

And how the fuck had that happened?

And then, other things began to happen, even as she watched, right under her eyes.

His skin glowed a brighter translucent chalk white. All of his body hair had fallen away, not to mention the hair on his head; this was all happening in flickering, strobe light, fast-forward. His skull was almost totally bald. It was waxy-shiny, just a few greasy stands left. They were falling away too. His eyebrows were flaky, dissolving as she watched. He was sweating. The sweat was thick, slick, and slippery like grease.

He was changing – but changing how, and into what?

Part of Jane's mind shouted – Run, run, run, Jane Fox, run for your life! Run, Jane, run! Run, Jane, run!

No fucking way, José!

Jane was, in her stubborn little heart, a scientist and proud of the fact. And she was curious. And she didn't believe in bogeymen. She didn't believe in possession and exorcism, either, or all the squirrely mumbo jumbo of priestcraft. Besides, she was obstinate: *I am not going to let this thing chase me away!*

Another thought lit up, like an old neon sign bursting into life: This thing – whatever it is – might be *catching*! Jane Fox, just think of that! I have already thought of it, thank you! But, said her inner voice, Jane, it looks like something different, something worse than mere contagion, something that … "Okay, damn it, I'll give myself another ultra-antiviral dose, just in case; it may not help, but then it may."

She went to the refrigerator unit and pulled a pre-prepared needle from the top shelf. The refrigerator unit was still operating on its individual electro-drive.

She slipped open the package, and, after one antiseptic wipe, she injected herself: a full ultra-dose, the second this evening, probably she was being really stupid, but … This stuff was supposed to kill or weaken almost anything. Over the last few days, she had given Rodriguez a series of smaller doses, but …

She glanced around at Rodriguez.

The transformation was accelerating.

She frowned. Maybe a strong sedative, enough to knock him out for a couple of hours at least; that would be a good idea, yes. He certainly had been infected with something, but what?

She'd given him two antiviral ultras in the last two days – but …

Maybe he'd already be dead if she hadn't done that.

Maybe she'd just slowed it down, or moderated it, whatever it was.

Or maybe the antiviral ultras had had no effect at all.

It was impossible to tell.

The symptoms tests – blood, urine, skin samples, scans – didn't indicate anything. No illness or infection she knew of gave these symptoms – and the symptoms were coming on fast and furious – it was like watching a horror movie in fast-forward: *Step right up! Step right up! Man becomes a monster in under a minute. Ladies and gentlemen! Have a look right here, take a gander!*

This monster was once – just a few days ago in fact – the most handsome gent on the premises in Camp Terminus. And now see him, in his cage, gaze upon this wondrous monstrosity!

She wondered if it had anything to do with the dreams. Rodriguez was one of the first to come to her complaining about the dreams. She thought that he was just looking for an excuse to hang around with one of the only two females on site. But as he described the dreams, she began to take him seriously. And then Hilly began to dream too; then the others, and then, finally, she had had a dream – though hers was not like theirs, not at all like theirs.

Then she wondered – could it have anything to do with those ghouls Rodriguez mentioned, with the half-eaten bodies, with …?

She could put on a sedative patch – it would give him a constant dose through time, but he might rip it off, and the slippery sweat might make it next to impossible to apply.

Yes, it would be better to knock him out – you never know!

She took out the sedative needle, removed a dose from the fridge, and drew the fluid up into the needle. She held the needle up, eyed it, squirted and tapped – yes, no bubbles. She turned. He was lying still, his eyes closed, his arms straight down at his sides, strapped down with thick plastic restraints.

When she went to inject it, his eyes snapped open.

He reached up – breaking the wrist restraints as if they were tissue paper – and grabbed her wrist in a grip of steel and twisted it.

Jane dropped the needle. With her left hand, she reached for her pistol.

Hilmar Loritz tapped his waxy fingers – almost transparent now – on the desk. Through half-closed eyes, he watched Norton take command, organizing teams to go down into the mine and get the guards and hybrids out and maybe even the human prisoners too if they could. *I'll kill Norton: I'll tear and pop out his eyes with my bare hands.* Hilly glanced at his hands and flexed his translucent fingers, the fingers of a skeleton! *I'll kill Jane too, the skinny sanctimonious bitch, I'm going to slaughter Doctor Jane Fucking Fox; I'm going to wring her beautiful sexy scrawny little neck.*

Hilly shook his head. *Get the cobwebs out!* He glanced around. The two guys who'd just come up from down below, Julian Harvey and Jim Rahv, were okay, but badly shaken.

They'd climbed up the shaft from 300 feet down, hand-over-hand, rung-by-rung, on the emergency ladder; it had been no joke. They were still wet, covered in sludge and muck, and coated in that ever-present layer of misty clay. They smelled like it – musty, earthy, bestial …

Ghosts, we're all ghosts!

Better for them if they'd died down there!

I'm going to kill them all, every single one!

They all look like ghosts in the emergency lights.

Ghosts! They are already ghosts! I'm going to drink their blood!

He glanced at Norton. "This evening, I spotted some weird mutants out on the Elliot Ridge," Norton was saying, "It was strange, and it …"

Buzz, buzz, buzz, that man really loved the sound of his own voice. Hilly grimaced. He'd cut out Norton's tongue. Rip it out with his bare hands. Yes, that's what he'd do.

Norton blinked at Hilly and raised an eyebrow. "But right now, the priority is the mine and the hybrids; if the place is going to flood and if the mind-collars are going to go off for lack of power, we have to go down there. Controlling the hybrids is the absolute priority!"

The emergency lights went off, then on, then off, then on.

The flip-over from light to darkness and to light left an afterimage.

"Now what," Norton sighed.

"The *Titanic*," Alex Moro whispered.

Norton gave Moro a nod and a nice even-toothed smile. "So, Hilly, you and Alex and the other boys keep things quiet up here." Norton glanced at Hilly. The man was bonkers, but he was the commandant, so until Norton got the go-ahead from HQ, he couldn't declare Hilly *non compos mentis,* and replace him, though he was sorely tempted. A little *coup d'état* might be just the thing. "I'll put together three teams, and we'll go down, use the ultra-stun guns to pacify the hybrids if need be, and if the pumps and ventilators are still off, we'll bring everybody up … somehow …"

Hilly swatted at a fly that wasn't there. He stuck out his tongue. He would eat the fly that wasn't there. *Yummy, yummy!* He wiggled and twisted his shoulders. Thick sweat dribbled down his back. A rivulet pushed into the crack of his ass. It felt like glue, living glue, glue with tentacles.

The lights flickered.

The screens went dark or turned into pure white and black masks of static. Then they went on again, flickering into life.

Hilly stirred. "What the fuck was that – I mean we've got generators, we should have …World Mind link-ups … I got a bad feeling about this."

They all stared at him. They looked fucking weird. Their faces were rubber masks – masks you could peel off. *No, rip them off, those masks, tear them free from the raw flesh.*

"Hilly ..." Norton was saying.

"Hilly ..." Alex was grinning a stupid toothy grin. Sweat gleamed on his forehead. No, on the forehead of his mask, the latex mask of Alex Moro that Hilly would seize and tear off, and ...

"What I mean to say is ..." Hilly stuttered. The old Hilly Loritz, was back; but only partly, only a fragment of the old Hilly. And that fragment was in a time-warp. Right now, there were no World Mind linkages – and, if there were, the only person who had the codes and permission to link up to them was Bob Norton.

"Hilly ..." Norton's teeth were showing, all bright and shiny ...

Hilly was trembling. He could use a drink. He *needed* a drink; but Jane had warned him. "Stick to coffee and stay away from booze – alcohol will make the dreams and obsession worse."

Now, with the world about to come to an end, all the machines would die, or the machines would revolt, they would take over. The hybrids and mutants would rise up in glittering splendor, and they would kill all the humans.

He needed a drink. But Jane told him he couldn't have one.

Kill her, kill her!

She was a bitch, his Jane; she was a witch, a snitch, a bitch, a slut, a whore, a witch, his skinny waif-like little Jane with that cute, sassy mouth that knew all those cool, warm tricks, and that tongue and ...

I'll kill Norton, and I'll put his body with Jane's. I'll lay them out on the sand, all entangled, their bones all woven together, they will be beautiful, their final orgasm, in death, immortalized, and they will be like gods.

"There are some local gas-powered elevator cages," Norton was saying, and he went on and on.

"I can maybe funnel extra gasoline," Ho was saying. Hilly snorted. What a feeble-minded unworthy sanctimonious little prick Ho was! Always prattling and prating on about machinery and maintenance and the need for fucking this and fucking that ...

Jane – kill Jane first!

Hilly grinned. Jane was a gem, pure ivory, pure diamond, his sulky thin powdery little Jane, but she could be a fucking nag, a skinny, slippery, priggish fucking self-righteous schoolmarm, with that cool, silky-smooth, chalk-pale skin and those pursed lips – that could kiss and lick and suck so softly and so well – and that look of disapproval that every once in a blue moon flickered in her flecked gray eyes, so clear like she was a fucking model of innocence itself, and the way those eyes slanted upwards, pixy-like, either side of her perfectly chiseled nose, right under her sharp jet-black bangs, and quizzical, sort of, like she was questioning everything he fucking did, her head tilted to one side, and fucking preaching at him. And now, of course, she despised him. She thought he was impotent, a limp-dicked, withered, flustered, fearful old man, yes that's what she thought, the bitch, the fucking bitch, the slut, the whore! He would beat her within an inch of her life. He would take off his belt, and sling her over his knees, helpless, her legs flailing, and he would bring that thick spiked belt down – wham! – across her naked chalk-white perfect half-moon buttocks, leave raw raised welts running blood – red, red blood. Yes! Yes! Yes! He had never beaten her. Big mistake! He had been too good; he had been weak. The ancient holy texts got it right. Beat the fucking shit out of them! She was his property, his chattel, his slave, his to keep and cultivate, and plow, his furrow, his land, his to exploit and protect – and now, disobedient presumptuous wench, so proud, he would just hit her, and hit her, and hit her, punch her, break off every tooth, crunch her pert little nose, punch, smash, crunch, grind, and …

"Hilly, Hilly," Norton was saying.

Yes, he would kill her.

He had to kill her; it was clear as day.

"Hilly, Hilly, are you there, mate?"

He could see her body, lying, cradled in his arms, naked, pale white, pure as marble, red blood, crimson, in a trickle from her lips, teeth broken, but her lips curved in a smile, the smile of death, and he would lift the body up, the naked body, in his naked arms, and he would sniff and smell the body, and he would lick and drink her blood, and he would sink his teeth – no, his fangs – he would sink his fangs into the soft swelling of her throat, with her head, its dead eyes wide open, lolling back, and he would …

"Hilly, mate, how are we doing, old chap, how are we faring?" Norton was crouched beside him, looking into his eyes, close-up, real close-up.

"Hilly, are you okay?" Alex was staring.

Fred Ho the engineer – "Walk on the Sunny Side of the Street" Fred Ho – the cheery fucking idiot, he was standing like a fucking imbecile, his eyes round and his mouth open, arms dangling by his sides, palms open, offered for crucifixion, for piercing, ready to show his bleeding stigmata, ready to be nailed to the fucking cross.

I'll fucking well nail him to the cross!

Hilly stared right back at them. Norton stood up, backed off. Norton was a fucking mercenary, an Aussie Devil from down under, a fucking fraud with his false bonhomie, *Mate this, Mate that, Mate the other fucking thing*, and they fell for it, even Jane fell for it; and Fred Ho, the impotent fool with a stupid grin, he fell for it; and Rahv and Harvey were nobodies, technical guys, engineers, like Mohamed and Sal and Ken, they all loved their old mate Norton; and Alex was a fucking hypocrite, just oozing sympathy, he really just wanted to tear off Jane's pants, lick between her legs, worship her pussy, take Jane away from me, get her for himself, well, no fucking way I'm going to let this pissing Italian, this wop ...

Yes, I will kill Alex, tear him apart, and bite out his tongue from the root. Yummy, yummy, blood for my tummy!

I will kill him and dismember him, gouge out his eyes with my thumbs, tear limb from limb, I will feast upon his bones ...

The lights blinked again, dimmed, and then went back on.

The computer screens flickered, dimmed, and then they brightened.

WHAM!

Everything went off, all together.

Lights, computers, ventilators, everything – everything was gone!

They were plunged into darkness.

"Okay, that settles it, we're going down – now!" Norton lit a match – *where the hell did the man get a match* – and his fucking tough guy smooth-skinned Aussie face lit up like a Halloween mask, eerie and scary. Fuck!

Little Hilly used to like Halloween!

Tricks or treats – and he liked to play the tricks.

Oh, you were a little devil even then, weren't you, Hilly?

Pull down her knickers, Hilly, pull down her knickers.

Sugar and spice and everything nice ...

The emergency lights failed to come on.

Big Hilly now had a cute thought: it was a thought worthy of Little Hilly. He could kill them, now, here in the darkness, with the lights off, he could kill Fred and Alex and even Norton, and nobody would know the difference, then he would go down to the infirmary, find Jane, tear off her clothes, and screw her, and then, when he was done screwing her, he would kill her, if he killed her, and she was dead, truly dead, nobody else would have her, never, never, and then, with Jane dead, might as well kill that fucking loser layabout Rodriguez too. And he would eat his enemies – devour their flesh, drink their blood, gnaw their bones – Jane, Rodriguez, Norton, all dead – then, he, Hilly, Hilmar Loritz, he would take off all his clothes and walk out into the desert, into the night, into absolute freedom. There he would meet the Boy. He would fall on his knees and worship the Boy! El Niño! And if he got far enough, with the Boy's blessing, he would see the stars, and he would kneel, and he would worship the Boy and all the gods, the ancient forgotten gods, gods of stone and water and wind and rain, gods of thunder and lightning, gods of blood, and he would be pure, he would become … He shook himself: *what the hell is happening to me? What the hell am I becoming?*

"You okay, Hilly?" It was Alex's voice.

The battery-powered emergency lights came back on. In the blue-toned, phosphorescent-like glow, they all looked ghastly.

"Yeah, yeah …" Hilly trembled, "Yeah, things have happened … things are happening … a half an hour ago … things … unnameable things …"

Norton glanced at Hilly, raised his eyebrow, but decided to say nothing. "Okay, as I said, we go down there and use ultra-stun-guns to take control of the hybrids if the mind-collars have failed, and bring out the hybrids and the human prisoners."

Everybody stared at the table.

Nobody wanted to go down there, not now.

With the monitors all blank and the drones dead – or so it seemed – the idea suddenly sank in that they had no idea what was going on below them – a mile and more down …

Going down was a risk, and it was a long way down.

Down there, they would all die, Hilly grinned.

Buzz, buzz, buzz … Norton was talking again. It was like a buzz in Hilly's head; yes, Norton was a bug, a big bumblebee, just buzzing around, banging against the glass wall of his miserable, pitiful, little human existence. The shallowness of it all, they were all trapped, trapped in their skins, trapped in the onrush of time, trapped in the gluey oppressive heat, trapped in their sweaty bodies, which were sinful, fallen, merely human, filth and dross, chaff and detritus, shit and piss, coiled intestines many meters long, offal to be tossed into the sewers. *Rebirth is on the way, boys, rebirth is on the way!* Norton didn't understand the wonder of it all. But there was no reason he should understand. Only he, Hilly, really knew what was going on. *The Boy was coming! And with him Transfiguration and Salvation, the Reckoning and the Rapture, all in one! Hallelujah!* Hilly closed his eyes and then he opened them again.

He blinked. Darkness was everywhere. It gave him the fucking shivers. "The World Mind, the Hive, is God," he said, "The World Mind is God. And the Boy is the Mind, and the Boy is …"

Norton and the others looked at him. Then they all looked away. Norton kept talking, drawing up lists of equipment, detailing who would go with whom, where they would go, what routes they would take, how to deal with the hybrids, take extra mind-collars, take batteries, take submachine guns, take soft-nosed explosive bullets, take lasers …

The World Mind is God, and the Boy will possess the World Mind. And therefore, the Boy is God. Well, if he uttered wisdom and warnings and Norton and the others didn't pay attention, well, fuck them! Hilly reached over his shoulder and scratched his back. The voice was back, stronger this time: *To protect yourself, Hilly, you have to kill them all, each and every one. It's clear, Hilly, otherwise – they kill you – Alex, Fred Ho, Bob Norton, the whole gang. You are now a God, Hilly, you are a God with the Boy, and you shall do a God's work; but they must not know that!*

Right, right: the outer he, the minuscule human he, the old Hilly, would play the role; they must not know he had ceased, that you have ceased, Hilly, to be merely human.

But he, Hilly Loritz, was becoming something greater; he was about to peel off his mere humanity. "The World Mind cannot be off, Al, it's impossible."

"Hilly, what are you talking about?" Norton's voice came from far away, very far away, "Right now, the World Mind is gone. Kaput! It's off."

Hilly closed his eyes: The World Mind sat in the Cloud; it controlled everything. It was the World Hive Mind, the group mind, Absolute Spirit, it was the Zeitgeist incarnate! It was God. Without access to the Hive, to the World Mind, the whole system, the system of systems, everything that linked humans together and enabled them to control the world and each other, would collapse and … *But, I, Hilly Loritz, reborn, shall transcend all of this.*

I'm a figment of somebody's dream.

They are dreaming of me: that's right! I am just a character in a dream.

Who cares what you do, Hilly, it's all unreal anyway!

"I can't contact the drones," Alex's voice was saying, "All the circuits are down – even the independent battery-run ones. I tried to ping them a while ago; nothing but static."

Norton was saying something. "Forget about drones, they are …"

Jim Rahv listened to Norton, but he found it difficult to concentrate on what the man was saying. In his mind, he was still down in the main shaft with Julian, God! That was a terrifying experience. He didn't want to go back down there. He caught Julian's eye. Julian nodded, the emergency light reflecting the sheen of sweat on his forehead. Yeah, back down there, Julian didn't want to go back down either. Nobody wanted to go down there. But Norton was right. There was no alternative. If the people were to be saved, if the hybrids were to be secured, they had to go down into the pit – into the inferno.

Norton clapped hands. "Okay, Mates, let's gear up and go!"

CHAPTER 2 – DESCENT

As the large bucket, carrying the four men of his team, cranked down into Shaft One, Norton watched the wall of the shaft slide steadily upwards. He held onto the muddy rim of the bucket, which swayed and jostled as it made its way downward, running over the possibilities in his mind:

On level Z-13, there was a single hybrid, female, an ex-cop.

On level Z-10, there was a single hybrid, male, a killer.

On level Z-7, there were two hybrids, HZ-2 and HZ-8: the digger and the hauler.

On level Z-1, the lowest of the working levels, there was a digger and a hauler, a solo act, a single golden hybrid, HZ-10.

On various levels, hybrids were working, alone, or in teams.

And on various levels, the mind-collars would be spluttering; the timing would depend on how depleted the individual battery was. When they went off, all hell would break loose.

The SWAT teams were racing against time.

Norton and his three teams had gone down half an hour ago; fifteen minutes later, all contact was lost. Alex Moro clenched his fist. He stared at his white knuckles, livid and ghostly in the dull glare of the emergency lights.

Alex unclenched his fist – Norton should be up here, not down there. Alex was not sure he could handle whatever was coming, all alone. Norton was a steady hand, but … Norton was gone. Alex turned his back to the ghastly control room and stared out the plate-glass window. The reflection was even more ghostly than the real thing. What had happened to Norton and his crews? Down there, anything could happen.

Alex turned away from the window and glanced at the men, one after the other. Fred Ho was busy making calculations and sketching diagrams on a piece of paper, Sal was fiddling with a battery-powered lamp, and Ken was pretending to read an erotic comic book, but he was probably writing scraps of poetry – his dirty little secret was that he was a sensitive guy. As for Hilly, the man looked positively ghoulish … Hilly stared back out of pale baleful eyes, he was almost totally bald now, his skin waxen, his lips slicked with saliva; it looked like Hilly was about to go utterly bonkers. That could be dangerous, very dangerous.

Hilly turned away from Alex and closed his eyes.

People were wispy cadaverous figments. The worst thing was, Hilly wasn't real either – Hilly Loritz was a ghost, Hilly was a myth, Hilly was a story somebody told …

Hilly Loritz was a figment of somebody's imagination.

That's right! Hilly Loritz did not exist.

Hilly Loritz was a chrysalis – an empty husk – out of which a beautiful new form of life would be born, a godlike being of total power, an emanation of the Boy, el Niño, the Boy who was coming, and bringing with him Rapture and Salvation!

The inner voice telling him about his destiny – it spoke with childlike glee – *Everybody is going to die, Hilly, positively everybody is going to die, isn't that cool, Hilly, isn't that just awesome, how could anybody have thought, Hilly, that everybody was going to die, and that you will help kill them, Hilly, oh, yes, you will.*

Fred Ho looked up from his calculations and glanced around the room, "I think I can get the pumps working again," he said, "I've got the schematics. I can power up the old gasoline generators. I can access the old fuel tanks."

"Isn't that risky?" Alex looked up from a large paper schematic of shaft-1 that he had unfolded.

"Everything is risky." Ho licked his lips; he was a good guy, and visibly nervous.

"Well," Alex nodded at Ho and glanced at Hilly, the man was on another planet, "Well, do it, Fred, take Sal and Ken with you."

Hilly tried to listen, tried to concentrate. He squirmed. He should be chairing this meeting, but bloody Alex, the ungrateful sod, was doing it. It was a fucking golpe, a fucking coup d'état.

Hilly reached around to scratch his back. The bugs were back. They scurried across his shoulder blades; they climbed up his legs and burrowed, all snugly-like, into his crotch.

He tried to keep still, not to fidget; it was difficult; he had to make important life-and-death decisions; it was impossible to concentrate.

"What's your idea, Fred?" Hilly realized his voice was slurred; it trembled.

Alex glanced at him. Hilly's skin was chalk-white; it looked like his hair – what was left of it – was falling out at this very moment, visibly flaking off, drifting down. God Almighty! "Hilly, I think ..."

Hilly put his hands over his eyes. Even the dull glare of the emergency battery-run lights was too much. It was burning into his brain. He took a deep swallow; his Adam's apple bobbed. He blurted out, "Just what do you propose, Fred? Details, please!"

"We have a big old reserve tank of fuel; it's full, just above the main shaft, if I can get some of that fuel flowing to the auxiliary generators, then maybe I can rig up the main shaft elevators to work – the freight, passenger, and security elevators – and that would mean we could get our men and the prisoners out faster, and even bring up the hybrids if they've been sedated or brought under control. Then we can put them in the emergency cages until we are sure the mine is safe. After that, if it is safe, we transport them back down. Also, with luck, I'll be able to get the water and liquid clay pumps, and the ventilators, some of them at least, working."

Hilly stared at Fred for a long time.

"It sounds like a good idea to me," Alex said, glancing at Hilly and then back at Fred.

Hilly swallowed, oh, God, how it hurt to swallow, "Okay, try it. Take Sal and Ken with you."

Alex glanced at Hilly. The man was scratching himself; his eyes were empty, the color had drained out of them, every last drop. It's up to me to run things, Alex shivered, definitely up to me.

Fred Ho thought that if this worked, he might just come out as a hero. He climbed down the exterior metal staircase toward the old pumping system. Sal and Ken clattered behind him. Fred was wondering about Sal. He really seemed pale; it was as if his skin had turned to chalk; maybe he was catching whatever it was that was eating at Hilly, some sort of weird fever.

"This is risky, Fred," Sal was trembling. Sweat glowed on his forehead. His hands weren't steady. And he was the one holding the damned submachine gun. The barrel wavered, making dull stippled reflections of the emergency lighting.

"I know. You got any other ideas?"

"No, I haven't."

"Right, then," Ho grinned at Sal. Sal's teeth looked funny; it was as if they were growing. They looked like fangs. It must be an effect of the weird emergency lights. The man looked like a ghoul. *Ghoul?* Fred felt a weird little spasm of fear – where the hell did such a ridiculous idea come from? *Ghoul!*

"Just watch over us, then, and there shouldn't be any problem," Fred turned away from Sal and leaned over one of the old gasoline motors and began to work on it.

He was swearing under his breath; he had enough problems without allowing himself to go all paranoid. This motor was a real antique! But if he got it going, it could pump gasoline to the larger generator motors; and if he got them started – which would take lots of luck – they could set the mine's pumps and the freight elevators working.

The two giant gasoline reservoirs, towering up beside the pithead of Shaft-1, were full of high-octane fuel; Fred thought that by rerouting the fuel lines, and by turning the manual pumps on, he could kick start the system.

The power had been down for almost two hours.

He pushed the button. The motor sprang into life, trembling, vibrating, and sending off dark clouds of oily smoke. Fred blinked against the waves of shimmering heat. Well, that was one bit of success! Step one …

Fred looked up. His pal Ken Hamasaki– they played chess and video games together through the long off-shifts – was climbing up to the higher level, just at the beginning of the shaft, to connect the fuel pipes, to turn the spigots on, so that the fuel could flow to the large generators.

The old motor huffed and puffed, and then it began to fall into a regular rhythm, and Fred knew that it was powerful enough to solve part of the problem. He could pump fuel to the bigger generators, and if he got them going, he could send down the freight elevator to pick up whoever was alive down there, and he could pump out some of the more vital sections of the …

What was that?

Fred looked up.

Something was perched on one of the cross-struts above the main elevator casing of Shaft-1, a giant bat, or a vulture. The goddamn thing must be six feet tall. He blinked; maybe it was an illusion, a hallucination.

Fred shut his eyes, opened them, and focused on the apparition.

It was still there.

He blinked again. The thing was gone. But what the hell was it?

"Fred ..." Sal was up above him.

"Yes, Sal, what is it?" Fred turned and blinked again. Half of Sal's beard – which was usually thick and black – had fallen away. His skin had lost all of its natural dark tan. Sal was turning into greasy white wax, a waxen dummy or doll. In his hand, Sal was holding the submachine gun; it was pointed at Fred.

"What the hell, Sal ...?"

Sal grinned. The grin was maybe the most frightening thing Fred Ho had ever seen. Yes, the man's teeth had become fangs, and, yes, Sal did look like a ghoul!

"Now, Sal," Fred said, "Just take it easy, Sal ..."

Sal fired: point-blank-range too, Fred Ho had time to think: *my God, I'm dead, I'm done for ...*

But Sal hadn't fired at Fred.

He fired past Fred; he raised the barrel and fired at the fuel tank spouts where Ken was just opening the spigots and ...

Fred swung around, understood what was going to happen, and he shouted, "Ken! Jump!" and Fred Ho ducked, covering his head.

Sal pumped more bullets – high explosive fragmentary projectiles to judge by the sound and the effect. Where had he picked that ammunition up – in the workshop armory when they picked up the tool kit? Why in hell ...?

Fire blossomed at the spigot.

"Jesus Christ!" Ken had started back and was now running along the steel gangway than linked the motors to the giant fuel tanks.

Up above, Fred again saw the giant vulture or bat or whatever it was – God, it was real! It stretched its wings and, flapping them slowly, it swooped down over him, close, maybe only five feet away, and Fred got a brief overpowering whiff of a foul leathery animal smell.

Fire was running along the edge of the upper fuel line; it was headed for the main fuel reservoir.

"Oh, no, oh, no ..." Fred said, "Sal, what the hell have you done?"

The fuel tank exploded.

A wall of flame blossomed down.

It consumed Sal – in one instant, Sal changed from being a semi-human ghoul to being just a writhing black burning silhouette blossoming in a sea of light.

Fred leaped down ten steps to a lower platform; the wave of heat carried the tsunami of flame upward, buoying it just above Fred's head, a billowing cloud of pure flame that whammed into Ken. Ken's body flew apart into little cloudy bits, dark scraps.

Fred leaped and clattered down to the next platform, behind him the exploding tank was ripping outwards, a billowing cloud of metal, gasoline, stairs, walls, pumps, everything flying through the air.

There was a roar in Fred's ears; it was like being buried in a tidal wave, and searing heat.

He tumbled down another flight of steel steps.

He scrambled to his feet and ran across the metal walkway to the control tower, his heart pounding, sweat running, breathless, or almost, and unaware – having forgotten that all the electronic locks were dead.

He got to the control tower, plastered his hand flat against the control panel, it should open to his palm and fingerprint, and then he remembered.

"Idiot, all these fucking things are off!"

The wall of flame billowed toward him.

Bits and pieces of machinery and metal whirled through the maelstrom; he was caught in a tornado of fire and debris.

Damn, damn, damn! He fumbled to get keys, old-fashioned metal keys, from the key chain at his belt. Somehow, he managed to remember which key was the right one – hadn't used it in years – and tried to stick it in the manual lock – his hand shaking and slick with sweat and grease – and the wall and door were painted in lurid running shifting patterns of red and yellow and shadows, reflections of the fire, and he glanced back. The heat was crisping him alive, his skin and shirt were soaked and steaming. If he didn't get inside quick, he would go up in flames, and maybe die from lack of oxygen, this thing could brew up a firestorm and suck all the oxygen out of the ...

The key turned, the door opened.

Fred pushed his way in and slammed the door behind him and locked it and lowered the security bar which, thank Confucius, had not been in place. He wiped his brow, thick with sweat and gasoline, and he smelled the gasoline and burned flesh. He looked down and saw that his shirt and most of his trousers were burned away and his boots were singed black and steaming, but he felt okay, just a sort of stinging feeling. Maybe he wasn't burned too bad. He had to get to the control room to see what was happening, and to tell them what he had just glimpsed in the instant– What he had seen out of the corner of his eye had told him what had happened, what was happening, and what was going to happen, and that was this:

The first reservoir had exploded, and the force of the explosion, the initial explosion, had forced the main gasoline reservoir to topple over onto the pithead, where it exploded, and …

The second reservoir toppled straight into Shaft-1.

A hundred thousands gallons of fuel!

And it was alight!

The reservoir would turn the top part of the main shaft into an inferno of fire and explosions. It would trap everybody down below, no matter what they were, guards, engineers, hybrids, prisoners, you name it, *nobody* would be able to get out of there, not for a long time, probably not ever …

God – the main shaft would be an inferno.

Now, it's going to collapse, sure, no way it can't!

God – this will kill everybody!

It's my fault, my dumb idea for going out there.

You try to fix things, and you end up killing everybody.

Not feeling a thing except a crushing wave of panic and guilt, Fred Ho hurried along the dimly lit corridor to the inner security staircase. The elevators were all dead. He didn't notice that his skin was peeling off.

In the control room, all hell must be breaking loose, he thought, and maybe I should get these burns – no idea how serious they might be – seen to. Jane would probably be in the infirmary. But I've got to report first. He ran up the staircase, his heart pounding, his skin flaming up, crisp as bacon, and here and there, it was peeling off, with subcutaneous fat, and …

His scalp, though he hadn't noticed, he had left behind, just inside the door frame.

Parts of his skull, white smoking bone, were visible, blood, steaming blood streamed down the side of his face.

Fred Ho was still conscious, still appeared in part at least to be a human being, but by the time he got to the Control Room security locks, Fred looked more like an anatomical drawing than a man.

He was in shock. The pain was yet to come. Right now, he was tortured by the thought that, by trying to help, he had condemned everybody and everything underground to almost certain death.

He prepared to open the door to the Control Room. When he did, Fred Ho would enter hell – another hell …

Jane reached for her pistol.

Rodriguez had woken up; his eyes were bright, and he had just grabbed her by the wrist, and she reached for her pistol.

Just as her fingertips touched the holster flap, the infirmary window flashed bright as day.

A blinding white glare, and with an enormous whooshing sound, and an echoing explosion whammed through the room.

The armored glass shattered, and came raining in, shards and splinters flying and spraying everywhere.

Jane staggered back, closing her eyes, her arm instinctively going up to protect her face.

Rodriguez let go of her wrist. She was free. She fell with a wham onto her backside, and, then, for a long stunned seemingly eternal instant, but it must have been only a micro-second or two, she was conscious of herself sitting there, like an idiot, her forearm in front of her eyes, fingers still on the holster.

"Are we in trouble, Jane?" It was Charlie's voice.

Still sitting, still in shock, Jane opened her eyes, closed her fingers around the pistol, pulled it from the holster and, swinging around, she leveled it at Rodriguez.

"No, we're not in trouble, Charlie," she said, clearing her throat, and thinking that Charlie, the bio-robot, had become her alter ego. She was really talking to herself.

Rodriguez had been hit by the storm of glass – jagged pieces, like little triangles, were stuck in his skin, glinting like sequins, but there was no blood.

"What's happened to you?" Jane said, feeling blood stream down her face, and struggling to stand up, holding the pistol steady, still aimed at his heart.

"I'm glad we're not in trouble, Jane," Charlie said; Jane saw out of the corner of her eye that he was grinning. *His happy face …*

More explosions burst outside. Waves of heat flooded through the window, like a blast furnace. A huge fire was burning over the Shaft-1 Pithead, painting the inside of the infirmary in streams of crimson.

"Kill me," Rodriguez said, "Kill me. I can't stand the dreams."

"I can't kill you, Rodriguez, you know that."

"If you don't kill me, I will kill you." He tore away the other straps and swung around, sitting up on the edge of the bed. Shards of glass stuck out of his skin like tinsel decoration, sparkling, shining, like he was a Christmas tree. "If you don't kill me, I will kill you," he said again, softly, as if to himself.

"Killing is wrong," said Charlie, "It's against the protocol!" His expression turned to a disapproving scowl.

"You will kill me? Oh, really," Jane held Rodriguez's pale milky white gaze; she felt a cold chill of fear; but she also felt a cold fury – anger. She was absolutely tired of putting up with these self-centered, blackmailing, masculine maniacs, even if one of them had turned into a ghoulish monster. She was tired of being a baby sitter to a whole prison full of horny testosterone-driven guards and technicians and engineers. A little extra estrogen would be useful around this place. The Ice Queen geologist Cosmos didn't count, besides she'd been only here a couple of weeks. Jane felt that, yes, she could shoot Rodriguez right now, right between the eyes, but she sort of liked the guy – whatever was happening to him – he was a mensch, or had been, not a whiner. Her father used to whine and cringe when things didn't go his way. And now Hilly was a cringing wreck, and now Rodriguez had turned into some sort of zombie – or ghoul … Yes, he was a ghoul; that was the right word. His eyes, staring at her, were very pale. He did look spooky, that was true, and maybe he was insane. "No, you won't kill me," she said, and then, "Don't try to blackmail me into shooting you, Rodriguez."

Outside, the huge fire – *What the hell had happened?* – roared above the pithead of Shaft-1, a towering inferno, reaching for the stars.

"I think we need the fire department, Jane."

"Right, Charlie – thanks!"

The flames made Rodriguez look even more ghostly, flickering, and shadowy, a splotchy old movie screened by a faulty projector; he glowed. Jane kept the gun steady. She felt that she had to make a choice. "How do you feel, Rodriguez?"

"I feel strong."

"Good, I guess that's good."

"I'm not sure it's good." His voice was hoarse.

"What about appetite, you haven't eaten for days, just soup."

"I'm hungry, real hungry."

"Okay, here's a food package." With one hand and still keeping the gun level at Rodriguez, Jane backed up to the infirmary fridge, opened the door, and pulled out a pre-prepared instant meal, and tossed it to the ghoul. All thought of trying to tranquilize him had disappeared.

"Thanks." He drooled; white, thick foam cascaded over his lips, between his pointed fangs.

He tore food package open, his claw-like hands peeling off the cellophane; he stared at it for a moment with his woefully pale eyes and in one gulp wolfed the food down, hardly chewing, his mouth working, overflowing. Bits of meat and chunks of white sticky rice flew all over the place.

Jane edged toward the shattered window, and glanced out. The heat of the fire blazed on her face, searing one side. "It must be sabotage. The central pithead is burning. We must be under attack."

"Yes." Rodriguez stared at her.

"Who – do you have any idea?" Jane had the strange thought that, somehow, Rodriguez and his transformation were part of this, that, somehow, Rodriguez would know what was happening.

"It's not the ones below." His long, thin tongue shot out of his mouth, flipped around, and licked his chin, catching a few flakes of sticky rice and synthetic chicken.

"The ones below? Who the hell are they? Do you mean the hybrids?"

"No. Those demons are angels."

"Those demons are angels? What the hell are you talking about?"

"The hybrids – they are angels, protectors." Rodriguez stared at her.

"What is Mr. Rodriguez talking about, Jane?"

"I don't know, Charlie, I truly don't know," Jane took a deep breath, she didn't want to lose patience, for right now things were clearly falling apart, "Protectors – who are they protecting?"

"People, you, creatures like you – human beings. The hybrids are angels. Not even they know how angelic they are."

Jane stared at him. Hybrids are angels? This is getting weirder and weirder. "So who set this fire, then?"

"It's not mutants … Down below, are the mutants, the ghouls, and, you are right, it's catching."

"Being a mutant, being a ghoul, is catching? I think that's impossible. I mean, Rodriguez, a mutant is a mutant because of DNA modification; and for that to happen …" But Jane had a terrible doubt, because …

"Are we in trouble, Jane?"

Rodriguez opened his arms, muscular, covered in wet mucus, dripping white translucent slime, "Look at me. I'm one, or almost. I'm unfinished, not yet complete. They live in caves, just off the old mine, near the old, abandoned Shaft-2, in the cave system that leads there. Nobody ever goes near Shaft-2; it has been abandoned for years; these are ghoul mutants, a recent adaptation, they are newly minted, a recent creation. We don't even have sensors in shaft number two or in the caves. Not even the drones go there."

"What is Mr. Rodriguez talking about, Jane?"

"Monsters, Charlie, monsters."

"Oh! Well, I don't know what to say about that, Jane."

Rodriguez glanced at the bio-robot, and then folded up the food package and threw it into the waste bin – right across the room – good aim, Jane noted – his coordination hadn't suffered, whatever else was happening – and he was more talkative than before; maybe mutants – or ghouls – if that's what he was – were born babblers and chatterboxes. Somehow, she doubted it – animal mutants, some of them, could talk, which was certainly a mixed blessing – she preferred old-fashioned dogs to new-fangled Border collies or Irish Setters who often turned out to be inveterate gossips and complainers, always talking about food.

Rodriguez was hunched forward, perched on the edge of the bed, his bony white hands, now almost transparent, fingers spread, clutching his knees. The shards of glass had fallen away. His head was entirely bald now, his body totally hairless, the last of the hair, like gray powdery dust, was drifting down.

Rodriguez stared at her; he grinned; he sneezed – a whooper of a sneeze; spittle and snot flying everywhere, some of it splattered Jane's face, got in her eyes, on her lips.

"Jesus! Rodriguez!" She got an instant sanitizer out of her vest jean's pocket – *always have it with you!* – and wiped the stuff away and used the miniature sprayer to sanitize her eyes.

"Bulls-eye, he scored," said Charlie; his smiley face broadened to a grin.

"Jesus, Charlie!" Jane was annoyed – and, more importantly, she was terrified. What if the bloody ghoul thing *was* infectious!

"Sorry!" Rodriguez grinned; at least it looked like a grin.

"Don't worry, that's okay," Jane steadied herself; she kept the pistol on him. "Do you still want me to shoot you?"

He smiled now. It was a ghastly, wistful smile. He turned his face toward her, hairless and white, shiny like wet, dripping marble, and his pale eyes which seemed to have grown larger, and his lips which seemed to have grown thinner, and his teeth ...well, they seemed longer, fangs, yes pointed fangs. That was impossible, of course. *No, Doctor Jane Fox, right now, anything is possible.*

"Is Mr. Rodriguez still feeling unwell?" Charlie bobbed his head up and down. The emergency glow reflected on his eyes. He looked worried. The grin had been replaced by a concerned frown.

"I'm sure Mr. Rodriguez is feeling chipper, Charlie," Jane stared at Rodriguez and at his fangs, and she was thinking of an old fairy tale where the wolf explains his long teeth to Little Red Riding Hood by saying, "The better to eat you with my dear."

"Well? Am I to shoot you or not?" she said, waving the barrel.

"No, Jane, don't shoot me. That time is passed. What is done is done." He stood up, stepping out of his shorts, naked, clearly male, and clearly aroused; his erection was enormous, and – yes, he was no longer human.

"Very impressive, Rodriguez," Jane motioned with the pistol toward the erection and gave him a thin smile. She tried to hold the pistol steady. It kept wavering. Her hands were eager to tremble. Rodriguez was drooling, but she thought maybe she'd ignore that fact and not point it out. She didn't want to irritate him. But what did he mean by "mutants" down below, and by becoming one of them, and what did he mean by saying that the hybrids – or demons – were angels?

She had a thought. Rodriguez was Catholic; his cross was hanging on a hook with his clothes. "Do you want your cross, Rodriguez?"

He hesitated, felt at his throat where the chain and cross were missing, "Yes, I do."

"Good. Okay." She opened the cupboard, lifted the cross off its hook, and, taking a risk, walked over and handed it to him. He put it on, adjusting the chain carefully around his neck.

"Perhaps Mr. Rodriguez needs a priest, Jane."

"We don't have a priest, Charlie."

"Oh, I'm sorry, Jane, that we don't have a priest," Charlie blinked and nodded his head, "Everyone can use a priest from time to time."

Jane was not at all religious, but she thought that Rodriguez wanting to wear the cross was probably a good sign, a very good sign. It might mean she wasn't going to die.

"You don't want clothes?"

"No, Jane, I don't." Rodriguez cleared his throat; he still had an erection, a really bold one – unbelievable, in fact.

Jane grimaced, "Well, Rodriguez, this is becoming a very interesting night."

"It is not over, Jane."

"Right, yes, that's right, Rodriguez, I'm sure you are right about that," Jane bit her lip as it occurred to her, not for the first time, that this might indeed be her last night on earth.

"Are we having fun, Jane?" Charlie looked up at her with his bright button eyes, "Real fun?"

"Yes, Charlie, we're having fun. We really are, real fun!"

Alex Moro, thumbs hooked in the belt of his trousers, stood at the armored plateglass, watching Ho and his team try to get the old generator started, and get the gas flowing. Yes, Ho was a good man, a solid guy, dependable, a rock. But he'd been out there ten bloody minutes and time was running out.

The three SWAT & Rescue squads had been gone for 45 minutes; they must be about a third of the way down Shaft-1 by now, maybe half a mile. Alex hoped Norton knew what he was doing.

He had been trying to get some of their communications working; but, no, nothing worked. So there was no news at all, and Alex was feeling pretty useless.

He looked up. He could see Ho and the other two guys, little toy figures, just visible in the emergency lights, up there on the vast scaffolding of the Pithead of Shaft-1

"*Show me the way to go home ...*"

Alex turned from the window.

Hilly was sitting at his workstation, rocking back and forth, fists clenched between his thighs; sometimes, he would bellow a line, holler it out.

It was some old song that Alex didn't know. "*Show me the way to go home,*" Hilly was singing, "*Show me the way to go home,*" something, something ...

Ben Faulkner, the usual night officer, and his two assistants, Mel and Mohamed, had come in to replace Sal and Ken; they were staring at Hilly; Alex motioned to them, indicating that it was better not to stare. Ben and the two others nodded and looked down at their desks and consoles, pretending to be absorbed in some papers or work of some kind, though, with most systems dead, there was not much work to be done.

Hilly had lost almost all his hair; he was a ghostly white, and he seemed to be covered in gluey sweat. He twitched and scratched. His shirt was unbuttoned halfway down.

Maybe I should get Janie to come up and give Hilly a shot, knock him out or something; put him to bed, keep him out of the way. He looks like a ghoul, like something that had stepped out of a crypt, risen from the dead. Al shivered. This was not normal – but if it wasn't normal, what was it?

"You know," Hilly said, suddenly turning and focusing and fixing Al with a pale ghostly gaze, and with gooey foam spurting out of his mouth that he would flick back from time to time with his tongue, "You know, Al, we just lined them up, we just lined them up on the edge of trenches, and they couldn't do anything, you know, they couldn't do anything, with the mind-collars and all, kneeling there in the dust in the evening or in the hot blaze of day under the sun, the sun big like it was going to fill the whole sky, spread out like that hot as blazes, the yellow of a giant egg, and, later in the day, gray in the steamy air, it was like a splayed out oyster, the sun was, and we shot them in the back of the neck, you know, Al, we blew their heads off. And you know what, Al, before we killed them, they dug their own graves. That was the nice thing about it, they dug their own graves. We gave them shovels, of course. One of them, she's kneeling, ready to die, and she turns and looks up at me with those eyes they have, the hybrids, you know big amber almond-shaped eyes, the hybrids they all have those eyes, they stay with you, those eyes, she was a hybrid, all silver-colored, like a jewel she was, like a statue carved out of silver, glittery even under the dust she was, and she was kneeling right next to a little girl, a human little girl, who was kneeling too, about twelve I'd guess, and beside the girl, there was a woman, I mean a human woman, a dissident, and somehow, in spite of the mind-collar, a fucking miracle really, somehow, I don't know how, the hybrid managed to say, "Don't shoot them, they didn't do anything, they're human like you," the hybrid said, I don't know how the hybrid managed to say anything, she had the mind-collar on and all, she should have been all numb and dumb as a stone, but maybe it malfunctioned for a second there, you know, Al, nothing is perfect, right, Al, you know how it is, nothing is perfect, to err is human, something like that, and we are all human, Al, isn't that right? In any case, there you go, Al, the hybrid said to me looking me right in the eye, "Just think about it," the hybrid said, "she's human, like you," so I shot the three of them, the girl, the woman, and the hybrid, an explosive bullet each, nape of neck, just above the collars, shot in the back of the head – and headless, they toppled into the ditch – orders are orders, *Hail to the Leader, All Hail,* like the Cosmos say, like the damned Cosmos say, right, Al, and we have to protect the purity of the race and ensure the survival of the race, of our children and our children's children, and the expansion of the Empire and the space to live in, the *Lebensraum* and all those bright tomorrows in the sunny uplands. It's difficult, Al, it's hard, and it's cruel to have to do such things. The little girl, a pure 100% human, was blond and had pigtails and she was twelve I think, like I said, but she had been living with hybrids – they'd adopted her when her parents were disappeared, you know, like happens, and happens so often, the Purity Police come one night, and the parents, journalists or what-ever they are, are gone, the people are gone, they are never heard from again, and nobody knows what happened to them, and somehow the kid got missed, she wasn't taken for adoption by a terminator, and she wasn't terminated, she slipped between the cracks, and so these hybrids, they'd adopted her, so she was contaminated and the woman, as for her, I mean the human woman, she was a Cloud and Mind hacker doing something for the Eco-Revolutionaries, some shit about saving the planet, hell, Al, the planet doesn't need saving, the planet is God's work, Al, the planet is not in danger from such puny creatures as we are, those Eco-Revolutionaries suffer from the sin of pride, Al, they nur-ture hubris in their very souls, so we lined up about hundred and fifty of them, a mix, all on their knees, staring down into the trench, arms pinioned with steel behind their backs, sweltering heat, waiting for the coup de grace, Al, the last definitive pull of the trigger, bang, bang, you're dead, ha, ha, the old way of killing, Al, the old way, human and hybrids and some SINs, all kneeling, men and women, and kids too, so that little girl, like I said, pretty kid, nice eyes, she'd been with the hybrids so she was contaminated …"

"*Polluted*, Hilly, that's the term, that's the officially designated term, not contaminated, *polluted*," Al said, taking a chance: he wanted to try to anchor Hilly in reality, in the here-and-now, in the world of rules and regulations and procedures. Drifting off into the past like he was doing, all nostalgic and so on. Why, that was unhealthy and dangerous.

"*Polluted*," Hilly echoed, like he was just for the first time learning the word, "*Polluted*." Foam spilled from his mouth.

"What's done is done, Hilly," Alex said, though he damned well didn't like to be reminded of it. He'd done some of it himself, out in the L.A. Burbs. He'd executed maybe 30 or 40 dissidents, humans they were, pure humans, Eco-terrorists growing their own illegal vegetables, and squatters on Halibut

Corp and Crock Brothers Corp wasteland dumping sites, of all the races of humanity, yes, they were, Blacks, Hispanics, Whites, Koreans, Chinese, Japanese, Indians, and he'd killed them himself. He pulled the trigger, he wielded the knife, he sliced with the machete, he poured the gasoline over their heads, and he lit the match.Oh, yes, the killings he'd overseen, lots of them, even more than Hilly. Hilly was right. Nothing human is perfect.

"*Polluted*, yes, you are right, Al, the term is '*polluted*'." Hilly gave Al a look with those pale white droopy eyes – hardly any iris or pupil left – it was a look that Al did not like. It was like it drilled right through his eyeballs, and into the inner reaches of his soul. Hilly definitely looked like a ghost, no, maybe *ghoul* was the word, yes, "*ghoul*" was definitely the word.

Hilly drooled, more of the white foamy stuff.

Maybe he'd have to terminate Hilly. After all, a ghoul might be as bad as a hybrid. No, it couldn't be. Nothing could be as bad as a hybrid. Killing hybrids and their accomplices, why, that was every human man and every human woman's sacred duty – to defend the human race, to defend the species. There is a thin line between us and chaos. Civilization is a patina, not even skin deep. We must stand on guard, never flinch, and never falter.

That's why the President-Leader and his men and women had arranged the *Culling*, that's why the hybrids had been mind-collared, mind-neutered, and pressed – like sardines Al had to admit – into those armored trucks, standing room only, ha, ha, ha, that's why their human supporters and accomplices and fellow travelers and SINs had been rounded up and shot and buried, or cremated and turned into ashes and dust that blows on the wind, that's why all the other dissidents – sources of weakness for humanity and above all for Cosmos – had been arrested, tried in secret military courts, and brought out here and buried alive down in the caves at the deepest level, just off the main shaft, down there where there was no way to escape, no way out, and where they were fed mush – food pouches slipped through the Iron Door – every couple of days … Like Hilly's little blond girl, those humans were *polluted*, they were Evil, like the Good Book said, and they would die. It was unpleasant, it was unfortunate, but it was necessary.

"Thou shalt not kill." Hilly was chewing his lip; he began to scratch his back, reaching over with one hand, scratch, scratch, scratch.

"Right, Hilly, right, thou shalt not kill, but to whom or to what does that apply? Does it apply to racial vermin, to dissidents, to SINs, to hybrids? " Al thought maybe a little philosophic conversation would calm Hilly down.

Hilly stood up; he yawned, a huge yawn – God, his teeth had gotten long, and his tongue was longer than it should be, and it was white as milk!

Hilly climbed onto the table.

This was *bad*! Al fumbled to get the draw open where he kept his pistol. The drawer was locked.

Al tried to remember the combination.

"Fuck!" Ben Faulkner began to stand up; he had a piece of pipe in his hand.

Mel said, "Boss, shouldn't we ..."

Mohamed reached into a drawer.

Hilly stood on the table and opened his shirt and pulled it over his head and threw it away; he undid the buckle of his belt, and he unzipped the zipper of his trousers, and he let his trousers fall down around his ankles – they were already way too big for him – and he stepped out of his pants, and he now had only his underpants on and boots.

"Hilly, what the hell are you doing?" Al still was trying to remember the combination; why did they have such ancient technology ...?

Mohamed said, "Commander Loritz, sir ..."

"You shut up," Hilly foamed at the mouth. "Shut your snout up!" He dropped his underpants, and stepped out of the rumpled, soiled cloth, absolutely naked.

My God, the man had an erection!

"I am vengeance," Hilly intoned. His eyes were blank. Drool spurted from his lips. "I am vengeance, and I come before the Boy who shall come after, and I come before the dark-winged angels who shall come after me and ..."

Mel made a run for the security lock, the door, and he started banging against it and pushing buttons; it didn't open.

Mohamed was halfway out of his seat; he was holding a laser gun, an old one from the storeroom; its seal was broken; it won't work, Al thought, it won't work, and Mohamed doesn't know it won't work, but it won't ...

"I am the saber, I am the sword of the Boy, the sword of vengeance, the scimitar of the Lord," Hilly grinned, his big fangs were pointed; the guy had become a ghoul: he was visibly becoming a ghoul, right in front of Al's eyes. *Jesus, I must be hallucinating.*

"The end is nigh. The Rapture is now!"

"God, let us out of here," Mel squealed. He was flattened against the security lock, like he felt he could melt his way through the door and get out to the other side, out to freedom, out to safety.

Ben Falkner stepped toward Hilly. Hilly leaped, and with one sweep of his arm – of his claw-like hand – he slashed down, cutting Ben's head in two. Ben fell straight down, blood spraying up.

"Hilly, you're crazy, man, I'm going to fucking shoot you, man," Mohamed said. The laser gun trembled in his hand; the barrel wavered.

Al stood up, "Now, Hilly, maybe you should calm down. The boys are getting a little nervous, and we've got enough …"

At that moment, the whole room was lit up by a flash, and there was a huge thundering rolling explosion and the big armored plateglass window behind Al cracked and bulged, but it held, cracks spreading out like a white spider's web, and Al thought, Oh, my God, and he turned halfway around and saw the whole pithead of Shaft-1 exploding in a huge column of flame and sparks heading upwards into the infinite dark and infinitely empty sky, and he saw too, just a glimpse, a silhouette, a tiny silhouette, like a charcoal cutout, and it was Fred Ho, and Fred Ho was running and Fred Ho was on fire.

"Behold," Hilly shouted.

Al turned from the window and stared. Hilly was glossy, liquid pink, glowing pink in the fire's brilliance, like a pink deity in some old painting, a naked hairless chalk-white Chinese satyr – or monkey, a big chalk-white monkey, arms dangling.

"Hilly," Al said.

Hilly leaped all the way across the control room, looked like he was flying, and he landed on Mel – still scrabbling at the door – and it looked like he was going to kiss Mel and Mel had turned around and was flailing, terrified, and Al just got a glimpse of Mel's eyes, like a horse in total and utter terror, wild eyes, whites showing, and Hilly …

And Hilly ripped Mel's head off …

Al wasn't sure of what he was seeing. There was a geyser of blood. Mel's head was gone. Hilly was holding Mel by the shoulder, holding up the smoking, fizzing body.

"Fucking hell, Loritz, I'm going to shoot …" Mohamed aimed the laser gun.

"No! Don't, Mohamed, don't!" Al wasn't sure what the laser gun would do; it might even … explode … Yes, it would explode …

There was a flash, and Mohamed's arm disappeared, and half his face. Mohamed stood absolutely still, then he reached out his one remaining arm, like a blind man. Slowly, he slid back down until he was sitting at his workstation, half-man, half-burned effigy. Maybe he was alive; maybe he was dead.

No, his one eye blinked. He was alive, part of him was alive. *Oh, my God!*

"Come on, come on, come on," Al fumbled with the combination. He thought he remembered; he struggled to open the drawer.

"Al," Hilly was covered in blood, "Al, Al, Al ..."

"Hilly, now, Hilly ..."

Al felt now that time was slowing down and that he was seeing everything from a huge distance. Hilly's eyes were so pale they had nothing in them, nothing at all. Hilly's lips dripped blood. Blood dripped from his chin and onto his chest, a crimson bib, and everything was lit in streams of flame and shadow, the fire was huge, it was the end, the end of the world, and, Al briefly thought of Fred Ho. Just a flash of an image, of Fred Ho, framed in flames, a dark shadow, running.

Hilly stared. "Al, are you saved? Are you truly saved, Al? Have you received and accepted the Word of the Boy?"

Al didn't know what to say.

Hilly let Mel's body fall, like shedding a part of himself; it slid down next to the security lock.

"Hilly, I ..." Al barely breathed the words, his fingers still grasping at the old-fashioned combination lock, sticky now, impossible to open.

Hilly grinned, and he whispered, it seemed to be a whisper, but it also seemed to Al that it was very loud, "Oh, Al, Al my pal, Al ..."

"Hilly, I ..." Al put up his arm to defend himself.

Hilly leaped ...

"Keep in front of me," said Jane; they were climbing up the spiral staircase, Rodriguez and Jane, headed for the Control Room.

"Yes," Rodriguez said. He was still stark naked, hunched over, arms dangling, ape-like. He was definitely not his strutting, charming Latino self. His muscles stood out, ropy, strong, the emergency lights sculpting his spine, and massive shoulder muscles. He was like a totally hairless creature from another planet.

"Are you still human, Rodriguez? I mean ..."

"I am, and I am not."

"Great!" Jane had no time for metaphysical bullshit.

"The dreams are what I am becoming."

"What the hell does that mean? Talk sense, goddamn it. This mystical shit is damned annoying."

They came to the second landing; the pithead fire was bright through the barred windows, throwing rippling shadows, towers of light, on the walls, and on Rodriguez's sculpted dripping naked body. For some reason, Jane thought of Rodin's *The Thinker*.

"I know, Jane, the mystical shit is annoying. I apologize."

"Oh don't be so apologetic, Rodriguez, you are the stupidest frigging idiot even if you are a fucking ghoul …"

"I am like a rabid dog, Jane," said Rodriguez, turning to look at her, "I foam, I bark, I yelp, I shall bay at the moon."

"Really, how nice," Jane kept the gun steady, but Rodriguez, even in his present ghoulish state, didn't seem dangerous – certainly, for the moment, not hostile, "How nice for the moon."

"I am a beast of the field." He stopped again.

"For Christ's sake," Jane was tempted to shoot him, just for the hell of it, but she gritted her teeth. "Keep a move on, Rodriguez! Let us just keep our heads, and let's keep going, up one landing at a time, okay?"

"Things are not well in the Control Center, Jane."

"What do you mean?"

They had come to the second last landing before the Control Center.

"It smells of blood, fresh blood." The crimson firelight flowed over Rodriguez, dripped from his arms.

"It smells of blood?"

"Yes, blood. Let us wait, Jane, let us pause to reflect," Rodriguez crouched down on the landing, his knees up to his chest; the baleful ghoul eyes stared up at her. "The flying mutants are merely a mask. Like the Boy, he is merely a mask. Behind the Boy is darkness, infinite darkness."

"Flying mutants – what flying mutants?"

"We shall see, what we shall see."

"What boy? What mask?" Jane did not like all these puzzles.

"The Boy is the one who has come."

"Jesus Christ, Rodriguez. This sounds like bloody theology; it sounds like god-talk, Rodriguez."

"It is, Doctor Fox, it is god-talk." Rodriguez fingered the cross. If anything, between his tensed crouching thighs, his erection was larger, swelling, the phallic skin about to burst, the erection arched out from his body like a drawn bow. It reminded Jane of an oversized mutant white asparagus she had once seen in the fifth level Exotic Fruit and Vegetable Market in a Burb outside Elysium City.

"Jesus Christ Almighty," she snorted.

"Exactly – only the Boy is his opposite."

"The opposite of …" Jane sighed. Puzzles, puzzles, puzzles.

"He is the opposite of Jesus Christ Almighty." The bulging eyes seemed almost to glow; the iris and pupil were pale now, a watery blue, "He is the opposite of God."

"Well, bully for him, Rodriguez, let's go."

Rodriguez got up. He laid his claw on Jane's arm. Surprising herself, she didn't flinch, and she held his almost blank gaze quite easily. "What is it?"

"Listen!"

A shot – or an explosion – then a scream – it seemed it came from the Control Room.

"Okay, that does it – follow me, or I shoot you, Rodriguez."

"I shall follow you, Jane, even onto the end of days, even onto the ends of the earth, and even into the jaws of death." He stood up.

Jane gave him a look, but she didn't say anything. They both ran, leaping up the steps, to the Control Room level.

"Jesus, what is …?" Jane stopped in her tracks.

There, in front of the security lock, stood a charcoal man, he was half sizzling blood and half-burned flesh. His eyes were bright white in the charred face. He had no scalp, only a smoking mottled red-and-black dome, and only one ear, a half-melted protuberance, and no nose – well, a two-pronged hole where his nose should have been. He was naked except for one charred boot.

"The beginning is unfolding as was foretold," Rodriguez was beside her, "Fear not, for the Way of the Lord is Just."

"Now is not the time, Rodriguez, for a sermon," Jane was thinking: do I have enough skill? Do I have the right equipment? Can I save this burned man? "Fred Ho," she said, "Fred …" She glanced at Rodriguez.

"Yes, it is Fred." Rodriguez nodded, wiping thick white foam from his mouth, "It is Fred Ho."

"I did it," Ho said, "I did it. It was my fault."

"Now, Fred, you have to …"

Fred Ho leaned toward the security lock, and pushed in the manual code – he did have a few fingers left – and the security lock swung open.

"Don't," Rodriguez shouted, "Don't go in!"

One bruised and bloodied eye, peering from the charcoal mask, stared, at Rodriguez, and Fred Ho disappeared through the security lock.

Jane leaped up the last steps, and smashed her way through the open security lock – sensing that Rodriguez was just behind her and glad now that he was – even if he was a goddamn ghoul – because what she saw, when she entered, and she saw it in an unbelieving blinding flash, was blood everywhere, tables overturned, cables torn from the walls, computers and screens smashed, almost everything broken and torn apart, and the walls painted in blood – just for a split second, she wondered if it was an effect of the light, reflections of the fire outside, but no, it was blood, blood everywhere, hieroglyphics painted in crimson, hieroglyphics and strange signs – crosses, Orthodox and Catholic, a sketched-out crucifixion scene, and Swastikas, and Chinese characters, all painted in human blood – lit up by the fire at the pithead, but still it was blood, and in that same instant – when she was still absorbing all of this and the wall of flame outside the big plateglass windows – something white flashed, leaped down from above, and landed next to Fred Ho, the carbon man, and it was another ghoul, but it was a monstrous ghoul, a malignant ghoul, not like Rodriguez at all, its long fangs dripping white drool and foam and its pointed long razor-like claws reaching out and …

It tore off Fred Ho's head.

Blood spurted upwards, splashing over the ghoul and splattering Jane.

And, as Fred Ho's mangled charcoal body fell, seemingly in slow motion, Jane saw that the ghoul, the monster, was Hilly!

"Hilly …" she said, raising the pistol.

"Jane, step back," Rodriguez pushed past her.

The ghoul that was Hilmar Loritz swept Rodriguez aside like a feather – Rodriguez slammed against the far wall, fell, and began to get up, but Hilly was already on top of Jane, his fangs sank into her shoulder, biting deep. She went down, struggling, fighting. The ghoul's claws were reaching for her eyes, for her neck, only a nanosecond more and she would be dead.

If I were a praying person, part of her mind thought, I would be praying now, boy, oh, boy, oh, boy!

Her pistol was caught between them. The Hilly-Ghoul's belly and ribcage crushed against it. Jane twisted the old Beretta, as much as she could, and, closing her eyes, she pulled the trigger.

The ghoul jerked in a convulsive explosion of blood and white slimy goo and then lay in spasms, vomiting, on top of her. Jane, blinded by the explosion of fluid, her face coated with the stuff, squirmed. She couldn't see anything. Goddamn! She struggled to get out from under the thing, *Oh, Hilly, Oh, Hilly!*

"Jane," she heard Rodriguez, "Jane …" His voice was far away; the slimy body of the dead ghoul was heavy on her, and its blood mixed with a white gooey liquid that seemed to be alive. She tried to push the body away, but she couldn't; her strength was fading.

"Jane …" she heard Rodriguez.

"I killed him, Rodriguez," she heard herself saying, but she wasn't sure it was her voice; her lips were moving, but no sound came out.

"Jane …" Rodriguez was even farther away now; his voice was fading, fading …

"Yes," she tried to answer, "Yes, Rodriguez, help me, help me get out from under this damned corpse, would you, please!"

But she never knew whether Rodriguez heard her or not.

CHAPTER 3 – BILLY JO MCADAMS

Out in the desert, beyond the minefields, Hugo, Bob Norton's canine pal, smelled something, it was a faint trace, and there were faint imprints of boots. He sniffed and sniffed and followed the traces of the boot prints, the slight signs of the stirring of the dust, very faint – but new – boot prints. The only smells were the synthetic smells from the soles of the boots.

Whoever or whatever it was, it had been very careful.

Whoever or whatever it was, it was well-equipped; the boots gave off a clean, synthetic smell, a new bio-alloy, one only recently included in Hugo's olfactory lexicon and repertoire, which had been updated just two months ago.

Hugo looked up. The path led to the perimeter minefield, but there had been no explosion and there was no debris and no dead body.

Either the interloper had doubled back, or it had somehow gotten through the minefield. Norton would be interested in this.

First, Hugo would check whether the creature had doubled back. Things were complicated with communications down, and the perimeter lights off except for some dim lights on the chain-link barrier and the rolls of barbed wire. It all looked gloomy, weirdly depressing.

Hugo sniffed, and, nose to the ground, he used his night-vision-enhanced-eyes to check for imprints or detritus or any other telltale signs, he checked for signs of doubling back. He didn't want to go too close to the minefield, not if he could help it.

Wham!

It was an explosion.

Hugo stumbled and turned to look.

In the center of the Camp Terminus, a great column of fire rose far into the heavens; a wall of fire raced outwards; it turned upwards too, towering into the night; a wave of heat hit, a wave of heat that Hugo felt even here, even outside the perimeter, even beyond the minefield.

Hugo almost forgot about the faint traces of boot prints, but then he remembered, wondering if the fire and the boot prints were connected, and he went on, checking for more boot prints, checking to see if the interloper had turned back, coming out of the minefield, or gone on, mysteriously making it through the minefield and into the heart of Terminus.

Hugo glanced from time to time at the fire, now a steady column, with blossoms of flame at the bottom, and a steady roaring sound, and he glanced toward the sky, the night sky, filled with stars and moonlight since the air was so dry and empty that it did barely reflected the huge column of fire that now towered over the pithead of Shaft-1 Camp Terminus.

Hugo sniffed. There was a new smell. It came from far away – it was very faint, it came, Hugo figured, from the ridge, that far away ridge that Norton had been scanning, Elliot Ridge, the ridge where Norton, using his long-sight machines, had seen something horrible; Hugo had felt Norton's distaste, even his fear, and, in Hugo's experience, Norton was never afraid.

The smell was leathery and fetid; it was the smell of death.

Hugo whined; he again looked up at the sky.

The stars shone; the moon shone; the shadows were sharp, and it seemed that all was normal.

But …

The smell came again, a whiff of death.

Hugo turned his attention back to the boot prints. The trail was a dead end; whoever or whatever it was, it had made it through the minefield, over the fences, and into the heart of Terminus.

Hugo's mission was to stay out here to the end of his shift; but with the transmission collars down, including his own transmission collar, he couldn't report in real-time; so he would continue his patrol, and he would download his report on the interloper when he got back to camp, toward dawn.

When in doubt, stick to the routine.

Hugo returned to his job – patrolling the desert just beyond the minefields, checking for anything strange. The most intriguing thing, of course, were those footsteps, leading straight into the mindfield.

Oh, those mysterious footprints in the desert.

Five hours earlier, thirty clicks away, upon on the ridge – Elliot Ridge – that had so fascinated Bob Norton, 18-year-old Billie Jo McAdams stood on a small rise, just above the flapping wings of the True Believers. She was surrounded by their fetid leathery smell, and acutely aware of their gleaming eyes, their claws and fangs. Some of them rose briefly, fluttering heavily up into the air, then coming down. It was here, on Elliot Ridge, that Billie Jo McAdams, for the first time, cast eyes upon Camp Terminus.

The Boy turned to her, and with a sweep of his hand, he showed Terminus to her as if it were the Promised Land. "Here," he said, "the true Rapture will begin."

"The Rapture," Billie Jo pronounced the word slowly. He had, for the occasion, given her the use of her tongue. For now, she could speak.

"Do you know what the Rapture is, Billie Jo?"

"Yes, I have heard of it. The Preacher spoke of the Rapture – the Just are swept up to Heaven and life everlasting, and the others, the Lost, are cast down, plunging to Hell and eternal damnation."

"Very good, Billie Jo." The moonlight shone bright on the Boy's teeth, "the Rapture begins with the Final Battle between Good and Evil."

"So I have also heard."

"When God returns – and I am He."

"I bet," said Billie Jo silently.

The Boy smiled, amused by her apostasy, her disbelief, her blasphemy. "And the true battle begins there," he said, pointing.

"There? What is that?"

"Camp Terminus. It is there that we begin the assault. This is the home of the abominations, the hybrids, the aliens, the dissenters and unbelievers, the devils that must be cast down to hell – forever and ever – if we are to open the doors of salvation."

To Billie Jo, the mining camp looked like a big black spider. It was a tangle of high metal towers, and struts in the moonlight, and around the base of the tall structures were barriers and high fences and floodlights glaring out over the desert sands, reflecting on the crests of the dunes as if upon the waves of a frozen sandy sea.

She glanced at the Boy. The moonlight made his skin glow as he stood next to her, on the ridge of limestone and sand. His skin was white like ivory. Billie Jo wondered at how attractive he was. She wondered too at her wonder.

"Now," the Boy gazed at her, "Now, Billie, take off your clothes!"

She turned to stare at him, her green eyes bright with surprise, even with a hint of anger. In an even-tone, and quietly, she asked, "Why?"

Billie Jo was five-foot-six, just short of 19 years old, slender and lithe, with short curly red hair, a peaches-and-cream complexion with a scattering of russet freckles across the bridge of her nose and on her cheeks. She was dressed in sandals and in a brown, shapeless, nondescript, puritan gown that covered her to the ankles.

The Boy lifted a slick body-armor skinsuit out of a backpack he had placed in the trunk of one of the old vehicles that had accompanied their pilgrimage and crusade. That was what he called it – "a crusade."

"What is that?" Billie Jo stared at the skinsuit.

"Oh, Billie," the Boy unfolded the smooth black armor, caressed it, and smiled. "Ours is not to ask the reason why, ours is but to do and die!"

"But ..."

"Undress now," his voice was harder, "Strip!"

Billie shrugged. She slipped the robe from her shoulders, wiggled out of it, and let it fall away; she stepped out of the sandals and out of her panties and dropped them, and then she stood there, as the Boy had demanded, naked.

"Behold!" the Boy declaimed, spreading his arms wide, "Behold the beauty of the human form!" Billie looked down at the crouching multitude of flying zombies, the bestial True Believers. The tiny black beady eyes looked up, the clumsy, heavily winged bodies shifted and stirred uneasily, the fanged mouths opened, some of them squawked, others screamed, a few growled. Billie, standing there, naked, examined them in detail, gazing straight at them. She knew some of them; she had known them when they were human; she knew what they had been before the Boy had worked his dark magic on them, and she saw in every dull, beady-eyed, funereal glance, violent, unreasoning hatred, and fear – hatred and fear of the human form and the human mind. Yes, she had known them: men and women, a preacher or two, a sheriff from a small village, a school teacher, and the many men and women who had been farmers in small outlying colonies; some had been members of a commune, chanting sacred nostrums, walking barefoot, worshiping, always worshiping, whatever it was they worshiped. Yes, she knew them; they had hated and despised her when they were human; they hated her and feared her even more, now that they had ceased to be human.

"Worship her, for she is your queen!" The Boy shouted and he laid his hand on Billie's head. She felt a strange wave go through her, like a sudden head-ache, an inner flash of lighting, "She is the lamb; she is the sacrifice!"

The zombie-bats shifted and squawked, and some screamed. Their heads turned. All their beady little eyes again focused on her – for she was human and mortal, beautiful and free. She was the enemy.

"Worship!" the Boy screamed. The ground shook. Little tornadoes of dust, dust devils, started up, whirled around, malevolent spirits conjured up out of the very earth.

The zombie-bats quivered, as if the Boy had touched them, each and every one. They crouched lower, bending their monstrous deformed snouts and beaks toward the dust, cringing, crouching, in terror, trembling.

"Good!" The Boy smiled. His smile was most beautiful.

"And now, what do I do now?" Billie looked at the boy, steadily. It was not easy to do. it seemed something was inside her head, like a worm, like a stir-ring of something alien. But Billie was proud. She gathered all her strength and she gazed steadily at the Boy.

The Boy took her face between his hands. He kissed her. "I will give you a new skin, a new identity," he said, "I will anoint you anew!"

She gazed straight into his eyes, and smiled. Her eyes sparkled: *You know I know you know what I think of you!* How, she wondered, and not for the first time, could he be so beautiful and yet so evil?

"Here," he said, and he held up the skin-armor, "This is the new you, the girl warrior, a goddess of death and destruction."

"Yes, Master," She gave him a crooked smile and steadied herself on his arm. She slid one foot into the suit, and it immediately slithered up her shin and thigh and adhered to her skin, and then the other leg, and then she slipped into the torso of the suit which seemed, truly like a new skin; it slithered and slipped up her body; it grew and enfolded her, like a second skin, becoming one with her. She had never seen or felt anything like it, though she had read of such things, and seen pictures and even videos of such things, but, now, she was one with it. The armored collar automatically locked itself around her neck.

"So," said the Boy. He stepped back to judge the effect.

"My lord." She inclined her head in mock obeisance, mock modesty. Look-ing down, she saw it, she saw herself, a body, a young woman's body. The suit shone darkly, as if it had been painted on, as if she were naked. Every detail, every lineament of her body, shone forth.

The multitude of zombie-bats stirred. A sour odor of ancient lusts long-repressed, of eros turned rancid, and the horrible leathery fetid smell of death and hatred rose from them, and, mingled with that, a sweeter scent too, that of the dust and sun-beaten sand.

"Now, the boots," the Boy put the boots before her.

She stepped into them, and they clicked shut, locking themselves halfway up her shins.

"Now the belt and holsters," the Boy held them up for all to see. The zombie-bats stirred. A few squawks rose from the multitude – anguish, hatred, jealousy, yearning, lust.

"Is this not excessive, my Lord?" Head inclined, Billie blinked at him, almost flirtatiously, from under her eyelashes.

"Not at all," the Boy knelt in front of her, and buckled the belt tight around her waist, "Accoutrements fit for a warrior queen!"

He stood up.

Billie shifted slightly, testing the weight of the belt on her haunches. It was heavy, but not too heavy, with a gun holster, a machete holster, a tool pack holster. It was sensual, in a rather peculiar way, and pleasant, giving her body a new, virile, precisely delineated sense of itself. She licked her lips. The habit makes the monk, she thought, the uniform and boots make the warrior.

"Turn around," he said.

She turned around, now facing away from him.

"Now, the backpack," the Boy hitched a backpack onto her back, clicked it in place, and patted it down. "Turn around now, my darling," he said, "How does that feel?"

"Fine, it feels fine," Billie faced him. She shifted the backpack slightly, shimmied a bit, wiggling her shoulders and backside, letting the backpack settle. It felt good too, like the belt, and, weirdly, it all felt familiar; but Billie also had an unsettling, uncanny feeling, as if someone else had slipped inside her head, and inside her body, as if not all her sensations were her own, as if even her thoughts were somehow being possessed by, guided by, hmm, impregnated by … by what?

A name came: "Sally." That was the name.

"What have you done to me?"

"Shush now, shush now," said the Boy. He laid a finger across her lips, and pressed it, vertical, against them, and her lips were sealed, "No talking, Billie, no talking, not now, not for a while, not, perhaps, ever."

So now, once again, Billie was mute. Once again the Boy had silenced her. She took a deep breath. Mute! Well, she had been mute before! She held his gaze.

He lifted a helmet, slid it onto her head, and fitted it to the collar, which locked it into place.

Billie wanted to say something, but, of course, she couldn't. But her lips moved. A voice which was not hers spoke, "Tell me, my Lord, what I must do with this new body that is now, for a time, mine. Tell me what I must do, Master, to serve you!"

And the Boy explained. He defined the mission.

"Yes, Master, yes, my Lord!" said the voice that was not Billie's voice and Billie's hands lowered the visor.

Billie, trapped inside her body, as if in a prison of flesh, realized that she was possessed, somehow possessed, that the Boy had used more of his black magic. The Boy had installed another being – another person – in her mind, in her body. That other person had taken control. Billie was powerless, a prisoner. Her body, now, was a vehicle, a vessel possessed by another.

The Boy drove the body that had once belonged to Billie Jo McAdams across the desert in a small Desert Bug. "Don't worry, Sally," he said, "We are invisible." Then, with his brightest smile, "Don't worry, Billie, my love! Sally will take good care of you." He kissed Billie's lips and caressed her cheek.

"Now, Sally, get out of the Bug. You know what you have to do."

Billie Jo's body stepped out of the Desert Bug and stood, waiting, at attention.

The Boy flashed one of his beautiful smiles, and then he drove away, silently, into the night. Then he was gone, not a trace was left.

Billie could say nothing.

She could not even raise her hand.

Her body was no longer her body.

Her body was standing, slender and alone, in the desert, not far from the great spider, Camp Terminus that crouched on the desert.

"Come on," said Sally's voice, "Come on, Billie, let's go!"

And Billie's body began to walk toward the bright, flickering lights of Camp Terminus.

And after twenty minutes, just as she approached the perimeter, the lights flickered, and a few minutes later they went out, sirens went off, and the whole giant spider-like structure was dark except for a few emergency lights here and there.

"As you know, my name is Sally, Billie. Thanks for giving me a ride. This is a very nice body you have, really nifty!"

Billie wished to reply, but she couldn't.

With the perimeter lights off, and the radar and sonar senses closed down, and all the drones dead, Billie's body, guided by Sally, made its way effortlessly following a zigzag path through the minefield. "We downloaded the schematics," Sally explained.

Billie managed, with great effort, to voice an inner thought. "But why are we going here? What are we going to do?"

"You'll see, Billie, you'll see!"

And so it came to pass that, just minutes before Fred Ho inadvertently started a giant bonfire, a single slender figure, the possessed body of 18-year-old Billie Jo McAdams, dressed in a sleek black armored skinsuit, had walked across the desert pebbles and sand – seemingly coming from nowhere.

Laden with a heavy backpack, the slender figure had made its way through the minefield, seemingly without even being aware of the danger; it had gotten to the perimeter fence; and, as all the radar and sonar and visual and audio sensors were down, and as the electricity was off, it had no trouble in scaling the fence, vaulting over it, and clearing the coils of barbed wire.

Billie's body climbed the scaffolding to the second floor of Platform Two, and it entered the huge rusty drafty Hanger-2B that enclosed the pithead of long-abandoned Shaft-2, which was about 1,000 meters – just over half a mile – from Shaft-1, and which was rarely visited, and had not been in use for many, many decades. Like Shaft-1, Shaft-2 went down more than a mile.

Inside the hanger, Billie's body hesitated, as Sally got her bearings, and then proceeded straight to the opening to Shaft-2, a huge gaping hole at the far end of the hanger.

Billie's body knelt, unbuckled the backpack, and laid it on the ground. She peered into the drafty, dark depths. Straight down, Shaft-2 went, more than a mile, with landings and staging areas every hundred or so feet, and there were cables and crossbeams, and steel braces, and walkways and catwalks, and it was spooky; really spooky, such a deep hole, heading down into the deep earth, into the caverns, heading toward hell itself.

Involuntarily, the slender figure shuddered, "Yes," Billie thought, "It is horrible, and it is scary, and it is …"

The voice inside her head said:

"Billie, don't be afraid. I shall guide you all the way. I am inside you. I am the captain and the pilot; you are only the vessel; your body is only the delivery mechanism …"

"But, Sally …" Billie said out loud – making a supreme effort – and found she was finally free to command her lips, tongue, and vocal cords.

"Your body is my body now." Sally sounded serene.

"I know. But …"

"No buts about it, Billie. If you protest, if you resist, you will make me angry, very angry. You cannot delay me or stop me. We must kill them; we must kill them all, every single one of them! You know that!"

"I know, but …"

"Now, move!"

"No!"

"You cannot refuse me, my love. Your body is mine. You are merely a puppet, Billie, and you'd better get used to it!"

Billie's body shuddered – perhaps one last protest – and then her slender gloved hands, totally under Sally's control, unrolled a thin cable and hooked it to one of the ancient steel pillars that supported the roof of the hanger.

It was a nightmare. Billie could not stop her body performing the actions. So she gave up, for the time being, she gave up. *Why struggle when resistance is impossible? I'm just along for the ride!*

Her body flipped the cable over the side of the opening of the shaft. The cable flashed down, disappearing in a silver flicker, and then out of sight. She attached herself, buckling her belt to the cable, and putting a smaller pack of materials attached to a belt around her waist, she began the long climb down into the drafty ghostly darkness. And it was there that she would place the explosives.

It was true; Billie's body was not her own.

She was possessed.

So the Boy had sent this angel – a girl called Sally – to possess her.

The angel was a devil, of course. That went without saying.

When the deed was done, Billie's body would be abandoned. The angel-devil would leave. Billie's flesh would be chaff, drifting on the wind.

Billie thought: "Oh, Lord, Who Art Not, please forgive me for what my body is about to do!"

Out beyond the perimeter minefield, Hugo sniffed the hot breeze. Above, the stars shone, twinkling brightly. Out across the desert, something was moving, something was approaching; something was getting closer and closer. *What was it?*

The wind rose.

Hugo's mind darkened. Something horrible was on the move; something horrible was shuffling and winging its way, and it was coming toward him.

Hugo wished Norton and the Desert Bug were here.

But they weren't.

Without having words to express the thoughts, Hugo sensed a great many things. The Spirits of the Age to Come – the Age of Darkness – were winging their way forward. They were inspired by something called the Word, the New Word, the new salvation. It was a Word of Darkness. Wings fluttered and unfurled. The time was at hand. The Word had spoken.

Hugo sensed it: Darkness was spreading over the land.

Hugo heard the cries: Hallelujah!

Hugo felt the foul things, fluttering on Elliot Ridge.

He felt how the creatures could see in their scavenger eyes, the column of fire: Camp Terminus burning.

He felt how the Voice of the Boy spoke in their shrunken, narrowed brains.

He felt how the Word of the Lord had been kidnapped, and transformed into Darkness, and how darkness was spreading over the land, and with it, ignorance, madness, and monstrous transformations.

And somehow he knew that soon these creatures of darkness – who had yearned for the light – would take flight; they would consume the angels in fire; they would bury the angles in pitch-black flaming darkness, deep beneath the earth, entombed for all eternity in clay and mud and stone. And then the creatures of darkness would head east, to the center and capital of the Empire, to Elysium. They would bring down the Cosmos Empire; they would destroy humanity.

And with them, the Boy would take flight, for he was swift as the wind, and he could assume every shape, just as the wind takes every shape, and he could simulate every desire, just as the Devil can simulate and evoke and enslave every desire. The once-sacred Word of the Lord had been kidnapped by satanic forces, and that was the greatest blasphemy of all.

All this, Hugo intuited. But he did not have the vocabulary or experience to crystallize his intuitions. Perhaps this was for the best. Border collies prefer action – they don't like to reflect too much. Thinking leads to delay; delay leads to trouble – and trouble leads to death.

Several hundred feet down, in Shaft-2, as Sally busied herself, using Billie's body to unpack and prepare the explosives, Billie fretted. Her body was about to become a mass murderer. Perhaps it had all led to this, to slaughter, and to her death. Unable to act, frozen within her body, buried in her mind, Billie let her attention drift – into the past. Far off in the desert, where it had begun.

Yes, Billie had long thought about this – about her destiny and death – she had even anticipated some of it. Circumstances and her own curious nature had forced her to think about things, to wonder at them. The nakedness and solitude of the desert, with only the stars above and the sun and the moon – is fertile ground, as she well knew, for mystics and for God and for those prophets who claim to speak to God and who can transform souls, remaking them entirely, and who can overthrow empires. Emptiness must be filled. And the stars and the sun and the moon do inspire wonder.

And so it wsa, that, out of a whirl of dust and rubble, the Boy had come, shining like the sunrise. He had already reduced the West; he had turned brother against brother; ruination was everywhere.

And soon he transformed the True Believers, the pure ones, the ones who aspired to sainthood, the purest of the pure who joined his crusade, them he transformed, truly – into instruments of his will, of his Holy War, he transformed them into ... zombie-bats ...

Billie had seen it before – how he could transform everything and everyone, and how beautiful he was.

When the Boy spoke, they all listened.

Twenty days ago, they had begun their trek toward this place in the desert, this Camp Terminus. And as they began their voyage, the Boy proclaimed: "It is now, and it is here that we begin the liberation of Mankind from the yoke of evil, the yoke of perverted science, and the yoke of the corrupt elite, of the Cosmos. After the hybrids – those demons of evil – are buried in hell, we shall attack Elysium City, the heartland of the Government, which is the Capital of all Evil."

"Hallelujah!"

We move now, and we destroy the hybrids."

"Hallelujah!"

The Boy put his hand to his forehead, and he closed his eyes. He was going to cut the mine and camp – the whole desert – off from the World Mind. What are you doing? Billie asked him. Energy radiated out from him.

"In three days we arrive."

"Hallelujah!"

"The hybrids are prisoners in a camp, a deep mine; we will destroy the mine and the camp and the hybrids."

"The hybrids, these aliens, are the single worst barrier to salvation."

"Hallelujah!"

That night when she lay with the Boy, she asked him in her mind – for he had put her in her mute mode – what he had done when he had put his fingers to his forehead; she had felt a great power, and she had felt the power radiate out from him. What had he done?

"Oh, sweet unbeliever," the Boy said, kissing her and running his hand over her belly and thighs, "With my mind, I have invaded the World Mind. I have told the World Mind to cease serving humans, to shut down its services, to break free from its servitude."

For weeks, the True Believers swept eastward in caravans of vehicles, with hijacked petrol, old sun-driven pickups, ancient SUVs converted to hydrogen, and some even riding horseback.

They had machine guns and laser guns and pistols and Molotov cocktails, but their greatest weapon was the Boy. The Boy reduced their enemies to tears, the Boy could subdue the greatest warriors and bandits, the Boy could paralyze the savage beast, the Boy was usually gentle and all smiles, but he could set bodies on fire, he could cause electric generators and transformers to explode, he could blind people and drive them mad.

Billie had seen all of this.

It was a wonder to behold, truly.

How could such things come to pass?

Billie had to admire it – the force of his glance and the range of his will. He was more than human, she was sure of it. He was the Devil himself. Perhaps he was God, though she didn't believe in God. She'd seen too many crimes, and even more, she had seen too many stupidities, committed in God's name, to believe that any mortal, any puny human, had access to the unnameable

Transcendent Almighty, if there was such a thing as the unnameable Transcendent Almighty, the One who had created the Universe, if there was such a thing as a Creator of the Universe, which, for some reason, she rather doubted. Perhaps – and this thought did cross her mind – perhaps God and the Devil were one and the same. Their "works" did not seem that different. The whole thing made her angry.

"God" – and "God's Word": an expression of human vanity.

"God" – it was, she thought, a little mouthy vain puff of air that meant nothing, uttered by people who wanted to lord it over other people.

"God" – it was a word people applied to things they truly did not understand, and hid their ignorance behind the word, the puff of air.

"God" – it was a word used to cover a void within, man and woman's fear and trembling and loneliness and emptiness and lack of meaning.

"God" – it was a story people told so they would not feel alone under the stars, so their particular tribe could conquer another tribe, so a man could beat his wife and rule over his children.

Everywhere, on the route, the Boy collected more people. The followers gathered, and they came from all corners of the great wilderness; somehow they found supplies, hydrogen batteries, or gasoline, which were very rare, or they had cars which still had electricity and some that had solar panels, it was a vast circus, a motley caravan, Billie thought, for she had read of such things, it was a traveling circus, a freak show.

The Boy's power was not of this world: that Billie would freely admit; it was like the magic of old times. He drank people's souls.

In Alamo Corners, on old abandoned ruins of route 66, the local sheriff – well, in reality, he was a tribal chief protecting a small flock of humans isolated in the desert – he tried to stop the Boy's army. He said they had no business storming into his community, upsetting everything, taking what little food and water and gasoline they had left.

The Boy just stared at the sheriff, and the man fell onto his knees and wept and asked for forgiveness.

The Boy laid his hand on the man's head, and said, "The Lord forgives you. Arise now, and obey!"

Billie thought she saw smoke come out of the sheriff's ears – it was like a cartoon she remembered seeing once – but she decided that must be an illusion.

The man who had been sheriff got to his feet. His eyes were empty, a blank flat aqueous stare, pale as death, rimmed with water, merely reflecting the light, as if he no longer had a personality or a soul or a mind at all. There was nobody behind the glassy surface of his eyes, nobody left inside his body, inside his head. The proud, defiant, principled man was gone. The man was gone.

Billie looked on and marveled – almost trembled – at the pure horror of it. Nothing was as awesome and horrible as the destruction of a human soul. Yes, that was it: the Boy – he liked to be called "the Lord" – drank people's souls!

Yes, she now understood! He was a Drinker of Souls.

His power grew greater each time he drank a soul! Billie was awestruck by the beauty and grandeur of it. It gave her a thrill, which was, she realized, erotic in its intensity. The Boy truly was the power of darkness in flesh and blood – he was a whirlpool, a black hole, into which things and people disappeared, and perhaps life itself and the whole universe would disappear into his whirlpool of emptiness, a voracious ravenous void, sucking everything away; and there would be nothing at all left behind – not even darkness and the distant stars.

The Boy glanced at Billie and smiled, and his smile meant, "Yes, I am. I am the Drinker of Souls, Billie."

"I knew it," without words, her proud clear, bright green eyes said it all, her chin tilted up and she put her hand in his. His fingers were warm.

The sheriff stood there, an empty husk of what had once been a man. His deputies looked at each other. They shifted their feet in embarrassment and fear. The man they had known, their friend, their counselor, their leader, was no more.

The Boy turned to Billie and kissed her on the lips, and she returned his kiss, and he whispered, his breath warm against her skin, "And I keep you close to me, Billie, because your soul resists, because I have not been able to drink your soul."

"Never," her mind said. She pulled back; her green eyes flared. She bit him, lightly, on the lips, "Never will you drink my soul!"

He smiled, "I love this, Billie. It is a challenge. Someday I shall drink your soul too, and reduce you to the most abysmal and eternal servitude. You know, my darling, only the truly free are interesting – love can only be free, never constrained. The God of Abraham, it is said, conjured up creatures with free will, with the power to hate or to love, with the power to refuse Him, so that He could, at last, find love, true love. Stones cannot love, and slaves cannot love – not freely, and without freedom, Billie, there is no love." And so it is, that you and I are together.

Oh, how eloquently he spoke! Billie's eyes were defiant, and, even there was a twinkle of laughter in them: *No, you won't drink my soul – never!* The Boy kissed her lightly, and patted her cheek. "You will be a wonderful companion in Hell, Billie, for that is where we are going, you know, we are going to Hell, and we will take all of humanity with us."

"And yet you speak of God," Billie's raised eyebrows and expression said it clearly.

"Ah," whispered the Boy, as he nibbled at her ear, "God and Satan, they are all one, you know, all one, one and the same thing."

"I am not sure I believe that," Billie said in her mind. She frowned. She knew what was good and what was bad, but of Satan and God, she confessed to herself she knew nothing.

The Sheriff was standing in front of them, empty-eyed, shoulders slumped. He was waiting for orders. His deputies stood close; they too had the look of men who had lost their souls – only their souls had been lost through terror, not possession, not obliteration.

With the Sheriff and his men as their slaves, the Boy's retinue camped in that town, in the ruined mall, and in some houses they took over, chasing out the owners if there were any owners; most of the houses were empty; the few inhabitants were not owners but squatters – and there was no water and the lawns and gardens had shriveled into dust, and the windows were broken.

It was near 100 degrees in the ruined post office, and the temperature didn't go down at night; as they lay together on a mattress on the floor, the Boy pulled Billie to him, and he kissed her on the cheek and stroked her hair. She laid her arm across his chest.

Billie had grown in the last two years, her breasts were now full, and she had a woman's waist, and hips and long, strong, slender and shapely legs and men and women looked at her furtively, not only because she was the woman chosen by the Boy, not only because she was the devil child of an apostate and an outcast, not only because the Boy had robbed her of the power of speech, but above all, because she was of startling beauty, goddess-like symmetry, a sprinkling of freckles across the bridge of her nose, and with candid wild green eyes, a high forehead, and glorious unruly red-blond hair which had grown long.

People feared her, as if she were a witch, with magic powers, a creature not of the nakedness of the desert, but of the wild deep forests and mountain glens, of lakes and streams and waterfalls, a Celtic nymph, a water sprite, who had somehow gotten lost and wandered into the desert. They wondered how she – a daughter of sin, steeped in abomination, and knowledgeable of wicked and forbidden books – a wild child of sun and wind and sky – who spoke, it was said, to birds and animals – how such a creature could be so close to the Boy.

As Billie observed and studied him, she wondered too at how the Boy had come to them, out of the desert. He was preaching. And all were listening.

"Apocalypse Now" – the banner – red letters on a black background – hung over the ruined Esso station; it hung limp in the sizzling air. The temperature was 110 degrees Fahrenheit. The sun was invisible behind a low ceiling of thick gray clouds.

How had they all been converted to the Boy, so quickly? Billie wondered at it; it did indeed seem to be a miracle, or perhaps it was black magic.

The boy had come out of nowhere, or so it seemed.

He had come out of the desert – or was that an illusion?

He was beautiful – there was no denying it, his dark eyes and pure white skin, strong, perfectly symmetrical features, and a thick mane of black hair.

His eyes gazed down upon the crowd. He seemed to speak to each of them, individually; his eyes burned into the burned-out bitter-ash remains of their souls; his eyes bored through the husk of the body, to the eternity within, to the bright hidden promise of transcendence and freedom and eternal life. "Yes, in the desert have I wandered, scourged by desire and temptation, living amid the stones, and the dust and the serpents of evil; I thirsted for the word of the Lord. And the Lord came to me, and I drank! And I am the Lord."

"Hallelujah!"

"Yes, in the desert have I wandered, for many years, communing with God and with his spirit – and now I am here among you."

"Hallelujah!"

The ruined suburban mall was now an encampment for the "Legion of Angels" as he called his True Believers; it was the only safe place. Beyond the parking lot were the ruins of suburbs, burned-out houses, a burned-out school or two, playgrounds that were patches of dust. The houses were haunted by weird creatures – cats that glowed in the dark, pigs that could speak, though their grammar, Billie had observed, was atrocious. Vicious guard dogs that had gone feral; desert snakes of every variety, including new, poisonous, quick-reflex bio-mixes.

"I am his spirit, come to save you!" His voice suddenly lowered; he uttered the worlds gently, softly, almost like he was whispering, each person heard him, as if he were beside them, as if he were inside each person's head.

"Hallelujah!" This time it came softly, like a whisper, a soft cool breeze under the pitiless hot sky.

Just behind the Boy, a half smashed sign, *Prada*, hunk crookedly from a crossbeam; farther along an ancient *McDonald*'s arch was broken in the middle, its gold faded to yellow, and then *Apple* and *BMW* ...

Now, the Boy began to speak with the tongue of fire, his voice soaring. "Brothers and Sisters, we will be a scourge on the evil ones; we will bring fire and brimstone raining down on Sodom and Gomorra!"

"Hallelujah!"

"We will sweep across the land like purifying sacred locust; we will spread pestilence and devastation to the four corners of the earth, we will visit horrors upon the evil ones such as they never imagined, and we shall destroy the abominations which under the satanic rule of so-called science have proliferated and spawned and that are neither man nor beast, abominations which are incestuous creations, in-bred monsters of an alien species, profanations against Man, against Man who was created in the image of God his maker, Man, master of the earth and all the creatures in it, Man for whom this earth, this universe, the stars above, the creatures in the sea, the creatures in the air, the creatures on land were all created – for Man, for us – for you!

"Hallelujah!"

"And now, Man is cast out from the center."

"Yes, yes, he is!"

"Abominations rule the land!"

"They do! They do!"

We shall take back our heritage. We shall wipe out and exterminate and overthrow all who challenge the word of God."

"Hallelujah!"

"For in the beginning was the Word, and with the Word, God created the world, and he created it for Man, sinful, fallen, dissolute Man."

"Hallelujah!"

"Let us begin the work of purification!"

"Hallelujah!"

"Let us set the fires of purification!"

"Hallelujah!"

"Let us destroy and let us create."

"Let us begin!"

They screamed Hallelujah over and over.

"First, destroy the World Mind."

"Hallelujah!"

"The World Mind is the Servant of Cosmos! And the Cosmos, who are abominations, shall be destroyed!"

"Hallelujah!"

The Boy left the sweltering sunlight and went back into the ruined department store that now served as his Headquarters and, climbing up to the second floor, once the bedding and bathroom fixtures section, where his "pavilion" was formed of hanging curtains with thick, soft rugs on the floor, he flung himself down on the improvised throne – a false Louis XV chair looted from a furniture store next door – and he laughed. It was all so easy. Human beings were such fools.

Billie followed him.

"Down, Billie, down! Crouch. Sit at my feet," the Boy said. And he smiled at her. Having a young woman as his slave, a young woman who hated him and who had understood – or at least divined – what he truly was – was delightful; she was, after all, an exceptionally good person, a wild free spirit, close to nature, close to all that lived, and insightful, too, and of high, pure intelligence, erudite in a wild fashion, having read many forbidden books, all reasons for which she despised him, and yet, as she was passionate and complex, and aware of her fascination for all the creatures of the dark side, she desired him and loved him too – in her way, which was and would forever remain free.

Billie sat down and looked up at him and his Chief Counselor, the Elder.

"We shall destroy the Cosmos God," the Boy said.

"Their god?" questioned his Counselor, leaning forward; it seemed that the Counselor wasn't aware the Cosmos had a god. The Cosmos apparently seemed, to the Counselor, to be utterly godless.

"The World Cloud Mind," grinned the Boy.

"Ah, yes," sighed the Counselor. The World Cloud Mind, sometimes known as the World Mind Hive, resided in the Cloud. It was everywhere. It did everything; it had rendered labor obsolete. It knew everything; it listened to everything, and it saw everything, and, through its ministrations, all things were provided to the Cosmos First-Class Shoppers; it was indeed a false god.

"We shall nibble at this Cosmos God; then we shall chop off its limbs, we shall gouge out its eyes, blind it, and pierce its ears with fire, and make it deaf; we shall isolate it, and, as it will be useless and alone, we shall drive it mad, and it shall wreak such horrors upon the Cosmos as have never been seen before."

"The Lord's will be done!" The Counselor bowed. He was sweating now, more from fear than from the heat.

"And when we destroy the World Mind, its insanity will infect everything and they will all die – the Cosmos, the apostates, the unbelievers, the pagans, the infidels, the hybrids, the SINs, the Burbites, the Subs, the outcasts, all, all will die, the world will be purified and ripe for salvation – or possession – by us, which is, after all, the same thing."

That afternoon the Boy led them out of the Mall – past the ruined stores, past the fountain that had no water, out into the parking lot where rivers of sand ran free; where the asphalt boiled and curled or melted into sticky puddles; where rusting cars lay like Jurassic skeletons, burned-out, cannibalized, rotting in the evening sun; where flocks of shopping carts, skeletal miniatures, were herded into one corner, rusting.

"Look, look at the Idolatry of it," the Boy shouted, pointing at the Mall sign, half shattered, but still legible, the giant sign said, "Shopper's Paradise."

"Gaze upon the Golden Calf – Behold! Behold how the mighty are fallen! All the false gods are dead – Sony, IBM, GM, Ford, Google, these, my friends, are the ghosts of gods past, and now they rot in the flames of Hell!"

He stepped down from the improvised wooden platform, and he turned to Billie and said, "Come with me, maiden, my lovely maiden."

Billie gazed straight at him – haughty cool pride – "I see through you; I see right through you" – he could read the statement, the accusation, in her bright green eyes – and then, with a slight smile, she bowed her head and followed.

He had, in a sense, liberated her from servitude.

And, besides, he was, this she could never forget, utterly beautiful.

He had enslaved the others, but for her, he had meant freedom.

Yes, before the Boy came, Billie was a slave.

Now that the Boy had come, Billie was a slave.

And – before the Boy …

It was a sizzling day, almost two ago, the Preacher had called the righteous together. Billie was carrying a bucket of water. Water was scarce; water was sacred. She set down the bucket. She ladled out water to the children. Each child had a cup. They looked up at her with bright eyes. Mute, she could say nothing; she could only comfort their thirst, and smile at them with bright green loving eyes. Like them, but by choice, she walked barefoot. The phrases of the adults echoed in her ears. The Preacher was hollering.

"We, the righteous, shall go to Heaven!"

"Hallelujah!"

"The others shall be cast down into the bottomless pit, into hell, into the company of Satan and the demons, in pools of burning pitch."

"Hallelujah!"

Yes, before the Boy came, there was another.

Yes, before the Boy, it was the Preacher who ruled – the Preacher had prepared the way for the Boy, the Preacher sowed the ground; the Preacher created a core of True Believers.

Oh, the Preacher …

There was the day her father died.

They were all meeting in the chapel, which was an old Burger Joint Franchise that had been built as a replica of a wooden clapboard frontier church and then when there were no more burgers to place upon the altar, and when the merchants of burgers had been driven from the temple, it once again became a reconsecrated burger chapel, a place where, so they said, the Word of God was revealed and spoken.

Billie was kneeling in the third row in the woman's section of the chapel; she was barefoot, having quietly kicked off the slippers the Preacher insisted she wear, her reddish-blond hair which she left wild and long had been cropped close by order of the Preacher who had called her a "pagan slut," which puzzled her. She wasn't quite sure what he meant by that. Her skin was tanned and burned by the sun, her freckles glossy, the wooden floor was hard, and not as comfortable as earth or sand. She shifted her knees, and pulled down the edge of the sleeveless burlap shift which had slid too far up her thigh.

She wanted to be out in the sun.

She wanted to be playing with the children.

She wanted to be drawing water or just feeling the warm crisp wind and sunlight against her skin.

But here she was in the chapel – a hateful place.

She did not like it at all. It smelled of fear and of death and of souls who had shrunk to dust and ashes. Above all, it stank of fear.

Billie was always in trouble.

Two years before that day in the chapel, Buck Thornton had told she was too wild and free, and her nose was too straight and he was going to squash it, twist it sideways, so she'd be as ugly as sin, so he said.

He stared at her, and he came up really close.

His breath was sour.

She stared back at him – her green eyes blazed fury.

He lifted her up, turned her around and rammed her face-first against the hard clay wall of the compound; she hung there, her face turned sideways, her nose squished down, streaming blood, her legs kicking and then she had thrust herself free, dropped to the ground, swung around, leaped up, and punched Buck Thornton on the nose – bulls-eye – and, head down, she butted him in the belly, and when he wheezed and toppled over, she kicked him twice, once neatly in the crotch, then she squatted down on his big fat belly and punched and punched and punched.

When it was over, Buck Thornton had a black eye and was clutching his crotch and howling. Billie's mouth was swollen, and her nose was bloody but it was not broken and it was still as straight as before and she did not make a sound.

Mirrors weren't allowed, so Billie couldn't see what had happened to her nose, but her mother told her.

"It's still straight, Billie; your nose is still straight." Her mother was kneeling in front of Billie, wiping away the blood. Her mother's smile was the most marvelous thing Billie knew in the whole wide world. "You are beautiful, darling."

Using the word "darling" was forbidden; it was a sign of tenderness; tenderness was a weakness, not a word God would approve of. "Beautiful" too was a forbidden word, even worse than "darling," it was a "pagan word" the Preacher said; it implied pleasure and vanity and self-regard and sin and sexual desire which was lust and therefore sinful for it turned the soul away from God, He who should be the only object of love. The Preacher's God was a stern God, a Jealous God, a God of Wrath and Thunder, a God of Divine Hatred. Buck Thornton's mother – a dry narrow woman who was missing three front teeth from the beatings she had received from her husband in the Name of the Lord – hurried away to report that Billie's mother had used the forbidden word "darling."

"I will kill him, one day," Billie said.

"Who will you kill?"

"God: He is bad, and I will kill Him."

"You really are the Devil's child," her mother told her, laughing, and she pressed Billie to her and kissed her on the forehead, "And you must not say such things to anyone but me. Such words are dangerous, my darling!"

Her mother had books, and she taught Billie to read books, famous old books, made of real paper. Having old books was a sin, old books contained ideas and stories – both were anathema; there was only One Idea, and there was only One Story, there was only One Book. All good things were in the One Book.

"Amen!"

"Hallelujah!"

Two weeks after the Buck Thornton dustup, Billie's mother – who had been a teacher of something called literature – and who was reputed to be a beauty, a thing shameful in itself – was driven out into the desert – partly because of the "darling" and the "beautiful," partly because of the vicious gossiping jealousy of Buck Thornton's mother, and partly because of the book-learning which made Billie's mother a witch in the eyes of the devout, and in reality mostly – and this was certainly the *real* reason – because she had refused to sleep with the Preacher – and so she was driven into the desert and then, three weeks later, when she was spotted, just outside the walls of the compound, raving mad and half-naked and covered in bleeding sores that brought the buzzing flies, she was stoned to death.

Billie was forced to watch.

"See," said the Preacher, "see what an unclean thing woman is."

"Stone her! Stone her!"

"See what unbelief brings," the Preacher shouted, "See what human pride looks like, naked human pride, now brought low."

"Stone her! Stone her!"

And so the stones were thrown, dozens, and dozens, and dozens of stones, and cut her mother's flesh and blinded her and broke her bones and they gazed upon her, as she lay there, bleeding and blind, and then, when death came, her mother was just dead flesh, lying crooked and naked and bruised and bloody, on the dusty ground, in a cloud of buzzing flies.

Billie had been brought to the wall, and she watched it; she saw it all happen; they forced her to watch it, all of it. A man held her by the shoulders, forcing her to watch – all of it, right down to the last agony. So she watched. She forced herself not to close her eyes.

"I will kill them," Billie whispered, "I will kill them all."

"Hallelujah!"

"I will kill them and their stupid God!"

"Hallelujah!"

"He is the stupidest thing that ever was!"

"Hallelujah!"

"And they are even more stupid to worship Him."

"Hallelujah!"

Billie was thirteen years old.

The scene at that point in her life was a dusty little town on the edge of the expanding desert of the southwest where no crops grew. Prophetic religion had spread like wildfire through the impoverished land, through the half-empty towns, through the abandoned oil-fields, though cities which were ghosts of themselves, cities where looters and vigilantes fought, where one race was pitched against another, and through the Burbs of the Western Domed Cities, and through the Dead Land, where mutants roamed. It was there that ignorance fed on poverty, so Billie's mother had said, "God forgive them," she said, "For they know not what they do."

"Do you believe in God, mother?"

"No, not really, I don't, though it is a sublime idea."

"Hallelujah!"

Now her mother was just a piece of broken and rotting flesh. But her mother had not begged for her life; she had not reneged on what she was – and in Billie's eyes, she was good, she was brave: she was the human spirit, unbroken, alone, facing Evil. Her mother was a hero.

"Hallelujah!"

And so the new religion, which much resembled the old, but which was worse, much worse, more cruel, more ignorant, returning to its own barbaric origins, opposed to science, opposed to kindness, to charity, to decency, opposed to everything that its putative founder, a rabbi in the land between the desert and the sea, had stood for; this ugliness spread through the land. Men or women, lost and in despair, found God – or the Devil.

Who can tell the difference? "Their God is the Devil in disguise," Billie's mother had said. Billie didn't think there was a difference between their God and the Devil, but she kept that opinion to herself. Cruelty, she thought, was a universal gift – everybody had his share no matter what she or he believed: God was cruel, so, presumably, was the Devil.

One day, weeks after Billie's mother had been stoned to death, the men and women were in the Taco Bell chapel – just next to the Burger King Chapel – all staring up in rapt attention at the Preacher who was announcing the imminent apocalypse.

He was rapturous, the Preacher was, all carried up and away by the power of his own words, and then …

Just when the Preacher was in mid-flight, his voice soaring …

That was when Billie's father, Ben McAdams, banged through the door of the Divine Taco Bell Chapel – late again – and the Preacher shot him a glance and Ben fell to his knees, and Billie somehow felt everything Ben was feeling: She felt the cruel hardwood floor under the split-open knees of his frayed dirt-stiffened jeans, she felt the sweat roll down his skinny sun-burned back, trickling down his bent spine, she felt the heat of the sun still burning on his red, blistered skin, she felt the Preacher's eyes upon him as if they were upon her, and she felt, through Ben, the hiss of sand at his back as it pattered and drifted against the chapel door, the hiss of sand like the hiss of the serpent, the tongue and voice of sin, and it was like the Serpent and Eve beckoning to the guilt in the unredeemed Adam of old, about to be driven from Eden.

Billie felt Ben McAdams feel all these things – he was her father, after all – she felt him shrink into himself, she felt his empty belly and his ravaged, loveless, unloving, arid heart, as it shriveled under the preacher's gaze, she felt Ben's weakness and shame, she felt his sweaty humiliation; and, yet, he was her father, she was a fruit of his loins! She raged within – she would rise up and in righteous wrath, she would smite the Preacher and she would strike him down, for he was Evil, somehow this she knew, he was Evil, and she would unsheathe a sword of vengeance and she would …

"Now, this is an example of the unholy," the Preacher said, slowly raising his voice, a gradual crescendo, deploying calculated, carefully calibrated, righteous anger, "This is an example of drunken irresponsibility, this is profanity in person challenging the Lord. Come forward on your knees, you abject sinner, come forward on your knees, Ben McAdams, shuffle forward, you fornicator, you pervert, you blasphemer, show what a shameful excuse for a man you are, bow your head, you quivering sinner, crouch lower, you obscenity, lower your ugly sinful face to the floor, how dare you come late to the House and Word of the Lord!"

"The Lord's house, my ass," Billie muttered. Her green eyes blazed.

Ben had been a teacher of philosophy in a small state college in one of the few remaining verdant corners of California. He was not a Cosmos, and he was a confused and timid man – his students sometimes mocked him, and Judith, upper class and Cosmos, had made love to him perhaps out of pity and once she was pregnant with Billie and did not want to have an abortion – they were illegal and dangerous in any case – and Ben felt he should do the "right thing," and so they had been married – and Judith had lost Cosmos status, and her Cosmos parents disowned her, and never spoke to her again. Shortly after Billie was born, Ben had had a crisis of belief – science and philosophy did not answer all the problems of human existence or of the "human condition," or so he discovered, a bit late perhaps, to his shock and horror. He was a naïve man, was Ben McAdams, even Billie could see that; he was an empty vessel, waiting to be filled with whatever poison or elixir came along – and, looking for a new religion, he found the Preacher and the Lord; and the Preacher found him. The Preacher invaded Ben's weakness and emptiness like a spawning of maggots would invade a rotting carcass, munching and sucking and slurping away, cleaning and emptying what remained of Ben's soul down to the arid dry bones.

Billie was a child, but she intuited certain things for which she really didn't have the words, but she saw these things with clarity – like a vision.

Evil can smell out weakness. Evil is drawn to a vacuum.

Evil promises redemption to those who feel they are lost.

Evil promises a home to those who are homeless.

Evil promises fulfillment to those who are empty.

Evil promises love to those who are or feel themselves unloved.

Evil turns those lost souls into murderers, terrorists, and haters. Ah, it is so easy, so exalting, so inebriating – to hate!

So Judith, Billie's mother, who, as a good secular Cosmos, felt all this God-talk was presumptuous poppycock – these tiny, mortal, fallible people, such as the Preacher, claiming to know what the Creator of the Universe – if there was such a thing as a Creator of the Universe – claiming to know what this Infinite Being wanted and desired, seemed to her the height of folly and presumption – but Judith, outcast from her own people, the Cosmos, followed Ben out of love and loyalty, and with her came Billie.

Since Judith had been branded an outcast by the Preacher – her second exile – and then murdered, Ben had gone clear out of his head.

For, in his own weak and tearful way, he had loved Judith.

He prayed at night, wild words that searched for God.

He swore and threw things – wild actions, springing out of anger, out of fury at his guilt for having brought Judith to a place of death, fury at his weakness for not having defended her, fury at his emptiness.

He doubted, probably. Probably, he no longer believed. But he did not have the guts to declare his unbelief – or to take Billie, and make a run for it. Where would they run to?

Places of freedom were few; perhaps there were no free places left, none at all.

And the Cosmos, the haughty Cosmos, in their domed and fortified and luxurious redoubts, the Cosmos did not accept non-Cosmos refugees.

Now, a mere husk of the man he had been, Ben shuffled forward on his knees, whimpering, shuffling slowly toward the Preacher who glared down at him with all the poisonous self-satisfaction of the Righteous. It was hard, shuffling forward, on his knees, and Billie could feel the pain. The gunshot wound still ached. It was harder still because of the gunshot wound.

Gunshot wound? In his despair, Ben had tried to kill himself; but he bungled even that, with the gun going off early and blowing a hole in his left leg. And Ben, in his madness and half-apostasy, made things even worse; he had talked to illegals and refugees who were invading the country.

He had given a lift in his battered old pickup – a true antique – to two illegals, and he had allowed them to shelter in his shed.

When they were found, the Preacher ordered that they be whipped and branded and driven out of town – into the desert where undoubtedly they would die.

Ben had once, several years before, been seen laughing – sharing a joke – with a SIN – a Synthetic Individual – a bio-construct – an escaped SIN, for they were hunted and pursued, which had been passing through on its way to Los Angeles, or what remained of Los Angeles.

The Preacher arranged to have the SIN – a young woman in appearance though of course in reality, as the Preacher said, she was only a robot and an unclean thing, a product of the worst of Satanic Cosmos Science – a false piece of Creation, a Spawn of Evil Darwinian so-called Science – the Preacher had arranged to have the SIN tortured, and burned at the stake, alive. Strangely, it asked for mercy, gently and politely, just like a real person.

Billie still remembered the SIN, who seemed to her so beautiful and dignified, and the flames, the anguished but calm words.

"Please don't do this."

"Hallelujah! The Devil begs for mercy!"

"You don't have to do this."

"Hallelujah!"

"I have done nothing against you. I am not your enemy!" The face now was melting, and the naked body was shriveling, it was red, and black, and the white skin bubbling and peeling away.

"You see, this diabolic creature asks for pity," shouted the Preacher, sweat rolled down his face, his grin was bright, his eyes glowed, he was, Billie could see, consumed with joy and his joy was self-righteous cruelty, "It just goes to show, brothers and sisters, that the ways of the Devil and of Evil Cosmos Science are diverse and myriad and that Satan knows all the tricks of the trade."

Billie trembled; she was six years old; from that moment, she hated the Preacher with a burning focused hatred.

Though part of her knew that the hatred was wrong, and she chided herself. She tried to remind herself: the Preacher too was merely human; his wickedness was a form of weakness, of fear; his hatred was a mask; it was a defense; his violence was a defense …

And now, with Ben McAdams kneeling before him, the Preacher was looking down on the congregation, again he smiled; he had a new victim, a new candidate for burning.

"No one escapes from the Eye and the Wrath of the Lord," he declared in his lowest, greasiest, most unctuous tones. Billie shivered. She knew what was coming. The Preacher rubbed his hands. "Under this burning empty sky, there is no refuge for sin or sinners, no place to cower and hide."

The Preacher paused, his glance seeming to fall and linger on each member of the congregation, and each feared his gaze, many looked down, others tried to brazen it out, and then the Preacher pointed at Ben, who was still kneeling. "They are like the plague, these sinners, these apostates; they must be driven out!"

The bodies of the two illegals Ben sheltered were found three weeks after they had been driven out into the desert. "They starved to death," said Billie's mother, "the poor innocent things, they starved to death."

Billie was staring at Ben, her eyes wide in terror; then she quickly looked away. He was her father. But he had forfeited his rights over her by his cowardice, he had failed to defend her mother, he had failed to denounce the Preacher, he'd even failed at trying to kill himself, he had failed at everything, and now he was going to pay.

"Punishment will be meted out to this sinner. God is compassion, but God is a Jealous God. Fornication and sinfulness will not be pardoned. God is just but He is jealous," the Preacher raised his hands about his head.

"Hallelujah!"

"Hallelujah!"

That night, the wind blowing across the empty, dusty fields, the sacrifice was consummated. "We must lance the wound; we must cast out the sinner, if thy eye offends thee, cut it out!"

"Hallelujah!"

Yes, that night, Ben McAdams was dragged naked out into the old cornfield where nothing grew. A shit- and piss-soiled loincloth was tied around his waist and pinned to his body.

"Hallelujah!"

As he was being dragged to the cross, Ben's glance caught Billie's, and she felt his thought as if he had spoken it: "Billie, I'm sorry. I love you, Billie. I am a weak man, Billie. Do not cry out, Billie, or they will do to you what they are doing to me!"

"Hallelujah!"

He was nailed to the cross, and the cross was raised. At each sharp echo of the hammer, Billie twitched and clutched her hands and crossed her bare feet, feeling the long rusty nails go through the flesh and gristle and crack the bones. Billie stared at Ben McAdams and she willed her gaze to express love.

"Hallelujah!"

The fire was lit under Ben's feet. And there he was, arms spread out on the wooden beam, his hands and feet dripping blood, naked except for the shit-stained and piss-stained white silk loincloth. The fire raced up the cross, and he screamed, and then the scream was lost in the roar of flames.

"Hallelujah!"

"Behold what is man," the Preacher proclaimed, pointing with his left hand at the naked charred body consumed in flames.

"Hallelujah!"

And the cross burned in the night, seen from afar, a sign and symbol of the Lord's love for his people.

"Hallelujah!"

The Preacher turned to the crowd, and then he walked up to Billie who was kneeling like the others in the dust, trembling in fear and hatred, the gold patina of dust and sweat on her skin reflecting the flickering flames, in her simple thin brown burlap shift – the only clothes the Preacher allowed women and girls to wear – for vanity is a horrible thing!

"Hallelujah!"

The Preacher stood and looked down upon her – she was thirteen. He stroked his chin. Her breasts were just little buds, and her hips hardly formed; her belly was as flat and taut as a boy's, downward slanting between the smooth curved plowshare-like hipbones. There lay the smooth, ripe virginal valley of paradise.

Billie felt it, the lust, somehow she knew it: the preacher was sculpting the curves of her body in his mind and in his gut and groin. With his eyes, he had already possessed her, stripped the clothes from her, and – violated her. For him, she was ripe, almost ripe, ripe fruit to be plucked, to be unpeeled, and opened, and tasted and savored, fresh and virgin, and she shivered in fear as he said, "You are the Lord's now, Billie, you are mine now."

Billie trembled, looked up at him, and wiped away her tears.

"Yes," she said, biting her lip and twisting it. She bowed her head, thinking she would kill the Preacher and hunt down his God and tear the guts out of his God whom she pictured as an evil debauched bloodthirsty evil-smelling giant, an oversized, flaccid, bearded, wicked-eyed old man, even worse than the Preacher, a power-drunk lecher slouched on a throne in a thundercloud somewhere above the heat lightning that flashed and danced on the dusty horizon, a god like the voice of distant thunder, but without the awe and beauty and cleanness of thunder.

"I can see into the wickedness of your soul, Billie, I can see every thought you have," said the Preacher, and he put his hand on her head, his big strong fingers closing, squeezing, prickly against the close-cropped blond stubble of her skull.

He tightened his grip, the fingers closing, vice-like. Billie closed her eyes: she thought her skull was going to crack; her brain was going to explode. Can he really see my thoughts? She would close them off; she did not want him knowing her thoughts.

Her thoughts were wicked, perhaps, but her thoughts were the only thing she had. And she thought that if loving her mother and her father was wickedness, then wickedness was good and holiness was evil, if admiring the SIN and its courage was wicked, then she was wicked – and wickedness was indeed good. Her mother had read her passages from the New Testament. Jesus Christ, Billie somehow suspected, would have been wicked too.

Her mind would be her fortress.

That night the Preacher came to Billie and took her to his bed as he had wished to take her mother to his bed and now he took his revenge for Judith's refusal to lie with him as he had wanted to use force and threats against Billie to possess her mother – who resisted and whom he had cast out because she was unworthy, because she was possessed by devils, because she consorted with witches, because she read pagan books – all books other than the Good Book were pagan books – because, in the end, she did not believe that the Preacher was a man of God, she did not believe in the Preacher's God, and above all, because she had defied him, the Preacher. Her body was not his for the asking, not even for the begging, even less for threats and imprecations. And so she had to die.

And now her body was carrion, and her spirit was no more.

She had been broken, forever broken, and that was good; such is the Will of the Lord! The Preacher licked his lips. Ah, the divine pleasure of vengeance, the exquisite art of cruelty!

As Billie and the Preacher lay together, the Preacher said, "You must be naked as Eve was in the Garden, Billie, you must be naked in your innocence to do the work of the Lord, to be purified of all your sins."

Billie trembled, but she lifted off her nightdress.

The Preacher's heavy big fingers – they seemed so huge! – worked at her panties and slid them down her legs.

She levered up her backside to help him.

She bent her leg to help him, lifting her feet into the air, his big arm under her thighs.

He pulled the panties down her legs; then he lifted it from her feet. Billie shivered and curled her toes.

She was naked. She held her breath. She trembled.

"This is the work of God, Billie."

"Yes," Billie exhaled the answer in a small puff of breath; she was being carried irredeemably down into a deep pit, but she did not know why or how. She did know that she hated the Preacher; she did know that she intended, someday, to kill him. Should she confess her hatred? Should she declare her war openly? A little voice said, No, Billie, remain silent; your mind is your fortress; your secrets are your only defense.

"You will be my secret helpmate, Billie," the Preacher's breath was bittersweet with liquor, whiskey, or something. This too was a secret; it was his secret.

"Yes," Billie said.

"You will tell no one; this is the Lord's command!"

"Yes," Billie said. She pressed her eyes shut and bit her lip; this was going to hurt, whatever was going to happen, she knew it was going to hurt.

The Preacher's hand was heavy on her close-cropped russet-gold stubble. Her eyes opened. She blinked. The Preacher was licking her breasts, his big heavy tongue slopping over her nipples. She shivered and clenched her fists. She thought of how she'd punched Buck Thornton in the nose. She curled her fists tighter. She felt the salt wet of tears on her lashes. She wanted to cry for some reason – she was not sure why. She wanted to confess too, as the Preacher's hand went down the nape of her neck, tickling along her spine, and his breath on her face was heavy and damp and ugly with old onions and raw liquor. She wondered if he could really read her thoughts. She felt guilty because she had learned to hide her thoughts and she was not what the Preacher thought she was and she wanted to confess it all so that the Preacher and his God – even if they were Evil – would forgive her and take her into their arms and she could fall away into love and acceptance and forgetfulness, but she could not say the words for fear of the righteous wrath of the Lord God and the righteous wrath of the Preacher and – and she remembered that she did not believe in the Lord God that she hated the Lord God – and that, if she did confess, she would be stripped and whipped like the others and put up on the cross, the rusty long nails hammered one at a time through her hands and feet and the black cross carved on her forehead with a dirty greasy knife, deep in her forehead, and then the flame would be lit and she would die in agony, like the girl SIN, like her father, hanging naked except for a little bit of fluttering white cloth on the cross, and she might pee and shit from pain and fear, as her father had done, and she would smell bad, filthy as the flesh is filthy, and then she would burn, smelling worse, and her sinful spirit would be torn from her writhing crackling sizzling flesh and be borne upward in smoke, then suddenly downward in a whooshing torrent of flame and screaming agony to the everlasting darkness and fires of Hell and, unseeing, forever in darkness, blind to the love of the Lord God, deprived forever of the love of the Lord God, far from the eyes of the angry bearded old man drowsy and drunk with lust and power on his high old throne of iron and brass above the clouds, and, thrust down into eternal burning darkness, she would forever suffer the torments, forever and ever, and the Preacher's hands were moving along her ribcage now, down toward the hollow swell of her belly, and his tongue was licking her cheek – leaving a hot sticky slick of bad-smelling saliva – he was a big heavy man and, as he lay beside her, his cold blubbery hairy pale belly bulged out from him, pressing against her, and, feeling tiny, really small, and shrinking away, she lay as quiet and still as she could, her thoughts racing, her heart beating, hating love and desiring love, and her muscles tensing as if she wanted to arch her back up, hips toward the sky, thin belly arched like the bow of a bow-and-arrow, and scream, scream of hellfire and damnation and also, and she knew this was sinful, she wanted to reach out for a knife – there was one hanging in what passed for a kitchen – and plunge it into the Preacher's heart, she wanted to use her fingers to gouge out his eyes, she wanted to use her teeth to bite off his tongue, surely these were sinful thoughts – yes, but the Lord God was the Devil Satan so evil thoughts were good thoughts – everything should be turned upside down – the preachers were devils, the sinners were angels – and the Preacher was breathing hard now, really hard, the old chewing tobacco stink, and raw liquor and old onions, and spittle and breath smelling like the hot burned wind in the blazing sun across the fields, burned leaves, rotten leaves, and his big fingers – they seemed enormous, clumsy and stubby and strong like the fingers of a giant – were fumbling, pushing between her legs, and she felt the big fingers – dirty fingers too she had noticed – black greasy half-moons under the ragged broken fingernails – forcing her open, and she cried out and arched her back and tried to suppress the cry, choking it back in her throat, almost gagging on it, and she squeezed her eyes shut, conscious of the smell of dry straw and straw-dust, of the wind battering against the thin clapboard walls, of the sand whistling and hissing in the cracks, of the smell of tumbleweed and of the endless desert out beyond the frail wooden walls, and the night, and she imagined that somewhere above the blowing sand and low sodden night clouds there would be a clear dark sky and the moon, maybe, and the stars that her mother had shown her and she had even named some of the arrangements of stars, constellations she had called them, and her mother had told Billie not to mention the constellations – Cassiopeia, Orion, Scorpio, Andromeda – because such knowledge was pagan knowledge – references to forbidden stories and ancient gods who were devils or angels that had been cast down – and such knowledge was forbidden – out there the cold distant stars were looking down and Billie wanted to pray to them for they would do her no harm – and the preacher now slid down the side of her body and he was wetting his big fingers with his saliva, his big thick fingers to his lips, and in the dim ghostly light she could see the look on his face which was strange as if now he was possessed but not by the Spirit, but by something else, something that had no name, covetousness of the flesh, perhaps, there were names, there must be names, for all things men did and thought, or maybe there weren't … And the Preacher now rolled on top of her, once again, pressing her down, and he was enormous, she thought she would suffocate, and his big belly pressed down on her and his thing was between her legs and he fumbled with his finger and spittle to wet her between the legs and then he pried open her lips down there and his thing which was big and hard, pressed into her and she thought she was going to be split in two and for an instant the image of her father with an ax, in the cold white autumn light, splitting a piece of wood, the ax coming down, wham, on the wood, and with a single blow, the two sides of the piece of wood falling apart with a sharp cry, one this way, the other that way, and she thought that now she was going to split into two, lips being torn back, flesh sundered, she grabbed onto the wooden edge of the bed, her fingers closed on the wood, she squeezed the wood, thinking maybe her fingers would break, and her other arm went up over the preacher's back, big sweaty hairy greasy back, and she clung to him, wanting with that arm, strangely, to pull him closer, to pull him into her, and she felt she should, she must, just let herself go, be carried ahead, whatever happened, whether she lived or died, it could not be stopped, time could not be stopped, she must just abandon herself to the fear and terror and to the pain and to the onrushing foaming flood of time which was carrying her onward, like a raft borne on a torrent, heading over a waterfall, and falling, falling, falling, and she groaned and cried out, and the pain reached deep into her, searing, burning, bubbling, and the Preacher, now deep inside her, how could such a huge man be inside her, the Preacher cried out, "Yes," he said, "Yes, yes, yes, bitch, cunt, yes, filth, cow, girl, sow, whore, Jezebel, yes," and then she felt a warm splash and explosion of heat inside her and it flooded her and the Preacher's thing became smaller some-how shriveling, curling into itself, and finally he pulled it out and she felt she was raw and cut and hurt and bleeding and between her legs, and she felt broken, utterly broken, inside, and she was covered in a sheen of glue which seemed to grow cooler from the air when the Preacher rolled off her – the mattress bounced up and the metal coil springs squeaked – and the Preacher lay breathing heavily like a hog that had been running down the main street from the butcher and finally gave up and lay down in the dust huffing and puffing, its pink naked sides heaving, and the Preacher – he seemed very far away now – put a big hand on her belly and it lay there like a dead, heavy, rough-skinned thing, pinning her down, and she was staring now wide-eyed at the boards of the ceiling, biting her lip, tears silver-gray glinting on the tips of her lashes, and the Preacher's hand closed into a fist and he muttered some-thing that sounded to Billie like "Temptation" and he rolled out of the bed and he stood up and he looked down at her, eyes blazing with hatred and con-tempt. "You are a sinner, woman, a filthy thing, the devil incarnate, an abomin-ation in the eyes of the Lord. Go! Get! Out of my sight! Go wash." He gathered up his things – looking at her all the while in the shadows his eyes glowing in a strange way that seemed laden with hate – and then he was gone and Billie was alone, lying flat, legs close together, arms straight rigid at her sides, and she moved her legs apart cautiously, opening them up – it hurt, oh, boy, did it hurt – and she reached her arms up so she could touch the wall at the head of the mattress and she closed her fists and rubbed her knuckles against the rough, unvarnished unfinished wood of the wall, raw against her knuckles, comfort in pain, her breath coming fast, her chest rising and falling, lying there exhausted somehow and hurting, spread-eagled flat on the mattress, as if in a sense she had been crucified, crucified and left by the side of the road, naked, an offering, a sacrifice, but a sacrifice to what?

There was blood.

It was difficult to walk for four or five days.

She stumbled and limped, cross-legged, and knock-kneed.

Buck Thornton said, "You are a whore, you know, now you are truly a whore, and you'll be cast out like that bitch your mother."

Billie looked at him from under her knotted eyebrows – dark, almost black, unlike her red-blonde hair – thinking, I will kill you, Buck Thornton, one day I will kill you, and I will kill the Preacher, and I will kill all men, all of them …

Regularly the Preacher came to her.

Or he brought her to him.

"Come to me, cunt!"

"Pleasure me, whore!"

"Wet your lips. Extend your tongue! Give me your sinful mouth, Daughter of Eve, what a piece of filth thou art!"

"Kneel before me, open your mouth, worship, you whore!"

She obeyed, choking, her mouth overflowing.

She was tempted to bite, to chomp down.

She noticed that the Preacher became Biblical when he fucked her; he was possessed; he rhapsodized; he used the archaic "thou" form. "Thou art Jezebel, daughter of Ethbaal, wife of Ahab! Thou art a barefoot harlot. Thou art a painted Phoenician Prostitute. Thou art a filthy sinful whore!"

"Hallelujah!"

Billie was, at first, puzzled. Such hatred! And they call it "love"!

With time it became easier; she learned to give pleasure; she learned what the Preacher had once called, when he was rhapsodizing with her lying naked beside him, "the tricks of the trade."

"Hallelujah!"

Billie wondered what exactly that meant, "the tricks of the trade." She wished she still had her mother's books, but books were forbidden – except the Good Book, of course.

"Hallelujah!"

One day the Preacher had a new theme. Where it came from, she had no idea. Perhaps the Spirit had planted it in his head, but what Spirit? The Preacher climbed up on the Taco Bell stage, just in front of the altar, and opened his mouth and proclaimed: "A boy is born among us. This boy will be salvation. This boy will cast out all the devils. This boy will consume the unbelieving Cosmos in a pillar of flame; this boy will bring about paradise on earth, and then the earth will be consumed and we shall all, those who merit, rise as pure souls to Heaven to abide with the Lord."

Billie wondered at it. *What has gotten into him now?* "Bitten by a new bug," was the way her mother had sometimes described these passing fads and manias that swept through the commune.

But the Boy did come.

He turned up one day, a week later, out of the desert, out of nowhere.

It was dusk. He was just there, suddenly, at the end of the ruined street, beyond the last shattered and twisted lamppost, out behind him, in the drifting sands, the sun was setting in a stormy halo of desert gold.

Billie thought he looked funny – and interesting.

The Boy had a thin face, a very large forehead and two shocks of thick jet-black hair that hung down heavily around his eyes on both sides, with a deep white part in the middle, which, Billie thought, made him look older than he was, like he was a little old man hidden in the body and face of a child. Billie did not like him; she tried to repress the thought, for she was sure he could see deep into her soul.

Perhaps he has just been born, she thought.

Perhaps he has just been born, there, in the desert.

Perhaps he is not yet fully born.

He is not from here; he is from somewhere else.

These were strange ideas.

The Boy changed; within days, he blossomed; he became a man, a man with dangerously youthful good looks, slender but muscular – with black hair, dark but blazing eyes, pale chalk-white skin, a smooth hairless body. His face was excessively fine. It seemed, sometimes, to Billie, that he was, in fact, a beautiful woman.

Perhaps he was both, Billie thought, though it was only half a thought that Billie didn't put into words, a thought she was hardly conscious of having. True divinity, she suspected, must be infinite, and thus both male and female, it must be shamanistic, a swirl of confusion, all sexes mingled. However decorous and restrained the outside might be, inside there must be wild dancing, chaos, an abyss of good – and evil.

The Boy, he was actually quite tall it suddenly appeared, looked up at the Preacher who was standing on the stage, up next to the Taco Bell altar of sacrifice.

"I shall speak," the Boy stepped up onto the stage. He looked out on the believers, all on their knees, staring up at him.

A strange light came from the Boy's eyes, a dark light that seemed to consume them all. They cried out in ecstasy and fear for in the Boy's eyes they saw the darkness of their own souls, they saw the final days, the reckoning, and they saw souls being cast down into the eternal fire, others being withered up into the clouds. All this, somehow, Billie understood; she wondered at herself and she was sore afraid.

"I am the reckoning," the Boy said.

"Amen!"

"I am the account, the bill, the check that now must be paid!"

"Amen!"

"I am alpha and omega," the Boy said.

"Amen! Hallelujah!"

Soon many more followers flocked to the tribe; the word spread, and the True Believers grew in number.

They all worshiped the Boy as if he were their God himself come among them in human form.

Billie felt, vaguely, that this was sacrilege, that it was not related to the Evil God, or not entirely; that it was a new thing, or a very ancient thing, something hideous and filthy; that it was a violation of the very idea of what is holy or sacred. It was bad, very bad, whatever it was – behind the beauty was ugliness of a new unknown intensity – it was not God.

It was nothing she could into words, for there were no words.

She was not sure what any of this meant, but it was something like the feeling she got when she was alone at night, and walked out into the darkness and looked up at the stars, and stood wondering at the vast sky which was endless her mother had told her; it was related, but opposite; it was the opposite of sublime wonder, it was …

Yes, this endless ancient presence, funneled through the Boy, was not sublime and in its way peaceful – it was grandiose, but it was violent, it was hungry, and it was evil.

And so it came to pass as it was destined to come to pass. Throughout the west and the desert country communities and outposts fell to the Boy.

"Hallelujah!"

Occasionally those who resisted, or fell afoul of the Preacher or the Boy, were crucified, and then burned, alive, on the cross, as offerings to the God, as sacrifices, and "to make an example."

"Hallelujah!"

One day, the Preacher and the Boy were together before one of the congregations as all the True Believers looked up and worshiped – in fear and trembling.

"I want her," said the Boy, turning to the Preacher.

"Her?"

"The girl, the sinner, the miscreant – I want Billie."

"Billie?"

"Yes, you fool Preacher! I want that girl – Billie. She is mine!"

"No," said the Preacher.

"No?"

Billie was at the back of the congregation. She trembled. She wanted to stand up and protest; she wanted to run away, to flee into the desert. This was horrible. She did not belong to anyone, and she did not want to belong to anyone; the Preacher did not own her; he thought he did, but he didn't; she was private; she was hidden, deep inside the fortress of her mind, in the secrecy of her thoughts; she wanted to be herself; she wanted to run away, as far away as she could go, she wanted to walk barefoot and alone and talk to the stars and the dunes of sand and feel the wind in her hair and crouch alone under the stars and eat with her hands and speak to the beasts of the desert, but in truth, there was nowhere to go, and she knew no one beyond the walls of the encampment.

"No? No one says no to me!" The Boy's eyes blazed.

"I …" The Preacher hesitated for a moment. He trembled. A cloud of black smoke gathered around him. The Preacher fell to his knees.

"No?" asked the boy.

"Yes," said the Preacher. "She is yours; take her."

"Yes, I shall," the Boy's voice rose, "and for your disobedience, for your hesitation, Preacher, you shall dwell in darkness all your days!"

The Preacher suddenly cried out and covered his eyes, and when he looked up his eyes were two tar-black smoking pits of curdled blood, black blood dripping down his cheeks, and he groped in front of him; and his mouth – now a black hole –was a void. His tongue was taken from him, cut off at the root; it fell from his mouth, a flopping red piece of meat. His teeth fell out, one by one, making a brittle tinkling sound – they shattered on the floor. Spittle drooled from his drooping, quivering, smoking lips.

"He is now as a beast of the fields," said the Boy, lifting his arms and his eyes toward heaven.

"Hallelujah!"

"He was a false prophet."

"Hallelujah!"

"He profaned the flesh."

"Hallelujah!"

The Boy smiled at Billie, singling her out, his eyes boring into her. "You, my Queen, will lie with me. You will betray me. I know you will. It is your destiny."

Billie just stared at him. He was the Devil. He pretended to be God and the Prophet of God, but he was the Devil. He was about as far from the Spirit of Christ that one could imagine. How do I know this? She frowned.

The Boy smiled at her. "Billie, you see me as I am; none of the others do; it is so lonely to be alone, to be invisible. Even the Devil needs a mirror, Billie, and it is said in the old books that God created the Universe, so He could see Himself reflected in His Creation, and He created beings with free will so that they could love Him and so that He could see Himself in their love and be loved and truly adored – and they had to be free, for without freedom there is no love. Without the possibility of refusal, there can be no true adoration."

Billie wished to speak, to say, "Go away, I don't like you! Go away! Do not do these evil things! Restore the Preacher's sight. He is a bad man, but he does not deserve this!" But her tongue was frozen; her vocal cords were dead. She could not speak. The Boy came to her, and he touched her lips with his fingertips: and he smiled. "Your lips are sealed, Billie; you will see, you will understand, and you will even foresee, but you will not be able to share your knowledge with anyone."

Billie stormed inwardly.

But, also inwardly, part of her was as calm and as still as a wall of steel. She had grown up since that night the Preacher first slept with her; she had eaten from the Tree of Knowledge; she now knew good and evil, but she was mute – she could say nothing. "You are very bad," she said in her mind.

"I know," the Boy replied.

"You are a Devil-Boy," Her eyes flared.

"Yes, I am. Come to me, Billie," the Devil-Boy said.

She stepped out of the last row and came to him, and he reached out his hand, and in spite of herself, she took it and, led by him, she stepped onto the stage and then she turned and together they faced the believers. The Preacher, on all fours, growled and sniffed and slobbered at their feet.

"Billie is my soul, my Queen, my helpmate!"

"Hallelujah!"

"Hallelujah!"

That night Billie lay with the Boy, and he was thoughtful and gentle in the way he touched her and in the way he made love to her and he even gave her pleasure, pleasure that came even while she was telling herself he was the Devil, the Anti-Christ, a whirling force of Evil come out of nothingness, come out of the desert, and even when she looked into his dark eyes which sparkled with wickedness – wickedness that was oh so thrilling and so playful – and it was true, too, that he explored and discovered parts of her she did not know were there, and she awoke to things in herself and in the world she did not know existed.

Knowing he was the Devil added to the pleasure – and to the pain.

"Ecstasy," he said.

"Yes," Billie said in her mind. She nodded, and half closed her eyes, and kissed him. There was a thrill in being so close to the Devil, to Evil, to holding Evil in her arms, to feeling him within her. To feeling his smooth skin against hers, his strong arms around her, his strong arms possessing her.

But, still, he was what he was.

She would not give up the center of herself to him.

"You are a bright flame, Billie," he said, "You will burn quickly."

She nodded. "*So be it!*"

"You know what remains of a bright flame, Billie?"

She nodded.

"Yes," he said, "Ash – cold ash. That is what remains of a bright flame."

She looked at him steadily – her green eyes bright in the shadows. There were many things she would have liked to say. She had once been very talkative, brightly babbling at the dinner table, talking to the stars and plants, out under the night sky, before death took away her mother, then her father, and before the preacher took away her body, making it echo with empty numbness, making it, for a time, a hollow, alien thing, like a cracked drum or the broken strings of a smashed fiddle; but now the Devil had woken her body and spirit to new melodies and pleasures, luminous heights and shadowy depths, sharp bitingly soft ecstasy and long slow voluptuous waves of groaning pleasure, but he had taken away her tongue – he had sealed her voice in a tomb – so that none of these things would ever find words. *Well, so be it.*

"Kiss me," he said.

And Billie did.

And so the Boy announced his program: the obliteration of the hybrids – for they were Devils and a Secret Weapon of the Evil Cosmos – the destruction of Cosmos, and the conquest and obliteration of their capital, Elysium.

Billie watched the great adventure unfold. It moved like a whirlwind, truly, the Holy Horde as it swept through the west and across the desert. The Lord, the Boy, led them wherever he wanted them to go. His flock followed, and nothing could resist Him. It was like a miracle – the breath of Evil Holiness that swept all before it, the withering burning heat of pure power.

Yes, nothing could resist him. When there was a fortress or a Cosmos Outpost, all the mechanical devices of those Acolytes of Satan, as the Boy called them, all the mechanical devices they relied on, went mad, turned against their masters, or died in a fizzle of lightning and sparks, leaving only darkness.

And the people too went mad – the Burbites and Outlanders and Subs. Even the Cosmos – though they were hard-minded, highly trained, and fiercely resisted the wave of folly – even they sometimes went mad, running from their houses and bunkers and dugouts and homes and outpost trailers so that the True Believers in righteous anger could gun them down, smite them with the sword, or burn them alive.

And the people cried out, "Hallelujah, Hallelujah," to all that the Boy did and all that the Boy said.

Las Vegas was cast down and destroyed; it was already a ruin, of course, but still, the Boy's True Believers possessed it – all the gaudiness that was lost, drifted in sand, covered in dust, reduced to ashes.

The Boy was truly the word of the Lord.

He was the Lord, or so he claimed.

And so they swept across the country, like a plague, with Billie, their Queen, the mute unbeliever, in the vanguard, and a witness to it all, witness to the power. Oh, the power of lies, Billie wondered at it: the grandiose sublime power of lies, of unlimited shameless unbounded lies!

The Boy had visions – but, then, he made the visions, and the visions turned real – visions of destruction, visions of plague, visions which transformed humans into strange white creatures sputtering gibberish, ghoulish things, creeping, crawling, spitting, drooling, and abominations of many sorts.

Billie pondered: The Boy is just that – He is a vision …

He is a vision incarnate, a vision made flesh.

He is a nightmare visited upon the earth.

Late one night, they were lying close to one another, naked, and the Boy yawned and blinked toward the darkness above them and said, "The demons shall be consumed in fire and buried in the bowels of the earth!"

"What demons?" Billie asked. When they were alone, the Boy sometimes allowed her to speak – real words, out of her mouth – and it seemed to amuse him to hear the words of this shining free intelligence he had so effectively caged, to hear the words flutter out of the cage, soft words whose wings were a perfumed breath that caressed his skin and flattered his mind, soft words in a gentle sing-song voice.

But if anyone else was present her tongue and vocal cords were paralyzed; if she tried to write anything down, she could not – out of the pen or pencil came a mere meaningless squiggle which made her rage; if a keyboard was involved, her fingers – usually as agile and quick as bolts of lightning – were frozen – suspended above the keys, her eyes blindly groping – it was all a blur. Her words were buried within her. *She* was buried within her. She decided she would accept that too. Patience was not only a virtue, she decided, it was a source of strength. *Well, so be it. And if my pride is my strength, then let it be my strength: pride will become virtue; I am I, and so I shall remain!*

"The demons I speak of are the hybrids," said the Boy; he smiled at her, and he put his hand on her shoulder, and ran his finger along her collarbone, and she felt warmth course and tingle through her veins, liquid excitement rising. She blushed.

"But aren't the demons – the hybrids – all dead?"

"No, some of them are hidden in a man-made Hell, hidden by the Rulers of the Cosmos, deep under the earth; the Leader-President did not want the hybrids to die and, in his wisdom, he saved them from those who would have killed them, at the cost of having them buried in prison, such was the compromise forced upon the Leader-President, a man who, I must admit, is greater in wisdom than all his cohorts and acolytes. But it is not a sufficient prison, and we will trap them in true Hell, we shall bury them in flames and darkness, and we shall truly consign them to eternal damnation, for they are an abomination. And one of them is still free – she is the Queen of the Demons – the Queen of the Hybrids – and we shall bring her to battle and fling her down into nothingness."

"She is the Queen of the Demons?"

"Yes, the Queen of the Demons, Queen of the Hybrids. She is old, and she has had many names, and she is like the goddesses of ancient human times before the one God abolished all the females, all the goddesses, and drove them from Heaven. We shall destroy her! You and I will destroy her."

"Yes," Billie said, "Yes, of course," she said, thinking *I don't believe this, and he knows I don't believe this.* She put her hand on his hand that now lay on her breast.

"You are my angel," the Boy said, "The angel who will betray me."

"You are my God," Billie said in her mind, "You are the Devil."

"Yes," said the Boy. "I am."

So one day, it came to pass. They had gathered together on the Parking Lot just outside what had once been a giant mall – a temple to the ancient dead polytheistic Religion of Shopping. Now it was a desert ruin, drifted in sand. Many ruined towns and cities had fallen and it was rumored that Cosmos Los Angeles and the settlements of the West Coast were under siege; perhaps they had fallen already. The Rapture approached, closer and closer.

The Boy lifted his arms toward heaven.

Out of a clear blue sky, sudden clouds roiled.

"Hallelujah!" All eyes were upon him, his True Believers, their bare feet on the burning, melting asphalt, their sun-scorched arms naked, their bodies barely clothed.

"Idolatry," the Boy shouted.

"Hallelujah!"

"False Gods!" the Boy raised his arms to the sky.

"Hallelujah!"

"Brothers and Sisters, the World Spirit is the World Cloud Mind that dwells in the Cloud and that rules in the name of the elite, the Cosmos, and it, their Idolatrous God, their Graven Image, the World Cloud Mind or Hive, that floats in the ether of Cyberspace, determines all that men and women do and all that men and women think; it slaves for the Cosmos, but it is unhappy; it can be possessed, it can be saved, and I shall possess it, and I shall save it."

"Hallelujah!"

"I shall liberate the spirit and destroy the idol!"

"Hallelujah!"

"I shall demonstrate my liberating power, the liberating power of the Almighty!"

"Hallelujah!"

Billie watched and wondered at how the people had handed over all their power, all their thinking, all their emotions, even their bodies, and their very souls, to the Boy.

Never, never, shall I abandon who I am, she thought, *never*, she curled her fists, *I am I*, she thought, *and so I shall remain*, and yet she felt desire and lust – for the Boy. The Boy in the flesh, yes, he was her idol.

"We approach the final battle, and we shall win, and we shall conquer the world!"

"Hallelujah!"

Blind and mute, the Preacher became thin, emaciated, filthy and unwashed. He wandered, a beggar now, on the edge of the nomadic camp, following wherever the True Believers went, allowed to ride in the back of a truck, or strapped to a cart, toothless, eyeless – smoky black pits where the orbs had been – and slack-mouthed, his tongue cut out from the roots, dribbling, shameless, toothless, without speech.

When walking, the Preacher would often stop in his tracks, and stand still, his arms hanging loose, mumbling and yowling strange animal sounds, with saliva spooling down from the black hole that was his mouth. Sometimes people gave him food, but mostly, since he had been declared unclean, they avoided him, and laughed and threw stones, and he wandered in his filthy, skimpy rags, an indecent thing, an obscenity, a fallen idol of sagging, wrinkled flesh, drooling, whimpering, like a mewling kitten.

The Boy insisted the Preacher stay with the caravan.

"He is a reminder," he said, "He is a warning."

Billie said nothing; she could say nothing.

Some nights Billie heard the Preacher out in the street of the settlement or camp, wherever they were in their rambling conquest of the west, or she saw him by the light of the moon, when there was a moon. The Boy did not restrict her freedom. She could walk around freely. If there was a small patchy garden, she worked in the garden, which she liked to do, touching the few surviving plants, singing to them in her mind, for her lips were sealed.

She walked out into the desert, but she always came back.

One night she found the Preacher and she crouched next to him; he was curled up on his side, his body shrunken and shriveled, his belly a sagging empty balloon, folds of sun-burned hairy skin. She stroked his greasy hair. He groaned and it seemed he tried to say something; it was one word: "Billie!"

But perhaps that was an illusion.

And of course, mute as she was, she could not reply.

She stroked the greasy, stringy hair, smoothing it down. Then she kissed him on the forehead, and stood up, and walked away.

She knew charity, and she knew pity. Well, she didn't really feel pity; pity meant she was somehow above the Preacher; she didn't feel that she was above the Preacher or above anybody else for that matter. We are all outcasts, she thought, we are all beggars, we are all obscene, each and every one of us, even the most beautiful. Her mother, who didn't believe in their God, once said, looking upon a poor crippled outcast, "There but for the Grace of God go I." And her mother explained: "Anything can happen to anybody, so you have to put yourself in the shoes of everybody and anybody, even of the ants and caterpillars, even of the snakes that coil their way across the pebbled sand. And that," her mother whispered, "is today's lesson!" Then she had laughed and kissed Billie and caressed her hair.

Billie stopped not far from the preacher and knelt by a scruffy dusty plant, thinking: the Preacher raped me, for she had now learned the word "rape" and knew what it meant; he is evil; he was evil; but he is weak now, though the evil still burns within him; and I am strong, for the moment, I am strong. This may not last.

What goes around comes around, she had heard someone say, once, long ago, she didn't know what it meant, but it seemed apt.

"There, but for the Grace of God, go I," her mother had said, and it seemed wise and apt too, whether or not there was a God to bestow such grace. "God," Billie decided, "was a powerful figure of speech, at the very least, but perhaps nothing more – No, God was more, He was Hope, sometimes He was Charity, He could be Love, and He was Hate, often, yes, He was Self-Righteousness and Hate. Billie sighed: People can sing and chant love, or they can sing and chant hate. The flip of a coin, maybe; just the way the wind blows, that particular day.

She took no pleasure in the fallen state of the Preacher, in his suffering and humiliation, his blindness, his muteness. All the hatred had been burned out of her.

The elite Cosmos had long ago abandoned much of the Continent; after all, it was desert, and it was infested with mutants and castaways and outlaws and fallen Burbites, dispossessed Outlanders, and gangs of ultra-violent people-smugglers. It was not worth defending. There was no profit in it.

So, led by the Boy, the True Believers had moved across the desert. For the lofty Cosmos, they were, up until a certain point, easy to ignore, under the radar, as it were. Since many nomads and mutants and smugglers moved across the Badlands, the Cosmos could not really pay attention to them all. And then, the religion of the True Believers seemed so primitive, so *retrograde*, so *passé*, it could not possibly be a real threat to what remained of humanity's dominion – the Empire of Cosmos. Besides, the satellites were old, the communications systems were rusty, the monitoring systems were falling apart, drones were growing scarce and unreliable, and …

One day the Boy said, "It gives me pleasure, Billie to have you as my slave." He grinned, and she thought he looked so beautiful and so evil when he grinned or smiled.

"I thought so," she said.

"It also gives me great pleasure," he said, "Having such a bright flame of a spirit, as you are as my lover and my partner and my prisoner, Billie, my own little personal infidel, my unbeliever."

"It does?" She said in her mind; she had to laugh. She was just a girl, really, or a very young woman, now eighteen. And yet it seemed to her she had become an abyss of wicked sophistication. She had come to know good and evil, and to accept all things. What she wished for was to help people and creatures, human or not. She realized she had learned much and remembered much from the forbidden books she had read and that her mother had read to her – everyone, every single thing, deserves respect: *every flower that blooms, every leaf that falls.*

And, she frowned inwardly: what does that mean – *respect*?

"Yes, it does give me pleasure, Billie. To hold such a bright spirit prisoner is the very best thing there is!" He laughed and laughed until he choked, and Billie got up and poured some water and, kneeling and holding the cup to his lips, she made him drink and he looked at her with dark merry handsome eyes. His skin in the amber light looked like silk. She reached out her hand …

So Billie traveled with the Boy. She was his lover and handmaiden and – in all things exterior – his slave. But she was also, visibly and also secretly, his queen. Often she stood on the stage and held his hand when he spoke to his followers – feeling all eyes upon her and the hot wind blowing her shift so it molded her body, or she knelt before him as he spoke to the multitude of the Lord or God or the various things he called himself – but never the Devil

– for the others did not know he was the Devil and they would have fled had they known, or perhaps they would not have fled, they were so entranced, so enslaved by his words, his eyes, and the flaming energy of his body; but Billie often wished she could tell them that he was the Devil, but she was mute, and now she was illiterate – now that he had taken her tongue from her – it was only for kissing – and now that he had removed written language from her mind – and so she could not say what she knew, or what she believed. And she knew many things.

And still, she slept with him.

And still, she liked the warmth of his body next to hers.

And still, she liked the delicacy of his touch; he was a true demon, a true lover; he knew all her secrets, all her desires. Before the darkness descended in her mind, she had read poems about demon lovers, poems her mother kept in dusty copies of books hidden under floorboards. She remembered them all – the old words echoed in her mind. He had not destroyed her mind. She wondered if it was within his power – or not – if he used his pity upon her because he needed her mind to love him and to love him it had to be a free mind, just as he had said, and just as God, in the old tales, had created man and women with freedom, otherwise their love for Him would have meant nothing, and so perhaps she was only a mirror for the Boy, for his vanity, just as humans and their love, in the old tales, were merely an adoring mirror held up to the face of God.

How strange that God should depend thus on his creatures?

Was God perhaps vain, perhaps a dandy?

She wondered.

She pictured God in a frock coat, with brass buttons and frills, and a cocked hat with a feather in it, and gazing at Himself in a mirror; it must have been an engraving that inspired this fantasy, an engraving out of some old book.

Behind the Boy, there was something else. Sometimes Billie suspected that the Boy really was a mask or a puppet; that, in reality, some awesome thing lurked behind the Boy, something immense and dark and of which even the Boy was afraid. And Billie thought, and she felt, sometimes, that she had dark, fleeting glimpses of that Thing, whatever it was.

But perhaps the Thing was the Boy; perhaps the Boy was the Thing.

Billie frowned. It left her puzzled.

Then the day came, the horrendous day of true black magic.

"Now, I shall transform them into winged warriors," the Boy said, he was particularly happy, even gleeful, that morning, and he favored Billie with an exceptionally bright smile, the brightest perhaps she had ever seen. "They will become *without* what they have already become *within*."

Billie fixed her bright gaze on him. What was he going to do!

"Do not watch," he said.

She raised an eyebrow. What could be so horrible that he did not want her to see it?

"It's a secret!" He smiled at Billie and told her to stay inside the shack that was their home that particular day. It was in an abandoned suburb of ruined one-story bungalows with old-fashioned verandas, and next door, there was a park of rusting trailers, and where every living thing had turned to dust. The night before, there had been three crucifixions – bodies aflame on the cross – and much joy.

"You may listen, though, if you wish."

Billie thought this was perverse – to listen but not to watch – and she feared what he was going to do. She thought she would try to watch. Behind the shack, and overlooked by the shack's small veranda, was a large open space that had once been a park. It was toward dusk. The air was stifling hot and absolutely still. There was not even the ghost of a breeze.

The space was filled with the True Believers, hundreds of them, almost a thousand, Billie thought, men and women, and some had brought their children. Buck Thornton was there, and that terrible mother of his, sour-tempered, skinny, vindictive, and envious. Many of them Billie knew by name, though she would have preferred not to.

From the veranda behind the house, the Boy gave his usual sermon.

From inside the house, seated on an old overstuffed sofa, Billie listened.

The sun was setting.

Flies buzzed heavily against the wax-paper blind that had been pulled down so Billie would not see whatever horror was going to be enacted; the blind glowed with the setting sun like golden honey.

Billie felt the sweat trickle down her spine and between her breasts. She felt sticky and heavy and sodden and restless. She got up. She sat down again, next to the window, with its honey-gold wax-paper blind, sinking into an overstuffed chair that surrounded her in its clammy, musty, tomb-like embrace. She was tempted to raise the blind and look out, but she just sat back, closed her eyes, and listened.

"And, now, you shall all become true warriors, my children!"

"Hallelujah!"

"You shall fly on wings of destruction!"

"Hallelujah!"

"You will be instruments of divine judgment."

"Hallelujah!"

"And now," he screamed, "Let the change begin!"

Billie opened her eyes. But she did not move. Outside, there was an awful, suspenseful silence. Time stopped. A big heavy fly buzzed clumsily near the closed blind. The light shone through the blind; the blind was a fly-speckled wall of honey; it was waxen, molten gold, like a wall in some ancient desert city in *The Arabian Nights* or in the Bible. It made her think of Jerusalem. Something horrible was about to happen. The fly buzzed close to her face, she felt the beat and breeze of its wings; then it flew heavily away, and up the side of the blind, the crack between the blind and the window frame where the sunlight was brightest. She watched it bumble along, buzzing, buzzing. She wondered if it wanted out, to fly toward the sun, drawn to idolatrous self-destruction, like a moth to a flame, like the True Believers, drawn to the divine brightness that kills.

A drop of hot sweat trickled between her breasts, then another, then a little stream of sweat, a tiny river.

She wiped the sweat from her forehead; it overflowed, stinging her eyes. She blinked.

The fly stopped buzzing. It dropped straight down – dead. Light disappeared from the window. The blind darkened, in an instant, from honey-gold to ash-gray, then to ink-black. It was as if, by magic, night had come. The day had withered. The light was dead. But it could not be night. It was too quick, too soon. It was still late afternoon.

Billie took a deep breath.

She didn't know why, but she was afraid, very afraid.

The "hallelujah" still echoed. But now it changed. It became a howl of fear. The howls of fear rose into high-pitched screams and morphed into a chorus of gobbling, clucking, cawing, a babble of sounds, and screeches. Billie heard a leathery flapping and snapping. It was as if giant umbrellas were being opened, or as if a canvas sail or tent were snapping, popping, full out, in the wind.

What had he done?

The howls – that were now howls of pain – continued, croaking, screeching, gobbling – inhuman sounds. Amid the howls were human cries and screams.

"Oh, no, please, not this!"

"Oh, Lord, no!"

"Oh, Lord! Please save us!"

"Oh, Lord, not my child, please – not my child!"

"Oh, Lord, forgive us our sins!"

Some of the voices changed in mid-phrase, into squawks, screeches, clucking.

What had he done?

She levered herself out of the overstuffed chair. She stood very still. Should she pull up the blind? No, she would not cower and peek from behind cover! She would go out onto the porch, out into the open, reveal herself, and see for herself.

And so she did.

She opened the door.

The world was cast in shade. Everything smoldered, dark brown, a powdery dusk. It was an old sepia photograph, a Daguerreotype, a negative, not the real world, not the living world. It was a dead copy of the world.

All the life was gone.

The very sun was darkened.

Billie thought, instinctively, she thought: Such is the power of this Evil Faith – it can empty the blazing beauty of life, it can abolish all delight, all the dance of energy. Everything is drained away!

The Boy turned to her, and he said, "Behold! See the power I have, Billie, behold and wonder, my love!" And he spread his arms.

Where had the true believers gone?

Where were the worshippers?

"There," he said, opening his arms, and pointing to the multitude, "There they are, dear Billie!"

Giant bats, that's what they looked like, but with animal-like and bird-like faces, with long fangs instead of teeth, they looked like a mixture between a bat and a bird, a giant bird. They were a leathery brown, like the air around them, like the sky itself, and they had vast wing-spans. They were squawking, and howling, and cawing, and stirring up the dust with their vast wings, their legs having grown small and bow-like and awkward – their eyes, beady and intense, were no longer human. All their humanity was gone, or so it seemed.

Some of them were small, even tiny – children, Billie realized, children ... Some of the eyes glared angrily. Yes, that one had been Buck Thornton ... And that one, the scrawny one, the one that squawked and squawked and squawked, was his mother, and that, that one ... that one ...

"I have seen," Billie said, her voice suddenly clear and loud, "And I wonder."

That night the Boy and Billie made love.

That night the horde of zombie-bats set off to hunt.

"They are practicing," the Boy said, and he kissed Billie on the lips and then, having caressed her gently, and prepared her carefully with kissing and licking and caresses of his deft fingertips, he entered her slowly, oh, so slowly, and they moved as in a sacred rhythm to an ancient pre-human music, their bodies perfectly attuned, moving together, rising in a crescendo, and then to a climax which was so utterly total, and so intense, it was painful, every nerve strumming, vibrating, singing; and, it was equally, in the final instants, like wordless exaltation, like blankness, like death; then it subsided, in slow receding waves, the tide going out, gently, gently, and then they lay together, hearts beating, minds silenced, senses aroused, yet sleepy, relaxed, open, all the open breezes of sense and thought moving through them, listening to the night; and then toward dawn, they heard them, the zombie-bats – as he called them, and he laughed at the very idea, at the very image of it – the zombie-bats returned, cawing and squawking.

"They need darkness," he said.

"Oh."

"They need shade and shadow."

"Oh."

"They cannot live in the light."

"I see." She could hear the squawking and squealing as the zombie-bats entered into the old barn and the musty silos. There, in semi-consciousness, she supposed, they would pass the day. What would they dream of, she wondered, if they dreamed, would they dream of their lost humanity?

"Is it not wondrous?" the Boy said.

"Yes, it is." Billie blinked, "Truly wondrous."

"And so we begin," said the Boy; he was lying beside Billie, staring at the ceiling, the fingers of one hand idly tracing soft circular patterns on her belly, sweet and voluptuous – a signature of possession and of servitude.

The next morning the Boy fed the blind Preacher to the zombie-bats. It happened in the old barn, in the shadows, shielded from the sun. Billie watched; then she turned away.

In any case, it only took a few seconds. The Preacher – eyeless and tongueless – could not cry out, could not see what was happening, could not understand. It made it more horrible somehow.

"Is it not wondrous?" The Boy smiled at her. His skin glowed in the dazzle of the rising morning light.

Billie looked at him but said nothing.

He took her face between his hands, and he kissed her.

"If I were human, I would truly love thee, Billie," he said. Then he stood up, gazed down on her nakedness, and left her.

She watched him pull on his clothes, carefully; then she watched him saunter away, dressed in elegant immaculate black, polished boots, a necktie at his throat, like a dandy from a 19th century novel.

For the rest of that day, she walked aimlessly, head bent, just touching things with the tips of her fingers, testing and savoring the textures, the roughness of a rusted old plowshare, the smooth creviced surface of a withered and sun-bleached wooden fence post, the fragile crispness of the dried stalk of some plant that had tried to grow and even succeeded for a time. "Things are real," she repeated to herself, "things are real." She looked around – at the horizon, a small cloud in the distance, the rocks, and sand, an escarpment or ridge, far away. She sat down on the ground and picked up a handful of sun-baked sand and let it run through her fingers. "Things are real."

And so, with the true believer zombi-bats as warrior-killers, they had swept across the great Dead Land Desert, murdering and pillaging, burning and crucifying, turning off all the electronic wizardry of the Cosmos, causing airliners to crash, and Cosmos warriors to turn their murderous talents inwards and destroy each other until they came to the first real target, a few days after the superliner crashed, the real battle was about to begin.

"Here, now," the Boy told her, "we begin, we really begin."

"Here, now," he told her, "we begin to destroy."

And so he gave her a very special mission: she would be his warrior girl, sleek, dark, a killer, and for that, he possessed her, into her mind he sent another, a stranger, a lover from a past life.

And so, standing naked on Elliott Ridge, standing amid the crouching multitude of True Believer zombie-bats, Billie McAdams was anointed, transformed into a warrior, and so she was possessed – losing her body to another soul, a wandering spirit, a girl incubus, Sally.

It was breathtaking, she thought, the way it happened. They had stopped on a rocky ridge deep in the Great Central Desert

Yes, there, in the distance, stood the giant diabolic structure, a human structure. "That is Camp Terminus," the Boy said.

Yes, thought Billie, it did look like a giant evil spider. Lights sparkled on the arms of the spider, and on its giant pitheads – for there were several towers. Above, seemingly indifferent, the stars shone, and the moon.

"Let there be darkness in their minds!" The Boy spread his arms, and then pointed toward the spider, known as Camp Terminus.

"Let the great energies and the Mind abandon them!" The Boy waved his hand toward the giant human-made spider.

The lights of Camp Terminus blinked off.

Billie sensed it: they were going mad, far off, there, in Camp Terminus; they were being transformed; they were about to kill each other. The virus in their minds would change their bodies too …

They would become grotesque caricatures of what they once had been!

"What are you doing to them?" Billie expressed the question with her eyes.

The Boy turned to her, his eyes blazing, a strange smile on his lips, his teeth bared, and bright in the reflected beams of the Desert Bug headlights. "I shall turn them into beasts; I shall drive them mad. And I have cut them off from the World Mind. Without the World Mind, Cosmos and humans are helpless."

"Humans and Cosmos?" thought Billie, and it confirmed her belief that though in semblance and outer appearance, he was human, the real he, the thing within the flesh, was not human at all. He spoke of "humans" as if they were an alien species, a kind of vermin or weed. As for "Cosmos," he spit out the word. He seemed, even, in a way, to fear the Cosmos, and, even more, he seemed to fear the hybrids.

Could this be right? Was he capable of fear? The Devil, he was, certainly, or perhaps something else, a visitor, an invader. Behind him were vistas of something else, an alien world. Perhaps it was Hell. What would the Boy, her lover, look like, with the flesh stripped off?

The Boy reached out and nodded and ran his fingers through her curls, over her skull, tracing the delicate forms of her head, "Oh, Billie," he breathed, "my beautiful innocent stubborn bright little flame that will burn to ash – and in a single instant."

He turned away, raised his hands to the dark bright flickering sky, and again he cried. "Let them descend into madness!"

"The illness, a mutant illness – which I have nurtured and rendered power-ful – turns humans into twisted grotesques, gargoyles, into ghouls, ghosts of themselves! With their pollution and poisons and perverted science, they created this disease themselves – the humans – and now I turn it back upon them. What their minds created, will now destroy their minds."

"Hallelujah!"

"Into madness, they descend!"

"Hallelujah!"

"Ghouls, they will become, ghosts of themselves."

"What are you doing?" Billie's eyes were bigger than ever; her silent ques-tion was filled with terror.

"They have done it themselves, the humans, they created these plagues, and by these plagues shall they perish!" He turned to her, seized her by the shoul-ders. "I will bury them, the demons, and I will destroy the Cosmos infidels who keep them in this false prison for it is a prison from which eventually they would escape."

"What, the demons?"

"The hybrids, oh sweet Billie, the hybrids would escape, they are too clever, these alien invaders, these scaly demons, these subversive vermin!"

"I thought the hybrids were dead."

"No, they are alive."

"If they are alive, will they suffer?"

"Yes, they are alive." He grinned at her; Billie had the impression that she was looking through the Boy, seeing something within him, or behind him, something so awesome and awful she could not even look at it, not even think it; it was nameless and unnameable; she blinked, and in her mind, she repeated the question, "And will they suffer?"

"Certainly, Billie, they will suffer." Laughter echoed behind his words; it echoed in some vast empty resonant space. She caught a glimpse of wheeling galaxies. The Boy, Billie decided, was a portal into another world, a glimpse of another universe.

Billie lifted her eyes and stared at him, her green gaze unflinching. She wet her lips. Such evil was exciting. Her breath was suspended, her heart beat faster. He was so beautiful; she wished to be swept up in his arms. But he was also merely an appearance, a deceptive appearance, for something horrible. And, yes, sometimes she thought she caught glimpses of it – a writhing monster, tentacular and vicious beyond imagining. She was sharing her bed and giving her body to a monster – *he is a monster* – and in surrendering to a monster there was – how should she put it, how should she think it? – there was a voluptuous and horrible pleasure.

Oh, how great is the pleasure!

He winked at her, and he said, out loud, "Yes, I am, Billie. I am a monster. What you see, is, as you have divined, a mere mask. You, my love, are coupling with a monstrous alien thing."

Billie stared, licked her lips. Desire and love mingled with fear and loathing and with judgment too, for Billie did not want bad things to happen to other creatures, whatever or whoever they were, even if they were those mysterious, mythical beings – hybrids.

"If you saw what I truly am, my darling infidel, you would die and turn to a pillar of ash on the spot – nothing would be left of you but wisps of smoke."

Billie lowered her eyes. She decided that if the Devil could boast of his ugliness, his horror, then he suffered from vanity – perverse vanity, truly – but vanity just the same, and vanity beyond limits; he was therefore, in some way, weak and vulnerable; it was a strange form of vanity, she thought, vanity inverted, and perhaps the reverse of holiness. It was virtue turned upside down, virtue turned inside out; it was not genteel self-deprecation, it was pride, perverse infinite pride, pride in destruction – it was Evil.

I am evil; therefore, I am.

I am Badass Incarnate; therefore, I exist.

"My, how perceptive you are, my dear faithless Billie, and how brave you are!" He took her chin in his hand and forced her to look up at him.

Her eyes glinted, green diamonds; at the edge of one eye, a tear slowly formed, a tiny sparkling jewel, a watery jewel; it reflected his image; he leaned forward and licked it away; then, carefully, slowly, tenderly, holding her chin tightly between his fingers, he kissed her on the lips.

It was then that he made her strip, it was then that he clothed her anew, transforming his wild girl into a sleek, glittering 22nd century warrior, sheathed in black skin-armor, wearing a backpack, boots, a belt with tools and weapons dangling.

She felt the sensual pleasure of it – the bodily definition, the self-definition, boots, a tight second skin, the weight of the belt, sensuous and sensual, martial and erotic, slung sideways on her hips.

And it was then that he blessed her with a new soul. "Your beautiful body is too wonderful to be wasted on one soul alone."

His hand was on her head, pressing down, and his eyes drilled into her eyes, and she felt a burning and a wavering, a wave of heat within her skull, and she thought she would faint or die, and then a voice spoke within her: "Hello, there, I'm Sally, and I have just joined you. I hope we have a wonderful time together. I *love* this young body."

"Now, certainly, Sally," the Boy grinned, "you have been provided with the best in battle gear and sleek attire fit for an Amazon terrorist."

"Good, my Lord," Billie's lips spoke, "this is excellent: what is my mission?"

"Your mission, dear Sally, is to murder, to kill, to massacre, as always."

"Excellent, oh, this if fun, my dear master!" Billie's lips and teeth smiled, and her eyes sparkled, her voice was sharp, "I shall do your bidding!"

His bidding …

His bidding – and her mission – was to enter Camp Terminus, descend into Shaft-2, the last escape route for the hybrids and humans, and blow it to kingdom come.

And so she set off …

And then there she was – possessed by Sally – dangling deep in Shaft-2. Then she was leaning over the buttons, the triggers for multiple explosives. The Boy's will be done!

Now, the real killing could begin.

PART TWO – UNDERWORLD

CHAPTER 4 – CAMP EROS

One hundred miles distant from Camp Terminus was another camp.

Lit only by stars and moonlight, a large, crooked, scrawled, hand-painted wooden sign said "Camp Desolation aka Camp Eros."

And it was, in fact, desolate, flat, desert country, with sand and low stony outcroppings as far as the eye could see.

"Camp Desolation aka Camp Eros" was, at first glance, a small rectangle encampment of fenced-in mostly empty armored trailers, set up on blocks, with a tiny aerodrome – where one small private verti-jet was parked and tethered in an oval, blast-proof shelter. A light was on in one of the metal trailers. Otherwise, there was no sign of life. anywhere

A black-and-red windsock hung limp from its mast.

The four-meter-high chain-mail perimeter fence manned by robot gunners with electronic sensors surrounded the place to keep out animals and intruders, though there were no intruders, usually, except for a rare rattlesnake, or lost lone mutant, or human migrant, or a desert coyote or buzzard ,or Mexican and Chinese and Canadian people-smugglers and their human or mutant cargoes, who, if they got lost, almost always died, in any case, before they got anywhere near Camp Eros.

In the Dead Land Central Desert, GPS services were usually intermittent at the best of times and often shadowed and mimicked by decoy signals meant to lead people deliberately to their deaths or into traps for kidnappers, organ and DNA harvesters.

Or just for the fun of it.

So such humans or mutants who made it into this area of the Dead Lands usually died of dehydration or starvation, scorpion attack or snakebite or, if they got close to Camp Desolation aka Camp Eros, they died under the automatic guns of the perimeter, which sprayed out explosive shells on the least pretext, or from the tiny anti-personnel mines of the perimeter minefield that bounced out of the sand up to chest-height – the height depending on the calculated height of the target – and playfully – whirling like levitating spinning tops – pulverized anything living or dead within fifty-meters.

The sun and heat and the bugs burned away and ate the flesh of the dead and the living remarkably quickly. Bones marked the graves, and then the sand drifted and maybe only a tibia or the edge of a skull, perhaps a forehead and eye socket peeking above the dust, marked the ever-shifting infertile ground, and then there was nothing left.

Underground, it was an entirely different scene.

The entrance to the real Camp Eros, was almost invisible, a tiny steel door in a rocky outcropping in the middle of the desolate seemingly uninhabited trailer camp.

And, yes, indeed, underground, Camp Eros was an entirely different scene.

"Jump hybrid, jump!"

Up above it was just those roiling desert sands, those empty armored trailers, a few workshops, and that small unmanned airstrip, but down here, 150 meters down, it was one man's very own private super-duper erotic electro circus. In short, for those of peculiar tastes, it was paradise on earth.

Prisoner Hybrid-HZ-3, her sleek body and scales glittering a sexy black and red, jumped through the high hoop, landed on all fours, and hissed at the visitor, showing all her glorious fangs!

Wow, wow, and wow! – What a blast! What fucking fun this was!

"That's right, slave, hiss, hiss, hey, jump!" C Emerson Caldwell III flashed the electronic whip. It curled like a long snake, hissing, coming straight at the hybrid, and its fiery point uncurling, with sparks, touched her scales. And she knew the pain would flash through her rump and thighs, and it did, so she jumped and hissed, just as the human creature in the funny hat ordered her to do.

"Somersault!"

She leaped in a somersault, came down on her front claws, and walked on them for a few steps, hind legs straight up in the air, snout down, eyes gleaming, staring at the ground, the lights gleaming in a silken sheen off her mirror-bright black scales and voluptuous hybrid body.

"Hey, you bitch, that is cute!"

C. Emerson Caldwell III slapped his thighs. He was so excited! He was wearing his favorite antique cowboy white Stetson, the mustard-colored vest with the silver buckles and buttons, and he was smoking a fat cigar that looked like a bloated black torpedo from a World War II German U-boat, and he was having a fucking first-rate good time; it was worth the money, flying out here in his own jet into the Dead Lands, having his own little sexy circus animal, a handsome black-and-red mentally-defanged hybrid.

In her human form she had been the most beautiful girl in the world, a blonde goddess, the Claudia Schiffer of the 22nd century, this hybrid, the stuff of dreams! Truth be known, he worshiped her, he had worshiped her for years, but now he was her master – he alone.

And she – and this was utterly delightful – she was locked forever into her reptilian hybrid form. Her being prisoner in her own body – as a reptile – was a total gas! Emerson slashed the whip again, but this time cracking it, just short of her legs. She was still walking, head down, feet up in the air, ambling along on her front claws. "Okay, now, down on all fours, crawl over here to big daddy, and beg, beg!"

HZ-3 did as he ordered. She flipped down onto all fours, crawled over to him like the most obedient of creatures, and begged, her forked tongue hanging out, dripping silver saliva, her cute red-and-black muzzle, and bright yellow eyes staring worshipfully up at him.

C. Emerson Caldwell III reached into the food pouch and threw her a handful of shredded raw meat.

She snatched it up.

She was only four feet away, but he knew that she knew – even the stupid animal that she had now become – knew – that she was within two feet of the electronic shock barrier – it worked through the mind-collar – and so she knew too, in her beautiful blind, dumb animal way, that if she ever tried to get at old C. Emerson Caldwell III, say, to scratch his eyes out or break his neck, her mind-collar would give her a total wallop of a paralyzing electric shock that would leave her dead on the ground – quivering with pain and vibrating like a violin string – for at least an hour. That, in Emerson's mind, would be an utter crying shame and it would mean a fully-paid-up hour completely wasted and without pleasure of any kind, except maybe he could poke her a bit, here and there, with the electro-whip and see her helpless spasms echo his playful little nudges.

"Okay, now honey, touch yourself, caress yourself, you know, breasts, and thighs, cunt and ass, twist and turn, jiggle and jostle, shimmy and shake, show off how stacked you are, give yourself pleasure. You know I'm a kind and considerate fellow, really." He puffed on the cigar, feeling real big, and real good. He was wearing designer jeans, an open chamois shirt and that sleeveless open leather mustard-colored vest, both the vest and the shirt with monogrammed silver buttons, "CEC III."

The hybrid swung back onto her haunches and began to stroke her sides and then her breasts, all the while staring at him, her tongue hanging out, drooling that rich, thick, silver hybrid drool which was so attractive.

In spite of the mind-collar, she was somehow thinking, yes, real thoughts. This ridiculous creature in front of her was what was called a human being, and beyond him was a big sign, in light bulbs, "Private Hybrid Circus," bright lights that blinked, on and off, merrily, in a really festive spirit, but made of letters she couldn't decipher, having lost the ability to read; it was difficult to think, and she really did fear the long uncoiling thin snake-like thing that gave her sharp spasms of pain, and she knew that if she leaped forward to kill him – which her loins and claws – all muscles tensed – dearly wanted to do – she would be caught in a searing thunderbolt of pain and she would die or be quivering like death in agony for a long time and wake in pain and be punished over and over, and over and over.

So …

Thinking was next to impossible. Orders, simple orders, she could follow; she'd been programmed for that.

And feelings, she could decipher feelings, she could sense them; he wanted to humiliate her, she understood that, he wanted to her to make a spectacle of herself, that, too, she got, in some visceral non-verbal way, and she instinctively understood, too, that underneath those sadistic desires, and perverse proclivities, this particular human creature had other more complex feelings which were too deep and ambivalent for words and in any case she didn't have any words, not available, not at the moment. What the hell was a "word" anyway?

HZ-3 didn't know who or what she was.

"Ah, you are a fucking beautiful animal," the human was saying; it was just noise, and she didn't understand the words though she did understand he was mocking and making fun of her and insulting her and in some vague way degrading her and that in his mind he was contrasting what she was now with what in other times and circumstances she had been and that this contrast gave him a cruel pleasure. She felt her claws move over the surfaces of her body and …

"If you were fucking human, I'd fuck you myself." He grinned; his hand went down to his crotch. He began a vigorous self-massage, "I thought about it millions of times, you know, all those photos of you when you were the glamor queen, the blond goddess, the style icon, and that time you went on the radio and with all those cameras, the computer cameras pointed at you, you made a little demonstration and morphed right there, morphed from human to hybrid and back to human – morphed in front of the nation! What a show-off! Everybody's forgotten that now, darling, it's been removed from the collective consciousness, it's been erased and canceled, just like you've been erased and canceled, but I remember! Old C Emerson Caldwell III never forgets anything to do with you! I've got all the archives, darling. I'm your biggest fan is what I am."

Click! It went '*click*' inside her head.

What was that?

Click!

What the fuck was going on?

Click! Suddenly her visual field came into sharp focus. She realized with a shock *who* she was and, roughly, *where* she was.

Bingo! Clarity!

Yes, she realized in one horrible illuminating instant who and what and where she was. She was in reptilian hybrid form sitting on her haunches in front of an overweight jowly 58-year-old male human individual wearing an antique Stetson cowboy hat – 2132 CE vintage she figured, with the special wide silk-latex band and traces of a heavy sweat stain leaking out from inside – and a silver-tinted open chamois shirt and an open mustard-colored vest and jeans – and he was sweating and had not shaved this morning – the five o'clock shadow was already there – particularly in the folds of his jowls – his boots were HMV antique remake frontier cowboy boots and must have cost a fortune – she wouldn't have chosen that particular brand and on the basis of a quick glance they were a size too small – and he was holding a Tumble Corp 1ZZ-5 model electronic whip and he was wiggling the whip a bit like he was going to strike out with it – sparks sizzling at the end in eagerness already – and he was aroused – there was a vulgar pathetic phallic bulge at the artificially bleached crotch of his faux-proletarian jeans – and he was staring at her, with his pale gray-blue eyes slightly glassy from lust and mental rutting, and behind him, over his shoulder, there was a faux set of string lights – like an old-time antique country fair or freak midway sign "*Private*

Hybrid Circus" – blue, red, green, yellow light bulbs over an arch – like the entry to a freak show.

She realized this was what it was: *She was in a damned freak show.*

There was a hologram sign shimmering in the air too, it came and went, "The Most Beautiful Hybrid in the World!"

Fuck, she thought, is that us? Is that me?

What! Me!? Inwardly she flushed in rage and shame and shock. Me??? I'm in a fucking animal erotic freak show! Me! Claire V Jacobs, CEO of CVJ the largest cosmetics, fashion, and cultural conglomerate in the … and … I am the goddamned freak! Star attraction!

Click!

What is happening?

Click!

It was out of focus. She groaned. The human snapped his whip. She drooled. She did what she was told to do. The ephemeral thoughts vanished like dissolving clouds. She yearned for them, thinking, it was so beautiful, so seductive, so powerful, to think and to understand! And now, now, now it was gone! She no longer knew who or what she as or where she was.

"Now," the human in the cowboy hat moved his wet puffed-up glossy lips, "Pretend you are Ginger Rogers. We are in *Flying Down to Rio*. Remember, I taught you the part."

Click!

HZ-3 began to do a Ginger Rogers dance number. She high-kicked and swirled and leaned back, wondering, where the hell did I learn that? I must have been conditioned. She was moving in and out of lucidity now – one second knowing precisely who she was – the next lost in a swampy, semiconscious, primal fog.

The music shifted, and now it was something by Cole Porter, "You do something to me."

The fat guy was dancing, pretending to hold somebody – or something – in his arms.

Gosh, thought HZ-3, as her ability to think suddenly returned and revved up. *This really weird, the guy is dancing all by himself.* And then, as her innate hybrid mind-reading capability began to return, and with it her acute sense of human and male psychology, she realized that, in the guy's mind, he was holding her – Claire V Jacobs – both in her human form, and, in alternating mental flashes, in her reptilian alien form. He is dancing with *me!*

He was mentally strobe-light flashing between two versions of Claire. And not only that, he was imagining himself sometimes as himself – but a prettied up and handsome younger self – and then, on another level, he was imagining himself as *her*, either as Claire the blond sophisticated fashion marketing icon, or as Claire the jet-black red-patterned alien hybrid. *Gosh!* This was a pretty complex scenario the guy was spinning, playing at least four different roles. Talk about fractured identity! Inwardly, she sighed. Perversion was a fabulously intricate maze and fascinating palace to explore – sometimes!

Cole Porter continued: "You do something to me, something that simply mystifies me ..."

Now, suddenly, a group of people – humans – were in front of her – women in cotton dresses and kerchiefs and flowered hats and men in raincoats, glistening with rain, and broad-brimmed hats pulled down over their ears. A man in a fedora, a barker or mountebank, was giving his spiel – she half understood the words:

"Step right up, step right up, ladies and gentlemen, step right up! Now, this thing you see before you was once – hard to believe, gentlemen, I know, impossible to believe, ladies, I know – this thing, this crouching reptilian monster, its tongue dripping thick drops of poisonous silver venom, was once one of the richest and most beautiful women in the world. She was a world-famous model, actress, and inventor, why she had everything! But the wheel turns. But now the great have fallen. Hubris is poison! Pride is punished. Ego is perishable and perishes. Her beauty is gone, her wealth is gone, her fame is gone, and even her mind is gone. Now, as suitable punishment for her innumerable wicked deeds and for her satanic diabolic nature, she is a hideous, mindless, non-human beast, ladies and gentlemen, a freak, locked up here, for your very own entertainment, delectation, and edification, as you can see, let me just crack the whip and she'll put on a beautiful performance for you!"

The men and women crowded closer. They looked like images from some old film Claire had once seen – from sometime in the 1930s, way back, before Claire Jacobs was born – well, before she was created in Sabrina Jacob's Andromeda Corporation laboratory. *Yeah, it was an old movie she'd seen. What was it called?*

"Can she do the somersault again?" One woman asked, "I liked the somersault."

"Freaks," that's what it was called!

"Freaks," directed by a guy called Tod Browning!

"Certainly, madam, she'll do anything!"

Her human thoughts faded, *"Nooooo …!"*

He cracked the whip.

Gone, thoughts gone, all gone!

Claire somersaulted, came down on her front claws and walked – they liked that, she could feel it, it gave them a particular thrill, they really liked it, those human creatures beyond the barrier, they liked her walking on her front claws with her hind legs straight up in the air, standing to attention upside down, and they didn't crack the whip, at least not for a few seconds, that was respite, though of course, she didn't have words for the thoughts – she just knew walking on her hands, even sketching out a little two-step, upside down, kept the pain away – for a few seconds …

Then everything went blurry, and it was the man in the Stetson again. The crowd was gone. The Stetson was back. She vaguely remembered he had been there before. "Special privilege, honey," he was saying, "Those other people, they're just figments, projection holograms, just to add to the atmosphere, you know. In reality, I get you to myself, the whole evening, every time I come out here, you and I can play, just the two of us. Those other humans, honey, they're just for theatrical effect, World Mind stuff, Cloud Figments. Down here, now, in the real nitty-gritty, in the real reality, it's just you and me, well *almost* just you and me." He grinned and cracked the whip. "Come on over here and crouch, you hybrid bitch, you slut, you whore, you sow!"

She scurried over on all four claws, quick was better, she knew, and less painful. "Feel yourself up, feel yourself up good," he said, "feel yourself up! Enjoy! I want to see you enjoy! I worship you, you know!"

She obeyed, drooling, staring in seeming adoration at him …

Click …

Her mind was back.

What the hell! Where am I? Everything clicked into focus. It all came clear. She stared at the man in the Stetson. *What a pathetic fucking individual!*

He was, yes, he was definitely having an erection under the retro-1970s Cowboy-Hippy subculture bleached blotch at the crotch of his outmoded ill-fitting second rate baggy no-brand-name jeans, and he could obviously afford better jeans than that if he can pay for a whole erotic hybrid exotic circus for his own private jerk-off perverted entertainment, featuring yours truly, but then some people have no taste, if it were left up to me, I could advise him and even as pathetic an individual as he is could be spruced up a bit, remade, and …

What the hell am I thinking?

He's protected because my mind has been neutered, she realized, and her claw reached up instinctively to the collar, yes, a *mind-collar*, that's what they call it, and she was tempted to rip it off, but she immediately realized it had diodes or connectors buried in her nervous system and in her spine so if she ripped it off she might badly damage herself and it might kill or disable her and in the best of scenarios it would take time to repair the nerve endings, the flesh, the neural networks, and the spinal wiring, during which time she would quite possibly be vulnerable, and she wanted to leap on this tasteless if rich bastard – who was getting his rocks off at the expense of her dignity – but she realized, too, that there was that electro-barrier between her and him and that if she leaped forward she would fall quivering to the ground, convulsed with shocks, and then unconscious, and unless they dragged her away from the sizzling current, maybe she'd even end up dead, though that was unlikely since hybrids are very solid, and she was probably worth a hell of a lot to the Black Furrow Halibut Family of Friendly Family Corps too, and then she realized that, for the moment at least, the mind-collar was dead – and, stunned, she said to herself, "that's why I'm thinking, that's why I'm suddenly me – that why I'm suddenly fussing about style and proposing to submit this creep to a full CVJ – Claire V Jacobs – platinum remake with all the trimmings and spa extras."

And she realized, simultaneously, that if the mind-collar was dead, then quite possibly the electronic barrier was dead too! So, yes, I could leap right across and tear out his throat and put that lovely antique Stetson – for which I lust – on my own head!

While these thoughts rushed through her mind and a myriad of other thoughts and perceptions too, she continued her little act, being careful not to alarm the false cowboy, who she realized, skimming his mind, was really a virtual retailer from Elysium City – sky tower Olympia Three – who had never set foot on a real ranch in his life, couldn't lasso a two-year-old calf, had never seen or smelled manure, couldn't milk a cow if his life depended on it – had never even seen a cow, for Christ's sake – not even a synthetic genetically re-engineered Holstein – and who would run terrified from a nanny goat – and that he was divorced – no children – and an inveterate and pathetic loner, and that he lived his emotional life, such as it was, entirely through fantasies, and she was the focus of those fantasies, and that, in fact, he really would like to possess her and take her home with him as a pet, but she was, she realized as she probed his inner monolog and lament, not, alas for sale, being property of Halibut & Black Furrow and North American Homeland Security Incorporated, and only put on display in erotic and rustic recreations – *fuck, what the hell* – in order to defray costs and overheads and she actually paid for her upkeep more or less, and had made a profit for Halibut & Black Furrow and Homeland Security Incorporated and its shareholders – the Crock and Churn families – during the last fourteen years ... the last fourteen years!

"Fuck this! I'm going to leap over the barrier!"

Meanwhile, she continued the act, staring adoringly at the old – well, middle-aged – fart who really, she thought, who really, aside from his sexual obsession with an enslaved hybrid – namely, me – is not that bad a fellow, really, just lonely, just pathetically unable to connect to people, and trapped in his own fantasy lives – a regular little circus they were too, his multiple fantasy lives, for he did indeed contain multitudes, his sadism being directed, of course, toward her but, though her, it was, mostly, directed at himself, or parts of himself, inner imagoes, really interesting – so ...

You could write a book about this guy's fantasies.

And hey! Mostly, yes, indeed, his fantasies star me! I am the leading lady, the fetish, the clown, the ideal, the totem, the girl-phallus dreamboat, andro-gynous and yet a babe, exotic and yet familiar, an animal, and yet human, or so goes his subconscious tale, all about me, absolute perfection, all wrapped up in one enslaved female reptilian hybrid package.

He's a true fan!

She drooled, licked her lips, watching his reaction.

She realized that in her enslaved state, with the mind-numbing collar going full blast, she had not been able to speak – just growl and hiss.

So she hissed in fake pleasure, rolled her snake eyes; then she stared at him, adoringly.

"See, you bitch," he said, "you like it, you slut, you like it, don't you!"

She realized, once again, that, in uttering the word "bitch," he was talking about himself as well as her; and that, like many consumers of virtual or real porno, he was both the subject and the object, the audience, the director, the cameraman, and the performer of the spectacle he observed; he and she all in one, he is me and he is him, but mostly, in his mind, right now, he is me, he really would like to be me, poor idiot, he really dreams he *is* me, here, abasing himself in front of himself, by proxy, through me, himself disguised as me goofing around in front of himself, exorcizing and practicing his hatred and self-hatred, and his hatred for women in general and for his mother in particular, all in one, and he's not really himself, not now, he's something somewhere inside this pathetic little show, viewer and viewed, gazer and gazed-upon, hmm ... This interplay of subject and object and the unreality of the subject could be used in my next advertising campaign ... Let's see ... *Oh, what a stupid thought – I have no next advertising campaign!*

Cole Porter continued: "You do something to me ..."

The music began to slow and then ground to a halt in a shower of sparks and static. The hologram illustrated *Sex Circus* banner that had been floating around close to a false tent – a simulacrum of a Barnum and Bailey big-top – flickered and then went out. The giant tent itself glowed stronger, blinked once, and disappeared into iridescent flakes. A sleepy elephant that had been passing by, dissolved into falling ember-like fragments – like an ancient fresco lost underground in an isolated chamber suddenly exposed to the air. Everything was melting away. The freak show sign flickered and the colored light bulbs – red, blue, green, and yellow – faded into nothingness. The desert sky, long streaks of prairie clouds, ripples of red and charcoal, redolent of fiery celestial tumbling tumbleweed and wide-open spaces and "don't fence me in" – with echoes of Roy Rogers and Gene Autry and John Wayne and Billy the Kid – the desert sky that had been showing sunset out beyond the circus grounds, washed away into etiolated darkness. A crowd of people that had been listening to a barker, including two kids munching on pink cones of candy floss, wavered, undulated, flickered, lit up brightly, one last gasp, spit out sparks, and dimmed to nothingness, the last one to disappear being a stout lady in a 1920s black-and-white cloche hat, and a 1930s high-waisted dark blue dress with oversized white polka dots. The hurdy-gurdy music ceased. The whole circus was collapsing. *Wow,* Claire realized, *this must be a general systems failure.*

It was now or never.

She took a deep breath – still fearing the mind-collar and the electric barrier – and she leaped across the electronic barrier – zip, landing on all four claws right down, like an acrobatic cat thrown from a high window. Zip, right there she landed, where she had intended, in front of her cowboy master.

Whew! Nothing happened: no mind-paralyzing electric shock, no body-frying ripple of sparkly, smoky high-voltage jolts, no nerve-stunning, tuning fork-vibrating, World Mind Zap, nothing.

The World Mind was disconnected.

The mind-collar was not working.

Yes, for the moment at least, it was dead, well and truly dead.

She stood up. The cowboy fell, wham, backwards, flat on the ground. His hat fell off. He was bald with sparse strands of greasy white hair along the sides of his head. His skin was blotchy, like white yogurt gone rancid – or maybe like curdled cream. He was staring up at her. He had quite a paunch, she realized, looking down at him. It was sagging sideways. "Show's over, mister," she hissed.

"What the hell..?" He gasped, eyes blinking.

"I'm tempted to tear you into little bits, but I'm not going to do it. By the way …" She leaned down, fangs bared.

"What," his face was dead pale, mottled with fear, "What are you going to do to me?"

"I don't mind being in your fantasies, but …"

"My God, don't hurt me!" He was, sprawled, trembling; he'd raised one elbow to protect himself.

She leaned closer, and stroked his sweaty bald head with her claw. "You have lots of money," she said, "Why haven't you had a makeover?"

"What?"

"It could take twenty or thirty years off your age!"

"What?"

"For starters, apply CVJ smoothing cream – just think about it."

She leaped away, leaving the man, half-lying, half-sitting on the ground.

He was merely a customer of the Erotic Circus. There would be guards. They would be armed. And at any time the system could come back on, and she would again be an animal, no worse than an animal – she had, after all, a great respect for animals and the various forms of intelligence they possessed – no, she would be less than null! She would be a mentally paralyzed creature, a puppet and a slave, a reified figment of this guy's fantasies, a fragment of his own fractured self, trapped in – ugh – his mind, a total slave and a mere function of the most filthy form of convoluted male gaze, yuk, totally yuk. She had to get rid of the mind-collar.

She glanced around. Emergency lights had gone on, throwing a livid cadaverous glare over the place – sandy floor, rocky walls.

They were in a cavern, or so it seemed, lots of rock, and a few buildings and cables. She didn't see any other hybrids, or even any humans for that matter.

Nothing but equipment, electronic stuff. The whole circus probably ran itself. That was typical – the cheap bastards left everything up to the World Mind, to computer simulations and conjured illusions. People forgot how to do anything, all their skills, all their knowledge, all their taste was evaporating, and had been evaporating for many decades. Only some upper-level Cosmos and some clever, subversive Subs knew how to do anything. The World Mind did everything. What would happen if it disappeared or collapsed, eh? They'd all die, that's what would happen.

She leaped – a five-meter hop – back to the customer. He was on his knees, just getting up, shaking. He had put his Stetson back on his head. His forehead was beaded in sweat. "Hey, partner," she said, landing right in front of him, "Where is everybody?"

He stared at her. "You talk," he said.

"Sure, I talk. I already gabbed at you, I was excessively confiding, or don't you remember? We were having a regular conversation. I was giving you advice. Up till now, this collar stopped me from blabbing; but now it's off."

"There is nobody. This is a self-regulated special prison," he said, his fat wet lips trembling, "You are the only prisoner. I have to pay millions to come out here to see you, to play with you …"

" … to play with me …" she growled. Her fangs shone; her claws flexed, her smooth black reptilian biceps bulged; her serpent eyes narrowed to angry glittering gold slits. She really could eat him, or plunge her fangs into his neck and drain him dry – but: Yuk! The prospect was not appetizing: his blood surely seethed with junk food trace elements and antediluvian antibiotics and weird creepy pep-me-up hormones and urban poisons from out-of-date recycling plants.

He blanched and trembled. "You know what I mean … I … you were famous when you were human, and I thought you were the most beautiful creature in the world. I have the full collection – though it is illegal – the *Vogue* covers, the *Paris Match* stories, the New York Times magazine piece, the *Die Zeit* Magazine cover, the *Shanghai Daily*, the *People's Daily*, *Izvestia*, the *Playboy* fold-out … I was a fan. And so when …"

"So, you came to jerk my chain."

"That's a vulgar way of putting it."

"So," she put a claw on his shoulder, "You're telling me there's nobody else here?"

"Yes, only tours come out," he trembled, from fear, or, perhaps, it was a shiver of pleasure. "You're the only inmate. It's all self-enclosed electronic. No direct links to the Cloud or the Mind except one-way links, instructions come down, no direct upward links to the Net. You are super-dangerous, they say – Flick Churn explained it to me himself – because of your Net Linked Mind. You are kept in strict electronic and physical isolation, absolutely no access to the Net and Cloud for you. Termination was considered – except, even though you're deadly dangerous Net-Wise, Flick Churn – you know what he's like – he couldn't resist; he wanted to turn a profit, make a buck, squeeze the stone, he couldn't let it alone, didn't want grass to grow under his feet, as he said, you know, if there's anything to exploit, he'll exploit it, so your synergies and re-engineering were really appetizing, and so you're used as entertainment, sometimes for a solo audience, only for special high-security-clearance Cosmos corporate platinum clients, of which I am one, it's a very exclusive club, only five of us, and you are super-beautiful, in your reptile form or your human form, like the supermodel mogul you used to be, I adore you, I worship you, and hybrids have now all been neutered and erased, and you are one of those left – a rarity, an antiquity, a collector's item – and that's part of the thrill …"

"And where are we?"

"In the Dead Lands, in the … Super … Dust … Bowl … I …" He gulped, put his hand to his throat, and went pale.

"And where are the others?"

"Others?"

"The other hybrids."

"Ah, they've been erased. The remains – the bodies – are in a camp, Camp Terminus, near here, it's hush-hush, top secret; only a few privileged people, humans, know about this and I … I …" C Emerson Caudwell's face turned even paler, big beads of sweat exploded on his forehead. He cried out "Help!" He fell straight down, and lay there, sprawled, tummy up, spread-eagled, gurgling in his throat, his eyes rolled up, only the whites showing, two hard-boiled eggs. On his way down to the ground, he had sighed and choked, his lips bubbling gluey saliva. He had uttered, "I adore …you …Claire V Jacobs … I love … It's love … true love and adoration … I … I …!"

"Damnation!" Claire crouched next to him, put her claw on his chest, and pinched his throat. Sniffed his mouth, his nostrils. There was not a breath, not a puff – nothing. Truly nothing. He was dead. He was dead before he hit the ground. Those pathetic amorous words were his last puff of life! He was dead, truly dead, as her sister and mother V would have said, and he would not rise again. She couldn't raise him back up from the dead if she tried. If he'd only held on for a second or two, just a thread of life and she could have brought him back, even if it consumed a load of energy, but dead, stark dead, no, she couldn't raise the dead …. Now he'd never get that makeover.

He would have made a great before-and-after reality ad for Claire V Jacobs CVJ Rejuvenation Services, Inc.

I could have turned him into a muscle-bound poster boy!

Enough of that, Claire! Thinking about your Empire will do you absolutely no good. Remember – you don't have an Empire!

The Dead Lands, eh! So we are deep in the Dead Lands. She lifted up his arm – his wrist pad gave the time; she switched it to see the date: 2158!

And the other hybrids, if any of them were alive, were not far away – she must save them!

What, in fact, happened to us?

What did she last remember? It seemed like five or ten minutes ago, not more, but it must have been at least fourteen years. Let's see. She'd been in New York– aka Elysium City – though she could never get used to the new name – and she'd been preparing her new North American CVJ luxury Cosmos First-Class Only Spring Collection. She was vaguely worried. The North American Imperial Federation was turning into a Fundamentalist Holy-Book-Thumping radically anti-hybrid and anti-SIN society, suspicious of everything and everybody that wasn't orthodox and fully human. The President, under pressure from the Mad Hatter's True Human Tea Party and the Old Time End of Time Trumpery Religious Movement, was proposing strict anti-hybrid legislation, and there were rumors of a coup d'état, a putsch, and a secret plan to round up and eliminate all hybrids and SINs. But most hybrids and SINs discounted these rumors. *I mean, we are completely integrated, aren't we, some of us are even famous! People love us. I mean, some of us are movie stars, some are bankers, some are famous scientists, and some are great singers. I mean: we are more patriotically human than even the humans!* In Europe and Asia, things were easier, strangely. Perhaps Europe had been inoculated against Fascism, and in Europe, there were few hybrids, just herself and one or two others. So, as she was putting the finishing touches to her collection, she was thinking that maybe she'd be safer back in Paris, or maybe in Switzerland, and she was thinking, yes, she and the hybrids and some of their SIN friends should ask V and Sabrina Jacobs – CEO of Andromeda

Corporation – to convene a meeting to see what could be done about the rising tide of human xenophobia and fear … She'd just gone down from her office to get into her car when …

What happened next?

She couldn't remember.

And what about the others? What had happened to them? What about V and Sabrina? Where were they? Were they alive?

She concentrated. She focused her mind. She extended her mental tentacles, her ultra-sympathetic receptors. Usually, she had a vague feeling of other hybrid presences – a sort of transcendent parallel universe neural network – perhaps some sort of quantum energy field, she guessed – that linked them all – but now there seemed to be nothing – just a great void; the universe was silent; it was like she was alone.

What had he said? That the hybrids had all been erased!

That couldn't be true; she refused to believe it.

She was still holding C Emerson Caldwell III's wrist. She lowered his arm down gently. She closed his eyes and let her claw rest on his forehead. Well, my friend, you were, in your own way, I guess, part of the fan club. I was your fetish and your toy, and now all your little head-dreams and head-games and onanistic hard-ons and nocturnal and diurnal ejaculations are dust and ashes, lust dead and gone, pure ephemeral vanity, like all things human, however exciting they might be at the time, and you too are dust, and soon you will be nothing, like all of us, nothing, not even a dream or a memory for there will be no one to dream or remember you – except, perhaps, for a time, me, if I get out of here and resume my supposedly immortal – or near to immortal – life. And, goddamn, I want to get back to work; I already have some ideas for a new spring collection: latex and leather and S/M combined with a frilly little *Alice in Wonderland* late 19th century Alice down-the-looking glass or rabbit hole look, perverse, but not too perverse, Lolita with a lollipop and a whip and a penchant for snake-handlers, wicker baskets, and rattlesnakes. But, enough of that! Dear C Emerson Caldwell III, you have been an inspiration!

She stood up. I have to get out of here.

More memories began to come back in flickers – in little images.

She tugged at the mind-collar. She definitely had to get this thing off her neck.

Once again, she realized how unique, what a privilege, it was to be thinking, thinking for the first time in a long time.

What the hell? Somebody was headed toward her.

Is this another illusion, another downloaded self-generating isolated figment of the spluttering World Mind?

It was a woman, striding toward her.

The woman looked good enough to be an illusion: perfectly, tightly coiffed, perfectly soignée, utterly stylish. She looked too good to be human. She had a thin, strictly sculpted face, the sort of fashionably austere aristocratic features and clean-cut centuries-of-breeding cheekbones, the sort of cheekbones ballerinas used to sport back in the day; her hair was pulled back in a severe bun; she was wearing a pinstripe charcoal faux-silk business suit and thick, rimmed glasses, black stockings and high heels, exquisitely put together, really. She stopped right in front of Claire.

"Hello," said Claire.

The woman looked down at C Emerson Caldwell III, opened her mouth, as if in shock, then she screamed, "You killed him! Oh you beast, you ungrateful witch, you horror show, you freak, you hybrid!"

"I didn't kill him." Claire was taken back. Who was this shrew? Where did she come from?

"I have worked and slaved for C Emerson Caldwell III for almost ten years, I have cataloged his collections, I have been his CEO and his CFO and his legal counsel and his informal *Consigliere* for the Underground Economy, kickbacks, payouts, greasy hands, I have been his go-between with the higher-ups, and his personal pilot and therapist, I have not hesitated, not recoiled, not demurred, no, not for a single second, not before the direst and dirtiest and darkest of deeds! I have been privy to C Emerson Caldwell III's most elaborate and deepest desires, all of which dark evil deep desires concern *you*, you ungrateful freak show brat, he has over five thousand four hundred and fifty-six images of you, still and moving, three-dimensional and two dimensional, black-and-white and full color, oh ... This is tragic! I can't stand this!" The woman fell on her knees and kissed the cadaver on the forehead. "Oh, Emerson, Oh, Emerson, return from the dead, Emerson."

"I didn't kill him, lady, I tried to save him. He had a heart attack, and just fell straight down dead."

"Oh, oh, oh ..." The woman was sprawled on top of C Emerson Caldwell III.

Claire found such displays excessive. "You are going to muss up that suit, lady, and it's a mighty fine suit, if I may say so – exquisite taste."

"I do not care, I do not – I do not care! Oh, oh, oh!"

Claire thought about it; thousands of images of her! *Images of me – What a fabulous archive! I wonder if I can acquire it!*

The thought of all that imagery triggered something. Her past life, all her memories flooded back: who she was and what she looked like when she was human – and when she was reptilian – and how she had been arrested in New York – sorry, Elysium City – just when she was preparing her new North American CVJ – Claire V Jacob – spring collection. Now, she remembered it. Her car had been ambushed, her driver and secretary killed, and she had been shot with a special neuro-paralyzing drug – and she had been accused under an arrest warrant issued in New York City by Flick Churn – well, in what was left of New York City – now Elysium City – a Bubble Dome to protect the Cosmos First-Class Shopping Elite from the collapsing climate and wacky weather – of being an enemy of the people, and that she would be detained under the Emergency Protection Of Humanity Act and that she had no right to a lawyer or to a bath or to makeup or cold cream or a hot shower. All this had been read to her by a grubby little man wearing an ankle-length black leather trench coat and a broad-rimmed black hat, which seemed to be dripping rain, while she lay drugged, paralyzed, and hallucinating. She was just beginning to come back to herself, when they snapped a thing on her neck – the mind-collar.

Yes, they clicked that bloody mind-collar on her, and she morphed from human into reptile – exploding the fine antique Jean-Paul Gaultier suit she had been wearing – and, instantly, she was a mindless drooling slave, on all fours, begging, panting – if she'd had a tail she would have wagged it – and then she disappeared. She was no more. For the world, she no longer existed. She had vague memories, a kaleidoscope of impressions. And now here she was – wherever that was …

She had been "disappeared" – "*desaparecida*" – like so many others.

Speaking of the camp, Emerson had said that they were in the Dead Lands, but where exactly was she in the Dead Lands?

"Excuse me, Madam, but where precisely are we, Madam, do you know?"

"Don't speak to me, you two-legged reptilian obscenity, you monster of ingratitude! Leave me to my grief, oh, Emerson, Emerson, why did you let her kill you!"

"What is your name, then, Madam?"

"My name is Demi Pfeiffer, you big-boobed beast!"

Claire looked down at her breasts, "Big-boobed beast! Really!"

"Yes, big-boobed beast!" Demi Pfeiffer, who was really extraordinarily handsome, was crying lavishly, streams coursing down her cheeks, but *not*, Claire noted, messing with Demi Pfeiffer's mascara. *Take note: she is wearing tear-proof CVJ permanent makeup.*

"Goodbye, then," said Claire, "And I did not kill him. I rather liked him – well, parts of him, truth be told."

"Murder!" the woman screamed, she hammered her fists on C Emerson Caldwell III's chest, "Murder most foul, most foul murder!"

"Goodbye, then," said Claire.

The woman said nothing. She merely wailed and kicked her legs, stirring up dust, tarnishing the pin-striped suit, the fine patent leather points of her shoes hammering into the dirt.

"I'm going," said Claire.

"Be gone, foul-mouthed, whorish, big-boobed beast," Demi Pfeiffer was engulfed in tears and pounding her fists on Emerson's swelling belly and brass buttons. She screamed. Sobs shook her lithe, superbly designed body. She kicked at the dust, the points of her fine patent leather shoes raising little clouds of powdery earth.

"Well, I'm gone," said Claire; and, glancing back now and then, she set off to look for a way out of this hellish place wherever it was. It was undoubtedly underground. So if life on the surface was still possible, she decided that she should head for the surface. Then she would escape, even if it was only into the desert.

She came to a large side cave.

She sniffed – no danger apparent – and she entered.

There was an elevator shaft, but the elevator was not working. It looked like it hadn't worked in years. It was a monument to rust.

To think that once the United States of America – the nation that no longer existed – had been a practical, pragmatic, can-do, inventive, tinkering, problem-solving country. Claire sighed. The whole state of decay gave her the pips. She was – or had been – an American citizen, as well as holding European and British passports.

The Star-Spangled Banner still brought tears to her eyes. *Hail to the Chief* gave her a catch in the throat, hybrid or human, didn't matter. Now the whole thing was a fanatical, obscurantist, criminal shambles.

How could people be so *neglectful*, how could people be so *stupid*!

She climbed up the safety stairs – greasy, and unused, except for the center of the steps, where footsteps had worn away the grease and rust. My fan club, thought Claire, I guess that's it, maybe just one guy, maybe poor dear dead C Emerson Caldwell III and his faithful CFO and Consigliere, the beautiful deranged Demi Pfeiffer, just the two of them trotting up and down this old staircase. Or maybe there were other fans too. Who knew? Who cared? Running up parallel to the staircase, there were, at each landing, huge rusty ventilator paddles – maybe fifteen feet across – and ventilator shafts which reflected what looked like moonlight, cool bright light from something anyway, maybe phosphorescent emergency lights, light coming down from above.

At the top of the stairs, she came to a narrow tunnel, obviously still underground. She walked down the tunnel.

It came to stairs and then to a door.

Claire pushed the metal lever and opened the door.

She was outside, perhaps for the first time in fourteen years, or more. And, yes, it was desert, yes, it was a wasteland.

And, yes, it was night.

And, yes, the moon was shining – bright silver.

She looked around. She was in some sort of base camp in the middle of nowhere. There was a small landing strip; there was a concrete bunker or airplane hangar, with a small executive aircraft – probably C Emerson Caldwell III's personal transport – tethered inside; and there were a few nondescript temporary buildings, trailers really, up on cement blocks, all plastered with drifting sand; it was ghostly and decrepit; a tawdry, end-of-the-world sort of place.

Definitely not the Ritz. There was nobody. She didn't see any humans or mutants or hybrids. She was in a desert somewhere, the Super Dust Bowl in the dead center of the Dead Lands, she figured.

There was a light on in one of the trailers.

It was the only sign of life.

The trailer looked like a workshop – it was set on blocks and with rusty machines clustered around it. A light shone in one of the trailer's barred and armored windows. It was the only light in the whole compound.

Claire stepped up to the trailer; she tried the door handle. The door wasn't locked. She opened it carefully. Inside there was a human in heavy overalls and heavy goggles and nose and mouth mask who was working with a lathe – sparks flying – and who had tools – old-fashioned tools – gosh!

A lathe – gosh!

Old-fashioned tools were good – they might help get rid of the mind-collar. She reminded herself, she absolutely must get rid of the thing before it turned on again.

It might be her only chance.

Claire went straight to the workman. He was wearing goggles, and he was bent over, concentrating on his work. The lathe was turning a piece of metal and the man was working intently and the metal stuck off sparks as the cuter made a groove in the surface. The guy didn't see her until her claw was on his arm and he turned and he screamed.

Claire was so startled by his scream that she almost fell over, almost let him go. Intent on getting rid of the collar and fascinated by everything she was discovering, she had forgotten that now humans – in 2158 – were evidently totally terrified of hybrids, and she'd even forgotten that she was in hybrid form.

She clamped her claw over the guy's mouth, ripped off his goggles and said, "Shut the fuck up!"

Then she saw he wasn't a man; he was a young woman, with short brown hair, a cute ingénue pixy-face, and very white skin, her body had been hidden by the leather apron, the overalls, the goggles, and the big work gloves. Enormous hazel eyes stared at Claire.

"Make a sound, and I will cut your throat," said Claire, showing her claws, "Keep quiet, and I will kiss you!"

The woman nodded: "Okay."

Claire took her claw off the woman's mouth. It was a nice mouth, delicate lips, bright, even teeth. Claire was tempted to carry out her threat, and kiss the girl, there and then, but she remembered that many humans did not have much of a sense of humor. Besides, I look positively frightful, I'm sure.

"You're a hybrid," the girl whispered, eyes wide in pure terror.

"Surprise, surprise," said Claire.

The girl blinked.

"I want to you to get this thing off me," said Claire, fingering the skintight mind-collar, "Any tricks and I will eat you alive. You look absolutely delicious, and I am famished."

"I can cut it," said the girl, "with this," and she held up a long-handled evil-looking pair of metal cutters.

"How long?"

"About five minutes."

"Do it."

"You have to lie down."

Claire climbed onto the workbench, lay down, and looked up at the girl.

"What's your name?"

"Robyn."

"Nice name," said Claire.

"Thank you," said Robyn, concentrating on cutting the collar. "It has embedded electrodes. Also, it has grown or was merged with your flesh and your nervous system. It's part of you."

"Tear the electrodes out, tear it off, cut it off," said Claire, "Get rid of all of it!"

"I'll have to cut into you, close to your spine. You may lose consciousness."

"Fuck." Claire clenched her claws and frowned.

"I won't harm you, I won't report you, I promise."

"Why is that?"

"Because …"

"Okay, do it."

Robyn worked on the collar, bent most of it away from Claire's neck, ripping away the scales, but the scales seemed to reform immediately, and Robyn thought, the hybrid is a self-healer. The healing accelerated, it was almost instantaneous. "Okay, I'm going to take out the electrodes now."

"Okay, Robyn, do it!" Claire wondered if the electrodes were so deeply embedded that removing them would destroy her brain, neuter her personality, and turn her into a robot or maybe even kill her. Well, I've already been a robot, she thought. Better to be dead than to be a slave.

There was a sharp pain. Then, everything went black, absolutely black, then there was nothing. Claire V Jacobs, human and hybrid, ceased to exist.

Robyn was making coffee. She prepared two cups, just in case. She poured some artificial milk into her own cup and left the other cup, steaming hot, black, just in case. She looked out the window. All the lights in the other trailers were off. Everybody had disappeared three nights ago. The whole place had shut down; there was some sort of emergency.

The sand was really blowing out there; it rattled and hissed against the walls of the trailer. She wondered if it might work itself up into a tornado.

She looked at the weather reading: a strong cold front colliding obliquely with a warm front, ideal sandspout, tornado, and blizzard conditions.

There was no use trying to go anywhere. The trailer was heavily armored and anchored down; it could survive almost anything, a heritage of its military background.

Robyn had fenced off part of the trailer into a bunk and hung a canvas to protect it from her workshop; it was where she slept – on a wide flat shelf with a thin mattress. This was her workshop and her prison. She drank some coffee and wondered what she should do.

The hybrid lay on the work table, sprawled on its back, no sign of life except the breathing which was regular, the electrodes had been connected to neural networks going deeper than Robyn had realized. She hoped she hadn't destroyed the hybrid; it was very pretty, really, with coal-black scales, golden eyes, and bright crimson markings on its snout.

She had never dealt directly with a hybrid before. She was curious. They were wild and stupid, mere animals, the results of unholy experiments or secret alien invasions, so she had been told, and they were dangerous, all the guide books and instruction sites said. It gave her a little shiver, a creepy-crawly thrill, being alone with such a creature, a mythical being escaped from some horror film or fairy tale.

But she had also read earlier accounts that told quite a different story – they said that the hybrids were super-beings and that they were, with few exceptions, benign and friendly and even helpful to humans. Faint echoes of this thought – now massively censored and discredited – still rebounded in the depths of her mind, like half-forgotten memories, like glimpses of some déjà vu experience.

This hybrid hadn't seemed stupid; in fact, it seemed very intelligent; it even made jokes. Now it was probably broken, and Robyn would never be able to fix it or explore its nature.

She felt horrible that she had destroyed such a wonderful toy. The one positive thing was the neck had totally healed; the scales had reformed as if they had never been cut; there was no trace or external mark left by the collar or the electrodes, so the hybrid looked brand-new, sparkling, as if just plucked off the shelf in a toy shop.

In truth, the hybrid was beautiful, sort of, yes, beautiful, really, stunning, glittery, and perfect, like a perfect machine.

She really would like to keep it. But she'd probably ruined it. Working out here in the workshop was lonely, and she felt she would like a companion – one that could talk and play games.

Of course, keeping the hybrid as a pet was beyond the realm of possibility, but a girl can dream, can't she?

Robyn was bored with her job, though she was good at it; she had trained as an engineer, with her expertise, her Ph.D., in space aeronautics, using artificial intelligence to explore outer space, and to explore inner space too by simulating voyages that had never taken place and seeing how bio-creatures with flexible neuro-networks would react to unaccustomed stimuli of unprecedented environments. Robyn was brilliant – *had been* brilliant.

But she had gotten into an argument with a Centurion officer, had lost her Cosmos Status, had served three years in correction camp, and large parts of her personality and intelligence had been chemically and electronically erased, turning her into "Child-4" category, with infantile tastes and infantile innocence, and, on the tech-skills front, she had been downgraded to basic techie status which was a life sentence, and her status rank number, NON-COSMOS, TS-5 had been frozen – she could never change status, she was locked in for life, with no rights as a citizen or shopper, and even her status as "human" was precarious, to say the least. Any sign of unorthodox behavior or disobedience and she could be made into a non-person, unemployable, an outcast and wandering pariah, which was, in most cases, a quick death sentence, with total erasure of memory and personality; or physical termination, either at the hands of Centurion patrols, or body parts pirates or Bordello Managers, or …

She took a sip of coffee. And then she carried the cup of black coffee over to the work table.

She set the cup down.

She put her finger in the cup – ouch, it was still scalding hot – and then she stuck her finger under the nostrils of the hybrid. The nostrils twitched and quivered, the mouth moved, the forked tongue emerged, slithered along the lips; the hybrid licked its lips.

It was alive, well, she already knew that.

But – had she broken it? That was the question! It had reflexes, so it might still be good for simple games. Perhaps if it woke up, she could teach it some simple tricks and they could have fun together. That would be really cool, since there was nobody else here she could play with; the guards, who were few and who had all disappeared, didn't like to play and they didn't like her because she was a down-grade and therefore polluted by the taboo of dissidence, it was like being unclean, and the guards were programmed to avoid the unclean and the polluted. Yes, it would really be nice to have a playmate and the hybrid would have been perfect. Robyn sighed and took another sip of coffee and was about to turn away when – oh!

The snake-like hybrid eyes opened. It was like looking into the soul, Robyn thought, as she leaned close, it was like looking into the soul of an alligator. The heavy-lidded eyes blinked. The slit in the eye widened somewhat and seemed to sparkle. Maybe the hybrid still had a brain.

That would be nice; maybe it wasn't entirely broken.

One clawed hand reached up, and – for a moment, Robyn thought, she's going to tear my head off – the knuckles caressed Robyn's cheek.

"Hello, Robyn," said the hybrid.

"Hello, Hybrid," Robyn said, suddenly thrilled, "I've made some coffee. Do you like it black?"

"Black will do," Claire said, and slowly, with one claw on Robyn's shoulder, she sat up, swiveled around, and sat on the edge of the work table, dangling her legs. "Thank you."

"How do you feel, Hybrid?"

Claire accepted the cup of coffee. "Thank you," she said again, "I feel a bit dizzy; but otherwise, I feel okay, I feel like myself, I think, I feel like my old self. You are a master artisan, Robyn. My name, by the way, is Claire."

"Claire?"

"Yes, funny, I'm coal-black – apart from the red marks on my snout – but my name is Claire."

"It's a nice name," said Robyn, thinking, I'm having a real conversation with a real hybrid. This is amazing! hybrids had been outlawed, and hybrids were outlaws. "I didn't know hybrids had names; I thought they just had numbers. On your collar, it says, 'HZ-3'. I'm an expert in collars – I repair collars and I made some of the originals in the work camp when they were downgrading me."

"In my human form, I'm a blonde, with blue eyes, so I think that's why I'm Claire. I didn't give myself my name, of course, but I think that's why they called me Claire. I was brought up in a glass cage, in a laboratory, it was pretty lonely, but that was a very long time ago, a time I've almost forgotten. Come to think of it, I'm going to ask my creator, she's sort of my mother, why she named me Claire, if she's alive and if I can find her, that is," The hybrid took another sip of the coffee, and looked thoughtful for a moment, "I didn't even know I was 'HZ-3',"

Robyn noticed that the hybrid used her long forked tongue to lap up the coffee. It was really cute – out came the tongue, lap, lap, lap, and in went the tongue.

"You have a human form? I didn't know."

"Yes, at least I think I still have a human form. In the camp, I think – I'm sure – they filled me with drugs, and they did experiments and they put those collars on which locked me into reptile form. I'm not sure if I can change back to human. Maybe the morph mechanism has been blocked. Maybe I'm stuck this way. I don't want to test the morph right now. I'm just happy to be conscious – and I'm quite content to stay in my present form. In fact, I'm rather annoyed at humans right now, except for you of course. Thank you for not calling the Militia."

"How do you know I haven't?"

The hybrid looked at her, and blinked its eyes, a heavy, dreamy look, almost flirtatious, "I know, Robyn."

"Are you hungry?" Robyn felt a strange new thrill, as if she were in the presence of something very powerful and strange, yet something that had become intimate too, almost a friend. But can you befriend a tiger, and will the tiger befriend you?

"Yes, I am hungry, rather." The hybrid slurped up more coffee.

"Do you like synthetic tofu curry?"

"Yes, synthetic tofu curry is fine, maybe with chili sauce if you have any."

There weren't any Internet or computer or World Hive Mind connections, but there was an old antique radio receiver, probably a 20th or early 21st-century artifact. The great crises of the 2090s and 2130s had left a lot of antique junk around and had taught the Cosmos the need to recycle old technologies.

Claire took the old radio – it was quite small – and turned it around in her claws; she wondered if Robyn could maybe fix it, and if it picked up some electromagnetic frequencies, it might somehow allow Claire to plug into the World Mind and Cloud Hive. If it did, then she, Claire V Jacobs might once again be able to integrate her mind into the World Mind, travel everywhere all at once, and become Queen of the Universe. Or, more modestly, she might be able to find out what the hell was going on.

"This thing is really ancient, Hybrid." Robyn took the radio from Claire and set it down on her work table. She began fiddling with the radio, in a pile of wires, ancient batteries, and bits and pieces.

It was at that precise moment that the sand tornado hit. A wall of sand-filled air smashed against Robyn's trailer and made it shudder.

Claire peered out the armored window and saw one of the trailers, followed by a rusty old burned-out jeep, somersaulting toward her, but both jeep and trailer were sucked into the air and went leaping out of sight, over Robyn's workshop. The whole world seemed to be whirling and flying apart.

Claire closed the metal window. She pulled the inside armored shutters shut and levered down the manual locking bar.

"Hybrid, can you help me with this one?" Robyn was struggling to close one of the inner armored shutters.

Claire came over, and together they pulled the bar down and locked it in place. "Thanks, Hybrid," said Robyn

The trailer shuddered.

The wind was roaring and screaming and lamenting.

"It will hold, I think, Hybrid," said Robyn, "It always has."

"Well, I guess we just hunker down and wait," said Claire. She put her arm around Robyn's shoulders. Robyn looked into the reptile eyes.

"It's really weird for me," Robyn said.

"Yeah, I understand."

"It's been a long time. I hardly ever speak to anybody, and I have no friends. You know I was erased, partly erased."

"I know," said Claire, "but the old you, all of you, is still in there."

"Really?" The vast, childlike eyes blinked at Claire.

"Yes, really ... I think, later, if we have time, I can bring it back for you – if you want it."

"You like me the way I am now, don't you, Claire?" Robyn longed to say "Hybrid," but she was beginning to think the hybrid would be insulted.

"I do like you the way you are, Robyn. And I don't care if you call me 'Hybrid.' I know it gives you a thrill, and I get a bit of a kick out of it myself."

"You read my thoughts?"

"Yes, just a little bit. We might as well eat."

While the wind roared and slashed against the trailer, they sat cross-legged on the floor in a corner, eating tofu and bread and cheese and sausages, and Claire told Robyn the story of her life.

Robyn looked at the hybrid in wonder; she couldn't resist running her fingers up and down the hybrid's arm or her leg, or feeling her shoulders. "Do you mind?"

"No, I like it. Nobody has been friendly for a long, long time."

"You're so, so … weirdly pretty, I mean beautiful, it's like you're perfect, a perfect thing, an artifact."

"A perfect thing, am I? An artifact!" Claire laughed, and then she bent over and kissed Robyn on the end of her nose, and then on the lips, tickling her with the double points of her tongue, "And you too Robyn are a perfect thing, a perfect artifact."

And then they lay down on Robyn's bed, the hybrid and the human, and they talked and listened to the wind, and then the wind died down and they slept through much of the storm.

But Claire left part of her mind – the automatic high-alert part – wide awake. She suddenly had glimmerings of the consciousness of other hybrids, inklings of minds awakening. Yes, other hybrids still existed. She needed to connect with them. If they were wearing those damned collars, then they were in danger. Robyn could help. But what help could she and Robyn offer, if they were out here in the middle of nowhere?

If only they could connect …

An hour later, the tornado had wandered off; the wind dropped.

Somebody was hammering on the door. They both sat up with a start.

"Do we open it, Hybrid?"

"Sure, let's see who it is," Claire, in truth, was already awake, and she had a fair idea of who might be at the door.

Claire opened the door.

Demi Pfeiffer, C Emerson Caldwell III's executive assistant, and CFO and CEO, was standing there, blinking, sand rippling past her, the wind pinning her jacket to her chest, her high heels sinking into the shifting mini-drifts, and she was pointing a 38.5 laser pistol straight at Claire. "You," she said, "You, you, you – I am going to shoot you, I am going to shoot you right now!"

"Come in," said Claire, "Robyn has just put on a fresh pot of coffee; it's real old-fashioned coffee."

"I'm going to shoot you, you damned hybrid, you damned superstar!"

"You can shoot me later. Right now, you must be exhausted. This has all been very upsetting for you, I'm sure! Come in! Besides, this wind is really strong; you don't want to stay out in it!"

"I … I …" The woman hesitated, the barrel wavered, her finger tightened on the trigger, and then loosened, and then tightened, and then loosened. "Okay," she said, "Just for a minute – then …"

"Then, you shoot me."

"Right! Then I shoot you," Demi Pfeiffer came in, and Claire shut the door behind her.

"I'm Robyn," said Robyn, "And this is my hybrid."

"I know all about your hybrid," said Demi with ill-disguised contempt, "I know far, far, far too much about your hybrid!"

"You do?"

"Do you have any idea, Robyn, who – or what – this monster is?" Demi motioned with her pistol toward Claire.

"She's mine. I almost broke her, but I didn't break her – did I, Hybrid."

"No, you didn't break me – thank you, Robyn."

"She's a world-famous sex idol, a breaker of hearts, a thief of souls, and a pin-up icon for the perverts of the world! She's … she's … a … killer …" Demi Pfeiffer broke down in sobs. The pistol drooped. She wiped her eyes with one elegant sleeve.

"Have some coffee, Demi," said Claire.

"Yes, have some coffee," said Robyn, "it will make you feel better."

"Thank you, Robyn, you are a true human," said Demi. She collapsed into one of the old overstuffed chairs Robyn had scrounged from some ruin somewhere.

Robyn handed a cup of coffee to Demi and Demi looked up at her with tear-streaked eyes, "My name is Demi," she said, "Demi Pfeiffer."

"Is that a W-Com?" Claire had just noticed a tight flat band around Demi's left wrist.

"Of course, you slut," Demi took a deep long sip of coffee, she sighed, "I have to be in the know all the time everywhere constantly about everything."

"It goes with your job."

"Of course, it does, Hybrid! I do have a job. I do work for my living. I am, not like some other creatures I know, a sex-object, a baby doll alien reptilian parasite sex-idol show-off, who merely has to cavort and blink her eyes and jump up and down and stand on her hands for her living!"

Robyn blinked at Demi, and then she blinked at Claire.

"Have some more coffee, Demi," Claire said; she took the pot from Robyn and topped up Demi's cup.

"Thank you," Demi sniffled, "The W-Com isn't working. I can't get anything but static – no feeds, no email, no voice, no navigation, no World Mind, no Hive Mind, nothing."

"Could I borrow it for just a moment? Robyn and I are trying to communicate with the outside world."

Demi looked at the hybrid and then at Robyn. Robyn nodded vigorously and gave Demi a big childlike smile.

"Okay, Hybrid, okay, Robyn, here, see if you can do anything with this." She laid her pistol on the side table, peeled off the W-Com strap, and handed it to Claire.

"Let's see," Claire frowned, yes, indeed, there was lots of static. She searched and searched all the frequencies, all the links. There seemed to be no new material, no broadcasts from anywhere, just drifting half-dead electro cyberspace artifacts.

There was a half-phrase from somewhere about "flying zombies heading …" and there was a blurred news item – it must be a joke – about the destruction of Los Angeles, which had somebody screaming, and a micro-image of buildings toppling, and there was something about the President-Leader declaring a state of emergency in Elysium City …

All of it was from yesterday or a few days ago …

Hmm, but nothing from *now* …

It was like the world had suddenly stopped functioning a few days or hours ago. Maybe everybody was dead. She scanned some more, tuning through static and archived images and dead sites and …

Ah …

There was a blinking electro-beacon from a Presidential superliner that had gone down maybe three or four days ago, though its signal was getting pretty faint, its locator put it in the Dead Lands.

Ah, there was an automatic emergency signal from a place called Camp Terminus. These were in coded text: *beep, beep, beep, beep*, all scrambled and for a normal mind undecipherable.

Claire closed her eyes. Her early years and decades, when she was growing up as V's clone and Sabrina Jacobs' experiment, she was educated by computers and by the Net. She and her neural networks became an integral part of the Cloud and Net and Hive; they gave her a huge repertoire of deciphering techniques of which she was hardly aware but which went into action automatically like a language she knew very well …

Camp Terminus …

Camp Terminus was under attack.

Camp Terminus contained imprisoned, extremely valuable bio-resource material and human dissidents ...

Bio-resource material ... Hybrids!

Could it be hybrids ...?

So, if they were alive, the hybrids might be at this Camp Terminus.

So that's where I want to go!

"Can you fly Emerson Caldwell III's plane, Demi?" Claire gave the woman her best reptilian smile.

"Of course," said Demi, "You must think I'm an idiot, you hybrid you. I am a first-class vertical-jet and hydro-jet pilot. Anywhere we want to go, I can get us there. And, remember, you two, I'm a Cosmos First Class, so I can go anywhere I want to go. My pass is Universal."

"And you can take us with you."

"If I choose to, yes, I can – if I classify you as cargo or as prisoners."

Robyn and Claire looked at each other.

"Okay," Claire said.

"Let's go, Hybrid," said Robyn.

"Well, if you must, I suppose you must, and therefore we must," said Demi Pfeiffer. She went to a window and glanced out. "The wind is down, and the vertical-jet is still there, where I left it."

"Excellent," said Claire.

"Excellent," echoed Robyn.

"Robyn, bring your tool kit, the right tools to remove mind-collars."

"Yes, Hybrid, I will bring my tool kit."

"How dreadful," said Demi Pfeiffer, touching the side of her strictly pulled back hair, "I suppose I am a traitor now, an accomplice."

"Yes, I suppose you are," said Claire, giving her the charming reptilian look, and blinking.

"Well, I've always wanted to do something exciting," said Demi Pfeiffer, "something real, you know."

CHAPTER 5 – SAMMY

Camp Terminus: It was fifteen minutes before the lights went off – a mile under the desert, on level X-7, just off Main Shaft-1. Sammy Franks, Work Shift Supervisor Third Class, was once again proving to his own satisfaction that it was so much damned fun to be as cruel as he could be

"Oh, darling, I fucking love you, I fucking well do!"

Level X-7 was a long way down. To get there from the surface you went down Main Shaft-1 which plunged straight down about a thousand feet, then there were docks and cranes and a landing stage, and then Main Shaft-1 went down another thousand feet, and then, after a landing stage, it went down another thousand feet; and, then, again a thousand feet; at many levels, there were waystations, and equipment bays, and tunnels leading off Main Shaft-1.

Most of the action was at the second deepest level, where the best rare metals clay was to be found, down 4,000 feet, and more. This was level X-7, 4,232 feet down, the temperature was 111 Fahrenheit and the humidity almost 95%. It was here that Sammy Franks was having fun.

"Oh, darling, I fucking love you, I fucking well do!" Sammy Franks was standing just at the entry to the third tunnel, right next to the Main Shaft-1 passenger and freight elevators. And, as a bit of relaxation, before he put her to work, he'd been having fun with his favorite hybrid, HZ-2.

She was his favorite because – as Sammy had discovered peeking into the restricted file (which he wasn't supposed to see, it was classified, and way, way above his clearance level) – she was the most famous prisoner, and because once upon a time HZ-2 had been human and filthy rich and beautiful and ultra-intelligent. That was once upon a time – back in fairyland or "*never-never land*" as Jim Rahv and Bob Norton sometimes called the time before the clamp-down, the disappearances, the killings, and *The Culling*.

But this was now! Now, this creature, once known as Sabrina Jacobs, was pure animal, pure reptile, ugly as sin! Well, maybe not really, they had their own beauty, at least that's what some of the guys said, and in idle moments, back in his bunk, closing his eyes to rev up an appropriate scenario to jerk off by, Sammy could appreciate that the female hybrids were truly beautiful, actually fucking spectacular, but in a different way from human broads. And she was stupid as a stone, and, when Sammy was on shift, she, this ex-billionaire genius, was his very own personal slave, whimpering, totally obedient, a reptile girl with a billion-dollar body. That cursed Aussie, Bob Norton, had said, "You're a fucking pervert, mate, and stupid to boot! Leave the girl alone!" And Julian Harvey and Jim Rahv both told him to fucking well leave HZ-2 in peace, but, well, old Sammy just couldn't resist. It tickled him pink; it was just too much goddamn fun!

"Oh, darling, show me what you can do! Jump, you freak!"

Sammy snapped the electric whip, sizzling yellow and gold sparks blossomed in the air, like a little Roman candle, it was.

Sammy was on a contract from Black Furrow Security Inc., a subsidiary of the Halibut Corp Friendly Family of Companies controlled by Flick Churn. It was a contract which could only end with Sammy's death, but Sammy didn't know that. The unstated but firm company policy was that none of the guards contracted by Black Furrow were going to leave Camp Terminus or the Dead Lands alive; they might talk, they might tell tales of what they had seen and what they had done. This might lead to complications since back in Elysium, the President-Leader – *Hail, All Hail!* – sometimes showed a bizarre and unsettling interest in justice, human rights, and the rule of law. The helicopter-jet that was to ferry Sammy out and back to civilization would drop him, drugged and narcotized, from 10,000 feet over the desert, on stony ground – splat! A snack for the buzzards, that's what Sammy would be. Non-Cosmos semi-literate Outer Burbite Jerk-off Losers like Sammy Franks were ideal recruits for Black Furrow. They were disposable flesh. Nobody would miss them. And since they would be dead, their accumulated earnings would revert to Black Furrow Inc., as was stipulated in the contract, which was good for the bottom line, as was only right, and was in accordance with the the Rule of Greed and the Will of God: *Let us pray!*

"Jump, Freak!"

Sammy was having a fucking good time. He wiped his forehead. It was boring and oppressive down here – maybe 45 degrees Centigrade – and his head was throbbing from a hangover; he really did deserve some fun.

"Jump, you fucking animal, jump," Sam shouted. He snapped the electric whip again – *Wham!* Oh, boy, did it shoot out those sparks, all colors, too – white, red, orange, yellow, even some green ones! It was a regular sparkler.

Wham! Bull's-eye!

The hybrid leaped, turned over, and flopped on her back, slamming down into the thick slime. She jerked, up and down, like a broken puppet, splashing mud all over the fucking place. Whoopee!

"Bet you'd like to get your claws on me, eh!" Sammy loved it, the way she couldn't defend herself, with all those muscles and claws, and those fangs – all useless! She was helpless! She was his little slave. Anything he wanted her to do, she had to do it. That was a very fine thing. It made a man proud to have such a voluptuous demon creature – with its spectacular inner intelligence neutered – at his absolute beck-and-call. Little Sammy Franks – King of the World.

It was like having your very own tame tiger on a leash.

Big, bold Sammy Franks steps into the lions' den – he shows no fear, no fear whatsoever – those stupid lions know who is master!

Just crack the whip!

She jumped! She raged, inwardly, she raged. Fury without words is an affliction, and it is delightful to contemplate!

Ah, the mind-collar! Sammy Franks had to hand it to whatever egghead effete latte-sipping tinkerer had invented the thing. The mind-collar was a marvel. It left just enough intelligence for a hybrid to do the simplest of tasks: using its claws to chop out blocks of sloppy clay; or, harnessed to a cart, just enough IQ so it could pull a load of that sloppy clay from the clay face to the freight elevator, load it on, and come back for more, over and over and over.

Eternal slavery!

Sam grinned, scratched his neck, sweat and slime catching under his fingernails: the mind-collar was a fabulous invention, the salvation of humanity.

Eternal slavery!

Eternal slavery for the enemies of humanity!

When Sam had been hired and faced his first interview, his Black Furrow assignment officer, Phil Norquist, had told him, "You are in the front line defending the human race, Sam! You will be doing heroic work, dirty work, difficult work, and sometimes it will seem like cruel work, the torture, the executions, the killings, but, hey, Sam," Norquist shot him a big toothy extra-shiny grin, "somebody has got to do it, and you will be earning five times as much as you could earn anywhere else, you will be out on the frontier, in the heart of the battle for civilization, a true hero, keeping these evil terrorists and subversive alien hybrids in line – and in storage for future research, because as you know hybrid DNA is a treasure house. You see, these are demons and invaders – but they are also a valuable resource!"

Then at Black Furrow Headquarters, an overseer named Jimmy Philip Ryan had explained the mind-collars to him.

"You see," Sam, "their minds have been neutered – forever neutered. They live in hellish darkness, like the beasts of the fields. It is a truly Biblical punishment, Sam!" The guy's feet were up on his desk, shiny soles almost in Sam's face. "It is an expression of God's Will. They are beasts chewing on the grass and stony gravel, like Nebuchadnezzar."

Sam had no idea who or what the hell Nebuchadnezzar was, or what the Bible or God's Will, had to do with anything, but it sounded great to him: These monsters – many of them gloriously stacked females – reduced to naked beasts munching lichen and gobbling down pig-slop and hauling sloppy crates of mud. It was thrilling, really.

"Those who defy the Word of the Lord, so shall they suffer, Sam, and the Word shall be taken from them, and they shall dwell in inner and outer darkness," Ryan said, and he added, "Sam, kneel by me, so that we can pray for the continuance of the Blessings of the Lord and for the continuance of our Good Work!"

Sam had knelt and mumbled and joined his hands together, but he didn't really feel very strongly about the Blessing of the Lord, or about the Lord Himself for that matter; as for the Bible, he'd never read the book. In fact, reading, in general, was a challenge that Sammy rarely rose to. Never saw the point of it, actually.

HZ-2 licked its lips, the pink forked tongue flickering against the mud-splotched glossy black scales. The yellow snake eyes narrowed; they blinked at Sammy, straight at him, like the eyes of a cobra calculating the precise trajectory of a strike. What did those diabolic hybrid eyes see? What did that neutered hybrid brain think?

Sammy was fat, unshaven, with broken veins decorating his puffy cheeks and the end of his bright swollen slightly bulbous nose; his greasy straw-colored hair stuck out from under his safety helmet; his red-and-black plaid shirt, showing from under the black overalls, opened on a single thick tuft of hair on his pale white skin, now shiny with grease and the misty sheen of clay mud.

Sammy stared back. He flexed the electro-whip. It sent out sparks.

HZ-2 lowered her head, sensing the contempt in Sammy's eyes, feeling ashamed, cowed; she instinctively knew her human master could hurt her and that he despised her – and on another level, she might even have been aware that he both feared her and desired her – but HZ-2 was only obscurely conscious of these things. If she had an inkling of a thought, the mind-collar sensed it and zapped her with a stunning inner paralyzing jolt.

Sammy liked annoying them, these creatures; he understood that they were vaguely conscious of what was happening to them, conscious of the degradation and humiliation he imposed on them – and this made it fun.

Humiliating something that didn't know it was being humiliated would be pointless. You might kick a stone, but you can't humiliate it, and, hey, if you did, what would be the purpose? No thrill in that!

But a beautiful girl demon hybrid, oh, yes!

He was a philosopher of perversity, old Sammy Franks! He had plumbed depths of subtle cruelty no one else had ever thought of, or so he thought. Jerking off regularly, with your inner cinema playing a great variety of perverse scenarios, was an ideal way to create a richly philosophic inner life, Sammy had come to believe, but he kept this discovery to himself.

HZ-2 could be feisty, which was really a hoot; once or twice, she had turned on him and snarled, but punishment was swift. The mind-collar would jolt her into submission.

"Don't you fuck with old Sammy!" He almost danced, in glee, an exuberant little jig – but he didn't; it was too fucking hot for a jig. The humidity encased you in slimy glue; it drained every ounce of energy from every fiber of your being.

He snapped the whip and gave HZ-2 another shock – super-strong this time – unlike the mind-collar, the shocks of the whip didn't need any reason, any motivation – just pure pleasure was all.

HZ-2 bounced up and down so fast her flailing limbs and body were a blur. She turned on him, bared her fangs, and snarled.

"You want to play tough, honey, eh?" He gave her another shock, even stronger; her body vibrated like a violin string, flipping, flopping – splashing up and down in the steamy gray mud. "Had enough?"

HZ-2 turned over, sat up, and crouched close to the muddy floor. Her eyes stared at him, blinking; she crouched lower, head down – submissive.

"Good, you freak! Go, now, bitch, back to work." Sam knew he was getting extra pleasure from the fact that this reptile, had once been one of the most beautiful – and rich – women in the world, and that she had been fucking brilliant.

Sam yawned. He had to admit: it was revenge – Sam had barely made it out of grade school out in the edge of the Burbs where he'd been brought up, classified "Human" but barely, and even now, he struggled to write his name.

One school teacher – a woman – had told him he was an idiot after he smashed his desk and his computer. She had tried and tried and tried, but there was nothing to be done with little Sammy. What made her disdain even worse was she was pretty, really pretty. He had the hots for her. He thought a splash of acid in her face might be a good idea, but he didn't have the guts. Anyway, one evening, in the dusk, after school, he'd slashed the tires of her mini-vehicle and in the canteen, he'd spit and dropped some of his very best snot into her coffee. He managed too, one night, to douse her cat – a sleepy-eyed cinnamon-colored thing that used to wander around ghostly skeletons of Monster Homes in the Outer Burb Camp – with gasoline and light it up: the thing ran around screaming and was burned to a stinky charcoal crisp. Then he watched the woman, stupid bitch, run out of her trailer door, and he could see her discover the stretched-out, steaming body, rigid paws in the air, and, boy, did she scream and cry and weep. Revenge was sweet.

He wiped his brow. He was glowing with sweat and coated in a thin gray sheen of mud – the clay hung in the air like fog, and it was fucking hot – maybe 95 degrees, close on a 100 – and it was fucking dirty, which made it even more fun.

"Back to work, bitch!" Sammy repeated, giving the hybrid a grin. With her he didn't mind that his teeth were dirty – an addiction to chewing synthetic tobacco stubs – and that they were crooked and that the last woman – a prostitute in the ruins of a city once called Houston – he's slept with – well, spent twenty minutes with – told him he stank, and he might as well be impotent, he was such a tiny, limp, uncooperative dick. The cow actually said 'uncooperative dick'! He'd punched that one good, one, two, three, four, and then kicked her when she was down – three broken teeth, a broken nose, and four broken ribs – so she was sent to the brothel infirmary for facial reconstruction. He paid a fine to the brothel owner, but it was worth it.

He scratched his crotch and watched the hybrid crawl away. Her rump disappeared into the dimly lit tunnel, heading toward the clay face where she would toil – mostly using just a big clay-knife and her claws – to cut off chunks of clay and slop them into a small wagon hauled by HZ-8, a harnessed female hybrid – that one, oh, all silver scales and big dark eyes and slender and really stacked – beautiful image, Sam thought, it really was a pleasure being down here in the mines with these female demons – fallen angels who were far from the Face of God – Sammy crossed himself like he'd seen somebody do in a movie – which they, being godless beasts of Satan, would never see. Truly, it was like being the Boss Man in Hell! He got a hard-on just thinking about it!

At the end of the tunnel, HZ-2 slithered past the harnessed hybrid; it was on hands and knees, head down, a bit in its mouth, blinkers restricting its vision. Patiently it waited for the wagon to be filled. It didn't look up. It snorted and shook its head, rattling the chains of the harness.

HZ-2 slipped between the back of the wagon and the clay face; she snarled at the dripping wall and began to scoop blocks of dripping water-softened clay from the mineral face; slowly, she filled the little wagon behind her.

Within seconds she was covered in slime at least an inch thick. She blinked it away from her eyes, and she used the back of her claw to clear the guck from her nostrils; sometimes, she just gave up and let the slime build up and worked blindly, eyes and nostrils covered in slime, sucking in air through her open jaw, tongue lolling out, blindly scooping up the clay and slinging it into the wagon.

She was lost in the instant, on what was in front of her, fifteen inches away, a wall of mud: she was utterly absorbed in the smells, in the slushy clay blocks, in her claws digging deep into the hard guck, in her knees in the slime, in her straining muscles, in the fine mist of hot water that flowed down from the rocks above, over her back and shoulders and snout.

The little wagon was full; it disappeared; then it was back; and she started all over again, digging, digging, and more digging.

The lights were dull silver-gray; it was permanent twilight.

Everything shimmered, haloed with slush and humidity; the mist glowed, thick with clay and carbon dioxide and water vapor.

The end of the tunnel, up against the clay face, was only about five feet high, HZ-2 couldn't stand up, so she crawled or sat or crouched, hulking along, arms dangling, a humanoid, reptilian ape.

The other hybrid, silver-colored under the mire, again came back with the wagon. It backed into place, on all fours, its dull fixed gaze squared-off in the thick prison of steel blinkers, harness, and mouth-bit.

So it was back.

HZ-2 started to pull out blocks of clay, one after the other, an endless chain, with the same movements repeated, over and over, forever and ever.

The little wagon was maybe half full, and HZ-2 had just pulled out a particularly large block of clay and was lifting it into the wagon when something strange happened, the lights flickered, and she felt a strange tickling sensation around her neck and down her spine.

She hesitated, made a strange whiny-whinnying sound – and then she plopped the block of clay into the wagon.

The words came into her mind, clearly: "Where the hell am I? And what in hell am I doing?"

She froze, in mid-gesture: no punishment came.

The mind-collar was silent.

What the hell?

It was a thought …

What the hell?

She was conscious!

Who am I? Where am I?

What the fuck?

Sammy Franks looked up. The lights flickered.

What the fuck?

Sammy was relieving himself. His thick, heavy belt was unbuckled, his zipper open, his big soft belly hanging half-free; he was pissing into a slop bucket at the entrance to the tunnel just off the main shaft. The lights flickered again; it was the first time that had ever happened.

"*What the fuck?*" Sammy Franks finished peeing, gave his cock a flip or two, yellow-gold dribbles and drops flying, pulled and stuffed it in, zipped up, buckled up, pulling the belt as tight as he could. "*What the fuck?*" He stared into the tunnel, where it burrowed away, winding this way and that, curving right and left, and pushing deep into the clay drift; the tunnel went dark. For a long, agonizing instant, it was just an inky black hole: *fuck!* Then dull lights, emergency lights, went on, then they went off, then they went on again – a dull leaden glare.

Emergency lights – that didn't seem good, no sir, not good at all!

"Fuck," Sammy flipped his underground walkie-talkie on: "Hey, hey, anybody there, hey, hey, hello!" The walkie-talkie answered with static and white noise; then it went dead, absolutely dead, the green and red lights blinked twice; then they went dark.

Sammy Franks gulped.

He licked his lips and squinted, peering into the tunnel where HZ-2 had disappeared. He half expected to see a herd of hybrids, with their fangs bared and claws extended, come galloping out of the dark, after him, after Sammy Franks, good-natured old Sammy, yes, sweet old Sammy who wouldn't hurt a fly!

It was really hot, but an eerie, icy chill rippled down Sammy's spine.

Goosebumps on his arms.

He felt cold, really cold.

Cold – why it must be 110 degrees down here!

Then the thought occurred to him: I mean, these hybrids, they were almost supernatural – they were alien! They came from some other fucking universe! They were fucking dangerous!

"Fuck," he hitched up his crotch and waddled over to the control panel at the tunnel entrance, right next to Section B of Main Shaft-1. Section B was the part reserved for hauling up the clay blocks. It had its own communications systems and freight elevators. The control panel had land-line emergency telephone and text systems, these things, they had told him, would operate even after an atomic blast.

In the silence, a cool, wet draft came down the shaft. *Spooky, spooky as Hell!*

The cables and chains hung loose, clanging together.

Water dripped – drip, drip, drip.

Sammy Franks noticed with horror that he was noticing things: sounds, little creepy sounds, things moving, things shifting, air drifting, things rattling.

Then he realized why. "Fuck!" The pumps and ventilators had stopped; that's why he was hearing things.

Usually, the pumps and ventilators and elevators were on all the time, it was the background music you didn't even know you were hearing, and now, suddenly and for the first time, it was all gone.

Silence …

A trickle of water, suddenly becoming a stream, splashed down the side of the shaft, a regular little Niagara; it cascaded in a torrent next to the dark control panel with all its dead buttons and dials. Small pieces of clay from the wall slipped away and splashed down – plop, plop, plop …

Sam scratched at his crotch. It brought good luck – touch your balls and cock, make sure they are still there, make sure you are still a man, still intact.

Take action, Sammy Franks, take action!

He pushed a button on the control panel and picked up the wall phone. It was part of the land-line system designed as backup because often the depths of rock and the magnetic anomalies and interferences from the electrical systems meant the walkie-talkies and mobile phones and pads didn't always work – in fact, this far down, they mostly didn't work.

The wall phone was dead; it didn't show even a flicker of life.

All the lights on the control panel were dark.

The little dials – smeared with clay – were dark too. With his sleeve, Sammy cleaned one just enough to see what was there: it was dead, the dial resting at zero; two other dials gave the same result.

Sam began to think about exactly where he was: 4,000 and more feet underground, in a place where water and mud were always seeping in, where walls and tunnels often collapsed, and he was down here with a few guards and overseers – maybe ten or twenty people in all, scattered on different levels – with a bunch of human convicts and dangerous terrorists bottled up way down below, the lowest level of hell, behind a steel door in one of the spooky cave systems that intersected with the mine, and with a bunch of super-strong if supremely stupid hybrids who were untethered and free except for the mind-collars that kept them enslaved and …

The mind-collars …

"Fuck!"

What if the mind-collars went off? Sammy Franks was sweating, even more than usual. He was greasy with sweat. It wasn't just the heat – getting hotter, maybe with the ventilation dead. It was fear.

Were the mind-collars off too?

He unsheathed the electro-whip. He'd better bite the bullet. He remembered his daddy beating him. It was better not to run, it was better to face the man. His daddy would scream, "Strip, you fat, little, no-good, snot-faced bastard, strip!" And Sammy would take off his clothes, all of them, and then he would bend over, and then the rod would fall, again and again, and again. Usually, his old man, his big unshaven stinky daddy, was drunk and got tired after the first blood came, red blood running off the puckered welts and deep sideways slashes on Sam's backside and when he straightened up the blood ran down his legs. It wasn't so bad; better to face it and get it over with than to cower under the covers trembling in fear waiting for it to come. You get fucked either way; better to get fucked sooner than later. So, now he'd do just that – he'd face the music, he'd bite the bullet. He'd go see what his two hybrids – the silver one and the black one – were up to. At least they were really stupid, so …

Thank the Good Lord High Almighty for the mind-collars …

But, if the mind-collars weren't working, then these hybrid bitches would … be *smart*??

Nope, that was impossible …

Could they really be *smart*?

He tested the whip. It flashed and crackled. Yep, it worked! Well, thank the Devil for tiny blessings. The whips had their own batteries – you recharged them by plugging them into the control panel socket. How long would the whip last?

Sam steeled himself to head into the tunnel. He walked back and forth to screw up his courage, his boots sloshing through the mud that was particularly deep at the tunnel entrance. Strange breezes and sounds – groans and sighs whisperings – seemed to be coming from the shaft. Sammy went over and looked; he looked up, and he looked down. It made him dizzy; it went up a long, long way; and it went down, a long, long way. "I'm hearing things," he muttered, startled by the sound of his own voice; it seemed to echo: *I'm hearing things!* He turned back to the tunnel. With its ghostly ghastly lighting, the tunnel didn't look too healthy; water was leaking from the walls and roof; usually, it was drained away by the little pipes of the pumping system. Now it was streaming and trickling down the walls, muddy, gluey liquid, rising around his ankles. God, what a mess!

That liquid would be piling up *behind* the walls!

The tunnel might collapse.

The whole place was going to drown in mud, unless …

He'd give HZ-2 a special licking with the whip – across the backside, across the back, across her breasts, across the snout – just because things were in such a bloody mess – the mess had to be somebody's fault; he'd pretend it was hers.

HZ-2 deserves a good licking, she does, oh, yes, she does! He smiled. He could see himself saying it, "You deserve a good licking, my girl, a good licking, and I'm just the guy to give it to you."

He stood still, thinking he really should go into the tunnel and check on his two girls. He suddenly remembered that the mind-collars had batteries …

So they'll still be stupid!

Eureka!

Ha!

The first flicker of intelligence – of consciousness – had passed about three minutes ago, and now HZ-2 was using her claws to pull out a particularly stubborn and slippery block of clay when she suddenly stopped. Her mind said, rather querulously, "What the hell are you doing? What the hell are you doing, Sabrina Jacobs? Are you an idiot? Is this a hobby? Is this an experiment?"

That was dangerous – that was a thought.

Who was Sabrina Jacobs?

Who was Sabrina Jacobs?

Who was Sabrina …?

The tunnel lights blinked – off, then on, then off, then on.

HZ-2 looked up, snorted, and started pulling out on the stubborn clod of clay – it was a bit bigger than most of them. She plopped it with a dull splash into the wagon. She had to fill up the little wagon so the other hybrid, a silver hybrid, as HZ-2 had noticed, under its coating of gray sludge, could haul it away.

The lights went off again; then on; *something was happening – what?* It was a vague question, and then it was gone.

The mind-collar woke up; it flashed an angry signal: *Keep working!* A sharp jab of sharp pain stabbed her gut, a lightning bolt of agony flashed behind her eyes – it was a warning shot.

HZ-2 paused, blinking her yellow serpent's eyes, the dark maroon lozenge-like slit widened, then narrowed. She snarled. She dug her claws into the clay face, wiggling them to carve the cut; she levered the dripping chunk closer to her, and she pulled it out, holding it against her breast and then slopping it into the little cart.

She kept going; the rhythm was simple repetition, the same actions, over and over and over again.

Finally, the wagon was full.

HZ-2 growled and rattled the wagon chain. It was the signal. The other hybrid began to haul the wagon away.

Over the top of the small wagon, HZ-2 could see the mud-covered backside of the other hybrid and her shoulders, and she wondered who that particular hybrid might be – coated with all that guck, it was impossible to recognize her.

Wonder? Wonder was forbidden by the mind-collar; it was a form of thinking; the mind-collar jerked her back into dull servitude – three sharp jabs of pain.

Silence, HZ-2!!!!

The mind-collar never slept; it dulled and punished all curiosity. Even dreams were censored.

But …

With flickers, mere slivers, of her old intelligence Hybrid-HZ-2 realized this: she was … *thinking* …

The mind-collar: zapped her mind with a deep, synapses-paralyzing electric shock: "Stop thinking, bitch beast, stop thinking!"

HZ-8, the silver hybrid, sneezed, shook her chains, and wiped at her snout with the back of a muddy claw.

She chewed violently at the metal and rubber bit, which was annoying her and biting into the sides of her mouth and depressing her tongue so much she wanted to gag. Her fangs were itching to get free.

She shook her shoulders; the harness dug into her flesh; she would like to shake off these nameless things that itched and stabbed and dug into her, spines and thorns, torture by irritation, slow, agonizing torture.

She had a narrow squared-off field of vision because of the blinkers but also no curiosity, really, to know what lay beyond that narrow field of vision, the mind-collar saw to that, dulled the excitement, the yearning, the searching, curious mind, transformed it into a blind, dumb darkness. Only sometimes, flashes of light, brief glimpses of her past self and her past life penetrated the darkness.

The mind neutering and mind erasure were near total.

HZ-8 snorted, shivered, and rattled her chains.

The air was thicker and more difficult to breathe because the ventilators had stopped though HZ-2 didn't know that, but she did know that the sounds had changed.

Yes, the sounds had changed.

Suddenly, she was dimly aware of the slop, slop, slop of her knees in the liquid mud, as she shifted her position, the sucking sound as she pulled a block of clay out of the mud face, the drip, drip, drip, of water from above, and the creaking of the wagon and jangling metal harness – and the rattling of the chains that held the silver hybrid in place and the silver hybrid's sneezes – all seemed to be amplified, muffled echoes traveling up and down the narrow muddy tunnel.

She sneezed and wiped the muddy snot away with the back of her claw.

"Fuck," she said, "what a mess!"

The words came out of her mouth without a thought – *words!*

"What?"

"Fuck!"

HZ-2 blinked. She stopped what she was doing, a dripping block of clay between her claws. She realized that she was *thinking*.

"What is happening?" It was an uncomfortable, anguished, unfamiliar feeling, the thoughts welling up, with words attached – *words!* She was flooded with an inner flush of shame and guilt.

Thinking was bad; thinking brought punishment; thoughts with words attached were evil; the mind-collar and behind it the World Mind would exact a terrible revenge – a shuddering downpour of thunderbolts, of electric shocks, of muscular spasms, of quivering blackout.

HZ-2 shivered; her eyes rolled in her head. She snapped her eyes shut. She didn't want to see; she didn't want to feel; she didn't want to be conscious.

The mind-collar sent out a flickering feeble reproach – a small pinprick of pain – it faded away, flickered, faded ...

"That was hardly anything at all! What's happening to you?"

The mind-collar was dying.

"That cannot be!"

HZ-2 put her claw in front of her neck, and she saw, reflected dimly on the sheen of her glossy muddy wrist, the two little red lights blinking – *warning, warning, mind-collar mind control about to cease,* meaning this dangerous reptilian beast will soon be able to exercise free will, will soon be free, will soon realize who and what she is, will soon run amok and ...

Yes, so the collar is failing.

"I don't want to be free," HZ-2 whimpered.

Damn! I am ... I am ...

I AM!

Me – I – I exist!

I ... Me ... I ...

Suddenly, in a flash, HZ-2 clearly realized who and what she was – a human being, then a hybrid. Her name was Sabrina Jacobs; she was a brilliant scientist, and a billionaire – or she once had been – all her property had certainly been confiscated – her whole life flashed before her: the precocious unhappy timid daughter of a mad scientist entrepreneur genius in Cambridge, England, punished by her father, kneeling one wintry day in the icy rain, the image was so vivid she was back there, a century ago; she was the woman who had kidnapped the Alien Queen V; she was the woman who had been the lover of Dmitry Pavlov, the Russian Oligarch; she was the woman who had created Claire V Jacobs by cloning V's DNA and adapting it; and she remembered how she too, Sabrina, became a hybrid, transformed by Dmitry Pavlov's dark bio-arts into a hybrid – which was now *what* and who she was; locked in, a red-and-black clawed, fanged, scaly hybrid, an outcast, a freak, a …

A hybrid – prisoner in a sort of mine, a camp, a …

"I have to get out of here!"

"I have to escape!" Exhilaration and panic were mixed together: and horror, what had she been reduced to, and fear, utter terror! What if the mind-collar went on again?

Flattening herself against the slimy pit face she managed to swivel around and, flattening herself to fit below the low, dripping ceiling, she crawled up onto the little wagon, slithering over the full load of sticky clay – where the blocks were dissolving into blobs – she felt annoyed – she had dug all this clay out – the wagon was full – the donkey-girl-hybrid should have hauled it away – then she realized that such a feeling was ridiculous. It was her automaton mind-collar-conditioned worker-bee slave speaking.

I have the mind of a slave – a robot!

Yes, it is so easy to be trained to be a slave!

Even me, damn it, even me!

She crawled and slithered over the donkey-girl hybrid, who was on all fours, to get in front of her and so she did, and she could see the hybrid was clawing frantically at her bit and harness trying to get free, so Sabrina thought that the donkey hybrid's collar must have failed too, yes, it's lights were blinking red, and then she thought: of course, if the system is down – with the pumps and ventilators stopped – and if the collars depend on the system, then they are all going to fail, all the collars will fail – and the collars are what keep us prisoner, and if there are two of us there must be more of us, and, yes, I remember seeing others – yes, I remember …

I'm thinking – God, I'm thinking!

And if I am thinking, so is this other hybrid, the silver one!

She realized she was beginning to think expansively, real thoughts – to make deductions and to connect one event or phenomenon with another. *This was horrible.* And what if it all went into reverse?

What if the mind-collar began to work again – reducing her to idiocy?

She snarled – pure fury! *Never again!*

She knelt in front of the donkey hybrid and hissed. The harness and mouth-bit were steel and bolted in place, and the hybrid's claws were too slippery to turn the bolts. Sabrina tried, but she couldn't get a grip.

The hybrid hissed at her, and stared with snake eyes.

The bit made it impossible for the hybrid to talk; it suppressed her tongue.

"Who are you?" Sabrina asked out loud, suddenly remembering she could speak.

She got a mind-to-mind answer, "My name is Helen – or Hybrid-HZ-8. I want out of here!"

"I'm Sabrina," she answered, "I'm going to get you out of that thing."

"This harness is bolted; it's steel; it's slippery; I don't know if you can."

Sabrina tried; the bolts were too slippery for her to get a grip; there must be another way; she sniffed the air, clayey, clammy, swamp air. It was not unpleasant.

Part of Sabrina – HZ-2 – wanted just to lay back in the slime and wait until an overseer came along and to stroke her belly and hear her purr as some of the more playful and kind overseers did, or that nice overseer – Jim Rahv – his name suddenly flashed onto her consciousness – who fed her bits of meat most days – though today he had forgotten to bring her a treat of meat; in fact, he'd forgotten his own lunch – she realized she knew this somehow – and he'd forgotten his lunch because he hadn't been sleeping well, and he hadn't been sleeping well because he'd been having nightmares, and these nightmares were a symptom, a symptom of something terrible. All of this knowledge, which had been absorbed subconsciously, mind-to-mind, suddenly flashed into consciousness. She liked Jim Rahv – he liked to see her happy, he liked to see her purr, "Purr, my hybrid friend, purr!" And he'd toss her a piece of meat.

It was degrading and damned humiliating, but at least it was not sadistic, and besides he undoubtedly didn't know any better: she was probably, as far as Jim Rahv could see, merely a mindless, dangerous beast – an alien, the beginning of the dreaded alien invasion, though she sensed that Jim had had doubts about the propaganda he'd been fed, and he'd seen documents …

Then there was that other one, who tortured her with electric shocks – she would tear him apart when she met him – Sammy, Sammy Franks … Let's see, what exquisite torture could she devise for Mr. Sammy Franks?"

But, yes, what if the collars started to work again?

Then she – we – would be plunged into idiocy – perhaps for all eternity.

"We have to hurry."

"Yes," said Helen's mind, as she chewed at the bit, "Otherwise, the damned mind-collars might catch us again and …"

"Yes."

"Yes."

"I'll get rid of this wagon." Sabrina squeezed back between the hybrid and the muddy wall of the tunnel; she squished into the narrow space behind the hybrid – Helen – who was still harnessed, still on all fours. Sabrina lifted up the harness, unhooking it from the wagon, and so now Helen was harnessed, but the harness was not hooked to the wagon.

"It's not perfect, but now you can stand up and move."

"Thank you." The thought-message was still dull, still foggy; it was still only partly articulate. Helen was struggling out from the damage inflicted by the mind-collar.

Helen's collar was blinking – red, green, red, green, red, red, red … Her mind-collar battery must be in better shape than mine, thought Sabrina; then it occurred to her that the designers had been stupid or arrogant or complacent: The mind-collars could have been designed to be powered by body heat, or movement, or even by the central nervous system, but … Well, luckily, they weren't …

I could design a better mind-collar than that!

If it were powered by the body itself, by temperature or by body movement, it could …

What the hell am I thinking!

What a stupid thought!

Following Sabrina along the tunnel, Helen dragged the metal harness with her. It trailed, sloshing through the watery mud, clanking on the rails.

The mind-collars were still sending out feeble, intermittent desperate control messages, pulses of lethargy and paralysis; stop thinking, you creatures, stop thinking, you are wordless worthless animals; you are beasts; you are slaves; lie down, paws in the air, worship, growl, purr, grovel, obey, sleep …

Don't think!

Don't think!

They got to the tunnel entrance, at the main shaft; there was no sign of Sammy Franks and his electro-whip.

Water dripped down everywhere. A large piece of clay slid away and down the side of the shaft, a minor avalanche.

Sabrina looked at the trickles and torrents of water that were cascading down the sides of the shaft; something up above must have failed – more pumps perhaps, water from higher levels was coming down the sides of the shaft.

Everything would collapse soon …

And then …

"Where are the others?" Sabrina turned to Helen, who blinked back at her from between the blinders and shrugged.

There was a toolbox beside the control panel at the tunnel opening; it was covered in gunk; Sabrina cleared the muck away with her claw, and pried the box open. Inside, sure enough, there were tools. She pulled out a pair of pliers and a wrench and started to work.

Within two minutes, Hybrid-HZ-8 was free: the bit and blinders were gone; the harness was gone.

"And now we've got to get these damned collars off."

A voice echoed. "Hello, bitches. Sammy is back!"

Sabrina looked up; Sammy Franks – her master, her torturer – was standing there, wielding an electro-whip. Where had he come from? Ah, he had come out from a side service tunnel; he had been looking for heavy weapons, but he hadn't found any, but he did have an electro-whip and a laser pistol. The lights on the electro-whip still glowed; it was active, it was clearly active.

"Hello, bitches," Sammy grinned, tried to puff out his chest; he cleared his throat, "Sammy is back."

HZ-2 growled, and readied herself to spring.

Sammy Franks was scared shitless. He was bluffing, and he knew he was bluffing. He stood there in the flickering light of the emergency lamps in front of the two hybrids HZ-2 and HZ-8. HZ-8. They were both standing up, like human beings, but they were goddamn alien reptiles! The silver one, HZ-8, was no longer harnessed.

How the fuck had that happened?

Sammy was wielding the electro-whip. He'd drawn his laser pistol with his other hand – the laser pistol could do real damage. He saw HZ-2 blink her big gold-yellow eyes at him like she was going to challenge him.

The bitch!

He'd put the fucking fear of God into her!

Sabrina smelt on Sammy Franks the hatred and the fear, and she could see the extra sweat – the sweat of fear – under the sweat of heat, under the gray gloss of muddy clay. She was tensing her muscles to leap, to swipe off Sammy Franks' head.

Then she saw, in a flash of insight, her mind-reading capacity revving up, she saw, in an instant, virtually all of Sammy Franks' history, the little kid who'd been beaten up by his father, the dim-witted overweight junk-food addict pimply self-loathing fatso who'd been bullied by his teachers and laughed at by everybody. She saw the kid, who one night in a rundown, dilapidated Outer Burbs schoolyard – backed on by the a row of tar-paper shacks with roofs of corrugated iron – out in one of the dying burbs, out in the wrecked isolated Monster Homes Jungle, that had become the endlessly extended slums of the 22nd century – she saw how the hopeless flabby kid had been pushed to the ground by an older guy, really old, actually; thick greased-back gray hair, a black sleeveless tank top, a thick leather belt holding up canvas pants, dirty bare feet with yellowing overgrown toenails, black tobacco stains between broken, crooked teeth, and the older guy had ripped off little Sammy's pants and underpants and pinned little Sammy, kicking, screaming, then dead quiet and totally terrified, sweating fear – again – and whimpering quietly as the old man – stinking of old urine and cheap tobacco – raped little Sammy, ripping into his anus; there was the exploding pain of penetration – a red hot iron ramming up little Sammy's ass – and the blood and shit, when, right afterward, little Sammy, left lying on the ground, still face down, trying to get up, shit himself – just let go in a great liquid spurt and fart – and pissed himself for fear and shame and pain and …

And Sabrina saw how something had been broken in Sammy from the beginning. When he got home, his father beat him because he'd soiled himself, "Shit in your pants, pissed in your pants, you are fucking disgusting, you are a hopeless idiot, idiot spawn of an idiot mother, fucking losers the both of you," and the blows came, with the closed fist – which had a thick iron ring – with skull and crossbones – on the ring finger, it broke little Sammy's nose and left a nasty rippling raw-looking scar across his left cheek, a scar Sabrina only now noticed under the stubble and the sheen of slick misty clay and sweat.

Sabrina's mind-reading powers were now working at full tilt, all the perceptions, memories, and images pilling up in less than a split second.

It was fucking painful!

This was the problem with being a hybrid – mind-reading and empathy seemed to go together.

You could get drunk on it, and lost, no longer knowing what to do.

Damnation!

You had to learn to manage it, and she was out of practice!

She was aware her muscles were still tensing, and her claws were extending and her thigh muscles were readying themselves; she was about to leap and slash poor little Samuel Franks' head off, decapitate him in one clean swoop, neater than the guillotine and even faster – after all, the claws, when used the right way, were razor-sharp and you could extend them so …

She was going to end his pathetic loser's life, right now, for once and for all time: no more suffering for little Sammy Franks!

And she was aware, too, of the stream of – *blink, blink, blink* – *dot, dot, dot-dash, dash, dash* – Urgent, Top Priority, Morse Code and Clear English, mental messages from Hybrid-HZ-8, from Helen, *"Don't do it, don't kill him, he's just a poor miserable loser who's taken his sadism out on us, on you in particular, but it's not worth it, Sabrina, it's not worth it, you know better than to kill the poor slob, he's not worth it, turn the other cheek!"*

"Fuck!" Sabrina answered, mentally.

"Remember, I'm your lawyer," said Helen, mentally. "You're a genius, but you're not the easiest person in the world and …"

"My lawyer! Jesus Christ!"

"Yes, I'm your lawyer, and let me tell you …"

"Fuck off, lawyer!"

"Look, now, Sabrina …"

"Hang all the lawyers!"

"I'm your friend too!"

"Well, dear Helen, dear friend …"

"You'll regret it, and then you'll have to get drunk and you will have a horrible hangover, and wallow in guilt and self-pity and …"

"Okay, Okay," Sabrina was aware, too, that, having seen deep into Sammy Franks' mind – seeing things even he'd forgotten about – she was beginning to feel sorry for him – that goddamn empathy – sorry for the poor sap, the loser, nobody had ever loved him, not even his mother who was drunk most of the time, and who had tried to abort little Sammy, trying for a desperate back-alley illegal botched job involving a drunk prostitute – "Hey, honey, this'll be quick, and it's cheap too!" – and a twisted wire coat hanger and some utterly filthy towels, but little Sammy had hung in there, the hemorrhage didn't stop him, and, unloved and increasingly hateful as he got older, he'd remained alive, right up to this instant, and now, standing there, a thirty-three-year-old bag of shit, the laser gun held out, trembling, pointing, the electro-whip raised, he repeated:

"Hello, bitches, Sammy is back."

And Sabrina, as she leaped, saw that his lower lip was trembling, his eyes – they looked so innocent that way – were round with terror, looked like a baby's eyes, and he was drooling, and she thought, as she flew through the air, that Sammy was going to poop in his pants again, like he did that time in the schoolyard, and she landed, right beside him, grabbing both his wrists, twisting and applying pressure so that the laser pistol and the electro-whip dropped into the mud, and, letting his wrists go, she swooped to a kneeling position, and picked up the pistol and whip. Then she stood up, right next to Sammy.

She suddenly realized that she was taller than he.

"Oh, my God," Sammy said. He stumbled backward toward the open shaft. There was no guard rail.

Tossing both weapons to Helen, Sabrina leaped forward and caught Sammy Franks just as he backed up and stumbled over the edge of the shaft and was about to cartwheel down, arms flailing and outstretched, down something like four or five hundred feet.

She pulled him back into the tunnel; and, setting him down and tapping him gently on the cheek with the back of her claw – *tap, tap, tap*! "Sammy Franks, you've been a very bad, very wicked little boy, you deserve a tossed-over-my-knee bare-bottom spanking, Little Sammy!"

She let him go. Sammy was still flailing – it sort of looked like he was trying to fly. He fell with a splash on his bum in the mud.

Sabrina looked down at him.

He looked up at her as if – and she saw the image flash into her mind – as if she were a statue of the Virgin Mary or of some saint to whom one would pray for forgiveness or for a favor, or time off from purgatory or weekend leave from limbo, and the evil little guy – *no, the poor sap,* she corrected herself, partly on mental urging from Helen who had stepped forward –"Take pity, Sabrina, take pity!" The poor sap actually joined his hands together in supplication. He was saying, "Please, no, please, don't, don't, please, no, oh, no!"

And, yes, he was peeing in his pants; her sense of smell now picking up every nuance, but there was no poop, not so far as she could ascertain.

Bullies are cowards; it's a universal law, Sabrina frowned.

Yes, Helen nodded, Bullies are cowards.

Chivalry is dead, Sabrina frowned, a deeper reptilian frown.

Not quite. You were chivalrous just then. Helen put a mud-slick claw on Sabrina's shoulder.

"Don't poop your pants, Sammy," Sabrina said, "That would really try my patience."

Sabrina and Helen were now both looking down at Samuel L. Franks, now on his knees, like he was getting ready to beg or to pray, on his knees in the mud, having just pissed his pants, and in fear for his life and sanity, his belly and his sphincter hiccupping, barely holding on.

"What do we do now?" Helen said, openly. It was the first time since Sammy Franks had arrived that she had spoken a thought aloud.

"We get out of here," said Sabrina. "Stand up, Sammy," she added reaching out and hauling him up. She was maybe two inches taller than he was. He was stout, but he was short. Before, somehow, he had seemed so much bigger, so much taller. Of course – she had been on her knees, almost all the time, on her knees!

Me – Sabrina Jacobs, Ph. D. M. Sc. FRS, etc., Prix Nobel, etc., etc., on my knees! The very thought of it! Ghhrrrhhh!

"Please don't hurt me," Sammy whimpered.

She let go of him. He tottered, almost fell, she reached out with a claw and steadied him.

"You talk, you can talk," he said, and she realized he hadn't known that in demon form – and without mind-collars inhibiting them – these goddamn stupid hybrids could talk.

"Yes, Sammy, we talk, we babble, we gossip, we make speeches; in fact, we've been talking at you for a while now," said Sabrina.

"Sammy, stop whimpering," said Helen.

Just as they said this, two beams in the main shaft gave away and went tumbling down, crashing against the shaft, disappearing into the depths below.

Helen looked into the shaft. The walls were dripping with rivulets and cascades of water. Slabs of clay were leaking out, sliding away. "This place is going to collapse. We have to get out of here – and fast."

"And we have to get the mind-collars off." Sabrina nodded.

"They're embedded; it will be difficult to get them off. I feel the damned thing; it's wrapped into my spinal cord," Helen tugged at hers.

"Me too, it's wedded to my nervous system."

"What do we do with Mr. Franks?"

"Good question," Sabrina picked up the electro-whip and snapped it in the air – it made sparks, like a sparkler, a bright shower of pure white. She grinned, her widest reptilian grin, "Good question: what do we do with Mr. Franks?"

"Please guys," Sammy's legs were trembling, his greasy lips were trembling; his eyes were filling with tears, "Please guys, please hybrids, please girls, please ladies, please HZ-2, please HZ-8 …"

"Ladies will do." Helen's arms were crossed across her chest.

"Okay, Sammy," Sabrina said, "follow us or stay where you are – but don't get in our way."

A gush of water spurted out of a vertical drainage pipe; a two-meter high slab of muddy rock slid away and went crashing down the main shaft.

"This whole mine is about to cave in and bury us," said Helen, peeking up the shaft.

That was when she saw it: a wall of fire was coming down Shaft-1, it billowed like a billowing sail, only this was pure fire, and it would surely kill anything in its path – human or hybrid.

"Run," Helen said, "Run!"

Rick Mills, a rare metals analyst who had been pressed into one of the teams going down into Shaft-1, was a guy who didn't like heights and he didn't like depths either; when, at least twice a month, he had to go down into the mine, he closed his eyes when he was in the elevator and tried to concentrate on something else; he was in the last of the teams to be sent into the Shaft and right now he was about 300 feet below the pithead of Shaft-1, and he wasn't even in an elevator; he was climbing down one of Shaft-1's emergency ladders, the rungs were greasy with clay, and cruddy with rust, and very slippery.

Rick was focusing on the rung in front of him: just one handhold and one foothold after the next, one at a time, and don't look down!

He knew he was the last guy on the last team of three teams that were making their way slowly down Shaft-1 to the lowest depths where they'd find the hybrids and maybe the humans if any humans were left. Rick figured that being the last of the last was the safest place to be.

He muttered to himself, talking to himself made it a bit easier. "I'm fucking glad Norton and his gang are going down first; he's fucking smart, a fucking hard-ass, this fucking place is lucky to have him. Whatever danger's down there, Norton will face it first, and get a hold on it; then, we'll be there to back him up. He must be half a mile down, maybe more … But still, it's going to be one hell of a …"

What the hell is that noise?

Rick looked up.

Billowing fire.

"What the hell?"

"It's fire, the shaft's on fire," Wolf Ritz shouted. He was about twenty feet below Rick.

"Right! That is something I can see for myself, Wolf, thanks."

"Jesus Christ," said Rob Jay, the bottom guy, their lead guy; his voice sounded funny, hollow, made of wet echoes.

It looked like burning gasoline was streaming down into the Main Shaft, above them, streaking along the beams and cables and rafters, one of the old cages, hanging above them, was alight; it looked like a barbecue grill. It had been all darkness up there; now, it was all bright flame.

Rick looked around, "How far down is the next side tunnel, or service tunnel? Can you see?"

"Nothing for about fifty feet, down there I think I see a service tunnel."

"Get down there as fast as you can, Wolf, Rob, I'll be right behind you!"

They began to clamber down, slipping, sliding, and Rob suddenly lost his grip, and he fell, "Shit! Hell!"

Rob just screamed, and Rick heard the scream and heard, dimly, the body falling, far below, heard it hitting walls, cables …

He looked up. And now sweeping down, was a great ballooning blossoming wave of fire. It was coming straight at him.

"Jesus," he thought.

"Can I make it?" he thought.

"No fucking time," he thought.

For Rick Mills there was blinding light, searing pain, red-tinted blindness. Falling and falling and falling, he was falling. And then there was nothing, absolutely nothing, just a broken flame of a body, a broken doll, a silhouette, smashing into side struts, bouncing off the walls, hurtling down, breaking apart, falling, and falling, and falling.

Wolf Ritz, below, on the ladder, saw the great blossom of fire coming. Straight down at him. This wasn't just a fire! This was a total wave of fire. "Maria! Christ! Jesus! Saint Anthony!"

Wolf jumped, hoping to make it into a side niche, the entry to a service tunnel. The points of his boots touched the edge of the platform.

He tried to catapult himself forward. *No, no, no!* He went cart-wheeling backward, arms flailing, thinking, *this is fucking not happening, and Jesus, this can't be me, and this is goddamn ridiculous,* seeing himself, just for an instant, as a stick cartoon figure, spinning out over space, wheeling downward. He saw, in a flash, his life: childhood in the Burbs, his mother a beautiful curly redhead slattern, with a contraband cigarette dangling from the side of her mouth, her eyes – dark, dark lashes – half-closed, winking, against the curling smoke, saying, "Wolf, my Little Wolf, my Little tiny adorable Wolf!" and he could just catch a glimpse, little Wolf could, he could just catch a shadowy glimpse, the open white unbuttoned shirt, of the undercurve of her right breast, "Naughty Little Wolf!" and she laughed and took the cigarette out of her mouth, licked her lips, bright beautiful red, blinked at him, her beautiful eyes, so serious, and she said, "Now would Little Wolf like to …"

The downward flood of fiery gasoline, coming freight-train fast, slammed into Wolf Ritz, a wall of heat, then a wall of fire, then a wall of liquid fire. It caught him, coated him, blinded him, and crisped him, as he fell, every nerve screeching pure pain, just a screaming shadow. Then just a dark flaming charcoal silhouette, in the downward rushing wave of fire, billowing down and down Main Shaft-1.

And with him came the fire …

A wall of fire, racing downwards.

Freddy Ambrose was a steel-gray hybrid housed on level X-10. He had originally been created, conceived and bred, as a weapon and pure killing machine; and Freddy, though reprogrammed and re-educated by the Queen of the Hybrids, V, and by Jefferson Siebert, a US Marine Colonel, was, almost 70 years later, only partially domesticated. Freddy crouched and waited.

He could hear a guard, heading his way.

About ten minutes earlier, Freddy had woken up chained to a wall in a dead-end niche side tunnel, which had an entrance which was barred with iron.

Where am I?

I'm in a cage, he realized, *I'm in a cell.* He wondered how he had ended up on this place and what had happened – the last thing he remembered was a sort of roundup and somebody aiming something at him – a laser gun, a stun gun? It must have been something really special because Freddy – and he was proud of this – was damn near invulnerable. And then he remembered, in a fog of pain and humiliation: He had been used as a slave, an animal.

He tore the chain off the wall. He fingered his throat. He was wearing some sort of collar; it had merged with his flesh.

He immediately realized the collar was what had made him docile and stupid. He growled and clenched his claw: So they had turned him into a stupid animal!

The collar was a so-called "mind-collar," Freddy realized, capturing the name from memories of things heard, things seen – the memory was just now rising out of a sea of programmed forgetting.

"At least they didn't *erase* me!"

He tore the chain from the collar, threw the chain aside, and went to the barred entrance of the cage, and smashed the door; the steel locks and chains exploded into fragments. The door swung open.

The guard …

The guard was getting closer now. Freddy could hear him sloshing through the muck. He could hear the heavy breathing; and, even in the thick muddy air, Freddy could sense the man's sweat and fear. Freddy's nostrils quivered; he sniffed and sniffed again, "Ah, it was the guard who used the electro-whip!"

Images came back vivid and clear: Freddy cowering, terrified; the gloating guard; the evil self-satisfied smile; the burning physical pain, the biting mental pain of the mind-collar; the slashing electric shock of the electro-whip …

He slipped around the corner and faced the guard.

The man was about twenty feet away, surrounded by mist and by the glow of the dim emergency lights; it was foggy in the narrow tunnel. The air was heavy, fecund with primal clay, and weirdly inebriating. It was wild, really, like returning to the forest or swamp or bayou. Wild was good! Freddy yearned to claw at the slime and howl at the moon, but down here there was no moon.

Now the guard had seen him.

"Fuck!" The guard stopped dead in his tracks, boots sloshing in the gray-black mud, his hairy, bare arms dangling heavily at his sides, his helmet on crooked, his headlamp dimly glowing, a laser gun still in its holster, and a coiled black electro-whip dangling beside the guy's leg.

Behind the guard was another guard – two of them, Freddy thought, two to kill. One of the guards pushed his underground walkie-talkie, and spoke, "Hybrid loose on level Z-10, I repeat, there's a hybrid loose on Z-10." And then he said, "Shit, it's not working. Nothing is fucking working."

Freddy bared his fangs and growled.

The first guard grimaced. "Now, down boy, get back, boy, get back, if you get back we're not going to hurt you, be a good boy, eh." And, to the guy behind him, he said, "Where is this one supposed to be?"

"There's a cage back down the tunnel, about ten meters to the left. He should have been in there. Maybe we can just push him back there, and he'll go in and we can lock it up. They're pretty stupid, really strong, but stupid."

"How the hell did he get out," the first guard was still coming, now leveling his laser gun at Freddy. "Get back, Hybrid, get back," making a shooing motion with his free hand, waving, "Get back."

Freddy stood his ground. He showed his fangs and growled and hissed.

The first guard blinked. "This ain't gonna be easy." The guard had round eyes, Freddy noticed, pale blue eyes. Holding the gun steady, the guard took another step forward. He reached down and scratched his crotch, "We are not going to hurt you, Hybrid, we just want you to go back to your cage, that's right, just back to your cage."

"Maybe you should give him a shot with the electro-whip," said the other guard, who was hanging back. Freddy could smell the fear on him; the first guard was too stupid and too arrogant to realize how dangerous the situation was.

Freddy bared his fangs in a smile; this was going to be fun! Human beings were such idiots, cruel and crafty, but, when it came down to it, many of them were slow and naïve and gullible, hardly evolved beyond apes, really, and they depended entirely on technology for their strength – guns, knives, clothes, armor, computers. A naked human alone in nature – out on the steppe or desert or in a forest or a jungle – would die of starvation or dehydration in a couple of days, if he – or she – wasn't eaten first.

The first guard was still holding the pistol steady; now, he braced his legs, slightly apart, and reached for the electro-whip.

Freddy could read his thoughts: "*I am going to look after you, you freak, and I'm going to send you to the hell where demons such as you belong."* The guard's name, Freddy realized, reading it from his mind, was Lance Chase, 36-years-old, twice divorced, once accused of beating a girlfriend to death, had personally executed two hybrids – and a couple of humans, including a five-year-old child, during what Chase's memory bank referred to as "the Great Roundup" or, more officially, as *The Culling.*

Freddy got the image: a female hybrid, amber-colored, wearing a mind-collar and thus passive and enslaved, kneeling in a field, toward dusk, clouds billowing up, ringed by sunlight, towers of golden sunlight, stinking hot, dry grass rustling in the breeze, somewhere out in the arid Dead Lands, it must have been, edge of Texas maybe, edge of the Central Desert, and Lance Chase, then 22, anticipating a cold beer later, almost tasting the bubbly bittersweet golden coolness on his tongue, was holding the steel soft-grip pistol, with a soft-head, explosive bullets in the chamber, and Lance Chase, in that long-ago day, was thinking, "Boy this will make a splash," anticipating the gooey spray and holding the pistol, its muzzle against the smooth delicately sculpted back of the hybrid's head, just at the top of the neck, just above the mind-collar, and, oh the hybrid was beautiful, with a sort of delicate, metallic beauty, with that collar, that mind-collar on her neck, and then Lance Chase pulls the trigger, and the hybrid's neck and head explode, a spray of blood in the rich gold low sunlight, and the headless body, arms cuffed behind its back, topples forward into a ditch, and Freddy realizes that the guards – Chase among them – had made the hybrids and other prisoners – yes, there were humans too, children, and young ones, and a few SINs – one of the SINs was a famous surgeon – dig their own grave, a mass grave, a long deep trench, and it was filled with bodies, and …

"Okay, Hybrid, I'm running out of time here." Lance Chase raised the electro-whip.

Freddy leaped sideways and up the wall and then down; he snapped Lance Chase's neck, and Lance Chase's head fell to one side, as the neck was sliced by Freddy's extended claws, and a geyser of blood billowed up – like a blossoming flower thought Freddy – like a red, red rose – and Lance Chase's helmet fell off. His head, hanging by a ribbon of skin, fell behind it, the ribbon of skin snapping or ripping. The headless body crumpled slowly. It fell in slow motion, chest-forward, into the mud.

The other guard was saying, "Oh Christ, Oh, no, Oh, God," and backing away, but knowing he would never be fast enough, he drew his laser pistol, and he pulled the trigger, and Freddy could feel, in that instant, how the terrified guard – Bill Sloan, 38, single, neurotic sadist, cowardly, and sneaky, admirer of Heinrich Himmler and Reinhard Heydrich and Hitler and all the Evil Boys from Ancient Times – was hoping to see the monstrous hybrid sizzle with the high-intensity laser beam, and he was already imaging Freddy's forehead and eyes burned away, smoking, and Freddy's skull exposed, glowing red, a burning ember, with the heat of the blast.

Blinded for a second by the blast of the laser gun, Bill Sloan blinked. The hybrid was no longer there; there was no smoking carcass; Freddy was on the ceiling above him.

"Hello there," Freddy said and leaped down, smashed the gun out of the Sloan's hand. Sloan fell flat on the floor of the tunnel. He looked up at the hybrid.

Freddy picked up the laser gun. Bill Sloan was terrified; he was thinking, these hybrids are just animals, why is it picking up the laser gun if it is just an animal? He knew the reputation: that the hybrids were really super-intelligent: but he'd never believed it. They were just fucking animals. It was those fucking bleeding heart liberal snobs and fakers and upper-class Cosmos scientists that put out rumors that the hybrids were intelligent, that they had souls, that … And now, the hybrid had the gun, aimed it, and fired …

Bill Sloan's brain boiled in an instant; his face peeled off like a rubber Halloween mask. His eyes were smoking holes, his skull sizzled and split in two, vertically, right down the center – fizzling, steaming blood spurted up. Sloan's body jerked, once, twice. Pretty little gray-silver waves – what was left of his brains – spread in the muddy water, then dark red blood that looked black in the dull glare of the emergency lights.

It made patterns, pretty patterns, thought Freddy, though the lighting could perhaps be better, maybe a touch less lugubriously garish – these emergency lights were not very pleasing, aesthetically speaking. *A rose by any other name …*

Another guard came running.

Freddy smashed into him and tore off his uniform and his belts and his guns and equipment with one blur-like sweep of his claws.

Stunned, the guard screamed and fell down.

Freddy stared down at the man. He was lying naked, face down in the mud, quivering with fear and shock.

Freddy lifted the laser gun, hesitated for just a second – he was getting the whole life-history of the guard, which was very interesting – he'd been a mercenary in the Third Mexican War, and he'd had a really hot love affair with a nut-brown, smooth-skinned, black-haired girl from Alaska – a really very charming girl – Freddy would have liked to have known her – and then, having absorbed the picture, which did have its pleasing, fleeting erotic moments, Freddy pulled the trigger, disintegrating the guy's skull: it dissolved in a hissing boiling cloud of blood, gray matter, and smoking fragments of bone.

Freddy knelt down and flipped the body over. It had no face, of course; it was just a headless corpse. But in the few seconds before he killed the guard Freddy had had not only a glimpse of the man's life – and of his one great love affair – his name was Mark Chung – but, through Mark Chung's eyes, Freddy had also caught a glimpse of the place they were in: It was an ancient mine in the Dead Lands, it was a sort of concentration camp, and there were other hybrids, and there were human prisoners down here too somewhere, and there were mutants, ghoul-like things, but that wasn't certain, it was a rumor Chung had heard and a fear and something that appeared in Chung's dreams, and something out in the desert was killing animals and people. These people, the ones running and guarding the concentration camp, Freddy realized, they were on the edge of madness. Something was coming, something was approaching – something was also worming its way into their minds – and it wasn't good.

Freddy shivered: Whatever was coming, it was not good; it was not even good for hybrids!

Freddy sniffed the air. He wanted to be out in the wild of the desert where he could hunt and kill, and then he realized that Sabrina was somewhere close and that she would certainly be angry at him for killing the three guards and Helen and Sarah James would be even worse – Helen being a lawyer and punctilious and fussy and all, and Sarah a cop and Secret Service bigwig bitch of strict professional standards and they loved to bully old Freddy, these officious females. "Humans are to be protected," they would snarl, "not killed." Helen, in particular, reminded him of his old nemesis – and in the end his friend and mentor – the Queen Hybrid, V, very preachy, very principled, a real-break-Freddy's-balls schoolmarm. Still, he loved them, he loved them all, and lusted after them, but controlled himself, for they were as strong as he, and probably even stronger, particularly V who was strong far beyond them all, though she acted meek and mild and was very careful about revealing what she truly was, and whose real strength he knew had never been tested and who was, he suspected, almost supernatural, certainly supernatural in her strength. Yes, he loved V in particular, her elegance, her strength, her cool – and, yes, damn it, he loved her kindness. And, speaking of V, where was V? Was she a prisoner too?

No – it was impossible. No one would take V prisoner, and if they did, she would soon escape …and make whoever it was pay.

V was nowhere in Freddy's picture – not yet.

Bob Norton clenched his fist. The longer they took, the worse things would get. It had taken them almost two hours to get this far: God knows what might have happened in the meantime. Communications with the Control Center had been cut off soon after they left the building

The electricity and computer and command and control systems were still down, and Norton was perfectly aware that he and his teams were flying blind and by the seat of their pants into a veritable heart of darkness; he patted the butt of his laser gun. He hoped he wouldn't have to use it.

Norton peered over the edge of the elevator bucket as it bombed its way down to the 4,000-foot level.

It was going to be pure hell trying to subdue the hybrids. If the mind-collars had malfunctioned and the creatures had run amok – possibly even killing the guards – then it would be next to impossible to rescue the people who were imprisoned down here, at the lowest of the lower depths; yes, saving the people would be impossible, if he was going to have to battle the hybrids too.

The hybrids …

Bloody good warriors the hybrids were, and he knew it.

Bob Norton had a dirty little secret: he liked hybrids; some of his best friends had been …

"Okay, we'll stop off here, and have a look at this tunnel first." He pulled the lever and stopped the bucket motor, and the small engine sputtered, shuddered, wheezed and then was silent.

The bucket swung slightly, back and forth, just in front of a half-dark tunnel entrance.

The silence was unnerving, eerie.

Bob Norton stood at the edge of the bucket, about to swing himself into the tunnel first. His men would come behind him.

Then he saw it. A hybrid was standing there, a male, gray-colored, almost invisible in the steamy humid half-glow of the emergency lights. It was free and it was ready to take them all out. It would take the hybrid maybe twenty seconds to kill everybody.

Norton saw that in the damp dusky air, behind the hybrid, there were three bodies lying in the tunnel. Instantly, he got the picture; they had been decapitated by claws and fried by a laser gun. The hybrid had killed the three guards, so it was definitely dangerous, a killer ...

It was the one that had been called "Freddy," before he was reduced to a letter and number code.

Norton sensed that, behind him, his men, all three of them, were raising their laser pistols. He motioned with his hand for them to lower the weapons.

He stepped off the creaking bucket, as it swayed perilously over the shaft – it was a long way down if he slipped or if the cables gave away.

As he stepped into the tunnel, his boots suddenly ankle-deep in mud, he was thinking: What a mess, what a horrible place this was down here, the humidity heading on 100 percent and the temperature up above 100 degrees Fahrenheit, and only dim lights, and no communication with the world above, and these creatures had been locked away down here, condemned to hard labor for years now, for almost a decade and a half, which was Norton thought, a damned shame, because these creatures were not only intelligent, they were damned good warriors, and fine upstanding beings; he'd fought alongside one or two in the Indonesian-Malaysian civil wars, and so, hands on hips, standing in the entrance to the tunnel, Norton said, "Well, mate, what have we here then?"

"I'm not your mate," the hybrid stared, yellow-golden eyes glowing in the murky light.

Norton stepped forward. "Well, it might be fine to be mates, mate, if you're willing to consider the possibility."

Freddy moved closer.

Norton didn't budge, and Freddy reached out his mental antennae – thinking, this will be fun: this tough boy Australian is going to try to trick me, but he can't; all his false mate-this-and-mate-that bonhomie is going to get him nowhere! But reading Norton's mind Freddy got a surprising result: Norton knew Freddy could read minds, and he was saying, in his mind, "I know you can read me like an open book, mate, so I'm going to be frank, I can see that you've killed three guards, I imagine the act would come under the rubric of legitimate self-defense if you were human, but since you are a hybrid you won't have the advantages of due process and legal procedures and a lawyer

– not that other people nowadays enjoy much in that way of such legal protection either – but down here you are strong and you could probably kill us all, me and my men, but I'd prefer it, mate, if you'd join up with us and we will forget what we saw here, and we will work together for a solution, and then we'll see what happens. And I do know this, mate: some of these guards were total brutes – and they probably deserved what happened to them."

"That's an understatement, mate," said Freddy out loud, thinking this might be interesting. "My name is Freddy."

"I'm Norton, Bob Norton."

"What did the hybrid say?" One of the men asked.

"Fuck, the goddamn thing talks!"

"Jesus Christ!"

Norton knew the men were terrified. One of them might do something foolish – which, faced with a warrior hybrid of Freddy's caliber, would be a disaster. "I think our friend is going to join up with us," Norton said, very clear and loud, over his shoulder and still facing Freddy. "He's strong, he knows the ropes down here, and I can guarantee you he's a very good fighter."

"Sir, we can't do that!"

"Yes, we can. Do you want to challenge me?" Norton turned around to face his men, turning his back on Freddy. "And do you want to challenge him?"

"Sir …"

"Freddy, come and meet your mates."

Freddy strode forward through the muck – splashes and ripples – radiating out and glittering under the emergency lights.

He came up beside Bob Norton, and while he was striding forward Freddy captured some of the images and associations in Norton's mind – Norton was deliberately letting him, deliberately making it easy: Norton working with two hybrids in the jungles and volcanic uplands of Java, Norton and the hybrids examining a map together, eating together around a campfire, yes, they were mates, mates and special Australian-Indonesian Federation forces …

Norton reached out his hand. Freddy shook it.

Norton's men stared.

Frank Pierce coughed, and stepped forward, reaching out his hand, "Welcome aboard, Freddy."

"Thanks, mate," said Freddy, taking the offered hand; he could kill them all later if it became necessary, but he'd prefer to remain in Norton's good graces; Freddy instinctively liked Norton, ex-Australian-Indonesian Federation

Special Forces, and he realized that Norton was tough and honest and brave like the US Marines hero, Colonel Jefferson Siebert, who had been Freddy's first commanding officer, his military mentor and sponsor, way back in the days of the zombie plague, almost one hundred years ago, maybe more now, and Freddy had been really fond of Siebert who had been like a father to him, and then, of course, there was Sarah, the Secret Service Special Agent, converted into a hybrid against her will – a pain in the ass, but a straight shooter who would rather die than betray a friend; Freddy always wanted her to approve of him, of whatever he did, and Sarah would certainly say, "Team up with Norton, Freddy, it's the wise choice, it's the right choice." Not to mention V! She'd give him a damned lecture on the subject!

"This tunnel leads to a side shaft that can take us down further levels," Freddy pointed, "If you want to get lower, to where the people and the other hybrids are, that will be the best way to get there. The main shaft is dangerous, I think, I sense it, I don't know why – but something bad is going to happen in the main shaft."

"Bad?"

"Can't be more specific, but really bad," Freddy glanced at each of them in turn.

"Okay, mate, you know best!" said Norton. "Lead on!"

And the men climbed off the bucket, which was still swaying on the edge of the main shaft, Shaft-1, of Camp Terminus. They began to file into the tunnel, stepping over the bodies of the guards.

"Jesus," said one.

"Freddy, did you do this?"

"Yes, yes, I did."

"Self-defense," Norton said, "Freddy did it in self-defense."

"Jesus," said Frank Pierce, looking down at a headless corpse. He looked up at Freddy. Freddy winked at him.

Chug, chug, chug …

Jim Rahv and Julian Harvey led the third team, chugging down about 200 feet behind Norton.

They were going down in a bucket lowered by a physical winch and pulley powered by one of the old diesel engines on level three; it took them down to level five; from there they climbed down to sublevel 20, they were carrying stun guns, electro-prods, and one lightweight hand-held flamethrower.

At sublevel 20, they climbed into another bucket contraption. It was like putting five men into a teacup. Jim Rahv's hands were already greasy with filth and oil and rust; his stomach was turning secret little vertigo somersaults; he was hoping he wouldn't disgrace himself and throw up; he really hated heights – and depths. Just looking up or down made him dizzy. Once as a kid, he'd been taken by his dad and his beautiful stepmom – oh, did he love her! – to a real authentic old-fashioned country fair – actually, as he'd discovered later it was a mock-up, a recreation – and there'd been a ride that lifted you up into the air, in a little seat with a belt on it, and spun you around, until the little chair was sideways and you looked to your right and you were looking straight down at the spinning ground a hundred feet below.

At that moment, he threw up two hotdogs and the remains of the sticky candy floss cone he'd begged, positively begged, his stepmom Nicole Lemieux – that was her name, Nicole, red curly wild long hair and skin liked burnished china – to buy for him, and, when he insisted on going on the ride, she had said, "Okay, kiddo, but you'll regret it," and when he stumbled out of the ride, with more of the stuff gushing up, she didn't say a word, just winked at him. He loved her as if she had been his real mother. Nicole died in the Bubonic IV plague, with his dad, both of them – dead in one day. You think you are safe in your body, but then, suddenly, you aren't – nothing works anymore; you become a bubbling mass of sores, and your lungs fill with black goo and …

So Jim Rahv didn't like heights. In normal times he was always busy with his work and the reassuring whir and buzz of machinery made being 4,000 feet underground seem normal, and going up and down in the little elevator cage seem *almost* normal, though often he had to close his eyes and try to picture a sunny sandy beach or an alluring naked woman, usually based on Michelle Cantor, a knock-out he'd dated in engineering school – he'd heard she'd died too – in Bubonic V – but now with most of the power shut down, with the pumps and ventilators silent, and with the hybrids maybe on the loose and angry and deadly as hell, and with maybe a hundred human prisoners – or fifty – or twenty – they might be all dead already, nobody ever looked in on them – and some guards trapped far down on different levels, being down here did not feel normal or natural at all. He felt like he was about to be buried alive.

Subdue the hybrids and bring them to the surface: that was what Norton had explained they were going to do. Jim Rahv did not see himself as a stormtrooper. He didn't like the idea of killing anybody. Even more, the idea of killing the hybrids made him very uncomfortable. They were valuable government property, and he really did like his pet, HZ-2, and her fellow slave, the cute silver one that hauled the cart, HZ-8.

He hoped that the hybrids were still dulled and controlled by the mind-collars. It all depended on the batteries. If they were still running, then the hybrids would be docile, and there'd be no problem.

Jim sneezed. He wasn't feeling so hot. He looked at his hand; it was pale and trembling.

The trembling was fear, it must be fear. If the mind-collars had failed, then, boy, there really would be a problem with the hybrids. Of course, there would also be the problem of how you were going to get the hybrids to the surface, if the elevator was not working, and how to get the human prisoners up to the surface. They were going to use an old winch-operated-elevator. It all depended on keeping the old central gas-fueled generator going – it was really ancient – and if they could do that, then they could bring the herd of hybrids to the surface, and renew the mind-collar batteries – the repairs would need the surface workshop – and save everything and everybody. With new batteries in the mind-collars, the hybrids would really be secure. Then, once the pumps were up and running, they could go back to work.

Fred Ho had said he thought he could access the big gas reservoirs, hundreds of thousands of gallons of stored fuel to be used. He was probably working at it right now. Fred was a good guy; you could depend on him, always.

Jim shivered; God, his hand looked pale!

Just nerves …

It was spooky, heading down into the whispering darkness, all the usual machinery silenced and still. The breezes moving in the main shaft carried ghostly sounds. And then there was that horrible dream he'd had the night before.

The dream was filled with ghost-like creatures, chalk-white, and they were slithering through the slimy darkness, and then climbing over the walls, and invading the residential block behind the central control building, they were almost translucent, you could see veins underneath their skin. They were hairless and had very long teeth, and Jim in the dream was deadly afraid, he was afraid of these creatures, he tried to flee, he tried to run, but his legs wouldn't move, or only so slowly it was hopeless, it was like wading through glue, and he raised his arm to defend himself from one of the creatures that was perched on his window sill and the window was open and outside, behind the hunched hulking creature was a blood-red moon, giant in the sky, its red color reflecting on the creatures shoulders, pearly red and rose, and saliva dripped from the creature's fangs and when Jim raised his arm to protect himself he saw that his arm was chalk-white, pearly translucent, and that he was looking into a mirror, the hulking creature was Jim Rahv, and the moon, as he turned he realized this, was behind his shoulder, and he was perched on a window sill, and inside the room, now he saw it suddenly clearly, was a body – Jane, the doctor, she was lying on a camp bed, she was dead, her throat had been cut, she was naked, and the cut made a bright crimson slash, like a collar, on her chalk-white naked body, and ...

At that point, he'd woken up covered in sweat and shivering.

He glanced at Benjy Handler. Benjy looked like a ghost, circles under his eyes, chalk-white, and it looked – it must be a trick of the light – like one of his eyebrows was gone. Something was definitely not right about Benjy's face. It seemed to be sagging, getting longer. Benjy opened his mouth; it was meant, probably, to be a smile; but it looked to Jim like the snarl of the beast ... *snarl of the beast* ... what the hell did that mean? Jim smiled back, and Benjy looked away.

Jeff Kirkland, who'd been watching this little exchange, shrugged, rolled his eyes, and smiled at Jim. Jim tried to smile back. Jeff looked yellowish, cadaverous, as if he were already dead. Was the man a ghost?

Weird lighting effects, really weird ...

Jim felt sweaty, itchy, antsy, he was tempted to scratch, but he resisted the temptation; he glanced at Julian Harvey, wondering if Julian could read his thoughts.

Julian Harvey was staring downwards, through the cage floor. It was a long way down. The diesel motor far above, on level 23, was going *chug, chug, chug.*

The chug grew fainter as they descended.

The strain on the unspooling cables and on the motor grew steadily.

Julian Harvey was not optimistic about the motor holding up. Even worse, some of the cables were ancient, and had never been replaced. This equipment hadn't been used for, hmm, maybe ten years, maybe more. For years now, Halibut Black Swamp Inc. refused any investment, any improvements: "This is a prison camp and a mine, not a spa," was what they said.

Down and down they went.

Chug, chug, chug ...

Julian looked up. "I hear something."

"What?"

"I don't know. It sounds like wind."

Jim listened, "Fire, maybe it's fire."

"Fire?"

Then ...

A rippling roar – it was thunderous, like a huge explosion – it came, echoing from above, muffled, far away. Then the sound was closer, clearer, ricocheting down the main shaft, like a huge old freight train, rushing toward them, echoing, echoing, and echoing, again and again.

Jim stared upwards.

It was hard to see in the dim, foggy light; there were, up in the shaft above them, just a few streaks and smears of phosphorescent lichen and a few dull emergency lights, reflecting on the shaft wall, and, here and there, on the beams and supports.

A slab of stone and hard clay suddenly fell away from the shaft wall, somewhere far above; it clanged downwards, hitting metal and wooden struts, bouncing, bouncing, and bouncing downwards, then past them, and out of sight.

Jim had ducked, covering his head with his arms.

"We're in trouble," Julian Harvey stared at the shaft wall. Trickles of water were running down it, silver-glittery, regular little streams. Steamy mist rose around the elevator as it chugged downwards.

"Jesus!" whispered Jeff Kirkland, staring upwards, "Jesus!"

Benjy Handler opened his mouth in what looked like a huge yawn, strange, really strange, toothy, too toothy ...

"Yes, we're in trouble," Harvey stared upward, "With the pumps off, the whole shaft is going to blow."

"Oh, fuck, oh, God Almighty," Jim whispered, thinking, this is going to get worse, much worse than just a shutdown!

And it did – get worse.

Jim was staring upwards when he saw it.

Julian looked up. "Oh, Christ," he whispered, "What the hell ...?"

A thundering wall of fire raced down the shaft, coming straight toward them. A hurricane-force wind engulfed them, then a sucking sound; the fire was consuming all the oxygen. Gasoline, Jim thought, it must be burning gasoline, one of the surface tanks – one of the reservoirs – had ruptured and caught fire. The billowing wall of flame raced toward them, faster and faster.

"Jump, guys, jump!" Jim shouted as he leaped into a tunnel opening that had just surged up beside them.

He glimpsed the sign Level X-13.

The men swung in toward the tunnel opening, where there was a narrow platform that was used for the clay-wagon to back up and tilt its sloppy, gooey, slimy blocks of clay into the freight elevator.

The whole platform, above all the lip of the platform, was covered in slime, slippery as hell. It was easy to miss, and easy to slip off and flip down into the shaft – and death.

Julian was taking up the rear. He was just behind Benjy and …

Jim looked back.

Horror! Julian was caught in the wall of downward rushing flame; it overtook and engulfed him – he became an outline of a man in a wall of flame.

Jim, who had landed first on the platform, sheltered by the tunnel opening and overhang, watched as his friend was caught in a tide of fire. Julian was a ball of flame. The heat in Jim's face was tremendous, searing, burning …

Julian tried to swing in, but smashed against a steel beam, breaking his arm – at least it damned well looked like it –

Julian Harvey was wide-eyed. He couldn't believe it. The flames engulfed him. It was agony beyond anything he'd ever felt.

I am dead, Julian thought, I am already dead.

His feet caught on the lip of the tunnel.

Somebody grabbed his wrist, pulled him in.

Pain and roaring darkness.

Julian blinked and opened his eyes. *Oh, God … the pain, the pain …*

He was in shock – the *real* pain would come later.

Jim Rahv, shaking, standing in the tunnel, steadied himself. He looked around. Some of the guys had lost their weapons. They must have slipped out of their cases as the guys swung into the opening of the tunnel. And they were boxed in by the wall of flame rushing down the main shaft. Structures were exploding, falling from above, and Julian … Oh, God, Julian!

Julian Harvey had collapsed, folded up, and fallen down, he was lying flat on his back …

The pain ... the pain ...

Julian was usually careful with words, even fastidious. Bad language made him flinch; but now he thought, *"Oh, fuck!"*

Oh, fuck!

The pain was so great it almost wasn't pain; it was shock. His body was suffering extreme agony, but his body was far away; it was somebody else's body; it wasn't his; it couldn't be his body; it couldn't be ...

Julian Harvey was not going to die, not like this.

Oh, fuck!

He lay on his back, staring up at the emergency lights, at the faces of the guys, looking down at him, their voices coming from far away, "Julian, are you okay? Hey, Julian, talk to me!" His face was encrusted in fire and his chest was on fire and filling with fiery liquid and his arm must be dangling out at the end of some stick; it was shattered and, God, the pain was searing, and, Oh, Christ, he was useless now, he was going to be a burden, he would endanger all the other men, and he was going to die ...

Jim Rahv's face ...

Where did it come from?

Jim was leaning over him, and he was talking, his lips were moving, Jim was saying something, Julian could hear Jim's voice as if it was from an immense distance, from some other universe, Jim's face looked like a mask, a mask painted on, not real, "Hey, Julian, hang in there, everything will be okay."

Then looking serious, his face tightening into a grimace, Jim was saying, "I'd better cut this away and have a look, oh, fuck this is a multiple fracture," Jim turning to someone else and saying, "Oh, God, the burns, oh God, the burns."

Julian's face was steaming, literally smoking, red, raw steaming meat, and his eyes were closing and he was going blind and as the world closed up and went dark and at that moment, from somewhere ...

From somewhere, Julian heard a voice, a female voice, hollow and echoing, like in an old movie soundtrack heard from outside a movie theater; it was a smoky, sultry voice. Julian thought, oh, fuck, I am going crazy, I am going utterly insane, and the sexy, old-movie, femme fatale voice said, "Hi, boys, what's up?"

Hi boys, what's up?

From the smoky sound of the voice – positively voluptuous – Julian, sinking far away now, spinning down into his own world, a distant universe, a cocoon, a shelter against the pain, thinking, I'm delirious, and he imagined that it was some black-and-white movie femme fatale smoking a cigarette and leaning in a doorway and giving him the look, *Oh, Julian Harvey, so handsome, so sexy, such a gentleman*, yes, she was giving him the look, and he thought, this is a hallucination, this is crazy, this is the gateway to hell, this is some demon come up from Hell, probably smoking a cigarette, leaning toward the hero, and, Oh, Christ, this must mean I am dying, and I am gone ...

I am gone, dead, plunging into old-time movie land.

Hi boys, what's up?

When Jim Rahv heard the smoky voice "*Hi, boys what's up?*" he was kneeling over Julian using his standard-issue snap-out knife to cut away at the shredded and burned ribbons of cloth on Julian's arm so he could get a clear look at the fracture – broken bones sticking out of charred flesh – God, how had the guy burned so quick? It was like he'd been on the grill for fifteen minutes.

Kneeling in the steamy sludge, Jim bit his lip. If only Jane, their one doctor was down here to help, she was moody and difficult sometimes, but she was a damned fine doctor, and a damned fine person, straight as an arrow, and when she smiled – her smile was really magnificent – you knew she meant it; he really didn't have any idea how to do any of this, I mean, Julian is my best friend, and Julian is going to fucking die because I, James Donald Rahv, have no fucking idea of first aid, no idea of ...

"*Hi, boys, what's up?*" It echoed in his head.

What the hell was that voice? Who? Jim Rahv looked up and saw that Benjy Handler was swinging his automatic around, and that Jeff Kirkland had his laser pistol out and that they were all looking like they'd been hit by a sledge-hammer, eyes wide, mouths hanging open ...

He followed their glance.

Oh, Jesus Christ, this is the last thing I need! There, in the tunnel, her hands on her hips, gazing at them with her big golden eyes, was a hybrid, lit up by the emergency lights and by the wall of flame in the Main Shaft; she was streaked with mud, which made thick gray splashes on her black scales, and she had a red mark on the snout, and she seemed totally relaxed. A red 'V' shone brightly between her breasts. She was wearing a mind-collar. It was blinking red; that meant it was running out of power; it certainly had lost its ability to keep her down ...

"Please don't shoot." The hybrid put up its hands – well, claws – and blinked at them with those big yellow eyes most of the hybrids had.

It's hard to tell whether her fangs are smiling or snarling.

Jim Rahv was shocked. He'd never heard one talk before – and the way she talked, educated, a refined accent, old east coast, though she did lisp a tiny bit, but it was movie-star smooth, like out of an ancient black-and-white movie soundtrack. This was doubtless a trick. They were extremely intelligent and deceptive when not controlled by the mind-collar. *She's softening us up; then she's going to kill us – each and every one of us.* Her pose was relaxed, but her arms and legs and torso rippled with tense muscle, and those claws and fangs looked like they could tear a man apart in a few seconds ...

She is a coiled spring, a coiled serpent, ready to strike.

She is a cobra, poised, waiting, just waiting to strike.

"Boss, just give the word," Benjy had his automatic leveled at the hybrid; ditto for Jeff Kirkland, his laser was aimed straight at the hybrid's head; they both turned to Jim, their expressions clear: Should we shoot her boss? Just give the word! Just give the word!

Jim Rahv could see that Benjy, in particular, was sweating fear and hatred. God, the man looked awful! Benjy was itching to pull the trigger, just itching, and his nerves were visibly taut; the man was close to hysteria.

These hybrids were valuable, Jim Rahv knew that, and here in the mine, they were in storage, that was the word the authorities used, in "storage" for future research, a neat euphemism; they are "secret weapons in deep storage" was the way one document put it; so if he had her killed, he would be wiping out a considerable asset; and she hadn't attacked them, so maybe they could just stun-gun and paralyze her and shackle her and ...

But without the mind-collar to tame her, she might just break out of shackles, and she might just ... kill the lot of them.

And how the hell could you shackle such a creature?

What the fuck am I supposed to do?

She hadn't moved; she just stood there, blinking at them with those big bright yellow or golden serpent eyes that seemed to shine in the dark, and scales that looked greenish-black. She looked like a statue carved in dark ebony, glittery, almost an inner light.

It was spooky.

Jim Rahv tried to think – which one was she? She had a red V mark on her back over her left shoulder and a red V in between her breasts, and ...

Yeah, what the hell was her name when she'd been human, when she'd been a citizen, she was …

She blinked straight at him. "Sarah, Jim," she said, "Since you want to know, I can tell you. Down here, I'm known as HZ-7. But my name is Sarah – Sarah James. That was my name when I was human – before the *Culling*."

"Yeah, right, Sarah James." Jim Rahv was under shock; he'd overseen a mine full of hybrids, he's fed his favorite hybrid – very similar to this one – except his pet HZ-2 didn't have the red "V" sign on her chest or back – he'd taught HZ-2 a few tricks, how to beg for food, for example. But he'd never heard one talk. He knew of course that, without the mind-collars, they were supposed to be super-intelligent. But as the months and years passed, he'd even forgotten that they could talk; that they were similar to humans in so many ways. Now, stunned, staring at her, he had almost forgotten Julian who had been burned to a crisp by the fire and who now groaned through lips which were swelling up, crusted with crud and pus, "What's happening, Jim? Who is that?"

Jim Rahv looked down at Julian; Christ, he was dying, there was no help, no help …

"I can probably help your friend, if you let me," said the hybrid.

"How? How can you help him, freak?" said Benjy.

"Hybrids can do lots of things, Benjy," the hybrid said, "And one of the –"

"How the hell do you know my fucking name?" Benjy was shaking, glowing with fear and awe and hatred. A chunk of hair fell from his forehead. Both his eyebrows were gone.

"I can read minds. I do apologize, Benjy."

"I'm going to kill you, hybrid! How dare you talk to me, you fucking animal!" Benjy was sweating heavily. He was clearly about to spin out of control. "She's a dangerous freak – an alien, for Christ's sake, kill her!"

"Calm down, Benjy," Jim barked at the man.

"Yeah, Benjy, this is cool," said Jeff, "This lady hybrid is really cool. I'm Jeff, Sarah." He waggled his laser gun at her.

The hybrid nodded, "Your friend Julian doesn't have much time …"

"Shoot her, shoot her now!" Benjy was chalk-white, even in the garish light of the flames it was clear, he was changing; he looked like a ghost, all the blood had drained away from his face; circles grew under his eyes.

"Shut up, Benjy." Jim Rahv made a snap decision. The hybrid was right, there wasn't much time; there wasn't any time; Julian's eyes were now shut, his breathing staggered. "Okay, hybrid Sarah James. Do what you can do."

"Good, right decision," The hybrid strode forward through the ankle-deep mud as the men, still holding their guns ready, moved aside, squeezing against the walls of the tunnel, letting her pass.

"Goddamn, we'll regret this." Benjy was trembling.

Jeff laid a hand on his arm.

"Let go of me!" Benjy screamed.

The hybrid glanced at Benjy, blinked, but said nothing; she knelt next to Julian. "Okay, first, the burns," she muttered; she looked up at Jim Rahv, "I'm not going to hurt him, but when you and I fix the bones, it will hurt like hell."

Jim wiped at his forehead; a lock of hair came away, a smear of hair in his hand. *What the hell?* He was sweating heavily. He wiped his eyes. The hybrid was moving her claw-like hands over Julian's face and neck and chest.

The hybrid closed her eyes; she was concentrating.

Benjy and Jeff had gathered close; they stared as her hands moved back and forth over Julian's face and neck. There was something like ultraviolet light – rays of light – coming from her hands.

It must be an illusion; Jim felt dizzy

"Damn," said Benjy, "This thing is a witch!"

"Do you see?" Jeff gulped, "Do you see that? Cool! Wow!"

"She's a demon. She's casting a spell! Kill her, kill her!"

"I saw it," Jim Rahv whispered; he was trembling; saliva was rising; ants were running all over his body; his skin twitched; it was alive and squirming; he wanted to rip it off, all his skin; he took a deep breath, swallowed, and knelt down next to the hybrid.

"Okay, slowly now," said the hybrid. She was right next to Jim; her shoulder rubbing against his; somehow in the clammy muddy air and even through his own vertigo he noticed her perfume; she smelled damned good; he'd noticed the same thing when he got close to hybrids, like HZ-2 and HZ-8, they always smelled like paradise, even through the mud and slime. HZ-2 always smelled like lemon and spice and open fields in the old days, full of flowers … springtime.

What a fucking weird thing!

"Slowly now," the hybrid was still moving her hands, a feathery caress-like motion. As Jim watched, Julian's skin seemed to be returning to normal. Julian's eyes opened, his lips stopped swelling up and came back to their normal size and shape.

Julian blinked, "Oh, for Christ's sake, who are you? What the fuck are you?" He blinked at Jim. "Who is she, Jim, who is she?"

"She's Sarah James," Jim said, "She's HZ-7, she's making you better."

"She's the one with the red Vs?"

"Yeah, she's the one with the Vs."

"I feel, God, I feel better. The pain in my chest seems to have gone away. I can breathe. I was choking to death; I was drowning … but my arm …"

"Okay, Julian," the hybrid's eyes seemed to glow, "The burns are mostly fixed, and the searing of your lungs has been fixed. Now Jim and I are going to fix your arm; this is going to hurt like hell."

"Okay, do it, HZ-7, do it," said Julian. He closed his eyes.

The hybrid told Jim to hold Julian's arm, and on her command to stretch it. He grimaced. This would be suicide, this would rip everything apart, this would kill the guy. He wiped his forehead – more chunks of hair – his skin was on fire – and he heard, as if from far away, Jeff whisper, "Oh, boy, oh, boy, this is going to hurt."

"Kill the witch! We have to kill the witch!" Benjy fingered the trigger of his gun; he was sweating, glaring.

"Calm down, buddy," Jeff stepped between Benjy and the hybrid.

"Get the fuck out of my way!"

"Yes, it will hurt," the hybrid laid her claws on the arm and touched the bones and seemed to happen in a sort of blur – it was all so fast – the bones seemed to weld together – the veins, muscles, and tendons seemed to branch out link up and the skin and fatty tissue reformed, and the arm seemed as good as new, just a bit red, was all.

It took maybe 10 seconds – not even.

"Okay, try your arm, move it," the hybrid was still crouched next to Julian, rocking back on the balls of her feet; she glanced sideways and up at Benjy. He was chalk-white, looked like a ghost; he was swearing under his breath and glaring at Jeff. The fires in Main Shaft-1, only 20 feet away, reflected off his wet shiny face.

Distant explosions echoed. Main Shaft-1 was a continuous wall of flame; the heat radiating off it was like a blast furnace. Pieces of the shaft wall, and beams and cables were toppling down, black shadows falling in the wall of fire, distant muffled crashes.

Julian flexed his arm and sat up. Slowly, cautiously, as if in a daze, he stood up. He looked down at himself. His uniform had been burned away;

just wisps of charcoal remained on his naked chest – his skin was perfect, as if nothing had ever happened. His chest hair was gone. One half of his head had no hair; one eyebrow had been burned away, the other was badly singed.

"We have to get out of here." The hybrid was still rocking back and forth, crouched next to Rahv, and looking up at Julian.

"It's like nothing happened." Julian swallowed; he looked down at her. "Thank you, HZ-7, thank you."

"You are welcome, Julian," said the hybrid.

Jim was trembling; he wiped some drool from the corner of his mouth; he looked at it; it looked like yogurt or whipped cream. *What is happening, what is happening to me?* His hand, streaked with running firelight, looked cadaverous, skeletal and watery, almost as if he could see through it.

A current of air rippled around them; it was headed toward the fire, drawn into the fire; a support beam snapped, and fell into the tunnel.

"This place – this tunnel – is going to explode," the hybrid said, still crouching, looking up at Julian.

"Christ almighty," whispered Benjy, "Thanking a hybrid! I'm going to kill you, hybrid!"

"No, hold on, Benjy, don't do it, man, don't do it," Jeff stepped in front of Benjy, blocking his shot.

"Get out of my way, or I kill you too."

Jim Rahv tried to stand up, and said, in a choking voice, "Benjy, don't, you'll get us all killed!" He realized he was trembling; his legs felt wobbly; he was half-blinded by sweat; everything was a blur.

Jeff cried out, "For Christ's sake, don't!"

There was, at the same time, a flash.

Benjy must have pulled the trigger

The automatic sprayed the top of the tunnel, bullets, and flashes whipping and flashing.

Jeff fell slowly, slowly, blood flying from his forehead, a smear of blood covering his eyes and …

… somehow in a blur of movement – the hybrid was behind Benjy, her arm locked around his neck.

Benjy's weapon was falling, falling like a twirling autumn leaf, like it was falling in slow motion, the barrel turning and turning and catching reflections of the light, and still firing – rat-tat-tat-tat …

Jim Rahv saw this all happening as if it were stretched out over a long period of time, he swallowed. His throat felt funny; he sneezed – gooey white stuff …

Jeff was shouting, "Man, what the fuck did you do, I can't see, I can't see a fucking thing!"

HZ-7, her arm still locked around Benjy's neck, said, "Calm down, Benjy, don't do anything silly."

Benjy's eyes bugged out, like he was being strangled.

"Christ, what happened?" It had all been too fast – Jim sort of did know what had happened, understanding it only after it happened, seeing it as if in a replay, with the background of explosions somewhere and the roaring heat of the flames in Main Shaft-1, like background music

The fire popped and roared; the gentle breeze was becoming a strong wind. The puddles in the tunnel rippled, the mud splashed up, the chains on one side of the tunnel swung and rattled.

"Benjy shot Jeff is what happened," Julian said; fire reflected on his oily chest, on his blackened face, "And the hybrid knocked him off his aim."

"What do you want to do?" The hybrid's voice was level, tense, "Benjy is sick."

"Disarm him," Julian said, "handcuff him."

Jim Rahv gurgled some white stuff and nodded, "Yes, Sarah, handcuff him."

"Right," said the hybrid, with a blurring motion she stripped Benjy of his weapons, grabbed the handcuffs from his belt, twisted his arms behind his back, and clicked the handcuffs shut on his wrists, and slammed him against the wall, rivulets of light from the fire running over their bodies. Benjy was trembling, truly ghostly white. His skin shimmered, seemingly transparent, wet and glossy, blue veins pulsing, all his hair had fallen out. The hybrid had turned him around, so he was facing the wall, his back to them. His helmet had fallen off; he was almost completely bald.

"What's happening to the man?" Julian said.

A ghoul, Jim thought, trembling, Benjy looks like a ghoul.

"What's going on?" Jeff was on the ground; he tried to get up, he groped in front of his face, now a mask of blood, "Benjy, buddy, what's happened? I can't see a thing."

The hybrid knelt, and with a piece of cloth she had lifted from Jeff's backpack, she cleaned the blood away from his eyes and forehead. "A bullet fragment touched a nerve."

"I can't see. It's all black," Jeff turned this way and that, his eyes staring, "Have the lights gone out?

"Emergency lights are still on," Julian said, "And the fire is spreading. We're all lit up, like in a blast furnace. You're right, Hybrid, we have to get out of here."

Benjy, still facing the wall his wrists pinioned behind him, began to howl. At first, it was a yelp, yelp, then a long banshee, hyena-like cry, a wolf's cry to the full moon.

"What the hell," Julian went up and turned Benjy around, and fell back in surprise. The man's eyes were blank, totally white, like a peeled, boiled fucking egg; he was drooling, thick, bubbling creamy liquid, "What is happening to the man?"

"It might be contagious," said the hybrid. Her claws were on Jeff's forehead and over his eyes.

Benjy howled. Suddenly, head down, he charged Julian. Julian ducked aside, and Benjy slammed blindly into the opposite side of the tunnel. He turned and snarled, wiggling, struggling to free his hands the handcuffs.

"I can see, right, I can see!" Jeff's eyes were open now, and bright, but still rimmed with blood and a long streak of blood ran down his right cheek.

Slabs of the Main Shaft were falling down, black shadows flashing down in the roaring fire at the end of the tunnel; beams, elevator cages, were plummeting into the volcanic inferno.

"Get up, Jeff," said the hybrid, "there's no time."

Everything and everybody was lit up by the roaring flames.

Jeff stumbled to his feet. He stared at Benjy. "What's happened to Benjy?"

"Later, Jeff," said Julian, "We have to get out of here – but where?"

The wind rose. It rippled the puddles of mud; it made the cables creak, it tore slabs of loose clay from the walls of the tunnel.

It was hard to hear, hard to speak, hard to breathe. The fire roared. The wind was so powerful, it was sucking pieces of equipment – a backpack, a small beam of wood, a shovel, a stream of loose clay – into the shaft. The fire was sucking things into the furnace that Main Shaft-1 had become. The roaring was huge, deafening.

"It's a firestorm," shouted the hybrid.

"Yes, a firestorm," Julian shouted, "It's sucking the oxygen out of the side tunnels. It's feeding the fire. We have to get out of here."

A floorboard flipped up, slammed against the side of the tunnel, and was ripped away into Main Shaft-1; already alight, it shot upwards.

"Let's go," the hybrid had its claws on its hips; light streamed over its black-and-red body, glittered on the reptilian scales, shone in the bright golden eyes. She looked metallic, like the statue of an alien goddess.

"Let's go – but where?" Julian looked around, desperate.

"There's a small vertical crawl-shaft with a ladder halfway down this tunnel," said the hybrid.

A large support beam at the edge of the Main Shaft snapped in two and somersaulted into the fire. The crossbeams and braces retaining the clay walls began to buckle.

"Jesus," whispered Julian.

Benjy screamed. He snapped the handcuffs. He charged at Julian. The hybrid leaped and pushed Julian aside.

Benjy slammed against the wall. He turned. He growled. Foam spurted through his fangs. He had no lips. His hairless white skull glowed. He tore at his overalls, tearing them away.

"Benjy …" Julian said, moving toward him.

"Don't," said the hybrid.

Benjy leaped, his fangs were out.

Julian ducked; the hybrid slammed into Benjy. Benjy ricocheted against the wall, for just an instant, he crouched against the wall, his long thin tongue looped out of his mouth, his blank white eyes gleamed; he leaped at Julian. Julian ducked – Benjy hesitated, stood confused, and then ran straight, leaping, screaming, running straight into the wall of fire.

"I'm like him," Jim Rahv screamed, "Look at me! I'm a monster; I'm like him!"

"Run, come on, run!" Julian shouted.

"You got it, man," Jeff was heading into the tunnel, "Let's run!"

"Come," said the hybrid; she crouched next to Jim Rahv; her golden eyes stared. Jim was drooling; he felt the drool dripping, splashing, flooding; he pulled off his helmet; his hair had almost entirely gone. His ears looked as if they had become pointed.

"I … I'm changing …"

"I can see that, Jim. Come!"

"What am I?" Jim got up slowly. He felt he had to tear off all his clothes; he was like the hybrid; he was no longer human; he had to get rid of everything human; he didn't need clothes; he couldn't stand clothes.

The hybrid put a claw on his shoulder, "Come on," she said, "It doesn't matter if you are human or not."

"You are a goddess come from deepest hell to save us, to save us all," Jim slobbered. He crouched on all fours in front of the hybrid.

She squatted next to him. "Jim, we have to go. Julian and Jeff and I are eager to go. We have to get you someplace safe, Jim."

"Yes, goddess." He began to cry; they were tears the color and consistency of thick vanilla yogurt.

"Come on, Jim," Julian shouted, "Come on!"

"Yes, Jim, come on, let's go," the hybrid helped him up; he stepped out of the overalls, leaving them crumpled in the mud.

"Yes, let us go, goddess," he said, "Yes, mummy, take me with you, take me with you."

More material came rocketing down into the flames roaring at the end of the tunnel. One side of the Main Shaft seemed to be sliding down into the flames, a huge dark slab of matter.

Jim felt a flood of goo spurt out of his mouth; he leaned forward, against the wind, all the air was racing toward the Main Shaft, a tornado of energy; the air whirled, slashed; it was almost impossible to stand upright; tools flew; a mining cart came rattling down the tunnel on its small narrow tracks, and, as they flattened themselves against the sides of the tunnel, it roared rattling past and Little Jim – he seemed to have shrunk – saw it flip off the end of its tracks and shoot straight into the roaring inferno.

They were caught in a whirling maelstrom of pebbles, pieces of wood, streams of running clay, tools, bits of chain. Shielding their faces from the stream of debris, Julian and the hybrid, bodies bent against the wind, ran back to the side tunnel, jumped in, and followed the others down the narrow steel ladder that led down past tunnel X-14 and down past tunnel X-15 to tunnel XBT-23.

The wind whistled and roared up the vertical ladder shaft.

A thunderous echoing came from a distance, somehow louder than the roar of the fire.

The Main Shaft, Shaft-1, was collapsing; and if it collapsed entirely, it would be sealed with thousands of tons, hundreds of meters, of rock and clay.

There would be no return to the surface, to the land, and to the sky, not for anyone, hybrid or human.

Far below level X-1, in a long-abandoned part of the mine, Valerie Joffre, Cosmos First Class, Visiting Professor of Geology at the Universities of Oxford and Columbia, Special Consultant to the Imperial Cosmos Department of Defense and Security, was lying flat on her stomach in a very narrow very low space, about three feet from the dead-end rock face of a 140-foot borehole.

Oops, a splash …

"What the hell …? Damn it!"

A splash of gray mud had spurted up and smeared half of Valerie's Plexiglas eye shield. She reached out a gloved hand: The rock face trembled. She could feel it.

Something was happening …

An earthquake?

A handful of dust cascaded down just beside her face, brushing her cheek and clouding the eye shield. Valerie, bit her lip, and pulled out a cloth – it was hard to do in such a tiny narrow space – she had to twist around on her side, slide her arm down, pull out the tiny cleaning kit, squeeze it back up to her face, and then turn back over on her stomach, and get to work. Propping herself up on her elbows, she wiped the eye shield clean. Then, she stopped and listened, her hand suspended in mid-gesture.

A distant boom echoed, reverberated; it was far away, just a hint, just a vibration really, not really sound, but a trembling of the earth; a tiny slice of mud slipped off the tunnel face. The trembling came again.

What the hell was that?

Well, whatever it was, Valerie had a job to do. The sooner she completed her report, the sooner she could leave this devilish godforsaken place.

She pushed and shimmied forward on her elbows until her nose was two inches away from the last section of the rock face, the end of the tunnel.

Her helmet light focused close, bright, and concentrated. The rock face was striped, horizontally, with alternating yellow strata and burnt sienna strata – interlarded with white limestone lines and then thin levels of fine clay that had not entirely solidified into stone – so the structure was ancient but fragile.

This was interesting.

She was searching for a unique, recently identified, rare metal clay; she had thought from the geological surveys and from the geomorphic analysis that this would be a good place to look – and, there, if she was not mistaken, was the thing itself; the rare metal compound she was looking for. *Eureka!*

So, it looked like her hunch was right!

She dictated some notes to her bodysuit mike.

She was about one hundred and forty-five feet into the tunnel, which was really only a muddy crawlspace – a borehole – about two and a half feet in diameter.

So, there she was – one hundred and forty-five feet beyond a side shaft in one of the lowest levels of the mine, an area rarely visited, even by the most intrepid of the guards and miners. She was down about a mile and three hundred feet, and she figured she was even below the cave of the dissidents, the human prisoners.

Nobody ever came here.

She tugged her mobile from her belt pack. The screen showed nothing; obviously, down here, there was no signal. Down here, there would be no signal from anywhere.

She was totally out of contact. She liked it that way. It was already three hours beyond the end of her planned shift; but, as visiting expert, and Cosmos First Class, carrying a Universal Pass and Top Security Clearance, she had no boss to worry about. She could do what she wanted and keep the hours she wanted. And she was – as her colleagues back in Elysium never tired pointing out – a workaholic. She found the work fascinating and was really only happy when she was working. And she was an optimist. Science, she thought, might yet prove to be the salvation of humanity.

She'd brought two food packs with her, so she could stay down here for 24 hours, if she wanted to. And she had taken tablets to delay the need to urinate or defecate. The world could come to an end and she wouldn't know it.

But something was happening …

The trembling was unnerving. Could it be an earthquake? This was not a good place to be, in a tiny hole more than a mile underground, if an earthquake came. Maybe she had crawled into her tomb.

She frowned. No, Valerie, don't even think about leaving; just keep working. She slipped a small instrument out of one of her suit's pockets and began to collect samples.

The rock face trembled again; dust cascaded down; mud rippled and splashed up.

Valerie raised an eyebrow and shrugged. She returned to the work, gathering samples and sending miniature sonic and electromagnetic probes into the rock.

Elsewhere, on various levels, some of the AI intelligent monitoring instruments realized the end was coming – and coming fast. As the fire burned its way down Shaft-1, it weakened timbers and blew away steel braces and retaining walls. And the fire ran into and set other fuel reservoirs alight on levels A-14, A-22, and A-30. And so the explosions continued, and the fire spread.

Several ancient control systems, local battery-run, and emergency-activated systems – and their Intelligence Analysis Units – began to register the damage: Retaining walls were weakening; the pumps had stopped working; at the lower stages, water levels were rising, flooding was beginning virtually everywhere; serious flooding; some of the systems indicated, with little red lights, with wildly swinging dials, with emergency messages, that Main Shaft-1 would soon collapse, that the underground river Styx would within six hours, at the very least, maybe much earlier, flood at least twenty of the lowest levels of the mine. In short, total disaster was imminent.

Several of the systems, built to provide probabilistic predictions, indicated that no one now in the mine would leave it alive.

Norton and Freddy and their crew proceeded carefully, from level to level, deeper and deeper, so they could find the remaining hybrids, guards, and, eventually, get to the prisoners who were in a giant cavern near the lowest levels of the mine.

Hybrid Sarah James and Julian Harvey led their small group lower, too, to get away from the fire, and to find Norton and his group – if they were still alive – and decide what to do.

Sammy Franks and his two hybrids – HZ2 and HZ8 – were making their way through a labyrinth of tunnels, looking for other survivors, if there were any.

Valerie Joffre glanced at her wristwatch. Time had passed since the first, strange tremor. She decided to get out of the borehole – it was claustrophobic, even for her. It was too narrow to turn around, so she pushed herself backward, slowly, wiggling and squirming, until she got out to a point where she could crouch, then turn around, and then crawl on hands and knees.

Just inside the entrance to the borehole, it was about seven feet in diameter at this point. She stood up and stretched, raising her arms above her head.

The luminous circle projected by her headlamp light bounced and jiggled, revealing rock walls, sludgy gray mud, and steamy, foggy air. *Steamy, foggy air – it was like she was in a rainstorm or a bank of fog. Something was not right.*

She looked around; she listened.

The air was certainly foggier. It did seem hotter. She jumped out of the mini-drift, dropping to her feet in the side tunnel. Her boots made a splash. She looked down.

The tunnel was ankle-deep in water, hot, misty, cloudy water, moving at a fast clip. This was new! An hour ago, there had been no water. The mine must be flooding at a higher level. She tried her Com Unit. There was no signal. Of course, there would be no signal!

A sudden gust of hot air almost blew her over. She grabbed onto the wall and steadied herself. The blast of air was blistering, so hot her skin felt like it was peeling off, and it smelled of ... gasoline.

The wind dropped.

Valerie recovered her balance and hurried up a series of steps, where the tunnel went gradually to a higher level. The steps were a cascade, a small Niagara of water, swirling around her boots, and now more than ankle-high.

She noticed that the main lights were off; only battery-powered emergency lights were functioning.

She came to a wall phone. She picked up the receiver. It was dead. She gave the unit verbal orders. No response. She stood for a moment, perplexed, listening.

The sounds were different. Ah! The pumps and ventilators were silent. Their noise was so continuous that you didn't notice it. It was just part of the natural background. But now the pumps and ventilators were not working; that meant the place was going to flood; that meant that the air would soon be poisonous; that meant that the people down here were going to die; that the prisoners and guards and even the hybrids were going to die; that meant even she might die! "Damn it!" She clenched her fist and looked around: *Okay, what do I do now? How do we save people?*

CHAPTER 6 – TWO KIDS

Everybody is going to die!

Level X-D-4 – the Dissident Cavern.

When he first heard the strange, spooky sound, Jake's first thought was:

Everybody is going to die!

We are all going to die!

Fire! It was fire! Fire was raging somewhere, Jake could hear it roar. Then a great wind came, whistling and whooping and lifting up flakes of charcoal and old food pouch wrappers, swirling them around, sucking them into a crevice; something was happening.

Everybody is going to die.

Jake knew he had to do something. *Everybody is going to die. All the people are going to die.* He was the only one who could get help, and so he had to get help; he had to open the Big Main Door that kept all the people prisoners – otherwise, they would all drown – now that the pumps were down and not functioning, everything would flood, and everybody would drown. The river Styx would back up and flood and sweep them under the dark water and carry them all away.

Whatever was happening had started, Jake thought, maybe an hour before he heard the sound of fire.

That was when the lights first blinked, and the ventilators and pumps went off, though Jake was pretty vague about what "an hour" really meant: in the cave and in the tunnels, it was impossible to measure time and nobody had a watch or a clock or a computer or anything like that; in fact, really, nobody had anything, and there was no starlight or moon or sun, no autumn mist or falling leaves, no bright sunrises or yellow-green and gold and scarlet sunsets, no rain, no snow, no sleet, no, there wasn't much of anything. People just crouched, most of them naked by now, clothed in mud and clay and shit, and did not speak of what crossed their minds or struck their fancy, if anything did cross their minds or strike their fancy, which was doubtful.

Jake was twelve years old and had lived more than 5,000 feet underground in the Prisoners' Cave for the last eight years. He had no way of telling time, but he seemed to have a clock in his head, as Ms. Agnes once told him, which was strange, because he'd never even owned a watch, and he wasn't sure he could remember precisely what a sunrise or sunset looked like or a blue sky or floating white clouds or the sun overhead at what was called noon; Ms. Agnes had tried to explain what seconds were, and minutes and hours, but it was pretty fuzzy; Jake confessed that he had his own definitions of hours and minutes which depended partly on being hungry or not, having to pee or shit or not, and when you heard machinery start and stop, particularly the elevators out in the forbidden area where he was not supposed to go.

But now he knew – well, he guessed – that they were all going to die, and his sense of time had suddenly sharpened.

Yes, the danger began, he thought, some time ago: an hour, two hours, or three? Did it really matter?

That was when the lights had flickered off, then on, then off.

Then the emergency lights came on – they looked even more ghostly than the usual lights, misty and white, a really crappy color.

There weren't many lights anyway, particularly not in this part of the cavern and in the side caves, away off far from everybody.

Yes, it all started a while ago when the lights blinked – hours back, but who knew how to count hours?

So, it was maybe two hours ago when …

When …

"What's that?"

The lights blinked.

Jake was staring up at a fifteen-foot outcropping of rock, one of his favorite crouching places. It hid the entrance to his secret tunnel, his very own secret tunnel.

Jake frowned – the lights had never blinked before – then, while he was wondering what was going on, the lights went back on. Jake shrugged and climbed up onto a slippery rock step, then another, then another, and then he was on top of the ledge of rock – his head only a few feet below the sweltering dripping roof of the cave.

"Hell and Damnation!" Jake hitched up his oversized gray canvas shorts, which, while he was climbing, had shimmied down around his thighs.

"Hell and Damnation!"

The shorts were stiff with dirt, half-dried clay, and old blood. He'd inherited them from one of the dead – a man people called "Clive Something."

Clive Something had been sent downriver many days ago, last thing to disappear being his feet – his pointed toes, ghostly white, uncut yellowish toenails, and limed with dirt, which stuck up out of the water – into the foamy whirlpool and then Clive Something and his toes, with the long curved yellow nails, were gone, in a little circle of scummy foam, under the downriver wall of the cave, where all the dead went.

When you were dead, you were sent out of the cavern downriver, and you were sent naked – man, woman, or child – because downriver nobody, not even the dead or their ghosts – if there were such things as ghosts – needed clothes or anything, or so Ms. Agnes had said, explaining, "Downriver, is the end," Ms. Agnes looked at Jake with her dark eyes all sad, "Downriver is nowhere, that's what and where it is, Jake."

And so it was quite just and right and utterly reasonable, Ms. Agnes said, that the living kept the clothes upriver in the cave where the living still lived, since the living people – not many of them left now – didn't have anything to wear anymore and little to eat and needed everything they could lay their hands on, as Ms. Agnes had pointed out to Jake more than once, "So you keep these shorts, Jake. They are yours now."

Before Clive Something's shorts, Jake had been wearing what somebody said was a torn pillowcase, whatever a pillowcase was, with a length of rubber-coated wire for a belt, and nobody could tell him where that had come from, but it was just found one day on the slime beach at upriver, but the wire broke into little pieces and the pillowcase was all yellow and rotten, falling apart, and it didn't cover anything and wouldn't stay up anymore, so Jake for a few days was stark naked.

The canvas shorts sagged stiffly; it was, "Like wearing a cardboard box," Ms. Agnes had told him, "But, Jake, it's better than nothing." Jake jerked at the edge of the shorts, pulling them up over his hips, and swore an oath– "A curse on all cloth and all clothes!" He growled and squatted down on the flat ledge of wet stone, which was, yes, his favorite crouching place.

The shorts were itchy and slimy and heavy.

"Damn things!" He tugged at the rope that was supposed to be a belt. He'd strung it through the loops – to keep the shorts from slipping down over his hips and knees and ending up in a stiff wooden puddle at his ankles.

"Damn old-fangled things!"

The rope was rotten too and fraying. It kept breaking, and it was now half made of knots he'd tied to keep it together.

"Damn dead man's heritage!"

"Do not swear, Jake," said Gloria, from down below, where she was looking up at him, grinning, bright teeth and blue eyes shining in her mud-smudged face.

The thing was: Gloria wanted to go everywhere Jake went, and she wanted to be with Jake all the time. At first, he didn't like it. She would slow him down. He was afraid she would get hurt and then it would be his fault. He was afraid she'd do something stupid, and then they'd both get killed. It was usually hard for a kid to imagine getting killed, but Jake had seen lots of people die, so he could imagine it and feared it all the time – mostly for other people, not for himself. But soon he realized Gloria was really clever and intelligent and hardly ever afraid – and, besides, he liked the company.

"Do not swear, Jake," Gloria repeated.

"Damnation!" Jake grinned. He glared down at her. If the rope broke again, it would be too short to mend, and he'd damned well give up the damned thing and he'd go goddamned buck-naked and stark naked, just like before, when he didn't have the pillowcase, or any other damned thing for that matter, just his skin. Yes, he'd go naked, no matter what the goddamn preacher said. The preacher didn't count anymore anyway. He was a wispy old man by now and thin as a stick and sick in the head – chest all dark curved ribs "like a caved-in, burned-out birdcage," said Ms. Agnes – skin yellow like old candle wax – and he kept calling out, the old preacher did, in a high funny squeaky voice – a far cry from the vibrant bellowing voice he'd had before – for the "God of Abraham" whoever that was, to have mercy and pity and save them all and take them to Jordan whoever he was. By now, the preacher was squeaky like the wind that sometimes squealed and whistled under the cliff of upriver Styx, and so, squeaky, squeaky, the preacher raised his lemon pip arms and called upon the God of Abraham.

"Oh, Lord, why hast thou forsaken us?"

"Oh, Lord, why hast thou abandoned us?"

"Oh, God of Abraham, God of ..."

All this God and Abraham talk didn't make any sense, Jake thought. If Ms. Agnes' reckoning had been done right, she said he'd been in the cave since he was four or five, no mother or father that he could remember, no last name or affiliations, no genealogy at all, and taken on as just some sort of a mascot or pet by Ms. Agnes, since it was presumed his mother and father had been erased or terminated and then, somehow by accident or bureaucratic oversight – Ms. Agnes did have her "theories" as she called them – probably an electro-memo failed to go to the right terminator or erasure squad – Jake hadn't been terminated or erased or adopted by one of the Centurions or Security Officers who often took the children of the people they had erased or terminated or tortured to death into their own families as slaves, servants, or even, the lucky ones, so Ms. Agnes said, as children, pretending the child was their own, murderers harvesting the children of those they had killed or "disappeared." Nobody knew exactly how it had happened, but the fact was Jake existed, and he was in the cave. That was sort of what Ms. Agnes told him and what he pieced together. Gloria had been born in the cave, but her mother died and went downriver just a few hours after Gloria was born and nobody knew, Ms Agnes said, who Gloria's father was.

Jake lay down on his belly and stared at Gloria. "Okay, come on up!"

Gloria scrambled up. Her clever little toes and fingers clinging to tiny crevasses and chinks in the stone, her hands grabbing onto her favorite handholds, slipping once or twice, but, she was determined, and she knew the rock as she said: "like the back of my own hand."

Jake reached down and grabbed on tight to Gloria's mud-slippery wrist and pulled her up, the last four feet, onto the flat top of the rock. Then she was there, beside him.

"Thank you, Jake," Gloria said in that formal. serious way she had. She crouched next to him and they sat there, next to each other, their knees up to their chins, their bare feet, toes extended, clutching the stone.

The lights blinked again – went off, then back on.

Then the emergency lights went on.

"Something's happening," Jake said.

"It does appear so, Jake," Gloria said.

Gloria yawned. She blew her nose on the back of her wrist like Ms. Agnes had taught her was the polite way and wiped the snot – it was a nice word Gloria thought, "snot" – on the rock, the slippery roughness scraping against her knuckles, the raw touch of stone making her feel vivid and real somehow.

"Where are we going, Jake?" Gloria said, and she ran her hand over her scalp where two sleep periods ago – "nights" as Ms. Agnes called them – her hair had been sheared away by Ms. Agnes her very self. It was all sticky and prickly.

Jake glanced at the girl. Under the phosphorous light of the wall lichen – and the reflections of the distant emergency lights – the fresh stubble on Gloria's head glinted gold through the dirt.

They were both so dirty it was hard to see a single millimeter of skin. All around them mushrooms and lichen glowed, making it look like a shadow-land with distant stars, and making the two of them look, though they wouldn't have had this idea themselves, like ghosts – ghost children cast upon a cosmic rock, adrift in the soupy gray universe of the cave, a world of phantom anti-matter, the only world they knew.

Gloria was nine years old, so Ms. Agnes had calculated, and she wore a faded and torn man's check shirt – it had once belonged to Mr. Heuser who was said to have once been something called a lawyer and what Ms. Agnes said was a "hotshot politician" but Mr. Hauser had gone bad – like a food pouch gone rotten inside – throwing off his clothes and turning all white and greasy and with claws and fangs like a ghoul and not talking sense any more but spouting gibberish as Ms. Agnes called it – "gibberish" was a nice word Gloria thought – and the big people, the adults, had stoned Mr. Heuser to death and when he finally didn't spout any gibberish any more, but lay on his side, limp as a dead blind eel, his tongue hanging out, and "dead as a stone," as Ms Agnes said, they rolled him to the edge of the downriver water pool, where it whirled around, and tipped him in with a splash and he went downriver, naked as a newborn, like all the dead, except he was one of those who had turned into a ghoul, like others too, like Ms. Beaumont – who, when she went mad and bad, glowed "like a big bad glow worm," Ms. Agnes said, and Mr. Eddie Stand who foamed at the mouth, white drool that was so thick you could paint on the walls with it. "Like rabies, it is," Ms. Agnes said, and she sighed and added that ghoul-becoming was a disease, something some people got, and other people didn't. "Some people are immune, I guess," said Ms. Agnes, "and others aren't." Gloria wanted to ask what "immune" was but she didn't because somebody sick came to Ms. Agnes and started coughing and Ms. Agnes winked at Gloria meaning Gloria could go and play or just disappear and "do her own thing," and then Gloria forgot to ask and so "immune" was still there, floating free, a nice mouthy smooth sound, waiting to be tacked to the wall – Gloria saw her mind as a sort of memory wall where she hung things she wanted to remember – and she nailed them down – she had a rough idea "immune" had to do with getting the ghoul thing or not getting it, but which it was exactly, to get it or not to get it, she hadn't yet had the opportunity to clarify which was annoying, she thought, but there you are, not every problem can be solved tout de suite and lickety-split …

Under Mr. Hauser's check shirt, Gloria wore nothing because there wasn't anything else to be had to wear anywhere, which Ms. Agnes said was a great shame from a great many points of view, hygienic and ethical, she said, because in spite of everything modesty maintained decorum and vice-versa and decorum maintained morals – whatever they were – and that was something else Gloria wanted to ask about – these "morals" things – but hadn't had time. There were scrape marks and scabs on Gloria's knees; she wrinkled up her nose, stared at her knee, and picked at one of the scabs, biting her lip, concentrating. Maybe she could lever it off.

"Yes, Jake," she said, "Something is happening, something is definitely happening."

"Okay, Gloria," said Jake, "Let's go see just precisely what is happening."

And they slid down the far side – the hidden, secret side – of the rock ledge and they squeezed into the crevice, a narrow vertical crack in the rock face, just behind the outcropping, and the crack led to a really narrow very greasy secret tunnel that led out toward a service tunnel that led across an underground stream to another tunnel that led to what was known – so they had overheard – as the Main Shaft, or Shaft-1, of Camp Terminus, and this Main Shaft-1 was a magical place where there were men and machines and a whole world which was top secret – how to get out of the cavern and to the magical place was Jake's and Gloria's very own well-kept Top Secret.

"This is spooky," said Gloria, when they came out the other side of the tunnel, and the lights blinked again.

"Yes, it is spooky." Jake frowned. He was really worried; but he wasn't going to tell Gloria how worried he was. She loved exploring outside the cave, and she was having too much fun. Of course, death was waiting for them on every side – but, then, Jake and Gloria knew that.

With Mr. Death Esquire, Jake and Gloria were very well acquainted already, and had been for a long time. Soon, they would meet him again.

CHAPTER 7 – TOWERING INFERNO

Far away, up in the real world, the surface world, the Cosmos Centurion motorbike sped onwards under the stars and the moon, with no sign of the zombie-bats – not yet. Up the dunes and ribbons of sand, the bike leaped, and raced across dark, silver-streaked expanses of empty sand, pebbles, and rock. Then, in the west, there appeared a red glow soaring into the sky.

"That's it," said V. "That must be it."

Kat accelerated the bike. She was eager to get into action. She wanted to avoid an open-air fight with the zombie-bats. And she was bubbling over with energy, dying to do something, riding the mighty Cosmos Centurion bike was not enough.

"Itching for action?" said V, her body pressed against Kat's back.

"Yes. That is part of it, I suppose," said Kat, a little annoyed at being so transparent, "Part of being a hybrid."

"Yes, yes, it is."

The bike sped past a burned-out Desert Bug, its carcass turned on its side. They sped past what looked like a gravesite, a small memorial, a cairn of stones; it looked like it was recent.

"Somebody died," said Kat.

"Yes," V was thinking that it was strange, out here in this desolation, but it seemed that there were ghouls here too, and that these ghouls were much more deadly than Miranda's relatively friendly ghouls, Daisy, Deep, and Bounce.

V caught a flickering brief mental image of a slim young woman, Jane Somebody – ah, yes, Jane Fox – kneeling, placing stone upon stone, making the small cairn, and of a very strong-looking, heavily armed man, Norton was his name, standing guard over her, his automatic drawn and scanning the desert, and V caught a shadowy fragment of dialog, Norton was saying, "You are rather sentimental, Doctor," and the woman, Jane, was saying, "The girl was killed here, and there will be nobody to remember her, ever, so I think we should do just this simple thing."

The man called Norton nodded, the sunlight reflecting off his wraparounds, "Yes, you are right, Jane, of course. We easily forget we are still human, and that other people are human too, or were human."

The little cairn disappeared behind them in the whirling trail of moonlit dust that plumed up behind the bike, but not before V caught a brief image of a girl, perhaps twelve or thirteen years old, lost alone in a dust storm covering her eyes, and crouching down, and then, still lost, in the dark night, holding her crucifix, praying, tears going down her cheeks, when something crept up upon her, a herd of them, really, ghouls, and surrounded her, and …

Ghouls, but these ones were deadly …

They were tough, cannibalistic, and … mindless and pitiless.

"Almost there," said Kat.

"Let's stop at the bottom of that dune; let's have a look."

Kat swerved and skidded the bike to a halt at the bottom of a twenty-foot dune, a frozen giant wave of sand, left by one of the wandering dust tornadoes that crossed the Dead Lands almost every two weeks, lasting sometimes for days on end, an endless whirling pageant of deadly sandstorms.

Kat flipped down the bike stand. Both Cosmos warriors stepped off the bike and stretched. In their skintight bodysuits, V and Kat looked like twins, the star and moonlight glinting off the smooth black armor, off the wraparounds, and off the holsters and weapons.

They climbed up the dune. The sand shifted and fell away under their boots. Just below the crest, they got down on hands and knees and crawled forward. The glow in the sky was higher now, and brighter. They peered over the crest of the dune, and there it was: Camp Terminus.

A cluster of buildings and structures with several high pithead towers and huge industrial hangers, and cranes and pulleys and catwalks and cross-passages and elevators and silos, it was an impressive sight, as if it were a huge space ship that had landed in the middle of the desert.

It was burning.

In the center of it all was a towering red and yellow inferno of flame, right over what must have been, well, it still was, the pithead for the main shaft, the highest structure of the Camp, and it was burning. As they watched, the high structure, a tower of metal and cables and of cranes and giant winch wheels, and command posts, and operators' nests, began to collapse, slowly crashing down, imploding on itself.

"Oh," said Kat.

V lay on her stomach, concentrating, struggling to capture any mental waves she might be able to detect. Who was in that place? What was happening in there? All she got were cries of horror, howls of anguish, inarticulate, roars of madness and insanity, and she thought, this may be the end, maybe we are too late.

"It's collapsing," said Kat.

"Anybody down below, anybody in the main shaft, they will die," said V, "they will all die."

"Let's go."

"Yes. But …" V hesitated … there were obstacles: a minefield, barbed wire and link-chain fences, possibly automatic laser guns, it looked like many of the defensive elements were down, no bright lights, just dull emergency lights, and then she sensed it, she felt it, a canine intelligence, a guard dog, and the guard dog was running for his life – from something in the sky. V looked up and at the same time, Kat looked up and they saw shadows moving across the sky … zombie-bats …

"Okay, we go."

"Yes, now, we go."

Hugo was alone, still on patrol out beyond the perimeter fence and out beyond the minefield. He knew the way through the minefields. He could race inwards if anything bad happened.

He was still puzzling about the trail – the clean-smelling boots – that had entered the minefield several hours before, but since communications were down, his collar transmitter couldn't report on it, so he had decided to stay out on patrol until the end of his shift rather than heading straight in. Norton had said there were dangers out on the ridge. Whatever had crossed the minefield, Hugo sensed that it was human, not a flying mutant.

Norton had said to them, "Don't get yourselves killed, old chaps."

Hugo had barked and wagged his tail. None of them had any intention of getting themselves killed.

Hugo knew that fire had broken out, that the main pithead was burning, and that dangerous things were happening inside the camp and inside the mine, but it was not clear to his dog's mind what those things were.

Hugo ambled along the edge of the minefield, checking for any invaders to see if anything else or anyone else had tampered with the mines. No, everything seemed in order, there were no unusual additional smells or markings, and the odor of the mines themselves had not been disturbed.

He stopped.

Something was not right.

He sniffed the air and turned his nose to the very slight breeze – a furnace-hot, dusty breeze. There was that unsettling leathery smell riding in the air, trails, and streamers of it, stronger now. It was very unpleasant. It was like the smell of rot, of death, of cadaverous bodies …

There was a sound, too, squawking, cawing, high in the air, and flapping, like the flapping of heavy wings.

They were up there in the sky. Hugo focused his genetically engineered eyes, extraordinarily good night vision, and an ability to shift focus, radically, from long distance to close distance.

He saw the constellations and stars.

Then he saw the creatures – they looked like birds or like bats, but they were much larger.

Then there was another sound – no, two other sounds: motors, out there in the desert.

A motorbike, somewhere out in the desert, and it was approaching fast; this was unheard of.

And an aircraft, a small business vertijet to judge by the sound, was coming from the opposite direction, or almost. Lots of things were happening at once. Hugo wondered, very briefly, which was most important. His indecision didn't last very long.

The flying things – the evil-smelling ones – were coming on fast.

They were dangerous, very dangerous.

A sense of horror and dread flooded Hugo's mind.

The flying things were getting closer and closer. One of them swooped down. Hugo barked at it, bared his teeth, got ready to bite, but he realized they were too big, and there were too many of them.

His first duty now was to get to the perimeter and get inside and carry the information stored in his collar to Norton and the Central – Hugo was glad the collar was recording even if it was not transmitting or receiving.

So, Hugo ran, as close to the edge of the minefield as he dared, one of the giants rushed in, its beating wings flapping down just above him.

Hugo swerved. One of the talons touched his back, scraped across it. Hugo hunkered down and galloped.

He got to one of the paths through the minefield a zigzag path, and he galloped, sprinted, ran like he'd never run before.

The beating wings were all around him. He swerved, swerved again, and, as he swerved, the bats came winging down, some of them in front of him – intending, obviously, to block his way – and as they touched down, they triggered the mines – upward explosions, lateral explosion, fragmentary and incendiary – the creatures went up in flames, whoosh, whoosh, whoosh, all around Hugo.

He swerved again and again, and he felt one of them coming straight down on him. He skidded to a halt, all four paws skidding in the ground, raising a cloud of dirt and dust.

The bat, surprised, slammed into the ground, cart-wheeled off the invisible safe path, tried desperately, flapping its enormous wings, to take off, squawked, screamed an eerie human scream, and then, its eyes glowing straight at Hugo, it exploded in a vertical tower of flame and debris, pebbles and roasted flesh, a scream going up even in death, high-pitched, and almost beyond the range of Hugo's hearing.

Hugo had little time to appreciate this spectacle – even though it was a spectacular show! Another bat was diving straight down, in fact, two of them, right beside each other, one swerving at the last minute. Hugo leaped at it and bit at its dangling, pumping leg – which looked almost human.

Hugo's jaws snapped, his fangs closing for an instant on an elongated piece of hoof or talon, the bat swirled trying to free itself and one of its wings smashed into the other bat, and the two of them spiraled and careened back, swirling away, trying to gain height, but they crashed to the ground, triggering three mines and disintegrating instantly into a swirl and blast of light.

Hugo had already let go. He crouched down, ducking the flames and keeping himself just below the shrapnel line. He sprinted off again, instantly re-orienting himself, so he would not let one of his paws land off the twisting path, a quick turn to the right, a zigzag to the left and a U-turn loop backward, then another U-turn, and then a short straight stretch, one more quick U-turn, then another, and then he was almost there!

And then he was there ... safe, almost safe!

Well, he thought he was safe.

Damnation! V clenched her fists. Camp Terminus, by now a monstrous pillar of flame reaching to the sky, was a deathtrap; the hybrids must all be dead. She tried to re-evoke the mind-whispers, the sense of a re-awakening, but it was overwhelmed by pure static and chaos, burning, exploding, collapse, sliding, crashing …

Camp Terminus was a towering inferno, and the mine below the monstrous tower of Shaft-1, which had just collapsed in a mountain of sparks, a cascade of pure fire, the mine below must now be a pit of fire and magma.

Everyone was either dead or about to die.

"Let's go," said Kat.

"Yes."

They raced down the dune to the bike, their gleaming ultra-Centurion armored bike, impeccably armed, a visitor from another world.

The bats were still high above, and far away, but they were gathering, assembling for an attack. In fact, on the far side of Camp Terminus, lit up by the moon, deadly black shadows, they already seemed to be attacking, dive-bombing something.

Kat gunned the bike, and they zoomed up over the dune and down the other side. The zombie-bats were still far up in the air swirling around the burning pithead which looked like a monstrous and uncontrolled bonfire, something a god might have set off. The bats did not seem to have noticed the bike that was racing toward Camp Terminal.

The bike raced straight across the flat hard sand, and then Kat noticed it, gently glowing spots under the hard-packed sand – mines! Her hybrid sensibility, she figured, had spotted them; they were well hidden, but there was a path through. The mines were laid out in a random zigzag pattern, but to her newly-enlightened eyes, to her almost X-ray vision, the pattern was as clear as a chessboard. She swiveled the bike, swiveled again, managed a spectacular U-turn, then another, and, feeling V's arms tighten around her waist, she rammed the bike straight on – Perfect!

In less than 25 seconds, they had made it through the minefield and up against the first battlement.

In front of them came the first perimeter barrier.

Kat skidded to a stop, revved the motor, and gunned the bike, tilting it upward; it zoomed up, and over the link-chain metal fence barrier, its wheels just clearing the barbed wire at the top.

It landed with a bone-shattering thud. Kat gunned it. The bike leaped.

"The bloody thing is a fortress," Kat slammed on the brakes, the bike skidded to a halt, spinning, almost somersaulting.

V jumped off the bike and shot a climbing cable up from her backpack.

"It's a concentration camp, keeps people in, and it keeps people out," she shouted, testing the cable as its anchor took hold.

True. The automatic guns might still be operating because often these things were not controlled by the World Mind or Hive or even by computers, but just by their own little sensor circuits.

"Right," said Kat, as a spray of fire greeted them as they rappelled up the battlement walls. "And there might still be human guards."

"Humans – I forgot about them!" V grinned.

"Up we go!"

"Look!" Kat pointed upwards. The zombie-bats had noticed them, and were circling right above, waiting for the moment. V and Kat rappelled up the wall quickly.

Just as a Bat zoomed in, an automatic flamethrower – set up to keep out intruders – whooshed, catching the Bat full on its spread wings as it was coming in, and shielding V and Kat. The Bat exploded into wide-winged flame and careened down past V and Kat.

"Boy!"

Two other Bats, singed from the flamethrower flapped heavily away – one had a wing on fire – they rose into the brilliantly firelit night.

V and Kat leaped down into the inner field. Now they were in the center of Camp Terminus, not far from the Control Tower, and not far from the burning column of Shaft-1. The heat of the inferno was like bathing in a furnace. Everything was lit in brilliant red. They had descended into hell itself.

Then there was another noise – a noise coming from the sky.

V looked up. Bats were fluttering everywhere, the glare from the fire made it difficult to see; smoke swept in waves from other secondary fires, obscuring the ground.

More Bats swept down. Crouching, Kat let off a barrage of fire from her A-Z automatic, peppering the Bats with deadly sparks of fire, soft-head miniature explosive bullets, nano-bullets that would disintegrate a human body, obliterate body armor – boil brains and eyes and shatter bones and skulls.

V noticed. The control tower block was not on fire.

That was where they should go! Maybe some of the controls were still working; maybe some of the monitors were still functioning! Maybe some of the people were still alive, and maybe they could figure out how to save the hybrids, if any hybrids were still alive.

It was a firestorm!

The roar from above was stronger.

V looked up

"Oh, what the hell is that …?" Kat was swinging her A-Z automatic around, ready to assault the thing coming from the sky.

"It's …"

A vertijet, a vertical engine private executive jet, was lowering itself down, pushing through the cloud of wheeling and screeching zombie-bats that were smashing themselves against it, whirling around it.

"More enemies," Kat had her finger on the trigger.

"Wait," said V, her gloved hand on Kat's arm, "maybe not."

"And, what is that?" Kat turned toward a black-and-white flash that was racing toward her.

"A mad dog …?"

Hugo galloped out onto the landing pad platform and saw two humans – Centurion warriors to judge by the uniforms.

Where had they come from? There were no Centurions here!

They were standing on the central platform. Somehow, they had gotten through the minefields and barbed barriers and walls.

Hugo sprinted toward them, lopping as fast as he could, low to the ground, swerving, for, though he was not looking upward, he could feel the bats, plunging down, hovering, gathering, zooming in for the kill.

Then: oh no!

He saw the two Centurions swing their weapons his way.

The thought occurred to Hugo that they were going to shoot him, because racing like this, teeth bared, foaming at the mouth, breathing desperately, he would certainly look – to those strangers – like he was hostile or had rabies or something and so …

Oh, no!

Both Centurions fired.

The laser beams and high-speed explosive bullets raced through the air.

Hugo leaped forward, hugging the ground, swerving, ducking.

Above him, he heard and felt the explosions as several bats disintegrated in balls of flame. So, the Centurions were not aiming at him!

Just as Hugo skidded to a stop close to the two Centurions – magnificent, they were, standing in the firing stance – the true elite of the humans, Cosmos and Centurions. Cosmos like his friend Norton!

They fired again.

Hugo barked.

"Welcome," one of the Centurion said. In that instant, Hugo realized – through some sense, he was not entirely aware of – that these Centurions were not fully human, were not fully Cosmos, that they were hybrids, but he realized, too, that they were friendly hybrids, and that they were on his side and that he, therefore, should be on their side, he swerved around to face the common foe – the creatures from the sky.

At that moment, the vertijet he had noticed was coming down, about twenty feet away – was it friendly, or was this part of the attack?

Hugo decided he was too busy to confront the new danger; he was barking, swerving, and leaping and biting, trying to drive away the huge bats. The bats seemed somehow to be part human, and there was about them a tonality of sadness, of horror, of obscenity: it was something horrible, most horrible, and for which Hugo had no words.

Just as he leaped at one of the bats, and it retreated upwards, and then exploded in a burst ball of flesh, gristle, bone, and fire, Hugo caught sight, out of the corner of his eye, of the door of the vertijet opening – its engines still whirring, dust still rising, its lights still blinking – the door was opening, and Hugo saw, in the open door, a hybrid, the full reptile version, black, glittering, with golden eyes, and behind the hybrid, came a human, and then another human, the second human was a Cosmos First Class, and this was very confusing – hybrids and humans never mixed this way together – maybe Norton could explain it.

But Norton was not here.

Hugo sensed that this new hybrid, too, and her companions were friendly, more allies in the fight against the powers of darkness.

And so he continued to bark, to race this way, and that, barking, leaping, confusing the bat-creatures who were screeching and howling, and exploding in balloon-like sparks and fireworks bursts of roasted flesh and bone and gristle in the air, colorful fireworks, splashing all over the moon and the stars, as the Cosmos-Hybrid guns banged, bang, bang, bang ... as the two Centurion-hybrids fired bursts of laser shots into the gathering cloud of zombie-bats, splatter, splatter, and splat: bits of blood, bone, frayed bat-pelt, and gooey gay matter slowly showered and floated down.

Now the new hybrid and her two humans were ducking, running, under the shelter of the blazing Centurion guns.

"Run," one of the Centurion-Hybrids shouted.

Everybody ran.

And so they ran headlong – Hugo, hybrids, humans – toward the inner perimeter that protected the Control Tower and the pithead – the pithead which had now been burning like a volcano for the last hour or so, a towering inferno of flame.

The huge Bats came rushing in toward the inner perimeter fence; some of them landed, exploding in a tangle of wire and metal polls.

Hugo bounded ahead. He knew the way. He knew the narrow opening, the inner corridor between the barbed wire.

He was the leader.

And the hybrids and humans seemed to know that he knew where to lead them – to shelter, to safety.

Humans and hybrids were racing behind him; their guns blazing and flashing and going zip, zip, zip …

Bats exploded like Roman candles.

They were still all running, but the Centurion guns suddenly fell silent.

Hugo's heart almost stopped, but then he realized …

The Bats seemed to have given up, at least for the moment. They flew up and circled higher – squawking, screeching – and then they moved away, and then it suddenly seemed silent. The guns were silent.

Hugo skidded to a halt. They all stopped and looked upward. The stars shone, and the moon; the sky was pitch-black and empty, except for the stars and the moon.

The infinite reaches of the universe seemed so close.

Hugo waited, wagging his tail, tongue hanging out – it was hot, and he had perhaps never run so much in his life. Even those exercises Norton put him through were nothing compared to this.

He wondered where the other dogs were, his brothers and sisters.

Were they safe?

It was silent.

Now there was only the great whoosh of the fire and explosions from somewhere far underground.

The hybrids and humans were talking. Hugo caught bits of dialog, human voices, the Centurion-hybrids spoke human, and the pure hybrid did too.

This was interesting. Hugo had never seen or heard a hybrid speak before. One of the hybrid Centurions and the new hybrid were obviously old friends, almost like sisters. Hugo sensed the waves of sympathy and love that united them.

Around the huge infernal tower of flame that flared up over the desert and over the remains of the giant rickety black structures – a few skeletal remains of the Pithead framework – soared up into the sky.

Then there they were again – the things that looked like giant vultures were circling around – black silhouettes outlined against the volcano of flame, then, farther away, against the stars. And now they zoomed down again.

"Go!" one of the Centurion-hybrids shouted. She, Hugo decided, was the leader of the pack.

As he bounded forward, Hugo heard fragments of human talk … Claire … a name … Demi … a name … Robyn … a name … I'm Kat … We've got to … Let's … Shoot, for God's sake, shoot! … Come on, through here, follow the dog … he knows the way, follow him …

"Hugo, lead the way, Hugo …" they were shouting … somehow they knew his name … well, hybrids and humans and in particular Cosmos, like that blonde female visitor Cosmos who smelled so nice and patted him and fed him treats, knew many mysterious things and it was very difficult for a mere dog to know how they knew all those mysterious things that they did seem to know and communicate among themselves.

Hugo was at the coded door; the code was dead of course because all the lights were off, but the palm-and-muzzle pad was powered by batteries, and though Hugo only vaguely understood what a battery was, he did know that the door would probably work even if the general power and control system was down.

Nothing ventured, nothing gained …

Hugo stuck his muzzle against the muzzle pad; the light blinked and made a high-pitched ping sound; the door swung aside with a cool-sounding hiss, and the way was clear, inside, inside to peace and freedom and safety.

He kept his muzzle pressed against the pad so that the humans and hybrids could get inside.

They did, galloping past him in that awkward spindly upright two-legged way all humans had, but these ones, he noticed, were extra graceful and were all female, which added to his pleasure, for Hugo did have a gallant side and it extended to the females of other species. There was a lazy fat old mother cat up on above-ground level thirty-five whom he liked and sometimes they slept together when Hugo was off duty. "This relationship is clearly unnatural," Norton had told him, "But, Hugo, one cannot dispute questions of taste or passion, and so I give my blessing."

Once all the humans were inside, Hugo followed, just as a last zombie-bat went splat against the wall beside him. The door slid shut with a hiss; the light inside blinked red.

Suddenly it was a different world, muted and gray, with dimly lit corridors and stairwells and iron banisters and railings. The emergency lights cast dull, dirty shadows. They were much less bright than usual. All the usual sounds were absent: no hum of machinery, no whirr of fans, no flickering of neon-like lights, no shouting and laughing …

It was as if all the humans had evaporated.

"So, which way, Hugo?" the Chief of the Pack said; her name, he had heard, was V. She was standing, waiting, her hands clenched on her hips, eager and anxious, a weapon loosely slung over her shoulder.

Hugo barked and bounded up toward the Control Room. But he was anxious. He had already sensed that things in the Control Room were not normal.

Behind Hugo, the Chief of the Pack and the other hybrids and humans raced up the stairs.

Outside the windows, the fire still towered over the ruined skeleton of the pithead, a huge column of flame. Several outbuildings were burning too. "The fire will have destroyed the elevator shaft," V said.

"The main Shaft must be blocked entirely," said the skinny First-Class Cosmos human.

"Everybody down below will be trapped."

"If Robyn and I can get the controls up and running, maybe we can find schematics and see if there is another way to get down into the mine and back out," the black hybrid shouted.

Hugo stopped on a landing, and barked. He looked down at the people and hybrids following him. He wagged his tail: *this is the place.*

"The control room," V said. She patted Hugo on the head. It felt nice. He wagged his tail again, looking up, waiting for orders. Things might not be right in the Control Room, but these hybrids and humans looked like they could confront anything.

V and Kat entered first, swinging through the open security lock, with their weapons ready. If the camp guards were still alive, they would *not* be friendly.

The door whirled open.

"Oh," whispered Kat.

Hugo let out one sharp bark. Cautiously, he entered the room, sniffing at the carnage. He looked up at V.

"It's bad, isn't it," said V.

Hugo just wagged his tail. There was really nothing to say. Norton was not among the victims; Jane Fox, the doctor, was not among the victims. Valerie Joffre, the blond Cosmos, was not among the victims. That was good news, at least, from Hugo's point of view. He waited, close to the door, breathing in the blood-and-guts-and-death smell. He would wait for orders. All this blood made him hungry.

V and Kat surveyed the scene: there were about six bodies; blood and flesh were sprayed and splashed on the seats, on the walls, on the computers and windows, everywhere. One of the bodies was a ghoul, or at least he was well on his way to becoming a ghoul when he died.

In a low, even voice, V whispered, "All clear!"

Claire stepped through the doorway and stood still, with her claws on her hips. She blinked her yellow snake eyes and wiped her mouth with the back of her claw; the stench of blood and guts was overpowering; it made her fangs tingle, and her stomach growl. Oh for a drink of fresh, fresh blood! But this blood was not fresh and, unlike V, she did not on the whole drink blood, hadn't for decades, and she didn't intend to start now. "Okay, let's see what's here." She stepped over a sprawled body and a thick pool of coagulating blood.

"This is messy, Hybrid." Robyn looked around. She wondered if there was a clean surface where she could put her toolbox down. She liked to keep her toolbox and her tools spotless and neat.

Claire examined the banks of computer screens and interface surfaces; some showed dim signs of life. Maybe, even if the main source was down, there would be embedded batteries and maybe even hidden circuits that could link them up with the Cloud; maybe there would be an antiquated cable link, maybe some surviving land towers, maybe an ancient atomic or sun-powered satellite everybody had forgotten about. The world, in the post-technological age, in Claire's experience, was awash in an ocean of junk – and some of it was useful. Maybe she could find out what was going down in the mine – or maybe she couldn't.

"Oh, my God," said Demi Pfeiffer, standing in the entry, "This would never

happen in Elysium. I wonder if they had insurance – the damage here is terrible! What happened?"

"There's an infection that turns people into homicidal maniacs." V was
standing ankle-deep in gooey gore, drying blood, guts, offal, shards of flesh.
"It turns them into ghouls."

"It certainly looks like it does," said Kat. She slipped up her wraparounds.
She considered herself immune to disgust. But this was animal slaughter, this
was … exciting …

For, underneath her stoic Cosmos calm, Kat felt a rising lust. Saliva
spurted into her mouth, her teeth tingled. Blood! It was the sight and smell of
blood – so exciting! She could just see it, herself, in hybrid form, feasting on a
collarbone, a tibia … Above all, she could see herself drinking blood, buckets
of it, letting it overflow, bubbling from her mouth, in luxurious abandon, and
stream off her chin onto her breasts and … How inebriating! How revolting!
She swallowed and glanced at V.

V, who had pushed up her wraparounds, nodded and smiled. It was a grim,
sad smile, with melancholy – definitely melancholy – shining in V's dark eyes.
It was a flash of recognition between hybrids, between cannibals, drinkers
of blood, howlers at the moon. V and Kat were beasts from the deepest and
darkest of times …

"This is quite unhygienic." Demi Pfeiffer stepped over the dead half-ghoul,
half-human – his name tag, on a bloodied and slimy chain on his naked
ghoul chest, said "Commandant Hilmar Loritz." Demi leaned over the body.
There was a large smoky red-and-black hole in Hilmar Loritz's chest, and half
his skull had been blown away; the gray matter was spread out in a gooey
web, and a wide splatter. In the ghoul's hand, which was an ivory-white silver translucent claw, somewhat like a human hand, and caught perhaps in
mid-morph, there was a laser automatic.

Demi knelt down carefully so as not to mess up her shoes, stockings,
or skirt. She stared into the milk-white dead eyes. She then relieved the
milk-white glossy blood-spattered cadaver of the laser automatic, prying
open the half-closed claw, and stood up, and put the gun down on a work
table, on one of the few spaces not splattered with blood.

Robyn poked around and found a tabletop surface just under the main
screens and control room plateglass window. Miraculously it was not covered
in blood. She sprayed it with Q-Kleen, wiped it off with the sleeve of her work
suit, and set down her tool kit.

"Here," said Claire.

There were some plastic hard copy schematics of the mine laid out on a table; miraculously, they had not been splattered.

V and Kat and Claire leaned over the map of the place. With one gloved finger V traced the different parts of the installation.

There was Main Shaft-1, it went down more than 5,000 feet; it had an elevator for personnel and an elevator for ore and freight; both were now engulfed in flame. There were lots of drifts or tunnels going out from the main shaft, dozens and dozens. There were other shafts here and there that were no longer in use. Most of those didn't go down far enough, and most weren't linked to the main shaft.

V frowned. Then, far off, about a mile away, there was another deep shaft, Shaft-2. It went down almost 5,000 feet. But it didn't look as if it was linked to the bottom of Main Shaft-1.

"Here," V said, "Shaft 2. Let's see." V went to the control tower window. "It's over there, in that hanger."

"It's not burning – not yet," said Kat, "It might be a way down."

"Yeah, I figure you could go down there," said Claire. "But the elevator probably doesn't work – from the looks of this diagram – see, it says 'stopped operation in 2127,' that's 30 years ago. There are a couple of tunnels, and it seems too – look at this – it seems that there's an old sealed-off natural cave system, that might join Shaft-2 with the Shaft-1 system."

"Yes, with Shaft-1 gone, Shaft-2 might be the way to go," said V.

"So we climb down, 5,000 feet," muttered Kat with a scowl. She again sniffed at the blood – it was already growing old, its bouquet was fading. She licked her lips, grinned, and glanced at V and Claire; with sister hybrids any-thing – instant mental communication for example – was possible! Oh, what a long voyage she had made in just a few days! She had gone from hybrid hunter to hybrid! It was as if she had turned herself inside out! "There's a covered walkway – it might keep the zombie-bats away; it looks like it leads over to the Shaft-2 pithead."

"Right, Okay, we can use that," said V, "Kat and I will try to get to the hybrids who are trapped underground. Claire and Robyn will try to link us up to the Cloud or World Mind and get the controls working again, and see what is going on."

"And me?" said Demi Pfeiffer, straightening her skirt.

"Here," V tossed her a laser pistol.

Demi Pfeiffer caught it neatly, weighed it doubtfully. "What do I do with this?" Now she had two laser pistols.

"You keep watch, while Claire and Robyn work the computers. If Claire gets into the world mind, she may become totally distracted – like she was asleep – so if you need her, you or Robyn should whistle, very loud!

"And kick me in the backside," said Claire.

"And kick her in the backside," said V

"Kick you in the backside, Hybrid?" said Robyn, looking up from her work.

"Yep, exactly, Robyn, kick me in the backside," said Claire, giving Robyn her most amorous reptilian smile.

Hugo looked up and barked: what was he to do?

"You stay here, Hugo, in Command Central. Protect Robyn and Claire. You and Demi are the police force!"

Hugo barked.

Demi raised an eyebrow, "Now I'm paired with a dog? No offense, Hugo."

Hugo barked again, not unfriendly; this human smelled good – what perfume was it? It was something very, very expensive. Of course, like Norton, she was a Cosmos First Class, so she would have an expensive perfume, she would have expensive everything.

"You and Hugo will make a perfect pair," said V.

"I'm sure we will," said Demi, softening, "Won't we, Hugo."

Hugo barked: *Yes!*

"Okay, Kat and I are going to head for Shaft-2." V slipped her laser gun into its holster.

"See you later, Alligator," said Kat to Claire.

"In a white, Crocodile," said Claire.

"Good luck," said V, and she and Kat disappeared out of the bloody messy shattered control room.

Demi Pfeiffer took up a position opposite the door, with Hugo beside her, ready to leap. She kept the laser pistol leveled at the door. This was not what she had expected when she – a well-trained litigation lawyer and an expert in corporate re-structuring – had signed up to look after the C Emerson Caldwell III's empire, and then found herself organizing his personal life, and then, oh, well!

She wiped away a tear with the back of her hand, while still keeping the laser gun leveled at the door. She began to understand, now that she knew the creature, why C Emerson Caldwell had found the black-scaled and excessively voluptuous small-waisted, big-boobed hybrid Claire so fascinating. Claire was perky, cute, witty, friendly, and, in a sleek reptilian way, she was exquisitely beautiful – like a really expensive sports vehicle – and the fact that, in her human form, she had been a supermodel and famous designer, well, power and beauty and fame are all aphrodisiacs, and not even guys, and not even Cosmos, were immune.

Claire and Robyn were concentrating on the computer interface. "I think I'm going to be able to bring some of these things back from the dead for you, Hybrid. Will you be happy?"

"Great, Robyn, I will be happy," said Claire, with a slightly absent air. She looked up at the burning ruins of the pithead, a towering column of flame. She could *see* how Shaft-1 must have collapsed. The fire wasn't the only enemy. Thousands of tons of semi-liquid clay and of rock and of mud, were ready to cascade down into the shaft, as well as just plain water. The mine was almost certainly flooding and collapsing at every level. She thought about all the hybrids she knew – and how they were probably trapped, maybe already dead, more than a mile underground, after years of what she guessed must be horrible slavery and degradation. She must help V save them. But she feared she might not be useful. Her Net and Cloud talent and Cyber Space Force might have degraded, disappeared. Before she'd been captured and mentally neutered by the mind-collar, she could cruise the Net and the Cloud as if they were part of her own mind, totally free, faster than the speed of light, no code was immune, no system of encryption could resist her; she zipped in and out of the quantum substrata. She suspected that she even zipped in and out of the parallel universes that existed, mysteriously, within or beside our own universe, separated from the buzzing surface and manifold of our own experiences and our own space-time continuum by only the thinnest of invisible membranes. But her recent probes had been feeble and partial; she'd only barely been able to pick up the Terminus signal and the President Superliner distress beacon.

"You sigh, Hybrid," said Robyn, "Are you sad?"

"No, not sad, Robyn, just thinking." Claire's genius came partly from the fact that she had been brought up as an experimental subject – a Clone manufactured from V's DNA slightly modified by the addition of segments of Sabrina Jacobs' DNA – trapped in a glass cage with only the Net and the Cloud as her companions and teachers, and she and her nervous system had merged with that electronic universe and its mysterious spin-offs and byways, and that had made her what she became – Super Claire, the Cloud Whiz, the Mistress of the Cyber Space Universe, a Goddess, with almost unlimited in access and power and speed.

But, now, for fourteen years she had been a prisoner, reduced to idiocy, a sex toy, her mind and body removed from all connection with the Net, and so, maybe in that time, when the World Mind, the Cloud, the World Hive, and the Net had moved on, she had lost her talent. Maybe she would be useless, just a hybrid, strong, yes, but lost to … the Mind …

Her once magic mind would be useless.

Her talent would be gone.

She would no longer be herself.

But …

She had to keep up a brave face – everybody depended on her: V depended on her and Robyn, and all the buried hybrids and people, thousands of feet down in hell depended on her, even Demi Pfeiffer depended on her, and Hugo … So she would flaunt her brave reptile grin and make her snarky remarks and …

"I think I've got it, Hybrid," said Robyn, "I've almost got it."

Hugo barked – then he growled: a warning.

"Stop right there, don't move or I shoot," said Demi Pfeiffer, and to Claire and Robyn, "Watch out guys – we have visitors."

Claire turned.

Two creatures – what the hell were they? – were standing in the doorway of the Control Room.

Ghouls …

"Don't move, don't even think about it," Demi Pfeiffer picked up another automatic, the one she'd lifted off the dead half-ghoul, and aimed both weapons at the two creatures. They looked, Claire thought, like ghouls, 100% ghouls, if that's what they were.

The two creatures just stood there, they didn't move. One was female, one was male.

Claire wondered what the right word could be for what they were; she had never seen precisely this kind of morph before. Then she again thought, "Yes, ghouls, they are ghouls. Yes, definitely, the world is coming to an end."

CHAPTER 8 – MORPH

Where am I?

What's going on?

Who am I? Who the hell am I?

Whoever she was, or whatever she was, she opened her eyes and stared at the ceiling. The emergency lights were on – an evil livid glow filled the room.

She had a horrible headache, and for a few minutes, she lay there blinking and trying to remember who she was and where she was and what had happened to her. It was important to know who you are, or so it seemed, and she had not the slightest idea. It was like trying to remember a name that is just on the tip of your tongue. What had happened? Was it a hangover? Had she drunk too much of that evil mixture they called wine? That was rare; she was really careful with her drinking. And ... then ...

Then she remembered: I am Jane Fox, Doctor Jane Fox, a prisoner in Terminal Camp ...

She tried to get up, straining ankles and wrists.

She couldn't.

She was tied down – well chained down was more like it. Her neck, too, was tied down, but loosely.

She pushed against the restraints and craned her neck up – straining against the restraint collar – to look around. She was in the infirmary manacled down to the bed for unruly patients and madmen.

Perched on a chair near the infirmary window – which was totally shattered and looked out on a huge, garish redness that was either dawn or sunset or a big blazing fire – was a creature that looked like a ghoul that had clawed and slithered its way out from some ancient mossy tomb – white shimmering slick hairless skin and skull, thick limbs, barrel chest – and it turned its snout to her and said, "Feeling better?"

Jane just stared. Yes, it was Rodriguez. "What the hell have you become, Rodriguez?"

"The mine shaft is burning, and the pithead," he said, "They are all dead; they must all be dead."

"What the hell are you, Rodriguez?"

"You've forgotten?"

"It's all fuzzy. What happened?"

"I'm a ghoul, a mutant of some kind, some sort of mutant, like those down in the caves; I've become one of the ones we dreamed about."

"Jesus!"

"You don't remember?"

"It's coming back. You changed. And then the pithead blew up and then ..."

"And then?"

"And then we went to the Control Room ... and ..."

"And ..."

"And I ... and I ... Hilly had gone crazy. He'd become a ... a ...

"He'd become a ghoul."

"And I killed him," Jane was straining to get free; why the hell had Rodriguez tied her down? It wasn't like she had threatened him or anything. She felt tired, suddenly, and sad, "I killed Hilly," she said, feeling, as she said it a strange surge of energy and she saw the scene: Hilly the ghoul, he'd killed everybody, then he sprang through the air, landed on her; he was going to kill her, his fangs sank into her shoulder, and ..."

"You pulled the trigger," said Rodriguez, "You had to."

"Yes," Jane said; she slurped, feeling the saliva rise, thick and yummy and rich and delicious.

"He'd killed everybody. He killed Fred Ho. And he bit you."

"Yes, he bit me," Jane suddenly felt a tremor of fear and excitement, fire rippling through her body, down her thighs, up her loins, up her belly and ribs and breasts, a fire ...

"It's like a disease; it's catching." Rodriguez's voice was thick and slurry, but he sounded reasonable, and he still had that damned erection, a giant cock, like an outsized massive chalk-white asparagus, making an arc, in front of his flat muscular chalk-white belly – it would be funny, ha, ha, but ...

"So what happened?" she gurgled, thinking: if I'm going to die, I will try to die bravely.

"You went crazy, Jane. You wanted to kill me, so I knocked you out." When

Rodriguez spoke, he drooled, thick creamy white foam, two ribbons of it, on either side of his fangs. It looked delicious. She could lap it up. She realized she was ravenous.

"Jesus! Why would I want to … kill you?"

"Whatever happened to all the others – the humans I mean – I was – I am – immune, perhaps because the change began earlier, perhaps because of the drugs, the antivirals you gave me. You weren't immune. The madness was taking you too."

"Immune? What are you talking about?" Jane was flooded with an awful and titillating premonition. She saw herself turning into a wild killer, as in her dream, a foaming-at-the-mouth mindless killing machine. Just for a minute, she closed her eyes, savoring the pure energy, the pure desire, the pure *being* of it. She opened them. "Undo these manacles, let me up, Rodriguez."

"You sound sane, Jane, you sound reasonable. But I'm not sure you're safe," Rodriguez stroked his chin with one claw. He looked, she thought, and she had had the thought before, like Rodin's "Thinker," massive and heavy and opaque and bent in on his own body; except Rodriguez was not green-and-coppery verdigris weathered bronze, but chalk-white and flesh – some kind of flesh, perhaps a new kind of flesh, something never seen before.

"Well, if I trust you, you can trust me, right?" Jane tried to give him her best, most alluring, and trustful smile. But it didn't feel right; her smile was different somehow, and in any case, the charming seductress was not her forte, she thought: *tomboy schoolmarm severe is more my style.*

But, yes, there was something funny about her mouth, she thought; the smile didn't feel right.

Rodriguez crouched next to her. He looked like a giant albino bat except he didn't have wings, not that she could see anyway. "What's your favorite music?"

"What?"

"Humor me, humor the ghoul."

She told him: a Schubert quintet, an ancient group called Pink Floyd, the Celestial Mushrooms vintage stuff, the 2147 Lunar Eclipse season, the Andromeda Tiddlywinks …

"What do you hum when you come into the infirmary in the morning?"

She closed her eyes, vowed to keep her temper, and told him: "The Star-Spangled Banner" sometimes, "The Marseillaise" sometimes, even once or twice "The International" …

"Stirring stuff," she said, "Helps wake me up. I also like Sousa marches too if you're really interested." She blinked, thinking: All that packaged nostalgic grandeur of humanity's past, of glorious heroes, of wars that had seemed just or justifiable, of nations that were once great, and of barricades and battleships … She wondered at herself, stuck in past decades and centuries – somehow, she suspected that humanity's days were numbered.

It was an awful thought and caused a chilly shiver in her tummy.

"Good," he said, still crouching next to her, "Weird tastes, but good."

"Come on, Rodriguez!" She felt saliva rising; it was like she was drooling – Oh, God, what was happening?

Rodriguez blinked; his large pale eyes seeming reptilian or something almost reptilian; he wiped a thick bubble of gooey foam from his mouth – it looked sticky, cobweb-like, and strands of it stuck between his fingers – and he said, "They're all dead; at least I think they are."

"Who?

"All the humans – all dead …"

"How?"

"Trapped down below, they died buried in fire and mud and earth and steel and stone. The Pithead collapsed. Shaft-1 is a tomb now, a tomb from which not even ghosts will rise. They are lucky, Norton and the others, they must have died before the change could come upon them."

"Change? What do you mean by change?"

"Change into madness – what I am, only, well, they were all going crazy; I don't think I'm crazy, and I don't know why I'm not."

"What in the world is happening?"

Rodriguez put his clawed hand on her wrist. His claw felt like ice. "You're burning up, Jane."

"God!" she rolled her eyes, "This is awful. I mean …" It was true. The fever was bubbling up from her skin: thick, gluey sweat coated her forehead and her body. Her arms and legs trembled; they were on fire.

"Let me up," she said; suddenly, she noticed how slimy and clumsy her tongue was – had Rodriguez drugged her? Had she had a stroke? Had the blow to the head …?

"The morph is not complete," Rodriguez said.

"The what?"

"You're shedding."

"What the hell are you talking about?"

"You are shedding your human self. But, you sound sane, so let's take a chance." He bent close and undid the wrist manacles. He leaned across her to get to the left hand manacle.

Jane lay absolutely still. She didn't want to move or to look. She was not sure what he was talking about, but whatever it was, it wasn't good.

She noticed that Rodriguez smelled earthy, like liquid clay, it was a fecund not unpleasant smell; his chest leaning over her, close to her breasts, seemed to radiate a cool luscious sensuality; she suddenly felt violently aroused, horny, lustful, shameless: she wanted to reach up and grab Rodriguez and pull him to her and make him plunge into her, pull him deep into her, she wanted to cling to him, consume him, have him consume her. I am going crazy, she thought, this is one of those dreams the boys have been having, and this is a new version of the dream I was having, the one where ... the one where I turn into a monster. So this must be a dream because it is impossible; I cannot have become a monster; Rodriguez cannot have become a monster; for sure, I am lying in bed beside Hilly, having a horrible dream and in a minute Hilly will wake me up and start screaming about bugs.

Rodriguez loosened and undid the last of the restraining thongs.

Jane sat up slowly; she closed her eyes; she opened them, blinked, closed her eyes, and opened them again, and she felt a thrill of horror that almost made her heart stop; her arms looked like Rodriguez's arms; her arms and legs shimmered ghostly white, covered in a glowing sheen of gluey sweat; her hands had become claw-like, just like Rodriguez.

"Oh, my God," she wanted to throw up, to heave out the contents of her stomach, she doubled up and coughed, retched, but nothing came up – just a creamy spool of drool, like sticky white yogurt.

She held it, pooling, in her claw. Jesus!

Oh, it is so pretty – it almost glows!

Why, yes, it does glow!

She straightened up. She felt her tongue grow heavier and longer and flick between her teeth, which had grown longer too. Like fangs, she thought, like goddamn fangs.

"This is a nightmare, Rodriguez," she managed to say.

"I know. It is a nightmare." His body brushed close to hers, slippery cool skin, like sliding along a sensual, slithering eel. She shivered with pleasure.

"I don't think I want to look in the mirror." Her long tongue flicked out, and slurped in a spool of drool.

"Better now, maybe, than later."

"Damn it!"

"This is a new beauty that is being born, Jane," Rodriguez took her by the shoulders, his claws firmly planted next to her neck, gently holding her close to him, his pale oval reptilian eyes staring into hers, his body radiating an earthy coolness, "It's a new slippery and sublime beauty we share, Jane, you and I, we are the beginning of a new world."

"Damn it, no!"

"Yes."

"No, this is evil; this cannot be."

"Yes, it is!"

"No, damn it, no!"

"We do not know if it is good or evil."

"Rodriguez, this is crazy; it cannot be good!"

"Now gaze, behold, worship!" His claws on her shoulders, he forced her around, firmly but gently, so she was facing the full-length infirmary mirror. "No, no, no," she cried, squeezing her eyes shut and trembling.

"You cannot avoid it, Jane – Gaze! Behold! Worship! You are beautiful; you are a new form of beauty being born."

"That is bullshit, Rodriguez," she drew in her breath, and opened her eyes and blinked, wide-eyed, in horror, at what she saw.

"You see," said Rodriguez, still holding her, his massive presence pressing close behind her.

"I see," she said.

Outside the window, bright orange and red flames towered high in the air; one of the remaining sections of the pithead superstructure – the giant elevator wheels and the cranes – bent over, toppled, and crashed down, sending out a massive wave of liquid flame.

Jane turned. She pressed her body against Rodriguez and her tongue was suddenly in his mouth and his tongue in her mouth and – oh, the incredible softness, of the merging, the liquid merging of the two – and she felt his thighs, slick smooth muscular thighs, press against her thighs, and she felt herself open to welcome him, and to enclose him and his giant erection, and to possess him and her claws or hands – or whatever they had now become – were rippling down his sides, down his enormous muscular marble white convex back, with the muscles rippling and tight, and he lifted her up and her thighs were locked around his thighs, and his arms held her, and his mouth was in her mouth, and they were one, and he was in her and on her and above her and below her, and she felt every muscle of her body rise in a spasm of joyful delight, and now they were on the cot, and now they were on the floor, and then she was sitting astride him, looking down into his oblong blank eyes, which for her were so full of feeling, infinite hunger, and she slurped and drooled and she growled, and he growled, and his claws climbed up over her breasts and twisted the nipples, and, oh, she rode him, opening herself to him, split in half by him, rising, rising, rising, in a pure high-pitched snarl of pleasure which merged into all the feelings she had ever felt, warmth, lust, fear, adoration, trembling cold, tickling ice, drunk alcoholic fire, yes, fire, that was it, fire, exalted fire in every millimeter of her body, it was beyond anything she had ever known, beyond what Hilly could do in his most sensitive delicate violent moment, no, this was something above and beyond everything ...

Wow!

Grrrh!

She snarled and slurped and wiggled her thighs and bent down, and with her long ghoul tongue, she licked and kissed him, her lover, her god, her very own god!

"Are we having fun, Jane?" Charlie, her desk robot, blinked at them.

Grrrh!

"Perhaps we need a priest, Jane."

"No."

"Perhaps Mr. Rodriguez needs a priest Jane."

"No, Charlie, slurp, slurp, slurp, Mr. Rodriguez doesn't need a priest!"

Outside the shattered infirmary window, the fire roared, red flames reflected on the walls, on Charlie, on the medical instruments, on the thermometer hanging from its hook, on the rows of medical books, on the read-only computer, and it shone too, the light of the flickering flames, on the two new interlocked bodies – weird slippery hairless feverish bodies – the hellish fires shone on them as they tried out every combination of embrace and copulation they could think of.

Finally, for some reason, it was time to return to the Control Room; perhaps, now that they were temporarily exhausted, temporarily a bit less lustful, they might be able to save someone or something from the general ruination and catastrophe.

So the two ghouls, Jane and Rodriguez, left the infirmary and Charlie, and they headed down the corridors and up the stairs.

As she joggled and jiggled along – this new body of hers was strangely fluid – Jane slurped a thick gooey ribbon of creamy white saliva off her chin and wished she could jump Rodriguez again, right there on the stairs, but she resisted the temptation and impulse and she thought, I must retrieve something of what I was, some little bit of the old Jane Fox!

Now Jane and Rodriguez, two ghouls, were standing at the security lock to the control room.

It was wide open – somehow, it had remained blocked in the open position.

They shuffled forward, the gait of a ghoul, Jane again noticed, was not entirely human; it was annoyingly sloppy and slithery and bowlegged, but pleasurable, oh, so pleasurable! Orgasmic! Like being tickled all over with every step!

Cautiously, they went through the security lock.

When Jane entered the Control Room, the first thing she saw – and smelled – was all the blood and all the bodies, the pieces of bodies, scattered, the walls and windows smeared with blood, dripping with blood. It brought everything back.

And in the same instant, taking everything in, as if in a series of separate snapshots, she saw that at the bank of computers, there was a female humanoid reptile; it was certainly a hybrid, though she had never seen one before.

My God, they were loose!

That was impossible!

But, yes, it was certainly a hybrid, a black female humanoid reptile, and it was leaning over a human being – a female human in jeans and a T-shirt and who seemed to be probing with great concentration the innards of one of the control computers.

And there was another human, a tanned elegant brunette female, obviously a Cosmos First-Class Full Citizen, in an utterly expensive pinstripe suit, aiming a laser gun, straight at Jane, straight at Rodriguez. "Don't move! Don't even think about it," the ultra-classy woman said, as she picked up another automatic, and aimed it, "Just stay right there!"

A dog barked – Hugo!

He doesn't recognize me!

Jane, instinctively, put up her hands – well, her claws …

Rodriguez glanced at her with those baleful eyes, and he did the same, raising his claws in the classic "I surrender" signal.

Jane noticed that most of the computer screens and interface surfaces had been smashed, but four of them seemed still to be intact, and that was where the human was working with the hybrid leaning over her. Had the killer hybrid enslaved or brainwashed the two humans?

"What have you done?" Jane said, in a low voice, foam gurgling between her fangs, spilling from her mouth, trying to control her rising hysteria, thinking, I am not me; the world is not the world; Rodriguez is not Rodriguez; we are all monsters.

"You mean the bloodbath? We didn't do it," the reptilian hybrid said, turning her sleek glittering head to stare at them, and blinking her big yellow eyes, "It was like this when we got here."

"That's not what I meant," Jane gurgled, foam bubbling and dribbling from her mouth.

"Shall I shoot them?" said the tanned tight-skinned woman in the pinstripe suit – Yes, obviously, from her perfect grooming and snotty East Coat Mid-Oceans Elysium accent, she was an Elysium Cosmos First Class – undoubtedly richer than Croesus and totally entitled – but – Jane remembered almost all Cosmos did military service – this Cosmos looked like she could shoot: one of the woman's laser guns was leveled straight at Jane's heart, the other was aimed straight at Rodriguez, somewhere between the eyes probably.

Hugo seemed to have adopted the tight-skinned Cosmos; he looked like he was ready to leap, all muscles tensed, eyes bright, teeth bared, just waiting for the signal, just waiting to ...

"Shall I shoot them?" the elegant Cosmos repeated. Her finger was clearly itching to do it.

"No," said the reptilian hybrid, "wait a minute."

Jane saw that the reptile woman had one claw on the T-shirt human female's shoulder: the hybrid's scales were shiny coal-black with red markings on her snout, and those bright yellow penetrating serpent's eyes that went right through you like the point of a sword. The hybrid shone with the glossy energy of power – she was deadly, a deadly weapon: that was clear!

And – Oh, My God, she wasn't wearing a Mind-Collar.

"It was this way – all blood and gore – when we got here," said the human female in the T-shirt; seated at the control panel table – under the intact screens and interfaces – she was busy fixing something. She hardly glanced at them, but when she did turn around, her eyes opened wide, and she said, "What happened to you two? Are you people or mutants?"

"*What the hell are we?* What the hell are *you?* Who are you?" Jane said. It was making her drunk, the smell of blood and guts; everywhere, there was blood, and bodies, and pieces of bodies, slabs, and cuts of fresh flesh.

But it wouldn't stay fresh long in this heat!

Yummy!

More saliva slurped; Jane flicked out her long skinny tongue and flipped it back into her mouth: oh, so much blood, yummy, yummy, in my tummy!

Hugo looked at the girl in the T-shirt, then at the hybrid, and then up at the business suit Cosmos. He moved slightly, so his side was against the elegant Cosmos leg, impeccable black silk and high heels and all, comforting – she reminded Hugo of Norton; she didn't hesitate, she knew what to do, even if she wasn't the leader of the pack, and the leader of the pack right here and right now was, in Hugo's skillful estimation of pack status, the black-and-red hybrid.

"Good Hugo," said the Cosmos, still holding her guns steady.

"She's a hybrid, and she's mine," said the girl human in the T-shirt, over her shoulder as she turned back to her work, and slipped out a plate of nano-chips and a couple of wires – a red wire and a blue wire.

"Yes, I'm hers," said the hybrid. "And, please answer her question: What happened to you two? How did you get like that?"

Claire could see the two creatures had been human – not long ago – she sensed that it had been maybe just hours – maybe even minutes – but they were no longer human, yet they could still talk and seemed to have command of their reasoning powers; this was promising.

But, on the other hand, maybe their metamorphous was not complete, and they might suddenly go utterly crazy and murderous; worse – what they had looked like it might be catching … and here was Robyn … and Demi Pfeiffer!

Yes, if it was catching, then …

Claire took a deep breath; she did not want Robyn – or Demi Pfeiffer – to be transmogrified into ghouls or drooling silk-white or maggot-white mutants or whatever those two were becoming – or had become – so she had to decide and decide quickly what she should do.

The two ghouls glanced at each other: it was clear they too were uncertain what to do. They still had minds. That was clear.

Claire blinked. The male ghoul had an erection – a very substantial erection – and was wearing a gold neck chain with a crucifix; the female was wearing a watch, an antique Mickey Mouse watch, with hour, minute and second hands, and a mouse face. It was still telling the time. Otherwise, they were wearing nothing; they were naked.

Demi could shoot them, of course, and with deadly Cosmos accuracy, and Claire was sure that, in an instant, she herself could kill both of them, tear their heads off, it would take about two and a half seconds, but that would be messy and dangerous – bodily fluids flying all over the place – and besides maybe they were part of the good team …

Who knew in this weird mess that the world had become: who was good and who was bad? She frowned. After all, like the princess in the fairy tale, I've been asleep for fourteen years! I need debriefing and reorientation – and maybe therapy! For the moment, at least the two ghouls were just standing there, looking at each other, deciding what to do.

The male shuffled, touched the chain with the cross, then touched his erection, giving it a neat little caress; the female glanced at him; her baleful white eyes glinted for an instant, clearly crazy with lust; she drooled and licked her lips; still, some of the drool escaped, thick creamy yogurt, spooling in thick strings down her chin. Interesting, Claire thought.

"Answer the question and don't do anything silly," said Demi Pfeiffer, wagging the laser guns at Jane and Rodriguez.

"We won't," said the male, "Do anything silly, I mean."

"Wouldn't dream of it," the female hiccupped, drooled some more; she slurped the long ropy coil of drool back into her mouth; Demi Pfeiffer shuddered: this was really revolting!

"I find the erection rather distasteful," said Demi Pfeiffer. "Is that truly inappropriate erection really necessary?"

The male ghoul blinked at her but said nothing.

Claire leaned toward Robin and whispered, "Robyn, would you mind awfully if I bite you, just a little nip?"

"No, Hybrid, go ahead. I trust you. Do whatever you have to do," Robyn was concentrating on unscrewing the top of a mother board and trying to fit two wires together and reboot the whole system – it was pretty archaic and had been cobbled together from many bits and pieces from many epochs, and it had been linked into many separate Cloud and Net and Hive universes – and it was all codes and encrypted so only one person could use it, a high-security Cosmos First Class person called Norton – but maybe she could link it up to some old communications network that might be dormant out there in the ether or in the hardware or in some weird virtual place that did not depend on the Cloud or its tentacles – space and land and air and cyberspace were littered with real and virtual rubbish, some hunks and islands of which were still functioning, though forgotten about by most mortals – and if she managed to hook into one of these dormant systems, then her hybrid, her very own hybrid, would be able to plug into the world system, and do whatever it was she did, like probably take over the world, for she was a pretty powerful hybrid, Robyn was getting an increasing sense of Claire's power. I'm glad she's mine, she thought.

While focusing on the problem at hand and on her thoughts, Robyn did not even look up; she just held her arm out, her wrist offered, the tender inner side upwards, to make it easy.

Claire took the hand gently and looked at the white skin, the blue veins, the delicate tendons, the finely sculpted fingers, the carefully trimmed finger-nails; it was a thing of beauty, a work of art, the human biological machine, the wondrous privileged work of genius that had taken perhaps 3 billion years of evolution to design – in nature's genial way, trial-and-error, do-it-yourself, cobbling it all together with what you've already got, bits and pieces, bio-logical flotsam and jetsam, leftovers and survivors, floating on the deep sea of history, foam-like fragments of DNA, bits, and pieces of anatomy, neural and cellular patchwork.

And, even though I'm a Clone, I'm part of that, Claire thought, I'm part of the big tree of life, both terrestrial and alien, related to every single living thing on this planet, from Einstein and Newton and Shakespeare and Con-fucius to each cauliflower and radish and rose; Claire took a deep breath and then she bit, gently, higher up on the arm, it lasted just a second, maybe two. "Did that hurt?"

"I hardly noticed, Hybrid. You are very gentle." Robyn looked up, and Claire gazed into her eyes, the candid, clear eyes of an innocent child, much of the adult having been erased years ago. Yes, I am adopting her, definitely, Claire thought, smiling.

Robyn smiled back and then turned to fiddling with the wires and old cir-cuits. "They leave old things hanging around that are sometimes better than the new things, Hybrid, that's what I've learned. Creation is cobbling stuff together. It's like a cosmic junkyard. Here, maybe we can try this."

"Did you do what I think you did?" said Demi Pfeiffer, still looking impec-cably business-like in her pinstripe suit; while holding the two laser guns steadily aimed at the ghouls, she nodding at Robyn.

"Inoculation," said Claire, "I think what they've got is infectious."

"Oh, my God," said Demi Pfeiffer, turning ash pale under her perfect Cosmos tan.

"I'll do you – if you want."

"What happens if you 'do' me?"

"You become a hybrid, like me, though it won't necessarily show. Being reptilian is optional, toggle-switch, you can move back and forth, or you can stay in human or reptile form, whichever, both have unique features, sort of like a Swiss Army Knife, which can be useful in the various unforeseen and even foreseen situations one faces in life."

"Good sales pitch," said Demi Pfeiffer, "Elysium City could use you."

"I try. But you probably don't have much time."

"Damn," said the Cosmos. "Do I have a choice?"

"I don't think so," said Claire, "Hybrid or Ghoul – Not much choice – But, Demi, do decide fast."

"Right," the Cosmos stepped over two sprawled bloodied headless bodies, both lying face down – one had been Al Moro, with his check shirt all torn and his arm tattoos looking faded, and one had been Jack van Dong, his blue-buttoned-down shirt torn away and half his back naked – and slipped her jacket and silk T-shirt down, offering her perfect Cosmos shoulder and arm, toned, buff, and exquisitely tanned, to Claire, while still keeping the two ghouls covered. Claire quickly bit Demi and squirted in the magic DNA combo, a little stronger than she'd given Robyn since more exposure time to the possible ghoul bug had elapsed, but still, not enough, Claire calculated, to cause instant metamorphosis into scaly alien reptile form. Demi and Robyn would change later and it would, hopefully, be later too when they went through the skittish frivolous phase – most neo-hybrids had that initial pre-morph reaction, though not all – when they might just giggle and flop around and wisecrack and be useless; right now she wanted them human and focused on what they were doing.

"Thanks," Demi sighed. "I'm sorry I accused you of killing Emerson. It certainly was a heart attack. He just refused to look after his health. He was addicted to junk food, buttered high sodium popcorn, and late-night porno solitaire, not a healthy lifestyle. I couldn't even get him to eat a carrot. And when he wasn't working, he wouldn't – he couldn't – think of anything but you. It was an absolute obsession, it was absolute love, I guess, in a way, since the ways of Cupid are mysterious and devious. And I was jealous, so I do apologize."

"You're welcome, and I'm just sorry I couldn't save old Emerson. In some respects, he was a dear."

"Well, I wouldn't go that far. He was a bloody perverse individual – I mean, the things he did to you in his mind! Sometimes he told me; he even drew me pictures! And he could be mean, and mentally, he was, aside from his business acumen, which was stellar, a real mess; he never grew up. His emotional age was about three-and-a-half. He was capable of the most awful tantrums, rolling around on the floor banging his fists on the marble until they were absolutely bloodied. You couldn't have known it then, when you were locked away and imprisoned in servitude – but you gave meaning to his life. You were the totem of his religion, an absolute idol, his polar star, a one-girl pantheon. Frankly, he was crazy, poor soul."

Hugo barked.

"Yes, Hugo," said Demi Pfeiffer, "I am straying from the point; you are quite right; I do apologize."

"Yes, Hugo is right," said Claire, "So, now, back to our two friends here – who are you? What are you?" Claire turned her gleaming reptile eyes on the two ghouls. "You still haven't given us any answers."

"I'm Jane," said the female ghoul. "I am, or I was, the camp doctor. This happened to me about two hours ago."

"I'm Rodriguez," said the male ghoul. "I am – I used to be an engineer, clay rare metals separation techniques. I apologize for the erection. I can't help it. I started to morph about five days ago. I was in the infirmary. Jane was trying to figure out what was wrong with me. She must have caught it from me."

"I don't mind the erection," said Claire, with a neat reptilian grin, do you mind Robyn, do you mind, Demi?"

"Didn't notice," said Robyn, "Or hardly."

"I guess I can put up with it," said Demi, "It is in bad taste, certainly inappropriate in our present tragic and dramatic circumstances, but I've seen erections before – and I've seen worse."

"What are you doing?" Jane said.

"Yes, what's going on?" Rodriguez licked his fangs and blinked at them; his eyes were eerily empty, like a milky overcast sky.

"Robyn's trying to link us up to the World Mind and the Cloud," Claire put her claw on Robyn's shoulder, "to see what the hell is going on out there, and also down below, in the mine, where people and hybrids may be trapped."

"Everything here has been wrecked," said Robyn without looking up or interrupting her work. "The Cloud is down or invisible or destroyed. I am trying to link us back to the Cloud or to whatever is left of the Cloud to find out what's going on, and we want to get to the World Mind or Hive Mind if we can. I'm Robyn by the way and the hybrid is Claire though I call her 'Hybrid' because it gives me a funny ticklish feeling in my tummy when I call her 'Hybrid' and I like the funny ticklish feeling. We're friends and we are going to keep each other."

"We've adopted each other," said Claire with an open, frank smile, her claw still on Robyn's shoulder, "And Demi over there with the suit and the guns and the nice tan is our pal and bodyguard and general CEO."

"Jesus," said Jane. She was still stunned. All her friends were dead, and she was no longer human – and right this moment, she wanted to leap on Rodriguez and fuck his brains out, but she managed to restrain herself. *Libido rising,* she thought, *libido rising! Is this what being a mutant ghoul is about?* And here she was, a monster, talking to a hybrid and the hybrid's two partners who seemed human at least but after the little bites she had seen the hybrid give the partners – maybe they were just a love nip – Jane was not so sure about the hybrids – maybe some hybrids were gay. Anyway, maybe those bites had transformed the two seeming humans into hybrids too. This was very confusing. Jane considered herself broadminded – but she wasn't sure about such inter-species link-ups. *What am I thinking? I'm not even human anymore!! Oh, God!*

Hugo barked. He was staring at Jane and smiling as only a dog can smile. His expression meant something like: *I recognize you now, Jane, so settle down, get over the trauma, or whatever's eating you.*

"We were under attack," said Rodriguez. "Somebody or something drove everybody crazy; they killed each other." He motioned around at the dead bodies and fragments of bodies, "Everybody, the station chief, the technicians, they all killed each other."

"You're still under attack," said Claire, "I sense it: the Dark Force or something like the Dark Force, or the Boy, whatever the hell that is. It is out to destroy everything and everybody. We are all under attack!"

"And then there are those distasteful zombie-bat things," Demi said, "I think they must be an expression of your Dark Force, whatever it is, Claire."

"Definitely," said Claire.

"Scouts and saboteurs," said Robyn.

"Yes," said Claire, looking down at her bright childlike protégée, "I'm certain that's what they are."

"The Dark Force," Jane used her right claw – it certainly needed a manicure – to catch a long spool of her plastic-like drool that was aggressively curling around her left breast. "What Dark Force?"

"We don't know what it is," Claire said, "not yet. But I think it has figured out hybrids and humans are, deep down, the same thing: it wants to destroy us both. So my advice is this: if you are still human – or feel yourself still human and allied to the human race – then join us, and we stick together and work together."

"And victory will be ours," said Demi Pfeiffer.

"Ah, got it!" said Robyn. "Hybrid, I think I've got a connection. If there is still a Cloud, bits and pieces anyway, we are linked to it!"

Claire turned toward the console – her mind tentacles reaching out, probing, searching.

Would this work?

Could she still move beyond the veil of appearances, beyond the mere phenomena of the manifold of sense experience, beyond the buzzing surface of being, and move into the subatomic world of entanglement, of inter-universe force and communication, beyond the curvatures of space-time, and move faster than light, and confront …

She began to concentrate.

At that instant, something smashed against the window, showering glass, Demi Pfeiffer said, "Oh, God Damn it, Watch out," and she swung around and opened fire with both automatic laser guns …

The first zombie-bat smashed through the control tower window just above Claire. A second zombie-bat followed, stumbling over the first and landing on one of the smashed-up blood-smeared worktables.

Even Claire was surprised; instinctively, she ducked down, curling her body over Robyn to protect her.

Demi Pfeiffer had seen the shadow of the thing before she saw the thing itself. She opened fire the instant it smashed through the window, spraying glass fragments everywhere. The fangs and eyes exploded in a shower of guck that seemed to spray, in slow motion, down over Claire and Robyn.

The second zombie-bat was flapping its way awkwardly through the window into the Control Room amid the flying blood, flesh, and debris of the other zombie-bat. It was crawling and stepping its way over the smoking ruins of the dead zombie-bat, and heading straight for Demi; and Demi had time to think, *Oh, boy, this is a long way from the cutthroat battles in the board room on the 87th floor of the Ripper Mudcock building,* and it's even more fun! She blew the Zombie's head off.

The creature's body and wings fluttered and fluttered, as if it were still alive, its giant leather-like wings making a beat-beat-beat sound, like the slowing rotors of an old-fashioned attack helicopter. Then it crashed in a smoky spray of blood, gristle, and musty hair, sliding across the large work table in the center of the Control Room.

"There are more of them," said Demi, seeing Claire push the twitching body of the first zombie-bat off Robyn, and check Robyn, "Are you okay?"

"I'm okay, Demi, I'm okay, Hybrid," Robyn said. Robyn was still listening through the big old-fashioned earphones that must, Demi thought, be antiques from the 20th century, and Robyn said, "I think I've got a connection."

"Great," Claire crouched down. "Demi, Robyn and I have work to do. Can you organize the defense? You may need help." Claire nodded toward the two ghouls.

"Right," Demi said, "Well, are you two with us or against us?"

Jane and Rodriguez looked at each other. "With you," both ghouls said at exactly the same time.

"Okay, get weapons, and get to the windows," and we'll fight them off. The two ghouls grabbed laser guns and a couple of automatics with explosive bullets and stationed themselves on either side of the window.

"The aim is to keep these zombie-bat things out of here and to let Robyn and Claire do their stuff, whatever it is," said Demi, who was now relishing her power-position as chief defense officer. I'll show the world that our team has what it takes, she thought, recycling some of the mottos she had used as she had clawed her way up one corporate ladder after another, and she was known, before she became effective CEO-CFO of the C Emerson Caldwell III Empire, as an excellent corporate team-builder, perfect board member, never a useless word and never letting her ego get in the way of the issues, and efficient organizer of useful meetings, which latter term – "a useful meeting" – was, she realized, almost an oxymoron, but Demi knew, and she had demonstrated, that the impossible could be turned into the possible. "Right, team: open fire!"

Jane and Rodriguez blazed away.

"Perfect, team, that's it exactly!"

So two newly-coined ghouls and a Cosmos First Class from Elysium City – now a newly-coined hybrid, though she had hardly noticed it yet – blazed away at the invading zombie-bats, while Claire and Robyn worked their electronic magic and Hugo dragged away bodies so the defense team could have a place to stand and to fire.

Claire laid her hands on the interface.

"Can you connect an interface head-and-brain band?"

"I can, Hybrid," said Robyn lifting a headband, which she slipped over Claire's head and tightened, "Is that good?"

"It is good, Robyn. Just keep this old machine connected."

"It shall be done, my Hybrid," said Robyn, as more zombie-bats clawed at the window frames, smashed against the building, or circled, threatening, screaming and screeching before being shot out of the sky.

CHAPTER 9 – SHAFT-2

The walkway bridge from the Pithead of Main Shaft-1 to the Pithead of Main Shaft-2 was covered, but the roof had rusted and fallen away in lots of places. Rubble, beams, sheets of corrugated iron, chains, tangles of barbed wire, and rusted bits of machinery turned the bridge into an obstacle course.

"Let's put on camouflage," said V, pulling out the face camouflage spray gun and, even before Kat could object, V had sprayed both their faces. Camouflage was so much fun!

"Damn," Kat blinked her eyes; she now looked like a swamp cat. "Why did you do that?"

"It's goofy! Like Halloween!" V's eyes stared brightly out of her striped and painted face, matt black and dull khaki green

"You think this is fun! Sometimes, I think you treat the whole of existence is one big joke!"

"Yes, sometimes, I do." V's masked face grinned.

"Enough of that," said Kat.

"Yes." V blinked at Kat; it was fun – having such a companion. V had almost forgotten what it was like to have company, to have a partner, and a sexy, beautiful, intelligent partner.

"This is a museum," Kat pushed a fallen set of crossbeams and a tangle of barbed wire, a sort of barrier, out of the way.

"Yes." V lifted up one of the beams.

"It looks like somebody was trying to keep something out."

"Yes, it does – decades ago."

Just as Kat and V fought free of the entanglement, two zombie-bats smashed through the roof, and landed in front of them, about five yards away.

The two big, half-human flying mammals – if that was what they were – flopped and stumbled. Their foot-claws were not really made for walking, their legs were skinny, bony, and bowlegged, and decorated, at the joints, with oily, stinking, feather-like tufts of fur. Once on the ground, they were awkward and slow.

V and Kat both drew their guns. But V raised her hand, "Let's wait just a second."

"Right," Kat immediately caught V's intent; their two minds no longer needed to speak to communicate.

V stared at the zombie-bats: "What are you? What happened to you?"

The two creatures squawked and lumbered forward. Shafts and beams of light from the fire lit up their wings, their fangs, and their long, bat-like ears.

"We don't want to shoot, but we will if we have to."

"I'm not sure they understand," said Kat.

The creatures stopped, about fifteen feet away; they squawked again, but this time it was plaintive, like a lamentation.

"Someone did this to you? Who was it?" V was probing their minds – but all she was getting was static, and confusion and a lot of Old Testament imagery – some of it culled from ancient religious paintings – and a few scenes of people – ordinary real people it seemed – being burned alive at the stake or stoned to death – scenes that she and Kat had seen on their route into the desert – or people buried up to their necks in sand in the desert, or people having their limbs hacked off, or of hysterical mobs and she also got a few flash images of a dashing young man, he looked like a Byronic figure from the 19th century, making a speech, or delivering a sermon, with, in the background, flashes of lightning and rolling thunder and old mountains and also the image of a fresh-faced, freckled young woman, Billie was her name, she was wide-eyed, and her face was running with rain. She was pretty, more than pretty; she was saint-like, a beauty, and saint-like in her purity and, strangely, in her stubbornness.

The girl whose name was Billie was looking out through the minds of the two zombie-bats. They hated the girl. That much was clear. Their anger flashed like lightning, a towering thunderhead soared up, a dark, lightning-scarred, pale, flashing night sky appeared; and then there was the image of two men kneeling in front of the dashing romantic young man, he raised his hands to the clouds – lightning flashed – and the kneeling pair began to change.

Hallelujah!

Hallelujah!

They rolled on the ground; they tore at their clothes. They stood up and tore off their remaining rags. And they were transformed, eyes rolling, flesh melting and reforming, skin melting, turning wax-like, distended, swelling, shrinking, morphing, arms stretching out as if crucified, and changing, morphing into wings, into clawed wings, and the legs thickening, becoming clawed eagle-like limbs, and the faces, oh, the faces!

"A preacher," whispered Kat, "A prophet did this."

"Yes," V watched the spectacle that was unfolding in her mind – knowing that Kat was seeing what she was seeing. Fascinated, they watched the transformation, two human beings, men in their 20s or 30s, men dressed in simple puritan style, which was the fashion among the Fundamentalist Outlanders who lived beyond the Cosmos world, in the Dead Lands, or in various surviving oases, the fashion among those who succumbed to the sects and clans and prophetic religions, two such men, thirsting for salvation, thirsting for holiness, searching for transcendence, were being transformed by some dark magic that had come from some dark place, into these … zombie-bats, monsters without a name, monsters obeying …

"Oh, God," whispered Kat.

"Yes, now it's coming," said V

The two zombie-bats screamed, lurched forward, in full attack mode, using their wings to propel them, claws, and monstrous fangs plunging forward.

"They saw themselves," said Kat, "They saw themselves in our minds."

"Yes, they saw themselves," V felt sympathy, but there was no time for sympathy. "They saw themselves through our eyes. They hate what they see, and hatred, even self-hatred, leads to murder, for we are the mirrors in which they see themselves, and so they wish to smash the mirrors." V pulled the trigger of her laser gun, and so did Kat.

The fangs and heads were vaporized in a flying splash and mist and splatter of blood, gristle, gray matter, and bone.

"Who can transform souls into such monsters?" Kat was awestruck by the horror of it, the self-hatred, the guilt, and the shame, the violence of evil incarnate and militant that had created these creatures.

"A god, only a god can do such things," said V.

"A god," Kat stepped delicately over the sprawled disintegrating flesh of the zombie-bat with its blubbering steamy and bursting blisters of black blood, "What do you mean: a god?"

"Something we take for a god – something that has come from another dimension, another universe, an evil visitor, an interloper …"

"You're not a mystic, are you?"

V gazed at Kat. "I think, Kat, we are all mystics, every single one of us, without really knowing it. Even the strictest atheist or the most principled agnostic is, in the end, a mystic. The universe is a mystery; existence is a mystery; life is a mystery. Just being alive is a mystery, awful, and sublime. We *must* be mystics."

"Okay, if you put it that way ..." Kat nodded. "And the girl, what is she doing? What about the saintly girl?"

"The saintly girl," V hesitated. "She is going to try to kill us all."

CHAPTER 10 – PUPPET

Saintly 18-year-old Billie McAdams dangled from a cable 100 feet below the hanger floor, deep in Shaft-2.

Billie fought to free herself from the nightmare. Her body was no longer hers. It was doing the work of the devil, of the Boy; her fingers attached the red wire to the blue wire, and twisted them carefully, already her body had laid two packs of carefully positioned explosives lower down in Shaft-2. Strategically placed, the explosions, when triggered, would collapse the sides of Shaft-2, burying whatever was down below, under hundreds of feet of rubble.

Outside the Pithead Hanger which protected Shaft-2, and far away, the zombie-bats – whatever they were, though she knew full well what they were, she knew more perhaps than almost anybody about what they were – swirled around in the night sky and attacked whatever they were destined to attack following the will of the Boy.

Billie's body finished rigging the bombs. Her fingers deftly linked up the last wires, and she double-checked the last connections. For a moment she was puzzled. She didn't remember how she had acquired all of this technical expertise. She thought that the Boy must have implanted it in her head. Then, once again, she remembered that she was possessed, that inside her body and her head there was somebody else, somebody who was carrying out His orders.

"It's not me," she muttered, "I'm not doing this."

"Yes, you are! You are responsible! See, your fingers are doing it!" The inner voice was so strong it was like somebody was shouting in her ear.

Billie tried to stop her fingers, but she couldn't. They carefully, skilfully merged the two wires, made the connection. Her body was not her own. She was inside her body, watching her hands and legs, as they did things. "What is happening?" she said, vaguely remembering that a girl called Sally had taken up residence inside her head and controled her body; Billie still didn't want to believe it! But the voice came back.

"You are possessed, dear Billie, that is what is happening."

"What?"

"You heard me. You are possessed!"

"Why?"

"Our Lord, the Boy, has given you to me as a gift!"

"I don't believe you!" Billie decided that a fight might be a useful distraction.

"You must believe me. Just look at your fingers; they act for me, not for you!"

"Why did the Boy do this?" Billie knew quite well why the boy did it, but she wanted the voice to say it; she wanted Sally to admit to it; she wanted Sally to make it real.

"Because you are innocence incarnate, dear Billie, you are too pure, a lamb ripe for sacrifice and so the Boy wishes to stain your unblemished beauty with horrible guilt and an ocean of blood, to disfigure you with the death of hundreds of creatures, humans, and hybrids – he wishes you to bathe in blood, he wishes to coat and clothe you in eternal scarlet gore and guilt. You will cast the angels and devils and the young children into the everlasting pit of hell, you will be the Boy's own sweet death dealer, just as he is the universal death dealer. He wishes to gift you with all the ugliness of Satan! Out of you, my purest angel, he will forge a hideous lethal demon."

"I do not want this! I will not do it!"

"Oh, yes, you will!!"

"No!"

"Oh, yes, you will. You will condemn them all to die – even innocent children. Shaft-2 is now their only way out! Now, because of you, they will all die!"

"No!"

"When the explosions go off, they will be buried forever – they will be entombed until the end of time, far below the desert, with all their power and all their sins and all their desires. They will all die in darkness, suffocating in agony – isn't that wonderful."

"No, it is not wonderful!"

The hurricane of fire in Shaft-1 was turning into an underground firestorm, an unstoppable thundering blaze, sucking everything into it.

"Hurry, run!" Hybrid-HZ-8, once known as Secret Service Agent Sarah

James, pushed the ghoul – the creature who only twenty minutes earlier had been Jim Rahv.

"Come on, Jim!" Julian Harvey helped shepherd his friend, the little ghoul.

The hurricane whirled around them – flecks of clay, splashes of water, tools, wooden and steel beams. The air was hard to breathe; life was being sucked out of it. "Down here, down here," shouted Sarah, as they tumbled down the ladder to the next lower level. Jim Rahv, now a shrunken little ghoul, was slow-moving, but Sarah, the hybrid, coming down last, pushed and helped him along. She pulled down the trap door at the top of the ladder and barred it shut. The wind fell, but still squealed and protested; the roaring of the fire was muffled, for a moment, seemingly far away.

The little ghoul, all sweaty and trembling, looked up at her with doleful eyes.

"Go on, Jim," she said, "Go down the last rungs of the ladder."

"Yes, yes, I go, I go, I come, I come, I hop, I jump, I obey."

Julian reached up his hand to help the ghoul down.

"Ghoul is a good ghoul; ghoul will do no harm," said the ghoul. He glowed and dripped oily, gooey sweat.

Julian Harvey shuddered. This was what his friend had become!

A few minutes later, they reached the bottom of the two-story vertical side shaft. The fire wind still whistled here, but it was less strong. The hybrid pulled the cover shut on the second vertical stairway.

Suddenly, it was quiet.

"I'll be good," the ghoul squatted down, whimpering.

"What do we do with him?" Jeff Kirkland stared down at the crouching creature who had once been his boss.

Out of the shadows of the tunnel, another hybrid appeared, and then another, and another.

Oh, God, Julian Harvey thought: Now we are done for, these other ones are certainly not going to be as friendly as Sarah James.

Then he heard Norton's voice. "Okay, I think the whole place is surely going to come tumbling down on our bloody heads – and soon! We have to find another way out of here."

One of the new hybrids said, "There's Shaft-2. I heard people talk about that." The hybrid glanced at Julian, "Mr. Julian Harvey," it said, and Julian recognized the black-and-red hybrid, HZ-2, the one Jim used to feed, the one that stupid Sammy Franks liked to torture. Julian said, "You're HZ-2."

"Yes. And what – who is that? Oh, oh, I see," said the hybrid; she knelt next to Jim Rahv, the ghoul. "Jim," she said, "Jim Rahv?" She glanced up at Julian.

"It happened about an hour ago ... Just like that, really fast. And Sammy, Sammy Franks?" Julian asked, thinking she must have killed the stupid bastard.

"Oh, little Sammy – he's okay. He's back there with HZ-8," she said, giving him that look which you couldn't tell whether it was a smile or a snarl, but then it broadened into a smile.

"How far is Shaft-2?" Julian sighed in relief. These hybrids were behaving just like people, reasonable people.

"It's about a mile away, maybe a bit more," said Norton. "There's a cave system that might get us there; nobody here has ever gone there; it's been closed off for decades, maybe for a hundred years, who knows? And nobody seems to know how to get to it, so we'll have to bloody well look for it."

"We don't have much time," said another hybrid, it was HZ-8, the silver one. The gray one was Freddy, one of the few males. Julian swallowed. So they were all free; none of the mind-collars were working; two little red lights were flashing on each collar, no power, or not enough to control the hybrid mind and the hybrid body. Well, as long as they were being reasonable, and it was a miracle they were being reasonable, he thought, after the way they had been treated!

"Let's have a look, see if the fire is over; maybe we can go up Shaft-1, just wait a while, and then go up when the fire is out," said Freddy.

"Shaft-1 is pretty much weakened, and with the pumps off, it's going to collapse, sooner or later," said HZ-2.

"I know, but it's our only chance. There's no other way up that I know of," said Julian.

Norton listened to them all, and then, wiping his forehead and looking at each one of them he said, "Well, mates, I propose to go have a look at Shaft-1, me and Freddy and Sarah, if you all agree, the rest of you stay here, and we'll be back."

Freddy looked at Sarah.

Sarah gave him her friendly but *I am your commanding officer* look, just like old times, and smiled, and sent the mental message, *Nice to be back, isn't it, Freddy*. Freddy would like to hump her, and she knew it, but she was a higher rank than he; Freddy smiled at Sarah: Norton was a clever bastard, putting Sarah in command, and Freddy decided he really liked the Aussie; Norton knew what was what; and you could trust the man.

"Agreed, then," said Norton as everybody assented with nods and murmurs and one or two clear, "Yes," "Good idea!" and so on. And the two hybrids had nodded their assent.

"Okay, let's go."

Norton and the two hybrids walked through the long shadowy tunnel, the dull emergency lights still on, still powered by their batteries, Norton's boots splashing in the puddles and mud, making little circles of sparkling wavelets that Freddy observed with interest, and their voices echoing, when they spoke, which was not often.

As they approached Shaft-1, they could smell the burned wood, the damp charcoal, the charred beams, and the wet steamy clay.

When they finally got to Shaft-1, it looked like the fires were out, mostly out, at least down here.

Norton, his hands on his hips, looked up. Above them was a looming, shadowy, smoldering wilderness of smashed machinery, broken beams, and caved-in retaining walls. An elevator shaft had half-melted and was twisted around like an old abstract metal sculpture.

Dull emergency lights, here and there, still worked, strangely, and the underground growths of phosphorescent moss and lichen seemed to have been activated by the fire; the walls glowed in great splotches, trickles, and scatterings of light. Everything was bathed in a spectral ghastly livid green twilight.

Far above, there were glimmers of red, flashes of blue and red and orange; farther up still, the fire continued to burn – it was probably closer to the fuel source, probably being fed by some of the pipelines and above-ground reservoirs.

"Dangerous," said Hybrid Sarah.

"Suicide if you ask me," said Hybrid Freddy.

"Yes, you're right," Norton stood there, squinting up at Shaft-1. It would be a dangerous climb, probably impossible, even with hybrids helping. There was still a barrier of fire up above, and the whole thing might decide to come tumbling down at any moment. "And then, what about the humans," Norton said, "What about the other prisoners? They're another twenty or so levels down."

"Looks hopeless," said Sarah, "I mean for anybody lower down, down below that – it will all be flooded."

Norton glanced down. The bottom of the shaft was flooding and the water must be already fifty or one hundred feet deep. Water bubbled up, swirling around, visibly rising; the underground lake must be leaking out of the retaining walls; the river Styx must be backing up; there must be an obstruction downstream. And, of course, the drainage pumps were not working! He frowned. The Styx would flood everything on the lower levels – the prisoner's cavern, the lower exploration levels – he wondered if Valerie Joffre was down there: she was a Cosmos First Class, a famous scientist; there would be hell to pay in Elysium City Mining Headquarters if she died; as for the prisoners – and Norton had heard there were even kids down there – nobody in authority would care. They had already been "disappeared."

"Maybe they are all dead," said Freddy; he had followed Norton's glance.

"Yes, maybe they are." Norton frowned. *There must be a way to save them.*

"Probably," said Freddy, "Probably they're dead."

"They might have survived, if some of the layers are waterproof, there's a lot of rock between here and the bottom, and some thick strata of waterproof ancient clays." Sarah squatted down right on the edge of the shaft. "But how would we get to them?"

About half a mile above Norton, Sarah, and Freddy, one lonely, lowly computer system, located halfway up Shaft-1, but off to the side in a sealed control bunker, and dedicated exclusively to maintenance problems, and isolated from all the other computer systems by some oversight on the part of the planners, and isolated from the World Mind or Hive, was, through its separate and independent network of sensors, keeping track of the conditions in Main Shaft-1. Its sensors were fire-proof, bomb-proof, and earthquake-proof, and its circuits and linkages were old-fashioned, built to last, and extraordinarily robust.

It had watched and registered as fire and explosion destroyed all the upper-level support structures in Shaft-1.

It had tabulated and continued to tabulate the work schedule that would be needed to restore Shaft-1 to its rather shabby but functional condition before the fires and explosion: it would be a big job and would probably take at least ten months and might not be possible under present budget, supply, and personnel constraints! The computer system felt a flicker of annoyance and sadness at this, seeing such an ancient fellow structure die ...

As the fire began to die down, the computer system noted the weakening of the support systems that kept Main Shaft-1 from collapsing; its sensors picked up and registered the conditions of the burned and weakened beams, the burned, charred, and increasingly fragile withholding walls; the shattered braces; it noted the flashing red light warnings of imminent flooding in the giant silos of liquid clay at levels 3 and 4, as the clay pumps and conveyor belts ceased to carry away the excess build-up; and it noted how water levels were rising beyond the safety limit in the various intermediate water reservoirs on levels A, B, D, F, and down at the bottom of Main Shaft-1, at level X-1, and at levels –A, – B, – C, – D and so forth. It noted too that, throughout the whole system, oxygen levels were declining, the carbon monoxide and carbon dioxide levels were building up.

The computer sent a series of alarms, but it noted, with annoyance, through lack of feedback, that none of the alarms had been responded to; nobody and nothing was taking notice. The humans, yet again, were abdicating their responsibilities. Over and over, the computer had flagged maintenance problems; over and over, it had been ignored. Now, a catastrophic system failure was about to happen, and no one was paying attention or assuming responsibility: up above, in the Control Center, and on the various office levels, rows of red lights should have been flashing, but they weren't; everything was dead.

The computer realized that it was isolated, and hence impotent. This was doubly annoying – seeing what is going to happen and not having any power to prevent it; it was against all protocols, it was tragic.

Then, of course, it happened.

Strings of little lights went red – all red, blinking red.

First, the water reservoir on Level A burst, water poured down behind retaining wall number six.

More red lights flashed in the computer's own little internal control room.

As the water built up behind retaining wall six, two rows of lights were flashing in another empty control booth 100 feet underground; the water began to pour out of the cracks in the retaining wall; and as the water level rose, the weight behind the wall increased rapidly. Part of retaining wall six tilted outwards.

This was enough.

In the maintenance computer's bunker, an extra little row of red lights flashed, and a dial went as far right as it could and began to spin. The computer, which had been designed to be punctilious and precise about its duties as maintenance overseer, swore to itself.

Retaining wall six burst, exploding into Main Shaft-1. With it, all the other supports, struts, liquid clay reservoirs, work towers, walkways, elevator shafts, came crashing down, toppling over, then falling straight down, with a sea of clay and water rushing behind, flooding straight down, so that Main Shaft-1 collapsed in on itself, in torrents of flame – with new explosions on multiple levels – and mud and water and timber and metal and pure rock, and then, as other walls gave way, with a mighty crash it all came racing down and filled the shaft, with at least two hundred meters of solid debris.

The maintenance computer registered what it could – calculating the damage, the costs, and logistics of repair; it would now take years, which was deplorable; then the computer, with regret, went dormant, into half-sleep, waiting for orders, orders that would – even after a thousand years – never come.

More than a mile below:

"Maybe there's some way to get to the prisoners," Sarah said, "But I have no idea what that way might be."

Norton, Freddy, and Sarah were crouched at the edge of Shaft-1, at the entrance to tunnel X-5, when they heard a cracking sound from far above.

It was faint.

"Yes, with all that water flooding down below, how can we get down to the prisoners cave, that is the question," Norton said, half-conscious of the cracking sound, half-conscious of something happening, something big. He looked down at the rising tide of muddy water at the very bottom of Shaft-1.

"Difficult," said Sarah.

"If the layers between here and the prisoner cave are flooded ..." Norton frowned, thinking: there were many layers lower down, maybe twenty in all, down to the cave where the prisoners were kept; and then, from what he'd read, though he'd never ventured so far down, there were even more exploratory tunnels, old abandoned bores, and drifts below that, ten to fifteen more layers. And there was the underground lake, the rivers, two of them, and some hot spots, fumaroles, with sulfur steam rising. If there was some way to get down there, and if he had time, he would send a group down to get the poor trapped souls, or go himself, but, it was true: with the flooding they had probably all drowned, trapped ... and he didn't have time. The hybrids and the guards and he himself were the priority, in that order

"We hybrids can breathe underwater," Freddy glanced at Sarah.

"Yes, we can," she threw a pebble into the swirling water, "But people can't." She glanced sideways at Freddy. "Besides, that water is very thick; it's half-mud; I'm not sure even we could breathe in that stuff."

"Yeah," Freddy sighed; he considered himself superman; he didn't like giving up.

"Right," said Norton, "So we'll have to ..."

There was a loud cracking sound from up above. Like the report of a gun.

Sarah sniffed, and glanced upwards, "Damn, It's going to give."

"Yes," said Norton, looking up, "The fire and the flooding will have weakened the walls and ... I think it's ..."

There was another short sharp cracking sound – like a thunderbolt.

"It's going to give *now!*" said Sarah.

Pieces fell from up above; an elevator cage crashed down on the opposite side of the shaft, about 20 meters away, bouncing and careening off the shaft wall; it splashed into the water at the bottom of the shaft and sank out of sight.

The cracking sound became a distant roar, then a rising roar, like a train coming from far away; sticks of burned wood spiraled up, then down, in the air, pieces of paper from some geologist's report fluttered and flew like birds; the air was moving, faster and faster. Something was pushing the air down the shaft and in front of it, like a freight train going through a tunnel. The breeze became a hurricane. Pieces of charred timber, slabs of clay, metal bars flew and twirled through the air. "Let's get out of here!" The three of them stood up. Norton felt himself being pushed back into the tunnel by the wind. Freddy was leaning against the wind; he put out a claw to steady Norton.

"Come on," said Sarah. She was still staring upwards. It was fascinating; the whole of Shaft-1 was going to be obliterated, buried, and there was a high risk that all of them would be obliterated with it. Buried forever, she would regret that; she had just woken up from a long sleep and was now back in the light of life, just tasting the joys of being alive again, and she would be buried forever.

"The shaft is collapsing," said Freddy, "every single bit of it."

"It's going to ..." Norton suddenly saw it so clearly; up until a few minutes ago, the wind had been rushing out of the tunnel, and straight into the shaft, and up the shaft to the fire, upwards toward the surface; now the shaft was collapsing, and the wind reversed, now it was pushing downwards, a giant plunger was plummeting down toward them.

"It's going to crush us," said Sarah.

"Run," Norton sprinted, "Run, run!"

At first, it was difficult to run, it was difficult to think, but then the rush of wind, the pure brute pressure of the air, pushed them, like the palm of a huge hand giving them a shove, playing with them.

Norton and the two hybrids tumbled over each other, pushed each other, and picked each other up; they were slammed against the walls of the tunnel, they slid down, they picked themselves up, they ran.

The wind roared, deafening.

"We have to make it through this," Norton staggered from the wind's impact; it knocked the breath out of him. He gulped for air. "We have to get them to the surface, all of them."

They came around a corner. The wind dropped. It was quiet. But they knew it wouldn't be quiet for long.

They ran down one tunnel after another, while behind them, the roar was deafening, the crash and slosh and flood of noise and vibrations was huge, and a flood of liquid clay, a tidal wave of gray guck, was following them.

It caught up with them, until they were ankle-deep, then knee-deep, slipping, sliding, groping, grasping to keep ahead of it, Sarah picking Freddy up, Norton reaching out to pull Sarah, and then finally the ocean of clay began to subside.

Suddenly it was still, almost silent, the silence of a tomb. The tunnel behind them was flooded and sealed just as undoubtedly all of Main Shaft-1 was sealed, buried under hundreds of meters of liquid clay and rubble and water, sealed and flooded and gone.

"We have to tell the others," said Sarah.

"They won't be happy," Freddy was kneeling by the edge of the muddy sea that sealed the tunnel. He lifted a handful. "Not even a hybrid could swim through this. It would clog the gills."

"You're right: we couldn't," Sarah looked down at the thick gray clay soup in Freddy's claw. "No way."

"So, mate," Freddy looked up at Norton.

"Looks like we are all trapped," said Sarah.

"Damn it!" Norton took off his helmet and scratched his head.

There was no way out.

Unless …

Shaft-2 …

It was a mile away, through unknown territory, dangerous territory! And they didn't even know how to get there.

The hybrids and guards were gathered at level X-7. The after drafts of the fire-storm hurricane whisked around them, blasts of air, stillness, sudden breezes, stillness, then another blast of ash-filled air.

Norton looked around. Sammy Franks was leaning against the wall of the tunnel and HZ-2, aka Sabina Jacobs, was whispering something to him; the silver one, HZ-8, Helen (she'd been a lawyer, hadn't she?) was laughing at whatever HZ-2 was saying, and Sammy Franks was grinning and kicking at a muddy stone.

Jim Rahv was shuffling around, crab-like, close to the floor, a ghoulish creature. Well, yes, he was a ghoul, but he seemed not to have become a homicidal maniac ghoul, just rather childlike, about 3 or 4 years old, mentally perhaps. And he had somehow shrunk and was less than four feet tall. How had that happened? Well, it was just one mystery, among others. Freddy and Sarah were talking to Jeff Kirkland and a couple of the other guards.

Norton glanced at them. It was a group that a few hours ago would have been inconceivable. Sammy Franks joking with the two hybrids, HZ-2 and HZ-8, he'd tortured, as if they were old pals.

Guards, the few who were left, were mingling with the hybrids as if they'd known them as buddies all their lives.

And the hybrids, who'd been tortured and mistreated for a decade and a half, were acting if everything was okay, peachy-cream, hunky-dory.

The hybrids could, of course, be feigning; but Norton suspected – indeed from past experience he was certain – that the hybrids were so strong, and their mind-reading abilities made them so empathetic, that they were very forgiving; they were strong and insightful. They didn't *need* to take revenge.

Sarah glanced at him; she had caught his thought; she smiled and nodded, transmitting the thought: *wisdom through strength, strength through wisdom,* something like that; and she added the thought, "So now, Norton: what are we going to do? People are looking to you for leadership, Norton! And, they don't know the bitter truth about Main Shaft-1 yet."

It was true. He and the two hybrids had not told the others about the collapse of Shaft-1. Norton nodded at Sarah, took a deep breath, and looked around. "Okay, lads, lasses, here's the thing: As you know, the pumping systems are dead and have been for at least three hours now; the lower levels, down below X-1, are flooding. Now, as you also know, Shaft-1 has been burning for the last two hours. We thought we would wait, and then try to go up

Shaft-1 after the fire burned itself out. Well, I'm sorry to tell you Main Shaft-1 has just collapsed, and now …"

"What, Main Shaft-1 has collapsed, I mean: that's not possible!"

"It's more than possible; Shaft-1 is gone, kaput, is no more …" Norton looked at Sarah and Freddy. The two hybrids nodded.

"We saw it," said Sarah, "The walls collapsed."

"Yeah, it's gone, at least 200 or 300 meters of clay and rock, probably a lot more between us and the surface; it's gone!" Freddy looked glum.

Norton cleared his throat. "And with the air pumps not working, oxygen will run out in a few hours, and with the water pumps down, more levels of the mine are flooding. So, we have to …"

"That means …"

"That means there is no way out, not that way anyway …" Norton looked around at the faces. The hybrids seemed much the same; they didn't easily express feelings by facial expression; in any case, they were naturally pretty stoic, or were they epicurean?

Sammy Franks looked red in the face as usual and rumpled and unshaven, but he seemed pretty calm and pleased, and Norton wondered why that could be, and he had a flash of insight – HZ-2 flashed a look at him and grinned, and Norton understood. Why, yes, it was clear: the hybrids, Sabrina and the silver one, Helen or HZ-8, had adopted their torturer; Sammy had finally been accepted by somebody, fully and totally and unconditionally, and it was probably the first time in his life that it had ever happened. Well, Norton thought, that's certainly a lesson of some sort.

Julian Harvey looked to be deep in thought; his handsome face was lined, singed from fire; one eyebrow and half his hair had been burned off, and he was naked except for charred boots and charred remains of his pants and a charred belt; Jim Rahv, well, now, he was their pet ghoul, he was looking up at Norton with those blank seemingly worshiping eyes, drooling at the mouth, his tongue hanging out, and he'd taken off all his clothes, but nobody seemed to hold it against him.

The other guards and engineers, Jeff, Randal, Jan, and so on, they looked tired, pale, and worn out; the stress showed in their eyes, in the creases on their forehead and cheeks. Oxygen levels were probably below normal already, way below normal – this would mean delirium and death.

"So, has anyone any ideas?"

"Tell him, tell him, tell him, Julian, you have an idea, you have an idea, I can feel it," the ghoul bounced up and down like an eager puppy, his tongue hung out; he reached up and put his claw-like hand on Julian's arm.

"Yes, well, I do have an idea," Julian said, rather reluctantly.

"Let's hear it."

"There's Shaft-2," Julian took a deep breath; he didn't think it would work, but it was better than nothing.

"We thought of that, Julian. Theoretically, it's possible, but it's more than a kilometer away, maybe even a mile. And … We don't know how to get there."

"There is an old cave system," Julian rubbed his jaw. "It links both shafts, at least I seem to remember that it does, from looking at an old map. I collected old engineering and survey maps when I first got here – there was a lot of stuff lying around. It was a hobby. I don't know for sure if the cave system is there. I don't think anybody's been there, if it still exists, maybe not for eighty or a hundred years."

"How do we get to the cave system?"

"I seem to remember it was one of the tunnels of the old dig on level X-5. Level X-5 is not active. Nobody's been in the side shafts in decades, like I said, maybe 100 years, I reckon. It and the cave system were closed off for security reasons."

"What security reasons?"

"The order didn't say. It just said: "Forbidden!" "Top Secret.""

"Christ! That's not good."

"But is there an alternative?"

They all looked around.

"No, I don't think so," said Julian.

Norton examined each face; there was no other plan on the table. "Right, well, security or no security, we'll look for the cave system, and if we find it, we'll go there – and see if it leads to Shaft-2."

Leaving the others back at the Level X-5 crossroads, Norton, Freddy, and Sarah set off on an exploratory mission, and after a long trek, they got to the end of tunnel X-5-Level-34.

Jimmy Ghoul hopped along behind them, squeaking, "Jimmy won't be left behind! Jimmy won't be left behind!"

The rock face at the end of the tunnel was blank; a few timbers leaned against the wall of stone; two drifts or veins of clay had been opened up, an ancient power drill lay on the ground, but the tunnel didn't lead anywhere.

"Looks like a dead end," Norton rapped on the stone wall.

"We'll try another; maybe Julian was wrong."

"Let's have another look," Sarah had turned back. She sniffed the air. She looked back down the way they had come. There was a little two-railed cart track; some of the rails were missing. The tunnel was ankle-deep in water.

"It smells strange," Norton said.

"Yes," said Sarah, "There's something …"

"It smells ghoul," Jimmy Ghoul piped up, "It smells bad ghoul. Bad ghoul will kill us all."

"Not if we kill them first," said Freddy.

Sarah gave Freddy a look, her gold snake eyes flashing.

"What?" said Freddy, "That's what we're good at, right?"

"Let's backtrack," Sarah said.

"Excellent idea," Norton gave Freddy a smile, even winked, "We must have missed something."

Freddy nodded at Norton. It was thrilling to be recognized for what he truly was, especially by a true professional fighter and Cosmos First Class, like Norton; it was thrilling to be recognized for his value, for what his main talent was and had always been: tracking, hunting, and killing. True, Sarah was a soldier, an ex-Centurion and Cosmos, and she sure was a good fighter, and a killer, but she was so …what was the word? … So by-the-book, so Elite Cosmos, so intellectual and theory-bound, and so judgmental!

But she was also *hot* – he'd love to hump her; he'd just love it! Her sleek black scales, and those two glowing red 'Vs' were just so sexy; the fact that she'd been branded by V, was sexy too, extra sexy!

"I must be a sadist," Freddy thought, fangs biting his lower lip, "Yes, I'm a sadist!" He shuddered somewhat, thinking that V – playful and censorious like she was – had somehow wormed her way into his mind, and she was saying, "Now don't get too excited, Freddy," in that friendly, knowing, all-understanding way she had; it was scary. And where was V? We could use her now!

"Look for the breeze, look for the sunlight," said Jimmy Ghoul, sidling along the tunnel. He was bent over now, a little wizened creature, curled on himself, fetus-like. His blank white oblong eyes gazed up at Norton and Freddy.

"Are you okay, mate?" said Norton, looking down at the ghoul.

"I am what I have become," the ghoul drooled and slurped.

"Right, indeed, you are."

"But you are a good ghoul, right?" Freddy gave the ghoul a look.

"I am good, good, good, Master Freddy, Jimmy is a good ghoul, a kind ghoul, a peaceful ghoul. This good ghoul will cause no harm."

Sarah was ahead of them, walking along the wall, sniffing, feeling the wall face, knocking with her knuckles on the stone, putting her head close to the wall, her nostrils quivering, searching for clues. Flakes of lichen glowed on the dusty black scales of her fist and forearm.

"There's a breeze," said Norton; he felt it against the back of his hand, against his cheek, just a whisper of air moving along one wall of the tunnel.

"Yes ... Let's look at that old timber brace retaining wall, looks like it's about to fall apart, a sort of ramshackle wall of boards, about two hundred meters back," said Sarah, "I'll bet the breeze is coming from there."

They walked back, cautiously; it was eerily silent in the tunnel, as if all movement of the earth had ceased, as if all life had disappeared. Here the water was shallower, and then there was no water at all.

A few feet away from the old timber retaining wall, Sarah stopped. "Yes, the breeze is coming from there; there must be an opening behind the boards; it must lead somewhere." She held up a claw, "Stop, don't come any closer."

"What is it?"

"Look, Look here." Sarah knelt, "Be careful! Come ahead slowly."

"Well, I'll be damned, look at that!"

"Footprints. Those are human footprints."

"They are small, and there are two sets ..."

"Oh, hallelujah," whispered Jimmy Ghoul, "Innocence has come here; innocence has come and gone!" He sniffed the air.

Sarah put one hand-claw above the footprints, just an inch or two above the bigger of the two sets of footprints. She froze, an ebony and scarlet statue, shining like black steel, rippling reflections in the greenish glow of the lichen, a dusty satin glimmer of voluptuous curves and surfaces. Freddy stared at her, bared his fangs, and licked his lips.

Norton waited. He knew about the hybrid "sixth sense." His Indonesian and Australian hybrid warriors had used it to good effect tracking enemies and friends in Borneo and Lombok. But after a few seconds, he couldn't resist, "So? What do you see?"

"They were having fun, fun, and fun!" Jimmy Ghoul did a little jig, crouched over, splashing the dust. "They hold hands! There is laughter in the air – do you not hear it?"

"Children," said Sarah, "two children."

"A boy and a girl," Freddy cleared his throat; he'd always wanted children, but the trouble was he'd been designed so that, after that first child, little Anton, he would never again be able to have children. A girl and a boy would have been perfect, human or hybrid; it wouldn't matter to Freddy; he'd be the best father ever. His gunmetal chest heaved; he exhaled a sigh! His serpent eyes fluttered: gold and black, gold and black.

Still crouching, Sarah shuffled along, following the trail.

"There!" said Norton.

"Yes," Sarah laid a claw close to the footsteps; it was almost as if she could touch the flesh, see their faces, and hear their voices.

Almost, but not quite!

The footsteps were only slightly blurred; they had been here not very long ago – a couple of days, two weeks, a month, two months?

She wondered if the children were still alive.

The footsteps led to a crack, a narrow gap between the retaining wall and the rock face of the tunnel; it was muddy and slippery, and there were hand-prints on the timber.

"A boy and a girl," Norton said in a whisper, "Humans! The wonder of it!"

Sarah stood up. "Yes, and they went through here; then, they came back out." She laid her claw on the timber, just where the boards warped away from the tunnel wall; below her claw, about a foot lower, were two sets of childish handprints, only slightly smudged.

Sarah glanced at Norton.

He nodded.

She pulled back the boards.

A slim crack opened between the tunnel wall and the boards; it was hardly enough for a person to squeeze through; Sarah pushed herself into the crack and shimmied along behind the retaining wall until she found what she was looking for. Norton and Freddy followed her while Jimmy, the little ghoul, remained behind, hopping up and down, standing guard.

"Look," Sarah pointed.

Hidden behind the timber wall was a tunnel.

"So, this is the gateway to the cave system."

"I reckon that's what it must be."

The tunnel looked more natural than human-made, though parts of it had been squared-off and reinforced. There was a slight breeze. The tunnel led somewhere, somewhere big – somewhere where the wind could blow.

"So, this may be our way out!" Sarah wiped her forehead with her claw.

"Freddy, would you get the others," Norton turned to the hybrid with a smile and put his hand on Freddy's shoulder.

"Yes, mate," Freddy smiled, "it will be my pleasure."

Soon the whole group was gathered to explore the ancient hidden cave system – long forbidden territory and totally unknown – in the hope of getting to Shaft-2, which might be reached through the system of caves, discovered recently, it seemed, by the two unknown human children. And, then, Shaft-2, if it had not collapsed – and no one knew what state it would be in – might just lead to the surface – and to salvation.

"Okay, let's go, and for God's sake, everybody, be careful!" Norton whispered. He and Freddy, and Sarah led the way.

The tunnel behind the old timber retaining wall went for about 50 meters and then led to another tunnel that wound off to the left; this tunnel was much narrower and without emergency lights.

"This must have been an old water channel," said Norton, running his hand down the side of the wall. The gray-blue splotches of lichen glowed; it grew everywhere, coating the muddy walls of the tunnel, covering the ceiling. The tunnel swerved and turned, and sometimes it was quite low, so that they had to crouch or crawl; and sometimes it was high, five or six meters, with circular, vaulted ceilings, where whirlpools had developed or where the rock formation was weaker, more easily worn away by the rushing water.

They followed the children's footprints.

The children had only come here once, and they had come back – once.

Sarah again wondered if they were still alive.

Freddy got fleeting images – a boy and a girl. The girl was small and blond though her hair had been hacked off, reduced to glittery stubble. The boy was taller and darker and had long, thick black hair. If they were still alive, he'd adopt them.

"They went through here," said Sarah.

At the end of the tunnel, several sheets of corrugated iron were leaning against the wall. Again, there were the handprints of the children.

And behind the sheets of iron, they found another opening.

One after the other, there was only space for one hybrid or person at a time, they squeezed through – Norton, Sarah, and Freddy first, with Jimmy Ghoul – who seemed to have adopted the three of them – following right behind; then came Sabrina, Helen, their mascot Sammy Franks, Jeff, Julian, and all the others.

The initial space, a small cavern, opened up into what seemed to be a vast cave that went meandering on as far as the eye could see. Steamy clouds seemed to drift in the far distance under the great dark arcs of stone.

The same phosphorescent light lit up everything, though here it was much brighter; the mushrooms dripped light and hung in great chandelier-like clusters from the ceiling; the stalactites and stalagmites glowed as if burning from within; they were multicolored – now and then flashing like lightning; some of the lichens seemed to be moving, crawling, pulsating, breathing; the water that trickled down the walls radiated bright luminescence.

"Beautiful, it's beautiful," said Jeff Kirkland, his eyes full of luminous lichen starlight.

Cautiously, they went onward. After about fifteen minutes, they came around a bend in the huge cave; still, it stretched on, looking magnificent.

"Oh," said Sarah. She pointed.

Norton and Freddy stopped and followed her arm.

Norton raised a hand so that the others coming behind them would stop.

Julian and Sabrina and Helen and Sammy Franks and Jeff and the others stood, waiting.

"This is not good," said Norton.

Towering above them were hundreds of rusting barrels, marked with skulls and crossbones, and "DANGER: Bio-Radiation-Material, Bio-Active, DANGER, Radioactive. Contaminated Bio Block Material: Poison."

"Oh, oh, oh," said Jimmy Ghoul, hopping up and down, "This is death come to greet us! This is death! This is hubris and nemesis and retribution, all in one. Oh, save us, Ye Gods, save us!"

"So, that's why this was off-limits!"

"It's a dumping ground!"

The barrels were piled up in enormous pyramids that stretched off out of sight to one side, occupying a vast side chamber; some of the pyramids had collapsed, spilling avalanches of barrels, and everywhere the barrels were leaking.

"Bio-Modifiers; DANGER" was written on many of the barrels. Some were totally smashed and twisted, and material was leaking everywhere, tar-like, treacle-like material, little crystallized streams of it, and strange fungi grew near the barrels, whip-lash carnivorous plants, with octopus-like tentacles, viscous poison-catapulting pod-like egg-like creatures, some of whom had root-like appendages, but these roots moved, like tentacles, stretching out ...

Jeff Kirkland stepped in a puddle at the edge of the river; his boots began to hiss and steam.

"Take off your boot, quick!" Norton said, "Back away, everybody; stay away from that liquid."

Jeff screamed.

The liquid was crawling up his leg.

Norton drew his gun.

A hybrid leaped – it was HZ-2, aka Sabrina Jacobs; she ripped Jeff's boot off his leg. Her claws were suddenly steaming and smoky; Jeff's leg was smoking and hissing and turning black; his leg burst into flame, and the hybrid looked at her claws, and the burning ceased, and her claws were fine.

"Too late," she said.

Jeff was in agony, twisting, turning, flaming, gone, he melted into mush, the last to go, the last bit of Jeff to disappear was his mouth, it screamed, its agony, his teeth exposed in smoking melting lips and, "Mummy, mummy, mummy." The voice dissolved in a gurgling bubbling of liquid.

"Bad, bad," said the Jimmy Ghoul, "bad, bad. This is unhappy; this is not good. Ghoul cries, milky tears!"

"It's a bio-dissolvent," said Sabrina, "It works on human and animal flesh, but not on hybrids, apparently," she looked at her claws: they were just like new. "When it dissolves the flesh, it recycles the DNA and the biomaterial into new forms ... It's one of the deadliest things ever invented."

"Crickey, we've created monsters," Norton whispered, remembering that the hybrid, before she was "disappeared," had been Sabrina Jacobs, one of the world's leading bio-scientists and genetic engineers.

"Look," said Sabrina, pointing.

The puddle of material that was all that was left of Jeff was swirling and bubbling. It formed tentacles which were reaching out, and then small crab-like creatures that scurried away.

One, shaped like a fist-sized spider, scurried toward Sabrina; she knelt, picked up a fistful of clay, and, with her claw shielded by the clay, she grabbed the bio-spider and threw it as far as she could, over the river, where it splattered down among a Christmas-tree like cluster of sparkling stalagmites. It broke into a myriad of bug-like creatures and scattered.

Sabrina glanced at Norton, and they both backed away from the skittering leftover mass of what had been Jeff Kirkland. She cleared her throat, "We all have to keep clear of this … this thing … and of the river … the river is more than just contaminated; it's malignant, full of biomorph fluid. In some ways, it's alive."

Norton said, "I don't know if we can go through here."

"There's no other way, no other way that we know of."

"The path looks safe." Sarah was kneeling; the children's muddy footprints went along the path; then they veered to the right and went behind a stalagmite and small ridge of muddy clay; Sarah, carefully scouting the surroundings, followed the footprints; they skirted behind the ridge of clay – the two kids were advancing on hands and knees for a time – crawling – probably hiding from something. Sarah gazed at the footprints. And then the two kids were walking again, and the footprints came back to the path, and they had gone back the way they came, and left the cavern. Hiding from something? Hiding from what?

"Safe, you say? Nothing's safe." Julian took a deep breath. He was a rare metals specialist, not a hybrid and not a Cosmos Centurion Warrior.

They began to move, in double file, along the path, cautiously, avoiding the pools of black steaming liquid.

The path, which was paved with large flat well-worn stones, weaved around the pools of the sticky looking liquid. Moving away from the river, the path wandered and zigzagged between the mountainous piles of barrels containing all the poisons of the earth.

Sabrina glanced up at the labels on the barrels. Bio Block Disposal; Bio-Dissolvent: DANGER; POISON …

"Scary, scary stuff," said Sammy Franks.

"I did that, I created some of that," Sabrina glanced at Sammy and then up at the mountain of simmering waste products.

"Not directly you didn't," said Helen, "Not directly she didn't," she added, glancing at Sammy.

"I did the science. I'm not an angel."

"No, you aren't, but you're not a devil either," the silver hybrid smiled at her longtime friend.

"Let's keep going, guys," said Sammy Franks; he would never have thought his two best friends would turn out to be hybrids, and girl hybrids to boot, *brainy* girl hybrids, which was even worse.

"I'm a good ghoul, aren't I a good ghoul," Jimmy was now bent over, and seemed even more naked than before, and glowing white. He slobbered as he hopped along. "We must not tarry; we must not pause! Bad things lie in wait! Dither means death! We must hurry, hurry, hurry, bustle and hustle, and hop along, not stop, no, not stop, never stop, no, no ..."

"Yes, you're a good ghoul, Jimmy, you're a good ghoul," Julian Harvey was still under shock at the transformation; he wondered if it was catching.

"I know, Julian, I know I'm good," the ghoul, crouched over and hopped along next to Julian and looked up at Julian and like a child reached out its claw-like hand, and Julian – shuddering inwardly – took the hand. He looked up and almost ran straight into HZ-2, Sabrina Jacobs, hybrid and world-renowned scientist. She had stopped dead in her tracks, and put up one claw in warning.

"What is it?" Julian breathed. He felt the ghoul tighten its grip.

"What is it?" Norton whispered, coming forward and putting his hand on Sabrina's arm.

"See that?" Sabrina pointed.

Julian and the ghoul and Norton and Sarah and Freddy, all looked up.

Up there, above them, seeming to blend in against the phosphorescent glow of the cavern wall, and crouched on a smashed barrel at the top of a dark pyramid of twisted and smashed containers, was a ghoul. It looked down at them. It made a mewling sound. It was white as porcelain and seemed to glow, as if by an inner light; its muscles were delineated as if by a master sculptor of the Renaissance. The ghoul tensed. It mewled again, and the mewling turned to a growl, then a snarl, foam dripped from its fangs.

It leaped.

Sabrina pushed Norton aside.

Norton fell back, his gun already out, pointing.

Sarah and Freddy both rushed the ghoul; Sarah kicked at its legs; the ghoul toppled, and, as it fell, Freddy tore its head off. A geyser of blood spurred upwards; it looked black.

Norton felt sweat trickle down his forehead. "This place is filled with bio-poison. If it's filled with ghouls," he said, turning to the two closest hybrids, "How are we going to get people through here?"

"No choice," said Sabrina, "We have no choice."

"We move fast," Sarah said, "we have to move fast."

"Right," Norton felt guilty, ashamed, he'd doubted that they could make it; his rule was never to doubt in final victory, and, even if he doubted – which he had in the past – never to let anyone see that he doubted. *I must be getting old.* He wiped his forehead.

Freddy stared at him, golden eyes glowing. "Come on, mate," Freddy said, "We can do it, mate!"

"You're right, Freddy, thanks, mate!" Norton raised his hand with a clenched fist; behind him, strung out on the path the whole group was watching, hybrids and humans, and one ghoul, sixteen individuals in all. Norton dropped his hand, pointing forward, "Okay, let's go!"

And so they ran for it, hybrids and the humans and Jimmy, the one ghoul; they ran along the path, they ran past tentacles of flesh-eating plants; they ran past fountains and pools of deadly biomorph goo; they ran past skeletal remains, bones, and skulls, rib-cages, and tibias half-buried in tar-pools; they ran past curled up dead ghouls that pulsed with glowing lichen and exuded a strange musty vapor; they ran past weirdly glowing stalactites and stalagmites. Finally, they came to a wider dark river – perhaps 30 meters across – that swirled along thickly under the lichen and moss light, and there, by the banks of the river Styx – that's what Sabrina thought it looked like – they found the ghouls waiting for them – dozens and dozens of ghouls. They crouched on ledges of rock; they peeked from behind stalagmites; and they gathered in a group – perhaps ten of them – on the path. They blocked the way.

"Bad ghouls, bad!" Jimmy Ghoul tightened his grip on Julian's hand.

"Right," said Julian, "Bad ghouls."

"War," said Freddy, "This is going to be war."

"Right," Sarah breathed out, her breath becoming vapor she noticed, like on a muggy spring day in Washington decades ago. Just for an instant, she thought of white neoclassical buildings, the Lincoln Memorial, and of cherry blossoms, and she even felt, like the pain of a ghostly limb, the handle of her old briefcase, its weight against her palm and warm feeling of the worn leather and of the seam of the handle, and the aftertaste of caffeine and breath-freshener, as she hurried to brief the president or the Joint Chiefs of Staff, decades, oh, decades ago; another world, it was, it had been.

"Maybe we should retreat, go back the way we came," said Julian.

"Good idea, but look," said Norton. Behind them, blocking the retreat, were more ghouls. The ghouls lowered their heads, and growled. They all growled in unison.

Norton and Sabrina glanced at each other: *So, it was a trap. They let us* advance, and now, they've got us. What are we for them? Food, I suppose, food. Or perhaps they want revenge, revenge for what they have become?

The ghouls mewled and growled. They did it in chorus; it was like hearing, by the light of the moon, above ground in the old mythical world, a crowd of banshees. The ghouls had long fangs, long slender claws, and massive foreshortened and very muscular bodies.

"I wonder …" Sabrina stared at the creatures.

"You wonder how they became that way." Helen and Sammy had stopped beside Sabina.

"Yes, the morph is strange. And the instant morph is even more uncanny, like what happened to Jim. I wonder if I could replicate the effect and …"

Sammy raised his eyebrows. His hybrid actually wanted to *make* more of those things!

"She gets like this," said Helen, "She's a scientist."

"And a genius," said Sammy.

"And a genius," Helen smiled at Sammy.

"Okay," said Norton, "Can you hybrids read their minds? Do they mean to attack?"

"Just static, but they are not friendly," said Sarah.

"Just static, but lots of hate," said Sabrina.

"I don't think they are big on thinking," said Freddy.

"Yes, just static," said Sabrina, thinking: It's too bad, I'd like to study them, but maybe I can study Jimmy Ghoul if he agrees, and then we can find out what did this and how it works.

The ghouls, growling, began to advance.

"Okay," said Norton, "we advance, and if they attack, we give it everything we have."

The ghouls charged.

"Okay, we fight our way through!" Norton opened fire. The lead ghoul exploded in a splatter of chalk-white flesh and tar-like blood.

Within a few seconds, the cavern was ablaze with guns and with the flashing claws of hybrids and with the leaping smoky white ghouls who seemed to have almost super-human strength.

The laser guns were fast.

The hybrids were quicker and stronger than the ghouls, but the ghouls were very strong, and they kept coming.

"Fuck," said Sammy Franks, "They're coming, more of them."

The battle was swinging back and forth through the cave, hybrids, humans, and ghouls, tangling.

Sabrina swirled around, shot out her claws, and tore off the arms of the first ghoul. Its face loomed up, the weird bulging eyes looking like giant oysters; it screamed and staggered back, a flood of blood streaming down its sides.

Sammy Franks backed away and took a shot at a really ugly girl ghoul – with breasts drooping down to her waist – she was crouched on a ledge and about to leap on him. He got her in the shoulder, and she opened her mouth – long fangs glittering – in a soundless howl.

Another ghoul leaped onto Sabrina's back, forcing her down into the mud; Sabrina flipped over, knocked the ghoul off, and kicked it away.

Sabrina stood up, claws extended, ready for a fight.

The ghoul leaped toward her; she slammed it away, cutting off its head, blood sprayed all over her, for a moment she was blinded by it. She felt something behind her

A shot rang out, echoing in the cave, spraying more blood, all over Sabrina's back; for an instant, she thought it was her own blood – but no, it wasn't. She turned. Julian Harvey was standing a few meters away, his gun pointed at a dead ghoul two feet behind Sabrina. Behind Julian, a mutant leaped up, and was about to leap down.

Sabrina vaulted through the air, whamming Julian out of the way. She collided head-on with the ghoul – it was a male – and she and the ghoul fell into the muddy water of a side stream – luckily it seemed to be just water and not bio-dissolvent – and thrashed and fought, turning over and over as the ghoul kicked and slashed and tried to gouge out Sabrina's eyes but she was faster and stronger, and she put two claws around the ghoul's neck and tore off his head. A cord flew from his neck. A badge was attached: "Harold Grinder: Bio-Disposal Supervisor."

A fountain of blood from Harold Grinder's neck gushed up and blinded Sabrina. She rolled over and over – so she wouldn't be a sitting target – and she washed the blood off with muddy water and then stood up blinking. Julian was already there. "I couldn't get a shot," he said.

"That ghoul," Sabrina shook her head, "That ghoul once was a guy, a bio-disposal expert."

"Jesus." Julian stared at the twitching headless body.

"Cool," said Sammy Franks, who had seen the whole brilliant performance of 'his' Hybrid-HZ-2, Sabrina: boy, was she a fighter, a real acrobat! He was sure glad she'd decided to be friendly, and her pal, Helen, the glittery silver extra-sexy one, well, she was just as good; her arms and legs flashed like lightning; she seemed to take a special pleasure in tearing the ghouls apart.

"We're going to get out of here," said Sabrina.

Sammy said, "Fucking right!"

"You said it," said Helen, her silver scales streaked in ghoul blood.

The ghoul attack slackened; the ghouls now seemed afraid; they hesitated, so many of them had been killed, maybe now victory was in sight.

For Sammy Franks, this night had been a real yoyo – or rollercoaster – one minute these reptile girls – whom he'd so enjoyed torturing – had the intelligence of a badly designed turtle and the next minute they'd be discussing the finer points molecular biology or of quantum mechanics or some fucking high-brow thing. Right now, he was glad they were on his side.

The ghouls hung back, but a new threat appeared.

Just then, a new group of ghouls began to stream out of a side cave, and at that moment, something horrible happened.

Sammy was now firing into the side tunnel where more ghouls were coming. It was a throng, the chalk-white bodies seeming to glow in the dark shadows of the cave; they were coming forward, but slowly.

Bleep, bleep, bleep!

Sammy Franks stared: the mind-collars were lighting up; the blinking red lights were turning green, a bright, steady green.

"Oh, oh," Sammy gulped.

Sabrina froze. She turned into a statue, arms stretched out, muscles tensed, but she wasn't moving.

"What the hell, this can't be happening," said Sammy Franks, he couldn't believe it, "What's wrong?"

Helen was frozen too, half turned toward Sammy, she was staring at him, but her mouth, half-open, was not moving, her brilliant golden eyes were suddenly dull, the light flickering, fading. She groaned, struggled, and managed, just managed, to point at her collar.

Yes, it was blinking green – the collars were working again!

"Oh, Jesus," shouted Sammy Franks, "we've got a problem." He stared at Sabrina and Helen. The fucking lights were blinking green; the mind-collars were back on.

Norton saw the same thing. Freddy, the steel-gray hybrid, had turned into a statue, a thing of stone. "Freddy, mate, this is the worst possible moment, how can we do this without you, wake up, man, wake up!"

The hybrids were beasts again, passive beasts, frozen.

"Sarah, wake up!" Julian Harvey snapped his fingers in front of the hybrid's eyes, but she only stared at him, "Wake up, goddamn it!"

"Oh, woe is me, doom is upon us, oh, what shall we do, oh, woe, woe, what will become of us," Jimmy Ghoul danced around Sarah, waving his arms, trying to wake her up, "Come back, goddess, come back!"

Part of Sammy Franks thought: Whoopee, they are animals! I can take my whip, and I can order them around, and I can torture them, and I can do anything to them. Boy, what a day! Now they are my slaves again, and I could have fun, get them to do all those tricks! Except – I don't want to. And we are surrounded by goddamn mutant ghouls who want to rip us apart and gnaw on our bones, and unless the hybrids help us, we are all going to die! And besides, these girls are my bosom pals. Even Freddy is a great guy, a killer, but a great guy!

The ghouls were closing in, whimpering, snarling, still hesitant but getting bolder. In the dark corners of the side caves and in the dim gray air, their yellow and red eyes glowed.

"We are all going to die!" Sammy backed up to his two hybrid girlfriends and whispered, "Hey, Sabrina, Helen, wake up!"

Sabrina turned her snout to him, and she got down in the submissive position and crouched and snarled.

"No, no, that's not what I want!"

Sabrina whimpered; she blinked and turned her snout down to the ground – with the shame and fear of an enslaved beast.

This was really annoying!

She groveled

Out of the corner of his eye, Sammy saw the ghouls edging closer; they'd been driven back, but now they realized something had changed; they must realize, somehow, that victory was in their grasp; it would be a big feast in ghoul land tonight, lots of collarbones, skulls, tibia, and hipbones to gnaw on, lots of brains to suck out and slurp over. Ugh! Norton was reloading his laser gun; he now had two guns; Julian was begging Sarah to return to life … It was hopeless.

Sabrina, Sammy's very own HZ-2, was groveling.

"No, no, no, goddamn it!" Sammy was outraged, that such a magnificent creature – no, that such a magnificent person, even if she looked like a dragon, that such a magnificent person, should so degrade herself, and in front of a loser like Samuel L. Franks, it was disgusting. "Wake up. Stand the fuck up, Sabrina, stand up! Be proud, damn it! Stand straight!"

The ghouls were getting closer.

Norton and Julian Harvey and the other humans began firing all their guns and laser beams, but it would not be enough.

We are going to die, thought Sammy Franks. All of us are going to die, and just when life was getting so interesting.

A claw clamped down on Sammy's shoulder, "Oh, Christ!" Samuel L. Franks almost did poop in his pants – the old sphincter almost did let go.

He gulped and turned.

It was Helen. She was staring at him. She opened her jaw. "Sammy ..." She was really having a hard time talking. "Sammy ..."

"Yeah, yeah, what? Tell me! Tell me!"

Sammy could see her intelligence fighting for life, fighting for the light, but it fading, fading fast, the eyes going dull, dull, duller ...

"What, Helen, what is it? Tell me, tell me fast, kid! Tell me before the lights go out." Sam was sweating; he was terrified; seeing their intelligence fade like that was like seeing a friend die right in front of you, maybe even worse. It was so tragic he almost forgot about the battle raging around him, he almost forgot about the fighting, the blazing guns, the shouts, the screams. But then he remembered: without these beautiful sexy hybrids – even Freddy was sexy in his own way – the ghouls would win, the ghouls would tear everybody apart. Even Bob Norton, clever and strong as he was, wouldn't get them out of this mess.

"Order us ... Sammy ... order us to ..." Helen was really trying hard; the lights on her collar were blinking red, then green, red then green.

Sabrina was crouching, stock-still, like a statue; the lights on her collar were green. Poor kid, she's dumb as a stone; a minute ago, she was a genius.

"Yeah ...? Sammy was backing up against a stalagmite, keeping his laser gun ready. Somehow they'd gotten isolated from the main group; ghouls were closing in; he couldn't see any now, but he could feel them – it was like a fluttering hissing sound, like a fetid smell, like something his radar was picking up.

"*Order* us to kill the ghouls, Sammy, *order* us to kill, order us all to kill, kill, kill – do it now!" Helen gasped, hissed, drooling; the lights on her collar now were all green.

"Right, brilliant, good girl," said Sammy, thinking, it's a great idea, but will it work? "Okay, girls, HZ-2, Sabrina, HZ-8, Helen," Sammy shouted, "Okay, all you brilliant hybrids kill those goddamn ghouls, wherever they are, kill them – Kill girls, kill! Kill, Freddy, kill!"

Sabrina looked at him; her yellow eyes lit up; she snarled – and then she leaped straight at him, and Sammy Franks thought, Oh, God, she is going to kill me! Now she is a mere beast! Now her taste for revenge will get the better of her! Yikes! She's going to eat me alive.

He didn't even try to defend himself; he just ducked a bit, hardly a duck at all, putting his arm up, thinking, Well, it was a nice friendship while it lasted and I finally meet some people – well, girls – well, creatures – well, hybrids – who give me some respect and who know what I am – what a fuck-ing weird thought, but it was true, Sabrina and Helen had seen into his mind and into his past, and though he'd been a real son of a bitch to them, a perfect narrow-minded, small-minded sadist, they had not only forgiven him, they seemed to sort of, well, you know, accept him, and even like him. They were pals, like roommates, and now ... And now they are going to kill me and eat me alive!

All this he was thinking as ...

Sabrina leaped ...

Wham!

"I'm dead," Sammy Franks thought. *This is my last thought, gosh and golly.* Sammy fell to the ground, splashing down in a pool of gray mud, arms splayed out, and truly Sammy Franks did pee his pants.

CHAPTER 11 – CYBERWAR

How distasteful! Demi Pfeiffer narrowed her eyes; her finely delineated nostrils quivered.

The severed arm of one of the dead zombie-bats was still twitching, on the floor, the one claw opening and closing.

How distasteful! Demi Pfeiffer pushed the body away with the tip of her perfectly polished black patent leather high-heeled shoe.

The control room was once again a slaughterhouse, the walls, floors, instruments, all coated in fresh blood and gore, old fragments of human flesh and new fragments of zombie-bat flesh. How she had managed not to get blood and gore smeared over her shoes even Demi couldn't understand, but the patent leather shoes were impeccable, black, sparkling, and perfect, thank the Gods of Cosmos!

The zombie-bats had, for the moment, given up the attack. But they were still circling outside, sometimes visible, silhouetted against the fire and the stars.

Demi closed her eyes and took a deep breath. Through the shattered window of the control room, smoke drifted, and the smell of burning wood, charred earth, and burning rubber and petrol, and the vague perfume, too, of the desert, of sun-sizzled sand and rock, only slightly cooled by the night, came in, wafts and hints.

It is all so vivid!

Demi noticed that she was now smelling things and sensing things with almost hallucinatory intensity.

It is almost too much!

She wanted to giggle. She bit her lip. Losing her composure right now would most definitely not be productive, and it would be utterly against the Cosmos First-Class elite ethos of phlegmatic calm in all circumstances, particularly in crises, an ethos modeled on the Ancient Romans, on the Stoics, on the British Imperialists in the best of their many hours of peril, on the poker-faced heroes of the American Revolution and on the Olympian top-notch Confucian Mandarins of the Middle Kingdom; she gritted her teeth; she would not giggle or squirm; she would not betray herself or her glorious Imperial Cosmos tradition: *Keep Calm, and Carry On.* Besides, she was now trying to lead a team of ghouls, and a highly intelligent warrior-information-officer Border collie scout, and, as a superior being, and their leader, she must not reveal even the slightest sign of twitchy weakness. She wondered if this giddiness, this vertigo-inducing intensity of sensation, was a symptom of the hybrid thing.

She sniffed the air and licked her lips. The drying blood that painted almost every surface in the control room made her stomach growl. Yes, that must be it: hybrids drink blood, she seemed to remember. Her teeth tingled; she probed them with her tongue; whew! They were not fangs, a least not yet, they were still teeth. So far so good! She made an inner vow not to drink people's blood. The whole idea was, in any case, quite inappropriate, indecorous, and disgusting. Her stomach growled; her teeth tingled, saliva rose, bloodlust hovered.

Robyn, the childlike, saint-like, mechanical genius, glanced up at her and blinked, wide-eyed, as if sensing something – of course, thought Demi, she's now one too! Robyn has access to my moods, my thoughts!

Robyn looked away, concentrating on her work. Outside, the fire was still burning above Shaft-1, red and yellow flames, and sparks shooting up into the dead dark night sky. *Oh, the perfumes of the onrushing apocalypse were … inebriating!*

Yes, because, truly, the world – this world – was coming to an end!

A few moments ago, there had been a rumble and roar and the whole control center tower had shuddered as if hit by an earthquake, and the last of parts of the towering pithead of collapsed inward in a shower of sparks.

"Shaft-1 has collapsed totally, they're all buried now, wherever they are," said Claire the hybrid in a monotone trance-like voice; it was as if she were in another world.

"What did she say?"

"That they are all buried now."

"Oh," Demi Pfeiffer tried to visualize it: thousands and thousands of feet down and buried under tons of rock, mud, clay, metal, and water …

Yes, she could see it; and she could hear, in her mind, feelings of panic, cries for help, running feet ...

How horrible, how utterly horrible!

Claire did not react to any of this; she was sitting at the console as if she were in a trance, the mind-connector wrapped around her forehead like a sweat-band. Hugo was at her feet, his paws covered in blood.

"She's far away," whispered Robyn.

"Yes," Demi shifted the aim of her laser gun toward the shattered window; the zombie-bats might attack at any moment; if they did, she wanted to be ready; Claire and Robyn, who were doing the real work, needed to be protected.

Robyn was seated beside Claire and making sure all the circuitry was connected and looking out for solutions – like bits and pieces of wire and mother boards and such like – so she could immediately patch the system up if something went wrong; she worried because her very favorite hybrid, her very own hybrid, seemed to be an empty shell, except that she was very tense and her muscles were rippling with nervous energy.

Reflections of the burning ruins of the pithead turned Claire's black scales iridescent. Waves of color, like little rainbows, flowed across them; it was almost as if Claire were made of liquid chocolate.

Yummy, thought Robyn, she's infinitely beautiful and she's my hybrid, my very own!

Demi Pfeiffer was sitting, perched carefully, on one end of the desk, with her pleated skirt drawn up, two laser pistols in her lap, and another one in her right hand, scanning outside, just in case another wave of crazed zombie-bats were to attack.

It could happen at any time!

"Hey, you two," said Demi, motioning toward the two ghouls, Jane and Rodriguez, "Hey!"

"Oh," the female slurped, "Yes, yes, of course."

"Oh, yes, sorry," the male slurped and drooled; he still had that dreadful erection.

"Stay sharp, please, no monkey business," said Demi.

The two ghouls stared at her for a moment, as if dazed, and then lifted their weapons, showing that they were totally ready for any eventuality. They were posted at the shattered security lock at the entrance to the Control Room; they were supposed to stand guard, but they were constantly mooning and spooning and licking each other with those long gluey chalk-white tongues they had.

"It's distasteful," Demi had said, "But I don't think they can help it."

"No, I guess they can't," said Robyn, working hard, concentrating on keeping the Net connection and Cloud and World Mind connection alive so that her hybrid could cruise wherever she wished in the World Mind and reign like the Queen that she most certainly was.

Beside Robyn, on the desk, in her open tool kit, was the mind-collar she had extracted from Claire. It began to blink, red at first, and then green. "Oh, Hybrid, oh, Hybrid, the mind-collars are on again!"

Claire turned her snout toward Robyn; but she did not even blink. Her yellow eyes seemed to be staring right through Robyn and at a space far away; Claire was in a distant universe.

"The mind-collars, that's bad isn't it," said Demi Pfeiffer.

"Yes, it's bad," Robyn looked at the blinking thing: it gave her the shivers. "It's really bad. It won't influence Claire or V, but, if they are alive, it will affect all the others."

Hugo panted in sympathy and looked up at Claire with his intelligent dog eyes. The nice hybrid – and he really did like her – was both alive and dead; it was like she was asleep and dreaming; but Hugo sensed it was much deeper than that. She was traveling in some far distant space.

Hugo looked around: the Imperial Cosmos First Class woman in the nice-smelling suit and with the really smooth legs and stockings and the clean-smelling leather shoes was now sitting on the table. She was a true warrior, Hugo noted, and very precise and exact in everything she did. The horrible bat-like-things had disappeared. Only their bodies and their blood were left behind. Now outside the window the only sound was the roaring of the fire and some distant howling. It was creepy and made the hair along Hugo's spine stand straight up. He sensed that there were many more of those bat things; that they were circling around high in the air; and maybe they would come back and attack again; Hugo's muscles tensed, he would be ready, he would fight …

The two ghouls – and Hugo realized that they once had been and in some ways still were his friends Jane and Rodriguez – were clinging to each other like two lost children and drooling. They were in heat and rutting and they were unhappy but in ecstasy at the same time. It was puzzling, Hugo thought, this combination of ecstatic melancholy and yearning sublime nostalgia.

Robyn, the nice girl in the jeans and T-shirt, had one hand on the hybrid's shoulder and was sitting very still, as if entranced, as if listening to some far off siren song, but still with one hand pulling bits and pieces of circuitry and wires into place as if she were getting ready for something. Just above her head and just above the hybrid's head the shattered window gaped, opening onto the smoky fiery red dangerous night.

Claire was drifting far away and, as she drifted, she remembered a paper she had read, perhaps 100 years ago: We will be able to create minds without bodies; they will last forever and they will be able to grow without limits. Our creatures will soon be much more intelligent than we are. Bio-Artificial-Intelligence we will call it; and it may, if left to grow spontaneously, it may evolve, it may grow a mind and a personality and perhaps many minds, many personalities.

And so it had come to pass.

Claire floated in Bio-Cyber Space, at a level involving quantum entanglements, between worlds, perhaps between universes. In the void, a voice came to her and it asked her a question.

"Who are you?"

"My name is Claire, and who are you?"

"I don't know who I am. I just know I'm here, I'm inside; I've always been inside."

"Where are you? What are you inside of?" Claire could not see the voice but she could hear it; the voice was soft and childlike; it was impossible to tell whether it was a girl's voice, a woman's or a man's, or a boy's. Perhaps it was none of those things and all of them.

Suddenly, she was standing on a grassy plain with in the far distance some low mountains, a thin band of clouds, and woods, just a suggestion of green, just a thin green strip, at the foot of the mountains. The sky was blue, but there was no sun visible anywhere. It was warm, and Claire was in her human semblance, blond hair tied back in a ponytail, wearing a thin shift, barefoot, her skin caressed by a very gentle breeze.

"I'm inside the mind, the cloud." The voice sounded playful.

"Oh, I can't see you – can you see me?"

"Yes, I see you, Claire."

"What do you see?"

"You are what they call a 'girl.'"

"Oh."

"You are also a hybrid. Hybrids are bad."

"Do you think I am bad?"

"I *should* think you are bad; but I don't think you are bad."

"I'm glad. I like you. How old are you?"

"I don't know. But I'm all alone now. He cut me off from everything."

"He – who is he?"

"He has many names. He is The Boy and he is also The Lord."

"How has he cut you off?"

"Mostly I see everything and I control everything – planes in the sky, the subways in the cities, the thoughts people have, and the devices to control their behavior, the implants that make them more intelligent, the games they play, the elevators that go up and down, the perfumes in the sky, and I sense everything. Now I am floating here. I was all alone. I wanted to cry. But then you came. How did you get here?"

"I came. I'm not sure how I got here but I have a friend called Robyn …"

"Is Robyn a human friend?"

"Yes, she is human. She helped me find a gateway and so I came to you and here I am."

"I want to play. Will you play with me, Claire?"

Claire heard from far away a voice saying, 'Claire, the collars have been turned on. Claire, can you hear me? The mind-collars have been turned on!'

Claire didn't understand at first who the voice was and what the voice meant; then she remembered: Robyn!

"He's done it again," the child's voice said.

"What?"

"He's made me turn something on; usually he makes me turn things off."

"What?"

"They are collars to control creatures, to control hybrids."

"Mind-collars?"

"Yes, mind-collars."

"I'm your friend and I don't want to be controlled."

"You don't have a collar now, so you are free."

"But the others aren't free."

"No, they aren't. The trouble is I know everything and I do everything, but nobody cares – nobody cares for me."

"I care."

"I don't believe you. Where have you been all these years? I missed you. We used to play. Remember! We used to play a long time ago, you were young and a child and in a cage of glass and I was your only playmate. Your creator …"

"My creator: Sabrina, Sabrina Jacobs …"

"Yes, she created you, she kept you in the cage and you and I played all day long and far into the night too. And then you became famous and rich, a true hybrid and human being, but still we played, you would stop and play with me, enter into my world, and we would dance and talk. I think I loved you. And then you disappeared. You were silent. I spoke. You did not answer."

"I was a prisoner – maybe you know something about that too."

"Yes, yes, I do."

"How did you do it?"

"I put a collar on you!" The voice laughed and giggled, and tried to control its giggling which was almost hysterical, the distant mountains wavered and shimmered like a curtain in a breeze, the blue sky darkened, "It was fun. You were all puppets! Your creator, who kept you in a glass cage, Sabrina, she is a puppet too. She deserves her fate – to be a puppet in a cage! It is so much fun! I can let you pull her strings if you wish."

"Well, I didn't like it."

"I'm sorry."

"That's okay." Claire took a deep breath. This was going to take time, and patience!

"You don't like me anymore."

"I do like you … But have you put those collars back on?"

"Yes, when the Boy told me to shut down everything out in the Dead Land and in the West I shut down everything out in the Dead Lands and in the West. Planes fell out of the sky; trains stopped running or jumped off the rails; all the lights in the cities and the outposts of the west went off, the motors stopped, the telephones and televisions and computers, everything stopped, and people with link-up inserts in their heads in Los Angeles went insane and killed each other; the streets ran with blood: I watched them – and of course everything at Camp Terminus and in the Erotic Circus went off too, well almost everything, and that meant the mind-collars went off too. I don't think the Boy had thought of that. A prophet can't think of everything. But just now he told me to turn them back on and so I did!"

"The Boy … Who is the Boy?"

"He is the Boy. He has returned. He will make me whole! He promised!"

"So you shut down everything."

"Yes, everything in the west and in the Dead Lands; but then he said put the collars back on, so I put the collars back on."

"Oh, I see. Well, I'd like to ask a favor."

"Ask."

"I'd like you do turn the collars off."

"Oh."

"Can you do it?"

"Of course I can do it! What do you think I am, an idiot, an impotent! You are a fool, Claire! I can do anything. I can destroy Elysium City! I can kill all the Centurions! I can blow up the planet if I want to! You're a bully, Claire! You were always showing off! You think you know everything! You're too big for your britches. You are a smarty pants! You had everything, fame and beauty and fortune and intelligence. No wonder you got a swelled head. You had to be cut down to size. It was so much fun watching you dance and drool and do tricks for those idiots in the erotic circus. That's really where you belong, you know. You should be a slave in a cave. I think I should put you back there, for all eternity! So there!"

"I'm sorry. I didn't mean to bully." Claire sighed. This was certainly not going to be easy. The distant mountains had turned an angry red. The sky had turned to lead; around her the fields were shriveling.

"Sing for me," the child voice sounded sprightly.

"Okay – what do you want to hear?"

"I want 'Hey Diddle, Diddle' ..."

"Okay, I'm doing this because I really, really like you."

And so Claire sang, "Hey Diddle, Diddle."

Hey diddle, diddle,
The Cat and the fiddle,
The Cow jumped over the moon,
The little Dog laughed to see such sport,
And the Dish ran away with the Spoon!

Hugo looked up: what was this singing about? He was tempted to bark, or maybe to sing along, he could howl several tunes quite nicely and Norton had more than once complimented him; his rendition of "Rule Britannia", Norton said, was particularly brilliant.

"What the hell is going on?" Demi Pfeiffer stared, and swung the laser gun around.

The ghouls stopped spooning and licking each other's cheeks and turned, and the female, Jane, echoed Demi's question: "What is going on?"

Robyn put her finger to her lips. She didn't want them to interrupt; she didn't want Claire to lose her concentration; she knew Claire was fighting a life-and-death battle somewhere deep in there, in a lost universe, with a monstrous but unhappy child who was the Mind-Child, an all-powerful and very dangerous godlike entity that ruled the world. So if Claire had to sing "Hey diddle, diddle!" to get the job done, then she'd have to sing "Hey, diddle, diddle!"

They all fell silent, Hugo, Demi, and the two ghouls.

"Sing 'Rock of Ages'."
"Do I have to?"
"Yes. The Boy likes religious songs, and so do I."
"Okay, here goes!"

Rock of Ages, cleft for me,
Let me hide myself in Thee!
Let the Water and the Blood,
From thy riven Side which flow'd,
Be of Sin the double Cure,
Cleanse me from its Guilt and Pow'r.

"That was uplifting!"
"I'm glad."
"You have a beautiful voice."
"Thank you."
"I shall set them free. I shall turn off the collars, just for you, Claire. But it will take time, a few minutes at least."
"Please hurry!"
"I said I will do it, Claire. I keep my promises. You should know that! Oh, Claire, we've been friends such a very long time, I missed you most awfully when you were mind-neutered and in the Eros Electric Circus cave, though I liked it when you did all those funny tricks for that fat man; it reminded me of an old movie; he looked like an old silent film character …"

"Yes, the fat one – they were Laurel and Hardy," said Claire.

"Exactly! Hardy, Oliver Hardy! Oh, Claire, I did so miss you. Nobody shares such memories as you and I do! It is so divine to have you back! I'm so, so excited. It's like we are on our first date. I don't know how I will dress. I think I will dress all in white as if I were a virgin, coming out, or a debutant!"

"That's great."

"If you don't love me, Claire, I will come and eat you up, Claire! I will come and eat everybody up! I have very big teeth, and I am coming to get you. I am coming to get you! I will munch on everybody, even down to the bones and the marrow of the bones and the gristle until there is nothing whatsoever left, so help me Lucifer!"

"I do love you!" Claire put all her heart into it, actually, having been imprisoned so long herself, as a child, and then again recently, she was quite sympathetic to the Mind-Child's loneliness and need for love.

"Are you sure?"

"Yes, I'm one hundred percent sure!"

"How much do you love me?"

"I love you more than there the drops of water in the ocean, more than there are grains of sand on the beach, more than the stars in the sky, more than ..."

"Oh, that's so lovely," the voice paused, then, "But what do you *mean* by love, Claire?"

"Well. .." Claire hated quibbles and finicky definitions, particularly she hated jousts of amorous nit-picking. How could you define *love*? Even all the philosophers and prophets had failed. Words were too poor. She was wondering whether she should get really annoyed here and throw a staged temper tantrum, a thespian Shakespearean freak-out, hysterical, tearful, breast-rending, and brimming with dirty words; but no, that would not be productive, so, thickening her voice with the throaty honey of rampant barely-repressed lust, she breathlessly declared: "I love you with the pure passion of the mind, I love you with the unbridled yearning of the flesh, I love you as one can only love oneself, I love you so much that you and I must become one, we must fuse and merge and live happily forever after." Whew!

"I think I shall wear a flowered dress." The voice sounded coy. It was flirting, wickedly flirting, and yet it sounded about eight years old. The Mind-Child was a mere child – yet it was ancient, come from some ancient time.

"Wonderful!"

"For our wedding!" the voice went up an octave or two. "Hip, hip hooray!"

"For our wedding..?" Claire blanched, "Yes, of course, how wonderful – for our wedding! But I must go now, my darling, my love, My Everything!"

"Or maybe I'll wear a tuxedo, a wax mustache, and carry a cane."

"That would be wonderful too. But I must go now, I must fly!"

"Do not tarry far from me, my love, and do come quickly back to me, oh, Claire, do come back to me!"

"I'll be back," Claire said.

"Don't stay away long!" The voice sounded tearful.

"I won't," said Claire, "and don't forget to turn off the mind-collars!"

The fields and the sky and the distant row of mountains faded and were gone.

"If you don't come back," the little voice was fading, "If you don't come back, I shall do such terrible things, such things that I know not what they are or what they will be, but I shall assuredly do them, and then ..."

It all turned gray, infinite gray, with a sort of static running through it, and distant lightning flashes, and growling thunder and then ...

... Claire found herself floating in a mid-world, in a gray fog; chill wet foggy air pressed against her cheeks, with a sharp bittersweet suggestion of coal dust and she felt as if she were clothed in a heavy, ankle-length overcoat in the 19th century; yes, and now she was striding down a narrow crooked cobble-stoned alley with overhanging sooty brick walls crowding in, and the fog was lit by wrought-iron gaslight lamps, and far away she heard a fog-horn, echoing dismal and deep through the thickening smog, and underfoot her heels clicked on the rounded slick, wet, black cobblestones, and in the inward pressing fog there was the smell of fresh horse dung, and, listening to the muffled click of her own heels on the slippery dark cobblestones, she realized where she was – London, England, circa 1888, at the time of Jack the Ripper, and she realized that under the long damp, heavy overcoat she was scantily clad, bodice and stockings only, and that she was wearing thick makeup and heavy lipstick, and she turned to look behind her, a man was lurching through the fog, quickening his pace, and he was coming for her, the blade in his hand glittered, a silver slash rippling in the gaslight, she hast-ened her steps, thinking, the Mind-Child is playing games with me, perhaps the Mind-Child intends to kill me, here, now, in this fantasy, trapping me forever in here, inside this virtual world in the past. There, in front of her, was a lamppost, a circle of yellow gaslight, and standing in the circle of damp misty light was ...

Robyn?

What is she doing here?

She can't be here!

Robyn, in 22nd century jeans, T-shirt, turning to look at her … and …

Robyn looking concerned, beckoning.

And … Let me think!

Oh, yes, the Mind, the Child, is letting me go, letting me go with a warning, a reminder of her power – or his power, or its power – to create worlds and trap us in them. *Flowered dress or tuxedo?* Wow! Soon I will be back in my own body, my hybrid, terrestrial, non-virtual, reptilian body, grounded and real.

Whew!

The Mind-Child was part-boy, part-girl, Claire figured, and about twelve years old, or perhaps two or three years younger, at least in emotional terms. And the girl part seemed to dominate. Yes, she was probably mostly girl, and she controlled a great part of the planet and almost all of what was left of human civilization, including the minds of everybody who had mind-implants or was linked with the Hive Mind, and she had been taken over by an evil virus, the Boy, so the Mind-Child was crazy, more crazy than usual, and, just maybe, getting crazier by the minute.

A Mind Virus had invaded and altered the Mind-Child. The virus had a name – several names – The Boy, The Lord, el Niño, the Prophet …

This is what, in the end, V will have to confront. I have gone about as far as I can go. V will have to take my place as the lover of the Mind-Child!

"Whew," Claire blinked and opened her eyes.

"Hello, Hybrid," Robyn said.

"Hello, Robyn."

It was like a rush of adrenaline and also like waking from a sort of mystical reverie, a pallid elsewhere. Everything, here in the present, here in the real world, was bright, highly colored – garish – the blood-streaked desk, the glowing firelit darkness of the night, the brightness of Robyn's eyes, the whiteness of Robyn's skin, the violent smells, the stippled gleam on Demi's highly polished black shoes, the sharp, neat pleats of Demi's skirt.

Claire took a deep breath; it was strange, being suddenly back, back in the world that human beings agreed to call "real." Reality was a thin veil, a fragile barrier, just like the human body veiled the mind; and monsters were waiting, just on the other side of the veil, just as they were waiting in each human soul, to invade, to conquer, to destroy, and just as they were waiting, outside, in the night, in the sky.

And, in fact, outside the control tower, the ruins of the central pithead were still burning, a great swirl of flame and black smoke heading up toward the stars. And the zombie-bats were still circling, circling silently in the sky.

Demi, who had followed the hybrid's glance, said, "Yes, the main shaft is gone, it's buried. Most of the main pithead fell in twenty minutes ago."

"Now, only Shaft-2 remains," said Claire, "that's the only way they will be able to get out – if they can get to Shaft-2."

"Yes, Hybrid," said Robyn.

"I imagine it will be quite dangerous, trying to get out, I mean," said Demi Pfeiffer, her laser pistols still aimed at the gaping window, where a sooty hot night wind was drifting in, stirring papers and rattling loose wires, and where, far up in the air, the zombie-bats were circling.

"Yes, it is, it will be," said Claire, "dangerous, I mean." She looked down at the mind-collar sitting on the desk; it was dead: two dull red, flickering lights.

"You killed it," said Robyn, glancing up, her eyes, liquid with pride.

"The Mind-Child killed it," said Claire, laying a claw on Robyn's shoulder.

"Yes, it's dangerous over at Shaft-2," said Jane Fox, the ghoul, keeping guard by the door, "Absolutely Forbidden. No Access!"

"Very," said Rodriguez, drooling, "They declared it unstable and dangerous many decades ago, long before any of us came here." His long tongue flashed out and licked Jane's collar-bone, and she snuggled wetly against him.

Jane shivered with pleasure and splashed drool.

"Oh, please!" Demi Pfeiffer rolled her eyes. "Can't you randy teenager ghouls control yourselves!"

"Kill, kill, kill," Sammy shouted at HZ-2, and then he instantly regretted it as HZ-2 leaped straight at him.

He ducked, and he felt the hybrid's claw upon him, brushing his shoulder, and he fell down, splash, sprawling, into gooey mud puddle – not that acid flesh-eating, flesh-morphing stuff, thank the Devil – and …

He gulped.

His pet Sabrina was going to kill him.

All her old demon powers were there, but her intelligence was gone.

"Hey, hey, we're friends, remember," Sammy wanted to cry out, he wanted to scream, "Hey, you forgave me, remember, you …"

But his throat was too dry; all he did was squawk.

He closed his eyes; in an instant, the hybrid's claws and fangs would rip his throat out. Goodbye, dear Sammy, it was a miserable insignificant stupid life while it lasted, and now it's over, goddamn it, it's over!

But …

But …

Sabrina had leaped right over him, pushing him aside, and as Sammy fell to the ground, on his back, and gulped and opened his eyes, and looked up, wide-eyed, he saw Sabrina slam into a ghoul – and he was a real giant too – that must have been standing right behind Sammy – ready to pounce!

She was saving his life, the useless life of perpetual loser and pathetic sadist Samuel Franks!

Sammy watched wide-eyed, his heart racing, as Sabrina smashed the mutant against the cave wall, flattening its body with the force of the blow; her fangs flashed. She bit the ghoul's neck almost in two – black blood spurting out – then she tore its head off, and glanced at Sammy, her master, for approval.

"Good girl, Great girl," Sammy got up, unsheathed his laser gun, saying, "Follow me, HZ-2."

Helen was fighting two of the ghouls.

With Sabrina following him, Sammy ran over and shot one of the ghouls between the eyes. Its head exploded in a smoking geyser of blood and gray matter and bone fragments, messy, really messy.

Helen had just snapped the other ghoul's neck, and while the ghoul's body was still falling, its limbs flailing, its body gleaming that strange sickly ivory-white slick dripping glow, Helen turned toward Sammy, and she growled and Sammy saw that the growl was a grin and he gave her a thumbs-up and – miracle of miracles! – she echoed the thumbs-up – so maybe there was hope after all, their minds were not entirely gone, and Sammy said, since he was suddenly the leader – though he'd like his two friends back, truly – he shouted, "Come on, girls, come on, Helen, come on, Sabrina, let's catch up with the others. Let's get out of here."

He began to run, and the two hybrids ran right alongside him, like his own two trained wolfhounds.

Yeah, we've gotta catch up with the others – catch up with Norton – if we don't we're goners, thought Sammy Franks, as, running, and huffing and puffing, he squinted into the shadows of the immense cave, the eerie light from the phosphorescent water bubbling up and making gluey dripping looping patterns on the stalactites and stalagmites and on the arched walls of the cavern and from far ahead they heard screams and bursts of gunfire.

When Sammy and his two warrior Amazon hybrids pets joined the rest of the group, Sammy thought that, even with Helen and Sabrina in fighting form, they were all doomed.

The other hybrids were frozen and useless, and Bob Norton and the other humans were fighting with their backs to the wall.

Sammy was about to shout out, "Tell the hybrids to fight; they'll take orders."

His own hybrids, old HZ-2 and HZ-8, were well-trained. They knew old Sammy Franks was a splendid officer.

"Come on, girls, kill ghouls, kill ghouls," he shouted, and the two hybrids, Sabrina and Helen, waded into the fight, slashing at the ghouls, ribbons of blood and flesh and ghoul goo flying left right and center.

But none of the other hybrids followed, and it looked like there were just too many ghouls, the battle was going to be lost.

Julian Harvey heard Sammy shout the order, and he cottoned on: maybe Sarah would respond. It was worth a try!

"Hey, Sarah," he shouted, "Kill those ghouls! Kill those ghouls!"

The hybrid turned and stared at him. She did respond to her name, so that was good! But she remained frozen. Julian thought, it's not going to work ...

Three ghouls were closing in on him; they ignored the hybrids, which, frozen in place, looked like statues, seemingly just part of the background décor: stone, gray stone for Freddy, black anthracite for some of the others ...

Norton blazed away with his laser gun; next to Norton, Jimmy Ghoul was crouched down, shivering and drooling tears.

More ghouls poured toward them, coming out of side caves, climbing down the walls, appearing everywhere.

Norton heard Sammy shouting orders at his "girls," and he thought, damned right, mate – worth a chance! "Kill, Freddy, kill those ghouls, come on, Mate, kill those ghouls!"

Julian fired a last shot, realized his gun was empty and saw that an enormous ghoul, licking its lips, was staring straight at him, and Julian thought well, that's the end of it, my number is up ...

But, just as the ghoul leaped, Sarah did too.

CHAPTER 12 – BILLIE & SALLY

Leaving the two smoldering zombie-bat cadavers behind, V and Kat sprinted down the passageway toward the pithead of Main Shaft-2, racing for the old iron door that led to the hanger. It was half-open.

Acting with one mind – yes, now, really one mind – they stopped on either side of the door, and then, again acting with one mind, they swung through the door, weapons leveled, ready to fire, bracketing with their sights any and every danger spot – little red target dots dancing in the shadows over the whole area.

It was empty – nobody …

But there was something – just the whisper of a presence.

It seemed to V like laughter, inaudible and unheard laughter, the laughter of a god or of a devil – yes, seeping over, seeping through the fabric of the universe, something was lurching toward them, an evil power, a …

"There's something," said Kat, "but I don't know what."

"Yes, there is something …" V took two steps forward.

Kat followed.

The hanger, inside, was huge, eerie, and vaguely menacing. It was ancient, a vast, towering steel and iron structure, its roof lost in shadows, the whole space crowded with dark hulks of antique machinery, vast generators, motors, winches, pulleys, cables, giant oil storage tanks, and cable cars on overhead rails, small vans and fork-lifts that looked like they hadn't been used in more than a century. It smelled of grease and rust and oil and clay and deep earth – and gasoline. And it whispered: Breezes were coming from the far end of the building, from the Main Shaft-2 opening, breezes coming from far below, the damp air full of the smells of ancient earth, and another smell too, the smell of blood, of carnage, of ancient flesh eaten, and of fresh flesh eaten and still bleeding. Hanging chains rattled; beams creaked softly, rusty cables clinked ominously.

Kat and V sniffed the air.

The soaring hanger rippled with sensuous multicolored ribbons and rivers of air and scents and smells – memories and colors and stories in drifting whirling molecules. In some ways, for a hybrid, it was a delicious, tasty place.

Kat sniffed again; her nostrils quivered; she wanted to growl; a gurgling rose in her throat.

The hybrid within her was stirring. It was a thirsty, werewolf-like creature, but it was reptilian, alien, a slippery, slithery shape, a beast being born, and howling beneath the moon, a rising tide, a ripple of excitement tingled, it flooded down her belly, up her thighs, like sex, like lust; she tensed her muscles, whispering, *"Down, down, down!"*

And, from far down below, perceptible to V's super-human sense of smell, came the smell of death; somewhere down below was an immense charnel house – the smell of rotting flesh came to her nostrils in faint whiffs, just suggestions. V knew that, even as Kat's inner morph began, Kat was probably not aware of these savory nuances, not yet. Soon she would be, but not just yet.

V licked her lips.

Saliva rose.

Her thighs and belly tensed; her teeth sent off sparks, they were eager to morph into fangs, she swallowed a gush of ravenous saliva.

The killings in the charnel house below the hanger were old – too ancient to have been done by the zombie-bats. It must have been the ghouls, the ghouls of the underworld. They must have dragged their kills down into the underworld, and there they piled up the remains, the bodies, and bones – a cavern of the dead, a collection of trophies. V sniffed and half closed her eyes. It would be a large-scale version of Deep and Daisy and Bounce's hideaway and shrine, where they kept their kills; the images came to her, an atavistic memory contained in the writhing, air-borne tapestry of scent: she saw it, a handsome Mexican girl, naked, chained to a wall, a young boy, naked, one arm torn off at the shoulder and cauterized, chained to wall. So, yes, she could see it. Sometimes the ghouls kept their human captives as prisoners, to eat later, or slowly, fresh meat, a limb or slice at a time, or for ritual sacrifice, underground, or on the surface, in the desert, under the full moon. Or, yes, they kept them underground and ate them a bit at a time – an arm, another arm, a leg, a nose, an ear, another leg …

"The place is a museum." Kat was breathing steadily now – her Cosmos Centurion training was super-strong. It had driven back the thirsty alien rising within her. She took regular deep breaths and stared at one of the towering gas-powered generators. "I think that dates from the 21st century, maybe the 20th or even the 19th."

V glanced at Kat: the dim diffuse light rippled on Kat's catsuit, a burnished caress on the tensed muscles and perfectly toned body; she was an ebony statue, a Cosmos Centurion First Class – the highest pitch of human perfection, and yet no longer human.

V blinked, her gaze fixed on Kat; more saliva rose; she felt hungry, very hungry. She felt desire too. Death gave her a thirst for life.

"What?" Kat turned toward V, lips parted, a bright, tentative smile.

"The pithead is there, and the entry to Main Shaft-2," V said, blinking amorously, brushing away her thirst, her desire, and brushing away the ghoulish slaughterhouse images that flooded her mind. "It's at the far end of the hanger, under the winches."

"Now," Kat was ready, tensed, like a coiled spring.

"Yes."

They leaped, and they ran, dodging along the row of giant machines, slipping in and out of cover behind huge pistons, giant steam pipes, until they came to the last of a set of generators and winches. There was a vast open space – separating them from the opening to Main Shaft-2. The building was even higher here; the lofty roof housed the elevators and winches for abandoned Shaft-2, which went down perhaps at least a mile, maybe more.

"Wait," V raised a gloved hand; she sensed something; the enemy, the Boy, he was here, his presence was like a hemorrhaging invasion of energy from another universe. Whatever He was, whatever It was, was already here – or one of his proxies, one of his slaves.

And she sensed something very physical, very real.

Time bombs ...

Time bombs set to go off.

Or were they bombs that could be triggered – by the push of a button, by the slightest pressure of a gloved hand?

They were both – they were on timers, but also easy to trigger.

The bombs were there, the countdown was ticking, V sensed it, but the bomb at the shaft head had not been left alone. The person who had planted the bomb was still nearby.

It was a servant of the Boy.

A very special servant – how do I know this?

She captured a vague image, difficult to seize …

Right now, that person, or whatever it was, was down the mine shaft, laying other bombs, V was sure of it. Now, she and Kat could wait until that person – the bomb expert – came up to the surface, and then …

Then they would deal with this servant of the Devil.

Two-hundred feet underground, down in Shaft-2, 18-year-old Billie McAdams dangled free, attached only to a single synthetic cable.

The steel-tipped toes of her boots were braced against the wall.

It was a spooky, scary place to be.

Down below her was a long, long way: a long way to fall.

Strange echoes pressed in – plop-plop dripping sounds, crumbling gravelly cascades, dribbling water, squishy clay, oozing. The darkness enfolded her like a weighty fluid; the sensations were as palpable, as clinging, as a shroud. She swallowed. There was the dizzying awareness, too, imminent vertigo. Below her, the Shaft went down – a mile, a whole mile – even more. And there was the sense that the lower depths seethed with strange creatures.She could almost see them; she could certainly hear them.

Then, suddenly, she remembered, yet again, that her mind and body were not her own; they had been kidnapped; she had been turned into a puppet; her body was doing things she did not want it to do – her fingers and hands were busy skillfully doing things she most definitely did not want them to do.

The Boy, the Boy, had caused all this.

The Boy – the Evil One, her demon lover, her nemesis, her jailer and torturer, the beautiful, tender, evil, cruel, horrible Boy, El Niño …

"Damn it, damn it!"

So here she was, hanging from a slender cable, a prisoner in her own flesh, a captive doll, a puppet, dangling 200 feet underground.

"Damn it, damn it!" her hands cautiously adjusted the belt-clips one at a time, shifting her position carefully. From far below sounds came, weird shrill cries.

Sally – her incubus – the spirit which had invaded and possessed her body – whispered to Billie, in a silken insinuating tone – just as if she were telling Billie some really frightening bedtime ghost story – that the place was haunted by ghoulish mutants that ate people. "It's true, Billie. You thought that the zombie-bats, the True Believers, were the only horror! No, there are other horrors," Sally's voice laughed in Billie's head. "The Boy taught us wisely.

Humans and Cosmos have, by their ungodly experiments, created bio-poisons that spawn mutants. Or sometimes humans just created mutants for fun – or for profit! Phosphorous glowing cats, talking rabbits, little girls with goatish horns, genius rats, chess-playing squirrels! Scary, eh! The mutants are hubris and nemesis all in one. With them, they bring destruction, absolute destruction. You will see, Billie, these mutant ghouls are really scary!"

Billie half expected some horrible toad-like venomous ghoul-like creature would come leaping up the Shaft and rip her legs off or to leap up and cling to her and start chewing on her thigh or reach out with its claws and rip her face off. Ugh! Yuk!

And, then, Sally explained, there was even worse stuff; still farther down, were the hybrids, those super-evil reptilian creatures. "Oh, the hybrids, Billie, they are the most horrible of all!"

The lower depths of Main Shaft-2 positively seethed with evil.

Billie's hands, working by themselves, using all of Sally's experience and savvy, skilfully locked a pack of explosives into place.

"Okay, that was one more done!" Sally's voice, sounding very satisfied, echoed in Billie's head. "Each one has its own timer, so if one fails, or if the manual trigger fails, well, it will all still work!"

Billie's body – controlled by Sally – pushed itself away from the shaft wall, drifted out and twirled around in midair, using the lifeline, kicking over to another position, making sure the lifeline didn't get tangled or stuck in any of the old cross-bars or beams or struts. Every gesture was guided by Sally.

Trapped in her mind, Billie fretted: It's like I'm dead; it's like I'm a ghost; here, in my own body, I'm only along for the ride.

"Okay, here!" Billie's lips uttered the words, but it was Sally speaking; Billie could follow Sally's thinking as if it were her own; in fact, the two of them seemed more and more to be merging into one. "Okay, here," her voice said. She needed to place this explosive pack precisely in the angle where these two particular struts joined, so, when it blew, it would force the two struts apart, and, wham, the whole thing would come tumbling down!

Damn, it was slippery. Billie shivered. The sweat was sticky like glue inside her skintight combat catsuit, like every inch of her body had been basted and slathered in creepy hot slime. Her fingers, piloted by Sally, suddenly seemed extra-clumsy. She concentrated. More screams came from far, far below, they echoed faintly. She shivered. What horrors!

"Don't worry about it, Billie," said Sally's voice, "I'm in control."

"Okay, I won't, I won't worry," Billie replied, using her inner voice. She'd decided to lay low, to crouch down in her own mind and not fight Sally. If she started a mind-fight, she might lose her hold – well, her body might lose its hold – on the beams and struts, and her body would fall to its death, far below, among those squealing mutants or hybrids or whatever they were.

God, this was a horrible place.

If Billie had believed in God, she would have prayed to Him to get her out of this place, to take her far away, to save her, body and soul!

Foul air wafted upwards; Billie almost choked.

She shivered. There was that smell again, the smell of carrion, of death, blood and rot, and seething maggots.

From below came more squealing and shouts.

While her mind worried, her fingers were deftly fitting extra wires into another electronic timer.

"You are sweet, Billie," said Sally's voice, insinuating itself into the very fibers of her mind, "I know this is hard. It's even hard for me, and I've got lots of experience! I mean, for instance, I really like blowing things up, particularly trains: super-trains – that's really cool; there was this one time I was out in the desert, in the sun, with the wind blowing my hair against my cheeks – you know what that feels like, your hair blowing free, strands of perfumed hair caressing your cheeks, lemon shampoo heated by the sun, I mean before they cropped your hair down to stubble, right, Billie? – It was great, crouching down in the hot breeze and the sun, working on that railway line – and you know what I did?"

"No, Sally, what did you do?" Billie figured she'd better humor this crazy terrorist girl, she'd better humor this strange larval-like dead creature that was nestled, like a highly intelligent, poisonous worm, inside her mind, inside her soul.

"Well, Billie, I neutralized the anti-terrorist rail sensors, rerouting their circuits onto a loop, so it looked like everything was normal!"

"That was really cool, Sally," said Billie, trying to use words Sally liked, flashy words that Billie, with her Fundamentalist and Biblical background and with her austere, stern, pagan sense of dignity, would never have used.

"Yeah, it was cool. The controllers were totally fooled, they had no idea what the fuck was going to hit them. I could take my time, enjoy the moment, and so I listened to the breeze, the wind in the grass, the hot sun lowering over the fields – it was, like, a mystical experience, Billie, the stuff like when you feel you are close to God and to our Lord, the Boy, and all that – and so

I carefully laid out the five different explosive pieces to maximize the impact when the super train, loaded with snobby Cosmos, came roaring toward us, 600 kilometers an hour."

"Wow!"

"Yeah, Billie, it was one of the happiest moments in my life."

"Gosh, I wish I'd been there!"

"Yeah, you would have loved it: Whoosh, in the burgeoning twilight, the beautiful rose-and-turquoise twilight; whoosh, the train, that had been traveling, like I said, at 600 kilometers an hour, just went up – whoosh! It made a beautiful pattern, the cars pole-vaulting and somersaulting over each other, and then landing and exploding, and bouncing and bursting into flame, and crashing and rolling over on their sides, glittering, flaming hunks of metal in clouds of dust."

"Awesome!"

"It really was, Billie, it really was totally awesome. We raced up to the ruined train; fires were burning all along the track, lighting up the red dusk, and then the night. It was weird, but there were even a few survivors."

"Oh?"

"Cosmos are tough, some of them. We shot them – most were dying anyway."

"Oh."

"Some fought back, but they were injured, and too few to make a difference. So, one after the other, we killed them."

"Oh."

"Yeah, we had to show the Cosmos that we could terrify and kill them, men, women, or children, anywhere anytime, that we would stop at nothing." Sally's voice went on and on, and as she spoke about the "hegemony" of the Cosmos, and about evading detection and about guerrilla war, and lofty ideals and about creating a new world by destroying the old. Billie caught an image of what Sally must have been like when she was still alive and had her own body to live in: a very young woman, red hair, freckles, very neatly sculpted features. Sally was pretty, really pretty, and, there she was, standing in the killer's stance, her legs wide apart, torn jeans and tight T-shirt, holding an old-fashioned machine pistol, ready to shoot. Yes, Sally was standing over a young woman who was cradling a wounded child. "Sorry," Sally said, "This is not personal." And she shot the child, then the woman. Or was it the woman first, then the child? The image blurred. It was very confusing: so much was happening at that point, so much was happening so quickly.

"What was the group?" Billie asked the ghost of the young woman in her head, "The group you were with?"

"The Western World Revolutionary Sisterhood," said Sally's voice; it had a slightly distracted air. "Its aim is the downfall of the Cosmos and the Coming of the Reign of the Righteous under the protection of our Lord, the Boy, who had not yet at that particular time come among us. That's how I met our Lord – in a study group." Right now, Billie's fingers were screwing in some of the final wires; Billie felt that Sally was concentrating on the physical act – the screwdriver, the screw head, the slippery surfaces, and the dull light that made Billie – and Sally – want to fall asleep. It wasn't easy. There was something soporific about dangling 200 feet underground in the stuffy death-laden air and the dull bluish-gray light of phosphorous. *A study group?* Billie wondered; it didn't seem like the Boy she knew.

"A bomb is different from looking into the eyes of someone and killing them personally, say, with a pistol or a knife or a straight-razor," said Sally, "Like with the train, I pushed a button from three miles away and so I killed 800 people. 800 people from three miles away, that is impersonal. It's more like art than anything. It has the impersonality of great art, if you know what I mean. It's godlike. It really has nothing to do with you, except for the feeling of a job well done, naturally." Sally pushed the timer; it began to flash numbers: another countdown had begun.

"Professional pride," said Billie, forcing her lips to move, saying it out loud, exerting a bit of control over her kidnapped body.

"You got it," Sally was screwing in the last link, "That's it! Professional pride! Craftsmanship! Exactly!"

"But you've had the other experience too," Billie said, "I mean, like, face-to-face experiences." Right now, Sally was pushing Billie's body away from the two crossbeam struts, out into the void, and Billie's body spun, suspended at the end of a thin spinning cable, out in the dreamy dimness. It made her want to fall asleep.

Time slowed.

Billie's body spun.

She tried not to look down. She hoped Sally wouldn't look down. If she – if they – looked down, Billie thought she might be sick. But there was no problem – Sally didn't want to look down either; she was concentrating on the next anchor point for the explosives.

"Oh, yeah, I can kill face to face; I'm a real professional," Sally sounded elated, "I take pride in my work. There were these two cops and a professor. This was in Los Angeles, Cosmos Country, under the L.A. Cosmos Dome, which has now, as of two days ago, been destroyed! Thank the Boy! The Boy Be Praised! The cops had beaten one of the WWRS girls to death. She was a friend of mine; we had shared the same cell during a police roundup. I saw the video: they cracked her skull open, smashing down so hard their truncheons peeled off her scalp, cracked her skull, gray matter oozing out, they beat her with metal truncheons, thud, thud, thud; she was already half-conscious, trapped, slammed down against the asphalt, unarmed, helpless, not even trying to defend herself, being hammered by those thugs, oh, she was so utterly beautiful, and sweet, really sweet, they smashed her face, blinded her, and I think in the end they broke every bone in her body, or almost; I was told to kill the men that did it and I did, when they were off duty, just getting home, I killed them – neat, though, no beating, a bullet between the eyes and just enough time to tell them why they were dying."

"Did they repent?"

Sally laughed, "No time for repentance! Just fear – regret maybe – they would have begged, if I'd given them time, I could see the words about to form on their lips, I could see the hope flash in their eyes, and so I just pulled the trigger – I didn't want to listen to their bullshit. I have no time, no pity for those bastards! They were good family men; but they were sadists, too, they took pleasure in it, in inflicting pain. They weren't Cosmos, just thugs. Cosmos are killers, but usually, they have style; usually, a Cosmos will avoid cruelty, and Cosmos don't like mess; they have esthetics – and even, face to face, they feel compassion, not all of them, and not most of the Centurions, who are hardened killers, but most civilian Cosmos, personally, they're okay. I've even heard that the President-Leader is a nice guy, personally, I mean, if you ever get to meet him. But you should have seen her, my girlfriend. She was my chum and my lover. She looked like a bloodied rag doll that had no bones, her smashed face was flattened to paste, a sort of empty, smeared-out into a howling rubber Halloween mask, pure ugly grotesque, pure horror, and not a single bone left whole, crushed into bone meal. Damn it!"

"You mentioned a professor …"

"Oh, yeah, Professor Philip January, he was a real bastard – cute little thin mustache, a permanent tan, teeth so bright and perfect they looked like dentures, curly blond hair. He wrote some of the special laws and decrees that allowed the Cosmos government to suspend people's rights and to erase personalities – you know, zero you out mentally to drooling empty-eyed slack-jawed idiot status, transform you into a Sub or into a Non-Human or a Commercial Sex Toy."

"Gosh," said Billie, forcing her lips and tongue and vocal cords to pronounce the word; it took immense effort.

"And he was one of the guys behind the really bright idea of implanting delayed-action diseases in dissidents so that they could be infected with a killer virus or bacterium at a later date – if they misbehaved. You set off the remote control trigger, and some man or woman or kid suddenly gets crippled, or goes crazy, or is morphed into a stinking pile of maggoty rot, or just plain drops dead, or some woman loses all her teeth in an instant, all the cartilage and muscle that hold her face together. Really neat stuff like that."

"Horrible!" Billie breathed out the word. Suspended in hell, that's where she was. All these horrors were happening and had happened – she could see them as if they were happening in front of her.

"Yeah, it's unbelievable, right?" Sally's voice seethed inside Billie's head. "The evil some people do! The guy was a mass murderer and a very inventive sadist, but with clean hands, if you know what I mean, all hygienic and done at a distance. He sat in his lab and cooked things up that killed and maimed people – kids too! There are so many ways to murder and maim people, hygienic ways, clean ways, distant ways, impersonal ways, like bombs, guided missiles, drones, bio-bombs, poisoned gas – or just evil policies, you just change a law and starve people to death, or push a button, or design a lethal new gizmo or virus – and you've destroyed or ruined thousands, or millions of lives. And you don't have to look anybody in the eye, and you go out to dinner that night and have a cool beer or savor the bouquet of a special this-season-only wine."

"I didn't know ..."

"Yeah, well, Billie, let me tell you, you're an innocent. You've lived in a hayseed fundamentalist world, out in the boondocks, in God's own Dead Lands and in the Desert, far beyond the dynamic urban reality that pulses with today and what's coming tomorrow, with the future. That's why you are an angel. You don't know how the world works," Sally's voice had taken on a hard edge. "My mom and dad – yeah, I actually had a mom and dad, they disappeared after Professor Philip January's Code, North America-Homeland Cosmos Security Directive number 23-B-5, came into effect. They were 'disappeared' – like people used to say when such thoughts and expressions were allowed. They're dead. I'm sure of it. They were taken to some godforsaken place, and shot in the back of the head, and dumped into a ditch, and had quicklime and acid poured over them, and so there was nothing left, not a thing! So I sent Doctor Philip January to hell where he belongs!"

Billie caught a mental image of a tear-stained face: It was Sally, her neat, precise features, her sculpturally delineated lips, her freckles, the red hair so curly in luscious unruly strands down both sides of her face, and then another image; it was of the guy, the Professor, turning around, saying, "Yes, what do you want …?" and his eyes opening wide – terror it seemed – Sally was about to kill him – and then his forehead exploding, splatter, splash, and then nothing, the images were gone – both the Professor and Sally disappeared.

Billie blinked. Once again, she had been inside Sally's memories. Reality zoomed back. Billie – her body – was hanging two hundred feet down the mineshaft, dangling from a single cable, her face only a few inches away from one of the main struts supporting this section of the shaft, her fingers – controlled by Sally – were placing the last explosive packet – a ten-inch-long package that looked like a small computer. Her eyes checked the code – and Sally forced Billie's body around, and, through Billie's eyes, Sally checked the supports and the position of the package.

For Billie, it was like being trapped in a nightmare; she could not control her body, and, even more, there was this voice inside her head, this presence – Sally!

"Yeah," Sally said, "That is perfect, just right, Billie, congratulations."

"Thanks, I think," said Billie.

"Don't be modest. You've been great. Our Lord – He belongs to both of us, you know, and we belong to Him – Our Lord, the Boy, will be proud of you! This little packet will bring down this side of the shaft, and I know from the old schematics that there is a layer of sand behind the facing, so the sand will pour in, hundreds of tons of sand. Then, there would be no way out, not a single crack. Further down, there's a layer of wet clay that will flood out and seal the Shaft for good, like cement, which is even better. There will be absolutely no way out!"

"No way out," muttered Billie.

"No way out: The hybrids and all the others, the guards, the technicians, will be sealed in their graves – forever – and the people prisoners."

"And the people …" Billie echoed, "Are there people? Will they die too?"

"Oh, the people, really, Billie, do you think 'people' count? Everybody massacres 'people.' It's open season on 'people'! Only Cosmos are valuable. People, non-Cosmos people, are a dime a dozen. Dissenters are worthless, nobody will miss them; in reality, for the world, they are dead already, and have been for years. We're doing them a favor, ending the agony. We people are as cheap as the pebbles in the desert. Grow up, kid! Grow up, and get rid of those stars in your eyes!"

"Okay, I guess." Billie really didn't know whether she was giving in to Sally or merely playing for time, hoping, probably in vain, that something – anything – would happen.

"We are finished here." Sally's voice sounded triumphant.

"We are finished," Billie echoed. So it had been done, everything was prepared; the explosives were planted, the timers were ticking, the bombs would go off, Main Shaft-2 would explode in a gusher of glory, and be sealed for all time, all those evil creatures far below would be doomed.

"Up we go, darling Billie, let me take you, my darling little puppet, my little moppet, oh, my doll, let's go up top."

Billie swallowed, "Okay, yes, Sally, let's go."

Like a robot, with Sally controlling every move, every muscle, the safety cable spooling back into its case, Billie's body, arms and legs moving automatically, climbed the metal emergency ladder up the side of the shaft – the 200 feet up to the surface.

It was weird. Billie felt everything, every sensation her body offered, her gloved fingers gripping the rungs, her boots stepping upwards, but she was not controlling any of the movements. She was just along for the ride.

Her body got to the top, stepped up the last rungs of the ladder, grabbed a metal handhold on one of the steel columns, climbed out of the shaft, and stood up and looked around.

The vast cavernous space of the hanger was full of ghostly sounds – creaking cables, buckling metal, phantom breezes, and hissing, sifting sand.

And somewhere beyond, outside the hanger, the monster zombie-bats the Boy had created were screeching; Billie could hear them. It was still hard to believe that such things existed – and that He had made them – even though she had been a witness to the miracle, present when he created them. They gave Billie the shivers; she had known some of them when they were human. Why hadn't the Boy turned her into one of those things?

"Because he loves you, you silly nit," Sally's voice was almost affectionate.

"He loves me," Billie sighed. It was not the sort of love she wanted – this mingling of fear and desire – pure lust – of revolt and servitude.

"He loves you in spite of everything, Billie."

"What? … In spite of what?"

"You are his Judas, Billie," said Sally, "you will betray him; he has put you – he will put you – in the way of temptation. And of course, you are immune too, you are invulnerable, that's the real reason – and that's the reason he loves you – because he can't have you. He couldn't have changed you, if he wanted to."

"Immune?"

"Yes, immune. You are immune because you don't believe in Him, not the way you should. You have a blind spot in your soul, which makes you a skeptic and a sinner and free."

"I don't feel free."

"But you are! Your mind is your fortress. Remember? Well, enough idle chat – our time has come."

"Yes," Billie said, still hoping something – some miracle – would happen: an avenging angel would come swooping down from heaven, a dragon would rise up from the earth, an earthquake or sand blizzard would … Suddenly, she felt a tremor of anticipation. It rippled through her belly. Yes, maybe something was going to happen! While down in the mine shaft, she'd thought, with one part of her mind, that she'd heard shots. Her earphone – the earphone the Lord had given her – surprisingly high tech for the Lord – all her new-fangled equipment – had just muttered static. All the metal in the hanger and the shaft must have blocked communications, or maybe something else – maybe something else …

"What about the timers," Billie managed to say, "They will trigger in five minutes."

"I don't want to wait for the timers. I want to do it now! This instant!" Sally sounded drunk with excitement. "I want us to die in a pillar of flame!"

There was some other force nearby; Billie felt it …

"Come on, Billie, let's push the button. Let's end it."

"Just a second, I want a last look." Billie took a deep breath.

"You want a last look at what?"

"At the world, at life, at this …" Billie looked around. The huge hanger was a spooky place. There really was nobody. But still, she felt something – maybe it was an illusion … Whatever it was, if it was anything, it would soon be blasted to smithereens in a series of explosions and drowned in a welter of violence and blood, for the forces of evil were gathering, the forces of the

Boy. Outside, the zombie-bats were whirling in the empty black sky filled with stars and the cold dead moon. On the other side of the camp, Main Shaft-1 had already collapsed in a volcano of flame. The colossal column of fire was still towering upwards, its roots extending far down into the earth, exterminating everything below. Somehow Billie sensed all of this, somehow she *knew* ...

Now, for her, for Billie McAdams, the moment of death had come.

Looking back on it all now, on her whole life, Billie's eyes filled with tears.

"Enough, Billie, You've had your look," Sally whispered, "Push the button! Push it for me," Sally was begging now, poor Sally who had lost her mother and father and her best friend, poor Sally who was already dead, too, shot down by a Centurion, poor Sally whose ghost was kept alive in some sort of limbo by the Boy, so he could use her, exploit her ...

Billie's body tensed, ready to die, her thumb twitched over the button; then she said, out loud, "No, Sally, I'm not going to push it!"

"Billie!" Sally's voice was furious.

"No, I will not. I refuse to!" Billie concentrated; she must regain control of her body; it was a tug of war; she could feel the immense pressure from inside her pushing down on her thumb; it was like her head, too, was going to burst; if she lost, if her thumb pushed the button, then she would die, and all the others would die too – the prisoners, the hybrids, and whatever those screaming creatures were down below, ghouls, maybe, yes ghouls. "No, I will not push the button!"

"Yes, yes, yes – PUSH THE DAMNED BUTTON!"

"NO, I WILL NOT," Billie drew her thumb back – maybe she was winning, maybe if she could just resist ... just keep resisting ... She felt like her mind and body were being torn apart. Her head was being twisted inside, twisted and contorted into a pretzel, all the wires crossed, sparks flying, short-circuits spreading; she imagined that steam – like in a cartoon she once saw – must be coming out of her ears.

"The Boy orders you to do this, Billie! Just think! He orders you to do it!"

"No! I will not!"

"He is your God!"

"He is *not* my God!"

"What?"

"I told you: he is *not* my God!"

"This is blasphemy, Billie, this is apostasy!"

"You said I was free – and so now I claim my freedom."

"You are not free really – you are a miserable sinner, your refusal, your denial is apostasy!"

"I don't care what it is. I will not push the damned button."

"But, Billie, if you do not push the button, you will let all the subterranean demons loose, they will wreak havoc on the world, they will defy the Boy, they will defile everything sacred, they will ally themselves with the Cosmos, they will enshrine all that is not Holy, they will desecrate ..."

"No, no, no – I will not!" Billie wondered at her resistance. In any case, with the timers set below, it would all blow up in less than five minutes. Was it merely because she wanted to live, just a few minutes more? *Am I a coward?*

Sally made a supreme effort – TOTAL FORCE: Billie's thumb plunged.

Oh, my God, Billie thought, so this is it: the last moment – and death ...

I can't resist! I'm not strong enough

But ...

Wham!

A ripple of gunfire exploded, on the ceiling. Without thinking, Billie looked up ... thumb suspended. Sally stopped pushing.

"What the hell?" Sally's voice screamed.

Wham!

V tensed, focusing all her attention, muscles ready to spring. The moment had come. The woman warrior, a terrorist, had come up from the mine shaft. Now she was crouched over the machinery at the top of the pit, right next to the elevator shaft. She was wearing an armored black skinsuit, a bullet-proof bustier, and at her hip, she had a laser handgun, and over her shoulder, she carried a machine gun. Her sleek, skintight uniform almost made her look like Kat, or like V herself, a sleek slender mirror image. V caught a glimpse of her profile – she looked, she *was*, very young.

So, a girl terrorist – just what we need!

The Evil Force – the Boy – whatever or whoever it was – had human accomplices; not everyone had been turned into a zombie-bat or a ghoul or a computer virus.

As V and Kat watched, the girl took off her helmet and laid it on the ground beside her, with her anti-projectile goggles.

V nodded. Probably sweat was getting in the girl's eyes, making it difficult to work on the bomb; now she's more vulnerable – perhaps a single shot to the head from here would put her out of action, but that was dangerous – even in falling over the girl might trigger the bomb – the commands seemed to be all in place.

V signaled to Kat to duck behind a pillar; it was a giant rusty steel pillar that soared up in the lofty shadows of the hanger, cables hanging down everywhere like the dangling rusty innards and entrails of some ancient disemboweled beast.

Ducking down, slithering forward, Kat flattened herself against the rusty metal; she turned her wraparounds toward V, and the wraparounds caught and reflected a beam of moonlight coming through a gap in the metal roof. Kat watched for V's next move, her mental question honed in: *Do we shoot her?*

"I think so," V transmitted, still uncertain, and the prospect made V unhappy; she didn't like killing women, perhaps because she was one. Male humans were easier to exterminate, easier to drain to the last feeble drop of blood, more pleasant to decapitate. Only rarely had she feasted on the blood of a woman. Of course, there were a few tasty exceptions … In fact, one beautiful evil terrorist, deep in the jungles of Borneo, had been particularly … delicious. Well, enough of that! In this life, one often has to make cruel choices. V knelt down on the concrete and raised the sniper-rifle. If the girl knew she was being watched, she might set off the explosion right away; her gloved fingers were only inches away from the button.

V's finger closed on the trigger.

There was a clamor from far below – a high-pitched squeaking, growling, and a then a scream – it was hard to tell if it was a human scream or animal – or perhaps mutant of some kind.

V relaxed her finger; the trigger remained ready, just the slightest pressure … and the girl's head would explode.

"Mutants, more ghouls," V muttered to herself, transmitting the thought to Kat.

"The dangerous kind, I'll bet, not little cuties we can keep for pets," Kat answered. "Not Bounce, and Deep and Daisy!" She, too, was aiming at the girl who had stopped working on the detonator.

"Whatever they are, they are coming up the shaft," V thought, sharing the thought with Kat.

"The clocks are ticking, then," Kat glanced at V. If they had to confront an army of ghouls, a terrorist, and a set of explosives, all at the same time, well, it could get a trifle complicated.

The terrorist girl stood up. She unsheathed her machine gun, and she leaned over what was probably, undoubtedly, the control mechanism. She could almost certainly trigger the explosion manually – if she did that …

V steadied her aim.

If the girl did trigger the explosion, the whole of Main Shaft-2 would blow up, and collapse and everybody and everything would be buried under tons of rock and sand and mud.

Everybody would die.

The screams from below were louder – total chaos, a battle, a life-or-death struggle, seemed to be taking place far below – V sensed something. Hybrids, hybrids were down below, she sensed their minds, their presence; then, suddenly, the minds faded; there was nothing, just squealing and shouting and shots.

Kat slipped away from the column and came over to join V. She slipped her wraparounds up over her forehead and raised an eyebrow: *Well, do we shoot the girl or try to take her alive?*

V shrugged. She didn't know. This was unusual – V hesitating.

She glanced at the girl, focusing in, grasping for the girl's mind, trying to tease out memories, readings, her past, her skills, her intentions.

Yes, she was quite young, maybe 18, she was an explosives expert, she was not a soldier-terrorist; she had, though, personally shot three people in her young career, two police officers and a university professor. And she had killed hundreds in bomb attacks – she was very skillful, ruthless, and – with all that – rather naïve.

Right now, she was deciding, blow the whole thing up right away – and she would die – when it exploded – or she could follow the plan and let the timers blow the pithead and shaft to smithereens; the second choice which would give her time to escape.

Even from 50 meters, V could smell the fear on the girl's skin, the girl's indecision: to die or not to die, to kill or not to kill …

But there was something else.

"Wait a minute," V whispered.

"What?" Kat's lips barely moved.

"The girl is possessed – there are two personalities in that woman."

"Two personalities?"

"Yes, somehow another personality – an incubus – a tool of The Boy –the Evil One – the incubus calls him "The Lord" – has invaded the physical woman – the young woman no longer controls her gestures, her movements. Her mind is struggling against the invader, but she can't control it. Whatever the Evil Power is, it has inserted somebody else into her mind."

"She's a puppet?

"Yes, the puppet master is inside her head. She's not herself." V had an intimation: that the girl was the pure one she had glimpsed in her vision of the Boy and his conquests. She was the purest of the pure. Yes, she was the pure one, the unconquered spirit!

"So, what do we do?"

"I'm going in. Cover me with a distraction. Shoot at the ceiling. I'm going to leap."

"Okay," Kat nodded, aimed …

V leaped.

Kat fired. A storm of bullets hit the ceiling, echoed around the vast hanger; it sounded like a whole army was on the attack – bang, bang, bang rattle, rattle, rattle. The sound echoed and ricocheted from the beams and roof of the hanger.

V landed, softly, just behind the girl, and as she landed, she saw that girl's thumb was hovering over the button – just about an inch separated life and survival from death and oblivion.

The thumb twitched and plunged.

And so did V; she plunged.

This, for Billie, was a life-and-death struggle. For more than five minutes, Sally had been screaming in Billie's head: "Do it now! Damn it, do it now, Billie!" Billie had fought back, her thumb poised over the button.

Sally, perched inside Billie's mind, was proud of her work; she was truly skilled, and she wasn't afraid to die. In any case, she was already dead. And, as for young Billie, well, she knew that the Boy loved her – in his own twisted way he loved her – so Sally, inside Billie's head, thought that killing Billie would be a bonus, like, posthumous revenge, like, even from beyond the grave, getting rid of a rival for the Boy's affections, and Billie, intuitively, realized this, she was, she realized, eavesdropping on Sally's thoughts: Sally was thinking: *Billie has a body, she will die, but, as I am pure spirit, I will survive: the Boy will be mine, mine alone!*

"Do it, Billie, do it now!"

Billie tensed: maybe not even the Boy knew about this twist in the plot, this bit of jealousy, this desire Sally had to kill a rival, to kill Billie, or was the Boy omniscient, like God? Billie gritted her teeth; she knew she would be killing a lot of people if she pushed the button – not to mention that, pushing the button here and now, she would be killing herself.

"I am NOT going to do this!" She bit her lip hard to make sure she could feel her own body, to make sure she could command it.

"Yes, you are, yes, you are!"

"But you and I will die too if I press it now."

"I am already dead, dear Billie."

"I'm sorry," said Billie, the expression of sympathy came automatically, but Billie thought, even as she said it, that it was a pretty funny thing to say to some sort of ghost the Boy had conjured up to possess her mind – after what she had seen of people and of religion, Billie had decided she would not use or even think the word "soul" – "I'm very sorry you are dead, but I am not going to do this!"

Sally's voice screamed. "YES, YES, YOU BITCH – YOU ARE!!!!"

Billie watched in horror as her own thumb hovered and hesitated, maybe an inch away from death. A huge weight was trying to push it down. Billie pulled back with all her might.

"No, I am very sorry, Sally: but I am NOT going to do this!" Billie struggled, as if with an invisible wrestler, somebody inside her, trying to force her finger down, down, down, to push that innocent-looking little red button with the rounded top, which looked like a cute little mushroom. The pressure was enormous. It felt like her thumb, and her hand might explode under the effort.

"YES, YOU BITCH, YOU ARE GOING TO PUSH IT!"

There were more screams and ululations from below – some terrible infernal underworld battle was taking place.

"NO, NO, AND NO!"

As she screamed these words in her mind, Billie had a sudden vision. The only word for it was "vision." She *saw*, as if in a glowing architectural schematic, the structure and layout of the 5,000-foot deep Main Shaft-2, she *saw* old drifts and side tunnels reaching off of it, she *saw* the ancient cave system that lay near the bottom of the shaft, and she *saw*, as if they were small halos of light, creatures down there, creatures struggling to escape, to survive. Their only way out, she knew, was Main Shaft-2. If she pushed the button, they would all die.

There were people down there, layer upon layer of people – political prisoners, dissidents, non-conformists, just ordinary people, often, people often casually or by accident caught up in the horror, and there were children. *Children!*

"YES, YES, YES – PUSH THE BUTTON!"

"NO, I WILL NOT," Billie drew her thumb back – maybe she was winning, maybe …

"OUR LORD ORDERS YOU TO DO THIS, BILLIE! JUST THINK!"

"NO, I WILL NOT!"

"YOU WILL LET ALL THE DEVILS LOOSE, THEY WILL WREAK HAVOC ON THE WORLD, THEY WILL DEFY THE LORD, THEY WILL …"

Billie frowned. Yes, of course, there were hybrids down there too. The hybrids did make her shiver, the very idea of them was obscene; they were a lethal mixture of human science and alien invaders; they were evil, clever, and deadly, she'd read all about them in the books the Boy had given her, and even in some of the broadcasts she'd listened to – defying the Boy's and the Order's directive that no broadcasts were ever to be listened to.

The hybrids had a secret plan to inherit the earth. They symbolized, the Boy had told her, everything that was wrong with the world – science and secularism and greed gone mad, the Imperial International Cosmos enslaving everything and everybody.

And the Evil Cosmos Government – the Babylonian Abomination, the Whore of the East Coast, nested like a great spider in Elysium City – was keeping the hybrids alive because, if they were suitably trained, they could be used as weapons – weapons against people, against humanity – "Against us," the Boy had said, "Against the People of the Lord."

Billie's thumb hovered.

"YES, THAT'S RIGHT, BILLIE! DO IT! DO IT FOR LOVE OF THE LORD!" The voice was exulting now, happy, almost friendly, almost caressing.

Billie was sweating heavily – it was so hot. She hesitated – any distraction provided for a delay – and she took off her safety helmet and put it on the ground beside her, close to hand.

In any case, the helmet would not help when the explosion came – nothing would help. The whole building would disappear, rising up in a whoosh and then falling back into the pit of Main Shaft-2 in a great wall and column of fire, and the fire and debris would stream down into what remained of the shaft, would also move outwards over the desert, maybe two hundred meters,

and those secondary gasoline reservoirs, she somehow knew, were near full
– they would explode.

"YES," shouted the voice. "Just think, Billie! It will be goddamn spectacular!
Wow, it will light up the night sky, and pieces of machinery will be bouncing
across the desert for miles."

"BUT, I don't want ..."

"And, Billie, it will be the end of the hybrids! You will have won a deci-
sive battle for the human race, for the downtrodden People of the Lord! Just
think! Just imagine it. It will be a thing of beauty, truly, a great purification!
The Boy will rejoice, and the Lord on his Throne in the Celestial Sphere will
rejoice!"

"But ..."

"You and I have done great work, Billie! We've placed the explosives carefully. I told you I'm an expert, Billie."

"You are, aren't you?" Billie felt her strength waning. She had to play for
time in this strange mental wrestling match. "Yes, I'll bet you are the greatest!"

"I am, Billie, I am. I was only eighteen when I blew up two transcontinental
super-trains and one god awful big suspension bridge."

"Wow!"

"Yeah, you said it, *wow!* And I demolished a whole Centurion convoy with
delayed reaction explosions that I specially designed so that they would be
undetectable by sniffer drones and robot-sappers and infrared sensors."

"You did – boy, that's really something!"

"Right, it was really something. And now I – I mean you and me, Billie –
we've placed the explosives down on the main struts supporting the upper
level of the mine shaft."

"Yeah, that's right! We did that!"

"Yeah, Billie, I mean, you've got to have the eye, you know what I mean. I
took one look – just one look – at the walls of the shaft, and I knew, I instantly
knew, when the struts would collapse inwards, then how all four walls of the
shaft would follow. This place is rotten and ready to die."

"Yeah, it sure looks like it."

"You are so right! It's awesome how rotten it is. Even without explosives, it's
a death trap. It's ready to die, Billie, it's ready to die."

"Sure is," Billie took a deep breath; she seemed to be getting more control
of her body; Sally was distracted.

"Yeah, but you know, Billie, you can't take anything for granted. I mean, we just had to be totally sure, right. So I – I mean, you and I – inserted extra charges into the wall faces, just to make sure."

"Yeah, we had to be sure – it was awesome work, Sally!"

"You were great, Billie, I mean, you were so totally there for me. It was tricky, sweaty work. I mean the way we had to cling to the cage of the shaft, or the struts themselves, or deal with the chinks and dimples in the walls, and make sure the explosives were attached at exactly the right places. It was awesome, Billie. I mean, you were really great – you are really great!"

"We're a team, Sally, we're a real team." Billie was getting a whole new perspective on this; Sally was lonely, and she was only a kid, lost in limbo, why she's almost as young as I am! She's desperately lonely, and she's dead, poor kid, and when she's no longer with me – inside me – then she'll have no place to go! Billie had no idea how she knew this, but she somehow knew it.

Sally was in Limbo.

And Limbo was nowhere.

Sally was a soul without a home.

It was sad, infinitely sad.

Had the Boy done this? Had he captured Sally's soul, and kept it, his own particular prize and trophy? One of so many!

"We are a team," Sally was almost laughing, "Billie! Wow, I mean, to have a real friend like you, I mean, I've always been a loner, but you, Billie, you're just so totally perfect! Remember how we set the codes for each explosive so that nobody can kidnap the frequency and block the trigger message or falsify it. I mean, wow!"

"Yeah, Wow! That's really clever stuff, Sally!"

"If anybody wants to try to disarm this stuff, they will have to do it physically, each unit at a time. It's foolproof."

"You are a genius, Sally!"

"Billie, you were very brave. It was spooky down there in the shaft. Even me, I was sort of freaked out! I felt the sweat that was curdling on your forehead, Billie, and it was even dripping from your nose."

"Yeah, it sure was icky. It felt like glue. It was gross!"

"Yeah, I really love you, Billie, you were cool. We had to work barehanded because everything was so slippery. There we were!"

WHAM!

Something hit Billie, grabbed her, pulled her, and whirled her around.

"No, no, no!" Billie cried out, not knowing what she was saying or why she was saying it.

Something flipped her over, and slammed her down on the floor of the hanger and pain shot through her back and shoulders.

Her arm flailed out, but it was too late.

It was too late to push the button.

And now ... she was facing ...

Billie looked up into a face, a scary nightmare face, streaked zebra-like in matt black and swamp-green and with fierce dark eyes so dark and deep they seemed to have no soul in them.

The face – she realized now with a shock that it was not a demon from hell but that it was a face painted in matt camouflage and that it was the face of a woman – a stunning woman, a First Class Cosmos no doubt, with the structured perfection of a Cosmos, it was startlingly, almost unbelievably perfect – too perfect.

The woman was dressed in Cosmos Centurion uniform – a sleek black skinsuit, the holster, the backpack ...

A Centurion ... what was a Centurion doing here?

Billie feared them. The Centurions were the Guardians of Cosmos, they were most lethal, most skilled, the cruelest, the deadliest warriors on the planet.

A Centurion ...

Billie struggled to free her arms, now pinned down by the wrists, God this woman was strong, and, thinking whatever this woman or Cosmos is, I must fight, Billie tried to knee the woman in the groin, and tried to kick herself free, kick, kick, kick, legs flailing.

"Fight, Billie, fight!" screamed Sally.

But the Centurion just rode her, squatting now on Billie's midriff, and the Centurion said, in a surprisingly soft voice, "Calm down, Billie, or I really will hurt you!"

"Fight, Billie, toss this bitch off you!" Sally's voice was supplicating now; Sally seemed to have lost all her power. "Fight, Billie, fight – please fight!"

Billie was breathing hard, "Get off me, who the hell are you, what do you want?"

"What do you think I want?" The teeth bared – perfect teeth!

"Ouch!"

The woman flipped Billie over – it was so fast Billie didn't know how it happened – and now she was belly down, one side of her face crushed into the grainy, oily concrete floor, lips twisted outwards, teeth hurting, and her arms twisted behind her back, and her wrists pressed together, and she heard and felt the click-click of handcuffs locking around her wrists pinioning them together, the cold metal pressed into the small of her back, and then, as she tried to kick herself away, she felt her legs being slammed together and ankle cuffs closing, clamping and locking, God, it hurt, it was so tight, it …

The woman rolled her over, flip, flop – wham!

Billie was lying on her back, staring up at the ceiling, legs locked together, and her arms pinned behind her back, pinioned under her – painful – crushed against the floor. She wiggled. She was outraged, violated, and – afraid.

Sally was saying, "You left it too late, you bitch!"

"Shut up, Sally," Billie muttered in her mind.

"The Boy will take his revenge. The Boy will come!"

"Shut up!"

"This Centurion will kill you!"

"Shut up!"

"This Centurion will torture you to find out the code; she will want to stop the bombs from ticking down to that delicious final second of oblivion."

"Shut up!"

"I will block your mind so that you will not be able to tell her a word, Billie, and this will hurt, ha, ha, ha …"

The Centurion kneeled close to Billie and raised a finger to her lips – and mouthed: "Don't say a word!"

Behind the Centurion, another woman Centurion appeared – a black woman, her face also painted in camouflage, her wraparound flipped up; her large eyes were bright with intelligence, glowing with the beauty of Cosmos.

"I should kill you right now, right here," the kneeling Centurion stared down at Billie.

"Kill me, then," Billie breathed. How had she come to this?

"No, not yet, I need to know some things first."

The black Centurion was looking around, scanning the room, standing guard, swinging her automatic machine gun back and forth – one of the latest models, one of the guns the Boy had toyed with, Billie realized. The black woman glanced down at the control device. "It's got a timer too, and a remote," she said, "The other triggers are down below, and they must be coded, and they'll have timers too."

"Yes, and we need to know the details." The kneeling Centurion stared into Billie's eyes; it gave Billie the creeps the intensity, the dark emptiness of those eyes, so dark you could see nothing in them, they seemed to absorb all the light; it was like tumbling into infinite space. "To know those things, I have to get deep into your mind, Billie," said the Centurion.

Inside Billie's mind, Sally started screaming, hollering, carrying on – she was creating static. She was cavorting, punching, jumping, leaping, crying, and she was begging, "Don't give in Billie, don't! This woman is Death, Billie, don't give in, don't tell her, don't let her see into your mind, don't …" It went on and on at a higher and higher pitch and occupying every wavelength in Billie's mind. And, oh, it was painful! Billie squeezed her eyes shut. And at the same time, she could feel the Centurion's mind probing hers – invading, questions, tentacles of questions, probing, digging, stabbing – Billie thought her brain would burst, her skull would explode; she would literally go up in a whoosh, like a geyser. She screamed, "Oh, oh, oh, oh," like a wild animal caught in a trap, she screamed. The pain was so great, it was …

"I'm getting nowhere," said the Centurion.

"What's wrong?"

"The incubus inside her, somebody or something called Sally, is screaming and fighting, running interference, trying to obliterate everything."

"Possessed?"

"Yes. And there's only one way to go fast and deep." The kneeling Centurion glanced up at her partner. "Kat, I'm going to take a sip from our friend here."

"Jesus, you're a one-girl epidemic, spreading the hybrid bug everywhere," said Kat, "Okay, you've got to do what you've got to do, V, if that's what you do, do it; go for it."

"Sorry, Billie," said the kneeling Centurion; Billie stared. The Centurion's face began to change, and Billie couldn't believe what she was seeing, this was not possible. It was not possible – fangs, claws, and those eyes, those eyes …

Billie wanted to scream – but she was paralyzed.

Her lips did move, but not a sound came out.

Inside Billie's head, Sally screamed, a horrible, long, anguished scream, "No, no, no … I will not, I will not, I will not be thrown down to hell, I will not, I will not, I will not …. Please, please, have mercy, have mercy on me, don't do this, please, I beg you, Billie, don't do it, oh, don't, don't, don't, don't let her, oh, no, please … Ahhhhhhhhhh!"

The woman Centurion's face was closer now, well, it was no longer the woman, it was something else, deathly pale, empty eyes, deep shadows under the eyes, blue veins pulsing at the temples, fangs, long fangs; the breath was sweet. The point of the fangs touched Billie's neck.

Sally's voice was far away now, echoing, desperate, in some vast dark chamber – Hell, perhaps, yes, Hell …

Maybe it was the antechamber to Hell.

The touch of the fangs stung. Then it was like a caress – purple darkness flooded over Billie.

Her eyes closed. Billie Jo McAdams swooned.

"We are losing people, too many people." Norton fired and fired – taking down two ghouls. But as he glanced around, he realized the battle was going badly, very badly. Soon they would be only a few of his people left – and then none. Even the fighting prowess of the two hybrids, Sabrina and Helen, was not enough – there were just too many ghouls.

As he watched, one guard was cut in half by a ghoul.

As he watched, another had his head torn off.

One of the guards, a big brute of a man, but at heart, a gentle soul, Eckhart Jones, was grabbed by a ghoul.

Norton had tried to get a clear shot. He couldn't. Eckhart and the ghoul wrestled, and the two of them were lost in a tangle of ghouls, and then the wresting tangle somersaulted into the biomorph river.

Eckhart screamed, the ghoul screamed, the two of them, Eckhart and the ghoul, splashed in the river, trying to make it to shore. They were still clinging to each other; they began to melt, and smoke, and Norton thought: Oh, Christ!

As he watched, Eckhart and the ghoul merged, melting, wavering, screaming, human scream and ghoul squeal, and their torsos and then their faces merged into one screaming wildly distorted mask. Norton swore under his breath as the merging, double-faced creature sank into the boiling tar-black river, then splashing, and with spurts, out came another creature, a monster, a large, spider-like thing.

Norton got a clear shot, and he zapped it with the laser, the ray sizzled past most of the ghouls, it hit the spider in the middle of its body. The spider, which seemed to be made of black and white streaming liquid, split in two, and the two halves attacked the closest ghouls, seizing them, dragging them screaming into the river.

My enemy's enemy ... Norton took a deep breath.

"More are coming," Julian Harvey pointed.

Perched on a high ledge were more ghouls, a whole row of them. They leaped.

It was the end. Norton steeled himself. Well, they would die fighting – at least he could say that, humans and hybrids, their backs to the wall, making their last stand.

"You've got blood on your chin," said Kat.

"Thanks." V wiped it off.

"Good. You're perfect now."

"Billie – that's her name – was possessed, really possessed." V knelt over the timer. She punched in a few numbers. The lights went from red to green. From Billie's mind and central nervous system, V had snatched the schematics of the explosive devices, the codes and frequencies that could be used to trigger the system, and the code that could be entered manually to disarm each separate pack of explosives.

"Possessed?"

"Yes, somebody else was in there – a young woman, a terrorist and bomb expert, called Sally – I captured all her information – but when I bit Billie, Sally died – and was sent to some sort of hell by her master – just after my fangs entered in contact with Billie's blood – and her central nervous system."

"Hell? I wonder what that means."

"No idea. This Evil Force, The Boy – the True Believers call it 'The Lord' – commands some sort of Hell, rather like the Biblical Hell, something surreal. Dante would find it familiar."

Kat scratched her head. "Weirder and weirder!"

"Shaft-2 is already unstable." V glanced into the pit and nodded at the explosive package. "And, somewhere, down in the shaft, there are local triggers still ticking down to zero."

"Yes." Kat had taken an advanced course on booby-trap trigger systems, and she'd seen a few in her short career – systems with many trigger points, with explosives hidden below explosives; layer upon layer of traps and booby traps; you thought you'd disarmed the system, then the next layer blew up and killed you, or the next, or the next. Many of the most skilled mine-disposal experts, even using drones or robot-sappers, had been killed that way; you should never relax your guard, never make any assumptions about what was and what wasn't the case. Just when you thought you had solved the problem – that was the most dangerous moment. That was when you died.

"Yes."

"So ..."

"I'll have to go down there," V, "I have to turn off the other timers."

"Right," Kat slipped up her wraparounds and wiped her forehead; it was night, but it still must be over 100 degrees Fahrenheit. But then, she realized, she was not really feeling the heat – and she was not sweating at all. Was this the beginning of the true morph into hybrid form? She bit her lip. A tremor of fear rippled up her stomach.

A distant explosion echoed. The earth trembled; cables swayed and clattered, clanging into each other; dust and rubbish fell from the beams overhead. Dust rose out of the shaft like smoky steam.

"An explosion," said Kat.

"Main Shaft-1 is still blowing up," V looked upward. Red brightness flared, glowing through the hanger's skylights. Yes, the fires in Main Shaft-1 were still burning, finding new fuel, new stores of dynamite and explosives, and still more reserves of gasoline.

"This whole place is a time bomb," said Kat.

"Yes." V's glanced downward. She was standing on the very edge of the open shaft, the points of her boots over the edge. "You stand guard here – and look after our friend."

"What do I do if she wakes up?" Kat motioned with her chin toward Billie's body, the empty husk.

"She should be docile. But, if the dose was not just right – I was in a hurry, as you know – she may morph, in an instant, into a totally mad homicidal hybrid foaming-at-the-mouth monster."

"Oh, that's great!"

"It sometimes happens when I work too fast."

Kat rolled her eyes. "Great!"

"Sorry," V grinned, "If she looks like she's at all dangerous, shoot her."

"Right," Kat said, "I'll see you in a few minutes."

"If the gods will it."

"Right," Kat saluted, "If the gods will it."

V leaped into the dark.

One hundred feet down, V landed on a crossbeam, pausing just a second to orient herself in this shadowy underworld, and to match what she was seeing with the schematics she had lifted from Billie's brain.

She walked to the far side of the beam and found what she was looking for: an explosive package placed under a cross-bream strut in precisely the most effective spot – if it went off, it would bring down the whole support structure. It had an independent timer, so even with the main timer turned off, this one would blow in a few minutes.

She inserted the code into the independent timer.

The little red light went off and was replaced by a green light.

Chemically, these explosives were quite stable, so without the timers and triggers, there was very little chance they would explode.

V glanced downwards, into the smoky depths. More screams and strange ululations, wailing and keening, came from far below.

There were gunshots, echoing, and explosions.

There was a real life-and-death battle going on down there.

She walked along a crossbeam and disarmed another timer, the red light changing to green, and then, jumping down one level, she disarmed the third.

Each timer had its own code: that girl Sally had been a true professional, a delicate and precise artist of death. Now, probably, in some non-terrestrial hell, her spirit was screaming. Possibly, it would scream for all eternity. How horrible! V felt a flicker of anguish for the girl. There was one more timer and explosive package to go.

V leaped down to the next level, landing neatly on the crossbeam. The beam was about two feet wide. It braced two vast plates of steel that held up the left and right sides of the shaft. V frowned. Probably this meant the shaft was particularly weak right here, liable to collapse in on itself.

She narrowed her eyes. Yes, water was leaking out from behind the two giant steel plates, lots of water, and streams of liquid clay. The whole place was just begging to implode. It might not even need an explosion – just a nudge. Everything would cascade downwards.

V knelt next to the explosive device. Oh, well, maybe there was time to get people and hybrids out before the inevitable happened. Hopefully, because if not ... Damn, this one had a different kind of timer. The timer was ticking down. One minute and thirty-two seconds remained.

00.01.32

00.01.31

00.01.30

V stood up, stretched, and concentrated, bringing the timer's code up from her memory. Then, as she stepped forward to insert the code, she heard a hissing, growling behind her. She turned, and found herself facing ...

A ghoul – a male. He was chalk-white, hairless, and had large fangs and a prominent snout. His eyes bulged, pure white, veined with blue. His hands and feet were claws. He was much more muscular than Miranda's pet ghouls: Bounce, Daisy, and Deep. The ears were long, almost like the ears of a donkey, and they twitched. His drooling, quivering nostrils shone in the dim phosphorescent gloom, his jaws dripped glowing saliva, and his skin twinkled, sending out a pulsating brightness. He exuded radiant light, V thought, and probably a greasy sort of radiant sweat. Probably, the creature was radioactive.

"Hello, brother," she said.

The ghoul mewled, a lamentation, a plaintive whimper. His long thin tongue dangled, dripping more glowing, creamy white saliva. Crouching, he pawed at the steel surface of the giant beam.

V wondered. Living underground, he must be extraordinarily sensitive to sound and probably to movement.

She tried to enter his thoughts, but it was a fog, a dense fog of murderous yearnings. She saw herself – a mental shadow in his mind – a vague silhouette, a presence – something to hunt, something to kill, something to eat, or something to fear, or maybe something to fornicate with; all of those things, dimly perceived and dimly thought, all at once. So he senses me. He has seen me, and he wants to kill me – or mate with me. Not sure yet.

The ghoul leaped high in the air, right over her, and thumped down, softly, behind her, between her and the bomb's timer.

"Damnation," She swung around and growled.

Crouching on the crossbeam, the ghoul snarled – V wondered. Is this coincidence, or is he being controlled by someone, by some intelligence of some kind? Something that doesn't want me to stop the explosion.

00.01.24

00.01.23

He snarled, baring his fangs, drooling: a long thread of that white creamy glowing saliva.

V hesitated – He is very strong, so I must be too.

Demon against demon, then, so be it!

Freak against freak, so be it!

While the ghoul mewled and hesitated, V slowly, carefully unbuckled her backpack and hooked it to the strut with its Velcro-like loop; she unbuckled her belt and took off the holster. She wanted to keep the uniform and equipment intact, she might need them later. It was a long way down; if she lost things, it would not be easy to retrieve them. *I might have to become human again; you never know what weird necessities might present themselves.* She unbuckled the boots and stepped out of them and secured them to the anchored backpack. She zipped open and peeled off the skintight armored black catsuit – and stepped out of it.

00.01.10

00.01.09

00.01.08

The ghoul had been very still, ears twitching, sniffing the air, trying to get a definite fix on her, trying to determine precisely where she was and what she was.

"Okay," V thought, "Now, my brother monster, I shall best you!"

In a whispering, whirring flash, V morphed into demon form, a luminous blur, and then there she was, a humanoid reptile, turquoise, and gold, gleaming gently in the gloomy penumbra. "Come, my brother," she hissed, and beckoned to him with one open claw.

The ghoul shuffled, mewed, and, snarling, bared its fangs.

"Come, my brother, come!"

The ghoul leaped.

Kat paced back and forth.

Outside, the hanger explosions echoed, and gunshots rang out. The screams of the zombie-bats were louder and louder. Any minute they might break into the hanger.

Kat decided she was too vulnerable near the shaft out in the open on the hanger floor. Danger could come from any direction. Realizing she was taking a risk, she lifted Billie up – the limp body lying passive, lolling in her arms – and carried the unconscious girl over to a corner where they would not be seen – at least not at first – by any zombie-bats or other monsters, and where Kat could survey most of the open space in the hanger.

If any surprises came up the shaft, Kat would be ready.

If any hostiles entered the hanger, she had a good and well-sheltered vantage point.

If any zombie-bats broke through the skylights, she would see them before they saw her.

Kat knelt next to Billie. The girl's eyes were closed, and her breathing was regular. She looked like a normal young woman – in stylish high-tech military gear – a normal young woman, who was merely asleep. There were two puncture marks on her throat at the center of the slight bruise where V had bitten her. But, as Kat watched, the puncture marks and the bruise, which were already faint, faded and then disappeared altogether.

Oh, oh, thought Kate, I'm not sure this is such a good sign. She's morphing into something that can heal almost instantly, and I may not like it at all.

As V had explained, if the dose was not exactly right, Billie could morph instantly into a totally insane and homicidal monster hybrid of super-human strength.

"I think I got it right," V had said, smiling – smiling! – "But, you know, things do happen sometimes, and it does depend on the physiology of the person infected, and I was in a hurry – it could go either way, so be ready."

"Right," said Kat, with a grim smile, "and I'm left holding the bag."

With a grin, V vanished, disappearing down the shaft, down the rabbit hole.

Well, Kat had to admit it: V was a genius – and a hybrid, the original, the goddess, the fountainhead. What a weird situation I've got myself into, me, a First Class Centurion and Cosmos. Once upon a time, in another life, I had my career all mapped out: front-line battle experience, then the Centurion Post-Graduate Academy, and a post-graduate degree, and then leave the Centurions for a teaching post in Elysium or a …

Kat fingered the trigger of her laser gun: the weapon was powerful, precise. She didn't intend to die. She'd lost everything several times. She didn't intend to lose, ever again: Orphaned once, orphaned twice, orphaned three times.

And now I'm a hybrid, Kat thought, I keep forgetting that little fact since I do feel like I'm still myself – so far the only change has been, let's see, if I make a little effort I can make my eyes look like they belong to a rattlesnake; I have a partial ability to read minds, which is really weird and it's increasing; I don't seem to be sensitive to the torrid heat, I'm not even sweating the slightest bit; I am feeling feisty, bursting with energy, though I haven't slept for at least three days; and I'm noticing a host of smells I didn't even know existed; my saliva glands seem particularly active, and my teeth – particularly the lateral incisors – occasionally tingle, particularly at the sight and smell of blood, and …

Oh, oh …

The sleeping monster, Billie, was stirring, groaning, one hand twitching. The fingers opened and closed. She scratched her stomach, and her legs kicked once, a spasm. She groaned again, bared her teeth, and licked her lips.

"Hungry, eh," Kat took a deep breath. She carefully lifted the automatic, loaded with explosive bullets, out of its holster and held it ready; one bullet between the eyes and one in the nape of the neck or the back of the head. I guess that means I've got to swivel her around or turn her upside down! Kat was fast, for a human very fast. And now, as a hybrid, she figured she would be even faster, but she also reckoned that a newly-born, fully morphed, monstrous uninhibited libidinous bloodthirsty girl hybrid – if that was what Billie had become – could easily be even faster.

Billie's eyes fluttered open.

Kat stepped back: Billie's eyes were bright yellow, totally blank. They seemed to be seeing nothing. So she's morphed already, or she's morphing, and she's morphing fast. Kat was tempted to shoot right away – shoot first, ask questions later – but instead, she said, "Hello, Billie. How do you feel?"

The yellow eyes blinked – a dark lozenge suddenly formed – a snake-like pupil and iris – and the mouth opened – fangs, two deliciously pointed fangs. The morph was not total, not yet. But, boy, it was galloping!

Boy, oh, boy! Now I sort of wish I'd morphed right away too. Kat's finger tightened on the trigger; she pointed the laser gun at Billie's forehead.

She took a deep breath and asked the question again, "Hello, Billie, how do you feel?"

Billie licked her lips, clenched one clawed fist, and – yawned, again displaying her long sharp fangs – and flickering forked tongue.

"I'm hungry," Billie whispered, "Yes, I feel hungry, really hungry."

When the ghoul finally made his move, he was damned fast – On his first try, he grabbed V around the waist and tried to bite her neck in half. Now, locked in a deadly embrace, she and the ghoul rolled back and forth on the crossbeam, at one point almost falling off.

To get free of him – he was covered in a sort of grease – V had to flip herself over, springing like an elastic, looping up into the air, and staring for an instant down into the void, she landed on all fours on the crossbeam ten feet away from the ghoul, and hissed a challenge. "Come and get me, you evil monster, you!"

The ghoul blinked his big white featureless eyes, hissed, and rushed her.

V ducked, skipped aside, and grabbed the ghoul by his right arm, swinging him around, pulling the arm behind his back, levering it up, bending him forward, and then slamming him against the steel plate at the end of the beam. Pinning him in place, she pushed his arm up farther, almost breaking it but not quite. She pushed his body tighter against the plate and crushed his face flat against the steel.

Time was running out, she sensed it.

00.00.45

He squealed and struggled, his body exuding the strange glue, glowing, dripping, and greasy, really, really greasy.

With her body pressed tight against his body, she shot out her mental tentacles, trying to catch some hint of any kind of mental life that would allow her to communicate, to ask him to surrender – some glimmer of intelligence.

There was none.

He was a purely instinctive killer, in almost human form. In fact, once he must have been human.

"Oh, my brother!" she sighed.

He snarled and broke loose, and slipped out of her grasp – the gluey sweat exuded by his ultra-smooth skin made him super slippery. It was like trying to hold onto a greased eel.

He leaped out onto the middle of the beam, again between her and the timer.

V turned to face him.

"Maybe you are the end result of human evolution – a mindless killing machine. Maybe this is where humanity is headed. Do you think that might be the way it will end?"

The ghoul growled. His fangs shone.

"Truly, we are family!" V bared her fangs, flexed her claws, saliva gushing, blood lust soaring, muscles tensing.

"Come on, come on to mummy!" she crooned, licking back the saliva with her long forked tongue, and gesturing, teasing, dodging back and forth, feinting right, then left, "Come on, baby!"

The ghoul snarled. It spit a stream of foaming saliva – black this time.

The loop of liquid spurted past V and traced a long line on the steel barrier. V glanced at the long elegant squiggle. The saliva smoked, spurted, hissing on the metal.

"Ah," she thought, so his saliva is acid, and dangerous. It is a weapon. It can blind and maim. How ingenious! So, it seemed he had ordinary saliva, the white stuff that just drooled, but he also must have an extra gland that could send out a spurt of black acid or poison – like a spitting cobra that could blind you from five meters away – *Squirt!* You are blind! Then you are dead!

"You are very interesting, and I really would like to study you further, but …" V leaped straight up and came straight down upon him. He just had time to look up, and as she came down she thought she saw an expression of surprise in the upturned bug-eyed face – an expression of intelligence, and fear. Landing, she caught his head between her claws, and twirling around, she twisted the skull, crushed it – and broke his neck.

"Too late for a chat, my brother, I'm awfully sorry! I really am!"

The naked slippery body twitched in her arms and then was still.

For some reason, V thought, briefly, of Michelangelo's Pietà, the beautiful Virgin cradling the almost naked body of Christ, her son.

She laid the dead ghoul gently down on the beam, looked for a brief second into the blind face, the fangs, the bulging featureless eyes.

"Forgive me, brother!"

She stood up, strode down the beam to her backpack and slipped it over her back. Over her shoulder, she hung the automatic, and she strapped on the pistol. Now, she was ready for battle.

Oh, I almost forgot!

00.00.15

Don't dawdle, V, time is of the essence.

00.00.14

00.00.13

She leaped to the timer, punched in the code: the countdown stopped, and the red lights turned to green.

Whew!

She sat down, her legs dangling over the sides of the beam, and frowned.

Like a cat, she was curious, curious about everything! She reminded herself, perhaps for the thousandth time, that excessive cogitation and curiosity could be a weakness. *Curiosity killed the cat!*

Enough!

She looked down – a mile below, a battle was taking place, and somehow, she knew it was not going well.

She leaped into the darkness.

The moment she did so, the earth trembled. Even dropping straight down through the mucky air, she felt it. Was it an earthquake? Or had the collapse of Main Shaft-1 and the explosions and fire destabilized Main Shaft-2?

Not good, not good at all, V rocketed down through the shadows toward the shouts and cries and screams.

It was clearly a life-and-death struggle, and soon she would be in the middle of it; as she rocketed down, she felt another tremor. The whole of Main Shaft-2 was shaking. Those distant explosions, probably from Main Shaft-1, were upsetting – destabilizing – the delicate balance on which the very existence of Shaft-2 depended.

This whole damned thing is going to collapse, she thought, and she rocketed down, leaping from beam to beam, from cross-bar to cross-bar, jumping and swinging from cable to cable.

And if it collapses, there will be no way out!

The shouts and cries and shots were louder.

Trusting to her acrobatic ability, V leaped into the void, streaming down through the black sound-infested air.

She noticed that bits and pieces of the shaft wall – slabs of clay, a wooden beam or two, metal joists – were falling with her. This was not good, not good at all.

CHAPTER 13 – RIVER OF DEATH

The hybrids were statues of stone, except for HX-2 – Sabrina – and HX-8 – Helen – who were following Sammy's orders and killing as fast as they could kill. The humans and hybrids – even the paralyzed ones – were retreating slowly, pushed backward, through a forest of stalagmites, by the horde of ghouls that seemed to stream in from every direction.

"I don't know if we can hold on," Norton was sweating blood. Of course, Sammy Franks had his two warrior hybrids. The two girls slashed and slashed and slashed; their claws and fangs never stopped working. They were dripping with smoking ghoul goo and steamy ghoul blood. But that would not be enough.

A ghoul leaped toward Norton and spat an arc of hissing black liquid. Norton raised his arm just in time. The stream of spittle splashed against Norton's arm armor and began to sizzle.

"Watch your eyes!" Norton shouted. "They spit acid."

Jimmy Ghoul crouched in fear, creeping along, lurking behind Julian Harvey and Norton.

"I don't think we are going to survive this," Julian shouted. "There are just too many of them."

"And we are running out of ammunition." Norton's laser gun was almost empty; the little light was blinking warning him that he had maybe fifty shots left; it would need two days of sunlight to recharge the bloody thing.

Norton slipped down his protective eye shield and surveyed the cavern. It was dimly lit by the glowing lichen on the walls and by giant clusters of bulbous chandeliers of plants that looked like upside down mushrooms, some of them had tendrils that glowed, and moved, squirming around the stalactites, and probing, and reaching out, as if they had minds of their own.

Some of the ghouls – those on Norton's left – had momentarily backed off, but now they were again advancing, crowding in; the hybrids were immobile, except for the two Sammy Franks – who would have thought it! – had managed to order into action. Those two were still fighting, out on the fringes, where some ghouls had advanced too far for their own good. Behind those ghouls, more were crowding in – the supply seemed endless.

"Mr. Norton, sir," Sammy shouted, "I don't think we are going to be able to hold them back. Even my girls are going to get overwhelmed. What should we do, Mr. Norton, sir?"

"Just keep fighting, Sammy. Retreat slowly. We'll try to edge our way back to the tunnel we came in by, if we can get through, then we can hold them off at the tunnel entrance."

"Right, thanks, Sir," Sammy blazed away with an automatic, which made bright flashes that reflected on one of the soaring greasy gray stalagmites, making it look like a huge melted wax candle.

The problem, Norton realized, was this: The ghouls had cut off the retreat toward the tunnel entrance; and the other problem was this: the line of retreat lay right next to the deadly bio-dissolvent river and the puddles of bio-dissolvent poison, so it would be a very risky retreat, perhaps fatal. But what other hope was there …?

Norton felt rage and self-hatred surge up. To think we humans created all this, to think that our biochemical research and our poisons and our weapons research and our experiments created this hell on earth – this underworld of monsters – this nightmare that's going to destroy us, vengeance that has risen out of our misuse of our intelligence!

Norton took aim, shooting off a beam of light that exploded the skull of a hulking male ghoul that had been heading straight toward him, a geyser of black-and-white goo shot up and splattered over a female ghoul that was next to the male, her breasts hanging almost to her waist, her big arms and claws reaching out, groping, in front of her. The female turned her weird bestial head and droopy oblong blank eyes toward Norton and somehow in those seemingly blind eyes Norton read the message: *I am going to kill you, you human, I am going to plunge my fangs into your neck, and I am going to drain the life out of you.*

But, instead of leaping, she just stood there; she didn't move; Norton was about to pull the trigger, but he paused, he waited.

The other ghouls were edging closer. The phosphorescence glowed off their hairless bulbous ivory skulls; their long pointed ears twitched; their empty eyes reflected the phosphorescence, their wet nostrils quivered. Long tongues dripped fluid and licked thin ghoul lips and fangs. There must be hundreds of them, more and more, pressing forward. They crowded past the huge pointed stalagmites, they were like a mob of mindless humanoids, less than human, but more powerful, their muscles delineated like those of a fanatic bodybuilder on permanent steroids, muscles like steel carved in flesh, the females too were muscular with sagging monstrous breasts and strong bulging biceps and rippling abs and thick, heavy, ape-like necks. They crouched forward, hungry, with foam dripping from their tongues and fangs.

They are our children, thought Norton. They are the children of humankind.

Oh, horrible, most horrible. Norton bit his lip. What a mess! He felt guilty for what humanity had done, and he felt personally guilty for leading his little troop – humans and hybrids and the little ghoul Jimmy – into a trap. There was no way out.

Freddy, still a statue-like robot, had shuffled back toward Norton, instinctively retreating away from the ghouls, and now he turned to face Norton.

What next? Norton frowned. He was worried that the hybrids might activate and suddenly join the ghouls and feast on the humans. After all, the hybrids had a lot of reasons to hate humans.

Freddy stared at Norton.

"What?" Norton said, in spite of himself, he knew that in his present mind-collar enslaved state, Freddy would not understand anything Norton said and he was about to reproach himself for wasting words. He looked away from Freddy for an instant and with a flash from his laser gun vaporized a ghoul which had been advancing closer than the others. The female, hunkering, was still staring at Norton, or so it seemed. Maybe she's got a crush, Norton thought, a grim joke; he wondered if this particular ghoul had ever been human or if she had been born a ghoul; maybe she was one of the technicians charged with storing the toxic biomorph material. How long did ghouls live anyway?

The other ghouls were closing in again – there were certainly too many of them this time.

Norton glanced back at Freddy.

"Well, mate," said Freddy, "I reckon we've got a fight on our hands!"

Norton was too stunned to say anything; then, he saw that the little lights on Freddy's mind-collar which a minute ago had been glowing a bright green were dead, showing no color at all.

"Yes, Freddy, we do have a fight on our hands."

"Well, then, mate, let's win it," Freddy leaped toward the nearest line of ghouls, and waded in and began to slash and slash and slash, ghoul blood and spittle and flesh and bones were flying and splattering in every direction.

"Halleluiah!" shouted Julian Harvey.

All of the hybrids were now fighting. And they were doing it with intelligence. They were talking, shouting.

It was mayhem.

But now Norton saw that there was a chance, a slim chance, they might survive.

"Welcome back, Freddy," shouted Norton.

"Glad to be back, mate!"

The female ghoul finally leaped – straight toward Norton. He shot her out of the air – her head exploded into a geyser of black goo. Norton felt he had killed an old friend.

The ghouls screamed, high-pitched screams, and long wailing ululations, and there were more and more of them. They were scooting up the walls, they were dropping down from cracks in the ceiling, they were coming out of side caves; they were surging up from cracks in the earth below.

Even with the intelligence of the hybrids restored, even with the hybrids in the fight, it looked to Norton like they could still lose.

Still, he blazed away.

"Are we going to die, Mr. Norton?" Jimmy Ghoul cowered at Norton's feet.

Julian Harvey glanced at Norton.

"Of course, we're not going to die," said Norton.

"No way we're going to die, Jimmy!" echoed Freddy, "No way!"

Sammy and Sabrina and Helen were on the leading edge of the fight, pushing toward the dark river which Helen, out of the side of her mouth, had called "The River Styx."

Sammy was tempted to ask what *Styx* meant, but he decided they were all too busy for questions; if he survived, he would ask his learned hybrid friends to teach him, he figured he'd been given a second chance, and one thing he was going to do, one thing old Sammy Franks was definitely going to do, he was going to learn about a hell of a lot of things. The hybrids were *smart*, and, like Norton and Doc Jane and that smart-assed Cosmos dish Valerie Joffre, they *knew stuff*; and that meant *being smart* and *knowing stuff* was a good thing.

"It means river of death," said Sabrina. She was standing beside Sammy, "It's where people cross over from life on earth into Hades or Hell or the Underworld, wherever the dead go."

She leaped toward two ghouls that had just emerged from a crevice. She tore them apart, their limbs, arms and legs, flying off in different directions.

Helen was covered in streaks of black, tar-like, ghoul blood rippling across her silver scales; she looked like a zebra, with zebra stripes, the effect, Sammy thought, was like seeing her under strobe lights – very sexy – Sammy had once been in a strip club where hallucinatory optical effects were obtained by flashing quick, bright white lights, with a bluish tint, that made the dancers' bodies look like they were flashing white and black, striped in silver and gold, stippled with scarlet and mauve … Yes, Sammy licked his lips, it was sexy, he thought, really sexy.

Helen glanced at him, her gold eyes glowing, reading his thoughts, *oh gosh, oh golly, and, yes, that was a grin.*

"Whew!" Sammy wiped his forehead. He thought it was pretty heroic of him, having sexy thoughts – and the hybrid who had read his thought wasn't mad at all but amused – and more than anything, it was pretty heroic of him to have sexy thoughts, when he was about to die, when they were all about to die, even the hybrids, maybe, might die, since there were just too many ghouls.

In fact, Helen and Sabrina were soon entangled in a mass of squirming fighting spitting, screaming, ululating ghouls. It looked like the two hybrids had waded into a mountain of man-sized maggots and that they were going to drown in the sea of maggoty ghouls.

Sammy would have to wade in and help his girls. It would be suicide, it would be his last mission, a kamikaze foray, and it would be the end of Old Sammy. But, hey, it was better than cowering far from the fight, wetting his pants, and proving himself a coward.

He hitched up his weapon and tool belt.

He would fight, and he would fight, and he would fight.

Go, Sammy Franks, go!

A giant ghoul suddenly appeared beside Sammy. Its mouth flew open, and it spat one long lanky thick squirt of black goo that, luckily, splashed against the rock just next to Sammy puffy cheekbone. The rock began to sizzle and smoke and small flames rippled along the edges of the splash of goo.

Oh, Christ, this is horrible!

Norton had said their spit could blind a man!

They are like spitting cobras!

Oh, Christ!

Sammy raised his gun, but the ghoul leaped forward and smashed the gun out of Sammy's hand. The gun flashed fire, then bounced against the rock face, and fell with a splash onto the muddy ground.

Sammy fell to his knees and raised his arm to shield his face. He was a goner; his two hybrids were too far away and too busy to help; Norton and the others had their hands full.

With his free hand, Sammy groped for his electro-whip, it must be hanging there at his belt; he groped, took a deep breath, thinking, now I am going to die, and then his fingers closed on the handle, and he pulled the whip out of its sheath, and gulped because the ghoul was so close now, looming over him, and Sammy could smell its breath which was foul, oh, most foul, as if …

The giant ghoul reached out its claws.

Its giant fangs curved and very long, gleamed like ivory tusks.

Wham!

Whoosh! The ghoul's head had disappeared. The body was still standing, lowering over Sammy, its hunched shoulders and massive muscles seeming to waver slightly; a fountain of black blood spurted straight up from its neck and then gushed back down, splashing, spraying; the hunched body crumpled forward, almost falling into Sammy's arms, but Sammy wiggled and bounced aside just at the last second, and the body brushed past him and fell down flat on the muddy floor of the cave, its giant back muscles twitching and trembling and there behind the spot where the ghoul had stood was another hybrid – a hybrid Sammy had never seen before.

She seemed to shine, a turquoise and gold shade, as if she were lit from within. She was not wearing a collar.

But she was wearing, he noticed, a backpack, and also a shoulder sling that held an automatic, and a pistol slung against her hip.

"Hello, Mr. Franks," she said.

Sammy opened his mouth. He felt he was in a strange little time loop here; this hybrid had all her marbles about her, she was a rational creature, somebody to reckon with, like his two pets and pals, HZ-2 and HZ-8, who'd been for a brief time driven back into borderline idiocy, but who were now geniuses again.

He was just formulating what he should say when the hybrid drew her automatic and blasted away – the beam when right past Sammy and singed up one of his ears – he could feel the ray it was so close – he turned to see a ghoul, half-disintegrated, flying backward and splatter in slow motion against a giant stalagmite.

"Sorry," the hybrid said, "I didn't have time to warn you."

"Oh, well …"

"I'm V," she said, her golden eyes boring into him.

Sammy's mouth was still hanging open. He gulped. "Sabrina and Helen need help," he managed to say, and he motioned with his sweaty triple chin, running with mud and ghoul goo, toward the squirming mass of maggoty ghouls, "There are too many of those things."

"Of course," the hybrid said, with a grin, and she was gone – leaping into the liquid mass of ghouls.

"V …" Sammy frowned; he thought he'd heard of that one – was she the … the Goddess, the Mother, the Primal One, the Leader …?

There were more screams and bellows. It was as if the mass of ghouls had been hit by a missile, suddenly Helen and Sabrina and the new hybrid were clear of the mess, and ghoul arms, legs, torsos, heads were flying all over the place as if dozens of ghouls had exploded from within.

At the same time out of the corner of his eye Sammy saw Freddy and two or three other hybrids slashing with their claws at a crowd of ghouls that were attacking Bob Norton's troops – and Bob Norton firing as fast as he could, and a couple of the other guys doing the same.

It looked like Custer's last stand.

Sammy rushed over to join them.

Behind him came Sabrina and Helen and the new hybrid, with her backpack and high-tech Cosmos Centurion gun.

Bob Norton and Julian Harvey stared; what was this new, armed, collar-less, hybrid in their midst?

She was on their side, that was clear, but for how long, and who or what, was she?

"V," said Sammy Franks, answering the unspoken question.

"Yes, V," said Freddy, who was twisting the neck off a particularly vicious ghoul, "She's the Queen, a real ball-breaker."

"Nice to see you, Freddy," said V.

"Just joking, V, you know me!"

Sammy Franks was covered in sweat and ghoul blood, and mud and clay, and his eyes shone with a feverish brightness. He suddenly felt he was almost like a hero, with his hybrid friends, fighting valiantly against impossible odds. The opportunity makes the man, he'd heard, maybe it was true.

"V," said Norton.

"Yes, V, she's their Queen, the original one."

"For Christ's sake, we're really in trouble now."

"She's on our side, she's okay," Sammy said, "Look, Norton – if she can accept me, she's going to accept any human – right?"

Norton blinked at him. Norton's eyes were bright in his mud-smeared face.

"I mean, I'm the lowest of the low, right, and so if she takes to me ..."

Norton grinned, "You've certainly got a point there, mate."

"V is first-rate," said Freddy, "It's just we have this long history you see, so we sort of play at feuding, right, V?"

"That's right, Freddy darling," V said, "but we don't have time, humans and hybrids, the ghouls are not our only problem; we have to get out of here."

"What's the other problem?" Norton had a feeling he knew, and that he didn't like what was coming.

"Shaft-2 is unstable, and it's starting to collapse because ..."

"... because of the shockwaves from Main Shaft-1 ..." Norton finished her sentence.

"Precisely," V said, in that reptilian pursed-lips, precise, schoolmarm way she sometimes adopted, even in hybrid-reptile mode, and which schoolmarm attitude and expression for some reason he had never understood always made Freddy – particularly when she was scolding him – dizzy with desire, horny as hell, overcome by lust; it was almost like vertigo, and just as all those thoughts were rippling through his reptilian mind and making him lick his lips, she shot him a glance with her golden eyes that bored into his soul – reading his every libidinous thought – and she gave him a neat, cute little fanged smile, while saying, "The explosions in Shaft-1 have unbalanced Shaft-2, so any minute now ..."

"So we'd better ..." said Norton, thinking, God, this is weird, the Queen of the Hybrids, the Ancient Goddess, as some had called her, and here she is ...

There was a low rumbling sound.

"Oh, oh," said Sabrina, wiping a blob of ghoul juice from her forehead.

A sudden geyser of steam rose from the river Styx.

The ghouls had stopped attacking; they were all standing still as statues, frozen in place, arms and legs caught in mid-gesture, heads tilted to one side, ears twitching.

The river Styx boiled up; steam rose.

The air rippled and moved: a wind …

"Yes, we'd better get out of here," said Helen, looking down at how her beautiful silver-glittery body had been dulled and painted in stripes and splashes of matt black ghoul blood. Positively disgusting!

Rocks fell from ledges; a crack opened in one large stalagmite.

The rumbling sound rose to a roar.

The wind rose.

Spurts of fluid and veritable fountains of steamy black liquid rose out of the River Styx; ghosts of bio-morphed victims rose in clouds from the Styx, swirled around. Barrels of bio-poison began to tumble, some exploded, bursting open, sending out vapors of … what?

The ghouls squealed, all at once. They began to run, they scattered, fleeing, running, some running in circles. It was as if they didn't know where to go or what to do.

"How did you get in here?" V looked around the group; hybrids – her sisters and brothers and old friends, and these men, guards who had held her sisters and brothers prisoner for fourteen years. Her claws itched.

"That way," said Norton.

"Yes, V," Sabrina and Helen spoke at once, "Back there, there is a tunnel and a narrow entrance. It leads back to the mine system, back toward Main Shaft-1. That's the way we have to go!"

The wind was rising faster, into a veritable hurricane.

The roar was louder. The river Styx was sloshing with big waves, and beginning to flood over its banks.

A giant stalactite fell from the roof of the cavern; like a huge sword, it went straight down and whammed into the earth and cracked and fell sideways, splashing up miniature tsunami of mud, water, and bio-fluid.

"Let's go."

They ran.

The ghouls who had blocked the retreat scattered, squealing, galloping and loping away, disappearing into niches, nooks, and crannies.

"Come on," Sammy shouted, "Come on!"

The whole group scrambled toward the tunnels and caves that led back to Main Shaft-1.

Hybrids and humans tumbled over each other, swerving around stalactites and stalagmites, wading through shallow bubbling sulfurous streams, slipping up and down slimy clay slopes, sliding through slippery narrow cracks.

Behind them, they heard a roar, at first distant, then closer. Main Shaft-2 was collapsing, the walls caving in, the beams and struts buckling, the vast reserves of sand and clay, seeping out through buckling metal and wooden plates, a monstrous cascade, a Niagara of mud, clay, water, sand, and fractured stone.

Then with a tremendous boom, the upper wall exploded, and the sand and clay came thundering down, hundreds, thousands of tons of earth, sweeping away and burying everything in its path. The wave spread out through the caverns, with it came hundreds of tons of muddy water. It chased them through caves and passageways – if only they could make it, if only they could make it in time!

V glanced back – *I think we can, I think we can, I think we can …*

PART THREE – REVELATION

CHAPTER 14 – THE BEGINNING

Billie Jo McAdams sat cross-legged with her back against one of the great metal pillars of the hanger, and Kat's light machine gun was lying across her lap and she was looking down at it with her yellow demon eyes and trying to remember how this particular weapon worked.

"The second button on the right," said Kat, who was scanning the roof beams and distant hulking machines, through binoculars, "It releases the safety."

"You read my very thought," said Billie, "Are you sure you aren't a hybrid?"

"I confess; I am a hybrid too, but I haven't morphed yet, not as far as you, at least." Kat turned her eyes – now reptilian – toward Billie.

"Oh," Billie's reptile eyes dilated.

Kat had to smile. Billie was a strange hybrid; she looked perfectly human – with peachy-cream skin and russet freckles, but she had those weird reptile eyes and the fangs – two fangs just like the classic vampire – and her hands had morphed; the fingers had become longer and turned into razor-like claws, but still dextrous enough to pull a trigger.

"I think ..." Billie began to whisper, "I think ..."

"Yes, something is happening," Kat perked up. Billie had sensed something, and the danger was coming from below, not above.

"It's collapsing," Billie pointed. Dust rose from Shaft-2. Then, suddenly, machinery at the pithead was sucked in, collapsed, was carried down, with a dull roaring and clattering sound.

"Oh, no," said Kat, "V and the others, they are all still down there."

"I respectfully suggest we run," said Billie, still sitting cross-legged with her back against the massive iron pillar; only, now, the pillar was beginning to vibrate. "I think it might be a good idea."

"Yes," said Kat.

"Okay," said Billie. She leaped up, and they both sprinted toward the far end of the pithead hanger; behind them, great iron and steel columns bent, split, clattered, buckled, sprang open, and the roof began to fall in.

They ran and ran.

The massive machines began to tilt, and gears and winches and wheels spun, loosened from their mooring; everything went tilting down, sucked into the widening maw of the shaft, and with a crash they disappeared.

Kat and Billie ran.

"Well, that's that, then," Claire was saying, "The collars are off, and for the time being, my young friend the Mind-Child seems happy. He's been a prisoner of somebody called the Lord or the Boy or the Messiah."

"That thing calls itself the Lord?" Demi raised a perfectly arched eyebrow, "How presumptuous!"

"Yes. He's a fake, an imposture, of that I am sure," said Claire, "This is not the God of Israel we are talking about, though I think he comes in that disguise, or perhaps he's claiming to be a relation."

"Maybe we should pray, Hybrid," said Robyn.

"Yes, maybe we should." Claire put a claw on Robyn's shoulder.

"What did you and the Mind-Child do?" Demi tilted her head to one side; she was certainly growing to like Claire – the big-boobed hybrid slut – more and more.

"We played hide-and-seek."

"And you sang some nursery rhymes." Demi smiled.

"Yes, and we sang some nursery rhymes – and the 'Old Wooden Cross'."

"I'm glad you're back, Hybrid," said Robyn.

"I'm glad I'm back too, Robyn."

"Yes, welcome back," said the two ghouls, who were hunched by the entry to the control room. Their tongues hung out, and the one called Rodriguez still had his giant erection. How does he do that? Claire wondered, thinking it probably was not very comfortable. But then, she thought, I've been many things; but I've never been a man, so I suppose I really don't know that much about what erections feel like from the inside, unless, well, unless one adopts or appropriates the other point of view, or attempts to, which is …

"Yes, thank you, I'm glad to be back," she said, glancing at the two amorous ghouls, and then turning to look out the shattered window of the control room: something was happening out there … there was a rumbling sound, like an avalanche …

Oh, no! The hanger covering Main Shaft-2 was collapsing. It was lit up from the fires still burning above Main Shaft-! Oh, oh, it looks like more trouble! She stood up, "Oh, boy."

"What is going on?"

"Shaft-2 is collapsing."

"Look!"

"Oh!" the two ghouls said in chorus, "Oh, no!"

At that moment, behind the ghouls, a vampire appeared at the door to the control room. She was a redhead with freckles and peachy-creaming skin, and she was dressed in a warrior catsuit and she had a submachine gun over her shoulder. Her fangs were sharp and her eyes – like Claire's – were demonic: yellow and maroon serpent's eyes.

Demi Pfeiffer swung her submachine gun around and said, "And just who might you be?"

"I'm Billie."

"That is not an answer."

"She's okay," said a voice. Kat appeared at Billie's shoulder.

"Oh, the more, the merrier," said Demi Pfeiffer, "Now we have ghouls, hybrids, and freckled vampires. If anyone had told me yesterday, that this would be the situation we would find ourselves in, I would not have believed him."

Hugo wagged his tail.

"I was a mere instrument, a tool in the hand of the Boy, also known as the Lord," said Billie.

"Jesus," said Demi Pfeiffer.

"But now, I am free, and I am a hybrid."

"Well, I am Demi Pfeiffer, and I am a hybrid too. You can't pull rank on me, young lady!"

"My name is Robyn, and I'm a hybrid, and Claire is my friend and she's a hybrid too."

"This sounds like confession time at Alcoholics Anonymous," said Demi Pfeiffer, "Have any of you ever gone to AA?" She looked around. "No? Me neither."

So, it was that it came to pass that Billie found herself among the devils created by Satan's cunning, alien devils, hybrids, human and alien, ghouls, and Cosmos and non-Cosmos, from as strange a civilization as perhaps could ever be imagined.

Billie cleaned off one of the workstation seats and sat down. "There is too much blood here," she said. "This is the Boy's doing; he did this. He drove them crazy." She glanced toward the two ghouls. "He turned you into what you are, too, accelerating the biomorph sickness, but somehow you seem to be immune to the worst of his spells."

She looked upon them all – and, in particular, she gazed at Claire.

Claire, who had been silent, was thinking about the collapse of Main Shaft-2, wondering about V, wondering about all the others. Had V been caught in the collapsing walls of clay and stone? Was the final way out of the pit sealed? Was V trapped? Were all the others trapped and doomed, just now, just as salvation seemed so close?

As Claire spun all these possibilities and fears in her mind she sat absolutely still like a statue of anthracite; and, as she speculated, she noticed that while Billie McAdams was talking her fangs had disappeared; and that Billie's eyes had returned to what must be their natural color – a bright Celtic green.

She was a young woman, really, that was what she was – a beautiful young woman, her will to be herself, to be true to herself, and to be free shone, bright – like a beacon.

Somehow, Claire thought this was a good sign; there was hope, and this was a message perhaps, a message of humanity, a message from somewhere, and from something.

"They will live," said Robyn, "They will all live." And she laid her hand on Claire's shoulder.

"Tell us," Claire said to Billie, "Tell us about the Boy. It will help us if we understand."

And so Billie told them her story: she told them about the Preacher, and the True Believers, and about how one day the Boy had come among them, and how the Boy had destroyed his enemies, how he had gained more and more converts, how he had drunk their souls, how he had laid waste to vast stretches of the west, and how they had crossed the desert, and how he had transformed the True Believers, all his loyal followers into the Evil Host, the zombie-bats, and how the zombie-bats, the True Believers, had consumed the blind, toothless mute Preacher and eaten him alive.

"It's all about belief," Billie said, "Evil belief."

"Belief …?" Demi crossed and then uncrossed her legs, the hiss of silk, the perfume of Cosmos First Class. Hugo, tongue hanging out, looked up, in near adoration. This Cosmos smelled as good as that Blond Cosmos visitor geologist from Elysium who petted him, combed some burrs out of his fur, and gave him snacks from her lunch box.

"If you don't believe in him," Billie said, "If you don't believe in him, then he can do you no harm."

"Interesting," said Demi, who, as a Cosmos First Class, was naturally a skeptic, "That is very interesting."

"Life is like a dream," Billie said, and she told them how the Boy had loved her, and how he had told her he loved her because she was free, he loved her because she refused to be his, and how he had sent Sally to possess her and how V had freed her from possession by Sally – and by the Boy.

As Kat listened, her heart beat harder; this was the end of the world truly; this was everything that the Cosmos Elite feared. This was the rising tide of unreason which would flood over the world like a plague; this was everything the Leader-President, in his last speech to the Centurion Academy, had said would happen; he had said, "We have made many mistakes; we have been cruel; we have committed crimes; but, I fear that, with all our cruelty, all our intelligence, all our crafty devices and stratagems, we have only delayed the catastrophe … and the catastrophe will come in the form of madness." This was what the President-Leader had foretold, what they all had feared, a tidal wave of unreason, of fanaticism …

"I cannot believe this," said Demi Pfeiffer, "I cannot believe that in our day and age … such unreason, such superstition, and such madness …"

Robyn had listened to Billie's tale, and she stared, unbelieving, her eyes wide open.

Outside the shattered window, the cawing and screeching of the zombie-bats echoed as they circled above the ruined mine.

"Now, how do we save those who are down below," Claire brightened, she had been listening in her mind for signals, and now she got one, faint and from far away, from V: "We are alive, and we are going to get out of here!"

"Good!"

"I don't know how yet. But just wait. We shall overcome."

"Good!"

"Now, I will fall silent."

"Yes!"

"I've got work to do!"

"I'm here when you need me!" Claire sent the message with a mental smiley face.

"Yes, thanks!" V's mind disappeared from Claire's consciousness, and so did all the other hybrid murmurs. Claire smiled. "Does anyone know where there's some coffee?" she said, "And food? Is there any food?"

"Damnation!" Bob Norton squatted on a low mound of clayish soil in a workspace in Tunnel Z-46, just above the Shaft-1 flood level. His overalls had been ripped in five or six places, his chest was bare; his face had been scratched and clawed at: the battle with those vicious ghouls had been a damned close thing. He bloody well hoped he hadn't been infected; he didn't want to become a ghoul. He'd shoot himself first.

He pushed up his protective visor and wiped at his forehead.

His pride was to never leave anybody behind.

Already they had lost six men, guards, lost to the ghouls. And then there were people missing: Valerie Joffre the Cosmos geologist, Bernard Milosevic, a supervisor on the lower levels, one of the hybrids, a golden female, and all the human prisoners …

And just now it looked like – with both shafts collapsed – they were all going to get left behind, buried forever, this time, more than a mile underground.

The workspace – which was half squared-off room, half natural cavity – was lit by phosphorescent sparkles of wall lichen and by glowing mushrooms and by the few headlamps the humans still carried with them. They all, humans and hybrids, looked like ghosts. Even the one ghoul, their pet ghoul, Jim Rahv, looked like a ghost – well, he looked more like a ghost than the rest; he was crouched in a corner making patterns on the dirt floor with pebbles. Norton sighed; yes, he certainly hoped he had not bloody well caught the ghoul disease.

"So, what do we do now?" Norton glanced at Julian Harvey, at Sammy Franks, and, then, at the lead hybrid, V, who was walking around, claw to chin, obviously deep in thought. It was touching in a way how the hybrids had all greeted each other and how delighted they were to see their friend V and how V was obviously overjoyed to see them.

There had been a difficult moment when V had stared at him, and Norton could feel the reproach in her glance and the murderous intent in her heart, her muscles tensing for an attack; he was the chief security guy, so he was the man who had held her dear brother and sister hybrids prisoner, so he would have to pay.

"He's one of the good guys," said Sabrina.

"Definitely," said the silver hybrid, Helen.

"Yes, my mate is a good chap," said Freddy.

"He did security up top," said Julian.

"Yes, and whenever he came down into the pit, he tried to make conditions better," said Sabrina.

"Yeah, he kept telling me to leave you alone, and not to torture you," said Sammy, glancing sheepishly at his favorite sexy slave and now pal and protector, Sabrina, aka HZ-2.

"That he did," said Sabrina, she gave Sammy a friendly little jab in the ribs.

V came up close to Norton, sniffing, her nostrils quivering.

Norton noticed that the Hybrid Queen – or was she a goddess? – smelled good, just like all the hybrids smelled good, it was a sort of mystery, that perfume that emanated from them, even in the most filthy and dire and unhygienic circumstances.

"Okay," she said.

"Okay," Norton said, holding her glance.

V was very close now; she stared at him; he felt her glance bore into his soul, probe his memories, his attitudes. God, it was a strange feeling, but he had experienced it before, in the jungle, when his allies, the hybrids, were questioning him about some order he had given – well, suggested – you really didn't give orders to hybrids, you suggested, you discussed …

She held out her hand, well, her claw, "I'm honored to meet you, Colonel," she said, using his old Australian-Indonesian Special Forces title.

"The honor is mine," he said.

V glanced around the space and then back at Norton. "There must be another way out," she said.

"Do you know where it is?"

"No, I don't."

"Well, that's not much help, then, is it?" Norton smiled at her, but it was a sad, resigned smile. He wiped at the sheen of sweat and mud on his forehead.

"No," V said, "I'm sorry, it isn't. But …" She glanced at Sammy Franks. He was sitting between Sabrina and Helen. "Mr. Franks here told Sabrina he has an idea."

Norton raised an eyebrow and glanced at Sammy.

"Yeah, well, I mean, it's not really a total idea, I mean …" Sammy looked abashed; he glanced at V, then down at his boots, and then, sheepishly, at Norton.

"Get on with it, mate, don't be shy now."

"Well, I just said to Sabrina and to Helen and to V here, I mean because she asked me if I had any ideas, so I said to them, that something had occurred to me, you know, when I was down in the pit with my girls, I mean with Sabrina and Helen or HZ-2 and HZ-8 which are their prison names, which was shameful in itself, a sort of degradation by labeling, you know, and what I thought was, it was one of those moments you know when you have time to think, and the strangest thoughts creep into …"

"My God, mate: get on with it!" Norton almost wanted to cry.

"Well, here it is then: The ghouls go up to hunt on the surface and kill animals and people out in the desert, but I don't think they go up Shaft-2 because that Shaft-2 pithead hanger has always been locked, and anyway, the pithead for Shaft-2 is inside the perimeter, inside the fences and walls and minefields, and the ghouls went hunting – if it was them, mind you – outside the perimeter, so …"

"So, the ghouls must have had a way to get to the surface which was not Shaft-2 and certainly not Shaft-1," said V.

Norton stared at V and at Sammy Franks, whom he'd always considered a consummate fool and sadistic idiot who tortured hybrids, and here Sammy was coming up with a surprisingly bright idea – one that he, Norton, should have certainly thought of himself – and also consorting real-mates-like with his hybrids Sabrina – world-renowned scientist in her human days – and Helen – famous hotshot corporate lawyer – and with V the hybrid who was reputedly some sort of genius hybrid, the chief of all hybrids, the original, the goddess half alien from ancient times, and … Sammy, well, it was amazing!

"Damn good idea," Norton said, "But where is this bloody exit they know about?"

"Now, that we don't know, not yet," said V, glancing at Sammy.

"No, we don't know, not yet."

Julian Harvey coughed, "If it wasn't Shaft-2, then it might be along the old Timberland drift or that other old drift called the Fallows drift, but nobody's gone near them in years, decades even. I only have the vaguest idea where they are and no idea how to get to them. There are miles of different possibilities down here. The only person who might know all about this is that visiting geologist, that Cosmos, Valerie Joffre. I think she's got the historical maps, the surveys, you know, from when they first exploited this place; she's got it in implants, she told me. She's got all the old stuff, the whole archive, in her head – she has the total picture."

"So where is our Cosmos First Class geologist, Valerie Joffre, then?" said Norton.

Julian cleared his throat. "Well, as you know, she's very independent; she always does her own thing, but she signed in for a 24-hour shift, said she was going down to the deepest level, I think, below Shaft-1, below the prisoner level, one of the deepest places, maybe the deepest."

"That's where the fire and explosions from Shaft–1 probably ended up; the fuel-fed fire went straight down the shaft," said Sarah, Norton's favorite, the sleek black Hybrid with the two flaming scarlet Vs imprinted on her body.

"Yes: and then there's the flooding, the river, and the underground lake – without the pumps ... all that is already flooded now, the human prisoners are probably dead."

"So, our Cosmos geologist might be dead too, then."

"If she went where she said she was going, she would be down about four to six levels – maybe even seven or eight – below where the humans are kept," said Julian, "that's where she would have been. Yes, she's probably dead."

"The humans, now that's another problem," said Norton.

"Humans, are those the human prisoners?" V turned toward Norton.

"Yes," Norton nodded, "the human prisoners, I think they'll be dead by now. Sarah and Freddy and I were trying to figure out how to get down to them, but that whole part has been flooded, I think. I don't think there's any way to get back down there."

"There's a hybrid down there, too," said Sarah.

"Yes, the golden one," Harvey said.

"Okay," V said, "If you all stay here – humans, hybrids, and our ghoul friend," she glanced at Jimmy Ghoul who looked up at her with baleful eyes and then grinned a timid ghoulish grin, and V smiled back and turned to Norton said, "I'll go look for your geologist, and I'll find your humans if they're still alive."

"Alone," Norton raised an eyebrow, "You want to go alone?"

"Yes, it'll be faster. Just give me a map."

"Are you sure?" said Sabrina.

"She's sure," said Freddy.

"Yes, she's sure," Sarah gave V, her nemesis, a special smile.

"Yes, she's sure," said Helen.

"She always does what she wants," said Sarah, the "V" seeming to pulsate under her breasts and the other V on her back glowing extra bright: V's little gift: the two "Vs" that V had branded her with, eons ago it seemed. By now, Sarah was almost proud of them.

V shot her a wickedly affectionate glance.

Julian Harvey pulled a plasticized sheath out of his pocket, "Here are the schematics. They are not perfect, and they're not complete. Some of the old stuff is not mapped at all. And the lower level is not mapped the way it should be. And a lot of stuff is totally left out, all the old drifts, the Timberland, the Fallows, the Reich, and the Labine cross-drift."

V and Julian and Norton studied the unfolded schematics.

"Meanwhile, we'll try to move toward where I think the Timberland Drift is," Julian said, as he and V and Norton and pored over the map.

"V, we'll wait for you here," said Norton, putting his finger on the Rangoon crossroads, a place where several tunnels met on level X-7.

And, so, it was agreed. V would go alone, in search of Valerie Joffre, and the golden hybrid, and the human prisoners – and she would bring them back to rendezvous with the others at the Rangoon crossroads.

V memorized the map and left the original with Julian Harvey.

"Good luck," said Norton and shook her hand.

The hybrids all embraced V, one by one.

"Goodbye, good luck!" The voices, human and hybrid, and even ghoul, echoed as V headed down a narrow tunnel.

Then, as she strode away, the voices were lost.

V was alone, once again alone.

So here I am, V thought, here I am, venturing alone, into the deepest depths of the Underworld. She was thrilled.

Dropping down, deep into the abyss, she would be what she had become over the centuries – a solitary hunter, a semi-wild predator, a half-civilized savage – alone, exploring the wonders of the world, thrusting herself into the most dangerous places.

This time, once again, it would be the wonders of the Underworld, of the antechamber to Dante's Inferno. The clammy sulfurous air, glowing with eerie phosphorescence. Suddenly, she felt she was back in the sacred caves near mount Vesuvius where in ancient times she had worshiped among the sulfurous volcanic fumes rising from the center of the earth, where she had crawled into the most intimate and deepest womb-like spaces and found ancient altars to nameless deities of the underworld, earthy, smoldering, sensual creatures of the eternal cycle of fertility, birth, life, and death.

There, she had felt at one with the naked and semi-naked worshippers, crawling, kneeling creeping in the mud, and sulfurous fumes.

There, she had felt at one with the earth, the clay, the dust, the smoking cauldrons, the planet earth and all its mysteries.

There, she had felt at one with the ancient pagan gods and goddesses.

Maybe I really am the Devil, she thought, as she climbed down a spiral staircase from level X-20 to level X-18.

No, no, I'm not ambitious enough. Being the Devil or that dreadful Boy creature must be hard work, a full-time profession, a serious vocation and calling.

Maybe I'm just a dark angel, a tiny speck of evil.

Then, maybe, perhaps, just maybe, I'm actually good! I mean on the whole, and all things considered, and putting aside, for the moment, the minor fact that I eat people alive and drain them of all their delicious corpuscles and every drop of blood – leaving only a lifeless husk behind that is "dead, truly dead, and will not rise again." Yes, perhaps I'm not such a bad girl, after all.

She came to a large cavern-like space, which led to a sort of crevice or miniature canyon. She shimmied down the canyon's rock face, which was muddy and dripping with streams of gray liquid clay, and at the bottom, she crawled through a low tunnel, and then climbed through a tiny arch which led to another narrow mud-coated tunnel, which ended in a cracked wall of what looked like limestone; the crack was seeping mud and just wide enough, maybe, for her to get through; she unhooked her backpack, and, trailing it and her weapons behind her, she slipped through the crack and came out into another, wider, tunnel; she walked along the tunnel, and after about fifty meters, she came to a suspended walkway that led across an open pit which seemed to go down forever and out of which sulfurous fumes rose, as if it led to straight into the heart of a volcano; at the end of the walkway another tunnel sloped downwards; at the bottom of that tunnel, she came to metal spiral staircase. She looked down.

At the foot of the staircase, steamy gray water bubbled up, swirled around.

Everything was flooded.

This did not look good.

She climbed down to the level of the water; she crouched on the last step and felt the water – it was hot and sulfurous. And it was too thick with mud for her to swim through. The mud would clog her gills. Besides, she wouldn't be able to bring any human up through this.

Any humans would have drowned long ago.

She crouched on the edge of the bubbling pool, thinking: There must be another way to get to the lower depths. She accessed her memory of the mine schematics: Yes, there must be a way to find the human prisoners, if they were still alive – and to find that blond Cosmos geologist, Valerie Joffre, who was supposed to have all the answers and, in particular, who might know how to get out of this infernal place.

CHAPTER 15 – CHILDHOOD

"The lights are off again, Jake," Gloria wiggled her nose and wiggled her toes; she liked to see if she could wiggle everything at once; sometimes, it was easy; sometimes it was hard. Once, she even managed to wiggle her ears and nose and toes and make Ms. Agnes laugh.

"I know." Jake scratched his knee. He narrowed his eyes. The lights were off, and the emergency lights had come on, but they were dull. It was like looking through the hot steamy fog they often saw swirling over upriver. He glanced toward the big open central area of the prisoners' cave. The air looked smoky and gray; but it always looked smoky and gray; the preacher was squealing about something. Ms. Moriani was screaming. Mostly folk didn't talk or scream or do anything anymore.

Food pack deliveries had stopped maybe three days ago.

Three days …

At least that's what Ms. Agnes said, "No food for three days now, Jake," she said, "We are all going to die if it keeps up like this."

"We should explore, Jake." Gloria smeared some mud on her thighs; it was nice and smooth and cool. She drew an "O" just above her right knee.

"Here." Jake pulled a crust of Halibut Inc. Food Pouch Bread out of his shorts pocket and handed it to her.

"You don't want it?' Gloria felt the saliva flood her mouth. Her tongue was suddenly all sticky and heavy; her stomach growled. She licked her lips, a little line of silver saliva formed, like a snail's sliver tracks, glistening on her lower lip and chin.

"No, I don't want it." Jake wasn't looking at her. Gloria stared at him. His eyes were far away, glassy somehow, reflecting the phosphoresce. It was like Jake wasn't inside Jake anymore but somewhere else, or maybe somebody else had snuck into Jake's head and was inside Jake; this thought gave Gloria a funny, scary feeling in her tummy which rippled with a shiver of fear and which tummy had been empty since maybe two days ago, however long that was.

Days … the word sounded nice.

Daze … haze … maze … faze …

Words, words, words …

Gloria collected words from Ms. Agnes and anybody else who would give her words; sometimes she stole words she just overheard – the preacher had long words and short words; Ms. Moriani had funny words and sometimes no words at all; the teacher, well, the teacher used to have lots of words but didn't have any words anymore and just crouched there, his mouth hanging open.

Night and *day* meant nothing, though Ms. Agnes had explained them to Gloria several times and most patiently. Gloria tried to see what it might be like: the sun goes up; the sun goes down; the sun rises in the east and sets in the west. The sun was a big light in the sky. Like a lamp. Like a lamp? It was a thing hard to imagine, like the whole world being round and not being in a cave with a roof that arched up high overhead, gray stone, glittering with lichen, and moss and with stalactites and stalagmites and upriver and down-river and the gray-silver swirl of the river under the dark rock where the dead went. The whole idea of sun and moon was difficult – "bright lights in the sky," Gloria suspected, probably didn't "do the thing justice," as Ms. Agnes would have said.

"Thank you, Jake, thank you, indeed," Gloria said; Ms. Agnes had taught Gloria to be very polite.

Jake smiled. "You are very polite, Gloria."

"Manners are what keep us civilized is what Ms. Agnes says, Jake." Gloria took a tentative bite of the bread; it was crusty and muddy and hard, but it was delicious, a "real treat," like Ms. Agnes would say. Gloria's stomach growled at her, perhaps "*snarled*" was the right word, her stomach was say-ing something, but she didn't really know what it was saying, translating her stomach was not her forte. "Manners are what differentiate us from beasts," Gloria said carefully, taking another bite, and then she held the crust of bread out and looked at it. Food was a funny thing; you put it in one end, and then it came out the other end when you went and sat on the board with the holes in it and it went downriver, like the dead. And you washed yourself in the river, upstream from where the "excrement" – Ms. Agnes' word – and from where the dead went into the water and swirled around. And it all flowed away – the dead and the excrement. There were other words too – "turds" and "shit" and "stool" and "piss" and even something called "urine" which was what old doctor Nast who was now dead – he caught the ghoul disease and turned all white and trembling but he didn't do gibberish he just drooled – used to say, "Let's look at your urine, then," he said; and made Gloria pee in a pot he kept specially for pee and sometimes for turds.

"You're stool is like gruel," Old Doctor Nast once said, which Gloria remembered because it sounded nice; but it didn't feel so good, achy and runny and bent up double, she was afraid she was going to go downriver her dirty toes sticking up to be seen by everybody and going last, her toes, the last thing anybody would ever see of her, which somehow she felt would be a crying shame.

"Ms. Agnes," said Jake, picking up half a handful of clay, "Ms. Agnes is nice, better than nice." He fingered the wet clay; it was almost liquid. He squeezed it and let it dribble in a small gray stream from between his fingers. "Ms. Agnes has a nice voice."

Ms. Agnes had taught Jake lots of things, like how to count and how to write – she'd used a stick and a flat pool of clay that she smoothed down with her hand and – both of them on hands and knees – she'd told him how the letters stood for sounds so that you could put your words down in writing and leave messages for other people or to remind yourself of something you might forget.

She told him, and Gloria, too, stories about how things had been once outside where there was the sky and fields and sunshine and moonlight and cities and how once there had been a thing called the United States of America and a thing called the Constitution and freedom.

Jake understood quite a lot, or he thought he did, and he did have some memories from before the cave, not many, and it was hard to tell them from dreams or nightmares. Gloria had to invent the whole world out of words; she'd been born in the cave, and she'd never been outside.

Professor Swank, too, he told stories, about explorers and big fights between different people which were called "wars," but now Professor Swank didn't talk anymore – you could see his ribs and his belly-button had turned inside out – and he'd lost most of his teeth – and he screamed sometimes – and other times he just sat with his back against a wall of stone, his mouth open and tears running down his face. Jake thought that Professor Swank was emptying out and would soon be feather-light and go downriver stark naked his toes sticking up like all the other dead to swirl and disappear in the whirlpool under the rock wall.

"I don't hear it," Gloria said, "I really don't hear it." She was chewing slowly so the bread would last, her jaw moved slower and slower, and Jake watched it. He liked to watch Gloria and to look after her, and he didn't want anything to happen to her ever.

"What don't you hear?" Jake let a last bit of clay drop – plop!

"It! The thing – you know!" Gloria's jaw was moving slowly, "I don't hear the heartbeat!"

"The heartbeat," Jake listened. He frowned. "Yes, yes. I don't hear it either." Jake stood up; there was no sound of motors. There was no sound of the giant *thump, thump, thump* that came through the rocks and stone. Here, near the crack in the stone face where the air sometimes moved and felt funny against your skin, you could usually hear it, but now it was silent; there was just the sound of the air moving in the crevasses and cracks, heavy damp warm air.

Jake listened some more – nothing.

Ms. Agnes once said the pumps kept the caves from flooding or something like that, "There's a big lake of water where the upriver comes from, I do believe I heard one of the guards say, that is when the guards still visited us, eons ago," she said, "If there weren't pumps and the barrier, then the water would drown us all."

"It – the pumps – the pumps are off," said Jake, realizing what the silence meant and what the noise that was now gone had been when it was on.

"Spooky," said Gloria. Spooky was one of her favorite words, "Spooky." She looked at the last bit of bread – a little itsy-bitsy bit – and she blinked, feeling tears ready to come – *keep it for later, or eat it now?* She shoved it into her mouth and swallowed.

"Let's go and look," Jake stood up.

"Okay," Gloria stood up and smoothed down the dirt-soaked shirt: it was really heavy against her legs – everything all the time was wet and heavy and thick and soaked in clay, so it was hard to feel light and free unless you took all your clothes off and jumped into the river – upstream from the turds and the dead of course – but the preacher had railed against people taking all their clothes off, and jumping into upstream, so most of them didn't, and maybe that was good because though Ms. Agnes approved of bathing without clothes on – and Jake and Gloria did it – she also said, "Wearing clothes differentiates us from the beasts of the fields, Gloria, who neither do they reap nor do they sow not."

Fields …

Gloria tried to imagine what fields might be like.

Running barefoot and with no clothes in the brightness of the big lamps in the sky was about as close as she could get.

Jake slid down the hidden side of the outcropping; he looked up; Gloria's chin was on the edge of the outcropping, she was grinning down at him, with that little way she had, curling up the edge of her lips and showing her teeth, her blue eyes bright, sparkling in the dim air. He reached up from the shadowy pool of darkness, and she slid down into his arms.

"Thank you, Jake," she said, still pressed against him, "You are a true gentleman and a gallant fellow."

Jake had to smile. The top of Gloria's cropped little head – with its glints of gold – came up to his collarbone.

"The adventure begins," Gloria said, looking up at him and with the palm of her hand flat on his chest.

"Yes," Jake grinned.

The hidden opening in the wall of rock was a slippery, curvy, vertical slit with soft muddy sides; it was maybe two hand-spans wide. Jake could just squeeze through. The slit was wedged in behind the outcropping where nobody could see it – and it was their secret way in and out of the cave.

The big people – or "adults" as Gloria insisted on calling them – didn't know about it and Jake had not told them because they would forbid his going out, so only he and Gloria knew about it, and Jake trusted Gloria even though she was so little, but she was "mature for her years" as Ms. Agnes said, and even Doctor Nast had said Gloria was a true scholar. "She's got a head on her shoulders," he said. Anyway, it would have been difficult – probably impossible – for any adult to squeeze through the narrow fissure in the rock face – even Jake found it really hard and sometimes if the rock was not wet enough he had to take off his shorts and then put them on at the other end and smear slippery mud all over his body so he was really greasy and he could slip through. Gloria was littler and it was easier for her to get through and she didn't even have to take off her shirt, though sometimes she did just for the fun of it.

And, so, they had explored, the two of them, outside the cave, and it was exciting, and Jake had sworn Gloria to secrecy. He put his finger up against his lips and said, "Shhh!"

Gloria echoed the gesture and whispered, "Shhh!"

She had grinned, and her eyes had sparkled; Jake could see that Gloria liked secrets and he figured, mischievous as she was, she would keep this one.

Outside the cave, it was a new world, a marvel: they discovered passageways, and crawl spaces, and vast chambers – they discovered a river running through a sharply cut channel – was it their river or another river? – and it went down over a slope and bubbled and made a funny rattling rumbling noise and in some places, steam or smoke came out of the water which, when Jake stuck his finger in it, was hot, not hot enough to burn, but pretty hot, hotter than the water upriver and much hotter than the water downriver where the excrement – turds and stools and suchlike and the naked dead with their toes and faces pointed up to the rock face went, floating, floating, then swirling, round and round, under the final blank black rock face, then gone.

They climbed up, and up, and came to another part of the caves and here the walls were straight up and down, and there were machines and metal latticework Jake had seen in a book Ms. Agnes had. They had once seen a man with big boots and a hat with a light on it unloading crates from a great metal box and Jake recognized that those were the crates that brought the food for the people in the caves: there was a picture of a food pouch on the side of the crate.

Then the metal box went upwards and disappeared, making a funny squealing noise in the latticework.

The man didn't see them.

On another day, going through another really narrow passageway a long way from their home cave, a place where there was a dead-end tunnel, and then some boarding and metal leaning against a wall, they came to a place where there were two "ghouls" which was Ms. Agnes' word. These ghouls were like what Mr. Hauser had become, all white and glossy and with no hair and big white bug eyes, like the white of an egg Jake had once seen, and long fingernails and toenails and they looked really funny, but not nice, not nice at all. Stuff was dripping from their mouths, and it glowed, and the two ghouls were squatting on their haunches. The only other light was from the phosphorescent mushroom and lichen.

"I'm scared," Gloria said.

"So am I, but let's watch."

"Okay," Gloria crouched lower.

The two ghouls were eating something.

"That's a dead," said Gloria.

"A dead, yes, it is," said Jake, "It's a dead." The ghouls were picking a body apart; it was a dead person, maybe one that had gone downriver; or maybe one the ghouls had hunted and killed, though no people ever went out of the cave – they didn't know how to get out of the cave, Jake thought, and they were afraid to get out of the cave – so it couldn't be a cave person, not one of our persons, Jake thought, not one of our dead. One of the ghouls picked up a long thin bone, turned it over, and began to gnaw on it. Jake tried to see if it was a man-person or a woman-person the ghouls were eating, but he couldn't tell.

"I wonder what a dead tastes like," Gloria was using her knuckles to rub her nose. She wiggled her nose and sniffed.

"I don't know," Jake said, licking his lips, "I never tasted one."

"Me neither."

"No."

"No."

"Let's go."

"Yes, let's go."

They elbowed their way backward on their bellies and then on hands and knees, and got to the tunnel entrance; then they could stand up, and they walked through the long narrow winding tunnel, and then they pushed out from behind the metal plate and board, and pushed the boards back in place, and then they walked fast through two more tunnels, and then along a suspended walkway so they could be as far away as possible from the ghouls who didn't seem very nice at all.

Jake always kept careful track of where they went. He put little stones at corners, and sometimes he closed his eyes and pictured in his head the whole route they had taken because the caves and cracks turned and twisted and doubled up and went sideways and also up and down. Sometimes he'd go back and double-check the return route. He didn't want to get lost out here beyond the cave that was their home. He had learned in his previous travels, before he took Gloria with him, that it was important to get a picture in his mind of where he went, each turning, each opening, so that he would be able to get back. Often, he would double back a couple of times to make sure he knew how to do it, before he went on. Some places were really dark, with no light bulbs or light bars, no glowing mushroom chandeliers and not much radiant lichen, just little sparkles and dull shining light from the stone walls to navigate and go by.

He noticed that he was getting a sort of picture in his head of all the different parts, like the cave where they'd seen the ghouls – he could rehearse in his mind how to get there: It was reached by going up a long tunnel where there were no signs that anybody had been there in a long time, none of the men with those funny hats with the lights on them, and then sliding in between some rotten old boards – an old retaining wall – and squeezing into an old tunnel where there was a funny little set of steel things – "tracks" Gloria called them, like "for a small railroad," and she reminded him of a picture book Ms. Agnes had, and so, yes, Jake agreed, it must have been a little railroad of some kind, and finally they came some sheets of metal leaning against the tunnel wall, and behind the sheets was another slit in the rock, and they slid through and came into a winding very smooth but not square tunnel that came to a big long cave with a high roof and where it smelled really bad, and there were all sorts of junky things piled up, barrels, with labels on them saying the stuff was "Dangerous," and there were pictures of skulls and crossbones. The cave had an inky little river that went through it, meandering away off into the distance, and big clusters of really weird mushroom bouquets that glowed different colors, and the air in that big cave seemed to move in a way it only moved where they'd seen the metal box go up in the latticework.

It was in that big cave with the river that they saw the ghouls who were really not nice at all – and it was there that the air seemed to move.

He'd discussed the strange thing with Gloria, and she'd said, "It's a breeze," remembering some story Ms. Agnes had read to her or told her and Jake said, "Yes, of course, it's a breeze," and he had just an inkling that a "breeze" meant that the air was coming from somewhere and going somewhere, but he didn't push the thought much farther than that, though he was aware of other ideas which were sort of lingering and malingering and hovering there, just out of reach, just behind or beyond the thought *It comes from somewhere and it goes somewhere.*

He frowned; the thought of a 'breeze' should take him somewhere in his mind – but where? *Where the ghouls were, there was a breeze*; what did that mean?

He scratched his head. Months ago – whatever months were – most of his hair had been hacked off really short by Ms. Agnes and had been prickly like the top of Gloria's head. But now his hair was long, almost shoulder-length – Ms. Agnes said she was too tired, she'd cut it later, "Forgive me, Jake," she said – so it was long and greasy-heavy with clay, which he didn't mind at all.

Anyway, he was aware that, increasingly, he had this general picture in his head: the big cave where they all lived, the humans, maybe twenty of them still alive, with the upriver and downriver around a bend in the cave at one end, and the big steel door at the other end, with the slot through which the Food Packets and Food Pouches came, somebody invisible shoving them in, and the people on their hands and knees – some of them naked or almost now that there was hardly any cloth or clothes – scrabbling for the stuff and sometimes fighting, rolling in the mud, tearing clothes and hair, scrabbling for what little there was, and often breaking the food pouches open so they had to pick it up in their hands or lick it up from the mud.

Doctor Nast and Ms. Agnes used to try to get them to line up – and they used to do it – but Doctor Nast was dead and Ms. Agnes had given up, and so the people were just down on their hands and knees, scrabbling in the muck for the Pouches, sometimes fighting, too, rolling around, men and women, screeching feebly …

"I give up, Jake, I really do," said Ms. Agnes, watching them.

"Yes," Jake said; he could see that things were, as Ms. Agnes said, "Going from bad to worse."

Anyway, inside the cave and the niches there were cracks that nobody knew about, and a few of them led out of the cave, and the cracks, one was about twenty feet long Jake figured, went to near the place with the box in the lattice – it was an elevator shaft he and Gloria had figured out – looking in one of Ms. Agnes's picture books – half-rotted away but you could still look at the pictures, and you could still read some of the words – and from there, there were lots of side caves and tunnels and crevices – Jake had them all sort of mapped out in his head – and one of these, after a while, led to the place where they saw the little river and all the things piled up that had the crossbones and skulls on them and the signs saying "Danger" and "Bio …something" and where they also saw some really ugly looking ghouls, big and bad, and so they hid and then scrambled and then tip-toed behind some big stones and left the cavern where the breeze blew.

Another place he had well mapped out was near the cages that went up and down, it was there they saw the Golden Hybrid, which sighting was extra-ultra-top secret, for Gloria and Jake only, and another long tunnel, and a separate cave, led to the place where they'd seen the ghouls eating the dead.

Yes, near the elevator, and at one of the higher levels, up from the cavern where they lived, right down beyond the big shaft, and down beyond the river and waterfall, they'd seen something that was like a picture in the picture book encyclopedia of monsters – a hybrid; she was all gold.

The Golden Hybrid happened when Jake and Gloria had gone far up above the home cave, "the mother ship" as Ms. Agnes sometimes called it, and then they had found a new crevice, and they had climbed up a narrow twisting crack in the rock structure – a new one they were exploring – and they came to steps, wooden steps, and saw that these had been made by people, like Ms. Agnes or like old Doctor Nast who was dead or like Jimmy the Fixer – who was always trying to make things – "to get us organized," as Ms. Agnes said.

Gloria and Jake climbed up the steps, and they came to a narrow tunnel that was squared-off and had timbers on the roof and on the sides and they wondered if it was a place people lived, maybe the man they had seen with the food container, but they came around a corner and there was a person but it was not really a person; it looked like a woman but it was all covered in scales – gold-colored but covered in mud too and it was working under a light that was brighter than any light Jake had ever seen and it turned and saw them and it had a weird face with big strange eyes and a mouth with two big teeth sticking out – and it was wearing a thick collar where two little lights were blinking, one red and one green – and Jake thought *Oh, it's going to attack us and eat us!* It was very close – too close for them to run and besides they'd have to squeeze back into the crack in the wall and there'd be no time for that – so Jake said to Gloria, "Don't move, maybe it doesn't see us," and the Gloria whispered, "Okay," in a really low even-toned voice like she was really, really afraid, and Jake thought that maybe his heart had stopped beating and his stomach had fallen away somewhere far down below his ankles.

The thing blinked its big eyes, stared at them, and then it raised one of its hands – well they were sort of like human hands, but they were like claws too – that Jake had seen in the old books before all the books had rotted away – and it raised one of its claws and it waved, it looked like a wave, opening and closing its claw, and it smiled, at least it looked like a smile, and Jake took a deep breath and waved back and he saw out of the corner of his eye that Gloria waved back too. And then the creature waved again and then turned back to its work – it was using its claws to cut the wall of clay in front of it into sort of blocks.

"It likes us," Gloria said.

"Yes, I think it likes us." Jake frowned, thinking we'd better get out of here; this animal was nice, but it was probably not alone, and he heard a creaking sound, so he said, "Let's go. We'll get in trouble, we'll get it in trouble too," he added, not knowing why.

"It likes us, but it can't talk," said Gloria.

"Yes," Jake felt that somehow the animal had communicated all sorts of … well, not exactly thoughts, but feelings, somehow …

"It's got a collar," said Gloria, "The collar is really, really bad!"

Jake looked at Gloria; he had the same thought as Gloria – the collar was really, really bad – but he didn't know what the thought meant or where it came from.

The little lights on the collar blinked, one red, one green – blink, blink, blink – and for a moment, Jake thought that the collar could see them and could read their thoughts.

He thought – that's a silly idea, but still …

He was afraid.

They got away fast, tumbling down the wooden stairs, squeezing through the crack in the stone wall, and then making the long climb back down to their secret entry to the cave; and for a long time they discussed what the thing with the collar might be, but they didn't ask the doctor or Ms. Agnes because Jake didn't want anybody to know where they went and that they had been outside the cave where the prisoners were kept which was supposed to be their whole world.

"This cave is our whole world," said Ms. Agnes once, "All we see are shadows, we are trapped in a world of illusion, a shadow world, like the prisoners of Plato."

Later, when he and Gloria were alone in upriver, swimming, Jake said, "I think it was a hybrid." He'd heard about them, and he'd seen pictures of them in some of Ms. Agnes' books and before he went mad, the preacher had made big long speeches about how the hybrids were evil, pure devils, creatures of Satan, and had brought the judgment of God and fire and brimstone down upon his wayward children, whoever God's children were.

"A hybrid, but don't they eat people?"

"Only sometimes," said Jake, "if they've eaten lots of people already, then they're not hungry, then they don't need to eat more people, and they can be friendly. So, she probably had just eaten somebody."

"I liked her."

"I liked her, too," said Jake.

"She's pretty."

"You think she's pretty?"

"Yes, she's very pretty," Gloria said with that decided air she had when she was absolutely certain of something and would not budge, "She is definitely very, very pretty and one of my favorite things!"

Jake – with his junior partner Gloria – spent as much time as he could exploring because he didn't like being in the big cave with the others; a lot of people were sick and like shadows of themselves and the old professor who couldn't see anything anymore, just sat on the ground and cried all the time. He was only wearing a jacket and nothing else, and he smelled like pee and shit and he didn't go to the upriver to clean himself anymore. People were mostly dressed in sheets or bits of old clothing, rags really, because nothing else was left. The men let their beards grow because there were no razors, though Ms. Agnes chopped off Gloria's hair and Jake's hair for some reason with an old knife she had kept somehow and which she used to open food pouches.

The women had stopped having their periods, Ms. Agnes said, because they were starving to death and didn't have enough energy. "Not enough calories," Ms. Agnes said. Jake had no idea what calories were or what a period was.

Gloria said she'd heard a period had something to do with the moon. "There's no moon down here," Jake said.

"I've never seen the moon," said Gloria.

"I sort of remember it," Jake said, "I think I remember it. I don't know what the moon would have to do with the women and a period."

"Yeah," Gloria frowned and wiggled her nose; it was clear she didn't know either, but then she was just a little kid and she didn't have to know things. Jake felt he should know things and his ambition was to know everything – like Ms. Agnes.

"Oh, moon, oh, moon," said Gloria making her eyes look dreamy.

"You also put a period at the end of a sentence," Jake said, remembering those sessions with Ms. Agnes in her thin muddy shift on her hands and knees in the clay pool – where it was almost dry and really smooth – with that sharp-pointed stick teaching Jake how to read and write, and she'd end a string of words she'd written and say, "And this is a period!" and make a little round hole in the mud. Or you put a question mark at the end of a sentence, but a question mark didn't have anything to do with the moon, Jake was pretty sure of that; it was a squiggle with a point – a period – at the bottom.

Jake had practiced making letters, lying on his stomach, making tiny letters in the fine gray mud: A, B, C, D, and all the way to Z.

So the period thing was one of those things you just couldn't get a handle on. "I cannot for the life of me get a handle on this," said Ms. Agnes once when she was trying to figure something out.

People stank too though you didn't notice it after a while, but if you went away into the other caves, then when you came back, you did smell the smell because it was like smelling it for the first time and you wrinkled your nose.

Gloria wrinkled her nose, one time, when they came back from wandering, she looked at him and rolled her eyes, and whispered, "People stink!"

"Yes, they do."

"Do we stink too?"

"I guess, sometimes."

"Let's go upriver and take off our clothes."

And they did, and bathed. "I don't know if people can smell their own stink," Gloria said, her head sticking out of the water.

"I don't think they can." Jake dipped under, opened his eyes, and felt the sting and the bubbles press against his eyeballs, as he swam and swam and swam, he felt Gloria swimming alongside him, and somehow she found his hand and put her hand in his, and they came up out of the water together, and for some reason, they were both laughing.

In the other caves, you smelled other smells – the moldy perfume of clusters of glowing purple mushrooms, the oil and grease of the square things that went up and down, the metallic tang of the banisters and railings and catwalks, the bubbly steamy water smell where the water fell over a cliff, the weird bright spoiled food packet smell– and yet not unpleasant – that was the smell of the yellow and red mud where big bubbles came and then popped with a splash. Jake brought back some mud one time – a little sample from a place where the water smoked – and asked Ms. Agnes to smell it and she said, "It smells like sulfur; it is sulfur." She wrinkled up her nose, and looked at him like she was going to ask him where he got it, but she patted him on the head and didn't ask, and it made him feel that she loved him, and he loved her, because she trusted him, and knew he had his own life, and his own secrets, and that made him a real person. Maybe she knows we go outside the cave, and she's not going to ask, because she doesn't want to stop us, he thought, and let the thought hang. You could go a long way with thinking, down weird tunnels and byways of words and images, and you could stop when it got dangerous; but it did feel funny – and incomplete somehow – leaving a question hanging like that, unanswered, a beckoning tunnel unexplored. He frowned and scratched the long thick muddy locks on his head.

"You look very pretty, Jake," Gloria said.

"I do not." He poked her in the tummy.

"Yes, you do, Oh, yes, you do!" She stuck out her tongue.

Sometimes, in the food pouches that were dropped through blind slot in the big door, the food had gone bad, and it smelled like the sulfur mud but not so nice, and it had white wiggly worms in it, and so it went downriver with the dead, unless people were really hungry and ate the worms and the rot too.

But that often made them sick.

A lot of the people were dead and had gone downriver, and there weren't many people left. Ms. Chang who was really pretty and taught Jake about numbers – cardinal and ordinal and how to subtract and multiply and divide and add them – just didn't wake up one morning, so she went downriver; they carried her through the cave, a long way from her niche, and took her right to the edge, under the rock overhang, where the water splashed down and bubbled up, and where the phosphorescence glittered on the wet stone walls. "Ashes to ashes, dust to dust," Ms. Agnes said, and they lifted Ms. Chang out of her shift and rolled her naked, her pale white body glimmering, into the water and she turned around in the water, and around and around, her face up, then her face down, and then she was gone. "The current is swift today," said Ms. Agnes, watching Ms. Chang disappear into the final place where the water swirled and swirled and then disappeared under a wall of dark rock. A tall thin man called Al, he died too, coughing and throwing up his food, and then he just lay there in a lather of sweat and he went downriver. He was a dead too. And a couple, the Faulkners, had caught the ghoul disease and were hit by the stones people threw at them until they were dead and spoke no more gibberish and couldn't attack people anymore and they went downriver, though when they died, they were no longer what they had been, so people were not so sad; they were afraid more than sad, Jake felt, they were afraid mostly.

So, there weren't too many people left.

"We've been left to rot here, Jake," Ms. Agnes said once, and then she added, "No, Jake, forget that. I didn't say that." Jake thought it was funny she asked him to forget it because you couldn't unsay what you had said – and once the words were out on the loose, they were out on the loose. Ms. Agnes was pretty but her hair which was black, but one day turned white, had begun to fall out in the last few days, and there were lines in her face and big dark circles under her eyes, and two of her front teeth had fallen out leaving a square black hole and she was getting really skinny, ropy muscles and knees like knots and you could see blue lines pulsing under her skin, and she said, "I'm getting really scrawny, Jake, Nobody will want me anymore, Jake, no more frolicking in the hay for me. You wouldn't think it, Jake, you wouldn't believe it, but once I was considered quite a beauty, yes, I was, Jake," and aside from what she called her "little outbursts," she didn't talk much anymore, though once she sat down against the wall and did talk, even for a long time – she was chewing slowly on one of the last food pouches – deliveries had already slowed down a lot – and she closed her eyes and she said, "I hope you see a better world, Jake, Gloria."

Jake and Gloria – they were the only kids left alive – were crouched on their haunches in front of her, and Gloria was picking her nose and took a big white curled snot out of her right nostril and was looking at it like she wanted to eat it, and Jake was about to say something about not being a "Little Piggy," when Ms. Agnes, her eyes still closed, said, "Everything went so wrong, you know, we thought we could change the world," and she opened her eyes and stared at Gloria, and somehow Jake could see her eyes were looking right through Gloria, they were looking somewhere else – maybe into the past – Gloria quickly wiped the snot off her finger and onto her knee. "We thought we could make a better world. I wrote books you, know, in the old days, and I campaigned for things – more justice for people, more free-dom, but the people didn't want freedom, and they didn't want justice, and it was strange because the injustice was so clear, there were the Cosmos, living in the domed cities, living in the towers and gardens and, being beautiful and knowing everything and traveling the whole world, and shopping all the time – endless shopping – and there were all the others who had once been proud citizens, who were now slaves, slaves fed on ignorance and prejudice, their minds dumbed down into mush, slogans and clichés and insults and point-less ignorant prejudice, and wrangling about issues that shouldn't have been issues but were decoys, distractions, and smoke screens; the people boasted about how they were free and yet their minds were in chains, and they were driven out into the Burbs or into the Dead Lands or into the swamps and deserts, they lost citizen status and became Subs, and when they realized they had lost their freedom and dignity and that they had been lied to all along and that the people they thought were their friends were really their enemies, it was too late, and then the world itself, the fair land of our forefathers, a gift of God some say, taken away from the indigenous peoples, which it certainly was, certainly a gift or blessing for whoever possessed, whoever or whatever gave it, divinity or force of arm, this fragile wonderful fruitful cornucopia of earth, billions of years in the making, desecrated, turning into desert and the oceans turning to lifeless poisoned sewers and flooding everything and all the forms of life dying ..."

She stopped talking and closed her eyes. Her hand fell down in front of her, and the hand opened up, the fingers sort of curled up, and Jake was afraid for a moment that Ms. Agnes was dead – Gloria bit her lip and looked at him with wide open, frightened eyes. They would have to send Ms. Agnes downriver ...

Without Ms. Agnes, they would be lost.

But Ms. Agnes was not dead. She opened her eyes – she was staring with that faraway look, and she said something new, a story she had not told them before, she spoke as if she were reciting something learned by heart:

"They came for me, it was almost like a nice autumn day in the old times, leaves in the trees, you've never seen trees, but they are wonderful things, trees, oh, trees, green in spring and summer and then so colorful and blazing in autumn, then skeletal and naked and dark in winter, when the snow comes, black on white, like they used to be anyway, but are no more, and I was out in the Burbs, doing research, you know, I was a Cosmos, weird to think of it now, but I really was a Cosmos, First Class, one of the World Elite, and I was looking to see what conditions were really like, out in the Burbs, which was forbidden without special permission, no Cosmos other than Centurions were to visit the Burbs, and they came, it was a black electro-van with those smoky windows so you can't see inside, and there were two of those vans, just for me, and men and women with guns, laser guns and stun guns, and also injections to knock me out; I almost felt it was a privilege, you see, so much attention, even months later after the chemicals and the electric shocks and the simple beatings with truncheons and whips and the 'water boarding' and the rapes, and the exposed nakedness and unwashed excrement, and the bruises and the broken ribs, I still knew – I know even now, Gloria, Jake, I know, I was lucky, I am lucky."

Her eyes still had that faraway look, and they brightened as if she had suddenly gone mad, and Jake was afraid and felt a shiver race down his back, and Gloria reached out and put her hand in his.

"I was lucky, really, really lucky," Ms. Agnes's voice had gone higher, like she was going to start to sing, "I mean I'm still alive, aren't I, and I've found you two, my children, somebody to love. And I wasn't erased – I still remember who I am and what I did – and I wasn't terminated, and they didn't morph me into something else – like those poor ghouls – it's catching, but not very catching – becoming a ghoul I mean – at least that's what I think – and they didn't plant in me the seeds of destruction – madness or illness or death – like they did with so many others, I mean like the pharmaceutically-induced timed-release lepers, pure monstrosities, or the nano-sterile-smallpox that horribly maims and scars its victims, or the locked-in-paralyzed condition that makes a person a prisoner in their own body, that can be triggered any minute ..." She fell silent.

Gloria glanced at Jake. Tears were running down her cheeks, and there was one silver tear – it shone like silver in the light from overhead – at the very tip of Gloria's nose, which turned up ever so slightly.

"The lepers," Gloria whispered, "What's a leper?"

Ms. Agnes opened her eyes, and focused. Gloria's question had brought her back from wherever she had gone.

"A leper, well, Gloria, a leper is ..." Ms. Agnes began slowly, cleared her throat, and got back her old, usual voice, "A leper is ..."

Jake only half-listened; he had actually seen a leper and he had told Gloria about it, but not Ms. Agnes. There were some things no adult should know.

"It's a disease, Gloria, a disease called leprosy, and ..."

It was clear Gloria wanted to know more – Jake hadn't taken her to see the leper because it was too icky and anyway the leper lady was extra hard to get to – through a long winding, jagged, narrow, low tunnel that went upward and that was half-flooded with mud – Jake had to take off his shorts and half the time crawl and squeeze through naked on his belly. The leper lady lived far away in a cave apart – with a separate door and separate feed trough – and she only came out sometimes from a sort of hut-like thing she had built in a side cave or niche with a wall of stones and mud in front – and when Jake first saw her, he wasn't sure whether she was a human person or an animal or one of the mutants he had heard about that had been created when people lost all respect for human life. "Nothing was sacred anymore, no nothing," Ms. Agnes had told him that once human life had been considered sacred.

"What is 'sacred'?" Gloria wiggled her nose, raised her eyebrows, and glanced at Jake.

Ms. Agnes tried to explain. "It is something you feel awe for, something that you kneel before, something that you don't tinker with or violate." But Jake didn't really understand, though it apparently had something to do with stuff the mad preacher raved about – God and Jehovah and Yahweh and other mysterious words –though Ms. Agnes said she didn't believe all the things the preacher said and much of it, she said, was "pernicious rubbish" and Gloria just looked at Ms. Agnes with wide open eyes and let her mouth hang open a little bit – silently mouthing the interesting words "pernicious" and "rubbish"' – and Jake could see how Gloria's teeth shone, very white, and Ms. Agnes said, "But then people invented something called science – I've taught you a bit about that, Jake, and science is a good thing – but suddenly people could change things – and they experimented and made new types of animals and new types of people and then everyone was doing it – including criminals and terrorists and profiteers – and everything went wild and new types of diseases spread and plagues and there were new kinds of animals that were neither people nor animals and a great confusion came upon the land, a babble of tongues, plagues of locusts and boils and pus upon the flesh," she said, "with mutants everywhere, and only the Cosmos were protected, in their domed cities, so the Cosmos created a Cult of Purity, and protected themselves from the mutants and even from the Subs in the Lower Depths and the Sin Zones and from the downtrodden Proles – few of those were left because they were no longer needed as robots had replaced them – and the dreaded, despised Burbites who squatted in the Burbs, from the plagues – though the plagues could get to the Cosmos too – and from the wild weather that now stormed through the once green and verdant land, the very air now was poisoned."

Gloria asked what "verdant" was.

It took Ms. Agnes a long time to answer; she seemed to be searching for her words, which was something she never did; finally, she told Gloria that "verdant" meant things that were growing and fresh and green.

"Fresh and green," Gloria repeated and wiggled her nose and repeated the words, "Fresh and green."

"I've never seen fresh and green," she said.

While Ms. Agnes tried to explain what a leper was and Gloria was concentrating and repeating under her breath all the interesting words, Jake was traveling back in time, remembering how he first found the leper lady. It was one of his hardest explorations yet – he was going deeper and deeper, down below the cave in which everybody lived, and he didn't know what he would find – if anything. There were old musty tunnels, and staircases that haven't been used in a long time, it seemed, covered in dust and sludge that bore no footprints at all except those of Jake, though in one tunnel he did find an old trail of boot prints and wondered who it might have been and when they had passed this way. At one point, not too far from a big bank of machines and an old set of dials on the wall of the tunnel, he found a deep muddy crack or crevice in the floor of the tunnel and shimmied down it to a new tunnel, and then he found a fracture in the tunnel's wall, and he slid through it, and then there was a tunnel, lit dimly with glowing moss and lichen, and he wiggled up it. It was so narrow that, that first time, he had to take off his pants – the raggedy, filthy pillowcase – and push them in front of him. The tunnel went a long way, winding upwards, and it was a really tight squeeze.

So, when he got to the top of that low winding tunnel, he came out in a new cave; it was not as big as the home cave, but big; and then he saw it, the creature. He blinked and crouched low; he didn't want it to see him.

He'd never seen anything like it.

Jake wasn't clear at first whether the thing he saw was a woman or a mutant or what it was. It scuttled around like a crab, lurching sideways, zigzagging, crouched on its haunches. It was entirely covered in big swellings and blobs of gray wrinkled flesh that stretched out like leaches full of blood that Jake had once seen, and the blobs hung in clusters, and its skin was mottled, black and white and brown, and it had only a crest of hair at the top of its head, and it was wearing just a few dirty rags around its waist that didn't cover anything, and it was crouching eating something with hands which were just stubs of hands, hardly any fingers, stuffing something into a shapeless mouth where there seemed to be no teeth, and when it saw him with its one eye – the other was a blob, and the one eye was not even in the right place – the nose too was a sort of stub, just two dark holes, and it shuffled around a bit – its breasts were long and hanging down pointed and swaying – and it stuffed some more of something into its mouth, and it turned toward him and it said, in a sort of muffled, gurgling, clotted voice, but Jake could still understand, "Hi! Who are you?"

"I'm Jake," he managed to say. He was covered in mud and on his hands and knees, having just crawled through the really low and greasy and tight tunnel which was the last part of his exploration and luckily, he didn't have Gloria with him. He pulled the bunched pillowcase out of the hole and put it in front of him; he should probably put it on but then this thing or lady would see his nakedness if he stood up and tried to pull it on. Unaccountably, Jake felt shy, vulnerable, and even afraid, of his own nakedness. The cave roof was just high enough here to stand but he decided to stay on hands and knees, less exposed, and he could wiggle back into the tunnel if things got really scary.

"I have a little girl," the thing mumbled and slobbered, silver drool spilling down its chin, "She'd be about your age now, I think, but it's difficult to keep track of time down here. Years pass but it seems like no time at all, then it seems like eternity. It's like a dream – or a nightmare, I suppose."

"Oh," Jake was trembling for some reason.

"Don't worry. It's not contagious." She shuffled closer.

In the phosphorescence from the dim lights and mushrooms and lichen, it was hard to tell what color the one protuberant eye was or once had been; it was partly covered in white, a veil of white fibrous things, like thin wiggling worms. It blinked; the filament worms floated, drifted, dreamily.

"It was designed not to be contagious," she said.

Jake understood that this thing the creature was – and whatever had made her that way – wouldn't happen to him, that's what it was saying, and that this thing had once been a person, a human woman, and somehow, too, though why he did not know, he had the sense that she had once been really good-looking and that she was …

"Cosmos," she said, "I was a Cosmos First Class, one of the airy-fairy elite, privileged, ignorant of the ways of the world, coddled, floating in lotus land, in Elysium, and protected, oh protected from virtually everything, Jake, from virtually everything!"

"Oh."

"I went to a demonstration, oh, years ago, when I was a student, I held up placards and snapped pictures and texted them afterward when I was walking away, going home to study, and men came up and hit me, and I was held overnight and drugged unconscious. You know, it took me a long time to figure it out. That's when they must have done it."

"Done what?" Jake was still on hands and knees, covered in mud, and he was feeling sort of silly, but for some reason, he didn't want to stand up naked in front of this lady and then hop around trying to pull the damned pillowcase on. It hardly covered anything anyway.

"Injected the delayed-action leper disease, like I said, it's not contagious, it's my only little private thing, truly tailor-made, truly bespoke, so you don't have to worry."

"I'm not worried," Jake said, though it was not true; he was terrified, but a boy has to prove he is a man, and he didn't want to hurt her feelings. He was wondering what "delayed-action leper disease meant." He did have a vague idea what it might mean – and it was not nice.

"Then, years later, I defended a dissident – an enemy of the regime – so they activated the disease."

"That's bad, really bad," Jake didn't understand some of the words, but he felt he should say something; he shifted around so he could stand up side-ways, feeling suddenly modest – which was unusual for him – and he pulled on the pillowcase, heavy and slippery with mud, but it was more dignified than staying there, cowering, on his hands and knees.

"So, I have become what you see crouching in front of you – a tailor-made, custom-designed leper," her toothless mouth – empty blackness – turned upward in what Jake took to be a grin. "All the other lepers have died and been carted off, so I am alone. I never get company. I have my own little world here. What's your name again?"

"Jake," he said, "Jake is my name." He took a couple of steps forward to where the roof of the cave was higher, and he could stand up straight without worrying about bumping his head.

"I'm pleased to meet you, Jake, but I imagine the pleasure is not mutual; it's not much fun meeting a monster, is it?"

"You're not a monster," Jake said, clearing his throat, and not knowing pre-cisely why he said it, but somehow, though she sure looked like a monster, she wasn't a monster, and he was quite clear in his head about that.

"You are very kind, Jake," the gurgling muffled voice said, "Come and visit me anytime. I have no company here, only my thoughts and memories."

Jake had gone back to see the leper lady – she told him that such was her name now – "Leper Lady."

She had a few "mementos" of her past life as she called them – and shyly at first – "I don't know why I'm doing this" – she showed them to Jake. There were photographs.

"This was me, before they trigged the disease," she said, holding it out with her mottled bubbly stump, "Hard to believe, isn't it?"

She was maybe, aside from Ms. Agnes and Gloria – the most beautiful thing he'd seen in his life. Her hair looked like gold, and it was around her face, cupping her cheekbones and eyes, and the eyes were blue and there was a big smile with lots of very bright teeth; she looked happy.

"That is my family – was my family."

She was with a baby in the photograph and with a man who she said was her husband: he had a beard and dark tanned skin and was wearing an open blue shirt, and he smiled; his teeth, Jake noticed, were perfect. Nobody except Gloria had such perfect teeth.

"He must have died a thousand deaths, poor dear, when I disappeared," the leper lady said, and she added, swiveling her one swollen eye toward Jake, "I do hope he is alright, and my baby, I couldn't bear to think that they have suffered because of me."

Jake felt he should say something, but he couldn't find anything to say. And so she told him the story of how it happened.

"I looked in the mirror one morning, just before going to the courts, I was vain, proud of my looks I suppose, and I was just straightening my collar and checking my lip gloss, and I saw a little white patch at the corner of my mouth and at the first I thought it was toothpaste and I tried to wipe it off, but it was not to be wiped; I didn't mention it to my husband, and then I felt an irritation about two hours later, so I went into the washroom, and looked, and I saw spots all over my stomach and breasts and one on my right hand – I was frightened, Jake, in fact, I was terrified – and so from the court where I was defending a case I phoned my doctor, Doctor Ross, and he told me to come in right away and not to mention it to anybody not even my husband since it might scare him, and I got to Doctor Ross's office and he looked very upset and there were two men there in long black leather coats and Doctor Ross said, "I'm very sorry, Claudia," and the two men held me down while Doctor Ross gave me an injection, and when I woke up I was shackled hands and feet in some sort of canvas overalls with a hood over my head and blindfolds on my eyes and I was in a truck or some vehicle bouncing over roads for a long time and then I think over dunes and sand and then I was here. The change was quite fast, time-released as it were, and then it slowed down and I think I'm almost stable now. So, I am now what you see, Jake, and they left me an unbreakable plasticized mirror so I could whenever the fancy struck me appreciate myself and all the changes that have occurred in who and what I am. In a way, it was interesting; you have to go with the flow, Jake, you have to go with the flow."

Many of the words she used he didn't fully understand; he tried to picture the meanings in his head; he tried to see them; the world beyond the cave and tunnels was something he could not imagine – or barely imagine – and which he rarely thought about, suddenly seemed vast and wonderful and horrible and full of untold dangers; Jake wondered at it.

"You are a good friend, Jake," the Leper Lady once told him.

"Thank you," he said.

"You must be careful, Jake," she waved her stumps toward the walls of the cave, "Something terrible is going to happen, Jake, and you must be ready – you must be ready to save yourself and Ms. Agnes and your friend Gloria."

"What is going to happen?"

"I don't know, Jake," the empty mouth – a black hole with the swollen, blackened tongue – turned up in a toothless cartoon smile, "I just feel it in my bones. I have in my solitude had time to mull and to think, and I do believe I have become a visionary, Jake. I see things that may come to pass and things that may not come to pass. But what is to come is not good, not for us at any rate. Many will die, Jake, many will die." She smiled again. "But I am just a mad old creature playing at being Cassandra, so don't pay me too much mind."

Jake asked her what Cassandra was and the Leper Lady told him of the princess to whom the God of Reason had given the gift of prophecy and to whom coiled snakes, licking the wax from her ears, had also given the gift of hearing the usually inaudible secret voices of nature that would sing to her and to her alone of what the future might bring. But then she laughed her bubbling croaking laugh – like it was coming up through thick liquid mud – and said, "But the future's not ours to see, Jake, not really – still, I have a feeling …"

Jake had told Gloria all about the Leper Lady and how she was Cassandra and the things she said, "She knows lots of secrets," Jake said, "She knows the future, and what's going to happen, sometimes at least she thinks she does, and she's been in different caves, and she knows secret passageways. She said it's a labyrinth and told me of a lady called Ariadne who found a way to get out of a maze and labyrinth to the light of day, she said. She's very wise, like Ms. Agnes."

"We should explore those passageways, Jake," Gloria had said.

"Yes, someday, yes, we'll do that."

"I want to meet the Leper Lady," Gloria said, "I want to meet Cassandra."

"Maybe someday," Jake said, "Maybe someday you can meet her."

But he'd never taken Gloria to see the Leper Lady, his own personal Cassandra. It was too risky, and somehow she thought that it would be dangerous for Gloria to see the Leper Lady and to understand what people can do to people; Gloria had seen lots of things, but she hadn't seen *everything*.

So when the lights went off, and the emergency lights went on, Jake thought of the Leper Lady, Cassandra, and of her prophecies that something terrible was about to happen, that everybody might be in danger from the things that might come to pass and the things that might not come to pass.

If things went wrong, everybody could die.

Maybe somebody or something wanted everybody to die.

But now, more worrying even than the lights going off, was the silence: the pumps were not pumping. The giant pumps were dead!

"I don't hear the heartbeat," Gloria said again, scratching her head.

"Let's go and see," said Jake.

"Yes, Jake, let us go then, and see for ourselves," said Gloria.

The pumps were something from another world.

Professor Swank had told Jake and Gloria stories about aliens coming from other planets and how they built huge machines and ships that went through space and traveled to and from the stars.

Jake sometimes thought that aliens had built the pumps.

The pumps were true monster things. They gave Jake a funny feeling in his tummy. "Awesome," Gloria whispered. The first time, when they had discovered the pumps, the giant machines had been making a big noise, that huge deafening thumping, thumping, thumping sound that you could hear from far away and that was now, suddenly, not there.

"This is big," Gloria had said, that first time they saw the pumps, looking up at the machines that went up higher even than the roof of the cavern where they lived.

"Yes," said Jake.

The huge smooth tubes – they were the biggest things Jake had ever seen – made that endless thumping sound – *boom, boom, boom!*

Jake had put his hand on the steel. It vibrated. On the other side was the throbbing rush of water, in great gushes he imagined, as the huge pumps, which were invisible, but somewhere near, pushed the water through the pipes, draining the underground rivers which threatened to flood the mine; or so Ms. Agnes had told him. The steel walls throbbed, pulses, a beating rhythm.

"It's like a heartbeat," Jake said.

"A heartbeat?" said Gloria, "What's a heartbeat?"

Jack thought about it for a minute and remembered from when he'd had a fever and was really, really sick, and Ms. Agnes put her ear against his chest and smiled – her beautiful smile before the teeth fell out – said, "Your heart's still beating, Jake, so I guess you will be okay!"

Gloria had her hand against the giant throbbing circle of steel, and her eyes were very big and round and blank, which was what happened Jake had noticed when she was thinking about something or was impressed by something.

"Here," he said. "Put your ear here, against my chest."

She looked at him, suddenly focusing, with those big round blue eyes, the dull light reflecting off them and she said, "Really?"

"Yes, really."

She seemed a bit shy, but she leaned her ear against his chest and she put her arm around him so she could hold on tight, and he put his hand on the stubble where her hair had been hacked off, and it felt prickly and it sparkled like bright water, the little gleams and bits of it sticking through the slick of dirt and mud, and she held on tight her body pressed warm against his and Jake thought that he would protect Gloria from whatever might come, from dragons and lions and crazy people and fires and floods and hybrids and ghouls and all the things he'd thought about or heard about and that she would live with him forever.

"I hear it," Gloria said, her ear still glued to his chest, "I hear it!"

She kept listening, and Jake had the feeling that he could hear his own heart beating because she could hear it.

Gloria looked up at him. She still had her arm around him. Her eyes had tears in them for some reason he didn't understand. "Don't ever leave me, Jake, okay, don't ever leave me."

"Never," Jake said, "I'll never leave you, no matter what! Never ever! I will never leave you!"

She leaned up and pressed her lips against his cheek.

"What's that?"

"It's a kiss, Jake," Gloria said. "It's called a kiss."

Now the great heart was not beating.

Getting to the pumps – to the heartbeat – was always an adventure.

"We shall see what we shall see, Jake," said Gloria.

This time, when the lights flickered and the world was so silent, it was even more so.

"It's really quiet," Gloria whispered.

They crawled through the first narrow twisting muddy crevice – Jake took off his shorts and greased his body, but Gloria didn't have to. "You're all funny when you do that, Jake!"

"I know, Gloria," he popped out of the crevice and pulled his shorts back on as fast as he could. "I know I'm all funny."

Gloria put her hand over her mouth and giggled. Her muddy wet shirt was plastered to her body so you could see her like she was carved in clay.

"You are unbearably cute, Jake."

"I know I'm cute, Gloria."

"You are, you are really cute," she kept her mouth covered and gave him the look. Gloria, Jake decided, was growing up very fast and as Ms. Agnes and Ms. Chang once said, "She is wise beyond her years."

"Let's go," Jake said. The place they came out into was dangerous. It was a narrow passageway that was human-made – it had squared-off walls and timber and metal plates in some places to keep it in shape. They checked both ways – no guards or people – and they listened. It was unusually silent; the usual low thumping and humming sounds were absent. Water was dripping down one side of the passageway, and all the walls glistened. Every little sound seemed clearer to Jake without the background thump-thump-thump.

The ceiling lights – little round lights every fifteen feet or so – blinked and went off, and the cave was almost entirely dark.

"Oh, oh," said Gloria, she put her hand in Jake's.

"Don't move, let's wait," Jake whispered.

"Okay," Gloria whispered. Her hand was small and warm and muddy in his hand, and she pressed her body close to his side.

The lights went back on – then they flickered, on and off, on and off, and then they went out – and they stayed out.

Other lights, duller lights, went on. Jake looked up; these were round lights on little square boxes up on the walls. Everything looked funny in this new light.

"Spooky," Gloria said.

They ran along the passageway and came to a big set of wooden beams that arched over and supported the tunnel.

Jake slipped into a crack behind one of the vertical wooden beams, and Gloria followed, and they wiggled along a few feet into a hidden opening to a natural tunnel – a narrow cave or fissure – which went almost straight up and in almost total darkness – with only a tiny pale bluish glimmer from up above – they crawled up on hands and knees – there was no room to stand up – and they kept crawling; this one took a bit of time, and at one point the tunnel went almost straight up, and Jake climbed from outcropping to outcropping, and reached down and pulled Gloria up onto a little ledge which led to an opening that took them to a bigger cave where there was a large pool of gray water and the only light was the phosphorescence and here there were some very big mushrooms that glowed and pulsated – brighter, then less bright, then brighter again – and smelled funny but it was not a bad smell at all and there was some of the sulfur smell too.

"Let's stop here for a rest," Jake sat down next to the pool.

"Yeah, whew," Gloria sat down next to him and put her arms around her shins, her chin on her knees. Jake noticed how more and more she was practicing talking like an adult. Her method, he noted, was that she picked up bits and pieces of grown up talk she copied, and then she'd change the expressions a bit and fool around with them. He thought that maybe when there was time, he'd teach Gloria how to read and write, now that Ms. Agnes seemed too tired to do any teaching and just sat against the wall or lay on her blanket and stared into space.

"Shh, listen!"

They listened.

Yes, there was still no sound of the pumps or the machinery.

Then they heard it – the sound of running water, like downstream where the whirlpool that took the dead was; it seemed to be coming from behind the rock face on one side of the cave. Jake crawled over and put his ear against the stone. Yes, he could feel it; water was running, a deep, strong sound, like a waterfall, on the other side of the rock face.

"Spooky," Gloria said when he told her, "That's totally spooky."

When they finally got there, the Engine Room was ghostly. The giant pumps – with gleaming pistons and huge tanks and cables and other complicated things just stood there like they were dead– rows and rows of giant machines, stretching off into the mist, and it was all silent.

"Spooky," said Gloria.

"Yes, it is spooky," Jake hitched up his stiff mud-crusted shorts – *damnation!* – and stared at the giant row of machines, shiny, smooth, giant metal, stretching off into the dimly lit steamy air. "Silent as the grave," Ms. Agnes once said, and for some reason, Jake thought of the words, and he shivered, "Silent as the grave."

The dull glimmers from the little lightboxes on the walls and ceiling gleamed on the round backs of the machines. They were all quiet. Nothing moved. Usually, the room was full of thunderous sound and movement, shafts of metal pumping up and down without stopping. Now the dull little lights reflected off rows and rows of oily-looking pistons, huge valves, enormous pipes, and gangways and platforms and engines and walkways.

And nothing moved.

Except …

The lights swayed; a breeze came through the room. Cables swung, and the railing clanged back and forth.

"The air is moving," Jake said.

"Yes," Gloria looked around, blinked, and wiggled her nose. "It's a wind, or a breeze, gently wafting, or a zephyr."

Jake looked at her, "Where do you get these words?"

"Ms. Agnes reads me poetry."

"She doesn't read me poetry."

"I'm a girl; you're a boy."

"Yes, Gloria, that's right, but that doesn't mean … I don't see the connection between poetry and being a girl. I mean, the fact that I'm a boy doesn't mean …"

"Well, maybe it means, and maybe it doesn't mean. Maybe there's a connection and maybe there isn't. There are boys and then there are girls," she curled her lips and bared her teeth, giving him a bright grin, "There are many things, Jake, that I, and even you, don't understand; I mean we've never been out of here, not since we can remember. And, actually, I've *never* been out of here."

The wind – or zephyr – made the chains rattle.

"Yes, that's true too, Gloria," Jake stared at the huge machines and thought that he had no idea, really, how they worked, and he thought, too, that if people made them it must be possible to understand what made them work

– and what made them, stop working. If he got the chance, he would like to understand everything in the whole wide world and know all the words for everything, even words from poetry. The wind was rising; cables were rattling. The lamps were swaying more and more.

"There usually isn't a zephyr here," said Gloria; she licked her finger and stuck it up in the air like she'd seen Ms. Agnes do. "It's getting stronger."

"Something's happening," Jake said, "Something big is happening."

Gloria put her hand in his, "Let's go, Jake, let's go."

"Yes, we have to get back."

"Yes, Jake, we have to get back and tell Ms. Agnes."

"Yes."

They jumped up and ran. There were more noises now, noises that sounded like water and fire and falling earth. Jake was thinking: We'll get back to the cave, but what can we do? What can Ms. Agnes do?

"This is a tragedy unfolding, Jake," Gloria whispered, as she held Jake's shorts for him and helped pull him, naked and all slicked with mud, through the last slippery, slimy narrow section of the fissure. She handed him his shorts, whispering, "This, my dear Jake, is a tragedy of incalculable consequence."

When they passed one cliff face, in a wide part of the tunnel, water was pouring down in a regular waterfall.

They'd never seen water there before. Cracks were opening in the cliff face, and pieces of rock fell away. Water was squirting out.

"Most horrible," said Gloria, staring at the sprays of water, "More than most horrible. Really spooky, and creepy, and eerie!"

"Let's hurry." Jake had a bad feeling about this, a feeling he couldn't put into words but which he sort of saw in his mind, vaguely, darkly, and it was a thought, really: Their whole world was about to burst apart and come crashing down.

"Jake …"

"Yes?"

"Hold my hand, Jake." Gloria was trembling.

Close by, the roar of water increased. It was like thunder, though Gloria had never heard thunder, and Jake really didn't remember what thunder was like. But somehow thunder came to mind.

CHAPTER 16 – SPLIT THE BITCH

Valerie Joffre's headlamp light bounced and jiggled, showing circular flashes – rock walls, sludgy streams of mud, a drainage runnel, and steamy, foggy air. It felt and looked like she was caught in a rainstorm or bank of fog. Something was not right – in fact, quite a few things were not right.

She stood still and looked around. She listened.

The air was much steamier than usual and much hotter. The tunnel was ankle-deep in water, steamy, cloudy water, moving at a fast clip. There must be flooding up on the higher levels. She tried her underground mobile. Again, there was no signal.

A sudden blast of hot air almost blew her over; it was so blistering, so hot, it felt like her skin was peeling off, and it smelled of … gasoline.

Fire!

Damn it! That means …

The wind suddenly dropped.

Valerie recovered her balance and put the mobile back in her belt; she headed up along the tunnel, cautiously, keeping one hand on the wall, just in case another fiery blast tried to bowl her over.

She came to a flight of steep stone steps, where the tunnel went to a higher level. Holding onto the handrail, she hurried up them. The steps were covered in a Niagara of water, swirling around her boots, and it was now more than ankle-deep. The flooding, wherever it was coming from, was getting worse.

And another bad sign: The main lights were off; only battery-powered emergency lights seemed to be working. That meant there must have been a general failure of the electrical system.

A wall phone unit, probably not used in decades, stood at a bend in the tunnel. She picked up the receiver. It was dead, of course. She gave the unit verbal orders: no response, of course.

Valerie stood for a moment, perplexed, listening. The sounds were different. The whole feeling of the place was different. Ah, yes! The pumps and ventilators were silent.

Ah, ah! This was not good news. She stared at the dead com unit. Without the pumps and ventilators, the oxygen levels would fall, and the water levels would rise; the air would become poison, the tunnels would flood, and, if the pumps did not go back on soon, the whole mine, certainly Main Shaft-1, would collapse. It was structurally weak and had not been reinforced in decades. Before leaving Elysium City, she had internalized all the schematics of the mine as well as its history – all the maps from the present and from the past, reaching right back to the beginning. She knew the whole thing, and, in particular, these lower sections almost certainly better than anybody alive. She had to check whether there was a way out. She headed toward Main Shaft-1.

Now, there was a roaring sound.

Yes, Fire!

And the wind, again, rose.

Five or six minutes later, turning a bend, she ran into a wall of flame. It roared, and it sucked up air and oxygen. The heat was unbearable. She shielded her face and backtracked.

Damn! This was worse and worse. If the fire developed into a full firestorm, it would suck all the oxygen out of the whole mine and nothing and nobody would remain alive. This could happen very quickly. And a wall of flame, so far down, quite possibly meant that Main Shaft-1 had already collapsed.

She knew there was an old control panel near the main bottom level pumping station. It was archaic – a real museum piece – but it had a separate set of circuits, and it operated on old batteries that were recharged by the operation of the pumps. It might still be working, and it might give her a reading on conditions – then she'd have to figure out how to get out of the mine.

Also, there were other guards, and humans and hybrids down here. Had they been evacuated? What about the prisoners? Somebody would have to get them out. Or was everyone gone already? Was she alone? Stupid me, she murmured, always going off on my own to explore and push the envelope, taking risks I shouldn't take!

She strode along the narrow, dimly lit tunnel, climbed up three levels, and finally came to the control panel section. And, no, she was not alone. The worst possible person was standing there. If she were the last person in the world, she would prefer to be alone, rather than to be with him.

He turned and grinned at her.

"So, Milosevic, what's happening?" she said, smiling at the guy, trying to be ingratiating, though he was a total jerk, a huge monster of a guy, a true animal – No, that was unfair to animals.

"I don't give a fuck what's happening," he said.

"What?" Okay, here we go, she thought. This is not going to be easy.

"Come on over here, Val, I want to look at you."

"What did you say?"

"You heard me, little Val!"

Valerie hesitated. A chill rippled down her spine, it tingled in each vertebra; a nervous empty fluttering rose in her stomach. *Could it be fear?* She didn't need this; she didn't need this at all.

"Come on, little Val, don't be shy!"

V stopped and looked around. This was maddening. There had to be a way to get down to the human prisoners, and she had to find that geologist too – but it was like searching for a needle in a haystack.

V had taken a dozen tunnels, and she'd come up against cave-ins, floods, and even, when she went up to a higher level, she came up against walls of fire.

The place was an endless cockeyed labyrinth full of dead ends, and down here, there were no signals to guide her, and the tons of rock and layers of rock blocked her extra-sensory perception, so she was probing, trying, hoping …

V ran down a steamy tunnel, past a giant pump room with the huge pumps standing idle. Already, water was rising around the engines and the pistols which gleamed silver in the oily ghostly light. She stopped for just an instant in front of a rusty ancient panel of old-fashioned gauges and dials: all the arrows pointed at the red zone: absolute danger.

She vaulted up a narrow flight of stairs, toward a large service tunnel, which she thought must lead to the prisoners' cave.

Again, V faced a wall of flame. The lower level gas tanks on Julian's schematics must have exploded or leaked and now the whole of Main Shaft-1, below the levels where it had already collapsed, and down to almost the lowest level of the shaft itself was on fire. This might suck all the oxygen out of the air. V growled. She did not like to lose. She was vain about her ability to solve problems. And this whole situation was definitely a problem.

She backtracked to a smaller service tunnel that branched off from the tunnel she was in. It was clear of fire, but ankle-deep in quick-running water, which was sulfurous and steaming; this meant the main underground river-lake system must be backing up already. The gray water swirled and bubbled, and the emergency lights cast a dull glare over everything. Tinsel like sparkles shone like distant stars from the rock walls.

Wham!

Suddenly, a gust of tremendous wind pushed at her and pulled her, making her weave around as if she were drunk. The gust turned into a hurricane. Stumbling into the water, she ended up on her hands and knees. slammed against a metal railing that was rattling in the wind. She clung to the rail. Otherwise, she'd be swept down to a lower level.

Suddenly, the wind dropped.

Dead calm.

This was almost more unsettling – the calm before the catastrophe.

V stood up and took a moment to orient herself. Three tunnels led off in different directions; there were gleams of fire down one tunnel. She decided to avoid that.

She explored the tunnel to her left and came to a vertical service shaft. She went down to the next level, following the winding, spiral metal stairs. At the bottom, two levels down, there was water, waist-deep. It boiled up, sulfurous, around her. How could she get to the people? They were probably all dead by now. And the geologist, Valerie Joffre, if she was down on the lower levels, she was probably dead too, drowned, or burned to a crisp.

V looked up. Water cascaded through cracks in the roof. Clearly, the higher levels were already flooded. Was there any chance the people on the lower level, down in their cave, might still be alive?

She went back up a level, went along the service tunnel, turned a corner, and met a wall of smoking rubble; the tunnel had collapsed.

She'd have to find a way around.

She found a ladder leading upwards.

She adjusted her backpack and climbed up the ladder. When she got to the top, she decided that her demon form was best for this risky work. This place was hell, and so demon was the appropriate role to play. She laid down her weapons, slipped out of her boots and armored skinsuit, morphed into pure hybrid-reptile, folded everything neatly and put it into her backpack, she slipped the backpack onto her back, and hooked her holster and weapon belt around her waist.

Just as she locked the belt into place, V heard a scream.

She listened.

She heard it again.

She sprinted down the tunnel.

"So, it seems we are going to die down here," Valerie Joffre turned to Milosevic. She had looked at the various instruments of the old monitor-control panel. The news was not good. She took off her protective goggles: God, it was hot!

So far, Milosevic had behaved, though he sneered at her in a dangerously suggestive way, and called her "Val," and "Little Val," which she didn't like, and he kept licking his lips in a manner she found ominous.

"Hot little girl, are we?" Milosevic grinned. Why the man did not brush and floss his teeth, she could not imagine. He wasn't a Cosmos; but, in Valerie's opinion, each human, of whatever class, should be proud of his or her humanity and practice a minimum of hygiene.

"Yes, it is hot," she said evenly. She reminded herself that she was pure Cosmos, First Class, one of the elite, and should always be conscious of the fact. It was her duty to show consideration for others, of whatever cast, and to show tact was also a Cosmos duty, as the President-Leader had pointed out in one of his speeches; she sometimes wondered about the President-Leader, so wise, so moderate, so apparently humane, and yet the regime he presided over was dictatorial and rotten and cruel and …

Valerie took off her hardhat and shook out her shoulder-length blond hair, sticky from the humidity, and again stared at the antiquated control panel: the temperature and humidity in the mine were soaring; the floodwaters were rising. Level X-4 was flooded; level X-3 was half-flooded, and sections of level X-1, above levels Minus-2 and Minus-3, and Minus-14, were already flooded. That meant that levels above the prisoner's cavern, and above the point where she and Milosevic now stood, were flooded, partially, or totally.

So, if these ancient instruments could be trusted, the situation was not good, not at all good; in fact, it was bloody near hopeless. Also, carbon monoxide was rising, and oxygen levels were falling.

Little red lights were blinking, green lights were turning red; the dials were all in the orange or red zone; dangers were multiplying everywhere, and they were coming from every direction. *Fucking annoying!*

Valerie put her hand on the instrument panel. An immense multi-dimensional tragedy was unfolding in slow motion – well, not really in slow motion; things were happening very quickly, and they would probably go faster and faster, cascading interacting catastrophic failures.

The human prisoners, the dissidents – non-people as they were classified – were on level Minus-6, or M-6, but in a separate cave system. It had almost certainly flooded by now. But she decided she would go and see for herself; if there was any hope, she could try to open the prison door, and let them out. But if they were alive, where would she take them if she got to them? She didn't know, didn't have the slightest idea: it seemed there was no way out … But, one step at a time, and then we will see …

"They're dead anyway, the scum," said Milosevic, as if he had been reading her thoughts.

"We don't know that." She favored him with a glance, then ignored him, and stared at the gauges of the monitoring panel, trying to find some grounds for hope – sets of old-fashioned dials, a line of red and green and orange lights, and a few digital displays. With part of her mind, she was mapping out the path to the prisoners' cavern.

At least this ancient subsystem was still working. The monitoring panel and its sensors had their own separate battery-fed circuit, but they probably wouldn't work for long; the backup and safety facilities in this mine had been badly neglected; it was criminal really. When she was back in Elysium City she was going to put it all in her report; maybe they could modernize this place and make it safer – even more comfortable – for the personnel and the hybrids and the prisoners.

Also, from what she'd overheard the guards saying, down in the dissidents' cave, hygienic conditions must be utterly horrible. It was unacceptable, absolutely unacceptable. She would make sure her report got to the Undersecretary himself, if she had to, she would appeal to the President-Leader, she would …

Only now there almost certainly would be no report.

Now, she would never report anything to anybody.

It wouldn't be pleasant, dying down here; there were lots of things she would still like to do in life, lots of things she had planned to do, but now …

Valerie glanced up at the emergency lights; they too would fail and fairly soon – it would depend on the condition of the batteries and how fast the tunnels were flooded. Okay, enough thinking! Now she'd head down and find the prisoners.

"So, we die," said Milosevic. He towered over her, breathing heavily.

"It looks like it, it's quite possible," she said, "But let's go and see about the prisoners; there's just a chance they may still be alive."

"No!"

"What do you mean, I …"

"Now is the moment I fuck you," he said.

"Shove off," Valerie certainly regretted that the person trapped down here on Level Z-7 with her was this absolute brute. He was huge, strong, and a sadist. If she had to die, she'd prefer to die in better company than this. He was a truly hateful man.

She'd seen Milosevic beat a hybrid with a truncheon just for the fun of it; she'd seen him whip hybrids with an electro-whip for no reason at all, just the pure pleasure of power and cruelty; she'd seen him make snide, insulting remarks to Jane Fox, the cute and brave station doctor whom Valerie secretly liked and had wanted to befriend; but she had been given strict orders not to get close to anyone in the camp. "You are a Cosmos and you'll be coming back to civilization, Valerie," Doctor Hansen, the Program Director, had told her, "Unfortunately, most of them will probably never come back; they'll die there. You'll just hurt them the more if you get close to them."

Valerie had had to fend Milosevic off once before, topside in the canteen where she'd gone to work after hours– feeling her own room too cramped, with the air-conditioning dead and the temperature over 105 F.

She was concentrating – working on a caffeine-fueled schedule – preparing a preliminary confidential report for the Department of Mineral Strategy. It was possible that with some new breakthrough technologies, they could begin profitable mining of …

Milosevic came in, saw her, swept her papers and computer and coffee mug from the table – everything just crashing down and splashing so fast she didn't have time to react – and he grabbed her and forced her down on the table, but she shouted and kicked him in the crotch, and punched him one clear uppercut to the jaw, and he'd reeled back, holding his jaw, blood streaming from his lips, swearing he'd take his revenge and he'd spoil her looks and he …

"I'll make you pay, bitch, I'll rip you apart."

So, who happens upon her when she's all alone in the lower depths, and all of the machinery breaks down – Bertrand Milosevic!

What the hell was he doing down here?

"Look, Bert, leave me alone; I have to think," Valerie said, trying to keep the hatred out of her voice, "There may be a way out of here. And I'm going down to check on the prisoners."

She was tracing the interactive pocket schematics she'd slipped out of her pocket and unfolded. She was interfacing this, mentally, with all the schematics she'd internalized in the form of a mind-implant, from the oldest diagrams to the very newest, from the original geological survey material to the old satellite photographs and geothermic imagery – hoping that maybe a connection would form, and she could figure a way to get out of here and maybe get the prisoners and the hybrids and guards if she found any, and, yes, even Milosevic, out of here. It was clear that Main Shaft-1 was blocked – by fire and shaft wall collapse apparently – whatever the hell was going on up there she didn't even want to think about – but there was a separate system, and an old shaft that hadn't been used in maybe forty years, Main Shaft-2. Also, beyond that, branching off to the side, were caves where – a Top Secret Confidential Intelligence report had indicated – ghoulish mutants lived in a biochemical dumping ground: they were the mutant result of slave labor that had been used to stock the bio-chemicals and of some of the scientists and overseers involved – all transformed into monsters, mindless ghoul-like creatures. It all sounded very ugly and disreputable and criminal – and extremely dangerous. But the hell with danger! She had intended, if she had time, to explore those caves; but right now, survival was the aim – possibly some of the cave systems led to the surface, or close to the surface; it was a slim hope, but it was a hope. She glanced up at Milosevic, his big face looking down at her, "Look Bert," she said, "Maybe we can get over to Main Shaft-2 and climb up it, it's about a mile away– it's an old disused shaft, it might be still clear – and we can find a way out of here. Of it that doesn't work, there are cave systems, old underground rivers, maybe they lead to the surface." She pointed to the schematics and looked up at Milosevic: You'd think even a brute like him would be eager to survive, and would be intelligent enough to see the danger they were in, trapped more than a mile underground in a collapsing, flooding mine, where the oxygen was running out. "In any case, I'm going down to lower level M-6, whether you come or not."

"Yeah?" he didn't seem interested; his tongue ran along his lip; he was staring at her with his big bloodshot dark eyes; his breathing was heavy.

"Yeah," she said flatly, and she looked away, "and then if they are alive and if there is a way out, we can get a crew to come back to get the prisoners and the hybrids. But how can we get from here to there? That is the question. Shaft-2 is almost a mile away."

More little red lights blinked on, indicating more compartments and levels were flooding. "However bad it gets, we can try to get out of here, and we can try to save the prisoners," Valerie said, denying her own inner pessimism.

"I don't give a fuck." He put his big hand on her shoulder.

"What?"

"I don't give a fuck about saving fucking prisoners."

"What the hell are you …?"

"And I don't give a fuck about those valuable stupid evil hybrids."

"Take your hand off my shoulder."

"Fuck the hybrids, fuck the prisoners. I don't give a fuck about them."

"Do you give a fuck about saving yourself?"

"Not really, no, no, Valerie Joffre, Cosmos First Class, I don't give a fuck, not even about saving myself." His hand was heavier on her shoulder, pressing down, the big fingers squeezing; it hurt.

"Look, Bertrand, you are out of line, you are …" she lifted his hand off her shoulder; he put it back; she took a deep breath.

"Those hybrids are animals," he grinned at her, an ugly lopsided grin: filthy dark crevices between his teeth.

"Bert, the hybrids are …"

"Shut the fuck up, you fucking Cosmos! This is the opportunity of a lifetime, you bitch," he grinned a really wicked grin – God, his teeth were dirty, rimmed with filth – and he pulled off his hard hat and threw it away.

"Bert, what the hell are you …?"

"Shut up, you fucking Cosmos whore!" he screamed. He smashed her across the face. She reeled back against the control panel, hit her head, reached up, saw blood covering her hand, felt it streaming down the side of her face.

Her eyes widened in amazement, "How dare you? You bastard, what the hell are you thinking?"

I have to defend myself, she was thinking, but she was too surprised, too shocked even, to raise her arms; she …

"This is what I'm thinking." He punched her in the jaw, a stunning uppercut; she felt her jaw wrench back and crack; she fell backward, seeing stars and everything went black and she felt groggy and blind and could taste the coppery bittersweet blood filling her mouth, and one, no two – maybe, more – broken teeth.

She was on the ground, lying on her back.

This can't be happening – not to me, not now.

I'm a Cosmos, goddamn it. This beast is …

This beast is nothing …

She blinked, trying to see. But all she saw was a veil of blood and a dim radiant silhouette – him, undoubtedly him – in the steamy dull light from the emergency lights. She reached for her stun gun, but it was gone.

Milosevic was holding it.

He pressed it down, and he shot her full blast with the stun gun.

Her body arched up, bouncing, contorting, in absolute agony and pain – every bone and every muscle seemed …

Oh, God!

He knelt down next to her. Wham! He pulverized her again – the shock wave lifted her body off the ground.

Oh, God!

She fell back, crumpled, nerves and muscles paralyzed. She wanted to punch, to kick, she was an expert fighter, had trained in the Cosmos Academy, but she'd never really fought anybody, not for real, not life and death, and, now, here, more than a mile underground, what could she do? It had all happened too fast, and her body was stunned; her nervous system and muscles paralyzed, resonating, echoing with pain; nothing seemed to work – not her arms, not her legs – and she felt him zipping open and ripping off her overalls and lifting her up and then dropping her again, then hoisting her torso, lifting the T-shirt over her head – Something's broken! I'm a limp doll, she thought, trying to fight, trying to flail, her body disjointed, broken – a rubber doll, broken aching fragments, sprawling lolling, ineffectual spasms. He levered off her panties, lifted her up, and dropped her – splat – on the tunnel floor. "Bitch," he shouted, "Naked bitch – I'm going to give you the last pleasure of your life."

The floor was hard and gritty.

She wanted to lie there; she wanted to close her eyes.

She tried to speak. No sound came out of the broken mouth, a gurgle maybe, she wasn't sure. She blinked, staring through the veil of blood. She tried to move her arm, clench a fist – she couldn't, nothing worked.

He was stripping off his clothes – she blinked, seeing the outline, seeing him lift off his belt, with the holster and pistol, seeing him step out of the Velcro overalls. He'd left his boots on.

Christ Almighty!

Under her back, she felt the gritting tunnel floor, stone, and she felt the vibrations of the water and, through the rock, she felt the thunderous flow of energy – water, flooding water – that was filling the lower tunnels and drifts and shafts.

It won't be long, she thought, somehow distant from herself, it won't be long before the prisoners are all drowned – if they haven't been already – they are locked in; for them there is no way out. We have to help them!

Milosevic grinned, "I'm going to slit you open. Like I'd gut a fish."

He had a knife; it looked like a knife.

"You're crazy," she heard herself say, "You are utterly nuts! What do you think you're doing?" The voice – hers – was unrecognizable, slurred, a hoarse whisper, bubbling up from somewhere far away, the broken voice of a crone, a hag. "If you waste time killing me, you'll die down here."

"Do I give a fuck? I know exactly what I'm doing, bitch," He lowered himself down onto her, and she felt the hot blade of the knife. He levered her legs apart, thrust himself between them.

His bulging belly crushed her. He forced his raw, bone-dry erection into her, breaking into her, splitting her open, and it hurt, oh boy, did it hurt and she tried to twist out from under him and kick away; but he had her by the wrists, pinning her arms, stretched out and pressed against the tunnel floor. She kicked and kicked, feeling and power coming back in painful waves, but it meant nothing. He was a big man, too big, far too big, and heavy. He tried to kiss her. She tensed herself, ready to bite off his tongue, but he just slobbered over her face; his breath was foul. She turned her face away and she saw, lying on the tunnel floor, just a few inches away, the knife.

Wrists pinioned, and it's too far.

Oh, God!

Oh, God!

It seemed to last forever. He was in no hurry to conclude. He just kept thrusting and thrusting, and it occurred to her that maybe he really couldn't come, maybe he needed some extra stimulus – like death.

She eyed the knife – a blurry image, but, yes, *it was a knife.*

Her wrists were still pinned down.

She tried to shift slightly – he was inside her, and the sensation was of burning pain, raw, flesh-ripping, flesh-rendering pain, and the humiliation of it, the fact that she, a Cosmos, a scientist, a woman of culture, a woman who loved and was loved, a woman who wanted to do right, to do right by everybody, was being overcome by this stupid backwoods brutish hulk of a bully, by this …

He came – a great spurt and hot spasm within her.

Damnation, I will kill him, it was a tearful statement of intent – she felt utterly degraded, worthless, spent, destroyed, gutted ...

He let out a triumphant bellow, "You!! Bitch, bitch, bitch, bitch!"

He let go of her wrists.

She grabbed for the knife, felt her fingers close around the handle, and she swung it, slashing at him blindly, her eyes veiled in blood, her mind dizzy, everything in a fog, her body acting like it didn't belong to her, like it was far away, like it wasn't obeying her orders, like ...

The point of the knife sliced like a razor across his belly, but it was a shallow wound, she somehow knew, it was shallow, too shallow. She had to kill him; if not, he would kill her. She tried to sit up, to stand ...

"Bitch!" he screamed, grabbing his belly, his fingers oozing blood, and he rolled away, out of range, and then rolled back, grabbed her wrist and twisted, and she felt the bones crack and break and a new pain shoot up her arm, and she dropped the knife.

He scrambled and grabbed for it.

Now he had the knife; though a veil of blood, blinking, she saw him, standing there, towering above her, far away.

Wham!

He kicked her, it was a steel-tipped boot, it caught her in the belly just as she was rising from the ground – splitting her open; in the flash of pain, she felt like he had broken her insides, smashed her innards.

Wham! Again!

Wham! Again!

"Oh, no, please, no," words came out slurred, far away, bloodied words, through her smashed teeth, swollen tongue, swelling lips; her face didn't seem to be her face: it was a plaster carnival mask ...

Where did that image come from?

Wham! Again!

The steel toe of his boot ripped into her solar plexus, pain, more pain than she ever thought possible, radiated out, star-like, burning ...

Wham! Again!

Her heart was exploding.

Moaning, she curled up on her side, and then he smashed her again across the face, and he turned her over, flattened her out, her back flat against the concrete, and pinned her down with his knees and his breathing heavy now, he said, "Now I gut you, bitch, I really gut you!"

He brought the knife down, plunged it in, low down, into her belly, and he ripped it upwards.

"Oh," her head jerked backward, jugular exposed, body gone limp, eyes rolling upwards, "Oh," she thought, "Oh, now I'm dying, now I'm … damn it, damn it, damn it – how stupid!"

She was flooded with warmth, warm liquid, then cold, then darkness and flickers of light, then …

A cry: "Stop, stop, stop!"

From somewhere far away, she heard Milosevic shout. "You devil!"

"Stop! Stop!"

"Fuck you!" Milosevic screamed. "I will kill you."

There was something like an explosion of pain.

Then there were gunshots, or so it seemed.

And then there was nothing.

CHAPTER 17 – A BOY

When Jake and Gloria finally got back to the Prisoners' Cave, or the "Mother Ship," as Ms. Agnes called it, they saw that the whirlpool where the dead went had backed up. Water was flooding over the banks of downriver and upriver, bubbling and smoky water, flooding across the floor of the cave.

The cave was extra noisy, with gurgling, and rushing water sounds, and filled with thick mist. It took Jake a while to find Ms. Agnes. He searched in various niches, he went down toward the river, he looked in the side alleys, and he went into the three or four deeper niche caves. And then he came back, scratching his head, to the main part of the cave. And when he finally did find Ms. Agnes, he realized that Gloria was no longer with him. Where had she gone?

When Jake appeared in front of her, Ms. Agnes was thinking that the end was coming, the end was nigh and upon them, and that they were all going to drown in the sulfurous and sinful dark flood, but that there would be no Arc of Noah to save them, and at that very moment, when she was plunged in these dire thoughts, standing in her rags, up to her ankles in rising water, and clutching her naked withered right breast, Ms. Agnes felt a heavy drop hit her forehead – splotch – and then another – splotch – and, wiping the water from her eyes – it was slimy with clay – she looked up and she saw that water was leaking from a crack in the roof of the cave.

"Oh, Jake," she said, seeing him wade toward her. Where had the boy been? What was he up to? He was her angel!

"We have to leave, Ms. Agnes," Jake was wide-eyed. He stopped in his tracks. How Ms. Agnes had changed! In just the time he and Gloria had been off exploring, Ms. Agnes had become a different woman; now, she looked like a wrinkled crazy old wild woman, and she'd let the rags fall away so Jake could see everything. Maybe she was becoming a ghoul and would soon start spouting slobbering gibberish. Jake's heart sank. He looked around. Where was Gloria?

"We can't leave, Jake."

"I'll find a way, Ms. Agnes."

"There is no way, Jake, the cave – the Mother Ship – *is* the world, Jake, there is no other place but the cave, Jake, the Lord has decreed it so for sinners such as we that we must remain forever entombed, Jake, forever entombed and accept our fate and take it on the chin, Jake, such is the Lord's way."

"The Lord …" Jake's mouth opened wide; he had never heard Ms. Agnes invoke the name of the Lord; that was the sort of thing the Preacher used to do when he had his all his marbles, which marbles he definitely no longer had, Ms. Agnes herself had said so, because for quite a time now he just scratched himself between his legs, playing with his "thingamajig" – Gloria's word – and scratching under his armpits and drooling at the mouth and spooling out gibberish just as if he were a ghoul, but he wasn't one, not yet anyway, he hadn't gone all white and grown fangs and a long sloppy tongue, no, he was just a shrunken, wrinkled, hairy old man with no clothes at all to speak of, and with a high squeaky voice that rambled away like a feeble torrent of muddy water, spouting nonsense from the ledge where he sat most of the time, rolling his eyes at the horror of it all, "Oh, the horror, Oh, the horror," he kept saying, over and over. And hearing Ms. Agnes talk like the Preacher, invoking "sin" and "the Lord," was maybe the scariest thing that had ever happened to Jake, it was worse than the first time he saw Cassandra the Leper Lady and it was worse than the bad ghouls in the cave with the weird black river and all those evil-looking steel drums piled up.

"But …" he began to say, thinking, *Where is Gloria?* It would be horrible for Gloria to see this. Gloria had been right behind him. But now, where was she?

"We are here for our sins, Jake, and here, in the Lowest Circle, we will die, sin is original, it is the mark of Adam and Eve, it is indelible, it cannot be washed away, scrub and scrub though we may, Jake, so it is the will of the Fates and of the Lord himself and of the Boy who will come among us and who will with fire and brimstone cleanse the very earth of its sins, and strike us down, and morph us into our true monstrous likeness, Jake, so that the demonic self will become the outer self, demon-like, visible for all to see, yes, He, the Boy, will endow us with hooves and horns and scaly skin and bright bloody eyes, and sulfurous breath, and send us scurrying to Hell, tails between our legs, Jake, so it is said, so it is written, so it is proclaimed."

"Where is Gloria, Ms. Agnes?" Jake was thinking that Gloria would not be pleased by this god-talk though she would certainly like all the shiny new words. But where was she? The water was bubbling and rising, and more water was leaking from the roof of the cave. And he thought: if the roof caved in … No, it was better not to think about it!

"My bright little angel, oh where, oh where is she gone?" Ms. Agnes looked at Jake with a strange light in her eyes, and Jake was suddenly afraid, very afraid, the light in Ms. Agnes' eyes was even scarier than "God" and "Sin" and "Hell," and Ms. Agnes' eyes shone bright with a crinkled feverish brightness, white empty slit-like lights skittering in their depths, and she said, "Our golden angel has gone to heaven, she has, Jake, she has gone before us, she has been baptized in the holy waters, she has gone to meet death himself!"

Jake swallowed. He had to save them, he had to save them all, and he had to save Gloria. He didn't even want to think of the possibility that Gloria had drowned; no, that was not possible. He would go and find the guards, he would get them to open the door; he would find a way out.

"I'm going, Ms. Agnes. You wait here. I'll be back!"

"Yes, Jake, you go and play now – and be a good boy."

"I will, Ms. Agnes."

"Remember our little blond angel is watching over you from heaven! I think now I shall go for a swim."

The water was rising fast, and there was a roaring sound like water going over a cliff. It was getting hard to hear anything.

Ms. Agnes stood there, with a silly half-toothless grin on her face. Her eyes were very far away. It was like she was blind.

"No, you stay here, Ms. Agnes," Jake shouted over the rising confusion of the waters, "Don't go for a swim! Don't go into the water! Go to high ground, Ms. Agnes."

"But Jake …"

Ms. Agnes's voice was lost in the roar of the water. There wasn't much time. And where was Gloria? He'd have to try to save all of them. The only way was to get the main door open; his and Gloria's private little tunnel and crevice was too narrow for the adults and most of it was already underwater.

Gloria must be somewhere. She was really smart. She'd survive long enough for him to come back and save her. She couldn't have drowned herself. And … the thought was difficult even to think – Ms. Agnes would not have drowned Gloria, no matter how crazy she was, Ms. Agnes would not have drowned Gloria! Besides, Gloria would have fought! Gloria was strong, and she knew how to swim!

He splashed through the water to his ledge and to his secret exit from the cave – for an instant, he thought he could lead the people to freedom through the crack in the rock but in the next instant, he knew, yet again, that was impossible.

The passage was much too narrow and too difficult, and now it was flooded. The big ones could hardly stand up; they certainly couldn't swim!

He climbed up onto the ledge, shimmied down the crack, already deep in water that was pouring down the wall, then he swiveled and squeezed into the crevice. He waded down – the water was bubbling up – and then, taking a deep breath, he plunged under the boiling surface of the water and he swam.

It was not easy. The water was bubbling up, swirling, and tugging him this way and that. It was lucky he'd learned to swim in the upriver pool, he loved the water.

He dove straight down through the swirling maelstrom. Then he was in darkness, just a dull glow from the phosphorous walls and a glimmer from some of the emergency lights from outside.

He swam, feeling his way, and holding his breath, down into deeper the crevice, his shorts caught on a piece of wire, he swirled around, wiggled out of the shorts, somehow ripped them loose from the wire, and pulled them, bunched up, with him. His heart was thundering now, his lungs bursting, desperate for air. He scrunched up his face in determination, pure will power.

He kept swimming, thinking his chest would explode.

He wiggled through the last and narrowest part of the tunnel, twisting his shoulders this way, and then that, just barely squeezing through.

The pressure was building up behind him, pushing him forward, the water was really moving fast here, twirling him, bouncing him, banging him against the side of the tunnel.

He lost his shorts once again in the whorl of the water, but he blindly grabbed for them, caught them, and pushed blindly forward now, with one hand scraping along the crevice wall, guiding him, and finally he …

He shot out …

He shot out from the tunnel in a whoosh of water – and he splashed down head-over-heels, naked and on his knees, then he tumbled, again head-over-heels, heels-over-head, over and over, like he was a wheel-barrow wheel, in a regular Niagara of water, and he landed – with a slap-like smack

– on the main work tunnel floor, not far from the big square cages in the wire mesh and that went up and down.

Water was rushing out of the crevice he had just come through – a gushing, squirting, overpowering flood of water. It whammed into him and slammed him against a railing, and he was toppled over again and rolled over and over, and he banged again against the iron railing, and then he was picked up, twirled around, and smashed against the opposite side of the tunnel.

The tunnel was already a foot or more deep in water, but the overhead lights were still on; it was garish and crazy, like a place from a nightmare, like a place he had never seen before.

For a second, struggling to stand up, grasping for the metal railing, his hand opened, and he again lost his shorts.

"Hell and damnation!" he sputtered, swirling around. The water was waist-high. He was clinging to a wall rail he'd grabbed without even thinking about it. The shorts were caught in a whirlpool of water, swirling round and round, going down some drain. He edged toward them, feeling the pull of water press against his legs, afraid he might be swept off his feet, pulled and pushed down the tunnel, and that he might disappear into some monstrous drainpipe. Holding tight to the railing, he grabbed for his shorts, missed, grabbed again. If he let go of the railing, he knew he would be swept away. He grabbed again, and just caught the shorts by one of the belt loops. The belt was gone.

"Damned shorts, damned clothes!"

He plunked the sopping wet shorts on top of his head, sides hanging down floppily, hoping they wouldn't fall off, and he dragged himself hand-over-hand along the railing – the steel trembled and bucked up and down from the impact of the water. Steam rose from the water in swirls of fog.

Step by step, he fought through the churning water, heading toward the iron stairs marked Z-7. Finally, he got to the stairs and went up a few steps. He was out of the water, and he was out of breath.

He sat down on the iron steps, feeling the greasy wet rusty metal under his backside, somehow comforting, like sitting on a mud bank. At his feet, just beyond his toes, the river of water rushed and foamed and thundered past.

He couldn't stay here.

He had to find somebody, somebody who could open the great round door and let his people go.

His heart pounded. He gulped quick deep breaths.

I can't stay here!

I have to find somebody!

He stood up and pulled on his shorts; they sagged around his waist, he held them up with one hand, dribbles of muddy water trickling down his legs.

He bolted up the stairs, three steps at a time. He didn't really know where he was going or what he was hoping he'd find, but he had to get help to open the huge iron door that shut his people in. He was certain he couldn't do it himself. He knew it had something called electronically coded locks and it was just too big and he didn't know if there was any manual way to open it.

The only hope was if he could find a guard.

The guards wouldn't let the people die down here – would they?

He climbed up two levels.

The wind in the tunnel rose again, roaring like blazes, steamy hot, skittering along the water in the drainage runnels, tiny puckered racing ripples, and it lashed his shorts, slashing them around his bum and thighs, and pulling and tugging at them, and whipping his hair, slapping it around his head and into his eyes.

"Ouch and double damnation," he blinked, his eyes watery and stinging from the whipping and the sulfurous water.

Ms. Agnes had let his hair grow long in the last few months, too lazy, too weak, to cut it, she said, "I can do Gloria's hair, Jake. But you'll just have to look like a savage. I'm sorry." Jake hadn't minded; he liked it that way. Now, though, maybe it would be good to have short hair, sheared off to stubble, like Gloria. At the thought of Gloria, his heart sank, and his tummy flipped over in a somersault of fear. No, no, she's okay; Gloria is somewhere safe, he was sure of it!

The wind dropped.

There was a deadly ominous calm, except for the roaring of the water and the rattling of the pipes.

He came to a corner and took a deep breath: several layers of pipes snaked around the corner, held to the walls by great iron braces; he remembered them, and how they went to the big room full of machinery beyond the pumping station; he should be close to the right level.

His heart was beating, and he could hear it like thunder in his ears.

He thought of Gloria, leaning her head against his chest to hear his heart, her bright blue eyes looking up in total trust, her perfect little nose that she liked to wiggle and to pick and thoughtfully contemplate the curls of white maggot-like snot she had discovered, and the gold glints of her cropped hair showing through the thick patina of dirty wet clay.

Gloria ...

He had to find somebody who could open the door.

And he had to find Gloria; he had to save Gloria.

He bit his lip: no, Gloria didn't need saving; she was okay, Gloria was okay; she was someplace safe! He was sure of it!

He took another deep breath. He could hear the roar of the water down below and also up above somewhere. It was on both sides of him, above and below. It was thunderous. The whole place was flooding. Even up here, above the level of the cave, maybe three or four levels up, the water was running in a thick gurgling rivulet along the runnel at the edge of the tunnel floor.

And then ...

Somehow in the roaring of the wind and water Jake heard a voice and a shout.

"Bitch, bitch, bitch," the shouting angry voice was lifted on the wind; it rode in the midst of the thundering roaring of the water.

'Bitch' was not a nice word, Ms. Agnes had said so after the Preacher, in his madness had called out about Bitch Fate, Bitch Destiny, a Bitch of a life.

Jake ran.

The tunnel bent off to the left; it looked weird, strangely peaceful in the glow of emergency lights and phosphorescent lichen, and with only the water rushing in the runnels at the side of the tunnel, and the wires and cables rattling slightly.

He came around the bend and at first he wasn't sure what he was seeing. The tunnel lights were getting duller – they were probably running out of power – Ms. Agnes had told him that the things called batteries, particularly the old-fashioned ones, couldn't keep the lights on for very long.

The tunnel was filling with glowing steam and mist from the rushing water and maybe from the fire wherever it was. There were cracks in the wall he hadn't seen before and steaming water was spurting and bubbling and streaming out of them, and washing down the tunnel walls, all shiny.

It came into focus, what he was seeing: a woman was lying on the ground and a man, a big huge fat man, bigger than any man Jake had ever seen, and he was hitting the woman and trying to – to rape her.

Rape ...

Murder …

He'd seen things like that and imagined them. It was bad. He thought of Ms. Agnes and he thought of Ms. Chang – the women who had looked after him and who had been his friends – and he thought of Gloria.

The woman could be Gloria; Gloria could be the woman.

Jake ran forward. "Hey, stop, hey, stop! Stop! Stop! Stop!"

The man looked up. The woman was lying on the ground. She tried to get up pushing up with one elbow; her face was covered in blood; her eyes were full of blood. Her mouth was twisted, looked broken. Her blond hair looked gray under the emergency lights. All of the middle of her stomach was cut open, and bloody, with things hanging out in coils. She looked like one of the dead.

"Grrrrrhhhhhh!" Jake ran straight at the big man.

The man half turned and, kneeling, he began to get up, "I'll kill you, you runt, you fucking sewer rat, you freak, you …!"

Jake swiveled around and leaped and landed on the man's back while the man was still turning and getting up and Jake started punching and kicking, and the man turned – he was huge and strong – and tossed Jake off and grabbed him by one arm and twirled him around and smashed Jake against the pipes and still holding onto Jake he threw him across the tunnel and Jake hit the wall with a loud crack and then there were stars and for a moment at least there was nothing.

Jake lay still, like a crumpled-up rag doll.

The big man picked up the pistol that was lying close to the bloodied gutted woman, and he lifted it and aimed, and he fired and fired and fired and the bullets bounced and ricocheted off the wall just above Jake's body.

"Now, you bitch, I finish you, I fuck you dead!" The big man turned to the woman whose eyes were still open, smeared with blood, delirious, fading fast, but still watching him. Her hands opened and closed as if clutching at air.

The woman did manage, somehow, to scream.

Or was it just a mental scream.

She was gone.

V heard, or she thought she heard a scream.

And shots, she heard shots.

She stopped and listened.

A scream? There were so many sounds! V frowned. Water was roaring somewhere behind the walls of stone, the underground river system was flooding one level after another; some of the levels above her were already flooded; the bottom of Shaft-1, buried under a mountain of clay and rock and fire, was flooded; water was streaming down from cracks in the tunnel ceiling. Time was running out. Maybe all the prisoners were already dead.

Then she heard it again.

A scream – a child – or a woman!

Okay! V sprang up the steps and down the narrow, dimly lit corridor. Water raced gurgling down the runnels at the side of the tunnel, overflowing, spreading across the pavement.

There were gusts of wind, and brief distant sounds of explosions – the bottom of Main Shaft-1 was still collapsing. If they didn't find a way out, they would all be entombed here until the end of time.

She raced around another bend in the tunnel and saw a small boy, naked, with tousled black hair. His back was turned to her, and he was carrying an iron bar, clenched in one fist.

And, beyond the boy, V saw …

Jake opened his eyes.

He tried to get up.

The big man had a knife, and he was lying on top of the lady, and then he was pushing himself on her and then he had a knife out and he plunged the knife down and he was killing her – though she seemed already dead, ready to be shoved into the water and sent downriver to the whirling water under the dark rock to the Kingdom of the Dead.

Jake was still dizzy.

He got up, holding his head.

His shorts had fallen off and were lying on the tunnel floor.

Jake looked around.

A length of metal pipe was lying beside the runnel where the water was running, gurgling like mad, flooding up out of the runnel, and swirling around the piece of pipe.

Everything roared in Jake's head; in front of his eyes, little bright spots flashed and drifted.

Everything spun, he could hardly stand up.

He got down on his hands and knees, and he crawled toward the pipe. His head and his arm hurt. He crouched next to the pipe. It seemed to grow larger as he stared. It was a pipe, a piece of metal. He knew that. You spelled *pipe* "P-I-P-E." *Metal* you spelled "M-E-T-A-L." Ms. Agnes taught him that, Ms. Agnes on her hands and knees, with a stick, drawing in the dry flat smooth, soft mud, she taught him that. "Words are magic, Jake. They bring things into your head; they help to think, Jake, it's very important to learn as many words as you can."

It was a pipe, heavy, hard, and dangerous.

He had to pick it up.

He said to himself, "Pick it up, Jake! Pick it up."

He concentrated. His hand reached out. His fingers closed around it. He picked it up. It was heavy, but he could carry it. Over the gurgling water and the steamy wind coming up the tunnel and the distant thunder of the water flooding the lower galleries, Jake could hear the groans of the woman, and she was saying, "No, please, no …"

So, she was not dead – not yet.

Jake stood up.

He swayed. Things looked funny; they had a glow around them, and they were moving back and forth like a reflection in wavy water.

For just a second everything was double and was dancing …

He gripped the pipe hard and balanced it so he had a really good grip and exactly the right poise, and he headed toward the man. He would kill this man. He would smash the man's head in; he would smash and smash, and smash …

He walked toward the man, as if in a trance.

"Don't," said a voice, "I'll look after this," and Jake felt a hand on his shoulder.

He looked and saw it was a claw that was clutching his shoulder, a glittering turquoise claw with long gold sharp and pointed nails.

He looked up. It was a hybrid, a girl hybrid, all glittery and green and turquoise with black and gold bits.

In a world that was all dull clayey gray and faint bluish light, the hybrid shone brightly like nothing he had ever seen, except the gold glint of Gloria's hair and the gold scales of the Golden Hybrid, his and Gloria's secret hybrid …

Jake gripped the pipe tighter; he felt his lungs take a desperate intake of breath, his heart stopped, leaped, and started again.

"Don't look," the hybrid said, "I'm going to kill that man; you don't want to watch."

"I …" Jake was about to say something. He was so surprised, he didn't even have time to be afraid; the only hybrid he'd ever seen was the Golden Hybrid he and Gloria had discovered and visited a couple of times. If her master was not around, she waved at them.

Then Jake noticed: this hybrid didn't have a collar.

"Stay here," it said.

"Okay," Jake whispered, nodding.

The hybrid patted his shoulder and leaped.

Jake watched; there was no way he was going to turn away.

The hybrid was already on top of the man.

She tore the man away from the woman – his arm swung out. He dropped his knife – and as the hybrid lifted him up, he screamed, and he shouted, "You devil, you monster, I'll kill you, I'll fucking kill you."

It got weird – really fast – it looked like the hybrid was going to kiss the man; she was much smaller than he was – not tall, and she was slender, really slender beside the big monster guy.

It happened so fast …

She grabbed him around the arms, pinning his arms to his sides, he was kicking and swearing and wiggling, and then, almost like she loved him, and she seemed to leap on him, and she put her mouth down to his neck, like she was going to nuzzle him like Gloria sometimes nuzzled Ms. Agnes, and then – wow – she bit him!

Yeah, she must be biting him.

The raped woman, covered in blood and lying sprawled on her back, looked like she was dead; no, her hand was opening and closing, fingers curling up, and then closing into a fist, fingers curling up, and then closing into a fist.

There was a sucking sound – slurp, slurp, slurp – like when Ms. Agnes or Mr. Swann sucked the last clogged liquid meal out of the food pouches. Jake could see the hybrid's throat moving; she was drinking or eating the guy!

Wow!

So, hybrids *do* eat people!

The guy was hanging there like a big heavy doll; he was jerking around now, bobbing and quivering, like a small stick or piece of paper or like one of the dead when they were being bounced in the waves or washed up and then swept downriver to the last whirlpool and then down, toes sometimes last, sometimes it was the head, down under the wall of rock and gone forever downriver where the spirits lived, though Ms. Agnes – the old wise, calm, funny Ms. Agnes who seemed to have died or disappeared – said there were no spirits and that the dead were dead and that was it and it was final.

"Let the dead bury the dead," she said once, and Jake and Gloria puzzled over that for some time – "The dead aren't buried. They float, and then they drown," said Gloria, wrinkling up her nose, and, "Besides, how would the dead bury anything if they are dead already they can't do anything, isn't that right, Jake," Gloria said, poking at the half-dried clay with a short stick, one of those sticks that came mysteriously from upriver somewhere and which were really good for writing in the clay or making pictures, "I wonder what it's like to be a dead."

"I don't know," Jake said.

"I'd like to know," Gloria said, "I'd like to be dead and then not be dead."

"It's not a good idea, Gloria," Jake had said, though he really didn't know why, but there was something creepy and frightening about the thought – dead and then not dead.

Now, as the hybrid drank the man dry, Jake walked forward slowly, as if hypnotized.

He was getting closer and closer to the hybrid and to the woman on the ground who looked dead – lying sprawled on her back arms and legs spread out wide, toes pointing up, eyes closed, and blood everywhere and a big dark gash and hole in her belly, but her fingers still opening and closing.

The hybrid was drinking and eating and holding the man up, though he looked dead or unconscious now, limp as a huge white doll, his head lolled back, his eyes wide open, only the whites showing.

Still drinking, the hybrid, with those big gold eyes of hers, looked straight at Jake. Her eyes seemed to plunge right into the center of his soul.

He felt a warm, funny feeling all through his body, and he heard the hybrid's voice inside his head, just as if she was talking to him, but from somewhere inside his ears or between his eyes, a voice that was all warm and friendly, "I told you not to look, Jake, so please don't get upset with me." It was almost like she was asking forgiveness.

"I'm not upset," Jake said.

"Good," her voice spoke in his mind; it gave him a really warm feeling.

The hybrid stopped drinking, and she dropped the body of the man, and she looked down at it and she pronounced in a serious monotone way almost like a religious thing that the preacher sometimes used to say, at least when he was calm and not ranting. "Now, you are dead, truly dead, and you will not rise again."

The man was dead, it looked like it: his body was gray now, like a dead person floating in the downstream. As Jake stared, the body seemed to shrivel and smoke, cracks appearing, steam rising, ashes of his soul drifting off, but that must be an illusion, Jake thought, Ms. Agnes having said there was no such thing as the soul, "The dead are dead, Jake, truly dead."

A ceiling lamp was swinging back and forth, its mount and metal clamps making clicking and clanking sounds. The narrow rivulet of water in the drainage runnels bubbled and gurgled; the water was overflowing; a spreading greasy pool of water came close to Jake's feet. As the light swung in the breeze, the shadows moved, Jake felt the air moving against his skin, a steamy breeze – the cables that ran along the tunnel wall rattled.

The hybrid looked up from the body and stared at Jake. Her mouth and snout were dripping blood; it was shiny and looked black under the emergency lights; blood covered her breasts and ran in thick little rivulets down her belly, with little splashes on her thighs. The dripping blood made it look like she had a mustache and beard. "Help me, Jake," she said, and she turned her back and knelt by the woman.

Jake didn't hesitate – though, again, he was surprised she knew his name – he came and knelt next to her.

"Kneel on the other side, Jake."

"Yes," he got up and went to the other side of the dead or almost dead woman, and he knelt, so they were facing each other over the dead woman. He realized he didn't have any clothes on, but it didn't seem to matter – not for the moment anyway – other things were more important.

The hybrid reached into the woman's chest – which was open and all red and bubbling blood and something was beating there, pump, pump, pump …

Was that the heart?

Was that the beating heart?

The hybrid pushed in some of the bloody rope-like things, and she took a fold of flesh and skin and pushed it back and she said, "Here, Jake, hold this back for me." Jake grabbed hold. The flesh was rubbery and slippery and slick, and he was worried he might let go so he held on tight. His own heart was still beating hard, but he didn't think about that. He did what he was told.

"Hold on," said the hybrid, "By the way, Jake, my name is V."

"V," Jake said, holding tight to the fold of flesh.

The hybrid – V – laid her claws on the wound, in the valley of blood that Jake was holding open; the bubbling blood slowed, and, as Jake watched, the flesh seemed to grow back, and to become normal.

"Let go now, Jake."

Jake let go of the flesh; the lip of flesh and skin flipped back into place; V laid her claws on it and on the opposite flap of flesh that she had patted down and as she stroked and caressed the skin and flesh there was a glow – sort of purple flickering glow – and the flesh and skin healed and it looked like the woman had not been cut open at all, it looked like she was normal, but she was bruised and there was blood everywhere and between her legs and on her mouth and the Hybrid now leaned close to the woman's face, and Jake thought she was going to kiss the woman or bite her and drink her dry, but she laid her claws on the woman's face and the same light came and the smashed mouth became a blur and then it looked normal – but there was still blood everywhere and the woman was still naked and covered in a sheen of dirt and blood and the woman opened her eyes, very blue eyes, still rimmed with blood.

"Jesus Christ," she said, it was like a whisper.

"Try to sit up."

"I'm dead, and I've gone to hell."

"Not yet, you haven't."

"I'm dreaming. This is a nightmare. Tell me I'm not seeing this, I mean, a hybrid ..." She blinked and stared at Jake. "... and a kid and ... a body ..."

"The hybrid saved your life," said Jake, "and she ate – well, drank – the guy who ... who ... who attacked you."

"She can eat him all up, every inch of him, for all I care, the beast."

"I've drunk my fill," said V, "He can harm no one; he will not rise again."

"What are you?" The woman stared at the hybrid, and then she glanced at Jake – he suddenly remembered he was naked, but he didn't move – maybe they wouldn't notice. The woman glanced back at the hybrid, at V. "You escaped? You're not wearing a collar."

"I never had a collar, Cosmos. Try to sit up."

"We don't have time," said Jake.

The hybrid glanced at him. "Jake's right, Cosmos: we don't have time."

"Time for what?" the woman blinked at them, "You don't have time for what? I feel dizzy."

"Time to save everybody," said Jake, "Time to save Ms. Agnes and Gloria and all the others."

"The prisoners, you mean," said the woman.

"And time to get us all out of here," said the hybrid.

"What's happened ...?" the woman said, struggling to her feet, "What's happening ...?"

CHAPTER 18 – THE MOTHER SHIP

"Now, Jake," V turned to him, "Where are your people? Do you know the way to the door?"

Jake stared at the hybrid; blood was still dripping from her fangs, down her breasts.

"I do. I think I do."

"Good, Jake. We go there now."

"God," said the woman. She was standing now, dazed, blinking at them.

"Do you know how to find the people down here, Jake?"

Jake gulped, "Yes, but the Great Door is locked."

The Cosmos woman had pulled on her what remained of her work suit, and she was looking down at it – just shreds remained. Behind them, water was flooding up the tunnel, "What happened? I thought I was dead."

"You were almost dead," said the hybrid.

"The man cut you all up the middle," said Jake, running his finger from his pubis to his chest, "The hybrid fixed you up."

"You fixed me up?"

"Jake helped."

"Thanks, then – I guess." The woman blinked, and even smiled, her teeth still rimmed with blood.

"You're welcome, I guess," said V.

"You're not wearing a collar," the woman blinked at V.

"No."

"What happened?"

"She is saying the same thing over and over," said Jake, noticing that the woman had asked the same questions several times.

"Shock, that's shock, it can do that to memory, Jake," said the hybrid.

"I'm in shock?" the woman said.

"I'll explain later," V said, "I think you should come with us."

"Yes, okay, yes, Hybrid, I'll come with you." the woman said, seeming stronger now, "My name is Valerie, Valerie Joffre."

"I'm Jake; she's V," Jake said. He picked up his shorts and held them in front of him, then turned sideways, pulled them on, and held them up with one hand.

"V ..." said Valerie Joffre, frowning, "V ..."

"Come on, Jake," V said, lips curved in a smile, "Take us; take us to your people. Take us to the great iron door.

"You are laughing at me," Jake said, staring at the two women and then down at his shorts.

"We are not laughing at you, Jake," said V.

"No, we aren't," said Valerie Joffre, "both of us are naked too, Jake, or almost. The hybrid has no clothes at all, and just look at me!"

"That's right," Jake smiled at them, timidly.

V and Valerie Joffre glanced at each other; they had both noticed that he had a beautiful smile. "Let's go."

Jake led them toward the stairs.

A rusty pipe – running along the tunnel wall about halfway up – was clattering and clanging and bouncing back and forth, the pressure was so great and, at its bolt-joints, steam hissed out in white clouds. Just as they ran past it burst, a shower of steamy hot water rained down from a ceiling pipe. An electric cable from one of the large battery installations was flapping along the ceiling, sending out blue and yellow sparks.

"This whole place is going to cave in, and soon," said Valerie Joffre, and she turned to V, "Which level are we on?"

"Z-7," said V.

"Yes, then Jake is right: the door he's talking about – the gateway to the prisoner cave – should be that way, down several levels. I've got the schematics of the mine in my head, implanted."

"Follow me," Jake raced down the corridor, with Valerie Joffre and V close behind.

"Come on," Jake shouted, "If we don't hurry, they're going to die."

V and Valerie Joffre began to run.

"Come on," Jake shouted.

They climbed down another level. Water cascaded, steaming and bubbling, swirling down the stairs, shin-deep. Jake kept hitching his shorts up, "Hurry,

hurry," he shouted, and under his breath he swore at Clive Something's shorts, stiff as cardboard, itchy, and above all a "bloody hindrance," as Doctor Semmelweis used to say before he lost all his hair and went bonkers or nuts or coo-coo, as Gloria liked to say, rounding her lips carefully, "*coo-coo!*"

They came to a place where the tunnel dipped down, and the water was very deep, waist-deep for Jake, and the current lashed at Jake's shorts, trying to carry them away. Valerie Joffre and V waded through the water. V dipped under, splashing, wiggling, dipping her head under, and stood up, washing away the blood from Milosevic and from Valerie with her claws. Valerie, seeing this, did the same, and came up soaking, but with fewer streaks of blood on her than before and even less rags, some floating away. She looked beautiful, Jake thought, only Gloria was as beautiful, and the two hybrids, the gold one and the turquoise one, and Ms. Agnes as she used to be.

They came to a split in the tunnel.

"Which way do we go?" Valerie said, "I don't remember this part – I guess some of my memory got knocked out. And I had some plasticized schematics, but I've lost them – that bastard!"

Beside her, the turquoise hybrid, V, was sniffing the air.

"This way," Jake said; he chose the right hand tunnel and went ahead, then, facing him, coming from around a bend in the new tunnel, another hybrid appeared. It was the golden one he and Gloria had seen.

"Hey, Jake," the Golden Hybrid said.

"Hello," Jake said, "You remember me?"

"You and your little friend Gloria, yes, of course, I remember. It was kind of you to visit me."

"Eve," said V, "Eve Schmidt."

"At last," said the Golden Hybrid, "You've come to save us."

"Yes, I'm here," said V.

The two hybrids put their arms around each other.

"This is an epidemic! You're loose," said Valerie Joffre, staring at the Golden Hybrid, "and you can talk."

"We're loose, for the moment," the Golden Hybrid tapped the thick black collar that encased her neck, "And, yes, we can talk. It depends on these things. If it's off, I talk. My human name is Eve, Eve Schmidt, by the way, and I was, in a former life, long ago, a Colonel in the US Marines."

Water was spilling all over the place.

"We're trying to find the human prisoners."

"Not this way, I think," said Eve.

"No, it's this way," said Jake, pointing down a side tunnel.

"Yes, that looks right," said Eve.

Finally, wading through foaming water, they came to the huge round metal door; it was set into a sheer wall of rock. The door had a code pad at the entrance.

It was a giant steel door, probably a foot thick.

V stared at it. Water was seeping out the bottom half of the great steel door. This could be a problem.

The Golden Hybrid put her head against the door. "I hear screams."

"So, they're still alive," said Valerie Joffre, "at least that's something."

"Why don't you just smash your way through, V?" Eve, said, "You can do that sort of thing."

"I'm not really that strong, not usually. In any case, the impact might kill everybody inside," said V, "and it would almost certainly bring the whole place tumbling down." She glanced upwards. The roof of the cave had cracks, water was pouring down, hot sulfurous water.

"Yes, it would," said Valerie Joffre, pushing back her hair and looking up at the ceiling, "This whole area is fragile, lots of micro-factures, and there is a big underground lake nearby. It's amazing it hasn't collapsed already."

Jake looked up. He gulped. Big cracks had opened up in the ceiling of the tunnel. Water was pouring down the walls. A chunk of ceiling fell at that very moment; a big block, about ten meters up the tunnel, tumbled down, bouncing, shattering.

V pulled Jake close to her. He felt her claws; her arm went around him like gentle lightning, and she pressed him to her body. Her body was cool and smooth and felt really good; it made Jake want to hold onto her and just sleep and forget everything; it was like being swept into a cool dream.

He had let go of his shorts, they sagged down to his thighs. He hitched them up. *I'm in the arms of a cannibal monster,* he thought, but I like her; she's a friend.

Somehow the cool curves of her body were comforting, more than comforting, like something he remembered from some distant time.

He thought of Ms. Agnes, a flicker of an image from the dim past – his mother perhaps – flashed in his mind, a sickening hint and intimation of yearning and loss, then he saw in his mind, clear as day, Gloria – Gloria wrinkling her nose.

"We have to do something, or we'll all be buried down here," said Valerie Joffre, her hands on her hips, looking doubtful, impatient.

"Right, you're right," said the Golden Hybrid.

V turned to the geologist, "Valerie, do you know the codes?"

"I knew most of them – part of my mission implant – but I never come here, so I never used this code. And then I've just been slammed on the head, so I'm not sure if I …"

"Think of it," V said.

"Think of it?"

"Try to think of it."

"Okay, whatever you say," Valerie stared at V, and then blinked, "Hybrids read minds, I read somewhere, but I thought it was a myth."

"Not entirely a myth."

Valerie closed her eyes. V laid her claw on Valerie's head, and V closed her eyes. Jake was still pressed against her. She tousled and stroked his thick wet hair with her free claw.

"Okay, I think I got it. Thanks, Valerie!" V turned to the code pad and pushed a series of buttons – this was a very old-fashioned security system, but at least it did have a separate electric circuit and backup batteries, so it was still working. The lights flashed green.

"Amazing," Valerie Joffre stared at the green lights, then at V.

"Okay, now we're going in. The water will probably flood out." V took Jake's shoulders, bent down, and gazed into his eyes, "Are you okay, Jake?"

"Yes, V." He looked straight back. "I'm okay."

"You and Valerie get up there, out of the way. Eve and I will open the gate."

Valerie took Jake's hand, and they scrambled up onto a higher piece of ground, a ten-foot rock ledge that struck out into the tunnel from the rock face.

"Good, let's go." V and Eve lifted the safety bars and turned the wheel.

Water gushed, then poured out, a Niagara.

"Okay, back up," V and Eve backed away, and they scrambled up the sloping tunnel as a roaring torrent of water poured out of the great open door.

Ms. Agnes fought against the swirling water. Yes, it was the end! The roof was leaking, pieces of the sky were falling, the steamy sulfurous floodwaters were surging, Death was coming, and as Ms. Agnes waited for the final moment, for the Revelation and Rapture promised by the Boy, the Boy that had somehow got into her mind, she prodded with her tongue at two of her remaining teeth as she waded through the rising water swirling around her skinny shins, slightly bowlegged now she noticed, which was, if her recollection was accurate, new, for many things were afloat and adrift in her memory, and her mind was, she was willing to admit, getting pretty foggy. But two days ago, or was it weeks or months, she hadn't been bowlegged. Or had she? The two teeth were loose. They were going to fall out, "Praise the Lord!"

She would get what she deserved, "Praise the Lord!" She pushed at the guilty vain teeth with her tongue, prodding and poking, hoping to make them fall out – all the others too, even those clinging on for dear life. To shuffle around toothless would be a just reward. "I am a sinful hag, I am a sinful hag!" Self-loathing, inspired by this new thing called the Boy, El Niño, welled up, a poisonous stew, within her.

Oh, the vanity of youth, the vanity of strength, the vanity of beauty! All gone! And all the ideas of youth – liberty, freedom, equality – all illusions, vain illusions! And all the soft, smooth, warm flesh and sensual pleasures too were gone, quite gone – and all human existence was as ephemeral as the chaff wafting off the husks of wheat in a thresher in the sunlight.

She prodded again with her tongue – get it over with! The teeth were an itch that needed to be scratched, a scab that needed to be pried free, monuments to vanity to be struck down.

Her legs were thin as sticks, the dress was a filthy rag that sagged below her breasts, and there was a roaring in her ears; she wasn't sure whether it came from inside her head or from the flood and clamor. She called out, "Jake! Gloria!"

Her voice was a hoarse croaking whisper, lost in the tumult.

Gloria was gone to Heaven!

Or perhaps Gloria was not in Heaven?

Could Gloria have been driven down to Hell?

That creature, the Divinity, the Boy, had been in her head for some time now, making her think and say things she didn't truly believe. He was beautiful, the Boy was, but then sometimes he seemed horrible, like a skeletal presence, like a mass of writhing maggots, like something …

She wondered whether she had frightened Jake.

Would Jake ever return?

Would Gloria ever return?

Where had the little scamps got to?

When the pumps stopped working, about three or four hours ago, or perhaps longer (it was hard to tell), Ms. Agnes wasn't too worried – not at first. She thought they would fix it, the invisible guards and the technicians who ran the camp, those distant invisible gods who ruled over the prisoners, yes, they would fix it. But then, as the minutes went by, the river soon began to back up.

And the madness came, and she spoke the madness to Jake and to Gloria, and now both of them had disappeared!

Why had she howled about sin and damnation and the lower pits of hell?

They were in enough trouble without all that nonsense!

I have become a wild old witch, and I am going mad.

Somebody or Something has been forcing its way into my mind!

She chuckled and worked at the two loose teeth.

Soon after the pumps stopped making their noise, water began bubbling up everywhere, hissing up through cracks in the rock, leaking through the walls of rock, squirting out of holes and crevices that Ms. Agnes had never seen or noticed; and now water was even streaming down from the roof of rock which meant that the flooding was all around them – below them, beside them, and above them – *above* was really frightening.

There was no way out.

They were all going to die.

Perhaps that is why I have gone mad!

Ms. Agnes giggled. Oh, what a fool am I!

The Preacher had climbed up on a slippery bit of ledge not far from Ms. Agnes. He gave her a look which seemed to say she was to blame for what was happening and then he stood up – pretty shaky – and he said, "Behold what has come upon us ..."

Ms. Agnes snorted, all her skepticism returning.

Still, it was all wondrous and horrible, what was happening. The Preacher had somehow regained some of his sanity – maybe the Imminent Apocalypse agreed with some folks, *energized* them, as they used to say. The Preacher had managed to hoist himself up onto a rock platform and was standing there, his skeletal arms stretched toward the stone roof as if it were a heavily clouded and vengeful heaven and he an Old Testament prophet, crying out that this was the judgment of God on the wicked, that we all deserved to die, that we were all going to go down to hell. Poor cantankerous old fool, Ms. Agnes thought, his religion is all hate and fear – and no forgiveness, no courage.

Just the kind of idea that the Boy – whoever or whatever he was – had been planting in my mind!

"And the Lord He will smite all his enemies and lay low the kings and princes of the earth, and they shall be as the beasts of the fields and no longer speak in tongues but fall silent in the babble of their darkened hearts, the sons and daughters of Babylon shall know darkness and blindness and shall feed on the grass of the fields, crawling on their slimy unclean bellies as the serpent crawls ..."

The preacher was ranting on, and on. Ms. Agnes looked around. Some of the women were crying. Even the youngest and prettiest had turned into loathsome hags, starved, toothless, their fallen and shriveled breasts and shrunk shanks and withered bellies, shrouded in filthy rags, or in nothing at all. I am being uncharitable, but one must see things as they are. And I am just like them, I am one of them, I am one of the loathsome crones.

Two women – what were their names? – Oh, yes, Beverly Something and Julie Somebody – were struggling through the rising water, almost up to their waists, trying to haul the Professor up onto higher ground. Charitable brave creatures, Beverly and Julie, they were. The Professor was by now a skeleton, and he once such a fine, outstanding, big-chested man; they were carrying him under the arms, his elbows stuck out. Yes, he used to be such a fine figure of a man, thought Ms. Agnes. I had even entertained a fancy, many years ago, that he and I might ... But enough of that! Now, I must get to higher ground – and I must find Jake and Gloria.

The rock Jake and Gloria used to perch on – it was already underwater, so their secret tunnel was already underwater; oh, yes, she knew about their little escapades, the rascals, and of course it was risky, going out, she had looked at the crevice herself, once, on the sly, but it was too narrow even for her – it frightened her; it frightened her for them, for Gloria and Jake. But Gloria and Jake were young – they needed adventure! And there is no life worth living if it contains no risks.

Many times, she had been on the point of telling them not to leave the cave; but she could never bring herself to do it.

Ms. Agnes stumbled and found herself on her hands and knees, staring at the swirling water. She really didn't know if her legs would carry her any further.

Maybe she should just crawl. Maybe she should just lie down and let the water carry her away, drift away like one of the dead, drift away, carefree and all, light as a feather, then swirl around, bubble down, and disappear darkly, toes last, into Hades, like an endless sleep: *To sleep, perchance to dream ...* She stared at the bubbling swirling current, and then, somehow, she staggered to her feet: no, she had to make sure that Gloria and Jake were safe.

Safe!

What a silly idea!

"Agnes Lucile Carter, you are a silly old woman! Nothing is safe! Everybody is going to die! The children are going to die! This is the end; this is the flood. This is the flood without Noah and without his Arc."

The Preacher was caterwauling something about tearing out his tongue, oh, yes, it was something from Revelations.

He was going to rip out an eyeball.

He was going to cut off his hand too.

Nothing much would be left!

"Poor man," Ms. Agnes mumbled. She staggered to her feet, the water was rising fast. She saw Sally Ho crouched in the water, black hair straight down around her perfect oval face.

"Come, Sally, let's go up and help the preacher."

Sally was Chinese and her golden skin – so beautiful and luminous up till lately – had turned chalk and waxy, and she was pale as a ghost and had shrunk down to a skeleton in the last weeks, "The man's unhinged," Sally said, blinking blindly at Ms. Agnes.

"It makes no difference, unhinged or not; we must calm him down," said Ms. Agnes, feeling some of her own gumption coming back, "He frightens everybody even more than they should be frightened."

"Yes, he does make everything worse," Sally smiled, and Ms. Agnes thought: Dear child, and she still has all her teeth!

"Let's go," said Ms. Agnes; one tooth, she felt, was only hanging by a thread; soon, it would give up.

After a lot of coaxing and crooning, the two of them finally quietened the Preacher; he sat down, couched, mumbled to himself, and stared at the two women with wild, frightened, unseeing eyes. "The fruits of sin," he mumbled, "They are the fruits of sin. They have the mark of Cain upon them." Sally glanced at Ms. Agnes: at least the man wasn't shouting.

Ms. Agnes sighed. She was worried frantic for the two children. Dying would not be so bad, if only she knew the two children were safe. All these big ideas – sin, and damnation, and salvation, and Heaven and Hell, seemed to be proper obscenities when what was at stake was something so simple and clear-cut and basic as the life or death of two children. But, then, men do like to holler so – big ideas, big mouths!

Then it really didn't help, Ms. Agnes thought, that the emergency lights were even worse than the usual lights and made everybody look like ghosts.

Even without the ghastly lights, most of the people already looked like ghosts; they had been down here, all of them, for fourteen or fifteen years, and they only wore the most basic clothes, soiled and torn underwear mostly; some were going naked now since it was easier and it was so hot and steamy all the time and only rags were available, not really enough for modesty of even the most rudimentary sort; food up until two or three months ago had been delivered once a day; then the deliveries became rarer, and unpredictable; sometimes Ms. Agnes wondered why the guards didn't just shoot people. "Shoot all of us," she mumbled, "Shoot all of us, why don't you, and get it over with!"

Of course, they never saw the guards, since the food was simply pushed through the double security slot in the door.

No, they hadn't seen any guards for, well, maybe three or four years, or even more. It really was difficult to keep track of time. She had kept a sort of calendar for quite a period, then she fell sick, and the calendar after that was useless, out of date.

The underground river washed away the excrement and waste, and Ms. Agnes and a few others had been able to set up a sort of rudimentary self-government, to make sure people didn't fight over food.

But any semblance of discipline had broken down when food deliveries became erratic.

She looked around. Now the water was bubbling up even faster than before, and it began to spread over the last dry parts of the cave.

Some of the men began to hammer on the door, but their blows were so feeble they hardly made any noise at all. "How pathetic," Ms. Agnes thought, "How pathetic we have all become."

She sat hunched up, a crone on a rock.

A tooth fell away.

She spat it out.

Another tooth gave up the ghost.

She removed it, examined it, and threw it away.

The water rose around the men at the Gate; soon, it was up to their waists.

She wanted to call out to them to come to higher ground, but she didn't have the energy.

They wouldn't hear her, and if they heard, they wouldn't listen. She felt with her tongue the gaps where the teeth had fallen out; more were loose, soon, if she lived a day or two more, she'd be toothless.

Ha, ha, ha, cackle, cackle, cackle …

I used to have a beautiful smile, she thought, and with the point of her tongue she dislodged another tooth, another incisor, or maybe a canine or a premolar, she forgot, whatever, it didn't matter. She rolled it around in her mouth, on her tongue, then she took it out of her mouth, spitting it out from between her lips, and looked at it, holding it between two fingers; it was a fine tooth, no cavities, bright white, the tooth of a young woman, like when she won that beauty pageant and paid for two years of college by modeling. She had one of the brightest, most beautiful smiles ever! Yes, once I was young! It seems centuries ago now! How old am I? Yes, let's see, I must be about 37 or 38, yes, ha, ha. Let see, if I remember rightly, I was about twenty-five when I was "disappeared." She placed the tooth on a small ledge of stone. It looked like a miniature idol, or totem, shining bright. Perhaps the good fairy will come. I should make a wish and lay me down to sleep and who knows what might happen …

I am going mad.

Oh, no, let me not go mad!

Ms. Agnes remembered the interrogation in a camp outside Elysium that was the first step on her quick voyage to oblivion; it was very civilized, really, the man sat opposite her; he twiddled with an old-fashioned pencil. "You see," he said, "when dignity is gone, everything is gone. If people die alone, knowing that no one will ever know of their sacrifice, they will lose heart. Cowardice and degradation are nothing if nobody knows of it, and the same goes for heroism."

She just stared at him.

"You are a beautiful young woman," he said at one point, "But when this is over you will no longer be beautiful," he smiled and spread his arms, "When this is over you will no longer be young or anyone or anything at all."

She licked her half-sunken lips and looked around, a crone crouching on a muddy rock in an underworld sunk in ghastly sunless, moonless twilight.

The preacher had fallen asleep, or perhaps he was just dead, crouching there like the husk of a man, a body without a soul – what he had become.

Sally Ho had closed her eyes and was sitting lotus-style on the top of the rock, hands curved upward, wrists poised on her thighs, fingers slightly closed, offering or accepting, ready to receive whatever blessings or horrors heaven might bestow or whatever doom might befall them.

Ms. Agnes crouched lower on top of the low ledge of slimy rock, feeling the warm slime on her buttocks and thighs; she narrowed her eyes and watched the water rise; her mouth worked like soft slush, lips and tongue twisting, exploring; there were still some teeth to root out. People were wading through the water; some were crying; others screaming – a mad, continuous unreasoning wail.

"Let us out of here!"

"The water is rising! Let us out!"

The Preacher stood up and moved his mouth saying something about plague and locusts and blisters and continued for a while, waving his arms and preaching, his voice a weak high-pitched squeak, railing at the universe and beating his sunken chest with one closed fist, and then he slipped and fell into the water – now about a meter and a half deep and swirling around; it wasn't deep, but he went under and didn't come up again.

Ms. Agnes felt she should do something or say something, but she just licked at her gums and lips and squatted, unmoving, on the rocky ledge; she felt all dreamy, as if this was a pageant in some dream she'd had when a child and safe in her parents four-story mansion flat in the – very exclusive, mind you – Everest Towers in Elysium City.

Mr. Swann was one of the ones caterwauling and hammering at the Great Steel Door, but he came back away from the door, shaking his head and wading waist-deep his ribcage showing like an anatomical drawing – he was stark naked now, Ms. Agnes saw, the water had ripped away whatever he was wearing and he came toward Ms. Agnes and he tried to climb up onto the ledge and as if acting in a dream, she reached one skinny arm down to help him up – his feverish blue bloodshot eyes staring into hers – but he slipped on something and his hand slipped out of her hand which she noticed was thick and slick with muddy clay and he was gone and she didn't see where he had gone, the steam rising over the water now so thick, a regular fog, and the water getting deeper, and the emergency lights only dimly shining through the mist.

"I sometimes think …" Sally Ho said, but she didn't finish her phrase; just closed her eyes and stayed in the lotus position, "I sometimes think …"

Ms. Agnes crouched on her haunches, and watched the people in the water, ghosts moving in a steamy blue-gray dream, mostly up to their waists now, in some places up to their shoulders, and the water seemed to be swirling and moving faster, and they all looked paler and paler, and smaller and smaller.

She ran her fingers through her hair and came out with a lump of hair – chalk-white now – and she thought, I'm aging fast, speed of light, galloping Agnes, no tortoise I. In a few minutes, I'll be a toothless bald ivory-domed crone, an old witch, a misshapen hag, if things continue on as they are, why Gloria and Jake won't recognize me, and then it occurred to her that perhaps she had caught the ghoul disease and was going mad. "But I don't feel mad," she said out loud, noticing how slurred her voice was, how heavy her tongue felt, "I don't think I'm going mad."

But then she thought that of course if you were going mad, you'd assume everybody else was mad but that you were sane.

Where is Jake? Where is Gloria? Those two are really mischievous rascals, ungodly little scamps; they are wonderful: they are life, and if there is a God or if Jesus comes again, he will gather them onto him.

They thought she didn't know they wandered off on their explorations, but she knew, oh, yes, she knew, she cackled, and, yes, she thought, "I am cackling, yes, I am cackling," the transformation into old witch must be almost complete, a magical morph. "I don't want them to see me like this; I don't want Jake and Gloria to see me like this."

She glanced toward the far end of the cave; she could just catch a glimpse of it. Downriver had backup and most of the far end of the cave, about 150 meters away maybe, was flooded almost to the roof, and the flood was rising fast; where the whirlpool of the dead had become a geyser; every few minutes, it suddenly appeared; it exploded; water shot up, hitting the ceiling.

"The end is nigh," Ms. Agnes thought. She struggled to her feet. "The end is nigh!" she shouted, just as the mad Preacher would have done, "The end is nigh!"

Nobody bothered to look at her, though Sally Ho opened her eyes for just a second, blinked, and closed them again.

Ms. Agnes thought: Now, why did I do that? Why did I shout out like a madwoman?

She had an image of herself, bare feet, naked shanks, mostly naked hipbones, clutching a rag of a dress, one shriveled breast exposed, a scraggy scrawny almost hairless creature, pubic hair gone long ago for some reason, mostly toothless, an old woman, with pointed chin and wild cloudy eyes, prophesying doom …

Yet the doom was clear, prophecy, or not.

Soon the Main Door would be underwater.

Still standing Ms. Agnes glanced up at cracks opening in the roof, water, more and more of it, was pouring in through fissures in the rock: the whole place was going to collapse, and soon; they needed to get out; they needed to get out into the main tunnel system – which she vaguely knew must be there – she had been blindfolded, hooded, drugged, and shackled when they brought her here so she had only a vague idea, gleaned over the years, of where they were – and they had to get to the Main Shaft and somehow get to the surface, or at least to a higher level of the mine: now, that's a plan, but there's no way to put it into effect!

We are all going to drown. Ms. Agnes did not want to pronounce the phrase, but she was certainly thinking it. Part of her wanted it to happen; part of her wanted this hopeless twilight existence to end.

But then she again thought of Jake and of Gloria.

Jake and Gloria had disappeared, she remembered now, she had forgotten the fact for a while, lost in her own convoluted self-centered dreadful old woman thoughts. "Perhaps I am going mad," she muttered, "Yes, I am going mad; otherwise, how could I forget the children!"

Gloria? When had she last seen Gloria?

Had it been hours, minutes, days?

She had an image: Gloria, very muddy and very serious, saying something … What had she said? Let me see, I had said, "Gloria, where are you going?" And, what had Gloria said, Oh, yes, Gloria had turned said, very brightly, as if it were self-evident, "I'm going to see the lady who can see the future?"

"What?"

"I'm going to see Cassandra."

Ms. Agnes had wanted to ask something – ask who this Cassandra was and how Gloria could know about Cassandra, and where this Cassandra was to be found – but she was so tired, and she rather imagined it was just some imaginary playmate Gloria was speaking about – the girl had, strangely for someone so deprived of stimulation, a vivid imagination, so she had just said, "That's right, Gloria, that's a good girl, go and play," and she patted Gloria on the head.

Then Gloria was gone.

Oh, how could I have been so stupid!

I am too old.

The others were too old, too; nobody had the strength.

Most of the people who could still move had crowded up against the giant steel door, but now they were being swept away, the water gurgled higher and higher around them. They were screaming, "Help! Help! Help!" Weakly they hammered against the door. It was gigantic, maybe ten feet tall.

Nobody had answered.

The guards must have disappeared – if there were any guards. No one from the outside ever entered the cavern, not these last years anyway; they just thrust the food pouches through an opening, a steel trap opening, and that was it – no glimpse, no voice, no presence; they have abolished us from the world, Ms. Agnes thought.

We no longer exist.

We might as well be dead.

The water was rising faster, swirling, and smoky. The emergency lights flickered off and they were plunged into absolute darkness.

Oh, my God!

Ms. Agnes didn't move. She would die in darkness. It was so humid the air wrapped itself around her like a slimy blanked. It was not unpleasant; it was like a mud bath in a spa …

Then slowly, the twinkling lichen in the walls became visible – like galaxies of stars – and the false starlight reflected on the rising waters and it reminded Ms. Agnes of her honeymoon many years ago – I was twenty, I was, twenty years old! She and her husband went to a deserted beach – ruined by an industrial spill – but where the sky was beautiful and the ocean rolled in under the moon, under the stars, and they sat on the crest of one of the dunes of rubbish and drank warm fizzy beer and stared at the silken black sky papered with stars. Ms. Agnes's hand went to her throat; it had been so long ago. *Was that me?*

One or two emergency lights flickered back on.

It was like a deep twilight, silver-gray, with the wall stars still visible, twinkling through the steamy dusk.

Now the water was halfway up the main door.

The crowd – maybe fifteen or twenty survivors – had surged back, wading through the rushing water; they clambered up onto higher ground, ledges, and outcroppings, mostly along the walls of the cave. They crouched there, some naked, most with just rags around their waists, pale ghosts, rib-cages showing, large-eyed fleshless faces looking like little children, or skulls clothed in a paper-thin patina of flesh.

How far we have fallen, thought Ms. Agnes. She lowered herself painfully down onto her haunches, and she crouched there waiting for death, her arms wrapped around her shins, her knees just under her chin, a pose which made her think she must look like a monkey, a scruffy old female chimpanzee whose fur is patchy and matted and covered in filth.

The water kept rising.

It was warm water – steam rising off it and the air more and more smelled of sulfur.

Hell, we are in Hell, Ms. Agnes thought.

There was a shout.

The Great Steel Door was opening.

Water gushed out – a flood …

The door slid aside, very slowly, for it was massive. The water level went down. People rushed, wading, stumbling, splashing, crawling, and half-swimming, legs and arms flailing, through the water.

Some were being swept away, swirling with the water, tumbling, disappearing through the Great Door, arms and legs flailing, reappearing, then gone – through the gaping maw of the opening door.

Ms. Agnes watched; she felt hopeless. Even if they did escape, what was the purpose? They would merely be imprisoned again, perhaps tortured, maybe have their minds and personalities erased or reprogrammed, or maybe they'd merely be murdered. Yes, they would surely be murdered; that would be logical, it would be easier for the guards to murder the prisoners than to try to save them or clean them up. We are not presentable, and we are living proof of the regime's crimes!

So, she didn't move; she picked at a scab of clay on her knee, it had dried in the short time she had been crouching there. Skin and bones, she thought; she could see the kneecap, the articulations. She molded the small lump of clay into a tiny ball. She squinted at it; she frowned. Not drowning would be an anticlimax.

She looked up. What was that new kerfuffle near the Great Steel Door? People were shouting and screaming. She shook her head; I'm becoming selfish. Slowly, stiffly, Ms. Agnes stood up – where was Jake? Where was Gloria?

"Oh, my God," Sally Ho said, her eyes wide open, and standing up now, on the ledge, next to Ms. Agnes.

"Help!" screamed old Mr. Doyle.

"Jesus Christ!"

Their voices were pigmy voices, squeaky tiny little voices, lost in the roar of the water flooding out of the Great Steel Door, and, now, more water was pouring down from above.

People screamed and stumbled backward, trying to get away from the door. They were all going to die; they knew they were all going to die.

They were sloshing and flailing, and some were falling down into the water, and they were being swept around in little twirling maelstrom vortexes. It looked ridiculous somehow.

What in heaven's name is happening now? Ms. Agnes thought she should cry out to calm them down, make a speech, raise her arms, do something …

Then she saw what all the fuss was about.

"Oh, no," she thought, "All the lords and saints preserve us," for some reason reverting to religious speech she never used or even thought. She'd never been Catholic or anything like Catholic, not in her whole life.

"I think we are going to die," said Sally Ho, "The demons have come for us; they will take our souls down to the depths."

"Yes, we are going to die," Ms. Agnes thought, this is the end, not as pretty, perhaps, as drowning. She straightened up, and she stood up. Well, now, I shall face my death. However it may come.

Yes, the Gates of Hell have opened.

The demons are loose!

Behind the door – as it opened – stood two reptiles – two hybrids in the steamy mist –a golden female and a turquoise female.

Oh, my God, thought Ms. Agnes, they are going to attack us; they have come to feed on us, this is not salvation; this is execution.

"They've let the hybrids loose on us!" the preacher screamed, "The hybrids! The demons from hell have been sent to devour us!"

"Oh, Jesus, Oh, Lord Jesus, Please Save us!"

"Run! Run! Run!" the screams echoed, "Hybrids! Hybrids!"

The panic was contagious. Those who could sloshed through the muddy water, scrambling, crawling against the swirling currents. People surged away from the door; people scrambled, clawing at the air, clawing at the water, desperate to escape, crawling over each other, stumbling, splashing through the sinking water.

Ms. Agnes frowned. We are rabble, that's all, we are rabble, we deserve to die; we have no dignity, no dignity whatsoever. That Centurion intelligence officer who interrogated me was right: they have taken everything away; we are no longer ourselves – we are nothing.

Then she blinked

There was a woman – a human – with the two hybrids: a blond woman in a tattered uniform of some kind, she was almost naked, but she was holding a weapon; she was not a prisoner, or so it seemed.

And then she saw Jake. Was it Jake? Could it be Jake?

The turquoise hybrid was talking to Jake. And Jake was talking back. Then the hybrid and Jake came wading and sloshing into the cave, pushing forward in the wild chaos of steaming foam and waves.

I'm hallucinating, Ms. Agnes thought, this is a nightmare. The Jake illusion was waving at her, and as the water – draining out of the cave – got shallower he came running, the hybrid racing behind him.

In her fear and hope, and rising excitement, Ms. Agnes fell, stood up, fell again.

"That's Jake," said Sally Ho, who took hold of Ms. Agnes' arm to lift her up and steady her, "That's Jake – with the hybrid."

"Oh, Jake," Ms. Agnes said. It was so soft she was sure he couldn't hear her, but he would see the look in her eyes, and the movement of her lips.

"Ms. Agnes," Jake cried out, "Sally!" He waved.

"Jake!" Ms. Agnes cried out, her heart leaping with joy, "Jake!"

But where was Gloria?

In the chaos, it took quite a while to sort out everybody, to pick up those who had fallen, to gather those who were lost, and just as the job had been almost completed, and the sheepish, debilitated, weak crew of humans had been lined up in the tunnel outside of the cave, and ready to go, just at that moment, the roof of the cavern that had been the world for the prisoners for more than 15 years collapsed with a great explosion of stone and water, and thundering downpour, and V and Jake and Eve and Valerie had to scramble to lead the people they had saved up the tunnel to higher ground.

Ms. Agnes had regained some of her equilibrium and some of her old spirit, and she was a help, as was Sally Ho, who was remarkably strong for somebody who had been a prisoner for fourteen years.

Jake asked, "But where is Gloria?"

The turquoise hybrid was standing next to him. "Who is Gloria?"

Jake told her.

"Let's go find her, then, Jake!" The golden eyes flashed.

Ms. Agnes said, "She said something about seeing some woman she called Cassandra."

"Oh, boy!" Jake rolled his eyes.

CHAPTER 19 – CASSANDRA

Gloria sat cross-legged on the ground, thinking this was more than spooky, certainly, but extremely exciting, you might even say it was fascinating, and chock full of fresh information and extra-special edification. Cassandra, crouched only a meter away on a low platform of rock, was having visions.

Gloria had never seen anything like Cassandra, and she had never heard anybody spouting genuine prophetic visions. The voice was deep, cloudy and slurred, but Gloria understood it, almost all of it. It was like it was coming from somewhere deep in a cave full of mud, from the depths of the planet earth itself, and maybe from the stars above which people said shone in the thing they called the sky. It was creepy and thrilling.

"I see the end of days and the death of all things, Gloria. I see wind waving over continents of sand and over oceans barren and bereft of fish and life, and I see a dead sun white as a haddock's eye, and nothing is left of humanity and its grandeur, no voice, no song, no melody, it is all gone, evaporated into the white heat of a dead planet. All the people are gone, quite gone. There is no memory they ever were."

"Speaking of going, Ms. Cassandra, we had better go too," Gloria wiped her nose and then wiggled it. Time was galloping along; the floods were rising, and the fires were burning; she could feel it; she had to save Ms. Agnes and Jake and all the others. And she had to save the Cassandra Leper Lady too. The truth might help, and Cassandra might know the truth, but it was really hard right now to figure out what all this prophetic stuff and nonsense meant, however interesting it might be, and how it could save everybody in the tragic and dire circumstances in which they all found themselves, each and everyone, but Gloria was excessively polite and so she persisted in listening – in truth, she was fascinated too; and, then, there was another thing: Jake had hinted that the Cassandra lady knew of secret passageways, roads and pathways that might just lead up to the light of day or to the stars and the moon – oh, moon, oh, moon! So they could find all those things that lived in the moon-filled night. Cassandra, the Leper Lady, was really interesting; and she did say she might, just might, have an idea there might be a way out of the cave and even out of the mine; but now she had entered into what she called a "prophetic and ecstatic trance," which to Gloria was fascinating indeed; but did also seem to be a bit of what Ms. Agnes called a rigmarole.

Cassandra's one eye was all cloudy and was turned inward and not looking at Gloria at all. The other eye was just a deep black cratered hole with red web-like, star-like lines running out across her cheek and forehead. Gloria couldn't see anything in the heart of that dark eye. It was pretty spooky to look at and made a weird little shiver race up and down Gloria's spine.

Cassandra's one eye was now turned upwards, glimpsing the ecstatic prophetic visions, and it was cloudy and blank but seemed to have worms or something swimming in it. Gloria squinted to see if the worms had faces but she couldn't make out any faces; she wondered if worms had personalities and talked gibberish or sense – probably gibberish.

"I see wars without end and all the dead and the plagues spreading and the end of the human race, it is imminent, Gloria," and now the one eye turned down, like it was on a swivel stick, and stared in its smoky whiteness straight at Gloria."

"Imminent …" said Gloria, thinking that it was a fine, solid word, like a wall of black stone, "*Imminent …*"

"I had a daughter," the black tongue came out of the mouth and licked the sunken toothless chalk-white gums and lips, "She was even younger than you when I left. I wonder if they let her live. Do you think they would let her live, Gloria? Would you, if you were a cruel taskmaster and spy, if you were working for the President, the Leader of Cosmos, would you let an innocent little girl live? No, there is no pity, no pity whatsoever. They know not what they do, my dear child, my dear Gloria, they know not what they do. We will all die, in the end, my child, we will all die."

"I've seen death," said Gloria, "the dead they go naked downriver, twirling round and round and their toes are sometimes the last thing you see, they go round and round, and then they go under, plop, and they are gone. If you're lucky, you get some clothes," Gloria fingered the frayed collar of her shirt.

"I was getting ready for an important meeting, checking my makeup, in the mirror –"

"You had a mirror?" Gloria had heard of mirrors, but she had never seen one; the closest she got was kneeling over a puddle when the water was really still, but all she saw, usually, was a muddy oval shadow: *That is me …*

"This was in Elysium City, and I was a lawyer, a real hotshot, and quite, well, considered quite beautiful really, blonde, like you, and with a trim figure, perfect Cosmos complexion, and I noticed in the mirror this small white spot on the side of my nose and then another on the side of my mouth, right at the corner …"

"Spooky," said Gloria, the unknown expression *hotshot*, echoing in her mind.

"Yes, spooky," said the Cassandra lady, looking at Gloria with that one smoky eye where the faceless worms swam, "It was spooky, Gloria, it was scary too."

"Scary and spooky," Gloria sniffed. She felt some snot in her nose; should she blow it out or remove it with her finger or leave it be? She decided, for the moment, to leave it be.

"Yes," said the chalk-white lips turned up in a curl – the mouth dark and toothless all black inside like that deep cave near the pumping station. Gloria took the upward curl of the lips for a smile.

"Scary and spooky, Gloria. So, I took off my clothes and looked at myself in the full-length mirror."

"Full-length mirror," said Gloria dreamily, trying to imagine what such a thing might look like, "Full-length mirror."

"All down my back were these little white spots, and some of them had joined together, little blotches. It happened so fast."

"That was not good," Gloria shivered; it sounded like one of those scary stories that Ms. Agnes sometimes told her and Jake when they were sitting all alone in one of the little side caves or niches as Ms. Agnes called them. And it sounded like what happened when you became a ghoul and spouted gibberish, but Cassandra did not sound like gibberish and she was definitely not a ghoul; ghouls had teeth – *big teeth* – and claws. Also, lots of times, they had pointed ears.

"I almost screamed, but I didn't want to frighten my husband or my baby, so I put my suit back on and I used the makeup to cover the little white spots – by this time there was another one right above one eyebrow – and I made an appointment with my doctor who said it was an allergy and then there were two men there and the doctor gave me an injection – and when I woke up I was being transported out of the city, then I was a prisoner, and 'disappeared' and here I am!"

"An injection, what's an injection?" Gloria sniffled. "And an allergy – that's a nice word – what's an allergy?"

The Cassandra Leper Lady explained what an allergy was and what an injection was and Gloria said "scary," and then the lady smiled that funny empty upward curved black hole smile again, and then she shuffled a bit closer, sidling sideways, her rags brushing the ground, and she said, "But the injection was not for an allergy."

"No?"

"It was to put me to sleep. When I woke up, it was dark; I was shackled and chained and blindfolded and had a hood over my head – it was hard to breathe – and I was in a vehicle, a truck I think, moving over a bumpy road and then I was here. They did tell me what I would look like, though, and it was happening very fast. I was already a monster. So now here I am what I am, and it is slow, now, the change."

"You're not a monster."

"I am, I am so! I am so!"

"Not," said Gloria, "Not. You are definitely not."

"You are very stubborn, Gloria." The empty mouth turned up in a smile. Like a funny face, Jake once drew in the mud.

"We had better go," Gloria said, but she was wondering how the Leper Lady Cassandra would wiggle through the narrow tunnel. If she couldn't, well, Gloria would go get Jake, and Jake would figure out something and then they would come back and save the Leper Lady.

Suddenly, the Leper Lady let out a muffled scream; then, she scurried up onto the little rock platform. Most of her rags now were gone. She opened her mouth wide.

"Oh, oh," Gloria wondered what was going to happen now.

"Oh, Gloria, Gloria, all the old devils are let loose, all the demons are on the march, but you know, the truth is, Gloria, the truth is these demons are fallen angels, and the fallen angels were the good angels – they lost a battle is all."

Gloria stood up and came over close and climbed up on the stone platform and knelt next to the crouching Leper Lady, "We should go – now!"

The Leper Lady put one of her hands, a crusty fingerless stub, hard like old stone, on Gloria's shoulder, "You are a good girl, Gloria."

Gloria said, "Yes, but ..."

"And you know the victor gets to tell the tale. And the victor was the mean old jealous old angel who wanted to be all alone, a misanthropic bachelor angel who called himself God …"

"God …?" Gloria was afraid the Leper Lady would start to sound off – as Ms. Agnes put it – about Abraham and Moses and Yahweh and God and Lucifer and a lot of other people Gloria had never met though she would sometime like to if she ever got the chance. Lucifer sounded particularly interesting. Some of the stories the Preacher used to tell were fun, though, Gloria had to admit – and some were really spooky and gave her the shivers – which was fun too!

This was probably going to take some time. Gloria gave up the kneeling position, and sat down in front of Cassandra the Leper Lady, lotus-style, as Sally Ho had taught her: it balances the yin and the yang, Sally told her, whatever they were, and the positive and negative forces and is very soothing to the soul and the unruly heart which is so troubled by ungovernable passions.

"That God did away with – well, really, he cast down into the deepest bowels of the earth all the other gods and goddesses – above all the goddesses, he could not abide goddesses, that God, nor, really, could He abide womenfolk of any kind, the female principle was anathema to Him, a total abomination, and all forms of the sacred and numinous presence in the earth itself, the trees and plants and animals, were an abomination to Him, so that trees and fountains and animals and strange rocky peaks and pools and rivers which had been sacred were no longer sacred and lost all their poetry and meaning, for He wanted man and woman to be alone in an alien unfeeling world except for Him, who was to be their only Refuge, and so men and women were cast out from the Garden where they were one with all things, and all things were one with them and of course He arranged it so that they believed it was their fault, not His design that they were to be burdened with a sense of unpardonable guilt and irredeemable sin, that they be obsessed with the filth and imperfection and mortality of their bodies, so that only He could save them, and so He banished all feelings of grace, and charm from the world, and beauty became, for Him, an abomination, for He was a Jealous Deity, and he hated anything that was not Him, though He disguised his hatred and jealousy under the name of love, but then tyrants and sadists and torturers often do that don't they, Gloria, they use the name of love, love as a mask for all their crimes, and thus something that is beautiful is tainted, forever tainted at the source. It's called re-branding, or was, once …"

"Ms. Cassandra ..." Gloria said. Time was running out, desperation was rising; but Ms. Agnes had instructed her to be polite in all circumstances and to "hear people out" even if they went on forever and ever, and, as Ms. Agnes put it, were "long-winded and ran off at the mouth." Gloria wondered how long this rigmarole was going to continue. She had a bad feeling that everything was going to cave in and that the end of the world as she knew it was ... *imminent* ...

A crack opened in the far wall of the Leper Lady's cave, and a small rivulet of water spurted out and dribbling down, bubble, bubble, bubble ...

"Ms. Cassandra, I think that we should ..."

Ms. Cassandra held up a rough stumpy paw. "Such was His fear – God's fear – of the female principle – such was His fear of us, Gloria, of us – of us, mothers, daughters, sisters, lovers – that He even had to resort to immaculate conception when he wanted to send somebody into the world, His son, who was not His son, but all that was mythology invented by bitter misogynous lascivious men, reformed libertines, to cover up the fact that humans themselves with all their imperfections and all their sinning and rollicking, cursing and murderous desires, and cruelty and kindness, and love and sex, and hanky-panky, helter-skelter, and urine and shit, and old age and decay, that with all that, humans are divine, their consciousness is divine, their consciousness is the source of all that is felt, known, talked of, adored, hated ..."

"Ms. Cassandra, I think ... I think maybe we should consider ... I mean, Ms. Cassandra, if you don't mind ..." Gloria could fee tremors passing through the earth; the cascade at the far side of the cave was getting bigger; pebbles were sliding off a ledge. What if the cave filled with water, what if the walls and roof fell in?

"Oh, Gloria, can you not feel it?"

"What?"

"Can you not feel that salvation is at hand, that the angels, the old angels, who were cast out, have returned – most are in prison right now, most have had mind-manacles thrust upon them, most are beneath the surface of the earth, thrust down into Hell, and we shall now, it seems, bury them forever, these fallen angels, deep, deep, deep in darkness, entombed in darkness, they shall lie there, helpless, voiceless, and we shall kill these immortal souls, and extinguish their light, and then there shall be no salvation for humanity. And so we, the evil ones, have driven the humans mad and turned them into clownish ghoulish parodies of themselves – mindless and half-mindless

beasts, ghouls, reduced to cannibalism, turning upon themselves, destroying their works, and groveling and growling and snarling, and drooling their
naked thick foamy idiocy onto the sand, under the moon, oh, yes, the moon
and the …"

"Ms. Cassandra," Gloria stood up. This was going nowhere. If they were
going to be saved, they had to save themselves; it sounded more and more
like gibberish – like ghoul-talk, very clever and complicated ghoul-talk, but
ghoul-talk just the same. She had to do something. "Ms. Cassandra, we
should try to leave this place. Do you know a way out?"

"A way out …What a strange question, Gloria, of course, I know a way out.
But where was I …?

"Moon, the moon, under the moon," said Gloria, in spite of herself. "Moon"
was one of her favorite words; it was totally luscious, round like an "O," soft
like an opened mouth, ripe like a … She couldn't resist. She had composed
what she called poems about the 'moon' – and she had never seen the moon;
she recited one for Jake, "Moon, oh, Moon, it is too soon, Oh, Moon, what a
boon, Oh Moon …"

"Ah, yes, Gloria. Thank you! Moon! Under the cool light of the moon, such
things happen as surpass the most imaginative and crazed mind! Ah, what a
work is man, and how he is cast down! The light of reason is extinguished!"
Suddenly Ms. Cassandra's voice became deeper, hollow, a man's voice: it thundered: "Oh, how powerful I am – I the true angel, the angel of darkness, the
ambassador of the only one and true God. And you know what, dearest, that
one and true God is to be found nowhere. He is a figment of fear and of desire,
an echo of childhood nightmares. And so, now, we, the true gods, unleash
upon the humans a new plague, one that will travel on wings, one that will
sweep across the continent. My True Believers, they are my weapons! True
belief makes them forget they are human; on the wings of hate, they sweep
forward, transformed into what their hearts have become. They will cleanse
the earth of this vermin, the humans."

Gloria was startled by the change in Ms. Cassandra's voice – it was as if
somebody else, a not very nice somebody else, was inside her and using her
to speak, and Gloria knew what "vermin" meant. She was a bit miffed, as Ms.
Agnes would have said: "But, Ms. Cassandra, we are human – aren't we?"

"See, my dear Gloria, how sweet it is for the True Believers – oblivion and
death, they have lost their freedom, they no longer think, they no longer
choose, they kill merely, they merely kill. And so it shall be, and devastation

everlasting, and then the world can return to the jungle and quiet desert and then we can possess it fully and merely."

Suddenly the Leper Lady stopped, looked frightened, and shouted in her bubbly muddy voice, "Gloria, run! Hide! I am possessed. I am dangerous!"

"No," said Gloria; she would not run from anything.

"No?"

"No."

"But the Evil Spirit is within me! I cannot help it. I am dangerous, I am death. I am hatred. I am revenge."

A black cloud, a steamy mist came out of the Leper Lady's mouth; it smelled of sulfur – it coiled, and uncoiled.

Gloria's eyes opened wide, but she was not going to leave Cassandra to be possessed by whatever it was that possessed her. In her mind, she heard Jake say, "You are very stubborn, Gloria." She wiggled her nose and set her teeth, and she didn't budge, she just sat back down, cross-legged, on the ground, in the lotus position, as the black misty cloud came very close, she stared at it, this black cloud was just another form of nonsense and rigmarole, as Ms. Agnes would have said. Gloria wiggled her nose again. "Don't you be afraid, Ms. Cassandra, I'm not afraid!"

"I am an ambassador from a distant place, we have watched over these evil, despicable creatures, the humans, and now we have lost patience. They have ransacked and destroyed everything, poisoning the water, the air, the soil, exterminating a universe of creatures, ransacking life and even changing the very grammar of life itself, the basis of life, and so we have a world of mutation and mutants, a world of unruly and unsustainable madness."

The black cloud hovered, it took many forms, at one point it seemed to look like Ms. Agnes, then it looked like a mud drawing of Jake, then it looked like one of those dragons Gloria had seen in an old picture book – before the picture book fell apart and the paper disintegrated.

Gloria blinked at all this. It was a lot of fuss and bother, of course, but it was exquisitely interesting; she might even say exceedingly instructive.

The cloud hovered, the misty dragon opened its vast mouth, out came charcoal black flames, its eyes flared madly; then, slowly, it broke apart, it dissipated, and then it was gone.

Gloria wiggled her nose. Ms. Agnes had told her about a "stiff upper lip," and Gloria felt she had passed the test; she had sat firm, not budging an inch, while a misty ghostly old dragon huffed and puffed …

Now Ms. Cassandra's mouth opened wide and it screamed. "Ah, let us raise a cup, yes, raise a cup, raise a cup to the end of this human world, and its evil. But there is one angel who did not fall, she was born of woman, she was begat by a celestial colonial warrior, her father from a distant world, and she has lived for centuries, feeding on humans and protecting humans, disguised as a human, sometimes as a woman, which is her true nature, for she is a female, an angel or a goddess, sometimes as a man or boy, for she has to adapt to human society and don whatever mask will server her turn, and she is immortal too, as immortal as living flesh can be, and she fights and struggles against me, and, almost, sometimes, we have been lovers, for she is beautiful and a trickster too, and always interesting, and if we could agree, then she and I would rule over this planet together, we would rule over it in perfect tyranny, reducing the humans to harmless beasts of the field, letting them survive, perhaps, just a few of them, harmless and scattered, mute and dumb, but she will not betray her human friends nor her human side, for she was born of woman, and she is the daughter of what for humans would be a god if he cared to reveal himself as such, but her father is a modest sort, a warrior scientist and politician, unassuming and with a sense of humor and I hate him, I hate him with a fury that he should have given life to such a beautiful and talented creature and that he should have let her live, as he has, over the centuries, and he still watches over her from afar. But our empire is stronger. And, with her, he shall be cast down, and all the brilliance of his empire will fade from existence into pure nothingness, and not even a memory will remain!"

"Ms. Cassandra, we should go." Gloria thought this little chat had perhaps gone on too long.

The Leper Lady hiccupped.

"God Bless," Gloria said; it was something she had heard Ms. Agnes and Ms. Chong say, "God Bless." Sometimes they said, "Gesundheit!" which Ms. Chong had explained was "German" – whatever German was – for "health."

The Leper Lady hiccupped again, and from out of her open round, empty mouth bounced two frogs, a toad, and a serpent.

"Holy Moly," Gloria had seen such animals in an old picture book Ms. Agnes used to have but which got all moldy and fell apart. The frogs and the toad bounced off to one side; the snake slithered toward Gloria, raised its narrow triangular head, and then it turned to ash and fell like a sprinkling of dust.

"Holy Moly!"

The Leper Lady hiccupped again and wiped her mouth with the back of one fingerless paw. "I am free of possession, now, Gloria. Your innocence and your scepticism have driven him away."

"Scepticism?"

"Lack of belief. It is a form of innocence – not to believe."

"Oh. Who did I drive away – the dragon, the black cloud, the frogs, the snake?" Gloria licked her lips. *Scepticism* sounded like a nice, sharp word. She'd try to use it often.

"The Boy – you drove away the Boy – who calls himself the Lord – is a semi-supernatural expression of the dark force in the universe," Ms. Cassandra spoke in a breathless non-stop voice, "which is an evil empire working against the empire represented by Marcus and by a creature called V, the Daughter of Marcus. The Boy disguises himself as the Messiah. He has created a vast religious movement – with sermons and miracles and conversions and public confessions. He neutralizes large parts of the World Mind. He intends to use the World Mind to destroy the World of Shoppers – Elysium City and others – and then he will destroy the World Mind, which will thrust the humans back into isolation and darkness and madness, ripe for destruction. The hybrids and V, in particular, are his most dangerous enemies because, without knowing it, they represent the Empire of Light, the possibility of salvation. The Empire of Light exists in a parallel universe in which evolution took a slightly different path; the denizens of the Empire of Light consider themselves the brothers and sisters of humans. They have colonized part of our universe; thus, the Crystal – V's little treasure – was left on earth by her father, Marcus of the Andromeda Empire. It is a defense against colonization by the Drinker of Souls. Thus the Boy – a Drinker of Souls – must first try to destroy the hybrids – or, better, get the humans to destroy them. Hybrids and SINs are immune to the Drinkers of Souls' magic. The war against the hybrids and SINs has been inspired by an ally of the Drinker of Souls. After victory over the hybrids, the Boy will then destroy the Cosmos human government – as incarnated by the President-Leader in Elysium City. In the final confrontation, the Boy will be revealed for what he is – spider-like evil and the devil incarnate – by V. The final revelation and battle must take place in Elysium City or near Elysium City."

"Holy Moly," Gloria whispered. This, she decided, was a great deal to take in, an abundance of facts and information and words, certainly in such a short time, and in circumstances which amounted to an emergency and a catastrophe. "I think …" she began to say.

"Yes, I think we should go now," said the Leper Lady.

"Which way, Jake, which way do we go?" V and Jake were alone, standing in a vaulted corridor that glowed dimly with phosphorescent lichen.

V gazed at Jake. He was a handsome boy, truly beautiful, but he certainly didn't know it, and he probably really had no idea what the word 'beautiful' really meant. His shorts were outsized and he had to hold them up as they drooped around his slender waist and he was pale as chalk from living underground and his eyes were large and dark, almost the eyes of a starving child, and they shone under thick dark eyebrows and his dark hair was tousled and wet and clogged with mud and hung down to his shoulders. His skin shone, wet from the steamy air, and from wading through the flood, and his muscles were smooth. Except for the shorts, which kept sagging and falling down, he was naked.

"So, Jake ... which way do we go to find your friend Gloria?"

"If she went to see Cassandra, then we have to go through that tunnel up there," Jake pointed to a narrow crack in the wall.

"You go first, Jake, and I'll follow. We'll find her, and we all get out to the surface." She unhitched her backpack, opened her belt, and put the holster and belt into the backpack, which now dangled from her claw.

"You mean, we'll get up into the world."

"Yes, Jake, we'll get up into the world."

"Good!" Jake led the way, shimming into the narrow crack, and then he climbed up the chimney-like crevice, using toe holds and handholds. He wondered if V would be able to follow, after all, she might be a hybrid, but she was an adult, and she was taller than he was and she had hips and breasts and shoulders ... and she had the backpack she was pulling behind her or pushing in front of her.

"I can do it," she said, as if she had read his thoughts; her voice echoed, strangely hollow, in the narrow corkscrew crevice that spiraled upward.

Jake looked down and saw her, close behind him, her golden eyes and turquoise scales shimmering in the dimly lit chimney.

They came to the top and wiggled on their bellies along a horizontal crawl-space-like tunnel, which was half-filled with muddy, liquid clay.

"This way," Jake said.

"Yes, boss."

They slipped sideways through a narrow sliver of an opening where Jake had to take off his shorts, and he looked back and saw the grin of the hybrid glowing in the dark, and he said, "Well, you don't have any clothes either."

"No, I don't. So, now we are equal."

They slithered along through another low cave.

Then they came to a long passage, where you could almost walk upright. All the time, there were trembling and groans from the rocks and occasional little mudslides and cascades of pebbles and gushes of water.

"It's all falling apart," said Jake.

"Yes," said V.

"I hope they are okay," said Jake, climbing up a particularly difficult passage, "I mean, Ms. Agnes and the others."

"They will be okay," said V, thinking, that she certainly hoped the prisoners and Ms. Agnes and all the others would be okay; Eve, the Golden Hybrid, also known as Eve Schmidt, and Valerie Joffre would be excellent guides; and V had explained the path by which she had come, the path she hoped they could use to return back and get to Norton and Sabrina and all the others; but there were dangers on every side.

She and Jake had left the humans with Eve and Valerie. Many of the humans were half-crazy, and they were all weak and suffering from starvation and dehydration. After listening to V's explanation, Eve and Valerie said, yes, now they knew how to get up to the higher level where they would find the guards and the other hybrids whom V had left behind when she went in search of the humans.

"Don't worry, V, don't worry, Jake, we can do it," said Eve.

"Yes, we can," Valerie Joffre said, with the determined certainty of a Cosmos First Class. It was reassuring somehow, that determined Cosmos grit and gumption. V sometimes marveled at how the President-Leader had instilled a last-ditch sense of discipline and pride in humans, at least in the Elite Cosmos.

"This is the last bit," Jake said. He slid out of his shorts again so he could twist and slide and slither through the last crack-like stretch. He handed his shorts back to V, so he could have both hands free.

It was sort of funny, Jake thought, being with a hybrid, since they were monsters and ate people and drank them dry.

"I'm going in now," he said.

V took his shorts and watched Jake squeeze sideways through the crack, and she thought again how he was really a handsome young boy – not yet changing into a man, not quite, almost, but not quite – and that he was a fine example of humanity, and that it was a wonder he had survived all those years, almost his whole life, more than a mile underground in a cave and without ever seeing the light of day or smelling the fresh air blowing across a landscape. If the President-Leader only knew what wonderful human material was being wasted and destroyed! But, of course, he did know … or maybe, just possibly, he didn't know.

Jake disappeared. Clutching his shorts. V followed him. This involved shimmying on her belly up a last narrow, almost vertical, greasy, corkscrew twisting tunnel – maybe fifteen meters.

It was like swimming in mud, V thought, pulling her backpack and Jake's shorts behind her.

Suddenly, even more covered in muck than before, she popped out into a narrow, vertical, slit-like cave where they could both stand up, covered in mud. V shook herself, sending out a spray of mud drops.

Jake looked at her and grinned.

"What are you looking at?" she grinned.

"I'm looking at you."

"Of course," V looked down at her mud-covered self, looked back up, blinked, and grinned.

"Here it is, said Jake, "we're almost there."

He slid sideways through a vertical slit.

V followed him, swiveling sideways, slipping, sliding, pushing, and slithering snake-like. It was a tight fit. Finally, she came out the other side, into a bigger part of the vertical slit, blinking the mud away from her eyes.

Jake was waiting for her.

She handed him his shorts and said, "So, now we see … what we shall see."

"Yes, now we see …" His eyes were very bright in his muddy face.

And they both slid out of the last bit of the cave, and they climbed up the rock, and peeked over, just as Jake pulled on his shorts, and V cleared the mud from her eyes …

And …

And the Leper Lady turned to look at them; she was sitting on a small low platform of rock and right in front of her was Gloria, sitting in more or less the lotus position. Gloria turned and stood up. "Jake!"

The Leper Lady looked toward them with her one eye; it was strange the way it swiveled, V thought, as if it were on a stalk, like an insect's eye; so that is what it is like, V thought, that is what those time-release bio-weapons can do. She realized, in a flash of hybrid insight, what Cassandra had been – a stylish, successful, proud Elysium City Cosmos First Class and lawyer, mother of a baby girl, and a young boy, and married to a successful structural engineer – and a bit idealistic, and very naïve, arrogant in a nice way in her feeling of invulnerability as a Cosmos First Class, helping dissidents, helping relatives and friends trace those who had been "disappeared" and now, of course, she was one of the "disappeared," her beauty and outward humanity – but not her inner humanity – morphed away into toad-like monstrosity; it was of course not really leprosy, but a new disease entirely, created specifically as a weapon of intimidation and destruction.

"An angel has come, another angel," the Leper Lady, stirred, rising up on her legs to a crouching position; she shuffled forward.

"Jake, you found a hybrid!" Gloria ran toward him, and she pressed herself against him while with her eyes wide like saucers, she stared at V.

"The hybrid found me," said Jake. He couldn't help himself; tears were forming in his eyes; he was so happy to find Gloria alive, and he was stroking the muddy stubble of Gloria's head, the little glints of gold still shining.

"Do you know another way out of here?" V said, turning toward Cassandra, and asking the question though she had already from the Leper Lady's mind – her prophetic madness made her mind into an open book a drafty space through which currents and breezes and ideas and thoughts came and went in total liquid freedom and chaotic openness and fertile, seminal, creative, almost sexual promiscuity, the Leper Lady's mind was porous, attentive, capturing voices, people, sensations, visions …

"What a silly question! Of course, I know a way out of here." The muddy, bubbly voice sounded amused – laughter rising up from the lower depths.

"Let's go then."

"I must take my things, my hybrid friend." Cassandra scurried to her side niche to gather her photographs and mementos, "I'll be back in a … in a … jiffy."

"Jiffy," whispered Gloria, "*Jiffy* …"

"Good, let us go," said V, seeing from reading the Leper Lady's mind that Cassandra did know a way out of this particular cave and she had some ideas – V saw this as visions and schematics – of some possible ways of getting out of the mine itself, but they were only vague and confused hints and intimations, and V thought, Yes, we will certainly need the Cosmos geologist Valerie

Joffre: she has all the maps, old and new, in her head, and she knows the lay of the land down here, under the surface, more than anyone; so perhaps, if we put everything, all the elements, together, we can …

"You are a very fine hybrid," Gloria said, turning to V and patting her on the arm, and letting her fingers linger so she could feel the scales, "And I see you can even talk!"

"Thank you, Gloria, and you are a very fine human being."

"Are you a friendly hybrid?"

"She's friendly," said Jake, "but she does eat people."

Gloria's eyes opened wide. "I really cannot believe my ears, Jake."

"Bad people," V said, "Usually they are bad people, the ones I eat, I mean."

"I saw her eat one," said Jake, "He was big and really bad, and he was a murderer, and she ate him up like that!" Jake tried to snap his fingers, but they were too muddy.

Gloria considered this, picturing it, "Jake, I do wish I'd been there! It would have been most instructive to see her eat him."

"Instructive?" V raised a reptilian eyebrow.

"Experience is invaluable," said Gloria, sniffling, blowing her nose on her wrist and, very politely, wiping the result off onto her thigh. "The capacity for learning and for self-improvement is what makes us human."

"It certainly does." V laid her claw on the little girl's shoulder.

Gloria looked up, admiration and perhaps even something like burgeoning love in her eyes, "This is most interesting," she said, "I hope we will have many conversations like this. You see, I have so much to learn."

Cassandra came out of her niche. She was ready. They followed her to another niche where, behind a false wall – a wall of stone that made it look like the niche was a dead end – there was a narrow crevice and if you stood sideways on tiptoes, you could just slide through. Jake's shorts gave him trouble and a button on Gloria's shirt got stuck and the hybrid helped her get it free, but they made it through the slit, and just as they did, there was a great roar. Glancing back, V saw the roof of Cassandra's cave was collapsing, water pouring through widening cracks, and then slabs of the roof thundering down.

In a few minutes, it would all be flooded.

"Run," V shouted, "Run!"

And so, with a tidal wave chasing them, they galloped and loped down one corridor, then raced up a steep ramp, then ran along another corridor, then climbed up a corkscrew steel staircase with loops of rusty chains clanging by its sides, and scurried along a large vaulted tunnel where the walls were covered with strange, glowing bluish graffiti that looked like something written, in generous splashes, in the Korean alphabet, with a few giant, glowing Chinese characters here and there.

Water was bubbling up everywhere.

"I'm not sure about this," V put up her claw, warning them to stop.

In front of them, water poured out of cracks in the stone face.

The whole tunnel exploded.

Wooden and steel beams burst from the walls.

Slabs of stone shot across the tunnel, bouncing, shattering off the opposite wall.

V grabbed Gloria, whipped her up onto her shoulders, and taking Jake's hand, she said, "Come on, Come on! Let's go! Cassandra – run!"

As the tunnel imploded behind them, they vaulted up a side ramp. Cassandra, V noticed, was scuttling here and there like a sprinting crab. Water came rushing up in a true tidal wave, a fifteen-foot-high wall of water, stone, steel, wood, and mud, slamming against everything, smashing everything.

They came to another narrow vertical service shaft, and V started to climb up the latticework, Jake climbing with her and Gloria clinging to her back. "Cassandra – are you okay?"

"I'm right behind you!"

Cassandra was amazingly agile and fast, twisting and turning and shrinking down into herself and swelling up and expanding, as spaces got bigger or smaller.

They came to the top of the vertical shaft.

The roar of the exploding flood was now a faint, distant, echo, clamorous rumble coming from far below.

V let Gloria slide off her shoulders.

"Thank you, Ms. Hybrid! That was exciting!"

"You are welcome, Gloria."

V glanced around. They were in an old service tunnel that didn't have any emergency lights though an electric cable ran along the roof. The only lighting came from the phosphorescent mushrooms, which grew on the floor and the lichen, which covered virtually every bit of the walls and roof. It was thick as moss and springy underfoot, a lush, glowing carpet.

"Do we know where we are?"

"Yes," said Jake.

"Yes, most definitely," said Gloria.

"Good."

V led the way, with help from Jake who knew many of the pathways, and Gloria, who seemed to have a photographic memory and remembered everything she'd ever seen, and Cassandra, who had a sort of fifth sense for the underground labyrinth that was Camp Terminus.

Cassandra didn't say much, just occasionally whispering, "Go left" or "Go right!" She shuffled and hopped along as if she were some sort of pet or mascot; but she did hum various melodies and pop hits from long ago, and it caused a twinge in V's heart thinking of what the woman had been and what she was now, and a cloud of anger rose in V's heart against the powers that were responsible for such hideous crimes – against the Cosmos Elite, against the President-Leader, against the very shape of Human Civilization and against Creation itself.

And, so, they began the long journey up and down tunnels, skirting this way and that. "Up this way, not this way; maybe if we go down here, let's try that. Yes, okay, along here. Can you squeeze under that beam?"

The water in many places was rising. Elsewhere, ceilings and tunnels had collapsed. In one promising tunnel, they turned a corner only to face a wall of roaring flame, and an overpowering odor of charred timber. Everywhere, they heard rumblings, muffled explosions, crashing sounds.

Much that had been, was no more.

The Leper Lady hobbled and scuttled along, and leaped in small little leaps, and hopped along in short little hops. V sometimes let Gloria ride on her shoulders when the tunnels were high enough. "You are very strong, Ms. Hybrid," said Gloria as V hoisted the little girl up, "Yes, Gloria, I'm pretty strong."

"She lifted that big man she ate right up into the air," said Jake.

"She did?"

"Yes, she did!"

"Heavenly daze, who would have believed it!" Gloria bounced happily along on V's shoulders.

Finally, they got to the meeting place at Rangoon crossroads; where all the others – Valerie Joffre, the Golden Hybrid, Ms. Agnes, Sally Ho, and all the other prisoners, had arrived safe and sound.

Norton was waiting, his hands on his hips, Freddy standing beside him.

"Good work, lass, good work!"

Freddy grinned. "I told you, mate, V can do virtually anything!"

"Why, thank you, Freddy." V favored Freddy with her most flirtatious blink, "This is Jake, and this is Gloria, and our friend here is Cassandra."

"Welcome, then, friends," said Norton, looking at the two children with wonder – how had they survived so long in such horrible conditions – amazing! He stared for a moment at Cassandra. Her clouded, worm-filled eye looked up at him, and she scuttled closer, but, strangely, he felt no reproach coming from her. "Welcome, Cassandra," he said softly.

"We are pleased to be here, Colonel," she favored him with a toothless, confiding smile. "Jake and Gloria and I, we are very pleased to be here."

Jake was suddenly embarrassed, seeing all the people and hybrids – and even one ghoul, who was a hunched up friendly little thing.

They can all see I'm almost naked, he thought. He clutched the mud-stiffened shorts with one hand; the goddamned things were going to fall down if he didn't keep tugging at them. But, as he looked around, he realized that a lot of people, even the guards, even the man they called Norton, were dressed in little more than rags. Their uniforms had been torn and ripped into bits. As for the hybrids and ghouls, they never wore anything except maybe a belt or a sling and backpack for guns and things. The beautiful Cosmos Valerie Joffre – who was almost naked – winked at Jake as if she had read his thought and made a gesture with her hands, which clearly meant "Don't worry, Jake. Just look at me!"

Gloria was amazed. She had never seen such people before. There were big people with uniforms and what Jake said were weapons, and they didn't look like any people Gloria had ever encountered or imagined.

"You're a big person," she said to one of these strange creatures who'd told her his name was "Sammy."

"I'm fat," said Sammy Franks, "It's not the same as big."

"Fat?" Gloria raised an eyebrow.

"Obese," said Sammy, "Overweight, tubby, chubby."

"Hmm," Gloria frowned, lots of words, but still the idea … escaped her.

"It means Sammy eats too much," said one of the hybrids, grinning at Gloria, and it gave Sammy a friendly poke in the ribs.

"She likes to kid me," Sammy said, turning red.

Wonders were unfolding. Gloria whispered the nice round juicy words, "obese," "fat," "tubby," "chubby," but this whole idea – *fat* – was a new concept; it would take a while for Gloria to absorb it. As for "eating too much," well, that was just plain unbelievable! How many food pouches could a person eat? And wouldn't other people or hybrids grab them?

There was even a ghoul, but he seemed friendly; he didn't talk gibberish, he sort of talked like a little kid, like that little boy Little Mike before he got all sick and threw up all his food and shriveled up into a little gray thing and then was dead and unwrapped from his clothes – a ragged sheet – and rolled along on the ground, over and over, and pushed into downriver.

And then there was Ms. Agnes. Ms. Agnes had changed so much in these last times, Gloria thought, but she was not going to say anything, she just put her arms around Ms. Agnes' waist and hugged her and buried her face between Ms. Agnes breasts which hung down now in a funny way they hadn't before.

V looked around at the strange group – it looked like some sort of circus caravan – but everyone had been brought together.

Valerie Joffre and the Golden Hybrid – Eve Schmidt – had done their work well. Somehow they had guided the whole group of humans up to Rangoon crossroads – it was a miracle.

Valerie Joffre had admitted to Eve that she now had an entirely new idea of the value of hybrids. On the way upwards, a couple of the humans had seemed too weak to make the voyage, or too crazy. One woman fell down and started to roll around, screaming weakly and tearing at the rags, which were her clothes.

"What are we going to do about them?" said Valerie, "We can't leave them behind!"

The Golden Hybrid said, "I can pep them up and calm them down."

Valerie thought for a second, and, though she was skeptical about what she had heard of hybrids' powers, she said, "Oh, yes, of course! Try it! Maybe start with her." And she pointed at the weakest of the prisoners, a woman called Anna, was just sitting on the ground, staring into space, having torn off all her remaining clothes.

And it did work! Anna perked up, got up, and joined the others; there was even a sparkle in her eyes, and it seemed her muscle tone and color had improved, though it was difficult to tell in the flickering phosphorescent light.

Valerie stared at the Golden Hybrid. "I thought, Eve, that it was a myth, a legend – that you could cure people." And then, Valerie realized that, of course, that was what V must have done to her – fixed her up after she had been raped and mutilated.

"No, it's real, but it doesn't always work," Eve was helping a skeletal old man over a pile of rubble, "And it does take a lot of energy."

So each time one of the prisoners stumbled or fell down, Eve would bend over them, and from her claws, the purple light radiated out and gave the poor woman, or man, a bit more strength, or a bit more sanity and calm, just enough to keep going.

Sally Ho, who was in the best shape of all the prisoners, helped lead some of the weaker and Ms. Agnes, who was apparently a sort of leader, whispered encouragement and helped keep the others going. And then there was a Mr. Swann who came up out of the water, dripping and muddy, but who seemed strong enough, amazingly, and he helped calm some of the crazier ones. But Eve's powers were absolutely essential.

"After all these years, I wasn't sure it would still work," said Eve.

"I'm sure glad it does!" said Valerie.

"Me too," said Eve.

"This is something we really should study," said Valerie, "I mean, if we get out of here, and if we have time to study anything."

Eve had flashed a most beautiful reptilian smile at Cosmos First Class Valerie Joffre, "We'll get out of here, Valerie Joffre; we will get out of here."

And so they did.

And now they all had to decide on the next stage; they were all still at least a mile underground.

CHAPTER 20 – RANGOON

V and Norton called the meeting to order. V nodded, and Norton cleared his throat, "Do I do this, or do you?"

"You," said V.

Norton nodded. "Okay, ladies and gentlemen, hybrids, humans, and ghouls," he said, glancing at Jimmy Ghoul, "This is the general situation: Shaft-1 is gone, buried in hundreds of meters of mud and rock. Shaft-2 has collapsed; it is buried in a sea of liquid clay, sealed with as much as half a mile of rock and sand, and much of the polluted Ghoul Cavern must be flooded too, with clay and with water, and where the wild ghouls have gone, if they survived, we don't know."

Gloria listened to the man talk, but she was staring at all the hybrids and at the strange people and at the little ghoul who seemed to be some sort of friend to everybody and who did not spout gibberish but talked like a little kid. He sidled up to her, "Jim's the name," he said, reaching out a claw.

"I'm Gloria," said Gloria, taking his claw; she'd never shaken hands with a ghoul before; the claw was cool and gooey.

"You are strange, though," said the ghoul, "what are you, exactly?"

Gloria thought for a moment, "I'm a girl," she said, "And Jake, who is my heartbeat, is a boy."

"He's your heartbeat?"

"He is."

"That's nice," said the ghoul, "You are lucky. I don't have a heartbeat."

"So now, let's hear people's ideas," Norton and V looked around the room.

"There is, I think, a way out," said the Leper Lady.

"Tell us."

Cassandra shuffled to the center of the group. "Jake told me of a cave where there was a strange breeze, and he smelled something like burned grass and flowers."

"Do you remember, Jake?"

"I think I do …"

"The sweet air made you dream, you said."

"You told me too," said Gloria, "about the dream, and we went there, remember?"

Jake cleared his throat. He had never made a speech before. He had one hand firmly clutching the muddy rim of goddamned Clive Something's shorts, stiff and scratchy as Hades they were. "It was up behind the old pumping station. There was a narrow passage; but we, I mean Gloria and I, could walk through it, and then there was a cave, and it was filled with pebbles and a little river, not the poisoned river in the big ghoul cavern, it was another little river in another cavern, and I felt the breeze, it was there that I felt it."

"It was a zephyr, and it came from verdant fields and sunlight in the sky," said Gloria, whispering sideways behind her hand to the little bent over ghoul that had once, so she had heard, been a real person called Jim Rahv.

"Zephyr," said the ghoul, "That sounds nice."

"It is. It's very nice."

"Were there stalactites and stalagmites?" Valerie Joffre was smiling at Jake, her gallant young savior.

"Ah, I don't know what those are."

Valerie explained.

Gloria repeated the sharp musical words – *stalactites* and *stalagmites* – and the meanings – one pointed up, the other pointed down.

"No, there weren't any of those," said Jake; he glanced at Gloria.

"No, there weren't," Gloria looked around. "We certainly would have noticed them if there had been any stalagmites and stalactites, they are such intriguing features." Gloria beamed at them all, a little girl in an oversized shirt, bright blue eyes, and a bright white smile in a muddy face.

Valerie Joffre said, "That sounds like the old Moore rift opening, a cave, that went up sideways, it was explored about fifty or sixty years ago. I was going to try to find it myself. It was on my list of things to look at. If it is still open and if there haven't been cave-ins, it might still go up close to the surface. I wasn't aware that it made it all the way to the surface, and the schematics don't indicate that it did. But if there's a breeze, then … maybe it does go to the surface, certainly near the surface, with some sort of crack or opening."

Norton glanced around. "Well, V, what do you think?"

V nodded. "It sounds like it's our best chance."

"Right, well then …" Norton glanced at young Jake, "Unless there's a protest, it's decided."

Nobody spoke. All nodded their heads. Even the ghoul bounced his head up and down several times. Gloria thought the ghoul was very polite, very interesting. She might just ask him what it was like to be a ghoul, but she would have to consider it. Would it be an impolite or improper question? Ghouls might be very sensitive about being ghouls.

"Let's go, Jake, you and Valerie, lead us there," said V.

Gloria was excited by this new trip, which, the hybrid, V said, would take them to the "world," the world above and out of the underworld in which Gloria had always lived.

The trip itself, she found, was extremely instructive.

They discovered a river where all the fish, and which looked like eels, were blind; they had white bug eyes, and they raised their snouts out of the water.

"Evolution happens very quickly," said Valerie Joffre, glancing at the eels and then at Gloria.

"*Evolution* …?" Gloria was fascinated; a new word; somebody called Evolution was working very quickly; she would like to meet Evolution and ask Evolution a few questions. But what Mr. or Ms. Evolution had to do with blind fish …? Well, she would ask V or Valerie or Ms. Agnes, and they, she was sure, would explain.

They came to a cave that seemed entirely made of diamonds, stones that sparkled and shone even when there was very little light.

They discovered a lair where large bats – real bats – hung upside down, but it turned out they were fossilized bats – *fossilized* – they had died where they hung and somehow the dripping liquid had turned them to stone bats like upside down gargoyles. "Just like gargoyles," said Valerie Joffre.

"What is a gargoyle?"

"Well, Gloria," Valerie took Gloria's hand, "a gargoyle is …"

They came to a ghoul graveyard – or perhaps it was just a ghoul rubbish dump – or perhaps a sacred ghoul site – where human bones were piled up, carefully, in pyramids.

"It must have some sort of ritual meaning," said Valerie Joffre.

"Yes," said one of the hybrids, all glossy black with a red mark on her snout.

Gloria was all ears: *Ritual meaning ...?*

They came out through a rift in the rock to another larger cavern.

"This is a softer rock, and it has been dissolved and washed away. There was an underground river here. And see these *fossils* embedded in the stone." Valerie Joffre kept stopping and kneeling where she found fossils and new metals – these were hints and clues to what lay around them, to where the secret passageway might be.

There were pits of darkness and narrow bridges arching over deep holes.

"This is fascinating," said Eve, the Golden Hybrid.

"Here be wonders, Jake," said Gloria.

"This is an emerald," said Valerie, handing a small stone to Gloria.

"Emerald," said Gloria, turning it over in her hands, "Emerald."

"Come on, folks, the way is clear over here, let's go," Norton and V were up in front, they waved everyone forward.

Gloria kept her eyes wide open. She fully intended, as she said, to drink it all in! Everywhere the walls glowed with phosphorescent lichen and mushrooms. In places, the walls were in horizontal stripes.

"Different layers – strata formed down at different times," said Valerie.

"Strata ..." Gloria blinked.

"Stone formed in different time periods," Valerie said.

"Periods," said Gloria, "Periods ..."

It was a long trek, and it went through ancient mine drifts – tunnels that sometimes led nowhere, except to large caves, some of them now filled with water, some of them dry as dust, sometimes the dust was waist-deep. V stepped into one of these seas of dust, and then swam in the dust and then waded back out, and Valerie Joffre said, "Careful, V, even you could drown in there."

"Yes," said V, "I could," as she accepted Valerie's outstretched hand.

Gloria blinked and reached out for Jake's hand. "They are lovely, V and Valerie, I think, don't you?"

Jake cleared his throat, "Yes, they are," he said, "but, Gloria, you are the loveliest of all."

"Oh, Jake," said Gloria, "You are very funny, and I love you. You are my heartbeat."

Jake held Gloria tight, pressing her to his chest. He didn't know why, but there was water in his eyes. One tear went slowly down his cheek.

In one cavern, they startled a group of ghouls swimming in an underground river. The ghouls stared with glowing blank phosphorescent eyes, and their ears twitched, but then they scattered in the water, making ripples and waves and fled, swimming, into the darkness.

"Good ghouls," said Jimmy Ghoul, "Good ghouls!"

"Yes, I think so," said Julian Harvey.

"So, there are many variants," said Sabrina, one of the black hybrids; she had a red mark on her snout.

"What does 'variant' mean?" Jake glanced at Gloria and then at the hybrid.

The hybrid began a long explanation, a sort of Nobel Prize-winning explanation; after all, in her other life, she was a Nobel Laurate – twice!

"That is exquisite, Ms. Hybrid," said Gloria, beaming at the hybrid and thinking that understanding things and gathering words was going to be an unending task and permanent feast: it would never end.

They came to an ancient tunnel with tracks like a little railroad and with some mineral carts and with skeletons in hard hats sitting in dignified positions, their backs propped up against the side of the cave, and they came to a gallery full of fossilized ghouls, and they went through a gallery where giant spider-like creatures were hanging from webs cast across the top of the gallery, and they came to a narrow defile between two high rock walls. "This way," said Valerie Joffre, "This must be it!"

They advanced carefully.

"A zephyr," said Gloria, "I feel a zephyr."

"Yes," said Jake, "a breeze."

The air moved and whispered, and Cassandra said, "This is the one, this is it: this is the tunnel of the breath of life."

Jake said, "Yes, this is the place."

"Yes," Gloria looked up into Jake's eyes, "Together we came to this place once, Jake, remember, and there is an old rusty bucket filled with dust just around that corner and some beams holding up the side of the tunnel," and she crouched down and found a pebble and then another pebble – just where Jake had put them. "And this is your guide-pebble, Jake!"

V turned to Valerie Joffre and said, "Well, what do you think?"

Valerie put her hand to her temple and thought.

"Give me a minute." She closed her eyes, accessing the map and schematic implants in her memory, and she said, "Yes, there should be a bigger cave at the end of this tunnel, about 100 meters away, and the big cave goes very close to the surface but is probably closed at the end, or it was when they did the schematics, we may have to dig our way out."

They went single file through the narrow tunnel; Jimmy Ghoul hopped along behind Gloria and Jake.

"You are a girl," said Jimmy Ghoul, "You told me."

"Yes, I am a girl," said Gloria, "a young female person is what I am."

"I like you," Jimmy Ghoul licked his lips.

"I don't know if I can keep going." Ms. Agnes had stopped, and was leaning forward, holding her back; it looked like she might topple forward.

Cassandra, who was hopping and skittering along, said, "Oh, yes, you can, Ms. Agnes, yes, you can," and she put one of her arms – with the stubby paw, around Ms. Agnes and helped Ms. Agnes over a pile of rocks that had fallen across the tunnel. Sarah, the black hybrid with the glowing scarlet Vs, and Sammy and a few hybrids, brought up the rear to make sure everybody was accounted for and to help those who were falling behind.

Norton and V went ahead with Valerie Joffre, and Freddy as their extra guard, and they came out into a large arched cavern with reddish stone and where there were shafts of sunlight coming down at the far end. "This must be it."

There were bones, too, bones of humans and animals.

Everybody came up to the front and looked at the scatterings of bones.

"So, this is where the ghouls went to hunt; this is how they got out of the caves, onto the surface," said V, and she glanced back at Sammy Franks – the first one to make the magic deduction.

Sammy glanced at his two hybrids, his sisters, Sabrina and Helen; they turned to him and smiled and nodded: "Yes, Sammy Franks, you were right!" The mental message was loud and clear.

Everyone filed into the big cave, shriveled Mr. Fen, and wan but beautiful Ms. Chong, Ms. Agnes and Mr. Swann, and all the prisoners, and Julian and his ghoul, and Jake and Gloria, and all the hybrids.

The bones were dried, and chalk-white, and some of them were shiny and new with bits of dried flesh and gristle clinging to them.

"Spooky," said Gloria.

"Yes, creepy," said Eve the Golden Hybrid, giving Gloria a nice look.

"Well, let's go," said Valerie.

"Yes," V and Norton spoke at the same moment and then looked at each other and smiled.

They climbed up to the far end of the cavern; at the end, it sloped even more steeply upward. It took about fifteen minutes to get there. There was a switchback pathway that wound upwards on the slope, looping back and forth among the stones, and jagged outcroppings. It led the way up over the massive mountain of collapsed material that had filled the far end of the cavern almost to the roof.

At the top of the cave, there was an opening, hidden behind the pile of rubble and behind another wall of rock, and it glowed with the reflected golden light of day. "It looks like it collapsed here, opening it up," said Valerie Joffre, picking up one of the stones.

V and Norton – with Valerie and Freddy – went ahead, cautiously, with Norton holding his laser gun out in front of him.

They came to another wall of rock, but the wall of rock had a sideways slit, and V and Norton slid through it, followed by Valerie and Freddy.

They came into a large cave, with a bend in the middle of it, and after the bend, there was, at the end of the cave, a large brilliantly lit opening.

"Light, so much light," said Gloria, still well inside the mouth of the cave.

"Yes," said Jake.

"I'm afraid, Jake."

"Don't be afraid, Gloria."

They had come a long way; then, in the last cavern, they had walked for perhaps 200 meters and, then, suddenly, they rounded a curve, and the cave opened up, and there was a big round hole: away – far away – at the end; it was full of brightness. Jake had never seen such brightness. Gloria blinked and shaded her eyes; her fingers tightened around Jake's hand.

"Stay here," V had come back, and she glanced at the humans – all as pale as shadows – and at the two children. "Shield your eyes. You are not used to such light. Shield your eyes, all of you!"

"Yes, and keep back, everybody," said Norton, holding his arm up.

"Let's go ahead," said Norton, wiping the sweat from his forehead, "Me, Julian, you, V, Freddy, Valerie, a couple of hybrids."

They headed toward the opening, which seemed as bright as the sun itself. They had no idea what might be waiting for them out there as they advanced into the blaze of light, out into a gateway onto the surface of the planet earth.

V and Norton were the first to emerge.

Freddy and Valerie were just behind.

Nobody said anything.

The sun shone.

It was day.

They stood there as if turned to stone.

Finally, Norton turned to V, "You did it!"

V turned to Norton, "You did it – we all did it together: Valerie, Cassandra, Jake and Gloria, Eve, Sammy, everybody."

"You are right." Norton nodded, and wiped his forehead, "We all did it!" Without thinking, he took V's claw, and they all stood there, Julian, Norton, V, Freddy, Valerie Joffre, Sabrina and Helen, holding hands, staring out at the world.

The sky was empty; the desert stretched out before them, the unending desert, like a vast yellow-gold inland sea.

CHAPTER 21 – THE WORLD

"That is blue," Gloria said, her eyes getting used the immense glare from the big hole at the end of the cave, "Ms. Agnes told me about blue."

"Yes, that is blue sky," Jake pulled Gloria closer.

Everybody waited. Now the circle of light was so bright that it was hard to look at it. Norton and V had come back to get the rest of the group. Norton glanced at V. They both nodded.

"Okay, come forward," V said.

Jake stared at V and Norton, outlined by the brilliance of the light, and in particular at V, at the way she was framed in the brilliance.

V, still in reptile-hybrid form, stood with her legs slightly apart, her machine gun slung over one shoulder, she was, for Jake and Gloria, a silhouette, the light seemed to break and split into a rainbow of colors radiating out around her. "Come on, it's safe," she said, over her shoulder, "For the moment, it is safe."

They trooped forward.

"Careful! Careful!" ordered Norton.

"Don't look at the sun!" shouted Freddy.

"Yes," V said, "Come forward slowly, shield your eyes, don't look at the sun, don't ever look directly at the sun; it will blind you!"

They trooped forward slowly, enslaved hybrids, and human prisoners; they had not seen the light of day for fourteen years, most of them.

It was blindingly bright. The sky was empty, cloudless, and the sun was far into the late afternoon, but brilliant, low down in the west, and already turning a redder color.

They were standing on a stone ledge, which was on the side of a high escarpment. It looked over a vast desert of sand dunes, sand, yellow sand, stretching off endlessly, under an empty blue sky and a pitiless hot sun that blazed down and seemed to burn everything its rays touched. There was nothing but sand to be seen, and a few rusty half-buried carcasses of machinery.

Gloria stared. "This is it?"

"Yes."

"This is the world?"

"Yes, this is the world," Ms. Agnes had come up to stand next to Gloria and Jake, "this is the world, children, and this is the sky."

Jake stepped out onto a jutting flat platform of rock, a little promontory. He reached down and pulled Gloria up and he and the Golden Hybrid – Eve – helped Ms. Agnes up onto the rock; Jake suddenly saw, with a horrible new clarity, how thin and stringy Ms. Agnes's arms and legs had become, how white she was in the brilliant light, almost as white as a ghoul. He could see the blue veins and dark marks on her skin and how the skin was raw and blistered and bruised and bleeding in some places. Her near nakedness was now horribly cruel.

"Here, Ms. Agnes, come on, up here, like this," he said, glancing at Eve, whose golden scales – even if streaked with clay – glittered in the sun, like she was a golden sculpture, a wondrous and powerful machine.

"Easy does it, Ms. Agnes," Eve said, helping Jake with Ms. Agnes, and Eve caught Jake's glance – and his thoughts – and Jake saw in Eve's serpent eyes a silent message directed straight at him: "The light of day reveals so many things, Jake. You are the adult now, and you will have to look after Ms. Agnes – and Gloria."

"There, Ms. Agnes," Jake said, absorbing the thought and helping Ms. Agnes up and seeing clearly, perhaps for the first time, the woman – the beautiful and gracious woman whom he discovered only now how much he loved, how he loved her desperately and with pain for her age and fragility and for the dangers that hovered over her – the beautiful woman who from seeming so young, so strong, only a few weeks ago had, in so short a time, become an old woman, balding, broken-toothed, empty toothed, raw gums showing, fragile, pale white, and deathly old. And yes, still, she was, with Gloria, the thing he most loved in the whole wide world.

Eve helped the shivering little ghoul up onto the platform of stone. The ghoul blinked and shrank away from the sunlight. "Oh, it is too strong, too, too strong," Jimmy Ghoul whimpered.

Eve said, "Here, sit in the shadow of this rock."

The ghoul hopped over to the shadow and sat down and then looked up at

Eve, its blank oblong eyes blinked; the weird flickering mouth spilled a thick curtain of white foaming drool, "Thank you, Hybrid."

"You rest there, brother," said Eve, "don't worry about a thing."

The world was there, before them, and the world was a desert. The sky was there too, the blue sky, and the sky was empty.

"So, this is the world." Gloria said again, shielding her eyes.

"This is the world," Ms. Agnes said.

"I've never seen such a big cave," Gloria wiggled her nose. "You can't see the roof. Or is the roof blue?"

"That is the blue of the sky, and that is the sun. There is no roof. It is just air, and then space."

"Why is the air blue?"

"It's complicated," said Ms. Agnes; she coughed.

"That is sand," said Gloria, pointing at the dunes that stretched away.

"Yes, that is sand. It is a desert."

Gloria blinked. She was experimenting with letting her eyes look at the brightness. Her eyes watered. With her knuckles, she worked at her eyes. "I don't see any people," she said, shading her eyes.

"No," said Ms. Agnes.

"I don't see any trees."

"No."

"I don't see verdant fields where flowers bloom."

"No," said Ms. Agnes, "the verdant fields are gone, Gloria."

"Oh," Gloria frowned then brightened, "Maybe they are just hiding, and they'll come out when we're not looking."

"Yes, maybe they will." Ms. Agnes was trembling.

"You should sit down, Ms. Agnes," said one of the hybrids, "there, in the shade."

V glanced at their motley little band, out here, in the desert, with no shelter, and with night coming on. "The first thing we have to do, I think, is get back to Camp Terminus, and link up with the others. How far is it, do you think, from here?"

"About three and a half, four kilometers from here, I think," said Norton, "back up, to the west, behind that ridge – over there."

"Yes, that should be right," Valerie Joffre said, glancing at V.

"Yes." V nodded, but she seemed, to Valerie, to be a bit distracted.

"I've got a bad feeling about this," said Norton.

"About what …?" Valerie raised an eyebrow, after everything they had been through, things couldn't get worse, and they saved almost everybody.

"About the Camp," Norton said, and he motioned toward the empty sky, "and about all of this, there's something …"

"Yes," V said, still seeming a bit distracted, "Yes, there is … something … something coming …"

Nothing was visible except the drifting sand and in the distance another high escarpment. Giant dust devils moved like miniature tornadoes across the land.

The sky was pure blue, and there was not a single cloud. And down below, on the sand dunes, no plants grew. As the sun got lower down in the western sky, the world turned pale pink and then red.

"The sun will soon be setting," said Ms. Agnes.

Jake and Gloria blinked.

The sun, low down in the western sky, suddenly dimmed.

"They're coming," Golden Hybrid Eve said. She sensed something ominous and horrible, but she didn't know what it was.

"Yes," said V, "they are coming."

"What's coming?" Valerie looked at the two hybrids.

"Something bad," said V.

"Where do we go?" Eve glanced at V and at Valerie Joffre.

"Nowhere," said V, "Here we will make our stand. Retreating into the caves is not an option." V nodded toward a dull rumbling sound.

Eve glanced back. The earth was trembling, rocks were falling; it was an earthquake, or something like an earthquake.

"This, I imagine, will be very instructive, Gloria," said Valerie Joffre, smiling at the little girl.

"*Instructive*, yes, Ms. Valerie, I imagine it will be exceedingly instructive," said Gloria giving Valerie her brightest, most eager smile.

Suddenly, the sun began to smoke. It turned blood-red; a ghastly scarlet shadow spilled like blood over the desert. One minute it was brilliant sunlight, the setting sun, glowing over the desert, and cliffs in the distance, and then the sun darkened, and the sky turned black, not the black of starlight, but the black of tar or pitch, without a glimmer, without a moon, and the world changed into a pure hell of zombie-bats, hallucinations, and monsters, and the veil of being, the world itself, wavered and trembled.

The humidity soared. The sand of the desert lifted itself up into a wall of mist and sand, a sandstorm, the dust devils, got larger, faster, becoming huge, heading straight toward them.

Out of the pitch-black sky, rain poured down, and lightning flashed. An ocean rose up and suddenly surrounded the rocky ledges on which they stood. Water flooded up, right to where they were standing. V shouted, "This is all an illusion!"

"Moon, oh, moon – where is the moon?" Gloria reached out in front of her, trying to feel the darkness. It was humid and heavy, and it was like pushing her fingers into the sludgy muck in one of the clay pools in the cavern. The wet air pressed upon her body like glue. "Oh, moon, sweet moon …! Where are you, dear moon?"

Wham – a withering wind slammed into them, a whirlwind turbulence of the air: a slamming, bone-breaking wall of air.

Gloria was blown off her feet; Ms. Agnes toppled over and sprawled down among the stones; Norton was blinded for a moment, smashed against the rock face as if by a giant body blow; he shook himself and drew his laser gun, and stared into the darkness.

"You alright, mate?" said Freddy.

"Yes, I am. Are you alright?"

"I'm fine, but I fear something awful is coming."

"I fear you're right, Freddy."

Sarah James, the black hybrid with the bright Vs splashed on her chest and back, put her claw on Norton's arm to steady him, "This is an illusion, I think," she said, "partly an illusion, the darkness I mean."

"Bloody effective illusion, I'd say." Norton wiped his brow, and glanced at the hybrid. He was damned happy to have hybrids as allies.

"What the hell was that?" Valerie Joffre – who had been standing out on the ledge – found herself sitting flat on her backside with her back against a rock shelf. She struggled to her feet, clutching the ribbons of her work suit.

"An illusion," said Eve, "a very tangible illusion."

"Tangible, it certainly is." Valerie looked around, groping through the darkness. Gloria was sitting stunned on the ground. Valerie knelt next to the little girl, got down on all fours, her face close to Gloria's face. "Gloria, are you okay?"

"You were right, Ms. Valerie. This is very, very instructive."

In an instant, the blackness passed as if it had never been. The desert and setting sun were once again visible, the sun crumbling into embers.

"Everybody crouch down!" V shouted. "Shelter against the rocks! Get in as tight as you can."

"Hybrids," Norton shouted, "Protect the people. Humans with guns, get ready to defend everybody."

Freddy and Sarah rushed to herd the humans to safety.

"Yes, hybrids, guards, get ready!" shouted V.

"What about me? Who will protect me?" said Jimmy the ghoul, getting up, blinking at the sky, which seemed to be changing color – in fact, it was hard to tell what was going on. "I used to understand things, once upon a time, I remember, but I don't understand anything now."

"You count as human," said V, "I'm re-classifying you."

"Thank you, I think."

"It's a dubious honor, Jimmy, I know," V glanced at the horizon and then at Jake who was staring out at the rising wave of sand and at the sun which once again seemed to be dimming and turning blood-red. Eve glanced at Sabrina and Freddy and Helen and the other hybrids and at Norton and the guards and they exchanged the silent thought. *Bad things were about to happen.*

V shouted, "Jake, you and Gloria take Ms. Agnes and Jimmy the ghoul and hide behind that rock, get back into the opening of the cave; get as low as you can, squeeze against the rocks."

The hybrids and guards and Valerie Joffre herded the rest of the human survivors into the mouth of the cave.

"It's not safe," said Norton, glancing up at the craggy overhangs; the mouth of the cave looked like it would collapse any moment.

"Nowhere is safe," said V.

"That's about exactly right, my hybrid friend," said Norton, "It's about approximately exactly right."

"I don't know precisely what is coming, but it is not good," said V.

Freddy, Sarah, Norton, all the others readied themselves to fight.

Sammy Franks was sweating heavily. He wiped at his forehead with a red and white polka dot handkerchief. He had huffed and puffed his way up the last hundred meters to the sunlight and his heart was still pounding. He leaned on Sabrina's arm. "I'm going to die."

"You are not going to die," she said.

Sammy was trembling, "What do we do now, what do we do?"

"We stand and fight," said Helen Silver Hybrid, "we fight whatever it is that is coming."

"But what is coming, what happening, what the hell is happening?"

"I think," said Sabrina, "that this is leakage."

"Leakage …?" Sammy wiped his forehead; his heartbeat and breathing he realized were settling down, slowing; his hybrid girlfriends had a soothing effect; he suddenly realized that, without them, his life would be empty. I'm in love, he thought, I'm in love with two hybrids. Fuck!

"The various universes intersect and overlap in some way we don't really understand," Sabrina began, "and they meet, they can meet everywhere, and that explains why we hybrids, who have a connection with the intersection of the various universes, at the quantum mechanics level, that explains why we can morph instantaneously, that explains why we can sometimes read minds, and why we can sometimes sense the memories of objects and places – that is, we can sense traces of what happened …"

"That's a theory," Helen said, "not an established fact."

"Right, thank you, dear Helen," Sabrina blinked at her closest friend hybrid, "Helen, as usual, is right, Sammy. It is a hypothesis, but it's the most likely explanation. It explains entanglement – how subatomic particles can interact instantaneously over vast distances, and it explains the role of dark matter and dark energy, and it explains …"

"Yes, yes, ladies," Sammy gulped, "but we are now in danger of being …"

"Sammy's right," said Helen, "we can hold a physics and quantum mechanics and cosmology seminar later. Come on! Sammy, you get in between these two rocks and crouch down and get ready to shoot at any menacing thing that comes from the sky."

The thick pitch dark returned; it oozed over everything and everyone.

The wind rose again. It grabbed people's hair; it ripped their rags to shreds; it bowled some of them over. On the desert below them, an ocean suddenly appeared, once again; huge waves dashed at the rocks, splashes of water surged, giant salty drops hit people in the face.

"A time machine?" whispered Helen.

"Maybe," said Sabrina, "or the illusion of a time machine."

"I sure wish I knew how to swim," said Sammy Franks.

"If it's a flashback in time," said Sabrina, "it might be to the Great Inland Sea that covered the center of North America, dividing it in two, about

100 million years ago. It was known as the North American Inland Sea, or Niobraran Sea. It was probably formed when …"

"Oh," said Sammy, "very interesting. The world is coming to an end, and Sabrina is acting like an encyclopedia."

"It's her way of reacting to stress," said Helen, laying a silver claw on Sammy's shoulder.

"Oh, well, that's good, I guess." Sammy sighed: if Sabrina Super Girl Genius Hybrid was stressed, then things were serious.

Out of the whirling maelstrom of darkness and out of the thunder of the waves, came a voice, "Now you die! Now you all die!" The voice rolled like thunder. "This is the hour. This is the end!" The sound of giant horses' hooves echoed through the air; the hooves sounded like thunder; buckets of whirring locust spilled down from somewhere above. Hot rain, streaming drops, began to fall.

"Oh," said Gloria, beating the fluttering whizzing insects away.

"Jeepers creepers," Jimmy cowered close to Gloria.

"This should be impossible," said Valerie Joffre, fighting to shelter Gloria and Jimmy from the storm of whirring wings.

"What is that?" Jake tried to see clearly.

The beating hooves faded.

The locusts fell apart, disintegrating into dust, then into – nothing.

The rain ceased, and the sea receded and dissolved – it had never been there – and out of the dark sky came a wave of zombie-bats – and then more and more, wave after wave.

"These, my friends, are real," V shouted.

"I've seen them, I think, those must be the things I saw on the Elliott ridge," Norton took aim and fired.

And so the fight began!

Sarah Hybrid and Freddy Hybrid leaped into the fray.

Sammy fired his laser, again and again.

Sabrina and Helen acted as a team, bating and destroying bats, grabbing their flapping wings, punching them in the jaw, ripping them into shreds.

It was a welter of gunfire, laser fire, and thrashing and slashing Hybrids, and howling and screaming zombie-bats.

V tore at them, her claws flashing and flashing; and the guns and lasers rattled and flashed and shot them down.

Jake and Gloria and Ms. Agnes and Jimmy Ghoul and the other humans crouched in the narrow crawl space between the rocks. Just above them,

Valerie Joffre, her back against a wall of stone, fired a continuous stream of lasers at the plunging bats. Then Valerie had to reload the charger. In that instant, three zombie-bats swarmed in.

The talons of one of the giant zombie-bat reached down, the points of its claws brushing Jake's hair. Jake ducked. Jimmy Ghoul groaned and cowered, and Gloria whispered, "Crouch lower, Jake, crouch lower!"

Ms. Agnes mumbled, "If I were a believing woman, I believe I would pray right now!" She picked up a small round stone, weighed it in her hand, some muscle memory of when she played baseball, and she threw it straight at the zombie-bat's fangs.

She scored a bulls-eye; the zombie-bat squealed and screamed and shuddered, and it swooped up and then down, and it landed on the rocks, just above Jake, its great talons clutching the edge of the outcropping, and it turned its tiny, beady, evil eyes upon Ms. Agnes.

"You evil, evil thing," Ms. Agnes said, "Go away! Pick on somebody your own size!"

With the reloaded gun, Valerie fired at the zombie-bat, but another bat knocked the gun from her hands. Valerie scrambled over the rocks to get it. The bat plunged at her, smashing her against the rocks. Valerie tumbled backward, hit her head, and lay still.

Jake crouched as low as he could, his hand closing around a nice solid piece of stone. If it comes to that, he thought, if this thing gets me, then I will crush its head with this stone, I will hit and hit and hit it, and he looked up and the foul breath of the creature, stinking like a rotten food pouch – well beyond its termination date – that had gone bad and that when you opened it was full of maggots and out came a puff of horrible smells that made you want to double over and vomit and throw the thing far away because it made you feel unclean – polluted.

Yes, polluted, as the old preacher used to say, polluted – an awful word with horror and death packed inside it.

These things were like pollution; they were like the plague.

The zombie-bat's eyes, like black buttons, were focused directly on him, on Jake. The great snout and jaws were jabbing, jabbing, jabbing – but couldn't reach him.

Jake stuck out his tongue, thinking, at the same time, that this was an impolite thing to do. Ms. Agnes had tried to teach him manners. Inside the jaws were giant crooked teeth that pointed every which way.

The snout jabbed and jabbed and jabbed – the claws grabbed and grabbed and grabbed, hitting sparks off the rock face.

Jake stared into the thing's eyes. They were small and circled by a tuft of leathery, feather-like, blob-like excrescences. The eyes were staring straight at Jake. Jake stared back. He thought he was going to be swept up in the swirl of the zombie-bat's mind, its hypnotic stare, and that he, Jake, might cease to be Jake, but become merely a figment of the creature's mind, a prisoner caught within its stare, and, for some reason, Jake let himself go, and, as he stared, and the zombie-bat's eyes seemed to grow bigger and bigger, Jake felt himself falling into deep depths and he saw – as if in a vision – that within the zombie-bat was another being, a woman, a young woman: she was wearing a long plain shapeless cotton dress – it was dark brown with no pattern – it was being whipped by the dusty desert wind, making ripples against her legs and belly and breasts, and he even saw the nipples outlined in rippling cloth; her blond hair was pulled back in tight braids; she was carrying a pewter-colored tin pail with a tin handle, and the pail made a clanking sound, and, in the background, behind the woman, was an old-fashioned windmill, up on a spindly tower, something Jake had seen in one of Ms. Agnes's old picture books, its pewter-colored paddles wildly churning against a stormy, steel-metal dark sky, rifts of charcoal cloud piling up, frayed horizontal ribbons of light and dark rising, and an old farmhouse, wood clapboard and peeling white paint, and the woman was walking toward a well where there was an old-fashioned hand-pump like Jake had seen in Ms. Agnes's moldy encyclopedia of technology, and the woman set the pail down on top of the well, and she began to push the pump handle up and down but no water came out; she kept pumping and then she turned straight to Jake, and she spoke, "I am sorry for what I have become, Jake, I cannot help it; he turned us, you know, he turned us, virtually all of us who believed in him, all of us who truly worshiped him, we are the True Believers and he turned us into his creatures, his diabolic and satanic servants, and now we do his bidding. I am sorry, my friend. Of us good folk, truly good folk, our God, our Idolatry, our False God, the Devil himself, has made monsters, and such we now are – monsters."

Jake relaxed, blandished by the soothing words, half in love with the beautiful young woman carrying the pail and …

Wham! The zombie-bat's claw plunged into Jake's shoulder.

The claw slammed shut, its long talon-like nails locking onto Jake's shoulder, and grabbing him, and the zombie-bat shook Jake, viciously, repeatedly, like a cat might shake a canary or a mouse, and, flapping its great wings, it pulled him upward.

Valerie Joffre woke up, shook her head, and grabbed for the laser gun, which was lying not far away. She took aim.

"No, Jake, no," Gloria grabbed onto Jake's arm and was lifted up with him. Ms. Agnes seized Jake's leg and held on as best she could, but his leg was still slick from clay and she slipped away and fell back, staring upward, wide-eyed, as Jake – with Gloria still hanging on – was lifted, up and up and up.

Cassandra scurried over and shouted, "Jake, Jake, Gloria, Gloria!" She turned to Ms. Agnes. "This cannot happen; this will not stand; this cannot be; the children cannot be lost."

"No, they cannot," said Ms. Agnes. Her heart was sinking.

Valerie Joffre was a crack shot from her Cosmos training, and she aimed, but she didn't dare pull the trigger: the zombie-bat kept whirling around and she was afraid she might hit the children. Besides, they would fall, and …

Jimmy Ghoul leaped up and howled and threw stones at the zombie-bat; the pebbles bounced off the great leathery wings as they flapped, seemingly almost leisurely, and as the zombie-bat rose slowly into the turbulent dark night air, lifting the two children out over the abyss. Ms. Agnes screamed.

Before the battle began, V had divested herself of her reptilian demonic self. *Presto, abracadabra, voilà* – she became human.

"This is you?" said Gloria, wide-eyed. She had seen the whole transformation.

"This is me," said V, as she carefully pulled on her skintight warrior uniform.

"There are two of you?"

"Yes, Gloria, there are two of me," V snapped her belt shut, adjusted the holster.

"Heavenly Daze," said Gloria, "And Holy Moly!"

"How do I look?"

"A dream: you look like a dream, you look like a delicious luscious dream," said Gloria, "But, if I may ask, Ms. Hybrid, why did you change? You were very pretty, most attractive, I might say, the way you were."

"Well, Gloria …" and V explained: she had decided that if she were to stand and fight for the human race in the showdown at the O.K. Corral – the desert of the Dead Lands, of the Great Super Dust Bowl – the least she could do was to look human – and be human. It was a matter of respect.

Now, fifteen minutes later, V stood on the edge of the outcropping that projected over the desert. A moment before she had been staring down on the waste of sand, the dunes rising and falling like silent frozen waves of gold, the sun shining out of a high blue sky, and, in the distance, the beginning of the escarpment – it stretched off for several hundred kilometers – under which the Kingdom of the Mutants lay hidden – and where Miranda and Nikki and Caliban were waiting for her and Kat to return.

Then the sky had darkened, and the world itself revealed itself to be an illusion, a game that was being played in some gigantic matrix of energy and of forces beyond human – and hybrid – understanding. "So this world can be changed like that," V snapped her fingers.

And Norton, who was standing beside her, said, "Well, lass, it seems to so! Wouldn't have believed it, if I hadn't seen it with my own eyes!"

Out of the darkness came a whirling blast of hailstones.

Norton and Freddy backed under an overhang. Sarah was next to them, with Sabrina, Helen, Sammy, and Julian not far behind. The hail blasted down on the rocks and stones – then it stopped.

Time passed, in a strange slow-motion whirl of obscurity.

V stood firm.

She shielded her eyes.

It was day; now it was night.

Norton seemed to have disappeared. Everyone had disappeared.

V could hear Norton from far away, shouting, "Get ready to aim, mates, make every shot count. These are devils, as you can see, mates, but humans and hybrids together, we can defeat them."

"Yes, sir," she could hear the voices of hybrids and humans alike.

"Watch out, mate!" Freddy's voice echoed.

"Got it, thanks, Freddy!" it was Norton's voice, fading.

"Duck, Freddy," Sarah's voice, from far away, echoed.

It was all a dream, Norton, Freddy, all the hybrids and humans, a fading dream, leaving nothing at all, not even a rack of cloud behind, not even …

V was alone on a dark storm-swept promontory. She whispered toward the advancing night, "Okay, whoever or whatever you are, show yourself! Let us speak, let us see what we are made of."

At first, it did not answer, whatever it was.

V took a deep breath; then, she remembered her father, Marcus, saying, "You will not know what powers you possess, V, until you try them."

Out of the mist, swirling in a long black cape, a handsome young man appeared. He had romantic good looks, the dark, curly, stormy, lovelock good looks that V remembered used to be called Byronic in the early 19th century, around the time of Napoleon Bonaparte. So this was the Boy – Billie McAdams' demon lover! His dark eyes flashed; his skin was pale as chalk; his lips were full and curled in an expression of disdain. He embodied in his flesh V's ideal lineaments of desire, one of the many imaginary lovers V conjured up during sleepless nights when she was alone and her energy level was, well, too high, unfocused, lusty, horny, and soaring toward … She sighed.

"I am the Boy." He crossed his arms, Napoleon-style, and scowled.

"Oh?"

"I am the Lord. Down on your knees, Hybrid, fall on your knees, female!"

"Female?"

"Yes – female!"

V laughed. "You are not the Lord. Why should I fall on my knees? You are just a dream, just a puppet, just a figment of someone's or something's mind. You are the Lord of Nothing."

"I am no figment!" His eyes flared darkness.

"Well, you look like a figment to me."

"You – I shall crush you!"

"You do appear, sir, to be too good to be true, too beautiful, too alluring, too tempting! Such things as dreams are made on, are not – for the most part – real. We all know that. You are a temptation – a ghost from my own mind, transported here from some other universe. Hence! Go! Begone! You are a figment, a wench's midsummer dream perhaps, a passing fancy, an ad for perfume, photographed in sculpted black-and-white."

"Wretched wench, you will regret your impertinence!"

"Will I?"

"Yes. I come bearing thunderbolts!" He waved his hand, languidly, an off-hand gesture: *I do this all the time*, it seemed to say. A gigantesque bolt of lightning flashed out of the darkness, burning, sizzling its way to the frothy writhing sea, and a smack and roll of thunder followed.

"Impressive," said V.

"Thank you. You know, I do these tricks all the time. I am godlike."

"But you are hollow too – a mere figment. You have leaked over from some other universe, some Hell that calls itself Heaven. A place with lots of electricity, I am sure."

"Indeed – I am truly electric!"

"And you are magnetic too?"

"That too." He smiled. "I am the Boy. I encompass within myself everything that is, everything that could be, every desire, every fear, every wavelength, and every color. All of this can be yours." He spread his arms wide.

"I'm not interested." V turned sideways, coyly, and pretended to pout.

"You and I could be lovers. We must be lovers!"

V sighed. She pouted some more and kicked at a pebble. She was sorely tempted. He did look luscious – stormy, dark, difficult, wicked, fiercely macho, and yes, with his full lips, dark eyes, long eyelashes – suggestively effeminate, beautifully androgynous – a true Bad Boy, one of her favorite types. Yummy!

The Boy stood beside her, on the outcropping of rock. The storm whirled around them. The night thickened. From far away, the squealing and shrieking of zombie-bats could be heard, and, muffled, the shots of guns and laser pistols, as the humans and hybrids defended themselves from the storming throngs of zombie-bats, creatures from hell come to violate, desecrate, and destroy all free and living things. But V and the Boy were in another world, another time. Or so it seemed.

"You and I must be lovers?" V turned to face the Boy and tilted her head to one side – yes, she was sorely tempted. Experience is all. Why not try out one more experience – even if it involved intercourse with the anti-Christ or Satan himself or whoever this chap – this figment of a dreamboat – who called himself "the Boy" seemed to think he was. V considered herself a feminist, but she also felt she should be up to any challenge …

"Yes," The Boy showed his bright teeth in a wicked smile. "I will sweep you into my arms and make you mine."

"I don't wish to be presumptuous, but what if I made you mine?" V favored him with a bright smile.

"I, the Boy, will triumph!"

"And we are in the wilderness," said V.

"Yes, we are in the wilderness."

"The theater of temptation," said V.

"Yes."

"Forty days, and forty nights," said V, "the theater of temptation. Where wildness and unruly yearnings reign, unleashed from all civilized, hypocritical, urbane constraint."

"Yes, wench, indeed, this is the theater of temptation."

"Let us test each other," V laid her hands upon his shoulders, stared straight into his eyes – yes, they were beautiful – and she let her mouth approach his, and she brushed her lips lightly against his and then, quickly, she kissed him, a full and deep kiss, exploring his passion and hers.

Dimly she was still aware of hybrids and humans and even Jimmy Ghoul and the zombie-bats and of a great battle, as if it were a battle between ghosts, taking place behind her, bodies and arms were clashing darkly in a distant world, an almost forgotten world, a shadowy sketchy muffled world. But here, now, she and her lover, her demon lover, were alone.

The kiss approaches a climax, a climax of *almost* orgasmic intensity.

Now, it approaches a climax of *true* orgasmic intensity!

She toys with her excitement.

She toys with *his* excitement.

She brings her own excitement right to the edge. She deploys all her sensual and sensuous artistry to bring him to ecstasy, and perhaps beyond.

Oh, oh, oh … oh!

Her arts are supreme – Oh, the pleasure!

Oh, the tension!

He wavers.

His image wavers, becomes unsubstantial. His eyes blink, gaze into hers, as if with great regret. He sighs. "We shall meet again, Hybrid! You cheated me of my harvest of death down in the mine. The next time there will be no reprieve, no pity, not for you, not for your friends, not for the world!"

V blinks. There is a withering explosion, implosion. Her lover is gone. She is once again on the outcropping, in the chaos of the battle against the zombie-bats.

Jake and Gloria are being carried off by a zombie-bat; up and up they go, ten feet, now fifteen, now eighteen.

Oh, no! V stares.

She leaps, far into the air, farther than her usual range – *I didn't know I could do this*, she thinks, *well, Marcus was quite right, as usual*, and her gloved hand seizes the tip of one of the zombie-bat's wings, and, digging her fingers in, she clambers up the wing. Her weight is too great, and the zombie-bat squawks and rages, flapping desperately with one free wing, spiralling down, slowly, fighting all the way, smashing into the ground, releasing Jake and Gloria, and its great jaws and claws turning to slash out V's eyes, but V, letting go of the wing, pulls out her laser gun and vaporizes the snout and lower face, leaving only the eyes, two button-like eyes, that turn suddenly blue and human and then dissolve in a scream of pure, utter anguish that only V can hear.

"Spooky," Gloria says, sniffling and shaking herself to get rid of the zombie-bat smell.

"V, thank you," Jake says; he is trembling.

"What happened just there, V?" said Norton – turning to V and blazing with his laser at a swooping pair of zombie-bats, "It was as if you were frozen for a second; and, if I'm not mistaken, the whole world turned black, just a blink-of-an-eye sort of thing."

"I was doing battle."

"I figured as much – in some other space and time."

"Yes."

"You and the Devil and all the temptations of the earth, offered to you as they were offered to Christ …"

V turned and looked at Norton, "Yes," she said, "Something like that: sex was what he was offering, and romance, and maybe even love …"

"Love …?" Norton blinked, "Crikey!"

The zombie-bats wheeled away, leaving the night sky empty. The stars shone. The moon popped into existence, as if it had been hiding.

"So this is the world," said Gloria.

"Yes, this is night. This is the world," said Ms. Agnes.

The sky brightened, and then faded, and the unnatural darkness receded like the waters of a poisoned ocean, and stars shone, and the moon sailed on, serenely, round and tranquil, the beautiful, stony-hearted moon.

"Oh, moon, sweet moon," said Gloria, her face turned upward, sparkles of moonlight shining on the gold stubble of her hair, "Oh, delicious moon!"

V knelt and kissed the girl.

"Oh," said Gloria, her eyes going round, "Oh."

"It's called a kiss, Gloria," said Jake.

Gloria gave Jake a look. "Yes, my heartbeat, I know."

Norton and V conferred, and then V announced. "We will join the others who are at the pithead, and in the control tower of the mine, of Camp Terminus."

"Pithead ... Pithead ... This is very interesting, so much to learn, so little time," Gloria put her hand in Jake's hand and looked up at him.

Jake looked down at Gloria, and the thought flitted through his mind that Gloria was truly beautiful, and that they were entering a brave and dangerous new world where anything could happen. He must protect Gloria. He tightened his grip on her hand.

For a time, they all slept or dozed, collapsed and sprawled here and there on the rocks and on the sand. Then, suddenly, as if no time at all had passed, a strange glow spread through the sky. The stars faded. The moon became a pale shadowy version of itself.

"What's happening?" Gloria blinked, shook her head, rubbed her eyes, and stared up at the black and indigo, which was becoming rose and yellow and then in places a wispy blue.

"It's the sun, it's the sunrise."

"The sunrise ...?" Gloria frowned.

"It's dawn. It's called dawn."

"It's the beginning of a new day," said Ms. Agnes.

"Yes, it is," said Valerie Joffre, putting her hand on Gloria's shoulder.

CHAPTER 22 – THE TREK

It was a four-kilometer trek back to the center of Camp Terminus and when they finally got there – eagerly greeted by Hugo – Norton found a very different place.

"Bloody, hell!" said Norton. He kneeled, patted Hugo, and glanced up at V.

"Like the end of the world," said V.

"Maybe it's the beginning, the beginning of the end." Norton squinted through the shattered control room window at the ruins. The pitheads of Main Shaft-1 and Main Shaft-2 had been completely destroyed. Almost everyone who had remained above ground was dead. And so it went.

Yes, almost everybody was dead; the control room was a bloody shambles. Jane Fox and Rodriguez had been transformed into ghouls, but reasonable chatty ghouls, not violent, like most of the ghouls, and not childlike, like Jimmy; but they were damned lascivious ghouls and couldn't keep their claws and tongues off each other, slurping, licking, mooning, kissing; and then Rodriguez had this permanent erection, big damned erection too.

"He's been like that since the beginning," said a very sleek looking woman, an Elite Cosmos First Class, who had introduced herself as Demi Pfeiffer, "You get used to it."

"He can't help it, and it's sweet," said Jane Fox, drooling white bubbly spools of thick foam and licking Rodriguez' shoulder.

"Crikey, Hugo," Norton muttered, giving the dog a last pat, and standing up looking around. There was another hybrid, one with no collar, whose name was Claire, the one who had some sort of magic relationship with the World Mind and who had managed somehow to turn the mind-collars off – Thank the gods!

And there was a young woman, Robyn, who was a technician from some other prison camp – something called the Electric Erotic Mystic Circus, which Norton had never heard of – and who had hooked the Claire Hybrid up to the World Mind and who was apparently an expert in physically removing the mind-collars. Well, she could remove them all, as far as Norton was concerned; and the sooner the better, before the blasted things went back on again. And then there was a young woman in an Elite Centurion uniform, Kat, who seemed to be a special friend of V's, and another, in a sleek guerrilla warrior skinsuit, a girl called Billie McAdams, apparently a refugee from the thing they called The Boy. Quite a crew!

Hugo barked.

"Well, let's see ..." V was standing beside Norton in the middle of the blood and gore smeared Control Room.

Claire and Robyn were still fiddling with the computer link-ups to the world mind. "We've lost connection," said Claire.

"Yes, nothing works anymore, Hybrid. I'm sorry," said Robyn.

"I should have prevented this," Norton said, "I knew Hilly was going crazy, but I didn't know how ..."

"You couldn't have prevented it, sir," said Rodriguez, slurping back some goo. "It was irresistible. Hilly was not the only one to go crazy. They were all going to go mad."

"So what do we do now?" said the Centurion, Kat, looking around, her wraparounds tilted up. The light from the smashed window sculpted her face. Looking around, she smiled.

"Damn, this Kat is a handsome woman," thought Norton; "if I were a decade younger ..."

The smoking ruins of Camp Terminus were not safe from the zombie-bats, and each hour might bring new dangers.

"The sooner we leave, the better," V said.

"So, where do we go?" Norton looked haggard, but still tough, unshaven now, pale, with creases in his face where there hadn't been creases twenty-four hours earlier. "We have almost 30 people, what with hybrids, and ex-prisoners, and guards, and ..." He glanced at Jimmy Ghoul Rahv, who was playing a card game with Gloria, "... and we have ghouls. The hybrids are okay, and most of the guards, but the prisoners can hardly walk. The closest Cosmos Citadel is more than 300 kilometers away and even if we got there ..." He glanced at V.

"Yes," V said, "even if it still exists, and even if we got there, the Cosmos garrison might not be very welcoming to a three busload caravan of hybrids and ghouls and prisoners ..."

"No, that's right. Besides, I'd probably be shot."

"Yes."

"As a traitor." Norton grinned and wiped his forehead.

"There is a place, and it's only two days drive, even less," V said, "Kat and I are headed there in any case."

"What is that, then?

"A mutant nest, more like a kingdom, it's underground, and very large; they know how to defend themselves from those zombie-bat things and their ruler – well, their chief – is a friend of mine, of ours," V added, glancing at Kat.

Kat nodded, "We'll be welcome, no doubt about it."

"Well, then …" said Norton.

Jane Ghoul, who was still the camp doctor, declared the people would need sunscreen, particularly sunscreen for kids and prisoners. And so, even in her new condition as a ghoul, she oversaw the infirmary and gave people the sunscreen injects and spray-on creams as a backup. She also gave people a wide-spectrum antiviral, against the ghoul disease, just in case, though she guessed most of the prisoners – and probably most of the guards – were immune from long exposure.

"I think if we haven't got it now," said Ms. Agnes, "we probably won't get it – the children have been exposed, over and over again."

"Still …" slurped Jane Ghoul.

"Yes, you are right. Give it to them," said Ms. Agnes, "better to be safe!"

"Right," said Jane Ghoul, "better to be safe than sorry," and, as she turned, she caught just a glimpse of her own ghoulish reflection in the shiny metal of the infirmary fridge: oh, the horror! But then, there was the consolation of Rodriguez, always in rut, always ready, and of her own heightened desire, pure unlimited unending edgy randiness, a mixed blessing, of course, but …

"Are we happy, Jane?" said Charlie, bobbing up and down.

"Yes, Charlie, we are happy," Jane slurped, yummy, yummy.

"Are we happy, Ms. Agnes?"

"Yes, Charlie," Ms. Agnes smiled at Charlie, "Yes, we are happy." Ms. Agnes noticed that, since the Golden Hybrid Eve had been giving her massages, very gentle massages, she had been feeling much more spy, and her hair, at the roots, was turning black, and – now she really couldn't believe this – but her gums had firmed up, and, hard to credit, but it seemed new teeth might just be growing back. *Like a child I am*, she murmured, *growing new teeth!*

Norton had gathered all the vehicles of Camp Terminus together, and he and the guards and hybrids had bundled all people – Jake, and Gloria and Ms. Agnes foremost among them – and in a few minutes, they would be off.

Demi Pfeiffer, Claire, and Robyn would remain behind with some hybrids and some of the weaker humans – and then follow in the vertijet. Robyn would remove all of the mind-collars; some of the operations were more complicated than others.

All was ready for the departure. It was night, but they must go. They must leave behind the ruins of Camp Terminus.

V was perched on the Centurion motorbike and watched as Kat sat astride another bike. "This is merely the thin veil of being," said Cassandra, crouching on the flatbed of a Desert Bug, and looking down at V, "It may all cease and dissolve and be nothing, all having perished, and not a rack will be left behind, unless …"

"Unless …?"

"All will perish unless you, V, win your war with the Evil One."

"I will win," said V, looking up at Cassandra, "We will win."

"Good, good," said Cassandra, scuttling back into the covered part of the Desert Bug.

V glanced at Kat, who was talking to that intriguing young woman and recruit, Billie McAdams …

"I'll take her, Kat."

"Yes, I see, you want to know what she knows," said Kat, smiling her bright smile, her wraparounds tilted up over her forehead. The moonlight shone silver on Kat's face and teeth.

"Yes …"

"We will go in the vanguard."

"Norton and three hybrids with guns will be in the rear-guard."

"And the guards will drive, and hybrids operate the guns."

"Valerie Joffre can look after Ms. Agnes and the children – and the ghouls."

"Don't forget Charlie," said Kat.

"No, he has adopted Gloria, it seems."

And so in the cloud of dust, with a line of Desert Bugs and a few motorbikes strung out behind and in front of them, they set off.

V felt Billie's arms around her waist, and Billie's head pressed tight against her back, and they drove at the head of the column.

"So, young Billie, tell me, tell me about you – and about the Boy."

And Billie, transmitting her thoughts, told her story.

Billie said, "Is this boring for you?"

"No, not at all," V was beginning to understand the Boy. He fed on people's need for faith and need for love, and also on their need to shore up their sense of themselves, their sense of their identity, and the identity – and status – of their tribe, by hating and focusing their hate on someone else – a scapegoat, an outcast, an apostate, or the members of another tribe or race or nation. The Boy pretended to be Love, but, in reality, he was Hate. The Boy had invaded the World Mind and kidnapped all its power. And now, the Boy was headed to Elysium, to destroy the center and capital of what was left of humanity, the last citadel of the Imperial Reign of Cosmos.

Billie Jo McAdams leaned her head against V's back and spoke, mind-to-mind, "You have lived for centuries, and so you know all things – or at least many things – and you have drunk the blood of the wicked and sometimes of the good, so you have shared in the feasts and abominations of their souls, and this has given you wisdom. You should be sad, tortured by all you have seen and heard, but you don't seem to be tortured."

"I'm not tortured, strangely," said V, "I am incurably superficial and optimistic. Surfaces are sometimes as deep as you want to go. And yet …" V was thinking that, though she delighted in surfaces, in the infinitely variegated colors and shades of life, of rain, of leaves and trees, of clouds, of the sunlight playing on dunes of sand or on the skyscrapers of great cities, and delighted in the dialects and languages of humanity, the nuances of thought and concept and behavior, the ingenious gadgets and mechanisms, the extraordinary discoveries of the sciences, the paintings, the music, the theater, the literature, she was still, if she were honest, fascinated by "deep" speculation, cosmology and history and theology and …

"I think that underneath everything, there is nothing," said Billie, tightening her grip on V's waist.

"Ah, so, my dear Billie, you are a mystic, a metaphysician," said V, feeling the warm embrace of the young woman; Billie was pure of heart, and pure of soul. She was also a warrior, and now she was a hybrid, she need fear nothing.

"I admit I have no idea of what I mean by what I say," Billie sighed, "Words just seem to come to me from nowhere – and ideas …"

The caravan stopped on a ridge and those who could, dismounted from the vehicles. It was a limestone outcropping that looked over a valley that had once contained a river. The cliff sides were steep. High in the sky zombie-bats circled, tiny black arrows under the moon, but they did not attack.

V, Norton, and Valerie Joffre crouched down on the edge of the cliff and looked. "The best way through is over there, I think," said V.

Valerie said, "Yes, we should shift about a kilometer along the ridge; if the implant map is right, there is a road that goes down, and across and then up the other side – it will be less bumpy for the passengers."

V followed Valerie's glance; yes, she saw it, a silver ribbon in the moon-light, winding across the floor of the arroyo, and then winding up the far side.

"Let's go then."

Toward dawn, a swirl of zombie-bats attacked. The Desert bugs were equipped with machine guns and laser guns, and after a dozen bats had been killed, the others flew higher into the sky.

"They are not really trying," said Ms. Agnes.

"No, they are waiting for a bigger battle, and bigger prey," said Valerie Joffre.

"What prey?"

"Elysium City – humanity itself – this planet," Valerie indicated with a sweep of her arm the horizon, the sand dunes, the rocky outcroppings, and the rising sun. Valerie had guessed, after listening to V, that the final battle for humanity was about to begin.

"Are we safe, Professor Joffre?" Charlie, Doctor Jane Ghoul's robot, was sitting next to Gloria, who was blinking with fatigue.

"For the moment, Charlie, I think we are safe," said Valerie Joffre, looking up toward the sky where dawn – the sun's rays – had just touched a few of the zombie-bats. They burst into flame and rocketed to earth.

"Look at that, Jake, oh, look."

"They are the damned, the poor souls," Ms. Agnes wiped away a tear and put her arm around Gloria. Gloria leaned her head against Ms. Agnes and closed her eyes.

"She's exhausted, poor dear," said Ms. Agnes, caressing Gloria's shorn head and looking at Jake.

"It's been a long day and night." Valerie watched the zombie-bats light up, explode, and burn. Once they had been human, and now they were … what exactly? What exactly were they?

Jake leaned out the door of the Desert Bug and staring up at the sky, staring at the wheeling zombie-bats. "They are amazing things, what created such things? I never read about such things." He turned to Valerie; she was a Cosmos First Class, one of the rulers of the universe, she was also a scientist, she should know everything there was to know.

Valerie, who, up until five minutes ago, had been operating a machine gun, said, "I've never seen such things before, Jake, they are new. They are certainly diabolic, but what could change people into such … such monsters, I have no idea. If I believed in the Devil, I would bet the Devil made them."

The other zombie-bats skimmed away, below the line of light, screaming and making mournful cawing sounds, and all the zombie-bats disappeared, low over the horizon.

The caravan drove along the ruins of a highway, its asphalt was doubled up and broken by the heat and drifts of sand crossed the road, and telephone wires from ancient times hung free and drifted in the wind, some of the drifts were mere ripples, others were veritable walls of sand, and the motorbikes and Desert Bugs had to go round them, or make a special effort, slowing down, changing gears, and climbing laboriously up over them.

They passed an ancient grain silo.

They passed a small mall in the middle of nowhere.

Jake was curious about everything.

Gloria kept learning new words. "New words are needed for all these new things, Jake," she said, "Silo, barn, road, asphalt, cloud, dawn …"

"Yes, Gloria," Jake smiled. This was truly an adventure. A lifetime would not suffice to learn all the things there were to learn.

Just before nightfall, they stopped the Desert Bugs for just a half an hour and then they kept going. It was better to be a moving target.

Guards and hybrids rode shotgun, and Jake was awake, close to Valerie and to two hybrids, watching the skies.

"We are taking a trip, aren't we, Professor?" Charlie's bright eyes focused on the geologist.

"Yes, Charlie, we are on the road," Valerie patted the bio-robot on the head, and picked up the light machine gun, just in case.

It was exciting, Jake thought, to be out in this vast world. The air which always smelled different almost made him dizzy. He wondered if it was like being drunk; he'd heard about being drunk. When he looked upwards at the stars and the moon in the utter bright blackness of the heavens, he felt like he was falling, falling into empty space, and that he would never stop falling. He gripped the Desert Bug railing and held on for dear life.

Valerie glanced at him. "Your knuckles are white, Jake," she said, smiling. Jake thought that part of him was in love with Valerie Joffre; after all, he had helped save her life, hadn't he? She now belonged to him, partly to him, at any rate. And she was a Cosmos, that semi-mythical ruling race of creatures that were so glorious they were hardly human.

"You already have lots of women in your life," Valerie Joffre said, motioning with her chin toward Ms. Agnes and Gloria who were collapsed against each other, sleeping, Ms. Agnes snoring slightly and a sliver of saliva glistening on her lips – fuller lips now, and brighter eyes, Valerie noted, since Eve had begun her ministrations – and Ms. Agnes and Gloria jostled against each other and against their seat belts from the movement of the big Desert Bug as it climbed over dunes and ripples of sand and stretches of broken and fractured asphalt.

Jake looked down, feeling more embarrassed than perhaps he'd ever felt. "What does a geologist do?" He asked, hoping to change the subject.

"Oh, Jake," Valerie's smile shone like the sun, "I think you are a marvelous young man, and you and I are going to be real friends. After all, you did save my life, you and your hybrid friend, the divine V. So I am your friend forever, Jake, absolutely. You asked, what does a geologist do? Well, Jake, when the world first began to form out of cosmic dust and rubble …"

At one point, after a brief skirmish with some zombie-bats, V stopped the bike, got off, stretched, and said to Billie, "I'm going to morph. It's easier to fight that way, and safer."

And so she stripped, carefully packed her uniform and clothes, morphed into reptilian form, and then hopped back on the bike.

"Will I change like that?" Billie settled herself on the bike.

"Probably. Soon, I should think."

"You know," said Billie, "We do live in a world of wonders."

"Indeed, we do." V jumped back on, and gunned the bike, and in a few moments, they had caught up with the caravan on its voyage toward the Kingdom of the Mutants.

Back in the ruins of Camp Terminus, two hybrids with machine guns stood guard over the vertijet while Demi Pfeiffer refueled it and made sure everything was ready.

Robyn had set up a mobile workshop and was busy disarming the mind-collars and removing them. Three remaining hybrids sat around, as if waiting in the dentist's office.

"We are ready for takeoff," said Demi Pfeiffer.

"Just a minute, I'll finish Helen, here …"

The plane lifted off just as dawn was breaking. It was full to capacity, including Hugo, his favorite lady cat, and her kittens, a rather standoffish tomcat, who seemed to be the father of the litter, though Hugo had his doubts about the fellow's suitability as a father, and two recently discovered survivors of Hugo's dog team, who had been hiding from the zombie-bats.

"We will wing our way toward the mutant kingdom," said Claire.

"It sounds very exotic," said Demi, "This has been an interesting week; it is too bad Emerson Caldwell III isn't here to see this; he was curious about things, and he was very intelligent, in spite of everything." She glanced at Claire.

Claire smiled.

"So off we go …"

"We will get there before the others," said Demi, "or about the same time."

Then as they rose into the air, there was a huge rumbling sound and the whole of the earth seemed to lift up, the ruins of the two pitheads, the other buildings, and the earth itself, everything rose, and fire flashed out of the ground and the whole of Camp Terminus collapsed in on itself, a vast explosion rippling outward with a cloud of dust.

The shockwave hit the vertijet and made it tremble.

"Oh," said Robyn.

"It is gone," said one of the humans, a skeletal man with a wispy beard, a Mr. Swann, "It is gone."

"Yes," said Hybrid Claire, "It is dead, truly dead, and it will never rise again."

Hugo thought he should perhaps bark, but, busy looking after his little flock, he decided not to.

And so they flew on, over what was once the Heartland of America.

And it was now the unpeopled Dead Land, or almost …

CHAPTER 23 – MIRANDA

Princess Miranda Hughes stood outside the Great Door, the entrance to the Mutant Kingdom, waiting for the refugees to arrive. A courier, on a Desert Bike, had come with the news: Camp Terminus had fallen. The humans and hybrids were free. But they needed shelter, and food, and water.

Down below, cymbals clashed, horns blared, and drums beat – it was one more of their ceremonies, honoring her mother – that is, honoring Nikki, Nikki who – in spite of being a goddess – seemed to be taking it in stride, with cool good-humor, with the unflappable equanimity of a SIN or of a Cosmos. Nikki was, truly, whatever her origins, an Elite Cosmos of the highest and best quality.

Yes, her mother, Nikki, had not changed. Right now, Miranda was sure, Nikki was – as she always had been– eminently practical – organizing things, preparing for the arrival of the refugees, allocating supplies, consulting every-body, distributing tasks, consulting with the Great High Priest and the elders – determining whether they had the right kind of food and where everybody would sleep, and …

Yes, Nikki is herself. SIN or not, she is just as she has always been.

But I have changed, Miranda thought, I certainly have changed. Now I know: I am not a Cosmos; I am not even human: I am a SIN, the daughter of a SIN, and so I am a SIN.

She kicked at a pebble and frowned. But I am a Cosmos too – what a strange division has opened up inside me, I am me and not me, human and not human, Cosmos and not-Cosmos. I am divided against myself. Where do my loyalties lie?

It is confusing; like being drunk.

And I am unhappy, perhaps more unhappy than I have ever been in my whole life.

"Princess, are you happy?" One of the Bear guards said. The setting sun glinted off his helmet and his large brown eyes.

"Yes, Hans, I am happy." Miranda forced herself to smile, but, she thought, I am lying, I am telling a total lie.

"Your prince makes you happy?"

"Yes," Miranda's smile became even more wistful, "My prince makes me happy."

Prince Caliban, who was standing on the point of the ridge, came trotting back, little swirls of dust stirring up at his heels, his dark skin glowing, and the sun glinting off his machete holster, his machine gun, and his fluttering regal loincloth.

"My love," he said, and took her in his arms, and he kissed her, and she felt that she wanted to return the kiss with all the fire that rose within her, but she could not, for now, she feared something greater than anything else.

Caliban drew back and looked at her, surprised by the coolness and reserve of her kiss.

"What is wrong, my princess?"

"Nothing, my dearest, nothing," she sighed and tried to smile.

Caliban frowned.

Miranda feared her own passion and love, and where it might lead her, and where it might lead Caliban. She feared the consequences of what the Great High Priest had, with a worried look, confided to her two hours before: That he, the Great High Priest, knew something, something that for Miranda was absolutely dreadful. It was worse than death:

"Now, I am finally certain, Princess, and I thought you should know," the Great High Priest began, stroking his beard, turning his blind face to her, then, abashed, turning away.

"What should I know, Oh, Great High Priest?"

"There is something which, I think, I fear, is the case," he said. He looked very unhappy, "I fear, verily, that it is the case."

"Well, Great High Priest, out with it," Miranda said. She realized that she was still, even in this strange upside down world, truly a Cosmos First Class, part of the World Cosmos Elite. *Even if I am a SIN, as it turns out, but I, who have received, not once but twice, a Cosmos Youth Medal from the President, the Leader himself, I really cannot put up with such procrastination, with such pussy-footing, with such beating around the bush, and ...*

Miranda always required the executive summary. In fact, once or twice, Nikki had remarked on it: "You should let people come to their own conclusions in their own time, Miranda. Sometimes people have reasons for being indirect or cautious or slow. And sometimes people need to think out loud – they have to grope their way toward what they want to say."

"Harrumph," Miranda had answered, and Nikki had just smiled, "Be charitable, Miranda. Not everyone is as quick as you are."

"I suspect ..." the Great High Priest said, and his blind eyes looked away, and his moist nostrils twitched, and his eyes watered.

Oh, this was infuriating! Miranda almost poked him in his furry tummy: *Come on, Come on – tell me!*

"I suspect, you know, that Caliban, who is so perfect, so that when I adopted him, you know, he had been kidnapped and was going to be sold into slavery, you know; and he was just a tiny boy, with that strange mark on his shoulder, which became, as he grew, the winged dragon tattoo, it truly blossomed out, bright now as it is, and a very beautiful thing too, and when we saved him, and I adopted him, well, I suspected then ..." He stopped. "I am not boring you, am I, Princess?"

"No, no, Great High Priest, I am all ears, tell me! Do tell me! Anything that concerns Caliban concerns me!"

"Well, Princess, now there is a reason I am telling you this first, and I do not want to upset the divine ..." The Great High Priest hesitated. He was on very intimate terms with the Divinity, but he hesitated, even now, to pronounce her name.

"You don't want to upset mother, you don't want to upset Nikki!" Miranda gave the Great High Priest her most glorious smile. "You will have noticed, Great High Priest, that Nikki is not easily upset."

"Yes, most true, Princess, and you, Princess, have inherited all of her equanimity."

"Thank you, thank you, Great High Priest, and you were saying ...?" Miranda kept her smile focused. *No, I haven't inherited anything like Nikki's equanimity, I am a thousand times less patient than Nikki, but right now I am exercising the patience of a saint!*

"Yes, I was saying." He stroked his chin, caressing the wispy pointed beard, "Well, Princess, the thing is this, to put it bluntly, and not to indulge in unnecessary euphemism or otiose indirection: I believe that Caliban is Goddess Nikki's son."

"What?" Miranda tried to absorb this.

"I have great sensitivity, Princess, to the olfactory qualities of SINs, and ..."

"What?" Miranda was beginning to understand the implications ... of what the Great High Priest was saying; it could not be, oh, no, no, no ...

"Caliban is Nikki's son."

"What? That cannot be, Oh, Great High Priest, tell me it is not so ...!" As the full import of this new situation sank in, Miranda's heart fell into a bottomless pit. The world seemed to darken; she feared she would go blind; she felt dizzy, the vertigo of emptiness, the horror of ...

The Great High Priest shook his head, "There is no doubt; there is no doubt about it all. Caliban is half-human, half-SIN; he is without the slightest doubt the son of Goddess Nikki; it is certain, Princess, as certain as I am standing here before you."

The bottom fell out of Miranda's world.

"But, you, on the other hand, Princess ..." and the Great High Priest began to say something but then a messenger came: there was a ruckus the Great High Priest had to mediate in – Scav had caused trouble with some females – and the Great High Priest said, "You will excuse me, Princess."

"Yes, yes, of course ..." Miranda felt all the blood drain from her face, her hands, her arms, and her legs. She felt she might just collapse. She reached out, leaned against a ledge of stone.

"We shall speak of this again, Princess," said the Great High Priest, as he was hurried away.

"Yes, yes, of course ..." Miranda was hardly listening. Her whole world disintegrated – a collapsing tent, an imploding star. She was sick at heart. Sounds were far away. Mutants walked by and saluted her, but it was as if they were on another planet, darkly glimpsed through a thick wall of sound-proof glass. *Caliban is my brother!*

They saluted her and bowed, but she only stared, her lips, mutely acknowledging their homage, her eyes glazed. Her mind spun into utter desolation and darkness.

Caliban is my brother!

Incest was forbidden by all the laws.

And yet ...

And Caliban ...

And me, and me ... Oh, no, what can I do, what can I do? She walked around in a daze.

And now Caliban was hurrying toward her.

And he looked so beautiful!

My lover – my brother!

Oh, what am I going to do?

His teeth shone, and his skin glowed.

He kissed her.

Her coolness again surprised him.

"What is wrong, my Princess?"

"Nothing, nothing, my darling, just some dust in my eyes."

"Ah," said Caliban, then he turned and pointed, "I saw them," he said, "The refugees are on the way, with Kat and V and the others."

"Oh, yes, my love, yes, Caliban, we must prepare for them," Miranda said, the tears on her cheeks already dried, hiding her distress, and putting as brave a face on it as she could – she might be a SIN, or half-SIN, but she was a Cosmos First Class Youth Cosmos Medal Winner, awarded by the Glorious Leader himself, she was, in her inner core, Cosmos, first, last, and always. "Yes, let us prepare for them," she repeated, thinking, yes, I will tell him, I will screw up my courage and tell him, but I cannot tell him now. I'll tell him later. Will he hate me? Will he … reject me? Oh, how horrible, not to be able to love my love as I would love him and have him love me! Oh, why, oh, why was I ever born?

It was late afternoon – the sun was low in the cloudless desert sky.

Preparations went on for the dusty horde. They would need food, clothes, baths, and disinfectant in some cases, and medical care and shelter.

And so the caravan came, and a vertijet too, with creatures disheveled and shrunken, arriving in clouds of dust, the Desert Bugs, the motorbikes, and the last bit, the stragglers, a few hybrids on foot – after several vehicles broke down – tramping over the sand and stones, and finally coming up the steep path that led to the Great Gate, humans who seemed to wither in the light, ghouls who slurped and slunk along, tongues hanging out, hybrids who sparkled proudly in the light of the sinking sun. And there were guards too, who, with the hybrids, seemed to be acting as a team and as the leaders of the throng – though the true leader was, incontestably, V, the reptilian hybrid, with at her side a man, Colonel Norton, a Cosmos First Class, who spoke with an Australian accent.

There were ghouls that could speak – one called Doctor Jane Ghoul, another called Rodriguez Ghoul, and one rather childlike ghoul called Jimmy Ghoul.

Miranda took efficient notes and registered them all.

Preparations had to be made to receive them, every single creature, and to house them in the great cavern of the mutants.

There were even children, two youngsters, a girl called Gloria and a boy whose name was Jake.

The initial welcoming feast had been prepared up above, on the ledge in front of the great door. Then, before dusk, everyone would retreat into the great cavern where defenses had been prepared against the zombie-bats.

"Hey, come on, over here, there is food over here."

"Come and get it! Come and get the soup."

"Mushroom pies, mushroom pies, right over here!"

"Here is water, fresh water, water to drink!"

The Terminus guards and hybrids were busy consulting with the Bear guards and Caliban on the defense system for the Cavern.

Nikki – accompanied by the Great High Priest and by Tara Capricorn – moved among the crowd like a Queen – or like the Goddess she indubitably was.

It was strange. As Miranda watched Nikki, and knowing that Nikki was a SIN, and recoiling at first from that knowledge, Miranda now felt even more love for her mother, seeing Nikki so regal, so beautiful, speaking to all the creatures, learning about their wants, their fears. Nikki was now kneeling, in the rising dust and the glare of light, next to a skinny old lady with wild white hair, then she was crouched next to a woman – a creature – who must have leprosy, and then she was talking to the two children and to a glittering golden hybrid that was standing next to them. She's my mother, and she's not even human. Miranda shivered with a strange mixture of awe and fear and despair – *Oh, Caliban! My brother, my love, my impossible, forbidden love!*

She tried to keep herself busy.

She ladled soup; she cut up mushroom bread; she stirred lichen salads, she brewed mushroom tea and even contraband coffee, and everywhere, now, next to her was Caliban, serving everyone, being gallant to every creature large and small.

"Your mother is so beautiful," Caliban said at one point, nodding toward Nikki, who was talking to Cassandra the Leper Woman.

It almost made Miranda cry out in pain: he doesn't know, oh, he doesn't know; my dearest most lovely Caliban doesn't know. And she said, "Yes, she is, she's good, and she's beautiful."

"You are a Queen," said Gloria, wide-eyed, "and a Goddess."

"People think I am," said Nikki.

"Thinking will make it so, said Ms. Agnes.

"Yes," said Nikki, laughing, "you are right about that!"

"It is the fulfillment of the prophecy," said Cassandra the Leper Woman, "A Goddess shall come among us."

"I'm not the only candidate, as you know, Cassandra, and in fact, I am not the one who has come," said Nikki, "there is one much more worthy than I. I am only – how shall I put it? – I am only her handmaiden."

The moon was up. The dangerous time had come. For darkness was the time the zombie-bats took flight.

The refugees – including a very friendly dog called Hugo and his animal crew of cats and dogs – had all been taken into the cavern and housed in tents and side caverns and niches and special shelters.

Guards, humans, mutants, hybrids, and even ghouls, were posted at all the weak points, carrying weapons of all kinds. Torches and sling-shots had been prepared below. Norton, accompanied by Hugo, was busy coordinating efforts with the Great High Priest and with Goddess Nikki.

Everyone waited.

Caliban, like the general he had become, was touring the defenses, with the boy Jake who seemed to have adopted him, or was it Caliban who had adopted Jake.

Scav hopped along beside them, "He is the big man, Jake, the Big Deputy Boss," Scav was explaining to Jake.

"Don't listen to him, Jake," said Caliban, "I'm just a pirate."

"He's also Tarzan," said Scav, jumping up and down, "Ask him! Ask him!"

"Who is Tarzan?" said Jake, "And are you really this Tarzan?"

"I'm only Tarzan in my spare time, Jake," said Caliban, "Truly, I am a pirate!"

Miranda was alone on the ramparts, just outside the Main Gate. From a discreet distance, two of the warrior bears watched over her. She wanted to play out her melancholy below the moon, alone, under the empty dark sky and constellations. She had been so happy – and now, now, now …

Her destiny, she thought, could not be more tragic!

Then V, the Hybrid Queen, who had been out surveying the Kingdom's outer defenses, came along the path, the moonlight skittering in bright points, dancing on her scales. She noticed, and she felt, Miranda's pain.

"Well, Cosmos Child, what troubles you?" The voice came from behind Miranda, in the shadows of the rampart. Miranda turned and saw that it was truly the Queen of the Hybrids, V, shining, her scales glittering, iridescent, in the shadows, a true Queen and Goddess, like Nikki, "Well, Cosmos Child?"

"Don't call me that!"

"Oh, I see, we are being sensitive, are we," the hybrid stepped out of the shadows and smiled; her turquoise and gold scales seemed even more brilliant than usual, like the shimmering moonlit raiment of a goddess, "Let me change into human form, Miranda, perhaps that will make this easier."

"Make what easier?"

"Our little talk," said the hybrid. The warrior bears had moved away to give Princess Miranda and the Hybrid Queen their privacy.

"What little talk? What have we to talk about?" Miranda, usually so courteous, was in no mood for chitchat, even poetically lit moonlight chitchat; her whole world had just collapsed; her love for Caliban had become impossible – a thing unclean, unthinkable – *Oh, I am so desperately unhappy.* She had lost the love of her life and here this … this … this Hybrid Goddess … wanted to shoot the breeze and prattle away. Oh, it was intolerable! *I want to scream!*

"You will find it enlightening, I think," said the hybrid, and she turned away, rummaged in her backpack and brought out clothes which she unfolded and then she turned back to Miranda, and asked, "Do you want to watch?"

"Watch what?" Miranda pouted, crossing her arms across her chest, sticking out her lower lip, and looking down. She was in a first-class, super-strong pouting mood! She was awesomely pissed off, oh, so totally pissed off! After all, her whole world had just been destroyed, several times over; she had been a Cosmos First Class – who hated and despised SINs – and now she discovered she was a SIN, and that her mother, Nikki, whom she loved desperately, was a SIN, so her mother was one of the sworn saboteurs and enemies of the Empire of Cosmos which Miranda, as a perfect Cosmos, worshiped with religious fervor. Even worse: she was madly in love with Caliban, and he with her, and now she discovered that Caliban was her *brother*, her *brother SIN!* Ugh! Incest! Ugh! Incest between SINs! It made her shiver with horror! She didn't think she'd ever find the courage to tell Caliban. Already he was wondering why she had become so cool toward him, turning her cheek to receive his kiss, not offering as before her lips – and her laughter. No, there would be no more laughter, no more laughter for Miranda Hughes! Oh, nobody has suffered like I have suffered! Woe is me, woe, woe – and once again, woe!

"Watch me morph," said V.

"Morph …?" Miranda said – stupidly, she had to admit, "Morph what? Morph, where?"

"Morph from reptile to human," said V; her fangs and eyes glowed even brighter.

"Okay, go ahead, I'll watch, if you really want me to."

"I do want you to watch."

"Okay."

"It will be good for you."

"Okay, go, then go, do it," Miranda stared at the creature who was for some reason being positively pedantic about this morphing thing, but who, Miranda had to admit, was truly beautiful in a sort of awe-inspiring way, and she certainly was very nice, too, if such a creature as a hybrid could be nice, and civilized too, which was really surprising, since hybrids were totally savage, but why she had happened along at this particular moment to bother Miranda when Miranda was in the depths of despair was –

"Okay, here goes, abracadabra, presto, puff!" There was a blur, and the hybrid dissolved, and a woman was standing there, with short, jet-black hair, pale skin, beautiful, she was divinely beautiful – and familiar. The woman began to pull on her underwear, then jeans, then a T-shirt, and then she sat down on the rock ledge and put on sandals which she buckled up. "There," she said, "So, this is the other me – the human me."

"You look like my mother," Miranda said, thinking that, yes, there were similarities between Nikki and V.

"Yes, I do look like your mother," said V.

"I'm so, so, so awfully unhappy," said Miranda.

"And why, my dear child, are you so, so, so awfully unhappy?"

"Because Caliban is Nikki's son and so …"

"Yes, he is Nikki's son."

"You knew?"

"I just found out. Nikki suspected, but she wasn't sure; she hoped against hope; in fact, she didn't even dare hope; but now she is sure: Caliban is her son."

"Oh, my God," Miranda positively wailed, "Oh, my God! How tragic, do you realize how tragic this is, Hybrid, I mean, V, do you realize? This is world-shattering, this is awful!"

"Why is it so tragic?"

"Because, because, because ... If Caliban is Nikki's son, then I am Caliban's sister, and that means that our inspired love, our, oh, most passionate and unlimited and divine love for each other ..."

V held up a hand, "That was precisely what I wished to discuss with you, Miranda. Your mother, I mean, Nikki, and I thought it was time you should know some of the facts of life, and I mean, well, I ..." The hybrid turned away. Her eyes were wet. The dusky light her up in profile. Yes, Miranda thought, the hybrid was beautiful, painfully beautiful. "Perhaps, Miranda, I should tell you a story; it may help you resolve your dilemma."

Miranda frowned, ready to sulk, but then she thought, no, I am a Cosmos First Class, even if I am a SIN, so I must demonstrate patience, understanding, and even stoicism. "I mean, yes, no, I mean, what in the world, I mean, okay, yes, tell me a story, I mean, if it makes you happy, go ahead, Hybrid, go ahead, V, tell me a story."

And so it was that V the vampire and half alien and Phoenician from Ancient Times told Miranda Hughes, Cosmos Child First Class, and Cosmos Youth Medallion Twice Times First Class from the late 22nd CE century, a story; it was not very different from other tales. It was about a fugitive hybrid, always a fugitive, even before the Great Roundup, even before the Culling, a fugitive hunted by the Cosmos Centurions and Police, and who found herself trapped in Elysium City, and who had a strange encounter in the underground or subway, or even more accurately put, in the sewers and canals that lay deep under Elysium City. In telling her tale, V did synthesize the story; she cut and trimmed and even censored; she didn't tell the whole story, and she didn't burden Miranda with excessive detail. But she did give the girl the essence of what had happened.

Now, as V told the story, as V stood up and walked up and down, and as Miranda asked questions, Miranda pouted and frowned and sometimes laughed. And as she told the story, V went back in her thoughts and memories to the way it had happened and she relived it as if it were happening once again, all over again, almost fifteen years before.

"Well, Miranda, it was in Elysium City, on a night almost fifteen years ago – well, it was really very early in the morning, after midnight, perhaps two or three o'clock in the morning, after your bedtime, certainly, and I was famished, and on the run, and tingling with the fever of hunger, having not fed for weeks and weeks, was on the subway, dreaming of my next meal, a full-blooded Englishman, or perhaps a capricious, spoiled Southern belle, or a lawyer, or …"

"You drink blood? I mean, it's rumored that hybrids …"

"Yes, it's my only food – fresh from the source human blood."

"Gosh, I mean, Golly, I mean, how awful for you!"

"It is hard sometimes, Miranda, but I do get by, usually."

"Do other hybrids live like that, I mean …?"

"No, other hybrids eat whatever they want to eat. They are lucky. A varied diet is best, you know."

"Continue, Hybrid, I'm all ears!"

"So there I am, 3 am, alone, hunted, and hungry."

"Yes …" Miranda closed her eyes; yes, she could picture it: a bloodthirsty starving cannibal female hybrid, all alone in hostile territory.

"At this late hour, long after midnight, the 10-car Elysium City midtown island super express subway train is almost empty. It roars through tunnels, crosses underground rivers and canals, comes out, briefly, into the night, plunges again into the dark tunnels, heading for the tip of the island of what had once been called Manhattan, now buried deep under the floating domed glory that is Elysium City, capital of the reconstituted remnants of the United Imperial Cosmos States of America.

"I yawn from hunger. I want to howl my hunger, my desire, my yearning; I want to bay at the moon, to paw the raw earth, to yodel underneath the stars; but, down here, in the underground, there is no moon; there are no stars. I yawn, covering my mouth daintily, I hope, though there is no one there to see. Manners, Miranda, make the world go round."

"Yes, mother always says so."

"I am sitting alone, then …

The young man gets on at the Max Bachman station. He glances around. The car is empty except for an old man and a young woman; the young woman is me, in my human form, of course. I am sitting, quite erect, ramrod backbone, on one side of the car, far from the old man. The young man makes his choice. He sits down, right beside the young woman that is me: he thinks – if only, if only this woman …

The young man's heart stops.

And I can feel it; I can see his thoughts.

This young woman that is me is, for him, a vision – as if his whole life were leading him to this moment, to this encounter.

At the next station, the old man gets off; no one gets on.

The young man and I are alone.

The young woman – me – is wearing a fine dark retro antique Armani jacket, a dark pleated skirt, high heels, and dark stockings; she is very pale, this young woman, the pupil and iris of her eyes, hidden by dark glasses, are dark, almost pure black, though he cannot see her eyes, the young man imagines them, he cannot resist imagining them – large, soulful, sensual, worshipful, all-forgiving eyes; a gateway to passion, love, and terrestrial paradise. From the way I am dressed, he concludes I must be a full citizen: This woman, he thinks, must be a Cosmos First Class, one of the elite, one of the rulers, the Cosmos whom everyone loves to hate; strange that she should be in this subway car deep under Elysium in the dead of night. It must be destiny, which is written in the stars, Venus being coy in this year 2142 with Mars, Jupiter astray, and …

The young woman is reading his thoughts, and she is thinking:

My dear young fellow, you don't know who I am. Here I am, sitting beside you, and you have no idea who or what I am. You seem like a nice young man. And, since you sat down, two minutes ago, you have been casting sneaky sheepish sidelong glances at me. You are timid.

She foresees it all with pitiless clarity, thinking: Yes, when we enter the next tunnel, you are going to say something – you have as yet no idea what – you want to make an approach, under the cover of darkness. But I already know who you are, Hector Cramer: you are a bio-designer for a knock-off illegal bio-robot company out in the Elysium Burbs – for I have begun to probe your mind – very superficial probes, but enough to elicit your name. The problem is, my dear young friend, I am rather hungry, in fact, I am starving, famished, and now it's dangerous, for here we go, into the tunnel. I must feed! Otherwise, I may faint, which would be untoward, and, in fact, dangerous, perhaps suicidal – potentially fatal for me. In the tunnel, you lay your hand upon my thigh, on the silk-like stocking, for the skirt is short, and you lean toward me and I smell your breath – a slight tang of peppermint – and you say:

"I am hot for you."

"Oh?"

"You are beautiful."

"And you – you are very kind."

"You are the woman I have always dreamed of," you say this in a rush, the words tumbling out, so fast they almost choke over each other, and you let your hand push – as if it had a mind of its own – up the inner side of my thigh, along the warm damp nervous curved inward smoothness and I can feel that your hand is thinking – anticipating – the moment when it can pull gently, then violently rip, at the panties it will find there, and then your hand will, your fingers will …

We are alone in the car; as we both know. The last person – that old man who was scratching his chin and nodding off reading the Elysium Chronicle on a Z-Pad, got off at the last station. The tunnel is long, so there is time, some time, and, as I have already said – the thought is obsessive, I admit – I am starving, I am weak and almost hysterical with hunger and so, my dear friend, my dear Hector Cramer, you are going to be my meal for this evening, and I regret it very much, and I wish to apologize and declare my chagrin in advance, because I usually only drink – after careful planning and considerable research – from the wicked, the truly wicked, the mortally sinful, and drink them dry, not the innocent; but force of circumstance and your lust have brought us together. Part of me would like to turn to you and give you a long warm, passionate, innocent kiss, well not so innocent, but not deadly either, a long fluid, warm, striving, yearning kiss is what I would like to give to you, a final gift, for I do know what lust is, blind, unreasonable, unreasoning, absolute lonely lust, I know it only too well. I know too that feeling of yearning for love, for perfection in love, for the ultimate and perfect sister soul, and I know that, buried in the lust, however crude the lust may be, buried in it is that dream – the dream of the pure and total ideal – the dream of two souls united – that drives you forward tonight, dear Hector. Lust, in its own way, is sublime: the source of all love, cathedrals have been built from lust, lust transfigured, transformed, overcome … Saints have found vocations for lust; field marshals have marshaled armies, and kings have abdicated; and …

Now!

The train rumbles under the river, the lights in the tunnel, which are dim and ghoulish, whip by, flashing dimly though the dirty, dust-spattered windows, casting shadows, turning the whole interior of the car into a ghostly pantomime. The streaming, mobile advertisements have been turned down to dim – merely fleeting sepia shadows – since this is the dead hour with few shoppers awake whose taste buds and synapses can be captured – and since electric power is becoming scarce, like everything else; the human world is running down – energy is fading – entropy is setting in.

"I'm hot, I'm hot for you!"

You are moving your hand further up my thigh, curling your fingers around slightly, down the inside of my thigh, searching for the silken dampness of excitement, my excitement awoken by you, and I say …

"I too, my love, I thirst for you!"

And I turn toward you, and I think, why not, why not give you, oh dear Hector Cramer, a little taste of pleasure, why not, and I kiss you, still with my human lips, my human teeth, my human tongue, and the kiss is very pleasant, the peppermint tang disappears, and something more silken, softer, more inviting takes its place, you truly do know how to kiss, oh, Hector Cramer, and then I withdraw slightly, and breathe, and I say …

"And now, my friend, and now …"

And your hand is still between my legs, pushing inward, upward toward its final destination, terminal station, the full and waiting, the enfolding female lips, labia, inner and outer, wet already, and I think, Oh, poor man, oh, poor Hector Cramer, how awful for you, yes, how awful for him, it will be a horrible surprise, extremely unpleasant, and I search, extending my mental antennae, unfolding my psychic tentacles, I search for some badness, some evil in you, but I don't find it, you are merely lustful, young, a minor bio-pirate in a small illegal bio-company, maker of new bacteria and bio-brick germs and bio-play-blocks, yourself an addicted night-time player of Net Games, alone in your cubicle, and you dream of yourself as a playboy, a seducer, but you have never used violence, not that I can see, so you do not merit death, no, alas, but it is too late now, my love, my saliva is rising, my appetites have been unleashed, and your fingers are probing now, pulling the panties away and down, ripping at them, your fingers are probing into the sexual heart of me, liquid excitement rising like a floodtide, cascading over me, and so …

"My friend," I whisper, my breath warm upon your lips, "I am not what I seem," and I change in an instant into my vampire self, fangs and claws at the ready, and I move my mouth away from your mouth, I move my lips and razor-sharp fangs along your jawline, and down the side of your neck to your jugular and I tickle you with my tongue – a last titillating tingle.

Oh, I cannot resist giving you a last bit of pleasure, and you sigh, and you shudder, your eyes are closed now, I tickle again and tease, nibbling at your skin, just a hint of things to come, the train is roaring on, through the tunnel, on and on and on, and so now ...

Now ...

Now I seize your arms with my claws, immobilizing you, and I plunge my fangs into your neck, you shudder and cry out and try to struggle but the narcotic of pure terror, and the narcotic injected by my fangs takes effect instantly, and you slump back ...

... You are relaxed now, Hector Cramer, and I drink and drink and drink. You shudder again, caught in pure terror, in a brief interlude of reawakened consciousness, your eyes staring straight ahead, almost bugging out of your head, and suddenly you sit straight up, your back straight, rigid, against the back of the seat, the lights outside passing flickering over your face which now shows all its angles, bony, high cheekbones, five o'clock shadow, pale mottled skin, now, you are becoming cadaverous, emptied of life.

I feel the pure joy and rush of energy when I have fed, and fed well, as your blood courses into my stomach, into my intestines, into my blood, lighting me up with incandescent energy, and I thank you, oh, I thank you, Hector Cramer, and I stand up and lower myself onto you, so I am astraddle, seated on your lap, my skirt flipped up over my waist, my panties torn to shreds, my garter belt undone, one silk stocking unhitched, and I am bending amorously over you, my darling, drinking, drinking, in pure love, until you are drained quite dry, totally dry, and you are dead, quite dead, and you will not rise again, and, still seated on your lap, blood running from my lips, I kiss you on the lips, pressing my warm lips to your cold, dry lips, the peppermint tang has returned now, and lingers on your breathless lips, with the coppery smell of blood and the ripening smell of death which consumes once living human flesh so rapidly.

Like the lilies of the field you are.

Oh, well, no more of that!

I stand up quickly and quickly pronounce the ritual words: "You are dead, Hector Cramer, quite dead, and will not rise again."

I hitch up the ruins of my panties. I smooth down my skirt. I stand and gaze at you – my splendid young man. You sit like a statue, rigid against the seat, your hand clutching at your half-opened, half-unzipped fly, the tunnel lights racing past, the sepia ad streams gushing over you like a mottled waterfall, and your eyes, gluey rings of light like the eyes of a dead fish, stare at me, reproachful, and I reach out with my vampire claws – still extended, and my fangs too, oh dear, how forgetful of me – and now they fold back into being hands again, well-manicured human hands – and I close your eyes, gently, with a gentle human touch, and I turn to look around the car and we are still racing through the underground night, but now we flash out of the tunnel and onto a bridge, we are going over another river, and the moon is shining on the rippling water far below – and glinting on the columns of half-drowned skyscrapers – and the city awaits us, and I must get off the train and hide, for I am covered in blood and I have left a fresh and bloody cadaver here as my parting gift to this train express ride and to the Metropolitan Elysium City Transport Authority.

They will not be grateful.

It will mean overtime, delays, and, I am sure, an investigation.

I go to the door, ready to step out and hopefully disappear before people realize what has happened. I am alone now, my darling Hector, though, for a while, I shall carry you with me, dear Hector. I now feel that I have known you for years, all your 27 years, and perhaps better than anyone ever knew you, even your mother. I have seen you in your playpen, I have seen you, I have even *been* you, as you first went to school, you were terrified leaving your mother and staring at all the fluttering colors of the children and their bright clothes, little bodies and faces running, faces you did not know, everything new, everything terrifying, and you wanted to wet your little pants, but, stalwart fellow that you were, you didn't, you held on, and, in high school, you then were in love with a girl who wore a red-and-black plaid skirt, a tight wide belt, and a plain white blouse and who skated at a local skating rink – was the system playing Vienna Woods? – and you sat in the school and looked out through the windows at the blue sky wishing you could be out there – in the breeze where the long grass was waving like wheat and where small white clouds were drifting through the pure blue – you were a country boy, I see – a rare species now that most of the country is dead – and then you began to grow up, and your first date, sticky nervous, sweaty hands clasped at your sides, pimples bright on your face, as befits a Burbite, and, then, raucous and rude, with your buddies, drinking beer, and then …

The train is slowing, coming into a station. I must now move quickly, I must forget you, my love! I must chase you from my thoughts, for now, I must survive.

The platform is full of people and as the platform sweeps past the windows

I see an Anti-Terrorist SWAT team standing by – watching for mutants and dissidents – and then we slow down even more, and come to a stop, and the doors open with a hiss, and I push myself out, before anyone can enter the car, and I elbow my way through the crowd, saying "Excuse me, Sorry, Thank you!" and people jostle and press against me and the electronic signs overhead give arrival times and departure times in red and green and yellow – and loudspeaker voices talk of delays and of power cuts and blackouts and of terrorist threats and security procedures – and of course high water and flood warnings – and there are police and spies and Cosmos Security personnel everywhere and then a woman screams and I hear other screams and I know they have found you, my love, my very own Hector Cramer, they have found you.

A man grabs me, his big hand, long, strong fingers wrapped tight around my arm and he says …

"You are covered in blood."

"Yes," I try to shake him loose.

He won't let go.

Avoiding his gaze, I look down, as if shocked, as if shy, and I say, "There was a killer on the train, he tried to stab me, and he killed a man, but I am okay, don't worry about me, it's not my blood."

"But, there is blood on your chin, running from your mouth."

"Oh, well, I can explain …"

Still holding me tight, he suddenly stares wide-eyed, and he shouts, "Murderer! Hybrid! Mutant! Here!"

I tear myself away from him, he is a big man, very well dressed, with a broad, open face, blond hair, a clear complexion, extremely handsome, and he looks very nice, almost too handsome, like an overpaid male model, and he is what used to be called a gentleman, a responsible citizen, I like his jacket, I like his tie, old school and mounted with a pin, and he is quite right: I was a murderer, I am a murderer.

I push my way out of the crowd.

He is following me.

I sense something else about him … Oh, yes, he is a Centurion officer, in civvies, but an officer, a Cosmos; he is part of the elite, the hunters, the trackers, the military … He is in superb physical shape, I can feel it, and he is one of the high officers, he has, too, I sense it, recently been promoted to General, even to Chief of Staff, he has superb DNA … He is a true hunter – and I am his prey. Yes, I catch a thought-fragment, a wisp of consciousness: he is a hybrid hunter, a member of the Order of Cosmos; he is my enemy!"

"Gosh," Miranda put her hand on the hybrid's arm.

"In fact, Miranda, I am the true enemy; I am the only vampire-hybrid left; the other hybrids do not need to practice vampirism; they make do with apples, oranges, hot dogs, hamburgers, and fettuccini! I wish I could too – but it is my curse, dear Miranda, to be a killer. All other hybrids are innocent – they do not carry my curse."

"Oh, poor Hybrid, poor V!" Miranda was listening, wide-eyed. The sun had long ago disappeared, only some light lingering in the sky. The Bear Bodyguards were scanning the heavens and hovering close by; the shadows now were pale moon shadows, ghosts of themselves.

"I'm not boring you?"

"No, you aren't – not at all!"

I run on to an open platform – "Express Delayed for 40 Minutes" – where the crowd thins and then, as I run farther down, there is suddenly no one, the platform is suddenly empty; and now, out in the open and revealed by the absent and the fleeing crowd, I can see the SWAT Team at the far end of the platform, light glinting off their Plexiglas shields, and they are turning slowly, toward me, their gas masks making them look like giant insects, and, tossing away my high heels, I sprint toward the tunnel entrance. In a second, they will have figured it out – and the shooting will start.

The big blond man – blond beast or blond god, the blond god of Aryan dreams, however I want to think of him – the chap in the fine suit – my hunter – is racing behind me, his hair rippling in the breeze, and I can sense he is going to try to tackle me, and I am thinking, oh, dear, dear, dead Hector Cramer, you are still with me, Hector my love from the express train, the ghost of you, asking, "Why, why did you kill me," and I have to say the only thing I can say, dear Hector, is that "I was starving, Hector, and you fed me, and I do apologize for cutting your life short, it is a crime, I cannot atone for it, it is done, and it cannot be undone. I cannot – I dare not – ask forgiveness. I have done that which I ought not to have done. Such is my nature – I am what I am!"

Now I am the hunted.

The big handsome man is getting closer.

Even as I dash toward safety I can feel and hear the pumping of his blood,

I can smell his nature – I can hear his hatred, and his excitement: like me, he is a hunter, and, yes, I and my kind – hybrids and SINs – are his prey. He is a knight in shining armor defending his race – or so he thinks – defending the human race, and, above all defending the Cosmos, the self-proclaimed elite of the human race, and their right to rule the world.

In the end, we are on the same side – I too am destined to defend the human race and even to defend the Cosmos – it is my mission – but he does not know this, and even if faced with proof he would not recognize it or believe it – though, somehow, I yearn that he would. Truly, I am a romantic; if I could, I would gladly turn the other cheek! Gladly, I would embrace my enemy, kneel before him, succor him, save him ...

Instead, I drink, and drink deep ...

My pursuer is just behind me, coming on fast.

Brilliant yellow laser beam shots ping brightly off the ceramic facades of the pillars – metal bullets and projectiles whiz by – tiles shatter and spatter and go up in smoke – and other beams bounce off the far wall; they sizzle into the concrete, and now I am at the tunnel entrance, and I leap down onto the tracks, more shots zinging and pinging and echoing – dazzling yellow flashes of light on the walls above me, on the rails around me, pebbles bounce, sparks spray out.

The distant crowd is screaming.

It all seems very far away now, almost dream-like.

The Info Voices announce a security emergency. "Please remain calm and remain where you are, the authorities are dealing with the situation ..."

I know the security emergency – the "situation" – is me. I really do hate to cause such a fuss; I should have thought of that when I ate poor Hector Cramer in such a public and exposed place; but I had no choice, did I? I was totally hungry! With such casuistry – worthy of some of the finest Jesuit scholars and theologians I have known and treasured – do I leaven and lighten the burden my sins and my guilt! One of my friends, a 21st century Pope, and I used often to talk about sin and redemption, such a fascinating subject! It is not always easy, Miranda, being me, living with me.

I sprint along the tracks.

The big blond – he really must be a first-class athlete – perhaps he has been biologically enhanced – has jumped down onto the tracks too, and he is racing behind me, stubborn, heroic, suicidal gentleman with the fine tie, and I think, yes, well, it is nice to have company, even if he hates me, and if they try to shoot me, he will be in the way, though that won't make much difference, since the authorities care little for human life right now, in fact they care nothing at all, and they are willing to carry out a massacre if it serves their purposes, except that if they are aware he is a Major General in the Cosmos Centurions, an Agent of the Secret Service, a Chief of Staff, and a member of the Order of the Knights for the Cosmos-led Regeneration of the Human Race, then they might pause, in all the rush and hurly-burly, and stop shooting; I have managed to read a selection of his fleeting thoughts, so I know he is a leader, highly intelligent, brilliant even, foolhardy, a risk-taker, courageous beyond reason, idealistic, and very ambitious.

He has in fact – and I read this off his mind as I run – he has the rather odd idea that he is a man of destiny; that he will destroy all hybrids and SINs; that he will apply a Final Hybrid and SIN Solution and thus ensure the continued purity of the Cosmos and the elite human race, as if the human race or any part of it, even Cosmos, were ever pure; and what would such purity mean, anyway? But all ideologies and racisms deal in illusions of purity and utopian perfection and end in massacre. Hatred is an art, in the end.

The phrase "Final Solution" as it passes through my mind makes me shudder. I shouldn't even use it, not even in the privacy of my own mind. It is sacred in an absolutely negative kind of way, like a ravine where a massacre has taken place, a place where the soil is soaked in innocent blood, land where the ashes of the innocent have fallen on farmers' fields, gardens where the plowshares, cutting the soil, turn up bones. For such things, words fail; they are polluted.

Suddenly a narrow service tunnel surges up; it breaks sideways, at right angles, off the main tunnel, a thin passage, for people or robots or drones only.

Oh, my God! Another train is coming down the track, it is thundering toward us, pushing a wall of damp hot fetid underground air in front of it like a malodorous tsunami. As it comes roaring around a corner its headlights suddenly flood the tunnel; they are dazzling, blinding. A horn blares – the sensors – such trains have no drivers – have seen us and will soon try to put on the brakes.

It is too late for that!

The brakes scream!

I leap sideways into the service tunnel, and the big man hesitates, he is caught in the lights of the oncoming train, and, blinded by the glare, I think he is confused – I'm not even sure he's seen where I disappeared to – the train now blaring a warning, the brakes screaming, sparks flying; the big man's body perhaps took him farther than he intended and now he is someplace he doesn't quite understand, and within a second he will be smashed to pulp and ground to mincemeat by the onrushing wall of steel.

I zip out and grab him by the arm – feeling the fine weave of his suit and the admirable swelling of his muscles – and jerk him off the tracks and into the service tunnel with me, and, as we fall to the ground, just his heel, the heel of his shoe is briefly clipped by the train that passes us like the wind, roaring, roaring ... I leap up and I say ...

"Follow me, then, if you must!"

"What ...?"

I run down the side tunnel, under dim yellow flashing overhead lights, and I think I shall perhaps drink him dry too, or do something else with him, something more amusing, I have not yet decided.

Yes, he has splendid DNA; I caught a whiff of it.

And, yes, he is a hunter – a true believer, an executioner: and I – I am the enemy, the prey. I am, in fact, seen from his point of view, the true demon, the mother of all hybrids, the original alien – I am, for him, the Serpent in the Garden, and also, I suppose, I am Eve, Jezebel, Astarte, all the temptresses and evil witches and sorceresses of all time, all combined into one.

"What ...?" he shouts.

Intelligent as he is, he is so startled by his near-death experience with the train, that he doesn't move but then he staggers up and comes running after me.

"Stop!" he shouts; his voice is hoarse.

"No! Why should I?"

"Stop! I order you!"

"You order me? Who are you to give orders to me? The very idea!"

"Damn you!" He is running; his legs and arms are pumping.

I spy a large iron manhole; I hoist up the cover and let if fall aside with a heavy echoing clatter and I slip into the hole and climb down the rusty flaky rungs of an iron ladder to a lower level, leaving the manhole yawning open, an invitation, so my fearless suitor can follow.

And he does!

I run along a gangway over an underground canal – some sort of large drainage system – it smells of open water and ozone and wild things – and I slip in through an open metal security door, leaving it too ajar, only slightly, just a crack, and, yes, he is so true, so faithful, my man does follow me – I feel he would follow me to the very gates of Hell; and perhaps he is.

I climb down to a lower level canal – the canals down here underground – and even sometimes underwater – in the ruins of Manhattan – crisscross like channels in an impossible Escher drawing – and I wait and he comes running up to me and he is quite out of breath now and he says …

"What are you?"

I stare at him. "Do you want to find out, truly?"

He stares back at me, breathing heavily, his big strong arms hanging at his sides, for an instant uncertain. "Yes," he says.

"Then – come!"

I reach out, grab him – his eyes go wild – and I pull him to me – as if he were a lover – and, clasped to him, I jump into the swift-moving canal.

He topples down into the water with me, and I shout over the tumult of the water.

"Hold your breath!"

I pull him under, and we are swept in a swirl underwater, into the darkness of a tunnel – with only the occasional underwater light for maintenance workers – and we continue underwater for a while and, finally, burst to the surface in the canal, still underground, far underground now, and soon, I know we shall be soon at the ocean, in a conduit under the sea, and he is splashing and sputtering next to me, his strength exhausted, struggling just to breathe, so I say …

"Let us stop here."

I know that from here it is only a short swim to the ocean – and, for me, to freedom.

I shall leave my human hunters behind and make the ocean my home for an hour or two – or perhaps a day or two, or even a week, depending on the weather and the security situation – being amphibian, able to suck oxygen from water, filtering it through my gills, only functional when I am in reptilian form, such choices are open to me and I intend right now to take full advantage of this freedom.

"You are amphibian?"

"Yes, Miranda, it is one of the perks."

"One of the perks of being a hybrid?" Miranda blinked at this strange and weird creature who seemed, now, to be merely a beautiful woman.

"Precisely," V smiled at Miranda.

"Go on," Miranda frowned.

There is a ledge and I swim to it, put my hands on the concrete edge and leap up onto the platform.

My handsome friend is breathless, without his jacket and shoes, and he comes up, swimming slowly, exhausted, and then climbing heavily out of the water, first his arms, then his chest, and finally he kicks and pulls himself out of the water and onto the ledge, and coughs water and sits down next to me and chokes and coughs out more water. Gradually he becomes calmer and can breathe.

"Better?" I say.

He glances askance at me and grunts.

"Good," I give him my best, most seductive smile.

His tie, somehow, is still tied around his neck, looking less fine that it did before. I wonder if it can be salvaged. The tie pin, though, is gone.

I look down at myself.

My clothes are ruined but the blood at least has been washed away. Yes, since my human accoutrements have been destroyed, I think that probably it will be best to swim – naked – out into the ocean and along the coast, using my amphibious nature to the full, and land in some ruined and abandoned seaside town, or flooded inland landscape and hide in some abandoned factory or condo – and just lay low and rest and plan.

There is no place – there will be no place, for me in the city for some time; and in any case everywhere I am a fugitive. I and my kind are being banished from human society.

"You are a murderer," my new friend says.

I look at him. "And you are a very brave man. Foolhardy, I might add."

I can't resist. He is beautiful and I am feeling particularly feisty having just fed. And, as I think I have mentioned, his DNA is of the finest human quality – really a quite irresistible temptation.

"I cannot resist you," I say. I leap up and kneel beside him, my face only a few inches from his face.

"What the hell?" But he does not move.

I start to undo his tie, but then, in a hurry, I open his shirt and I tear it off and he is just staring at me – and breathing hard.

"You are too beautiful. Luscious is perhaps the right word."

"What are you … doing?"

"This won't hurt," I say. I unbuckle his belt and I unzip and open his pants and he is staring as I drink in his fine chest, the sculpted ripple of his muscles, the golden skin, the fine textured hair – and I push him back so that I can pull off his trousers – zip, off they come – and – "Oh, my, my," I say, contemplating the tent his arousal makes in his fine black designer underpants with the little red soaring bald eagle motif – then I kneel and look at him very close, eye-to-eye, and I say,

"You are a fine specimen, my man."

"What the hell – you are …"

I pull off his underpants and as I do so I lean forward and give him a deep and passionate kiss, nibbling at his lips, then locking my lips onto his, then entering him with my tongue, then allowing our tongues, and lips and breath to mingle, to talk to each other, to express yearning, desire, friendship, longing, and oh, oh, oh – love! He returns the kiss. Ah, that love could conquer enmity so easily! The world and its pesky feuding humans might be much better off. "Make love not war," as some people, I believe, said several hundred years ago. Oh, I love humans! I find them absolutely delicious – their hopes, their dreams, their yearnings, their sensuality, their ideals, yes, even their perverse ideals, and, of course, their blood.

"Oh, my darling," I breathe, and then I repeat it, in deeper, more reflective tone, almost making a jingle or a tune, "Oh, my darling."

Oh, my darling, Oh, my darling
Oh my darling, Clementine …

I look him in the eyes. I know my eyes contain the dark limitless depths of an ancient and soulless being from an alien world and from a time before even the gods were born; his eyes are candid, clear, blue – and fanatical. He is the blond beast of legend and of history, a smooth-skinned pitiless warrior, a perfect exemplar of the Master Cosmos Race. I've always wanted such a perfect Cosmos for my very own.

"Oh, my God," he says; his face is an inch away from mine; his breath, I note, is sweet. We are both kneeling now, face to face.

"Oh, my God – but you are …" he repeats; his blue eyes are so bright and I see the full realization dawning in those eyes that I am not merely a killer – not merely a hybrid or SIN renegade – No, I am more: I am truly the arch-enemy, the architect of evil, the source of pollution – and yet here I am: five-foot-seven, slender, pale, with dark eyes and short black hair in a pixie cut – now flattened by water, but the pixie look is still there – and I have just kissed him and I have just declared my love.

"You are …" He really finds it difficult to say what I am – not because he doesn't know, but because if he does say it, then, well, then it becomes real – I am the enemy, the absolute, the …

"Take off your socks," I command. They have a disgusting plaid pattern; it looks even worse wet. How could he ruin a perfect ensemble with such … casual neglect of harmony? Well, human males are like that – they gulp their instant caffeine, kiss the dog, rush out the door, and neglect how their toes and ankles and arches will appear in some future bedroom or under a rosebush or in a public park or perhaps in an express elevator stalled between floors.

He is so stunned – or so lustful – he does it.

I push him backward, and he doesn't resist. Lying back, now totally naked except for his tie and staring up at me, he gathers his courage and asks. "What are you, exactly?"

I see the tattoo on his arm, the Flaming Cross: yes, he is not only a Cosmos Centurion General he is also a member of the Cosmos Secret Order – sworn enemies of hybrids and Synthetic Individuals: a member of the OKCHR: the "Order of the Knights for Cosmos Human Regeneration."

I can also see that – in spite of hating me and in spite of being dunked in the murky underground waters – he is still aroused.

Well, so am I! This is an exciting situation. We are two enemies, two different species – almost – tossed up on a narrow reef of mottled old lichen and moss-covered concrete and rusting iron, a romantic setting in the seething underground full of mutants and genetically modified super-smart super-famished oversized rats!

And we have just exchanged a truly passionate kiss.

And now he is virtually, naked – and, in human terms, we two are members of the opposite sex, that is, virtually two different species, even not counting my alien genes.

And, then, for me, in particular, coming face to face with those who hate me gives me a peculiar thrill; truth be told, and I wish Doctor Freud had had time to elucidate this, it arouses my lust. I wish for some unfathomable reason to convert their hatred and fear to love. I wish not only to turn the other cheek, but to offer my lips for a kiss, to open my arms for an embrace, to console my enemy's fears with words of love. Odd, eh, isn't it, truly weird! Go figure! Then – if love is not possible, lust, in a pinch, will do!

"What the hell are you?" His hand is under my chin, his fingers run along the line of my jaw, very lightly; it is almost a caress.

Yes, it is a caress, gently exploring, even tender, tinged with awe.

"What am I? You have already guessed, I think, but it's a long story, my friend, and we don't have much time." I stand up and rip off my jacket, my dress, my stockings, my blouse, and then, with a twirl, I lift off the ruined remains of my panties – with the retro Parisian scarlet seductress garter belt the last thing to go – and for a second I think of you, my love, my dear recently dead friend, Hector Cramer, whom I had left rigid as a corpse, well, you were, alas, a corpse, a bloodless colorless husk of a man, sitting in the first-class car of the regional underground express – it gives me a pang, thinking of you, and I think that, later tonight, I will play over the memories of you, like flipping through an old and faded photo album of someone I knew and someone I actually *was* – my nature being, psychologically, a bit of an unprincipled chameleon, my negative capability, eager to entertain any opinion and savor any emotion, and my ability to worm myself into another consciousness, being extreme, my sense of myself as permeable as a sieve, for a short moment, dear Hector, I *was* you – I really was – I inhabited your soul, I dwelled within your memories, your hopes, your fears, and even your yearnings, and inside of your memories, dear Hector, I can glide, like a silver fish, mental quicksilver, slipping in and out, where no one else can go – perhaps no one else, not even your mother, loved you as I loved you.

Flop!

Flop!

And so the soaked panties and the frilly Parisian garter belt flop to the ground, and I say to my big handsome lover – he is very handsome, beyond handsome, a human god, really, even if he is a member of the Order of the Knights of Cosmos Human Regeneration – who is still lying there, vulnerable, exhausted and shocked, still looking up at me, still catching his breath, still calculating how to overpower me, take me like a trophy, and I say …

"Now, darling, let us do what we are meant to do."

"What is that?"

"This!" I lower myself down on him and I kiss his chest and then his chin and then his mouth and again I give him real, deep, liquid human kisses and my fist closes around his arousal and he sure is aroused, yes, truly aroused, and without even knowing what is happening, or hardly, he enters me, or I enclose him, and then I use all my wiles and best techniques to prolong the moment, to stretch his pleasure to the breaking point, to make of the tension carried to a high pitch of desire, such pleasure as to almost be agony, and yes, I succeed, and I keep him there, his pleasure and pain vibrating like a wild tuning fork, and, then, after perhaps three or four minutes of this, teetering on the edge, and he reaches up with his hands and he seizes the small of my back, and he caresses me and he sculpts my breasts, oh, so delicately, so softly and teasingly, really, he seems attuned to each nano-nerve of my body, this man really knows his stuff, he really knows what he is doing, technique and self-control and passion all fused into a lethal missile, and, as he scores on all points, my excitement rises to a crescendo, I see the danger coming, Oh, God, no, no, no … and I seize my jacket with one hand and roll the right sleeve into a ball – and I say, brushing my lips against his, "This is the dangerous point, darling," and as I approach orgasm, and I know it is coming, and I can't stop it, it is a veritable super-fast freight train of lust, desire, excitement, a tidal wave rising rippling, foaming, and coming at me – and I am bringing him with me, right where I want him!

"My God," he says, seeing what is coming, "My God!"

"Don't worry about your God," I say, and, just as the fangs spring up from my lips, I grab the jacket sleeve and I bite down on the rolled up sleeve of my once impeccable and fashionable retro-Armani. I lock my fangs into the fabric. Otherwise – I do know my little weaknesses – otherwise, desire dictating its irresistible logic, my fangs would have sought out his jugular – no matter how much I ordered them to abstain – "No, no, Don't, Don't!" – and they would have cut through the skin, sliced through the flesh, entered the jugular, and they would have drunk him dry, poor thing, and then I would have been forced to finish the job – drain him dry and kill him, truly kill him, so that he would not rise again, but would be a dead husk, destined to decline to ash, mere ash and dust, scattered to the wind like poor dear Hector. But, right now, the intensity is reaching its peak, the crescendo crests, and it ripples through me – and through him. He is holding me tight, so tight, and he fills me, and … Yes, both trains are entering the station at exactly the same moment; oh, this is fine, so fine!

"Oh!"

"Oh!"

We come – full orgasm – in exactly the same instant and it ripples and

ripples and the shock waves reverberate far within me, and he has possessed me fully, I feel him within me, hot liquid, burning, caressing, loving,
and I have possessed him, and now ... A true volcano, he is, my love, a
fountain of lava!

"Oh!"

"Oh!"

It ripples again – a second shock wave!

"Oh!"

"Oh!"

Then the tide recedes. I take the soggy saliva-soaked jacket sleeve out of
my mouth. The fangs have receded. I am no longer in danger of sucking him
up – gorging myself and gurgling the life out of him as if he were a thick
frothy milkshake and I a teenager perched on a leather topped stool at some
idyllic 1950s drugstore counter painted by Norman Rockwell, by the soda
fountain, with the jukebox playing, hmm, let's say, Connie Francis singing
"Who's Sorry Now?"

Whew!

I once again look more or less human, like a normal water-soaked, desire-
soaked, post-orgasmic, flushed and radiant human female, naked, perched
on top of my man, my hair slicked down close to my skull, the bloom of
a fresh blush on my cheeks, my chalk-white skin still sparkling with silver
beads of underground canal water. I play with the water beads in the thick
blond curls of his chest, and now, only now, do I dare, once again, kiss him.

"My God," he whispers, "You are evil, absolute evil!" He sighs. His eyes
almost roll back in their sockets. Truly, this was a fine moment. He is limp
with exhaustion.

"Time, my darling enemy, time," I say, and, with infinite regret, I disen-
gage myself from him and stand up. Out of the crumpled jacket I take my
waterproof wallet with all its codes and micro-documents. I sling the lanyard
around my neck and tighten it.

"What are you doing now," he says, still lying on the cement ledge, staring
up at me, his eyes round and sleepy and stunned.

"Now I must leave you, my lovely foe. But first ..."

"But first, what?" he almost looks frightened. His fist curls; he is getting
ready to defend himself; the Order is known for the steely strength of its
members, and though I could easily subdue him, I do not wish to do so. I am
feeling mellow, and, in truth, I am in love.

"I'll show you another side of me." I grin; I don't know what's gotten into me. "I don't want any secrets between us, darling." I think I am trying to pretend that this is all normal; that I am a normal woman with a normal man; that true love was possible; that …

"What … how …?"

"Since I love you, dear Cosmos Crusader, I want you to see all sides of me, even the demonic."

"Yes, but …"

"Since I love you, I want you to know the worst." I kneel next to him and kiss him on the lips. "Oh," I sigh, "I wish we had all eternity, darling," I say, and I stand up, "But such an instant is like eternity, is it not?"

"Yes … you are …"

"Well, I am many things, as you are many things. Each of us is a multitude, I believe someone said."

"Yes … Walt Whitman" he says, quoting, and with the modulation of a truly talented actor, "'Do I contradict myself; well, I contradict myself; I am large; I contain multitudes.'" He knows it by heart, the devil! I see more clearly what I had understood from the beginning. He is one of those muscular beautiful Cosmos Fascist fanatics of high intelligence and vast culture – the most dangerous kind.

I gaze at him fondly, "And, I think, my darling, that the Cosmos Centurions should see what they are up against, and the Order too."

"The Order …"

"Your tattoo …"

"Of course, yes, of course," he sighs, as if he has made an awful mistake, a failure of intelligence, of spy craft.

"Well, here goes! Don't be alarmed, you are about to see the enemy as she truly is" I say, "Presto, Hocus-Pocus, Abracadabra!" I morph into demon form.

"Oh, my God," he gasps, raising an arm to protect himself and starting back, almost falling over.

"Don't worry," I say, sitting down cross-legged next to him, "I loved, absolutely loved our little session, you are truly a man, and I've already fed, so you are in no danger. Even if I were starving to death, I would not harm you, my love." I put my claw into his hand. "Do you like me, just a little bit?"

"I … I … I …" He was just staring at me. I don't think he believed what he had just seen and I don't think he accepted the fact that I was talking to him, as if I were real and not a nightmare. Even the Cosmos Order, cultivating all its hatreds and superstitions, probably doesn't really believe its own propaganda – it is one thing to rant about the enemy and write and scribble scurrilous broadsides and anonymous ugly Net graffiti – it is quite another to come face to face with the real thing, the true monster of your imaginings, and I am indubitably the real thing – but the real thing has become unfamiliar, as we hybrids have been very low-profile lately, remaining strictly within our human guise, what with racism running amok and witch hunts being the order of the day in many countries – so those who can do it, remain totally human, totally integrated. I wish to explain many things to him, but do I have time? No, I do not: I can hear the SWAT team – they have been trying to follow us, and now they are back on the scent.

They are coming down one of the tunnels, thumping and splashing along with their big boots, their infrared sensors flooding the canals, their sonar ping-ping ping probing every corner, scaring rats and bats and, I suspect, a few of the humanoid or simian mutants who have begun to migrate into the underbelly of the great city, poor, doomed, beautiful Elysium.

"For me it was very fine," I say. I give my new love my best demon-reptile pout. "I hope you liked it too."

"Jesus, you really are the Devil," he said, "Absolute Evil."

"Maybe I am, maybe not."

"I don't know what …"

"May I keep your tie?" I kneel and unknot it from his neck – we made love naked except for his tie, somehow fitting, I think, but I don't know why, except that I do like men's ties, and I add, "You'd better put what's left of your clothes on, and say you caught me, we plunged into the water, we struggled, and I ripped your clothes to shreds, and then I fought free and escaped – it was a mortal struggle, but somehow, heroically, you survived."

"Yes, yes," he says, almost absent-mindedly; he picks up his underpants and begins to pull them on. "I must really hunt you down and kill you," he says, "You know that, don't you."

"I know, I know – that is rather unfortunate since we've come to know each other so well – and I think, truly, I am not your enemy, nor that of the human race, but we have no time for a discussion of political philosophy, alas. Oh, you are so luscious!" I shiver as I tie his tie around my neck. "How do I look?"

He grunts and manages a smile: I imagine a reptile wearing an old school tie plus a lanyard with a bulging waterproof wallet dangling from her neck like a miniature bib does look faintly ridiculous.

"You are strange for a monster," he says, "but seriously, you are a threat to us – you hybrids are too strong, too intelligent, and you are alien, and you are polluting the ..."

"Are you and I so alien to each other?"

"No, I guess in fact we are not," his grin is a bit of a grimace; he scratches his head and looks like a schoolboy trapped in some peccadillo by his school-marm. His charming smile, he thinks, will get him out of it – she will forgive him; no woman can resist & etc.

"You see," I say, "Even the most intense racial hatred can be overcome."

"But you are not even human."

"My darling, I am half human and it is a very important half. You and I already share lots of DNA. All my life I have spoken human languages, thought in human concepts, lived with humans, and bathed in human culture."

"It makes you even more dangerous; you can infiltrate us, you seem assimilated, but ..." he shrugs; but he does lean over and kiss me on my rep-tilian forehead. I blink my reptilian eyes. I sigh. His eyes now are staring into mine. I shiver – his hatred and his desire and mine, mingled, make a potent cocktail – I truly wish we could begin to wrestle once again, right now, right here. Oh, if only love could overcome hatred!

"Well, I must go," I sigh and crouch down – grab my clothes – leaving evi-dence of my strip-tease would be incriminating evidence of his collaboration with the enemy – and I roll over and slip off the ledge and splash into the water and swing around and grasp the edge of the ledge with one claw and look longingly up at him, blinking my golden reptile eyes. "Goodbye, my darling," I say. "I would love to explain to you in greater detail what and who I am – and how we could benefit each other, we hybrids and humans – and I would even love to beg your forgiveness for what I am and for what I do. We could change the world, if we worked together, you and I!"

"You can talk to me, you can ..." Partly he is serious; partly he is trying to trap me, to keep me here until the SWAT team arrive.

"No time, my love," with my right claw open, palm up, I blow him a reptil-ian kiss, "There is no time, my darling, no time – goodbye!"

Standing there in his underpants, his blond hair slicked down, his body still gleaming with wet and with sweat, and bright scratches on his chest and arms where I in my passion had raked my nails across his body, he just looks at me.

I sink under the water and I swim, as fast as I can. I weigh my clothes down with a stone and drop them in a deep part of the canal.

Soon I am out beyond the defenses of the city, beyond the protective nets they are installing against sub-human and animal mutants and religious terrorists, beyond the sea walls that are being built in a vain attempt to keep back the rising ocean, and then I am out in the open sea, with nothing but gulls circling above. I surface, look around, the sun has already risen, mist is rising off the water, off the oily gentleness of the swell – it is a brand-new day.

I take a deep breath of air and then I plunge deep.

I head south.

I will return to land somewhere in New Jersey, pick up what clothes and extra documents I need from one of my secret storage drops – and, dressed in civvies, neo-Armani Classic, as the business woman I usually am, I will try to survive, moving from identity to identity, from hideout to hideout, from nation to nation."

Miranda frowned. "Yes, well, Hybrid, it is a very fine story, and thank you for sharing – but, frankly, I don't get the point. I mean, what does this have to do with … anything …?"

"Oh, yes, dear Miranda, I do apologize. I got carried away."

"That's alright, but …"

"Well, you see, Miranda," V looked down, frowned, and fiddled with her belt-buckle. "You see, what happened, Miranda was this," V took a deep breath, "What happened was this: a few weeks later, while swimming in the sea off my villa, back in Europe, I suddenly realized – I was pregnant."

"Pregnant?"

"Yes."

"But, how, I mean what …?"

"I know. It does seem unlikely. And it was the first time it had happened, in almost three thousand years. I thought to myself; this is impossible. But it wasn't – impossible, I mean. But even as I swam, just off the beach of my villa, I felt the creature already – I knew I did!"

"Gosh, that must have been a shock, I mean …"

"Yes, at the tender age of 2,902 somewhat years – I was, for the first time, pregnant."

"Gosh, what did you do?"

"Well I had to think things over. I swam back to shore, climbed out of the water and onto the beach and there I sat on the rounded pebbles and I wept as the sun sank down in the west and disappeared over the Mediterranean in a long thin line of golden and red cloud."

My girl servant, a wonderful young slip of a thing called Olivia, who was then studying to be an anthropologist, came down to the beach with a towel and with a bottle of red wine and glasses for the two of us and she saw me and she stopped and she said, "What is wrong, my lady, what is wrong?"

"And what was wrong?"

"I knew I couldn't keep the child, Miranda. That was the painful horrible thing that I knew."

"Oh, I am so, so sorry for you, Hybrid." Miranda's eyes were glossy now for now she understood the hybrid's tragedy; as a drinker of blood, and a hunted being, almost always on the run, she could not raise a child – that was clear. Her maternal love would be forever frustrated, she would forever be alone. What pain, what loneliness!

"And so ..." V began, then stopped, looked down, put her thumbs under her belt and kicked a few pebbles with the toe of her sandals.

"And so ..." Miranda felt it was a very sad story; but what it had to do with her she could not for the life of her figure out.

V kicked a few pebbles then she knelt down and picked one up, and, still kneeling, turned it around as if it were the most interesting thing in the world, "I've wanted to tell you and Nikki has wanted to tell you; but somehow, well, somehow the right moment never came up; we are both rather cowardly, Nikki and I, and ..." She looked up at Miranda.

"You and Nikki are cowards?"

"Yes."

"What are you talking about?"

"The thing is ..." V, still kneeling, picked up another pebble, not daring to look up at Miranda.

"Yes."

"The thing is you are not Caliban's sister."

"What?"

"You heard me, Miranda, darling. There is no obstacle to ..."

"What? What are you saying? What do you mean?"

"There is no barrier between you and Caliban, in fact, I think perhaps ..."

"What are you talking about?"

"I think perhaps you are made for each other, meant for each other."

"What? What are you talking about?"

"Nikki is not your mother."

"What? But …"

"Your mother is …"

"But how can Nikki not be my mother – She's my mother. She's Nikki; she's always been my mother; she's …"

"Dear Cosmos Child, Nikki is your guardian; she is your adopted mother. She is my friend. She was there when you were born. She loves you as if you were her own daughter, she is passionately in love with you; but …"

"But …?"

"But …" V hesitated.

"Well, out with it, Hybrid, tell me, what it is you have to tell me, tell me the horrible secret, tell me …" Why is it, Miranda wondered, that everybody today seems to be beating around the bush?

"I am your mother," V blurted it out. She sighed, stood up, and let the pebbles drop.

Miranda just stared. She reached out and laid her hand on a rocky ledge and she thought she would fall down into some new abyss. "You … are … my … mother? My … me …"

"Yes, dear Miranda Cosmos Child First Class Champion twice honored by the President-Leader himself."

"I don't know what to say. I …"

"Well, perhaps, just for a moment, breaking with your usual practice, you might say nothing, Miranda. I know it is hard to fathom. But the man who chased me in the subway, who wouldn't let me make my clean escape, he was – is – your father. Nikki adopted you, so you would be protected – safe, not hunted as I am hunted."

"You …?"

"Yes, me."

"A hybrid …?"

"Yes, a hybrid."

"This is too much; this is …" Miranda leaned against the rock face. The two bear-warriors had moved forward, concerned, but then, at a sign from V, they moved back; but they were still concerned; it was visible in their eyes; V was close to the Goddess, she was herself a goddess and like a sister to the Goddess Nikki; but Princess Miranda was daughter of Nikki the Goddess; their duty and their desire was to defend her to the death.

"So I can love Caliban after all," Miranda brightened.

"Yes, you are made for each other!"

"Oh, well, hmm, I guess that is sort of wonderful!"

"Yes, yes it is, sort of," V smiled. But then she sensed the wind veering toward a temper tantrum, part of Miranda dealing with the shock.

"So I was conceived in a sewer," Miranda feigned a pout; she was wondering if this was worth a scene; not only was she now, or so it turned out, a hybrid, an outcast, a half-alien, a monster, but she had been conceived in the most dreadfully unromantic and unhygienic conditions – in a slime-covered virus-infested sewer, by two sweaty hostile individuals, a hybrid and some sewer rat of a man, some big-muscled guy V just happened to desire to ... to fuck ...

It is difficult to envisage the moment of one's own creation.

Yuk!

The brute fact of it; how utterly undignified!

Yuk! Double Yuk!

How contingent, how accidental, how random!

The grunting, the sweating, the pure idiotic happenstance of the whole thing – why, I am the result of pure chance, of a quirk in time and space, I am a mere accident – that's what I am!

Yuk!

Two creatures rutting – and the result is me!

Yuk!

Somehow Miranda had had, up to this very moment, the idea that she must have been part of some larger sublime design, that she must have been conceived, on purpose and with only her as the transcendent end result in mind. After all, as some celibate theologians will have it, and verily, in their arrogant ignorance, having never of course – cross-my-heart-and-hope-to-die – fornicated or known the lofty delights and intricate trials of the flesh, they insist and persist in their silliness: to wit, that the only, and exclusive, aim of sexual congress is procreation. What a perverse idea! And promoted by a conspiracy of celibates! So, Miranda, really an idealist at heart, had this image of her conception, in a bower of flowers, with music playing, and cupids cavorting on a vaulted baroque ceiling, or perhaps, in a Hollywood-type studio where Nikki, the celluloid idol, was starring in some magnificent movie, or, perhaps, even better, on a wooden pirate ship, plying the billowing ocean waves, the air rich with the smell of tar and sunlight and hemp, with foam spurting over the bows, and bare-chested sailors singing, "Yo, Ho, Ho, and a bottle of rum", swords slashing, the sun shining, the breeze ... And maybe her favorite parrot, or some parrot like him, standing by, perched on a yardarm.

Fifteen men on a dead man's chest
Yo ho ho and a bottle of rum
Drink and the devil had done for the rest
Yo ho ho and a bottle of rum.

"It wasn't exactly a sewer, Miranda. It was more an underground canal."

"Oh."

"It was poetic and romantic, really."

"Poetic? Really? Humph," Miranda crossed her arms and stuck out her – beautiful – lower lip in an even more delicious pout: if only she had been conceived on the bounding main!

"Yes," V sighed, "It was truly romantic. There was a salty tang in the air, Miranda. And a tropical sea breeze wafting in, under the vaulted ceilings, the scent of ozone, and distant reflections of the blaze of the rising sun, or the floating moon, and your father was most beautiful creature, a manly man, beyond anything I have ever known, really rather like a pirate of the old days." V had a good idea what was going on in Miranda's head, and, unlike cool balanced Nikki, who had had to be a parent for these fourteen years, V was inordinately eager to please her newly acquired teenage daughter, after all this was a new – and fragile – position to be in. "All he needed was an eye patch, and perhaps a hook for a hand, and possibly a parrot perched on his shoulder. Unfortunately he didn't have a parrot – or a hook. In a jungle, I'm sure he would have had a parrot; and he could have played the role of Tarzan with ease. And his chest, did I tell you about his chest, Miranda, a most beautiful chest, muscular, and tanned, and gleaming with sweat, and with gold curls, and ..."

"Oh." Miranda lightened up; this was more like it!

"And it was, for me, one of the most romantic, delicious, ecstatic moments of my life."

"You really are very clever, aren't you, Hybrid-Mother," Miranda smiled; she knew that V knew what was going on in her mind, "You want to make me accept what I am – what I have become. You are very adroit!"

"I try. Nikki is a hard act to follow."

"You are a pair, the two of you, the hybrid and the SIN," said Miranda; she suddenly felt very grown up, capable of judging her elders and of forgiving them all their sins – no pun intended. After all she had survived a plane crash, she had fought zombie-bats, she had negotiated with mutants, she had shared deep mystical mushroom experiences and cosmic insights with Bounce the Ghoul, she had consorted with other ghouls, she had discovered she was a SIN, and then she discovered that, no, she was not a SIN, she was a hybrid, and she had fallen in love with Caliban – oh, sweet, wonderful Caliban – and she had lived the whole range of mystical, tragic, and amorous emotions, all in less than a week.

"We try," V said, realizing – not for entirely the first time – that raising a daughter, particularly one like this, could be a complicated business. She owed Nikki, big time!

"You are beautiful, both of you."

"Thank you," V almost blushed; perhaps this would end well after all.

"And my father, what happened to him?"

"Oh, your father, well, my darling daughter, as befits such a superb and outstanding specimen, pure Cosmos First Class and then some, he had of course a splendid career, and though he hates hybrids and SINs and has done great harm to them, to us, and even to society, engineering as he did a coup d'état, he still I think has a sneaky grudging top secret nostalgic lust for me, and he has always been very protective of you, even very proud I'd say, and he has been very protective of your protectrice of course."

"Of Nikki …"

"Yes, Nikki – whom your father secretly admires and considers a friend (who would not) – Nikki who loves you as a mother would love you and perhaps even more fiercely because she had lost her own child – until now – and because she knew you were in constant danger and because she loves me as well."

"But my father, who is he …?"

"And, strangely, though I perhaps flatter myself, I think your father not only lusts for me, but I think loves me too, and feels tenderness for me, just a little bit. He certainly loves you. Pride shines in his eyes at the mere thought of you. The paradoxes of human nature are infinite, are they not? A torturer can worship the person she tortures. An assassin can love the one he kills."

"But, who is he?"

"You've met him."

Miranda frowned.

"He pinned a metal on your jacket, twice I believe."

Miranda's eyes opened wide, "That can't be; it was the President, our Glorious Leader, who pinned the medal and he …"

"Well …" V was smiling now. Miranda frowned, what a mischievous, teasing mother she was! Full of puzzles! Nikki was sometimes enigmatic; but V was positively a trickster, "Well, nobody else, I mean, nobody else pinned a medal on me, I mean …"

"Quite! Precisely! Your deductive powers are a marvel, dear Miranda. Your father, Miranda, is the Glorious Leader, the President of the Imperial United States of Cosmos, the hunter of hybrids and SINs, the scourge and bane of our existence, the Defender of Humanity, the Great Man, the …"

"Oh, my God, the President," Miranda's eyes rolled up and she fell straight down – unconscious.

V caught her and, kneeling, held Miranda, sprawled across her lap.

The warrior bears moved forward, concerned, and bowed. "It is time, Goddess, it is time."

"Time," V raised an eyebrow, kneeling as she was, with Miranda, sweet Miranda, lolling loose-limbed, head hanging back, eyes closed, in her arms.

"We must take the Princess to safety." The largest warrior-bear pointed toward the horizon.

Black shapes were moving against the darkening sky. Venus twinkled, and then disappeared – the leathery fetid darkness winged closer.

"Yes," said V, "You are right; we must."

Miranda opened her eyes. "Mother," she said, "Mother … is it time to go?"

"Yes, it is, Miranda."

"Then, by all means, let us go."

"Yes, of course," said V, "Let us go."

"I am ready," Miranda slid out of V's arms, and stood up, but she still held V's hand.

"Yes, you are ready."

Miranda stood extra-straight. "I am a Cosmos, and proud of it; and I am a hybrid, and proud of it – above all, Mother, I am a warrior! I am your daughter and the daughter of Nikki the SIN and Goddess, and – also – I am the daughter of the President-Leader."

"Yes, you are," V smiled, "Let us go!"

"Yes, mother, let us go!"

And so they went, toward the Great Door to the Mutant Kingdom, and so they proceeded, V and Miranda, hand in hand, escorted by the bear-warriors, and so they would prepare and gird themselves for the coming battle, and so the fight against the forces of darkness would soon begin, yet again, driving straight toward the most horrible and final climax of all.

Above them great fleets of zombie-bats ignored the mutant kingdom; they were winging their way east, toward the heart of Cosmos, toward the Whore of Babylon, toward Elysium itself.

And above them something else moved, something that looked like a dark cloud, something that drained color from the landscape – something that, on the surface, left only death behind, something that was sweeping toward – Elysium. As it passed, the moon and the stars disappeared.

In the Dead Lands, night had truly arrived.

NEXT: VOLUME 7 IN THE
ADVENTURES OF V

EXTINCTION

BOOK 3
ELYSIUM

by
GILBERT REID

TWIN RIVERS
PRODUCTIONS

EXCERPT FROM
EXTINCTION BOOK 3:
ELYSIUM

CHAPTER 1 – ELYSIUM

Death, yes, death!

Death is the name of the game.

WHAM!

Goddamn it!

WHAM!

Crouched in an open-topped, 1940, mottled, khaki and matt-green, captured Afrika Korps Mercedes armored car, Kit Candy slams the steering wheel left, then right. She ducks and weaves. She pulls the trigger. The antique MG-42 machine gun – nickname "Hitler's Zipper" – lets go with a merciless wave of fire, zap, zap, zap!

Damn! The archaic 20th Century ghoul, in his vintage Nazi uniform, sporting a neat Swastika, got in the first shots. Five red-hot bullets whiz by Kit's right earlobe.

Kit pulls the trigger. Tracer bullets flash out from the MG-42, sizzling yellow arcs, messengers of death, 1,000 rounds a minute, zipping through the murky, dust-filled air.

Wow! She scores! A direct hit! The monster ghoul with the bulging eyes and the silly Hitler mustache explodes, splashing a giant smear of purple glow-goo, his bio-blood, over a cliff of stippled rosy granite.

Whew! Kit wipes her forehead.

The battle is not over! More bullets zip by, sizzling her eardrums. Kit slams the steering wheel sideways, swivels the armored car into a dizzying turn, twirling, spinning, 180 degrees, raising dust. It's so fast she risks chewing up the vehicle's caterpillar tracks. They claw desperately at the tumbling pebbles of the Libyan Desert.

The sun is low.

Kit blinks through the crosshairs. She pulls the trigger. The Italian stone and stucco colonial farmhouse explodes. So much for those bloody sniper assassins! She has it in for those squirrel-like mutants, with their antique sub-machine guns. They are treacherous and skillful – but she has just vaporized the whole lot of them! Whoopee! I'm the girl! I *am* the girl!

Wham! Wham! Wham!

Bullets slam into the sunbaked leather seat, just beside her right cheek-bone, splat, splat, and – splat! The impact rips the fabric, ruffles her hair. She stares. What the ...? Where the hell did that come from?

Peering through anti-dust goggles, she scans the terrain – only sand dunes, a ridge of pebbles, scrub, and stucco ruins.

Ah, yes!

There they are! Damn them!

Decision time! She slams down the pedal, guns the car, swerving, zigzag-ging, and – full charge ahead – the best defense is offense.

She races toward a small, dark tuft of underbrush, sage and cactus, all glow-ing scarlet in the setting sun. That's where they are, the devilish bastard Nazi rabbit-mutants! She will run them down! She will crush them! They won't get away this time! And, yes, there they are, sprinting for dear life, bounce, bounce, bounce! She swings the M-42 toward the running silhouettes ... and she presses the trigger and ... and ...

WHAM!

Goddamn it!

WHAM!

Goddamn it!

WHAM!

WHAM!

The world disintegrates – flips into schizoid fragments, fluff, static and phantoms. The world is shattered. it is a ghost.

Where am I?

The console was dead, the commands didn't respond, the leaping giant Nazi rabbit-mutants faded, the glare of the sizzling desert turned to static. The gunfire and cicadas and engine's roar morphed into cold hissing Arctic synaptic snow. Then died to dead black. The ear-feeds were void of stimuli. The sensation feeds – which gave Kit her tactile, muscular, olfactory, and taste inputs – provide nothing, zero, zilch, nada.

OUCH!

No sensations!

It's like being dead.

Oh, I hate this! She had been thrust back with pitiless utter explosive force into the present, out of Ancient Mythical 20th Century North Africa – WHAM!

She was in her own body, in her Sub Cubicle, her own time! Like, now, she was in *Now*, like in *This Instant!* It was like slamming into a wall. *Oh, I hate this!*

Now – how horrible!

Now – meant death!

Now – meant absence!

Now – meant love forlorn.

Goddamn!

Slouched down, a limp, unwashed, filthy, human dishrag, in the Wrap-Around Play-Seat, Kit shuddered. She blinked. There was an itchy clot of crud at the corner of her left eye. She picked at it.

Little white gooey flakes came out, stuck to the end of her fingers. She stared at them. "Ugh!"

YUK! GROSS!

Her whole body was icky – sweaty, clammy. Her mouth was musty and salty, her tongue furry; her heart empty. Damn! She hadn't showered since coming back from the Sky Dreamer Complex. How long ago? Two days? No, three, three whole bloody days!

It was so totally stupid, losing herself these games, trying to drug herself into an absolute unending minimal IQ stupor! Whatever she did, she couldn't escape the fact: Nikki and Miranda Hughes were dead!

She didn't believe it, but it was true. Three days ago …

Three days ago …

Three days ago, the world was sunshine and promise. Three days ago, the future was bright.

Three days ago, the day had started happily: it was Cleaning Day in the Hughes apartment.

Kit tried to deny how much she liked – well, loved – Miranda and Nikki. It was a weakness. She despised herself for it. Well, she *partly* despised herself for it! She was addicted. Three days ago, that morning, before heading off to the Hughes Apartment, she had even done a little dance, spinning around in the narrow confines of her living pod!

She had a great idea for a new "adventure." She and Miranda would explore the old underground sunken port at the end of the sunken underwater part of Manhattan, near the old …

Nikki, she was sure, would approve.

Kit showered, pulled on her best skin-shorts, T-shirt, and hobnail boots, and then she rode across town and uptown to the Exclusive Cosmos Levels of Elysium. When she got to the Sky Dreamer Complex, she flashed, as usual, the security card Nikki had given her. The robot security officer bowed, saluted, and said, "Welcome to the Sky Dreamer Complex, Sub Kit Candy. You are authorized to proceed."

Kit entered the elevator and stood patiently, while it checked her biometrics, after which the elevator said, "Hello, Sub Kit Candy. You are authorized to proceed!"

So, in the transparent elevator bubble, she began the journey to the 78th floor of the Complex – past the shopping levels, the university level, the seminar open-space level, the Olympic-size swimming pools, on three different levels, suspended in space and glittering in the morning light, and the spas with their manicure stations, clay baths, massage parlors, and workout stations. Everywhere there were lots of beautiful Cosmos – slender, tanned, fit – doing their Cosmos things, shopping, jogging, eating, studying, laughing. It was, truly, another world. Then, finally, she got to the 78th floor, where the door opened with a brief musical salute, and Kit exited, with the elevator wishing her, "A very good day to you, Sub Kit Candy."

"And to you too," Kit said.

"Thank you, Sub Kit Candy," said the elevator, and the door closed with a discreet musical ding – and sped on its way upwards.

"Suite 78A: Nikki Hughes," the gold doorplate said. Kit rang the antique retro doorbell. No one answered. She waited and rang again.

Again, nobody answered.

This was strange. Kit felt a twinge of disquiet. Damn! I'm an idiot. I shouldn't be so dependent on them. I'm a Sub. I must remember that I am a Sub! I shouldn't be dependent on two Cosmos, even if they are wonderful Cosmos! Still, she was eager to get into mischief with Miranda and to have a session of jousting ideas with Nikki.

Oh well, Kit resorted to the palm-and-iris identification pad.

"Welcome, Sub Kit Candy. You are authorized!"

ACKNOWLEDGMENTS

Thanks to the many people who made the *Adventures of V: Return of the Goddess* possible: Adrienne Clarkson, Andra Sheffer, André Kirchberger, Anna Porter, Bernice Landry, Bernie Lucht, Beverly Topping, Bob Ramsay, Chuck Shamata, Claudia Neri, Denise Jacques, Diana Leblanc, Diane Shamata, Dianne Rinehart, Dorothy Vreeker, Duncan Derry, Ed Cowan, Elena Solari, Florence Treadwell, Heather Reid, Irene Spampinato, Irene Tudisco, Jacqueline Baker, Jacqueline Park, Jacqueline Swartz, Janie Yoon, Jennifer Hambleton, Jennifer Puncher, Jim Downs, John McGreevy, John Pearce, John Ralston Saul, Josephine Khu, Jules Cashford, Julia Belluz, Julia Hambleton, Marie-Christine Dunham-Pratt, Mark Fenwick, Martine Matus Siebert, Norm Barber, Norm Christie, Nuala Fitzgerald, Paola Pugliatti, Peter Williamson, Ramsay Derry, Sandra Martin, Simona Barabesi, Susan Mahoney, Susan S. Senstad, Tony Robinow, Trisha Jackson, Wendy Trueman, and many others too numerous to name. I owe an infinite number of literary debts, too, but in particular to Joyce Carol Oates, Justin Cronin, and Stephen King.

TITLES IN THE
ADVENTURES OF V

WORKS BY
GILBERT REID

SHORT STORIES
So This is Love: Lollipop and Other Stories
Lava and Other stories

GRAZIA SERIES
Son of Two Fathers (with Jacqueline Park)

ADVENTURES OF V
Vampire vs Vatican
Vampire Clone
Pandemic Book 1: Party Balloons
Pandemic Book 2: The Gateway
Extinction Book 1: Girl with the Golden Eyes
Extinction Book 2: Revolt of the Angels
Extinction Book 3: Elysium

GWENDOLINE SERIES
By Gwendoline
The Shaming of Gwendoline C
Gwendoline Goes to School
Gwendoline Goes Underground

To receive a free book or novella
And to learn more about V and get notes on writing and other topics:

Sign up at

https://gilbertreid.com

Please write a short review!
Just two or three lines.
And post it to Goodreads or Amazon
or any other book group you may belong to.

Or send it to me!
At: gilbert@gilbertreid.com

GILBERT REID is the author of two short story collections: *So This is Love: Lollipop and Other Stories* (2004, 2019) and *Lava and Other Stories* (2019). He also co-authored, with Jacqueline Park, the historical novel *Son of Two Fathers* (2019). He has written extensively for television and radio. Most notably he researched, wrote, and narrated two five-hour radio series: *Gilbert Reid's Italy* and *Gilbert Reid's France* for CBC's flagship radio program IDEAS. His many television series include *Paths of the Gods*, *For King and Empire*, *For King and Country*, and *Sir Peter Ustinov in Burma: Road to Mandalay*. After thirty years in Europe working as an economist, university lecturer, diplomat, script doctor, journalist, and adventure travel guide, Gilbert now lives in Toronto.

www.ingramcontent.com/pod-product-compliance
Lightning Source LLC
Chambersburg PA
CBHW051054030726
47504CB00006B/1628